BRUTAL BOYS OF EVERLAKE PREP BOOK 3

KINGS

OF

ANARCHY

CAROLINE PECKHAM   SUSANNE VALENTI

MW01287089

Kings of Anarchy
Copyright © 2020 Caroline Peckham & Susanne Valenti

Interior Formatting & Design by Wild Elegance Formatting

All rights reserved.
No part of this publication may be reproduced or transmitted by any means, electronic, mechanical,
photocopying or otherwise, without the prior permission of the copyright owner.

Kings of Anarchy/Caroline Peckham & Susanne Valenti – 1st ed.
ISBN-13 - 978-1-914425-46-2

This book is dedicated to cliffhangers.

May you be thrown from the cliff of this book and many others with the knowledge that your pain has not gone unnoticed (and the authors are laughing).

May your tears be shed with abandon and your kindles survive being thrown across the room (so you can come back for more suffering).

May your partner shrink away in alarm and debate your sanity (while you garble about the love of your life who just died and who was not them).

May you dive into the next book like a soldier returning to war, with battle scars on your heart and tear stains still dirtying your cheeks as you lift your chin and face another author eye to eye and demand, "More."

ACACIA SPORTS HALL

THE TEMPL

REDWOOD DINING HALL

ASPEN HALLS

PINE AUDITORIUM

HAZEL HOUSE

BEECH HOUS

EVERLAKE

CYPRESS GYM

MAPLE LODGE

TAHOMA MOUNTAIN

OAK COMMON HOUSE

THE SACRED STONE

CATACOMBS

SYCAMORE BEACH

ILLOW BOATHOUSE

THE HEMLOCK LIBRARY

CHAPTER ONE

Blood. There was so much fucking blood. My hands were painted red with it, my shirt soaked through, the leaves at my feet stained wet with it, the crimson colour catching in the faint moonlight from above.

"Tatum!" Monroe bellowed as he raced away down the dirt track, running at full speed, not even sparing a glance back at us as he chased after her.

"Fuck," I cursed as I pressed down harder, trying to stop the warmth which was still pulsing from Saint's body beneath my hands.

He'd passed out. Or at least I hoped he'd passed out. Because the alternative was a reality I refused to function in. There wasn't a world without Saint Memphis presiding over it as a self appointed god. There just wasn't.

My heart was leaping and pounding in my chest with a desperate frantic ache which made me feel like I was tearing in two. Tatum needed me. But Saint would most certainly be dead if I didn't stop this fucking blood.

Heavy footsteps tore towards me and I looked up to find Kyan running back my way, his face a mask of deadly intent which promised bloodshed and butchery.

"Keep him alive," he barked at me as he passed, refusing to even look at Saint, like he didn't want to have to admit that it might already be too late for that. "I'm going to get our girl."

"How?" I demanded as I leaned back just enough to rip my shirt off so that I could ball it up and press it down on the bloody wound and staunch the bleeding better.

"Make a bargain with the devil himself if you have to," Kyan snarled as he kept running past me, heading straight for the cabin in the opposite direction to the way that Tatum had just been taken. "That cloven hoofed asshole won't want Saint coming down to hell to steal his throne anyway."

I released a noise which was part strangled laughter, part enraged refusal of reality and part pure fucking grief, but Kyan was already racing up the blood-soaked stairs to the cabin before disappearing inside.

"Don't die on me you hateful bastard," I snarled at Saint as I looked down at his almost peaceful face. Shit, he didn't even look evil in that moment and it was disconcerting as fuck.

Monroe's desperate yells were fading into the distance as he raced away after Tatum and that motherfucker who'd taken her on foot and I couldn't even see him between the trees down the track anymore.

Kyan reappeared with a set of keys in his grip, sprinting across the wooden deck before the cabin and launching himself off of it before leaping onto a bike I hadn't even noticed leaning against a tree to the side of the clearing.

"I'm getting her back whatever it takes," he said, not so much as an inch of doubt in his words and leaving me certain that he'd do it, no matter the cost. He laid the bloody baseball bat across his lap and jammed the keys into the ignition.

"Rip his fucking head off for me!" I yelled just as Kyan started the bike up and the roar of the engine broke the silence of the forest.

"I'll do worse than that," he swore and with a spray of dirt, he sped off down the track, leaving me alone with a dying man.

"*Fuck*, brother," I hissed, gazing at Saint's lifeless face as I continued to press down on the bullet wound as hard as I fucking could. "Don't leave us now."

With a curse, I leaned forward pressing down on the wound even harder in a desperate bid to stop the bleeding. The bullet was still in there and I had to hope that was a good thing because there wasn't an exit wound for me to contend with too. I just didn't know if it had hit anything too important on the way in.

He needed a fucking ambulance but we were lost in the middle of nowhere, surrounded by corpses and well beyond the range of any cell signal.

My arms trembled as I fought to staunch the wound and cursed myself as fear took hold of me and locked me in its iron grip. I couldn't lose anyone else. I couldn't.

"You are not allowed to die," I commanded. "You hear me, asshole? That's a fucking rule and I know how much you love abiding by those. *You are not allowed to die.*"

The roar of the motorbike's engine being pushed to its limits faded away into the distance until it was just me and him, alone in the dark and bleeding. And I just had to pray that fate wasn't ready to fuck us quite yet.

Tatum was out there somewhere counting on us. And Saint was counting on me. We wouldn't let either of them down. The five of us had made our vows and sealed our fate. We belonged together and if I had to walk through the nine circles of hell to make sure we all stayed that way then I'd gladly do it.

Saint Memphis wasn't going to die on my watch. I fucking refused to let it happen. And when a Night Keeper decided something, not even the will of the gods could change it.

CHAPTER TWO

I stared at the man who'd murdered my father, who'd shot and run over Saint, who'd destroyed my world within minutes. He was my death. I could see it in the depths of his eyes, could see him working out the details already, his tongue whipping out to wet his lips as he thought over what he'd do to me first.

His gun was pointing at me across his lap, but his focus was waning now, lost to his fantasy. The car sped along a dark road and the silence between us was piercing. I let him fall deeper into a sense of security, let him think I'd given up. But fuck that.

His hand moved from his gun to rearrange the bulge in his pants and adrenaline pounded through my limbs. I twisted in my seat fast and kicked the gun from his lap with a yell of determination. It crashed into his footwell and Mortez swore, but I didn't hesitate before kicking him again, my booted heel slamming down into the centre of his crotch and crushing his junk, making him cry out in agony.

My pulse pounded harder as the car swerved violently. I spun around fast, grabbing the door handle, pulling and twisting and yanking it as it still refused to unlock and I cursed Monroe for his choice of vehicle and its dodgy fucking doors. *Open please, please!*

It suddenly swung wide, making my heart soar with victory and Mortez lunged forward to try and grab a fistful of my hair. He missed.

"No!" he roared as I flung myself out without a thought, needing to escape no matter what kind of landing awaited me. The car bumped up a verge and I slammed onto grass, praising my luck as I rolled even though pain still burst along my back. "Bitch!"

I got to my feet, panic making my breaths come heavily as I scrambled upright and took off into the dark trees beside the road. The car revved and headlights suddenly cut through the dark, illuminating me between the trunks and making fear wheel through me. I glanced over my shoulder, finding he'd parked the car, facing it towards the forest, the driver's door thrown wide as he got out.

A gunshot cut through the air and a scream of fear escaped me as I ducked instinctively. I felt nothing. No bullet tearing through flesh and bone, no heated metal driving into my body. So I ran like the hounds of hell were at my heels, but it was worse than that, far fucking worse.

"You wanna play with me, darlin'?!" Mortez roared, his boots crunching twigs and dead leaves beneath his feet as he took chase.

I veered away from the headlights, desperate to be swallowed by the dark, needing to get as far and deep into this woodland as I possibly could. My heart leapt as another bullet was fired and I swear my hair stirred in the air as it rushed past me. *Fuck. Too close.*

I made it to a steep hill, racing down it and leaving the light of the car far behind me at last. My breaths sounded too loud in my ears, even the drum of my pulse was like a claxon. Every footfall was a giveaway. I was sound embodied. He'd hear me, find me, rape me, kill me - *no. He won't. If he catches me, I'll fight. I'll win.*

I passed tree after tree, but his footsteps were still coming. My nightmare. My death. I could hear the heavy drag of his breaths even from here. Every one of my senses was alight. I was prey to a predator, but that wasn't right. That wasn't who I was. I wouldn't be hunted down in the dark like a frightened doe running from a wolf. *Not again.*

I darted behind a huge tree and slammed my back to it, pressing a hand to my mouth and falling entirely still. I needed to circle back, had to get to the Night Keepers. How far away were they now? Maybe they were coming, maybe they weren't far. Maybe all I needed to do was waste enough time until they got here. But my gut told me I didn't have long enough for that. The car had travelled too far from the cabin. I was on my own. And I had to be ready to face this monster who'd taken my father from me, carved a hole between his eyes. Eyes which had looked at me with love and pride and adoration. Eyes that would never see me again.

I stooped down and found a branch on the ground, hefting it into my grip before standing upright again and swallowing down my fear. I was a fighter, I was the girl my father had raised me to be and I wouldn't cower away like a rabbit in a hole. I was going to show this motherfucker exactly who he was dealing with.

"Come out here, sweet thing!" Mortez's voice made me wince. He was *so* close. I didn't dare move, didn't dare take a single breath no matter how much my lungs burned. "I promise you this, it'll hurt less if you give up now. If not...well, I'll make you suffer real bad, darlin'. I'll break a few bones before I find out what all those boys are chasing one pussy for. Then I'll cut off all your pretty fingers and toes before I even think about ending your sufferin'. So what'll it be?"

I heard him approaching the tree I was hidden behind and my fingers tightened around the damp wood in my hands. My muscles were bunched tight, coiled like a spring. Every ounce of strength I possessed was ready to be unleashed in this one blow.

The flashlight on his phone wheeled across the ground to my right so I angled myself that way, trying not to tremble as his footsteps closed in on that very spot.

One hard, furious blow could knock him to the ground. A second to the head could finish him. I just had to make the first one count. Once he was down, I wouldn't stop hitting until it was done. Until his blood stained the ground and he stopped twitching. I'd make him hurt, make him scream, make him *pay*.

My fear gave way to a pure and primal desire to avenge my family. This man had killed my father, killed Saint. He would pay for that. He would suffer and cry and no one would come to his aid. I felt the monster in me take over, a creature which had no morals, only a hunger for blood and death and revenge. I'd never felt its full embrace before, just a dark energy that had sometimes possessed me. I had a soul which matched those of the Night Keepers, that called to theirs in the way theirs called to mine. We were the same in this one, fundamental way, I just hadn't realised it until now. Not until everything had been taken from me and I'd seen my father bleeding on the floor beneath me. Lifeless. Dead. *Gone*.

"Come out, pretty pretty." Mortez stepped past the tree and I swung the branch, silent as the wings of death as it wheeled ferociously toward his head. It smashed into his face and he yelled out as he stumbled back, his foot catching on a tree root so he fell to the ground.

I went for his head again, but he brought up the gun and I was forced to change direction, smacking his hand instead with a yell of anger. The gun went off and the sound of the shot ricocheted through my ears. But I wasn't dead. The bullet was somewhere in the sky.

The gun tumbled over the ground and I brought the branch down again with a shriek of determination. Mortez flung up his arm and the branch broke against it, shattering in my hands.

He lunged at me with a feral growl, throwing his full weight forward. I tried to twist away, but his arms locked around my legs and I crashed to the ground beneath him.

I rolled over and tore at his face with my fingernails as he crawled over me, pinning me down with his huge body, his heated breath warming my frozen cheeks as he reared forward.

"You fucking whore," he spat and hot, wet blood dripped onto my cheeks from the wound on his forehead.

I shoved at his shoulders, clawing and writhing and kicking and trying to get him off me, but his weight alone was immobilising.

His hand locked around my throat and he squeezed hard to choke away my screams. He ran his tongue over my mouth, across my cheek and up to my ear. I squirmed as bile rose in my throat, my limbs locking tight in disgust at his touch.

"I'm gonna make sure it hurts now, sweet thing. I wonder if you'll scream for your daddy?" he panted in my ear.

He released my throat, reaching for his waistband and I reared up and headbutted him as hard as I could. Pain splintered through my forehead and my skull rang from the impact as he lurched back with a wail, his nose shattered and pouring blood.

"Fuck!" he roared, his hands flying to his face and I pressed my advantage, slamming my fists out, one snapping into his gut and the other into his throat.

He lifted enough of his weight off of me and I slammed my foot into his gut as I pulled myself free, knocking him back onto his ass in the dirt and buying myself a few precious seconds. I managed to get to my feet and I lunged towards the gun which was illuminated by the light of Mortez's phone abandoned beside him on the ground.

I snatched it from the mud, twisting around and aiming it at him with my heart leaping. He was on his knees, staring up at me with wide eyes and I took a step toward him as victory crashed through my body.

I pressed the barrel to his forehead, my upper lip peeling back as a cold, calm detachment took over me. I wasn't afraid to pull the trigger. I wanted to do it. I ached to fucking do it.

"You took away my only family," I hissed, my voice not even sounding like mine in that moment. It sounded terrifying. Merciless.

I clenched my jaw and thought of Dad. Then I pulled the trigger.

Mortez winced as a loud click rang out.

Fucking empty.

No.

Half a laugh escaped him before I cut it off with a furious blow to his head, using the butt of the gun as a club. He fell back in shock and I didn't stop coming, not hesitating for a moment, not allowing him any chance to get the upper hand again. I dropped down to straddle him, whacking and whacking while his fists pounded into my flesh. I couldn't feel the pain, I couldn't feel anything but that gun shattering his skull and the way his screams tangled in the air like the purest kind of music. I was filled with hate and vengeance and acid.

The fight went out of him, but I didn't stop there. I beat and beat and beat until blood coated me and there was nothing left of his face. It was only then I realised I was screaming. My throat was ripped raw as I let out every piece of pain this man had caused me tonight, let it tear through my body and fill the night with the sound. Tears mixed with the blood on my cheeks; I was soaked in his death, the scent of it everywhere. I looked exactly like I'd felt on the inside when Mortez had pulled the trigger against my dad, when he'd slammed the car into Saint. He'd taken too much from me and destroying him wasn't enough. But I still didn't stop beating the gun into his mangled face. I couldn't stop.

CHAPTER THREE

T he piece of shit bike that had belonged to Tatum's dad snarled and whined beneath me as I sped along the road, ignoring its protests as I pushed it to its limits. I didn't give a shit if the engine exploded beneath me so long as I made it to my girl before that happened.

Cold wind bit at my cheeks and chilled the wet blood splatters against my skin as I rode hard and fast but I was finally rewarded for my efforts by the sight of headlights drawing my attention on the road ahead of me.

I raced up behind Monroe's car, the 68 Mustang half up on the bank, its headlights casting the shadows aside between the thick trees to the left of the road.

My own headlight illuminated the empty seats inside it and the wide, open doors made it clear that no one was here.

An all too familiar scream caught my attention as I hit the brakes and the bike came skidding to a halt on the gravel at the side of the road, causing me to drag the heel of my boot along the asphalt to stop the whole thing from spinning out.

I cut the bike's engine, leaping off it and letting it drop to the road with a heavy crash before racing into the trees.

I could hear Tatum screaming somewhere in the dark, and it felt like my entire soul was screaming with her as my grip on the bat in my hand tightened and I raced towards her.

The ground sloped away steeply, the light from the car's headlights quickly getting left behind as I descended into the forest and chased after my girl. Every step I took felt like a torture of a specific kind, the raw, brutal pounding of my heart calling out to her with a desperate kind of plea for her to hold on just a little longer.

I'm coming baby. Just keep fighting for me.

It took everything in me not to call out to her to let her know I was coming, to keep my presence hidden so that I could sneak up on that motherfucker and end him before he even knew I was here. Because if he really thought he could hunt my girl in the dark and not fall prey to the monster in me, then he was about to find out exactly what I was made of when you cut away the bullshit.

Because once you dug beneath my skin, I was all deep, dark, primal violence and I fed my soul on the taste of blood. I'd been raised with the anger of a cornered wolf and the mercy of a starving viper. Nothing in this world could stop me from destroying him now.

I ran at full speed towards the sounds of her screams, and the closer I drew, the more my skin prickled as I heard something in them that was just as dark and brutal as the fury that lived in me.

I burst between the trees with my bat held high, ready to cave his fucking head in and found her instead. Tatum Rivers, the girl who'd sworn to be mine, who had made me hers through chains of passion and fate, who had never once backed down from a fight or caved to the evil in us, finally revealed to be the creature born of nightmares which I'd always known she was.

She was coated in blood, the bright red colour staining her skin and painting her as a queen of death to be worshipped as she stood over the body of the man she'd killed, her chest heaving and eyes wild as she looked up and

22

found me there. No doubt I was stained in death as heavily as she was, the two of us a pair of bloodied, broken souls who had found each other in the dark.

The body laying at her feet was clearly dead, the lifeless corpse bloodied and battered as she stood over him in victory and I swear I fell for her even more as I remained rooted to the spot, staring at her drenched in the blood of her enemy.

Her gaze met mine and a beat of silence passed between us as she realised I'd come to rescue her and I accepted that she hadn't needed me to. Not that it would stop me from coming for her again every time she needed me.

I dropped my bat and she dropped the gun in her fist as I took three long strides to close the distance between us and caught her jaw in my grasp.

Tatum sucked in a sharp breath as her bright blue eyes widened a moment before my mouth claimed hers.

A growl of pure, carnal, violent need swept through me as I tasted her, my tongue pushing between her lips and swallowing the gasp of surprise which came from her as I stole our first kiss. But if I was a thief then she was the most precious gemstone known to man and she was putting up no protest at me taking her.

I could taste her soul between the movement of our lips, feel her pain as she gripped my biceps and dug her nails in hard enough to make my own blood join what coated my flesh. She was pure and light and empty and dark, this fucked up little creature who was so close to breaking that I could feel it in every place I touched her. But she wouldn't break. Not now or ever. She was the fiercest, strongest, most defiant girl I'd ever met and there was nothing in this world or the next that could cast her to ruin.

Her teeth sank into my bottom lip and I wasn't even sure if the blood I could taste was mine or that of the men we'd just killed, and I didn't care. Because this kiss was more than just a kiss. It was an oath and a vow and a promise I intended to keep until death came and ripped me from this world kicking and screaming and cursing for the rest of time. I was her creature now.

I was a man on his knees in the rain and a monster hiding in the dark and I was hers to command at will.

She had taken ownership of my twisted, fucked up being and I would willingly dive into hellfire and beyond at her command, just to make her happy.

Her hands slid to the back of my neck until she was fisting my hair and pulling me closer, driving some of her own pain into me and claiming me as hers once and for all. There was no going back for us now and we both knew it. This was the final wall dividing us and we were tearing it down like it had never been constructed at all.

When I'd fought the urge to kiss her like this all of those times before now, it had been purely for her own good. She was better off away from me. Better off hating me and cursing me and aching for my pain. But now that I'd seen her in her darkest moment, I knew that holding out on her hadn't been doing a damn thing to stop her from owning me. And I was done holding back. I was her beast to use, destroy and punish and I'd give my life for hers before I'd ever see her hurt again.

We broke apart and she looked up at me with a feral kind of hunger which had me aching for more and more of her. I wished the world would fade away. I wished we could just put time on hold and forget about my brother bleeding out and needing us and forget about the dead men filling the forest so that I could claim her fully here and now. I wanted to bring our bodies together coated in the blood of our enemies and the pain of our grief. But if I did, it meant I was giving up on Saint. And I'd die before I did that.

"My monster," Tatum breathed as she looked up at me in the moonlight, painted in blood for her.

"Always," I agreed in a rough voice which I hoped conveyed to her the truth of that vow before snatching her hand and pulling her close to me.

I hooked the baseball bat from the ground and grabbed the cell phone which was laying amongst the dead leaves beside the corpse before switching it off and shoving it in my pocket. I gave the area another slow glance to make sure there was nothing else worth taking then grabbed her hand and set off

24

back up the hill towards the road.

We were seriously fucked. There was no way that we could cover this up ourselves, let alone get Saint the help he needed as quickly as he needed it...assuming the worst hadn't already happened.

But I refused to believe that, because I was sure I would have felt it if he'd died. The Night Keeper oaths we'd made might have seemed like bullshit sometimes, but one thing was for sure in my mind. They'd bound our souls together. And if his had moved on from this place then I just knew that I'd know it. I'd feel it in my gut like a piece of my twisted heart had been ripped from my flesh and burned to nothing.

"Saint?" Tatum asked as I pulled her into a fast pace and I could hear the fear in her voice.

"Alive," I snarled, daring her or the universe or whoever the fuck else might want to get involved to try and question me on that.

Her fingers tightened on mine and a choked sob of relief escaped her lips at my words.

I could feel her cracking, the adrenaline from the fight fading from her body and reality coming down on her hard and fast as she was forced to face everything that had happened tonight. And I got the feeling I didn't even know the half of it.

I turned to her and lifted her into my arms without a word, cradling her against my chest as I could feel her shocked gaze on my face, but I just kept moving back towards the road.

"Tatum!" Monroe bellowed as we approached the edge of the trees and I stepped out onto the road just as he sprinted up to the car.

"She's here, she's okay," I called back as his gaze fell on us and the frantic look in his eyes made me pause.

He was drenched in sweat from running this whole way and he didn't slow as he ran straight up to us and I let Tatum slide from my grip.

Monroe caught her face between his hands, tipping her chin back as he inspected her, his thumbs smearing the blood on her cheeks as he reassured himself it wasn't hers. Then he ran his hands down her sides, checking her arms, hands, waist, dropping to his knees before her as he inspected her legs, making absolutely certain that she wasn't injured before releasing a groan of relief and pressing his head to her stomach.

"I'm alright," Tatum reassured him, her hands stroking his blonde hair in a soothing motion that stained it with the blood of the man she'd killed.

He stood suddenly, his lips capturing hers as he wrapped her tight in his arms like he never wanted to let go again and my brows shot up as she melted into him.

I hadn't had a moment to consider why the fuck he'd been out in that cabin with her without his damn shirt on until this very second, but looking at them now made it undeniably clear. Apparently all of the Night Keepers were just as obsessed with our girl as each other and all of the protests he'd made before now to the contrary had just been bullshit designed to hide what was now painfully obvious.

Monroe pulled back suddenly like he'd just remembered I was here. That he was a teacher and she was his student and that was the biggest secret we would all have to keep after tonight.

I wanted to be angry about it. I wanted to roar and snarl and stake my claim and tell him to back the fuck off of my girl.

But she wasn't my girl, was she? She'd sworn herself to all of us and just because I was giving myself to her alone, didn't mean she'd be doing the same. I'd already known about what she had with Blake and I'd seen what lived between her and Saint. And if I really did want to buy into the story of who we all were and who we claimed to be then maybe I was going to have to accept that this was the way it was. The way it was always meant to be.

"That's how it is then?" I asked to confirm it, pinning Monroe in my glare as I dared him to make this mean any less than it had to if he expected me to share my girl with him.

Monroe swallowed thickly, his gaze slipping from me to Tatum as he held her hand tightly, clearly waiting for me to lose my mind over this truth.

But I could see it now, burning so bright that I must have been blind to miss it before. He was as captured by our queen as the rest of us.

"Yeah," Monroe said, raising his chin defiantly as he faced off against me. "This is how it is."

"What are you going to do?" Tatum asked and I blew out a breath as I pulled my cell phone from my pocket.

"Something I wish I didn't have to," I replied as I moved to make the call I'd sworn I'd never make. But all of the vows and oaths and declarations meant shit if they put my girl at risk and if they might equal the death of my brother.

"You can't tell anyone about us," Monroe snarled, catching my wrist in an iron grip like he was planning to tear my cell phone from my grasp.

"I'm not going to," I said, tearing my arm back out of his hold. "I'll keep your little secret, you can trust me on that. What I need to do now is sort this shit out. We've got a massacre and a dying man on our hands and I'm guessing you don't have any way to help us deal with that. So you can drive us back to the others while I make this call."

I stalked away from him and his suspicious looks and climbed into the back of his Mustang as I stared down at my phone like it was a ticking bomb about to go off in my face.

Monroe rolled the bike I'd ridden here out of the road and shoved it into the trees as I hesitated with my thumb over the call button. Why did doing this one simple thing feel like signing my own death sentence?

Tatum moved around the car and climbed into the passenger seat, turning to look over her shoulder at me with fear in her eyes.

"What are you doing?" she asked me as my gaze roamed over the blood on her skin.

"Fixing this," I said in a rough voice as I held back on the entire truth. *Selling my soul to the devil for you, baby.*

Her lips parted but I hit dial before she could ask any more and Monroe leapt into the car, starting the engine and turning us back towards the cabin.

27

It only rang twice before it connected and my uncle's amused laughter came down the speaker, sending a curl of rage dancing through my limbs.

"I knew you couldn't keep running from ya family, Kyan lad," Niall said, seeming like a jolly fool despite the fact that he was the most dangerous man I knew.

"I've never run from a thing in my damn life," I growled and Monroe met my gaze in the rear-view mirror for a moment like he'd just figured out exactly who I was calling. I'd told him enough about my family during our training sessions for him to have some understanding of how little I wanted to be having this conversation with them. But I'd do it for Saint. For her. This family of five I'd found for myself were worth any sacrifice I had to make. Certainly worth far more than the people who had brought me into this fucked up world.

"Pa will be so pleased to know you're back in the fold," Niall replied, ignoring my words as I felt the leash wrap tight around my throat like I'd always known it would again one day, no matter how much I'd ached to leave it behind.

"Well the price of my return is a doctor and a clean up," I said, swallowing down my hatred for my family with as much disdain as I could manage even though I knew I was losing the only shot I'd ever really had at escaping them.

Niall was the only one amongst them who I had even an ounce of respect for and that was mainly because I knew he only ever killed people he felt truly deserved it. Despite that prerequisite to his violent tendencies he was the most bloodthirsty and arguably the most deranged member of my genetically related family. He certainly had the most blood on his hands and would most definitely be the one sent after me if I ever pushed my grandpa too far and outlived my usefulness. Still, there was something about the psychotic bastard that I liked in my own fucked up way. And if I had to call on any of them for this favour then he was always going to be my uncle of choice.

Tatum was still watching me as we raced back down the road, but I didn't look at her. I didn't want her to see me selling myself out even if it was the only choice we had right now.

"How many bodies?" Niall asked, sounding more amused by the second as he realised I was buying my way back in with death.

"I lost count," I said honestly and he laughed louder, clapping his hands in excitement.

"I knew you had the O'Brien blood running hot in ya veins, lad," he cooed. "Just send me your location and I'll have it dealt with."

"The doctor needs to be fast," I demanded.

"Don't fret, lad. I'll forward the location of the best nearby when I know where you are and make sure he's ready and waiting when you get there. What are we dealing with?"

"He was hit by a car and shot," I ground out, fighting to keep my emotions locked down, though the fact that I was asking for a doctor for Saint would tell my family all about how much he meant to me anyway. But that didn't matter right now. I just needed to focus on making sure he stayed alive. All that followed would just have to fall on my shoulders when it did and I'd bear the weight of it then. There wasn't any price I wouldn't pay for my brother's life.

"Consider it done," Niall said happily. "And I look forward to seeing you and your girl for Christmas."

The line went dead and I dropped the phone into my lap with a curse of frustration. If there was any other way at all for me to have fixed this then I would have done it. But my family were the only people fucked up enough to deal with this shit for us effectively. And with so much of Saint's blood staining the ground I knew I couldn't risk law enforcement finding the scene of this massacre. There would be too much evidence available to link back to us.

"Who was that?" Tatum demanded and I looked into her blue eyes as I fixed an impenetrable mask over my features and shrugged.

"Just some people who can get rid of all this evidence for us," I replied evenly.

"What about my dad?" she asked, her voice hitching. "What will they do with his body?"

I opened my mouth to tell her he'd be disposed of like the rest, hacked up and dissolved in acid most likely. The evidence of everything he'd ever been destroyed and lost forevermore. But the look of raw pain in her eyes made something twist sharply in my gut and I hesitated. I might not have given a shit about my family, but it was clear that she did about hers. And if I was giving myself to her then that meant protecting her against anything that could hurt her, even if the pain wasn't physical.

"I'll make sure they give him a grave," I told her in a low voice, knowing that would only indebt me to my family further but feeling like it was the only real choice I could make. "A proper one you can visit. Somehow."

Her eyes filled with tears but they didn't spill over as she blinked hard and looked back to the road wordlessly.

I shot a quick message to Niall forwarding our coordinates and relaying the message to preserve Donovan Rivers' body. His response was instant.

Niall:

That'll cost ya, lad.

Kyan:

I know.

Monroe finally slammed the brakes on as we made it back to Blake and Saint and I leapt out of the car, my gaze raking over the still form of my brother as he lay dying in the dirt while Blake held pressure on the wound through pure force of will.

"Is he...?" Tatum began as she leapt out of the car, her eyes wild with fear while Blake looked up at her in clear relief. He didn't waste time asking about the motherfucker who had taken her. He knew full well that we wouldn't have left him breathing.

"He's alive," Blake growled. "Just about."

30

"I have a doctor waiting for us," I said, moving forward to take Saint's keys from his pocket. "Let's get his stubborn ass there before he bleeds out and comes back to haunt us for fucking this up."

No one laughed at my shitty joke and Tatum dropped down beside Blake to help him however she could. Monroe was looking at Saint with a dark intensity to his gaze which had my hackles rising, but as quickly as I thought I'd seen it, it was gone again.

"Take me to his car," I commanded as I moved back to the Mustang. "We hid it back by the road. We're going to need to keep pressure on that wound for the journey and there's no room in your piece of shit for that."

"It's a classic," Monroe growled but he didn't voice any further complaint as we leapt into the Mustang once more and raced away to get Saint's car.

Then all we had to do was drive to whatever off the books doctor Niall found for me and hope to fuck that Saint could pull through. But I wasn't going to give the alternative any space in my mind. Because Saint Memphis was as permanent as the rage in my soul and the violence in my veins. Besides, he'd never let some piece of shit nobody like that asshole be the death of him. He was far too proud for that.

CHAPTER FOUR

T he doctor had let us into a private clinic in some unknown town when we arrived several hours ago. I hadn't been able to focus on where we were, I'd only been able to focus on Saint and how still he was. The man had taken him inside with a bunch of nurses, all of them wearing masks and gloves. They hadn't let the rest of us into the building until they'd checked our temperatures and asked if we had any symptoms or been in contact with anyone we didn't know recently. None of us mentioned the group of armed men we'd all just been fighting and getting way too close to, and I didn't even want to think about the fact that we'd been put at risk of contamination on top of everything else. Or, I guess that wasn't entirely true, was it? Because according to one of the many bombs that had been dropped on my head tonight, I was actually immune. But I just didn't have the energy to think on that right now while I was so caught up worrying over Saint.

I stood in a white-walled waiting room with fluorescent lights beaming down on me, so blindingly bright that they seemed to blaze right into my skull. Worry ate into my chest like locusts feasting on my insides. I was in purgatory waiting to find out if Saint would live. To hear how bad his injuries were.

I found myself looking at Blake, Monroe and Kyan, their eyes locked on me like I was the centre of their world. I'd heard Monroe quietly explaining to them what had happened in the cabin, how Mortez had killed my dad and gotten a hold of me. And the way their expressions twisted at what I'd witnessed made me adore them even more.

A whimper of need escaped me as I moved towards them and as one they closed in around me, their bodies crushing me into the middle of them as they held and caressed me and I sighed as I just let myself have this. I couldn't process everything that had happened yet, I just needed to feel their warmth surrounding me. But through everything, my pain and grief spilled over and tears washed down my cheeks as the loss of my dad cut into me so deeply that I could hardly breathe.

The blood covering me was drying against my skin like a film. I wanted to wash and scrub every piece of my flesh until I revealed a new girl beneath it. But I was afraid of the one I'd find there when I did.

After a while, I was drawn out of the group and found myself being pulled down into a chair, wrapped in Blake's arms as he held me against his firm chest, murmuring reassurances in my ear. I buried my face in his neck as he shared in my pain. He knew this grief, he'd lived it himself not long ago. And it seemed only right to fall apart in his arms because he was a mirror to my soul right now.

Monroe pressed a hand to my back as he stood close behind me and Kyan's hand wrapped firmly around mine as he took the seat beside Blake. I cried until the tears wouldn't come anymore and my heart retreated into a hardened shell, my pain easing a little. I felt hollow and exhausted and somehow that was worse. Like I could feel the absence of my dad now. A new hole carved into my chest, widening the gap that Jess had left when I'd lost her. My entire family were gone. The memories of my childhood, of all the days we'd spent together now resided solely in me. There was no one left in the world who shared my past. No single person who would ever reminisce with me, who would know the jokes we'd shared, the fun we'd had, the life we'd led. It was mine to carry, to relive. Alone.

I slid from Blake's lap at last and Monroe moved back a step as I passed him by and walked to the window, staring out at the paling sky. Dawn was coming. And I didn't want it to. I wanted to go back to the last time the sun had set and change everything. Make a thousand different choices. It seemed like when the sun rose, this night would be set in stone. But right now, it all just felt like a terrible nightmare I could still wake from, if only I knew how.

The guys were talking in low voices, but I couldn't distinguish the words and didn't really try. There was a buzzing in my ears, a wall dividing me from the world as I retreated further and further into myself. I couldn't feel anything, not the wooden windowsill where my hand lay or the temperature in the room. I just felt...nothing.

"Tatum," Monroe spoke and the word seemed to tear through that wall I was vanishing behind, bringing me back to life. I didn't turn to him, but I felt him move close behind me. The heat of his flesh called to me and as he closed the distance between us, I leaned back against him, realising I was frozen to the bone once his hands encircled me. "We have to stay here for forty eight hours to quarantine, then we can go home."

Home. The word choice seemed so strange. Everlake wasn't home. Home was my dad, home was Jess, home was where my heart was content. Everlake wasn't any of those things. But...Monroe was.

"Saint," I murmured, a note of fear in my tone.

The doctor opened the door across the room and my heart jolted as I turned to him in panic. He kept his mask in place as he looked at us, his scrubs flecked with blood.

"He's stable," he said and the strength went out of my body.

"Fuck," Monroe breathed, but with no grit to his voice like I expected. Shouldn't he have been unhappy that Saint was okay?

My shoulders sagged with relief then my whole body followed and I crouched low, taking in long breaths as that news washed through me. Blake clapped Kyan on the shoulder as the two them shared a relieved hug.

"I told you that bastard was too stubborn to die, baby," Kyan said, barking a laugh.

"Can I see him?" I asked.

"He's unconscious," the doctor explained.

"I still want to see him."

Monroe moved closer, pulling me to my feet and keeping a hand on my back.

The doctor nodded. "You can see him shortly, the nurses are just cleaning up."

"What's the prognosis doc?" Blake pushed.

"He's got a hairline fracture in his radius in the right arm and three broken ribs on the same side. The bullet didn't go through, so we've extracted it from his shoulder and stitched him up and given him a blood transfusion, some antibiotics and some fluids. Frankly, he's one lucky guy."

"Maybe if the bullet had been made of pure silver there'd have been more chance of it killing him," Blake joked, jumping on Kyan in his joy and my heart lifted a little.

"Yeah with a priest tossing holy water on him and casting him back to hell," Kyan agreed.

"Even then, he probably would have refused to die. His skin could have melted off of his bones, but he'd just have hung around as an angry poltergeist shouting at us whenever we fucked up his schedules," Blake joked.

Their teasing banter almost brought a smile to my face especially as I could feel the relief in the room like a physical thing.

The doctor exited the waiting room again and I rubbed my tired eyes, leaning against Monroe for support as we waited to be allowed in to see Saint.

The minutes seemed to stretch on and on, but the doctor finally returned, beckoning us in. "Two at a time," he insisted.

"Come on, baby. I'll take you." Kyan took my hand and I let my fingers trail over Monroe's arm in goodbye as he led me away.

Kyan felt so strong, his body like armour. I wanted to slide into it for a while and pretend I was as unshakeable as him. But even as I drew on that strength in him, I knew it could do nothing to repair my shattered heart. Or heal the gaping wound left by the death of my father. Nothing could shield me from that.

The scent of blood still hung in the air as we entered the room, but it was dulled by a chemical tang that hit the back of my throat. Saint was shirtless, the wound on his shoulder bandaged along with his ribs and an IV was stuck in his left arm while a sling held his right against his chest.

He looked so un-Saint lying there, his features soft in sleep, making him appear young, vulnerable. I pulled away from Kyan, leaning down to caress Saint's cheek and the tears came again as I remembered the stand this boy had made for me, placing himself in front of that car, the apology he'd spoken to me, though I didn't know what he'd meant it for exactly. I traced his cheekbone with my fingertips and sighed at the heat of his skin, the confirmation that his heart was beating even though it was clear from the beeping of the monitor in the room anyway. But I had to feel it too. I ran my hand down to his throat and his pulse thumped there almost angrily like it was determined to show the world just how alive he really was. And that almost brought a smile to my lips.

"It would take more than a bullet and a car to kill Saint Memphis," Kyan growled in my ear, like he'd never been worried for his friend. But I'd seen the panic in him as clear as day. Kyan's heartless act didn't fool me anymore. He had a heart, and it held a deep and unwavering kind of love for his friends.

When we'd all spent some time with him, the doctor offered to look over our cuts and bruises. Despite my body being aching and sore, I somehow hadn't broken anything even when I'd jumped out of the car. In fact, no one had anything too serious and I had to believe that was nothing short of a miracle.

We were offered a private ward with a shower and some scrubs to sleep in and time stretched out ahead of us for the quarantine period. Amongst all the fears I'd had tonight, I'd barely had time to worry that the Night Keepers could be infected. They'd exposed themselves for me, another risk which I could never repay them for. They'd faced death in every imaginable way for me and I knew it changed everything.

I laid with Saint in his bed back at The Temple in cream pyjamas. His IV was set up beside his bed and a list of instructions from the doctor sat on his nightstand. It wasn't even close to ideal and the fear that something might happen to him in our care made me worry. So I'd stayed with him, never left his side for even a second since we'd gotten back here last night after the quarantine period was up. At least we'd evaded that one threat and I knew for sure that all of them would be okay. He was on a bunch of sedatives to give his body time to recover and he'd only stirred a few times in the night, but he was off them now, so it was just a matter of time before he came back to us.

As the morning crept on, I curled up against him, keeping my hand on his chest, the rise and fall of it assuring me that I could rest for a few hours. I was desperate for him to wake up though, stirring at any movement he made so it was hard to relax. But just as I was about to drift off, he groaned.

"Tatum," he said, his voice as soft as a whisper, his breath feathering against my cheek. We couldn't get a shirt on him, so he just wore navy sweatpants and socks.

I jolted upright, looking down at him and his dark eyes widened as his gaze dragged over my features, the bruises, the nicks and cuts, taking stock of all of it as I just drowned in the depths of his irises.

"That asshole hurt you," he said darkly, venom in his tone.

"He's dead," I said, lifting my chin a little.

He sighed, relaxing, but he didn't take his eyes from the injuries lining my flesh.

"You're okay," I told him. "You got shot and you've got cracked ribs and a fracture in your right arm, but you're alright, Saint."

"Mm," he grunted like he didn't agree with that assessment and he immediately tried to get up, his brow creasing sharply as he jolted his ribs.

"Lay down," I gasped, pressing my hand to his uninjured shoulder to try and stop him, but he kept going, sliding out of bed and getting to his feet. Except his legs didn't hold and he crashed to his knees instantly, making the IV jerk toward him on its wheels as he tugged it.

"Saint!" I jumped out after him, trying to help him up. "You lost a lot of blood, and you're on a lot of medication, you need to rest."

"I'm fine. I can get up by myself," he insisted, but it was clear he couldn't.

"Just let me help," I pushed, but he continued to try and shake me off.

"What's the time?" he demanded, panic in his eyes.

I glanced at the clock behind me on the nightstand and frowned as I saw it was three minutes to nine.

"Nine am," I said immediately.

"Liar," he hissed, trying to crane his neck to look at it himself, but I moved to block his view.

Footsteps came pounding up the stairs and Blake appeared in a pair of black sweatpants, his eyebrows jumping up as he saw Saint on the floor. He jogged forward, scooping him up and placing him back on the bed. "Here you go, buddy."

"I'm not your buddy, get the fuck out of my way," Saint snarled.

"Ohh, he's an angry little buddy." Blake grinned widely, clearly pleased as hell to see his friend awake despite his tempestuous mood.

"You have to stay in bed," I demanded and Saint turned to me with his forehead lined. "Please. Stay. I'll get you what you need. I'll do whatever you tell me to."

His throat bobbed as he realised I was surrendering control to him, allowing him to boss me about, get whatever he wanted. The man had nearly died to save me after all. It was the least I could do to help him heal from his injuries.

He jerked his chin once in agreement. "I need a piss."

"The doc gave you a special gift for that." Blake hooked up the bedpan from the floor, waving it at him and Saint scowled darkly.

"I won't be pissing in a plastic bowl. Ever." Saint swung his legs over the edge of the bed again and I shared a look with Blake, a nod of agreement passing between us as we moved to help him stand.

He muttered curses at us all the way to the bathroom as we helped him walk there, the IV bobbing along on its stand as I brought it with us while he insisted he could do it himself before tugging it inside and kicking the door shut in our faces.

I turned to Blake just as he reached out and traced his thumb over a bruise on my cheek. "How are you, sweetheart?"

He didn't want the bullshit answer, I could tell. He could see my pain like it shone out of my eyes, so I gave him the honest truth. "Exhausted, heartbroken and sort of...numb too. None of it feels real. But it is...I know it is." I dropped my head, biting back the tears which threatened to spill over and Blake tipped my chin up to meet his gaze.

"Whenever you wanna talk, I'm here. I've got you, Tate. Just say the word." He leaned down and kissed my cheek, but I turned into it, hunting out the heat of his mouth on instinct. He drew me closer by the waist, his gentle touches soothing my frantic heartbeat as he kissed me sweetly, saying a thousand silent condolences that helped stitch me back together. At least for a little while.

We parted just before the door yanked open and Saint stood there clutching his IV stand looking pale. He gritted his teeth, moving forward as if to barrel through the middle of us, but we stepped back and each looped an arm around his waist before he could attempt it.

"Stop fussing," he snapped, but mostly at Blake I noticed.

We helped him back into bed all the same and Saint dismissed Blake as I helped prop him up with several pillows.

"Just shout if you need help with anything, Cinders," Blake said before heading off downstairs, rolling his eyes at Saint.

When I was done arranging Saint's bedding, I met his frustrated gaze and dropped down to kneel before him on the end of the mattress in a silent offering that said *what do you need me to do?*

"I'll take a single day's rest," Saint said matter-of-factly. "You can wait on me today and then tomorrow things will return to normal."

"Saint..." I sighed. Things weren't going to be normal for a long time for him. The doctor said his recovery could take weeks. He wouldn't be able to work out or play football or do any of his usual activities until he was completely healed, or he could cause himself permanent damage.

"Tatum," he growled in warning and I looked up at him with my heart in tatters. I realised I needed this too, I needed Saint to take over and tell me what to do right now because I had no idea how to put one foot in front of the other knowing my dad was no longer in the world. I didn't know who I was without him. I didn't know what the future looked like anymore or where I belonged. I felt trapped in an endless shadow that stretched out forever before me. And I couldn't escape it.

"Let's just focus on right now," I compromised, fisting my hands in the sheets as I tried not to let my thoughts slip too far into despair again, back to the moment Mortez had shot Dad, how he'd fallen beneath me and I'd seen so much nothing in his eyes. No amount of time would ever be enough to erase that image from my mind. "Tell me what to do. *Please*," my voice cracked and I dipped my head, lost. I was so lost. I was going to split apart into pieces if I didn't just do something. Anything.

"Tatum...what's going on?" he asked, his tone soft and thick with concern. It didn't sound much like Saint at all.

"My dad," I forced out, trying to say it with detachment but I couldn't manage it. "Mortez shot him. He's...he's dead." Saying it aloud was far worse than repeating it in my head a thousand times. It was suddenly so suffocatingly real that I wished I could take the words back, force them down my throat and never utter them again. A couple of thick tears rolled down my cheeks and I wiped them hurriedly away.

Saint was silent for the longest time. "I can't...imagine how you feel right now," he said in a measured voice like he really meant those words. "But if you need me to take control-"

"I do," I said fiercely, looking up at him. This language was one we both understood, one we both got something out of. It centred us. Our lack of control in our current situations was debilitating and this answer was a gift to each of us.

He nodded firmly, a flare of fire in his eyes. "Fetch breakfast for everyone. I'll have mine on a lap tray here and you will eat yours here too. Oatmeal with raisins and warm milk. A sprinkle of sugar too."

Sugar? He never gave me sugar. But the instructions were clear and I grasped onto them, rising from the bed and padding downstairs, glad to have something to focus on other than what had transpired at the cabin. Kyan was asleep on the couch and Monroe was dozing in a chair with a strained crease between his eyes.

I made everyone's usual food and decided on toast and eggs for Monroe as I'd seen him eat that a few times at his place. When I was laying out all the food on the table, about to take mine and Saint's upstairs, Monroe stirred from the armchair and stood up, blinking the sleep from his eyes.

"What are you doing?" he asked me, an urgent worry to his tone.

"Saint's awake. I made breakfast," I said with a small shrug and his eyes turned to darkest pitch.

"Saint!" he boomed, looking to the balcony. "She's been through too much, you are *not* ordering her around!"

"It's okay," I said firmly before Saint could answer. "I want to. I *need* to."

Monroe's brow pinched and he moved toward me, shaking his head. "Let me help," he said in a voice just for me. "Tell me what you need and I'll give it to you." The sincerity in his eyes was touching and I gave him a

42

grateful smile.

"I need to keep busy. But you can wake Kyan and fetch Blake so they can eat some food?" I suggested and his jaw pulsed a couple of times before he nodded, giving in.

I headed upstairs as he walked over to Kyan, prodding him in the side.

"I wouldn't do it for all the camels in the world," Kyan murmured as he swatted at the place Monroe had prodded him like a fly had landed there. Monroe jabbed him again and Kyan jerked awake, lunging at Monroe with a vicious upper cut that Monroe deflected at the last second.

"Calm down, Rambo," Monroe muttered. "Breakfast is ready."

Kyan got up, his eyes finding me as I slipped away up onto the balcony and a longing filled his gaze that made my skin tingle. The kiss we'd shared had been so potent that I could still feel it lingering on my lips now. It had driven away any doubt I'd ever had about his intentions towards me. He'd offered me a piece of his soul in that kiss and I'd offered him mine in return.

I set up Saint's food on a lap tray and settled myself down beside him with the covers over us both. I didn't want any pauses between each instruction. I needed tasks for every minute of this day or I was never going to make it through.

Saint struggled to cut his food one handed, his irritation growing as he cursed and growled in fury.

"Let me," I offered as I finished my oatmeal and he paused as he considered that before nodding.

I cut up his food, moving to kneel beside him then holding the fork out and guiding it into his mouth. He watched me closely as I worked and I fell into the rhythm of it, feeding him one mouthful after the other.

"The man who hurt you is lucky he's dead," Saint commented conversationally. "Or I would drain his blood one drop at a time and cut him into a thousand tiny pieces for the birds to devour."

"Your heart is showing. I didn't realise you had one until you started bleeding so much," I mused.

"I'm bound to you, Tatum, dead or alive. And I would stand between you and the fires of hell to protect what is mine."

I tilted my head to one side as I took in his fierce expression, the raging inferno in his eyes. How had I thought he was so lifeless and cold when I'd first met him? There was so much fire in him right now, it was almost blinding. My stomach squeezed at his words. Words which I never could have imagined him saying to me, let alone imagine this warm response I had to them. "You already did, Saint."

I woke the next day to loud classical music playing over the speakers hidden behind Saint's bed. I must have somehow slept through it for a while because it was in the middle of a song I recognised as one of Saint's favourites. I pushed myself upright, finding the place beside me empty. Saint's IV had been taken out and my gut dropped as I realised he was nowhere in sight. On the end of the bed was a black pair of pants and a pink shirt waiting for me to put on and I cursed as I got up, hurrying downstairs through the empty lounge as I figured out where the sound was coming from.

I headed on down into the crypt, shoving the door open and finding Saint holding his uninjured arm over a bench as he did bicep curls with a heavy weight, cursing through his teeth as it made the muscles in the rest of his body tense up and jolt his injuries.

"Saint, are you crazy?!" I ran over to him in alarm, prising the weight from his hand and dropping it to the ground with a thunk.

"This is my routine," he snapped, a well of darkness opening up in his eyes as I dared defy him over this.

"You were shot and hit by a damn car," I said in exasperation. "If you push yourself, you're going to make your injuries worse. And then you won't heal right and your shoulder will be fucked up forever. Is that what you want?"

"I want things to go back to normal," he snarled, striding over to a weight rack and hobbling a little from the various cuts and bruises that covered his body.

"They aren't going back to normal. Not now. Not anytime soon. And not ever if you don't rest," I demanded.

He tsked, picking up another weight in his left hand. "I don't need rest, I need my routine."

Blake suddenly appeared through the door, huffing a breath of annoyance as he spotted Saint with the weight in his hand. He pointed at him with his teeth bared. "No working out. You don't get to almost die on us then fuck up your recovery." He charged over to Saint, wrestling the weight out of his grip and tossing it back in the rack. "Get back upstairs."

Saint got in Blake's face, knocking his forehead against his. "Don't tell me what to do, motherfucker." His threat was somewhat weakened by the paleness of his face and the shaking of his body. He really wasn't well.

"I'll *make* you do it in a second," Blake growled back.

"This isn't helping," I insisted, moving forward and pressing a hand to Blake's chest to warn him off before looking to Saint. "Why don't we go for a walk? We can keep to your exercise schedule. But you can't do this."

Saint's eyes moved to me and Blake's gaze seemed to say Saint shouldn't even be doing that. And I had to agree. But this was a compromise we could make.

"Fine," Saint finally gave in, taking my hand and guiding me towards the door, even though he was moving about as fast as an old man in need of a zimmer frame. If we really were going for a walk, he wasn't going to get far. But I supposed we just needed to walk for as long as his normal workout routine would have lasted for him not to lose his mind completely.

I left him in the lounge, hurrying upstairs and putting on the pants and shirt he'd left out for me before tugging my coat on. I kicked on my pumps and grabbed some headphones for Saint at the last minute, setting them up with his phone and hurrying downstairs to him.

"Here," I said, putting the headphones in for him and pressing play so his classical music blared in his ears.

He very almost smiled as I led him to the door and helped him into a warm jacket, guiding one arm into the sleeve and leaving the other one in its sling as I zipped the coat up over it. I glanced down at his sneakers, realising the laces were just hanging out as he'd obviously been unable to bend down and tie them. My heart tugged as I knelt down, doing them up for him and when I glanced up at him, he drew in a deep breath that said he was starting to relax.

I took his hand as I stood, leading him outside into the cold air and walking at his pace as he moved determinedly along the path.

After a while, he seemed to fall into a trance with the music in his ears and our slow but continuous pace along the lakeshore. I made sure we started heading back towards The Temple in time for seven thirty. If we didn't do this exactly to his schedule he was going to freak.

"You should go ahead and make breakfast," Saint said, taking one earphone out so he could hear my response.

"I'm not leaving you alone out here, you'll probably try running then fall over and break your good arm."

He actually released a small laugh at that, his fingers squeezing mine. "Okay," he agreed and my eyebrows arched in surprise.

"As easy as that?"

"None of this is easy," he muttered.

I nodded, wholeheartedly agreeing as my heart squeezed painfully.

"All of this makes me feel so fucking...mortal," he said with a grimace.

"You know you are mortal, right?" I teased a little, though it was hard to muster a smile. "Just blood, flesh and bone like the rest of us. I was surprised too."

He chuckled softly and the sound was new, warm, inviting. It made me want to lean closer to him, but I didn't.

"There's something I need to do today," I said after a while, my throat tightening. He remained quiet as he waited for me to explain. "My dad," I cleared my throat as the pain welled up again, moving hurriedly on. "He left me some papers. I need to look through them. He wanted me to get them to your father. I think it will prove his innocence."

Saint stilled and I glanced at him as his features pinched in confusion.

"His innocence?" he rasped.

"He didn't do it, Saint. Like I always said." I lifted my chin, staring up at this man who had punished me for the crimes of my father. But they weren't even his crimes. He'd never intended for the virus to be released and I wasn't going to let him take the blame for that, especially as he wasn't around to speak for himself now. "If you don't believe me, then-"

"I didn't say that," he cut me off, his tone gruff. "I want to see the evidence."

I nodded, my jaw locked as we headed back to The Temple and his face fixed into an expression of contemplation. Would he feel guilty for bullying me if he knew my father was innocent? Was Saint Memphis even capable of feeling guilt?

I released his hand as we stepped inside and turned to him, finding him struggling to get out of his coat with a look of irritation on his face. A twisted part of me wanted to watch him struggle for a moment, reminded of what he'd put me through over the Hades Virus, but he looked so damn infuriated that I sighed and gave in, tugging it from his shoulders. He didn't thank me as he stalked inside, his pride too important to him for that.

I walked after him, finding Monroe had arrived looking tired with bags under his eyes and a heaviness about his aura. He wore jeans and a white shirt which I realised was inside out, but I didn't have the heart to point it out to him. The tightness of his features said he was still worried about me and I wished I could just have a moment with him alone to fall apart in his arms. As it was, the only way I could focus was by taking orders from Saint and keeping myself moving from one job to another.

Blake pulled out Saint's chair for him as he made it to the dining table and Saint cursed him as he sat down but didn't lay into him any more than that. Blake shook his head at him behind his back before heading over to the coffee machine and setting it up.

"What do you think you're doing? That's Tatum's job," Saint growled and Monroe scowled.

"If you keep using that tone with her, I'll break one of your legs and triple your recovery time," Monroe snarled, a monster peering from his eyes.

I looked to Saint curiously and he pursed his lips.

"Tatum, do the coffee," Saint insisted and an endless pause passed where Monroe took a threatening step towards him. "Please," he bit out so harshly it almost sounded like a curse. I swallowed a laugh, surprised and kind of impressed by Monroe for managing to get through to the beast. But I guessed Saint wasn't in the best position to argue right now.

I headed to the kitchen, taking over from Blake, but he remained there, his hands brushing my back, his lips meeting my shoulder. He was all tenderness and sweetness since we'd gotten back here, and I couldn't deny how good it felt to have him comfort me like that. He never probed me for my thoughts, just hugged and kissed me in the moments I needed it most. The gap between tasks where I found too much space to think.

The hot press of his lips to my neck sent a blaze of desire down my spine and I sighed needily.

"Sit the fuck down, Blake, stop distracting her," Saint commanded and Blake laughed as he drew away from me, heading over to sit in his seat. Monroe dropped down beside him, leaving a space for Kyan between them. Did he even realise how smoothly he'd slid into their little group? He was like the missing piece they'd been waiting for.

I passed out coffee and received thanks from all of them before I set to work on breakfast. Monroe asked me several times if I needed help, but I insisted I didn't, wanting to stick to this routine just like Saint did. It felt normal. Like something to cling onto in this sea of fucking misery. My life wasn't the same anymore. But I could pretend it was and hold onto the last remnants of my sanity by doing menial tasks.

Kyan appeared just before I finished placing down plates and he scratched at his inked chest, yawning as he crossed the room.

"Morning, baby." He caught me by the waist, twisting me into his chest and nuzzling against my neck where there were fingerprint bruises from Mortez. He breathed in deep, raking his mouth across those marks in furious kisses and I shivered in surprise.

"Kyan," I gasped and he dragged his mouth up to my ear.

"Seeing these make me want to burn the world to the ground," he growled passionately, holding me flush against his firm body. "I need to fucking *destroy* something."

"You can go on a rampage after breakfast, Kyan," Saint clipped. "But right now, sit the fuck down. You're late."

"Naw, I'm here right when I meant to be." Kyan released me, moving around the table to Saint and scruffing his hair as he went by, making Saint swipe at him with his good arm, but Kyan was already out of reach.

"Fucking hillbilly," Saint muttered and my heart squeezed at the strangely comforting normality of this scene. I shouldn't have wanted to return to this life. Where I was a captive, forced to do their bidding, where I was owned by each of these beasts. But after what had happened at the cabin, it was hard to see them through a haze of hate anymore. They had killed for me again and again. They had put their lives on the line for mine and hadn't hesitated to do it. But why? What was it about me that drove them to those lengths? It had to be more than some old legend.

"So, Liam called again," Kyan said as he shovelled some of his fried eggs into his mouth. "He's expecting me home for Christmas tomorrow and you've gotta come with me, baby."

I glanced at Saint, uncomfortable about leaving him. "Are you sure I have to go?"

"I owe them big, there's no getting out of it," Kyan said and Saint's eyes flickered with shadows. "If I thought there was any way to do it without you, baby, I would, but it's actually safer for you to just give them what they want. I won't let them lay a finger on you while we're there though, so you don't have to worry."

"It is what it is, I don't need help anyway," Saint said and I looked to Blake imploringly. He gave me a small nod which promised he'd look after him and I knew he'd be okay. I didn't want to even think about Christmas without my dad in it, but it didn't sound like Kyan's family were the type to sit around the fire singing Christmas carols anyway.

When everyone had finished eating, Saint cleared his throat to get our attention. "We need to discuss some important matters. The first being the disturbing event that occurred the other night."

"My family have dealt with it," Kyan said calmly. "The bodies won't be linked back to us. Even *if* any trace of them are ever found."

"That's not what I was referring to." Saint looked to me then over to Monroe and pointed between us. "You two left campus in the middle of the night in secret. It's clear that you were going to meet with your father, Tatum, but there are two things which are still unsettling to me."

"And what are they?" Monroe drawled while I folded my arms, frowning at Saint.

"The first being that rather than sharing this information with all of us, the two of you upped and left in what can only be described as suspicious circumstances, and the second issue is Tatum's intentions." He looked to me and his gaze could have seared the flesh from my bones. "Were you planning on leaving us?" There was anger in his tone, but something more than that too. Something more fiery than rage.

Blake and Kyan sat up straighter in their chairs, looking to me for an explanation.

I opened my mouth, then closed it again, glancing over at Monroe whose jaw was tight. "I don't know if I would have left. But, maybe...if my dad had asked me to go then I would have considered it." I managed to say the words without my voice cracking, but Blake frowned over at Saint like he wanted to stop this conversation in its tracks.

Saint nodded, absorbing that. "And that's why you didn't tell us? Because you *might* have left?"

"I..." I sighed, straightening my spine, figuring I might as well be straight with them. "I trust Monroe. I knew he'd bring me there without question. And yes, maybe I would have left. And I knew you wouldn't allow it. Plus..." The next part wasn't so easy, my gut knotting as I prepared to speak about Dad again. "I wasn't exactly going to bring any of you near the man who you all believed had released the Hades Virus. Who you believed was responsible for so many atrocities." I glanced at Blake and a deep V formed between his eyes.

Before anyone could say anything in response, I jogged upstairs and got the pile of folded papers Dad had given me. My hand trembled as I spotted the blood stain on it that must have soaked through my pocket onto this. What if it was his blood?

A wave of nausea followed a crash of grief and suddenly I was falling, losing my grip on everything as despair took hold of me. I squeezed my eyes shut, trying to hold it all in but it was too much. *Oh Dad. How can you be gone? How will I go on without you?*

"Tatum, come downstairs," Saint called, the ring of an order in his voice. It helped me reclaim a little piece of myself and I took a shaky breath as I forced my pain aside.

I headed to the stairs, swiping at the fresh tears staining my cheeks. How long was it going to be before I ever felt okay again? I'd never truly healed from the loss of Jess and now losing Dad too...it felt like the world really was ending. And it was the kind of apocalypse my father never could have prepared me for. It was one I wouldn't survive.

I walked over to the table, my teeth clenched as I took a seat opposite them all and was glad when none of them commented on the redness of my eyes. I laid the papers down, unfolding them and finding emails Dad had printed detailing how Agent Mortez had manipulated him into giving him the virus samples. I read through each one, passing them to the others as I did so and when they reached Saint, he pressed them out neatly and made a pile of them in chronological order. The truth glared back at me from the words I'd read. How Mortez had gotten Dad to give him the virus and vaccine samples under the guise of protecting the country.

Saint drummed his fingers on the table as I looked at the other pages I had before me, detailing some of his work on the Hades Virus. "Did your father talk about Mortez with you?" he asked and I glanced at the others, figuring I had to lay my trust in them now. Blake's expression was dark, unreadable, like he'd retreated into his own mind.

I took a breath and relayed everything my father had told me about Mortez, how he'd said he was CIA and there had been real evidence that my father's boss had weaponised the Hades Virus and was looking to sell it on. How Dad had been offered large amounts of money to work for Mortez and gather intel on him and eventually sneak out samples. After that, he hadn't heard from him until the Hades Virus was leaked. Then Mortez had asked to meet with him and had tried to kill him.

"Do you think Mortez was really CIA?" I asked nervously. I'd killed him brutally. If the CIA came looking for him, found his body and my DNA...

"My family have covered our tracks, baby," Kyan said, evidently reading where my thoughts were headed. He hooked his foot around mine under the table and I relaxed a little. "They're the best at what they do. It doesn't matter who he was, he's nothing now and there'll be no evidence that links him to any of us."

Saint was still quiet in thought and he held out his hand for the rest of the papers.

"It's notes about the virus," I explained. "Looks like there's a login here to access his work files too. Can you get them to your father?" I felt nervous handing them over, this most precious thing that my dad had asked of me. The last thing he would ever ask of me. But after what Saint had done for me, I found it easier to place my faith in him.

"I will go through everything first and decide what the best course of action is to take," Saint said simply. And I guessed I should have realised that would be his plan. But maybe it was for the best anyway; if my dad's innocence was going to be irrefutably proven, who better to achieve that than Saint Memphis with his O.C.D. ways?

I pushed them across the table to him and our fingers grazed, a hungry pull in my belly drawing me to him.

Blake suddenly pushed out of his seat, striding from the room and a second later his bedroom door slammed so hard that the windows rattled. I gasped, pulling away from Saint and staring after him.

"What's his problem?" Monroe frowned.

"Beats me." Kyan shrugged.

"It's obvious, isn't it?" Saint said, seeming exasperated with the rest of the room who were unable to keep up with him. "These notes prove the innocence of Tatum's father. Blake has been punishing her brutally for those crimes. And it turns out he was innocent just like she said all along." Saint said it with no remorse, just a conversational tone to his voice. My heart thrummed harder at his words and I glanced at Kyan who was looking at me with a furious energy burning off of him.

He stood up, leaning across the table and gripping my face in both of his hands. "I'm sorry we were wrong, but I'm not sorry you're mine. I'll *never* apologise for that." He released me and I leaned back in my chair with my lips parting. I didn't know how to feel about that, only that my heart beat wildly like an untamed creature in my chest. I was hot and angry and hurt and confused.

I pushed out of my seat, looking from him to Saint with my lungs labouring. I glanced at Monroe, finding his eyes flaring with rage on my behalf and I drew on that passion, letting it fill me up. I turned my back on them, striding away to Blake's room without a word. I may have gotten even for everything they'd put me through, but I would always just be their little possession. Did Saint really care about keeping me so much that he'd put himself in front of a car for that purpose though? Or had Kyan wet himself in blood, incriminated himself time and time again for the sake of his precious Night Bound pet? Their ownership of me bordered on obsession if that was the case, but if it wasn't that, then it meant they cared. Truly cared. And that frightened me in a way I wasn't prepared to face right now.

I knocked on the door and when Blake didn't answer, I pushed it open. I found him sitting on the end of his bed, his hands fisted in his hair as he hunched over his knees.

"Blake," I said gently, knowing the feel of the twisting, writhing creature in him that was grief. It was too familiar an enemy.

"I hurt you, I fucking brought you out to that grave I dug in the woods... I can't live with what I've done to you," he gritted out and a chill rippled through my blood.

Did I forgive him? ...Yes. I did. I had sated my revenge and I'd seen the hurt in him. I'd destroyed the man who had killed my father. I could understand the hate Blake had aimed at me the day he'd stood above me with a gun in his hand. He hadn't seen an innocent girl standing in that grave, he'd seen his mother's death staring back at him and he'd wanted to avenge it.

I moved forward, pushing my hands into his black hair and forcing his own out of it, trying to make him look up until slowly, he did. I kept my hands tight in his hair and a magnetic, desperate energy twisted through the air between us.

"You already knew I wasn't responsible," I said.

"But thinking your dad was guilty helped me justify it still. If only a little," he rasped.

I lowered myself into his lap, wrapping my legs around him and brushing my lips against the corner of his mouth. "Hate is blinding."

"I never hated you," he admitted, giving in to my touch as he locked his arms around me and crushed me close. "I wanted to though, so bad that I convinced myself I did. But I don't hate you. I love you, Tate. I fucking love you. And I'd let you go if I was better, it's what you deserve. They say that's what love is. But it's not for me. My love is selfish and dirty and I will do whatever it takes to keep you right here." His mouth was suddenly on mine and I drowned in his kiss, soaking in the perfect heat of his tongue and the way the world faded around me. How everything was forgotten in that single, gleaming moment of light.

My golden boy was here with me now, the true soul that lived within this dark and monstrous exterior that had grown on him like a second skin. He was both light and dark colliding and every inch I claimed of him, it seemed more of the dark receded.

My hands slid beneath the hem of his shirt and I tugged it off of him, drowning in the feeling of his skin against mine. He undressed me slowly, dutifully, worshipping every inch of my body that he uncovered with kisses and caresses that had me panting and trembling in his arms.

When we were finally free of our clothes, our bodies slid together in this natural, perfect way and I could feel the depths of those words he'd spoken to me as he showed me how much he meant them with that act, making love to me instead of fucking me. Our souls collided and merged, and my heart swelled with that feeling of being worshipped as he built me up and up until I was seeing stars and coming apart beneath him in a galaxy of colour and heat.

He continued to kiss me long after we were done, holding me tight in his arms and promising me the world without any more words passing between us and I felt safe there in a way I'd longed to for so damn long that it hurt.

I couldn't say that I loved Blake Bowman. Maybe I did, maybe my heart was a traitor that had fallen for its tormentor. But deep down, I knew that if I fell for one of the Night Keepers, I would fall for all of them, no matter how terrifying that truth was. It meant the legend would come true. That I really was the Night Bound. They would own me in every way imaginable. I was afraid of letting that happen after everything that had happened between us. And I wasn't sure I ever could.

CHAPTER FIVE

T he O'Brien estate was only forty miles from Everlake, so I had no real excuse for how infrequently I visited my family home aside from the fact that I fucking despised everyone who shared blood with me. So there was that.

We'd taken my black, limited edition Harley Davidson, a couple of saddle bags loaded up with clothes for a couple of days on the back of it and my girl riding pillion behind me with her arms wrapped tight around my waist. I almost could have enjoyed it if I hadn't been dreading reaching our destination so damn much.

It was a picturesque ride down through the mountains and though it was cold, the sky was a bright and endless shade of blue, so we hadn't had to deal with much in the way of weather. The bike made it easier to travel through the city too, though with lockdown still in force, the roads were fairly clear.

We'd left at five in the morning which meant we were a lot less likely to be spotted by the cops, but Liam would have paid them all off anyway, so I wasn't really worried about getting caught breaking lockdown regulations.

We turned down the private road where my family pretty much all lived and started passing the O'Brien houses one after another. They were all huge, white monstrosities with multiple extensions, perfectly manicured lawns and ridiculously expensive cars parked on the driveways. Every single one of them was trying to out do the others with their obnoxiousness and yet not a single one even came close to competing with the main estate where Liam O'Brien lived alone, lording it over all of them in his eighteen bed mansion. My darling Grandpa, head of the family and all out King Bastard, living up on top of his hill like he ruled the fucking world. And I guessed he did. At least my version of it anyway.

Of course all nine of his children were eyeing him with hopes of taking his place as the head of the family when the old fucker finally croaked it. Well, all aside from Niall who didn't seem to have the slightest bit of interest in ruling an empire, though I was pretty sure that just made Liam more likely to select him for the role. But despite the fact that my grandpa was well into his eighties, I knew there was no way he was going to die any time soon. That said, conniving bastard that he was, he'd refused to publicly state which of his children he was naming as heir to his title as head of the family when he did up and die.

In fact, now that I was eighteen, it was technically possible that he might choose me for the position too. But I seriously doubted that. Because unlike every other adult member of this shit show they called a family, I spent absolutely none of my time trying to lick his ass and buy his favour. So there was no way in fuck he'd be picking me out of the ranks. Which was a damn good thing as far as I saw it. Maybe when he died I really would be able to cut ties with this horror show of freaks and fuck ups. The problem was that in the meantime I was clearly going to be forced to entangle myself with them as deeply as possible and I wasn't sure what kind of man I'd be once I came out the other side of that. But that was the price I'd agreed to pay when I'd asked for their help, so there was no point in me bitching about it now.

We pulled up to the gate and I lifted the visor on my helmet as the men on duty there gave me a once over before hitting the button to open it. They were armed to the teeth and had face tats and scars to prove how badass they were. I almost snorted a laugh at how hard they were trying to look intimidating and felt zero desire to quake in my boots for them.

I rode up the drive slowly, inching closer to the estate with a heavy heart and an aching weight in my chest. This was the last place on earth that I wanted to bring Tatum. Yet somehow fate had conspired to force her here. I just hoped seeing the monsters who had made me wouldn't change her opinion of me too much.

I parked up right outside the front doors instead of bothering to park around the side like I was supposed to and waited a moment as my girl released her grip on me and climbed off of the bike before standing myself.

I hung my helmet on the handlebars and she passed hers over for me to do the same with it.

"Once we're in there you don't leave my side, okay, baby?" I asked her in a low voice as I looked her over in the leathers she'd worn for the ride, pushing my fingers into her hair to tame some of the wild tangles she'd obtained on the way here. She looked pretty much like my ultimate wet dream right now and if I hadn't been half expecting one of my psychotic uncles to leap out of the bushes at any moment, I'd have been damn tempted to pounce on her.

"I know, Kyan, you don't have to keep reminding me," she replied, a snarky edge to her tone.

"Yeah, I do. Because no amount of warning can prepare you for them."

I tugged her close and stole a brief kiss from those full lips of hers, aching for more but forcing myself to pull back just as quickly. This was going to be rough.

She gave me a reassuring smile and I threw an arm around her shoulders as we headed up the steps to the front door.

One of my grandpa's butlers opened it before we could get close enough to knock and I tossed him the keys to my bike without even bothering to say hello. He caught them deftly, waiting for us to pass him before heading outside to get our bags and move the bike to the garage. He didn't mention the fact that I'd parked it in the wrong place and that was a clever move on his part because every step I took inside this house had the ball of angry energy inside me coiling tighter, hungering for release.

The scent of tobacco and whiskey filled the house alongside a spicy, Christmassy smell which I guessed had been added for the occasion by one of Liam's house servants. Certainly not the miserable motherfucker himself. But the place would look like Santa had vomited on it even if the only reasoning behind that was that he wanted everyone to agree he could pull off the best decorations.

No one was here yet, seeing as it was so early, so I led Tatum deeper into the house, heading for the kitchen where I knew Martha would be well underway with the Christmas feast.

"This place is stupid big," Tatum murmured as we walked down the long corridor past the sweeping staircase which led to the bedrooms upstairs and I turned her towards one of the doors the servants used to move about the place unseen.

"Yeah well, it suits my grandpa's head," I replied easily, trying not to show how fucking much I hated having her here, though I was fairly sure she could feel the tension in my posture as I held her close to my side.

We made it to the staff kitchens and I led her in, instantly spotting Martha amongst the workers who were in charge of all the cooking and smirking at her as she spotted me too.

"Coco!" she cried and I fought a cringe at that pet name. Though I supposed that this way, Tatum was meeting one person who I at least vaguely gave a shit about during this little adventure home.

I tugged Tatum over to her then we all had a moment of awkward pausing as we hit the invisible six foot marker and realised that we should be keeping our distance from the point of view of the damn virus. Not that I really thought any of the staff here were at risk of having it. I knew full well that Liam had banned any of them from leaving the estate since the Hades Virus had broken out, but I still didn't want to take any unnecessary risks with my girl.

"Who's the pretty little thing?" Martha asked, giving Tatum a once over as I let my hand slip from her shoulders down to her waist and tugged her closer.

"This is Tate, she's mine," I explained because as much as I'd wanted to hide Tatum from the prying eyes of my family, it was clear that they'd already figured out that she was important. So my only choice here was to stake my claim and keep her close to me to warn all of them away from her. If they sensed any kinds of cracks between us, they'd try and worm their way in to force us apart and then use her to hurt me in whatever way they could as a part of the power games they were constantly playing. "This is Martha. The only decent person in this shit pit," I added for Tatum's benefit.

"Nice to meet you," Tatum offered as Martha cooed.

"You too. Never thought I'd live to see the day Coco fell in love."

"Don't call me that," I said with about as much bite as I could muster for the cook who had actually seen me as a person instead of a commodity. I chose to ignore the love comment, but the curious way that Tatum was looking at me had me hiding a smirk with a thumb pressed to the corner of my lips.

"Why do you call him Coco?" Tatum asked, ignoring me as I growled to warn her off.

"Because he was always obsessed with chocolate as a boy. Used to sneak down here and pinch some every opportunity he got. He even used to trick me into making chocolate cake and then steal the bowl full of batter to lick it clean."

"That was *one* time," I groaned as Tatum smirked in amusement.

"I still have the pictures somewhere," Martha pressed, ignoring my pissy tone. "You two go and make yourselves comfortable in the smoking parlour and I'll whip you up some breakfast. With a bit of luck, I'll remember where I put them while I'm cooking."

I cursed her half-heartedly and tugged on Tatum's waist to get her moving again as she gave Martha a smile.

We headed out of the kitchens and down a long hall and I couldn't help but lean back to appreciate Tatum's ass in her bike leathers. Saint might have been one crazy motherfucker, but he knew how to buy our girl clothes alright. And as much as I was sure he hated the idea of her wearing these leathers, he'd done a damn good job of picking a set that looked hot as fuck on her.

"Stop staring at my ass," she teased as I blatantly checked her out and I chuckled darkly as I directed her into the smoking room.

"Or what, baby?" I taunted.

"Or I'll spank you," she threatened, her blue eyes flashing with the threat as she looked up at me and my heart leapt at the challenge in her tone.

"Oh no, baby. That's not how our power play is going to work out. I might be a slave to your desires now, but if one of us is going to be spanking the other then it'll definitely be me slapping that perfect ass of yours. And don't you forget that I've got you all to myself tonight too."

I wasn't entirely sure if she wanted me flirting with her or not after everything that had happened, but it was pretty fucking hard to stop and the way she was responding said she wasn't complaining.

Tatum licked her lips as she looked at me and I felt that move all the way down to my cock.

"Sometimes I think you're all talk, big man," she teased.

I was on her before she knew what was happening, flipping her around and snaring her wrists at the base of her spine before forcing her face down over the back of one of the huge leather armchairs beside the fire. She gasped in alarm as I transferred my grip on her wrists so that I was securing them with one hand before bending down and sinking my teeth into the perfect roundness of her ass through the tight leather covering it.

Tatum cried out, a moan of excitement laced with pain that had my dick aching as I straightened again and clapped my hand down on her ass right where my teeth had just been, making her moan again.

"Don't doubt me, baby. If you want to find out exactly what kind of animal I am then I promise you the ride of your life. But I'm warning you, I don't do anything by halves, so make sure you want it before you ask for it."

I stepped forward and ground my hard dick against her ass, half considering pulling those pants of hers down and making my point more thoroughly.

"And what if I do ask for it?" Tatum panted. "What if I want to ask you to spend tonight ruining me and making me forget all the reasons I have to cry?"

"I can definitely promise you that much," I growled, dropping my hold on her hands and flipping her around again as I lifted her to sit on the back of the armchair.

I leaned in to capture those full lips with mine, drowning in the feeling of them as she moaned into my mouth, her legs coiling around my waist and that blazing heat burning hot between us with a desperate kind of need for relief. It had been too fucking long in the making and I was so over waiting to have her in every way I'd been fantasising about.

"And there was me thinking you'd try and renege on our deal," Liam's voice came from behind me.

I fell still, drawing back and breaking our kiss as the sound of my grandpa's voice sent a chill down my spine.

"I'm a man of my word," I growled as I adjusted my dick in my pants before I turned to face him. I lifted Tatum from her perch and tucked her close to my side as I set her on her feet again.

Liam O'Brien was a tall man, his eyes sharp and his hair still dark brown despite his late years. He was turned out in an immaculate suit like always and a lit cigarette hung from the corner of his lips. I wasn't sure I'd ever seen him without one.

"And you brought the girl," Liam said in his lilting Irish accent like that was a surprise even though he'd made it abundantly clear that it wasn't an option.

"She has a name," Tatum quipped and I smirked even as my grandpa's gaze narrowed on her.

"This is Tatum," I added. "Like I know you know. She's my girl, so I won't put up with any shit tossed her way."

"I don't know why you're taking that tone with me, lad. I'm ever the gentleman." Liam moved across the room and stubbed his cigarette out before promptly lighting another. He left the pack down on the table before taking his usual armchair by the fire and I moved forward to claim one for myself.

I lit it up, taking a long drag and turned back to Tatum as I pointed her towards the couch. Instead of doing as I'd said, she reached out and snatched the freshly lit cigarette from my mouth and promptly stubbed it out.

Liam barked a laugh as I scowled down at her and she only raised her chin in defiance.

"I'm gonna need a few cigarettes to get through a couple of days in this house, baby," I warned her in a low voice. "You might wanna have one too."

"No," she said simply, arching a brow at me like she thought I'd just back down to her bullshit.

I held her eye as I reached for the packet again, took another smoke from it, placed it between my lips and lit up. I sucked deep on the butt and watched the reflected glow of the cherry blazing in her angry blue eyes before plucking it from my lips and blowing the smoke right into her face.

"Don't go getting the idea that you can tell me what to do just because I'm soft on you, baby," I purred. "I'm not the kind of monster who can be leashed."

I dropped down into the armchair opposite my grandpa and tugged her down to sit in my lap while she amped herself up to say something else. I clamped my hand down on her thigh and squeezed hard enough to warn her to back down and she narrowed her eyes on me, flicking the cigarette in my other hand a look that said this conversation wasn't done and then held her tongue.

"Nice to see she's got a bit of fire about her," Liam joked, but I could tell by the way he was looking at her that she really had caught his attention now and I didn't like that one bit.

"Well, happy Christmas," I said dryly.

"Good tidings to all," Liam replied casually, smiling broadly. But there were too many teeth to his smile which gave it the look of a predator eyeing a lamb instead of a man hosting Christmas for his family. I just wasn't sure if he thought I was the lamb his belly was rumbling for a bite of or if my girl was. He certainly wasn't above using her to hurt me. Her presence here alone was a threat in itself.

"How is business?" I asked, taking a long drag on my cigarette before hanging my arm back down over the edge of the couch to keep Tatum away from it.

"Ah, well there's been a downturn in the casinos obviously since lockdown," Liam replied. "But Dougal managed to get around some of it by continuing the fight nights in secret and live streaming them to members. Of course, he's having to take payments and hand out winnings electronically, so he's set up a whole roundabout offshore system to evade the authorities which I'm not too fond of. Either way it's his balls on the line so I guess the cards will fall as fate deigns fit."

I nodded like I gave a shit about that, but I didn't really care if my uncle Dougal was playing a risky game with the law. If he fucked it up and got himself carted off to prison, then that was just one less O'Brien for me to have to deal with. Besides, Dougal was a dick who'd made me watch him torture a man to death on my twelfth birthday as a gift. The guy had pissed himself and I swear the stench of it mixed with that of his blood had still been caught in the back of my throat when I was eating my birthday cake. He'd ruined red velvet for me for life. What kind of asshole ruins cake for people?

Tatum turned in my lap to make herself more comfortable, her hand dropping down to cup my balls where Liam couldn't see as she smiled sweetly at me. I had to fight not to react to that shit and forced myself to look back at my grandpa and keep the conversation going while wondering what exactly she was up to. Not that I was complaining.

"I'm sure he has it handled," I said with a nod. "What about product?"

I lifted the cigarette to my lips for another drag, but the second I inhaled, Tatum's grip on my balls sharpened tightly and I damn near leapt out of my chair, having to feign rearranging our position as I coughed the smoke back out of my lungs.

"Actually, sales are up on that front," Liam said, not seeming to notice that my girl had put my balls in a damn vice. "With so many people stuck at home, they're keen to dive into more of their recreational hobbies...at least they are for now while money isn't too much of an issue anyway. Dermot is running that with your mammy and as far as I can tell, the main issue is keeping the delivery boys out of sight when they're dropping it off to people's houses. I think it's become a mostly nocturnal practice to combat the police patrols."

I nodded like I was interested in that as I tried shifting to tug Tatum's hand from my balls. She'd gone back to caressing them instead of squeezing them but with the cigarette in one hand and my other wrapped around her waist, there wasn't an easy way to achieve that without making it obvious.

"Well, it sounds like you've got everything covered. Almost like you don't need me at all," I said, letting just a little disdain drip through my words and Liam smirked at me.

"Every piece of the puzzle has its role to play, lad," he assured me with that look he liked to shoot my way which said he thought he fucking owned me. The one that made me want to flip the fuck out and show him my worst as I painted his expensive walls with his blood.

I lifted the cigarette to my lips again so that I could concentrate on that and hide the flash of anger that tore through me, but the moment I tried to inhale, Tatum squeezed my fucking balls so hard my breath caught.

My grip on her thigh tightened in warning but her grasp on my balls just did the fucking same.

"Who'd like some chocolate cake?" Martha's voice saved me from Liam's scrutiny as she pranced into the room, carrying a large tray with coffee and cake laid out on it.

"You spoil this one, Martha," Liam said as he stood and took a coffee from the tray before heading towards the door. "I'll see you both at lunch."

Martha started muttering about us being love's young dream as she set the tray down on the table and bustled about the room while Tatum and I glared at each other.

Her grip on my fucking balls was unwavering and I grunted a curse as I slowly reached over and stubbed the cigarette out. She instantly released my balls, giving me a saccharine sweet smile as we fell into conversation with Martha over coffee and cake and I was gifted the treat of her showing photos of me as a kid with chocolate all over my face too.

I played along, mostly because Martha was the only person in this entire household who I actually gave a shit about and I watched Tatum as she let the stories and newness of this place steal her grief away for a little while.

I was glad she was distracted from the pain, but she'd ignited a heat in my veins with that little stunt which was only growing hotter and burning fiercer with every passing moment. No one got to hold me by the balls and get away with it. Figuratively or literally. So as soon as I could, I was going to make her realise exactly what kind of monster she'd been baiting with that little game of hers.

By the time we'd finished up with Martha and I'd given Tatum a tour of the house and grounds, I could hear more members of the family arriving and my gut was beginning to churn with the thought of spending the rest of the day in their company. I wasn't afraid of them as such, though I guessed I probably should have been. But I was mostly just so fucking sick of being forced to play to their tune all the damn time that I was worried about what I might do in their company. And I couldn't afford to lose my shit with them today. Tatum would be the one who paid for that. Her presence here was designed with that purpose in mind.

We'd been given a room in the east wing of the house and I'd taken a shower while Tatum got changed into whatever the hell Saint had decided was 'proper Christmas attire'. As I headed back through to the lavish room from the en-suite, my heart leapt at the sight of her.

She was wearing a full length navy dress with slits up both legs so that delicious skin of hers poked through as she moved. The front was panelled with white lace which was just transparent enough for me to see her cleavage through it in the mirror as she leaned forward to finish applying her makeup, painting her lips blood red.

I moved to stand behind her with the towel around my waist, my dick tenting it as I breathed in that sweet honey blossom scent of hers. I didn't stop until I was right up in her personal space, standing at her back as she straightened and looked over her shoulder at me in the mirror.

"You look fucking edible, baby," I growled, my hand snaking around her waist before sliding up over the silky material until I was teasing her breast through it and she gasped as I tugged on her nipple.

I continued to tease her until her pupils dilated and her back arched against me before suddenly shifting my grip to encircle her throat.

Tatum's big blues widened in surprise as my dick drove into her ass and the friction between us knocked my towel free so that it fell to the floor and I was left standing there naked.

"Did you really think I was going to let you get away with that shit you pulled downstairs?" I growled in her ear, my grip on her throat tight enough to hold her still though not enough to stop her from panting for me.

"I don't like you smoking, Kyan," she said stubbornly. "You only do it because you're stressed and I don't think you need to. It's a crutch you can go without."

"What is it that I need then?" I asked her, my other hand moving to her other breast as I teased that nipple though the material, loving the way it hardened at my touch.

She didn't seem to have an answer for that at first, but she licked those red lips and her hand reached behind her until she was gripping my dick.

"Maybe you just need an incentive to keep your cool," she breathed and my fingers flexed against her throat.

"Are you offering me your body in exchange for good behaviour?" I asked with a smirk. "Because I've got bad news for you, baby. I don't know how to be good."

"I don't want you to be good, Kyan. I like you being dark and dirty and rough, and I don't want you to hold back with me because you have some inaccurate assumption that I can't handle you at your worst. I've been to hell and back at the hands of you and the other Night Keepers and I've survived all the worst things a person can suffer in grief and heartache. So don't treat me like a china doll who might break if you push me too hard. I want to lose myself in you and I want you to do the same."

A growl of desire escaped me at the heat of her words and I groaned as I tugged her head aside and bit down on the side of her neck, sucking at her skin as she moaned my name and I left a mark on her for the whole fucking world to see that she was mine.

"You want to stop me from being mad at you for the duration of this fuck-fest of a dinner?" I asked her, my grip on her throat getting tighter as my anger rose in me again.

"Yes," she moaned and the heat in her eyes snapped the last of my restraint.

I twisted her in my arms and used my grip on her throat to tip her chin up so that I could kiss her with a brutal kind of passion that had me aching for more and more of her. I didn't know why I'd waited so fucking long to kiss her like this, but I was certain that she only tasted sweeter for the wait I'd endured.

Her hand curled around my cock but as her tongue swept over mine, I knew that wasn't what I wanted from her.

I used my grip on her to push her to her knees and she didn't even hesitate to slide that perfect mouth of hers around my dick. I groaned as I looked down at her, drawing the full, thick length of me between her lips, smearing my shaft with red lipstick as she went and drawing my cock right to the back of her throat.

I cursed as she pulled back, my hands fisting in her freshly curled hair and messing it the fuck up as I took control of her movements and drove myself into her mouth again.

Tatum moaned encouragement, the noises spilling from her sending sweet vibrations through my cock as she reached around to grasp my ass with both hands, her fingernails biting into my flesh as I fucked her mouth with a brutal demand to my movements.

I was hard as stone as she took me deep, her tongue swirling and full lips sucking in just the right way to make me her slave. It was almost enough to make me forget what she'd done downstairs, but I wasn't a man to roll over with his balls in a vice and she needed to know it.

I kept one hand fisted in her hair as I fucked her mouth good and deep and with the other, I snagged a cigarette from the pack sitting on the side and pushed it between my lips. It took me another moment to light it as my balls ached with the desire to finish this already beneath the punishment of her skills and I had to fight against it, wanting to prolong this moment.

I lit the smoke, taking a deep drag with a groan of satisfaction as Tatum growled in anger, realising what I done and made a move to pull back.

"Show me you own me, baby," I purred, keeping the cigarette in the corner of my mouth as I returned my other hand to her hair too and she used her teeth to scrape a line down my shaft in anger, but she didn't jerk away, taking me right to the back of her throat again like she had a point to prove.

That was all the acceptance I needed and I groaned again as I drove my cock deep and she took it like she was aching for it, moaning her own desire loudly and hungrily.

I wasn't a gentleman about it, gripping her hair hard and thrusting in and out of those perfect lips until I was coming hot and fast down her throat.

I held her tight as I remained deep inside her for a long moment, my head tipped back to the vaulted ceiling in ecstasy as I blew out a lungful of nicotine.

When I let her pull back, I stubbed the cigarette out then tugged her to her feet and kissed her, loving the taste of me on her lips and the way she curled her arms around my neck and pulled me even closer.

I walked her back to a heavy wooden dresser at the side of the room and lifted her up to sit on it, pushing her thighs apart and shifting her dress aside so that one of the slits in it bared her black panties to me.

I took her hand in mine as I continued to kiss her and guided it inside her panties, using my fingers to push two of her own inside herself and loving how fucking wet she was as I touched that sweet pussy of hers.

"You're such a fucking dick," she snarled, biting my lip in punishment for the smoke and I laughed against her anger.

"I think that's what you like about me. Fuck knows there isn't much else," I teased.

"You'll pay for that stunt," she swore, gasping as I used my fingers to guide hers in and out of herself again.

"We're late, baby," I groaned as I forced myself to step back. "If we're not down there in three minutes, Liam will lose his shit and believe me, that's not a pleasant experience for anyone involved. I won't put you at his mercy."

"So, what-" she began, moving to withdraw her hand, but I pushed it back down.

"I want you to come for me while I get dressed. And then tonight, I'm going to bring you back here and fuck you so good that you'll forget all about what a selfish fuck I've just been and forgive me for it." I smirked at her as I waited and she cursed me as she began moving her fingers in soft circles beneath her black panties.

I backed up until I could grab my clothes from my bag, tugging on a pair of boxers and charcoal grey pants before adding socks and lacing a pair of fancy ass shoes on my feet. It was made harder to concentrate on my task as Tatum moaned and panted opposite me, her fingers driving in and out of that tight pussy while she played her clit just the way she liked it and I took notes for later.

As I threaded my belt through the loops, I was gifted all kinds of ideas about how I'd like to string her up and ruin her and I had to re-buckle it as the thought of that and the sight of her working herself had me fucking it up.

I shrugged into a black shirt, hooking the buttons together over my tattooed torso as I approached her again and her moans got louder.

I watched the fucking perfect way her face contorted with pleasure as she worked herself into a frenzy and I pushed her panties aside just as her moans got louder. I drove two fingers deep inside her right as she came, her pussy clamping down hard around me as I kissed her to taste that fucking pleasure on her tongue.

"You're such an asshole," she panted against my mouth as I pumped my fingers a few times to prolong her orgasm before drawing them back out and fixing her underwear for her.

I sucked her wetness from my fingers and hers as I chuckled darkly.

"Yeah, baby, I am. But I promise that was barely even the warm up. Tonight I'll show you just how generous I can be when I want to. But right now, we need to run."

I lifted her back down from the dresser, straightening her dress and wiping some smeared red lipstick from the side of her mouth as she wiped some from my lips in return.

As soon as we looked near enough to respectable, we hurried for the door and I quickly tied my topknot into place before sweeping her off of her feet and tossing her over my shoulder so that we could go faster without her stilettos slowing us down. Saint had really been onto something with those shoes though. They were high as fuck with red soles which I wanted to look at while I bent her over and drove her to ruin beneath me. That shit would definitely be happening tonight.

Tatum gave me half assed protests as I jogged down the stairs with her slung over my shoulder and I slapped her ass to tell her off as I kept going all

72

the way to the huge dining room at the back of the house.

I placed her on her feet just as we reached the doors and tugged her inside where a huge oak table ran the full length of the enormous space. It looked like Christmas had thrown up in here; there were two tall trees at either end of the table and the fireplace roared with fancy ass stockings hanging around it. The table itself was laid out with red and gold place settings and bits of holly and shit looking all fancy. I would have made a derisive comment, but Tatum looked like she kinda loved it, so I decided to rein in the asshole in me for once.

Liam caught my eye from the head of the table where two empty seats sat waiting and inclined his head towards them. Of course all of my eight uncles would be here with their wives and I spotted my parents too, though they only waved at me from the far end of the table in acknowledgment of my presence. It might have seemed odd to some people, but I really had no relationship with my parents anymore. I'd been raised by nannies for the most part and had spent more time with Liam and my uncles than them once I was old enough to learn the joy of the family trades. I was just a means to an end for them, the heir they'd been required to provide and they were just DNA donors to me. I wasn't going to cry myself to sleep over it. I'd cut myself off from them after I'd been forced to initiate at Royaume D'élite and unlike Liam, they didn't have enough sway over me to force me back into the fold with them.

A few of my cousins had been invited as well, but there weren't many who had made enough of a name for themselves to get an invite. Let alone a plus one. Couple that with the fact that I was being offered pride of place at Liam's side and I basically had a whole table full of O'Briens shooting me less than subtle death glares.

That should have been terrifying, but I'd long since stopped giving a shit about the ire of my extended family. Because the truth was, we all lived and died by Liam's command around here, so even my uncle Niall who was a total psychopath, wouldn't do shit to me unless Liam ordered it. But the way they were looking at Tatum made my hackles rise. We might have had an unspoken law about never hurting our own family in any permanent way, but she wasn't family. Partners were always fair game until they married in. Which meant my cousins and uncles could do whatever the fuck they wanted to her and Liam wouldn't raise a single finger to stop them. If I wanted to keep her safe, then that was all on me. Luckily enough, I knew I was the strongest son of a bitch here so I was confident I could do it if I had to. But I definitely wouldn't be letting her out of my sight.

We took our seats, settling into the cloud of smoke which hovered over the table from my chain-smoking relatives and I leaned back in my chair as Martha and the other staff appeared with the food and began laying it all out on the table.

I noticed the seat opposite mine was empty and as I looked down the table at my assembled unwanted family members, I realised that my most dangerous, and favourite, uncle was missing.

"Where's Niall?" I asked casually as the rest of my family started up their posturing crap, boasting about the money they'd earned the family this year and trying to point score off each other while in ear shot of the head of the family.

Not that I ever got the impression Liam cared much. I was pretty sure he had every single dollar that had passed hands within his criminal empire marked down and accounted for and that he knew exactly which family member was responsible for bringing it in. But that didn't seem to be what he was looking for in those he offered favour to. I mean, why the fuck was I being gifted a seat at his left hand tonight when I'd literally tried to cut ties with this fucking family a few months ago and never look back? I certainly wasn't earning them any money either. The only money I earned came from taking part in the illegal fights I attended in Murkwell and I certainly never shared so much as a dime of that with this bunch of assholes.

"He's taking care of something," Liam said dismissively, letting me know that his youngest son had earned a free pass for being late with whatever

74

task he was currently performing.

My uncle Connor took up the chance to dominate Liam's attention with some rambling story about an enforcing job he'd carried out last week and I let him more than happily, relaxing back into my chair and digging into the food in front of me.

"So how much is Kyan paying you to sit there with him, sweetie pie?" Dougal asked from Tatum's other side, leaning in close and releasing a puff of smoke in her face. Every fucker at the table was smoking of course, though I didn't feel the need to join them just yet.

"Kyan doesn't need to pay me for my company," my girl replied coolly, stabbing her broccoli. "I'm his and he's mine."

"Well, property is always up for sale..." Dougal leaned forward and laid a hand on her thigh with a leering smile and she smacked it away with a snarl of rage, but I wasn't going to leave it at that.

I twisted my fork in my grip, shoved to my feet and slammed the piece of silverware straight down into his other hand which was lying flat on the table.

Dougal roared in pain, the cigarette falling from his lips and bouncing onto the table as he tore the fork free, clutching his hand to his chest and blood spilled down his arm.

Everyone at the table stopped eating to stare at us as I shoved my chair over and rounded Tatum to grab the front of Dougal's shirt and pull his face close to mine.

"Do I need to beat your ass in front of the entire family, or are you going to apologise to my girl?" I snarled in his face.

Dougal sneered at me as he clutched his bleeding hand to his chest before glancing around at the assembled family members and clearly taking a moment to figure out his odds. But I had about fifty pounds of muscle on him as well as the rage of a demon and he knew well enough that he was outmatched. The rules of the family said I couldn't kill him, beating the fuck out of him was fair game.

He barked a laugh as he yanked himself out of my grasp and sketched a mocking bow to Tatum who was still sitting in her chair. To her credit, she was hiding her shock well, looking up at us as she watched this drama play out. But in reality, this was barely even the start of the shit that would happen today if history was anything to go by. The more the family drank and smoked and talked shit, the more brawls would break out.

One year my cousin Aiden was stabbed so bad he bled out. But he had been fucking Dermot's girl, so I wasn't sure what else he'd expected to get. Liam let Dermot off for that death seeing as he'd only stabbed the fucker in the leg and it was really just bad luck he'd hit the artery. He had cut two of the fingers from his left hand in payment for it though, which had kinda ruined my appetite for the Christmas pudding. Of course, I'd only been nine then so my stomach hadn't been as strong as it was these days. I was pretty sure I wouldn't even bat an eye at some brain splatter while I ate my meal today unless some of it actually got on my plate. And even then I'd just have to dish up a new one.

"I didn't mean to cause any offence, pretty girl," Dougal said, dipping his head to Tatum and making a joke out of bowing too much. "Will you accept my apologies?"

"I can still beat the shit out of him if you want me to, baby?" I offered. "Or you can do the honours if you prefer?'

Tatum made a show of considering her options, picked up Dougal's dropped cigarette from the table and took her time stubbing it out in the middle of his plate of food.

"That's okay. No harm done," she said and everyone else quickly lost interest in us and went back to eating and drinking.

I dropped back into my seat and Dougal headed off to bandage up his hand.

"I'm glad I didn't have to kill you, lad," Liam said casually, aiming an appreciative smile my way which made my blood run cold. "Because you have a role to fill. As soon as you graduate, I think it would make sense for your daddy to start looking at retirement, don't you? And then you can step up and lead us from the front like you were born to."

His gaze slid from me as I clenched my jaw, to Tatum sitting at my side and I caught the not so subtle threat there. I was going to have to fall into line or she'd be the one paying for my disobedience. But I'd known that when I made that call to Niall and I'd done it anyway. To save Saint. To keep all of us out of prison. I was going to have to give up my freedom and bow to his desires for the rest of my life. Or at least the rest of his. And I knew deep down that that would slowly suffocate me, that I'd be drawn deeper and deeper into their darkness. That I'd be pushed to kill and bleed for them before long. The price always increasing. Because they had me now that they knew about her. And there was nothing I could do to protect her from them aside from bow my head and fall into line.

"Sounds like you've got it all figured out," I said in a flat tone. "You just say jump and I'll ask how high."

The sour taste those words left in my mouth were countered somewhat by the warm hand which took mine beneath the table. She ran her fingers over my scarred knuckles and soothed the beast within me with that touch alone, giving me the strength to bite my tongue and keep the rage locked inside me.

I moved my hand onto her knee and slowly teased the slit in the fabric apart as my fingers slipped over her butter soft skin.

More members of our family spoke with us as we ate and every time they pissed me off, I slid my fingers higher, loving the little gasps that passed her lips for every inch I gained. It was one of the best remedies to my temper that I'd ever come across.

The rest of the meal passed without too many incidents. A few punches were thrown, everyone got louder and louder. More cigarettes and booze were consumed than could easily be counted and Liam continued to lord it over everyone like he thought he was a god or something.

Tatum shifted close to me in her chair and I turned to look at her as her fingertips traced the line of my fly for a moment that didn't last nearly long enough.

The doors banged open and my uncle Niall finally appeared, interrupting us before I could find out if she might have been planning to do it again.

Everyone looked his way as he strode in dressed in jeans and a white t-shirt flecked with blood, his muscular, tattooed arms tensed and gleaming with sweat as if he'd just been working out. His dirty blond hair was pushed out of his eyes and his piercing green gaze dropped on Tatum instantly as a hungry grin captured his lips.

I tensed on instinct as he drew closer to my girl. I wasn't afraid to take on any of my relatives one on one. The problem with Niall was that he was so fucking unpredictable. I'd seen him laughing with a man one minute and stabbing him to death in the next and I'd never even found out what had made him flip. He was a wild card and you never knew when he was at his most dangerous.

He was Liam's youngest son and my mom was second oldest which meant he was actually only thirty two and he had a sense of youth and fun about him that most of my other uncles were lacking. Of course, his idea of fun usually meant someone was dying, but I had my own taste for bloodlust, so who was I to judge?

"Ho ho ho!" Niall called, swinging a red sack in his hands and pulling a Santa hat from his back pocket to shove down over his blond hair. "Who asked for a traitor's head in their stocking?"

"Is that really..." Tatum began and I sighed heavily as I wound an arm around her shoulders and tugged her a bit closer.

"Pretty sure it is," I muttered. "Sorry, baby. But I did tell you I was born of monsters."

Niall leapt up onto the table before my grandfather with a wide grin on his face as he shook the sack enticingly. "Have you been a good boy this year?" he asked as two round lumps pressed through the sack and dripped blood onto the tablecloth.

"Some of you may have been wondering why Patrick and his wife weren't invited tonight," Liam said loud enough to draw all attention his way and moving to lean back in his chair so that the blood didn't stain his clothes. "But they actually were. I found out that they were cutting an extra twenty percent of their take to keep for themselves. So, I decided to take the twenty percent back from them in flesh. I suppose Niall could have cut it from the bottom, but taking it off of the top seemed so much simpler somehow."

Niall laughed loudly and up-ended the sack over the table. I was on my feet and tugging Tatum behind my back before she had to look at the two heads which thumped down onto the dinner plates and her tight grip on my hand was the only thing keeping me still as I looked at the severed head of my cousin. He'd been a money grabbing dick, but still...

"Never forget where your loyalties lie," Liam called over the silence, his gaze cutting to me and letting me know exactly who this warning was really meant for. "Blood is thicker than water."

"Don't I know it," I replied, turning and heading from the room with Tatum's hand curled tight in mine.

"Merry Christmas, Kyan!" Niall called after us and I looked back to him with a big ass smile on my face like this had just been the most perfect day imaginable.

"Happy Christmas, motherfucker," I replied and he cackled like a mad man before kicking one of the heads off of the table like it was a soccer ball.

Tatum scrunched her nose up and I tightened my grip on her as I drew her along with me. I knew how this went, everyone was drunk and rowdy and ready to start talking shit as the party wrapped up and there was no need for us to participate in that bullshit.

Nobody made any attempt to stop us from leaving which let me know well enough that the point had been made and Liam believed I'd been successfully brought to heel. The worst thing about that was that I was pretty sure he was right.

We walked in silence all the way back up to the room we'd been given and when I finally closed the bedroom door behind us, I leaned back against the wood with a growl of frustration.

My fists were bunching at my sides and my jaw was clenched so hard I was in danger of cracking a fucking tooth. I needed to hit something. No, *someone.* I needed to feel the sweet relief of venting my rage on flesh and blood and pounding and pounding until bones cracked and blood poured.

"Do you want to tell me what part of that is upsetting you most?" Tatum asked, moving to stand before me with her chin high and no sign at all that she was freaked out by what she'd just been a witness to. Maybe she hadn't seen it. Maybe I'd spared her the sight of it at least.

"Upsetting?" I scoffed. "I'm fighting the urge to go down there and rip every one of those motherfuckers apart. Starting with my fucking grandpa."

"So what's stopping you?" she asked, moving closer instead of backing away which seemed like a dumb move considering how fucking angry I was right now.

"This family is like a fucking hydra. You cut off one head and two more will just sprout in their place. If I killed him, then the rest would come for me. And I might be good, but I can't take on every one of them. Though one day I probably would have done it. In fact I should have, before they figured out where to strike at me to actually make me bleed."

Tatum frowned like she didn't understand what I meant and I cursed as I turned away from the deep blue of her eyes and strode across the room, tugging open the buttons closest to my throat so that I could breathe easier.

But my blood was up now. I knew there was no relief to be found for me outside of the fight.

"You mean they'd come after me and the Night Keepers?" her voice came from too close to me and I stalked away as I muttered a confirmation.

It was fucking infuriating. It felt like being castrated. My whole life was going to be taken from me now. I'd be forced to become the puppet I'd always sworn I'd never become. I'd have to return to Royaume D'élite as well, even though I'd vowed I'd never set foot in that fucked up place again.

I yanked my hair free of its tie as I began pacing.

"You don't have the faintest idea of what these people are mixed up in," I muttered, mostly to myself as memories I didn't want to be having were forcing themselves in on me and making me take note of them and it was only making my anger rise.

I turned back and found her standing in my way as I moved to stalk forward again.

"So tell me then," she demanded, her eyes flashing defiantly like she was so sure that she wanted to know.

"You'd never look at me the same, baby," I said, shaking my head.

"Cut the shit, Kyan. You've put me through hell, tortured me with your friends, killed for me and *with* me and kissed me when I was painted in the blood of my enemy. Do you seriously think there's anything that you could tell me now that would change anything between us?"

"I don't know," I admitted as my gaze slid over her and I took in the defiance in her eyes and the pout of her full lips. "But I can't give you up, baby. Not now. And I don't know if I can cope with seeing the look in your eyes when you find out exactly just how fucked up I am."

Her knuckles collided with my jaw before I even realised she was taking a swing at me and I was knocked back a step as my lip split and blood coated my tongue.

"Don't you ever doubt how strong I am again, Kyan Roscoe," she snarled at me. "After all the shit you've put me through, the least I deserve from you is the truth. So give it to me."

The rage in me was a burning, throbbing thing and I whirled away from her before ripping a lamp from the nightstand and hurling at the wall where it shattered with a loud crash. I didn't have to worry about anyone coming to see what was going on though. No one in this family would do a damn thing to stop me even if I was in here carving Tatum's beautiful body apart piece by piece.

"Fine," I snarled as I paced away from her and moved to look out of the window over the yard below, fighting to hold myself together before I destroyed the whole goddamn room in a rage. "There's a club for rich, twisted assholes somewhere near Hemlock City called Royaume D'élite," I said in a low voice and the hairs on the back of my neck pricked up even as I mentioned that fucked up place.

"Tell me," she insisted as I hesitated and I cursed as I went on. Because maybe I needed to admit to this. Maybe I needed to stop worrying about what the fuck would happen if the people I cared about found out about it and just trust in them to still care once they knew or accept that they might not and know that that was up to them anyway.

"It's a place where people are put up for sale to the worst kinds of buyers. Sex trafficking, death matches, even just psychopaths looking for fresh victims can go there and place a price on human flesh."

She remained silent and I was glad because if I heard so much as an ounce of pity in her voice, I was pretty sure I'd rip this entire building apart. I'd made my choice. So I would own it. Even if I knew that doing so had carved a piece of my soul off which I'd never get back.

"Rich, twisted motherfuckers use the club as a place to do business. They watch the fights or fuck the girls or they just go there to drink and arrange whatever ways they want to carve up the country and use it for their own gain."

"So, it's kinda like a secret society?" Tatum asked, her voice sounding like it was coming from the bed, but I wasn't going to turn and look at her to confirm it.

"Yeah," I scoffed. "They could kill me just for telling you about it, but I don't give a shit about my own sorry ass. The only people allowed there are invited to initiate. Most of the rich bastards who participate buy a proxy to take part in the initiation - some poor kid who will jump at the chance to earn a couple of grand and take part on their behalf. All you have to do to gain entry is win or have a proxy win in your place. And if your proxy dies then you can just buy another and another and another until you back one that wins."

"Wins what?" she asked.

I swallowed down the bile that rose in my throat and shook my head.

"It's a...game I guess. We were put in this cage with weapons and tunnels and shit and told we had to be the last one standing if we wanted to leave with our lives. Once you're in there is no way out apart from winning. If you refuse to fight, they hang you from the post in the centre of the arena and gut you, leaving you to bleed out as a warning to everyone else."

"So, you had to kill people to win?" she asked softly.

"Yeah...but they weren't men like the ones we killed outside that cabin. They were just street kids who had been tricked into taking part for a chance at a better life. They weren't bad people. They didn't even want to fight. I resisted hurting the ones who begged for their lives and got through the first few hours by killing a couple of the more aggressive contenders. But it was so fucked up, Tate..."

I heard her moving off of the bed behind me, but I didn't want her trying to comfort me. I deserved to feel this rage and hatred towards myself and I wasn't looking for someone to try and tell me I wasn't the monster I'd discovered myself to be in that fucking place.

"You just did what it took to survive," she said firmly, and I was glad to find that there wasn't any pity in her tone. Just that fucking strength and bite that I loved so fucking much in her.

"There were people there in cages, being auctioned off for fuck knows what," I said as I turned to look at her. "Girls and guys who were whoring willingly to these fucked up old men because they were always promised this distant chance of more, a better life, an elevation to a higher tier where they'd be given more than they could ever dream of, but which didn't even exist from what I saw. Not to mention the unwilling ones. And you know what the worst thing about all of it is? When I gained my membership and they let me out of the fucking arena, covered in the blood of innocent fuckers who never should have been forced to die like that, I just left. I didn't try to help any of them, didn't try to go back and tear the place to the ground. I just thanked my lucky stars that I'd made it out of that fucking hell alive and went right back to my old life, trying to pretend that none of it had ever happened."

The silence that followed my words was so long that I finally turned to look at her, needing to see the disgust and contempt on her face for myself.

Instead I found her standing there looking up at me with her own rage in her eyes.

"Then let's find a way to burn it down, Kyan. If you hate the fact that you never went back so damn much, then fix it. Nobody forces the Night Keepers to do anything. So maybe you should figure out how to destroy that place and ruin all of the twisted people who run it in the process."

I almost barked a laugh, wondering if I'd failed to convey just how big of an organisation we were talking about here. The men and women who ran it were among the richest and most influential in the country. But that fire in her eyes said she'd understood that well enough. And she still believed I had what it took to burn it down.

"You think that's what we should do?" I questioned, because I knew that every decision I made now included all five of us. The vows we'd made were far more binding than any blood debt Liam imagined he held over me.

"Mortez told me that he was going to take me to Royaume D'élite when he kidnapped me. It didn't mean anything to me at the time, but hearing you say that name reminded me of it," she revealed. "This whole thing circles back to him. What if those are the real people who released the Hades Virus into the world? If he took it for them then it would make sense. And if they were the ones who did it then bringing them down could clear my father's name too."

My heart pounded at that admission and the rage in me grew to an almost unbearable level which had me struggling to hold it back. I was going to need to unleash this anger in me and soon or I'd lose my shit altogether.

"Let's destroy them then, baby," I vowed, because if they'd threatened her then that was more than enough motivation for me. I was her creature now. And even the slightest threat to her would find itself crushed beneath my wrath.

Tatum's blue eyes flared with a dark hunger at my words and she took a step closer to me. "You promised to show me your worst tonight," she breathed, reaching up to the back of her neck and tugging on the tie which held her dress up. She released it with a flick of her fingers and the silk dress fell to pool around her ankles, leaving her standing before me in her black lingerie and stilettos.

The monster in me was writhing with an energy so dark that deep down I knew I should have been refusing her, knowing that I wouldn't be able to hold back once I got my hands on her. But that was what a better man would have done. And I'd never claimed to be the better man.

I crossed the room in three long strides and kissed her hard enough to bruise, wanting to devour that faith in me which I could see burning within her eyes.

Her arms instantly wound around my neck and I gripped her ass as I forced her up hard against me. But she just bit down on the welt on my bottom lip from her punch, making me bleed again in answer to that.

"You swore to ruin me, Kyan," she growled. "Don't stop."

Any last efforts I might have made to restrain myself snapped at those words and I fisted my hand in her hair, tilting her head back and driving my tongue between her lips in a clear demand which she bowed to hungrily.

Her fingernails drove into my shoulders as she held onto me, but as her hand began to move down my chest, tugging my shirt buttons open, I pulled back.

I knocked her hands aside and looked around for a moment before spotting the red rope curtain tie hanging from a little hook on the wall beside us. I snatched it, spinning her around so that her back was to me before dragging her wrists together at the base of her spine and securing them there.

"You all good, baby?" I asked her, biting down on her earlobe as she shuddered beneath my touch.

"Yeah," she panted and I smiled darkly as I shoved her down face first on the bed, admiring the view of her ass in those little black panties as she wriggled up onto her knees for me, the red soles of her stilettos making her look even hotter.

I tugged my shirt off and kicked out of the rest of my clothes before moving after her, my hand sliding between her thighs so that I could feel the drenched material of her panties a moment before I gripped them in my fist.

Tatum gasped as the material was yanked tight then tore apart and a moment later, I was pressing the head of my cock to her entrance, loving the feeling of her wet heat against me.

I gripped her hip and drove myself straight into her, forcing her face down into the blankets so that her cry of pleasure was muffled by them.

I pulled back and slammed into her again, my hand striking down hard against her ass as I thrust in deep and she gasped as the breath was driven from her lungs.

I picked up my pace as I started moving faster, slapping her ass again whenever she cried out and thrusting my hips with a brutal savagery that had sweat rolling down my tattooed chest and her panting as she fought to meet me thrust for thrust.

The scream that left her as she came for me was almost enough to have me following her as her pussy clamped around my shaft and I cursed at the perfect tightness of her body.

But I wasn't done with her yet, I wanted more of her. Every fucking drop she had to give, and I needed it too if I wanted to tame this raging beast in my soul enough to stop its need for blood.

I pulled out of her, flipping her onto her back so that her bound hands were pinned beneath her before dropping down between her thighs and licking her sweet pussy until she was screaming again.

I gripped her ass tight enough to bruise as I devoured her, wanting to mark every inch of her flesh as mine in so many ways that she'd never get the feeling of me off of her skin.

Tatum was begging me for more as I licked and kissed her and just as I felt her drawing to the edge once more, I pushed two fingers into her pussy and my thumb into her ass. She bucked right off of the bed as she came for me and I bit down on the inside of her thigh just so that I could taste some of that pleasure in her flesh, leaving a ring of teeth marks on her skin.

I moved up her body, tugging her tits free of her bra so that the cups were crushed beneath them, pushing them up and into my face and I sucked and bit at them until she was begging me again.

"Can you take more, baby?" I purred as I moved to crouch between her thighs, looking down at her as she writhed, bound and at my mercy beneath me. It was so fucking hot that I wanted to take a picture of it and keep it forever.

I reached out to wrap my hand around her throat and her eyes widened as I tightened my grip just enough to keep hold of her and show her what I wanted.

Her tongue swept across those full, red lips and as I lined my cock up with her pussy again, she nodded, her pupils wide and gaze pleading.

I knew my smile was a dark and forceful thing as I drove myself into her again and my grip on her throat tightened just a little more. I slid my cock all the way in until my thick length was completely sheathed inside her and I gave her a moment to change her mind.

When her lips parted on a moan of pure need, my smile darkened further and I started moving.

Her legs curled around my back, her high heels driving into my spine as I fucked her hard and she encouraged me to go even harder.

My grip on her throat was tight enough for the thrill of it, but not enough to cut off her panting breaths which huffed between her lips with every deep thrust I made into her body.

I kept going, harder and harder until finally she cried out and her pussy gripped me so tight that I followed her into oblivion with a curse as pure, blinding pleasure tore through me and I collapsed down on top of her so that I could kiss that fucking beautiful sound from her lips.

The tension ran from my body like rain from a storm cloud and the frantic pace of our fucking melted into this deep and soul devouring kiss which had me never wanting to come up for air.

Her tongue danced with mine and I stroked her flesh, shifting onto my side and pulling her around so that I could loosen the rope from her wrists.

I trailed kisses over her throat, her breasts and the bite marks I'd left on her thighs. Every mark and bruise I'd placed on her skin, soothed and caressed as she caught her breath and pushed her fingers through my hair.

By the time I made it back up to her lips, she was smiling, her eyes hooded with a need for sleep as her fingers traced the devil tattoo on my chest.

"You really are an animal, Kyan Roscoe," she breathed with a smile that told me just how pleased she was to find out I hadn't been full of shit.

"I'm whatever you want me to be, baby," I replied as I kissed her again. "So long as you want me to be it."

CHAPTER SIX

We arrived back at Everlake Prep the following evening and my head was spinning with everything I'd found out about Kyan's family. I understood him better now and I'd been so off base with what I'd assumed about him that it made me feel like shit. I'd thought he was just another rich boy with a god complex, lording it around this school and beating down anyone who got in his way. But it wasn't that. Not entirely anyway. Kyan was a fundamentally good man. His morals guided his decisions. Those he punished deserved it. It wasn't black and white, but it was his truth. His need for blood and vengeance was born of the life he'd led with his family, but he turned that aggression onto deserving victims, or those who dared to challenge him in a fair fight.

He wasn't the demon I'd always thought him to be, he was a dark angel with no god. A vigilante who answered blood with blood. But the problem was, he punished himself too. He punished himself for being born of the O'Briens. He punished himself for the bad he'd done before he'd dared to leave them. I could see that hate for himself as clear as day now. He thought of himself as nothing, undeserving of love because he had never been offered it by the people who were meant to offer it unconditionally. Kyan Roscoe hadn't lived up to the name they wanted to brand him with. But what he didn't see was that that was because he was better than them. That he was worth far more in my eyes than a single one of those gangsters.

I wrapped my arms tighter around Kyan's waist as he parked his bike and killed the engine. Saint had bought me new leathers to wear a few weeks ago so I wasn't really cold, but there was a coldness in my heart now that never seemed to go away since losing Dad.

Kyan took his helmet off and I released him, doing the same as I slid off the bike. He took it from me, hanging it with his own on the handlebars and we headed down the path towards the main gate. He insisted on carrying both of our bags and I let him because I could see the need in him to do it for me. His hand brushed mine as we walked then he hooked it into his grip, squeezing possessively.

He led me confidently up to the gate and flashed a smirk at the guard on duty and he quickly let us in with a mumbled greeting. Kyan towed me up the gravel drive towards Aspen Halls, a drizzle in the air making droplets cling to my hair as we moved.

Instead of rounding the gothic building, he shoved me against it, leaning one hand above my head and caging me in as he looked down at me. I opened my mouth to question him, but he slammed his lips to mine, his hand clutching my throat in the same moment to immobilise me. I gasped, my back arching as he pressed his chest to mine, crushing me to the wall as his tongue slid between my lips and the taste of him set my heart racing. Every kiss from Kyan was like his last. Like the world was about to end and fire would rain down from the sky and devour us at any moment. But the fire that burned in me was entirely on the inside, making me hot and needy. I wanted to disappear into him and forget my pain time and again. Kyan wasn't gentle like Blake, he saw my pain and offered me a different kind. His answer to my grief was more darkness, but the type that made me forget, not the type that made me weep.

When he pulled away, we were both breathless and his eyes cut into mine as he stared at my swollen lips. He traced his thumb across them with a hungry gleam in his gaze. "One day I think I'll eat you up, baby." He gnashed his teeth at me and a smile curled up my lips.

"Not if I eat you first." I slipped away from him and he took chase, capturing my hand again and letting me pull him along this time.

"I'm not ready to share you again," he admitted.

"Greedy," I teased and he smirked, not denying it.

We reached The Temple and my heart pounded faster as we approached the door. A part of me was yearning to reunite with the rest of the Night Keepers. My tribe. The men who had come for me in my most desperate moment of need. But it was so strange to feel that way about them after everything. I just couldn't shake it off.

I pushed through the door and shouts and grunts caught my ear. I frowned as I kicked off my shoes and jogged further inside to see what the hell was going on. Saint was on the floor in the lounge while Blake knelt over him, trying to force pills into his mouth and simultaneously wash them down his throat with a bottle of water locked under his arm. It was squirting everywhere, soaking Saint as he fought Blake off with his good arm. As I watched, Saint's hand latched around Blake's throat tearing bloody nail marks into his golden flesh.

"What the hell?" I gasped as Kyan moved to my side, barking a laugh as he watched.

Blake looked up, but Saint's focus didn't waiver. He managed to get his knee between Blake's legs and jammed it into his balls. Blake fell off of him with a yell of pain, cupping his manhood and rolling from side to side on his back as the water bottle tumbled away.

Saint struggled to his feet and looked to me, his scowl lifting marginally in what very almost could have been a ghost of a smile. I noticed the place was generally a mess and Saint looked like he hadn't slept a single wink since we'd left.

"He won't take his fucking painkillers," Blake snarled as he got up, one hand still on his junk. "And I'm done trying to make him." He tossed the pills at Saint's back, serving him a sneer from the devil he'd engaged as he strode to the refrigerator, took out a beer and twisted off the cap. Blake threw himself onto the couch and started playing an Xbox game, ignoring the furious wraith that was Saint Memphis.

"This place has gone to hell," Saint snapped, his voice harsh and cold. "Rebecca is having time off for Christmas and Blake won't tidy a single fucking thing up. I can't keep up with the mess he makes because I've been too busy."

"Busy doing what?" I asked in confusion as Blake stood up from the couch, striding towards me confidently. "Wait," I gasped, holding up a hand. "I should wash my clothes and everything first and…" I looked to Kyan, the words on the tip of my tongue that I was immune from the Hades Virus, but what about him? "We should quarantine for forty eight hours." I found I hated keeping this secret, but my dad had told me in confidence and it felt wrong to just blurt it out.

"Right, yeah." Kyan looked between his friends in concern. "You'd better come bunk with me for two days then baby and Blake will have to cook for us and use Saint's bathroom until-"

"No," Saint hissed, his face twisting in rage. "I will risk the Hades Virus over sharing my bathroom with an ogre who will tarnish my clean space."

Blake scowled. "Well I'm not gonna continue waiting on Lord OCD. And anyway, I'm a Night Keeper. And I'm officially making a new rule of my own. If one of us gets sick, I'll get sick too." He shrugged like it meant nothing even though it absolutely did and Saint nodded his agreement.

"Don't be ridiculous," I gasped. "You can't risk catching the virus."

"We'll keep our distance from them, baby," Kyan assured me and I could see the decision in Blake and Saint's eyes like a solid wall. They weren't going to be swayed.

"Fine," I gave in, though I wasn't entirely happy about the compromise.

"Let me show you what I've been working on," Saint said smartly, striding to the stairs and I was glad to see that he at least seemed to be getting around alright on his own now.

I followed him up to his room and fell still as I saw what he'd done. One whole wall was plastered with each of the email print-outs my father had given me and the notes on the virus. But there were at least a hundred other pages with it now and there were more carefully organised piles on his desk too, looking ready to go into a black binder he had waiting at the centre of it.

"This is all of your father's work notes. I'm no virologist, but I am a fast learner so I took an online course on vaccines-"

"When?" I gasped. "We've only been gone two days."

"Forty one hours and thirteen minutes to be exact, and the course was fifteen hours so I had plenty of time to take it before I started reading through his work on the Hades Virus."

"*Saint.*" I turned to him, cupping his cheek to get his full attention. "Haven't you slept?"

His jaw ground and he pulled away. "That's irrelevant," he snapped, his tone harsh.

"It's not irrelevant, you're supposed to be resting. This is the complete opposite of resting," I said in exasperation. "And why won't you take your painkillers? You must be in agony!"

"The pain keeps my mind sharp," he said simply then strode over to the papers on his desk and started carefully using a hole punch to prepare them for the binder then placed them into it one at a time. I couldn't believe he'd spent Christmas like this. It made me sad that we'd gone at all.

I shook my head at him then strode downstairs and hurried over to Blake who was focusing on his video game.

"He's completely lost it," I hissed and he looked up, tossing his controller aside and dragging me down into his lap.

He kissed me hard and I blushed as he shamelessly pushed his tongue into my mouth. I tried to resist for a second longer, but I guessed as I was immune I couldn't pass the virus to him. I half wondered why he was so reckless though. It was his life he was taking into his own hands…was he that confident he wouldn't get it, or did he just not care either way? The idea of the latter made my heart hurt.

I moaned softly against his lips as he tugged me close and the knot in my chest eased a little. Blake's kisses always felt like our souls were bleeding into one another, becoming one, beautiful blazing entity that filled me up to the brim. He released me at last, rubbing his nose against mine and Kyan shot us a look from a chair across the room that I couldn't decipher.

"Firstly, hi," Blake murmured. "I should've said that when you walked in, but I was busy getting my balls crushed by our resident poltergeist. Secondly, yeah he's gone full Saint. I give up. I dunno what he needs."

"Didn't you have any fun over Christmas?" I asked with a frown.

"It was alright. Monroe came over and we watched action movies and ate pizza. Saint just stayed up in his room being Saint. He wouldn't eat anything until Monroe took pity on him and cooked him some pasta."

"Monroe did that?" I asked in surprise and Blake shrugged one shoulder.

"He's a surprisingly decent cook," Kyan chipped in, looking to me with a smirk. "He chops those onions *real* slow. And you should see him stuff a pepper."

Blake snorted and I shot him a subtle glare at his suggestive tone, though nothing he said could actually give away mine and Monroe's secret. Still, he didn't have to talk about fucking vegetables like that.

"FUCK!" Saint's voice split the air apart and my heart lurched hard.

We all darted out of our seats, racing upstairs to see what had happened. I was terrified he'd fallen or opened his wound somehow and panic blazed through me.

He was hunched over his desk as I got to him first, sliding my arm around his waist. "What's happened, are you okay? Did you hurt yourself?"

He was shaking, a single piece of paper clutched in his hand, his teeth bared and sweat beading on his brow as he stared at it.

"Shall I call the doctor?" Blake asked in concern while Kyan glanced around the room as if there might be danger lurking in the shadows.

"No," Saint breathed, his knuckles turning white as he gripped the page tighter. I realised the hole he'd punched into it for the binder clips had torn through the edge and my lips parted.

"Is this actually what's wrong?" I pointed at it and he nodded stiffly.

"We thought you'd hurt yourself!" I snapped. *Is he for real right now?*

"Get the fuck out!" he bellowed, twisting around and glaring at Blake and Kyan, waving the page at them like it was their fault there was a rip in it.

"Come on, Cinders, Satan needs a time out," Blake said, reaching for me, but Saint stepped into his way.

"Not her," Saint growled and Kyan folded his arms.

"She's not staying here while you're losing your shit, asshole," Kyan warned, holding out his hand to me in a command.

"It's fine," I insisted, knowing exactly what Saint needed. "Just go. Trust me."

"Baby-" Kyan started but Saint cut over him.

"She's made her decision now get the fuck out!" Saint snapped.

Kyan and Blake shared a look then gave in and left when it was clear I wasn't coming. I moved to Saint's nightstand, taking out the two types of painkillers and the antibiotic he was supposed to be on and popped them into my hand. I picked up the water bottle beside the bed and turned to him.

Saint was rigid as I approached him and I felt like I was closing in on a deadly snake in the grass. But I wasn't afraid. Saint and I had a strange understanding between us. And for some reason, I got past his defences easier than the others did when he was like this.

I took his hand, leading him to the armchair in the corner and encouraging him to sit down. He did so and I moved to straddle him, his throat bobbing as I settled my weight in his lap, careful not to put any pressure on his wounds. I pushed one of the pills between his lips and held the water bottle to his mouth. He tipped his head back and let me wash it down his throat then I did the next two. I pressed down gently on his uninjured shoulder so he rested back in the chair then reached towards the bandage covering the gunshot wound.

"Have you changed this since we left?" I asked and he shook his head.

I started unbinding it and he let me, his eyes on me the whole time as some of the cloying darkness left his eyes. I checked his wound for infection, but it looked clean and like it really was on the mend. Saint didn't even wince when I touched it, even though it must have been agony.

I soon had a new dressing on it and I helped him to his feet. He clutched his ribs as he moved and I hoped the painkillers would kick in soon. It hurt me to see him in so much pain.

"You need to rest," I said, leading him to the bed and pulling back the covers.

"No," he grunted. "I need more than that. I need to punish you."

I turned to him with my breath hitching even though I'd expected this. I nodded my agreement, waiting to see what he wanted and he eyed my damp hair and leather attire.

"Go to the bathroom," he commanded and I didn't hesitate, letting him take control of this situation. And I immediately felt the shackles of my mind releasing. I didn't have to try so hard to keep my mind from turning to my dad. I just had to focus on what he told me to do. Nothing else. It was so liberating.

I waited in the bathroom and he knocked on the door before long. "Can I come in?"

I released a breath of amusement. Saint sticking to the rules as usual.

"Yes," I called and he appeared holding a pale blue night dress with a black lace hem. He hung it on the back of the door and gestured to the shower with his chin. "Take your clothes off and get in. You can leave your underwear on if you want."

"What if I don't want to?" I said the words before I could pause to consider them.

"Then take them off," he said simply, but his eyes swirled with a thirst that made tingles rush down my spine.

98

I kept my eyes on his as I shed my clothes, pulling off each item and tossing it in the laundry basket as he watched. He gazed at me without blinking, like he feared missing a single millisecond of this. Saint and I were always dancing on this line of our relationship being sexual or not. I knew it was, deep in my soul, but at the same time...he wouldn't touch me. Before now that had felt right, I'd feared him touching me, my own desire for him something I'd longed to cut out. But that was before he'd almost died for me. Before he'd shown his cards and made me question everything. The fact was, I wanted him more than ever. Blake was my comfort, Monroe my rock, Kyan my strength, but Saint? Saint was my freedom. He had the ability to take over every hurt I had, every decision, every torment. He could bear the burden of it all and offer me time where I could just be free from it all. And I craved that more than anything right now.

I was down to my dark red underwear, standing before him and wanting to shed every piece of my clothing along with every emotion and hurt that kept me prisoner too. His eyes darkened to nightshade as he took in the marks Kyan had left on my body and his upper lip curled back as his rage spilled over.

"Kyan-" I started in explanation, but he cut me off.

"I know," he hissed, his gaze moving from one mark to the next like he was cataloguing them, from the bites on my thighs to the finger bruises on my hips. "Do you enjoy being fucked roughly, doll?"

I swallowed the ball in my throat as a blush rose in my cheeks. "Sometimes," I admitted. "Kyan knows I'm not breakable. I like that." I shrugged.

"I see," Saint said quietly and before he could continue this conversation I unclasped my bra and shrugged out of it, letting it fall to the floor.

Saint's features didn't even flicker, but his eyes gave away his lust and his silence spoke volumes. The dark ocean in his gaze was roiling like a stormy sea. His fingers flexed just enough to tell me how much he was itching to touch me. But he wouldn't. I knew that and yet I still ached for it.

"I don't like you calling me a doll," I said to him, raising my chin and staring him down. If he could ask me about how I liked to be fucked then I could ask him to stop disrespecting me. "It makes me sound like nothing more than a possession to you. Like my appearance is the only thing you care about. Is that what you want me to believe?"

I waited as Saint's eyes narrowed but he didn't do me the courtesy of responding to that request as he thought it over. Or maybe he wasn't thinking it over. Maybe that was all he thought of me, that I was just something to own and look pretty for him. But I found it hard to convince myself of that now that he'd almost died for me.

I slid my panties down my thighs, stepping out of them as my breathing became shallow.

"In the shower...Tatum," he said, his voice dry like sandpaper.

I tried not to flush with pleasure at the sound of my actual name on his lips, not wanting him to know how much I liked that and how much I appreciated him listening to my request, but I was fairly sure he could tell anyway.

I did as he asked, stepping into the large unit and waiting for my next instruction.

"Turn the water on. Cold," he growled, moving to the sink and resting his ass against it in prime position to watch me.

I bit into my lip as I turned the cold water on and gasped as it rushed over me. Goosebumps tumbled across my skin and I shivered in the freezing flow.

"Wash your hair first," Saint ordered and I reached for my shampoo. "No, use mine." He pointed to the products on the other side of the shower and I nodded, picking up his shampoo and squeezing some into my palm. I lathered the apple scented product into my hair, the icy water making my nipples pebble and my body pepper with tiny bumps. I knew this was another power play, a way to mark me out as his without ever laying a finger on me. Saint was creative like that.

When I'd washed my hair and it hung over me in a heavy sheet, he gave me his next command. "Switch the water to warm and use my soap to wash yourself."

I twisted the knob around and sighed as the warm water ran over me, chasing away the cold in an instant. I picked up Saint's soap, rubbing it over my body until a foam was bubbling over my breasts and running down my stomach between my thighs. My heart was thumping to a frantic, unknown beat at the feel of his eyes on me. It was so intense. I should have been ashamed or nervous, but I was neither of those things. I just felt present, focused on him and his orders and nothing else.

Steam was fogging on the glass and Saint suddenly opened the door so he could keep watching me. He wet his lips, his eyes burning holes in my flesh as he devoured me.

"Wash your pussy. Slowly," he gritted out, his eyes following my hand as I slid it between my thighs. My heart jack-hammered, my toes scrunching against the floor as I rubbed the bar of soap over my clit and a shudder ran through me.

He surveyed me with an intensity that made me want to grab him, pull him under the flow and feel his mouth on my skin. I wanted to fall to ruin for Saint Memphis. I wanted him to control my body and make me break and fall for him. I realised I was gasping for breath, my body tightening and clenching with need as I continued to circle that slick bar over and over myself.

"Enough," he growled. "Get out."

He stepped back and I dropped the bar of soap, trembling a little with the need for release as I did as he said, my eyes snagging on the huge bulge in his jeans. I froze before him, water streaming off of me as I waited for his next order, foolishly hoping that he might take this further. I was so close to him and his eyes on my body felt almost as good as his hands would as he trailed his gaze over each part of me. The air between us was electric, tangible. I could hardly breathe with how much I wanted to close the distance between us. And from the look on his face, he felt the exact same way.

"Dry off." He pointed at a large towel on the rack, stepping back again with an almost pained expression on his face. He schooled it fast, but I'd seen the transparency of his desire. He wanted this as badly as I did. But whatever it was that stayed his hand was still firmly in place in him. Maybe his need for control ran so deep that denying us both pleasure was another way to do it. I knew he'd had women before though, so what was it about me that made him resist?

I dried myself off with a towel and he directed me to put on the night dress hanging on the back of the door. I slid into it and he moved forward to arrange my damp hair over my shoulders and wipe a single droplet of water from my forehead.

"Perfect," he announced, inhaling to smell his own scent on me. "Now help me out of this sling."

I moved forward to help him take it off and placed it down on the basin as he slowly stretched out his arm which was in a cast, wincing a little as he did so.

"Does it hurt?" I asked, my voice strained.

"Not as much as losing you would have," he murmured and my heart thundered against my ribcage. "Go back to my room. Wait for me."

I nodded, turning and leaving him there as he wrapped his cast in a small towel one-handed. I heard him step into the shower as I closed the door behind me with a sharp click. I moved to the bed, sitting on the end of it and waiting, unable to help straining my ears, wondering if Saint was pleasuring himself over what he'd just seen. But if he was, I couldn't hear anything from here.

I thought over what he'd said to me and soaked in the undeniable heat in my chest it had left with me. I guessed it was hard to deny the depths of his feelings for me, whatever they may be exactly. He'd taken a bullet for me. What more could a person possibly do for someone?

He finally returned to the room with a towel around his waist, moving easier now that the painkillers had clearly kicked in. It brought a satisfied smile to my lips, but it was still hard to see all the bruising over his perfect body. He'd been careful not to get his dressing wet so it wouldn't need to be changed again and his cast was bone dry. Saint was born to follow rules. At least those he deemed necessary to follow.

"Can I help you get dressed?" I asked him as he made to walk past me and I slipped out of the bed to approach him.

Saint stilled as I moved closer, letting me walk right up to him as his eyes dragged over the thin nightdress he'd given me and he took in my hardened nipples pressing through the lace. I was still aching for the pleasure he'd almost let me have in the shower and looking at him standing there in nothing but a towel was giving me all kinds of ideas I probably shouldn't have been having about this cruel tormentor.

A bead of water slid down the dark skin of his bare chest and I bit down on my bottom lip as it rode over the swell of his pec and down his abs.

A low growl escaped him and his hands closed around my waist as he leaned down close to me, making my breath catch with his proximity.

"You never were a doll anyway, were you, Tatum?" he breathed, my name sounding sinful on those perfect lips of his. "You're a temptress, seductress, a damn siren sent to lure me in and make my body ache. You were built to test me in every way imaginable and sometimes, I think you might just make me forget every rule I've ever sworn to live by."

His grip on my waist tightened and a needy whimper escaped me as I reached for him, sliding my hands up his chest until my fingers were caressing his tattoo, inviting him to make good on that promise even though I knew I shouldn't.

"See?" he breathed, moving so close that I felt I might be consumed by his dark energy. "You're at it again. Siren."

I blinked up at him innocently, wanting to protest that I wasn't doing anything, but maybe I knew that wasn't true. Perhaps I didn't like to admit it to myself, but the idea of me tempting Saint in wasn't something I was against. This man before me might be a beast of the most terrifying kind, but there was an allure to him that I couldn't quite describe and I liked the idea of him feeling that way about me too.

"I need to get dressed," he said abruptly, using his grip on my waist to push me back a step before releasing me and walking away, leaving me reeling and aching for him to return. Why the hell did he keep doing that to me? And why the fuck did I keep letting it happen?

He walked into his closet and I frowned as I waited for him to come back. He could get out of his clothes fairly easily, but getting into them was a different matter. He returned in just a pair of boxers though, a crease on his brow saying he'd caused himself pain to pull them on.

"You're due to sleep in Blake's room tonight," he said with a flash of venom in his eyes. Was he...jealous?

"Screw the rules." I waved a hand dismissively. "I want to stay with you until you're better."

His eyebrows arched as if my suggestion was not only surprising but unsettling. I stood from the bed, taking his hand and drawing him towards his spot.

"Tatum," he warned. "The rules say-"

"I don't care, Saint," I said firmly. "I'm not going anywhere."

His eyes travelled to my lips and his adam's apple rose and fell. "Stay then," he said like it was his decision. "But when I'm strong enough to punish you properly, you'll pay for the rule break."

"Sure." I rolled my eyes, a smirk pulling at my mouth as I helped him into the bed.

I got in on the other side and Saint awkwardly tried to turn and get his book of Poe's dark poems off his nightstand.

"Would you ever just ask for help?" I teased as I leaned over him and got the book, placing it on his lap.

"I don't need help," he said simply and I tsked.

"Everyone needs help sometimes. It doesn't make you weak. Is that what you're worried about?"

A pause of silence passed. "No...my father always taught me to fight my own battles. To rely on myself and no one else."

"That sounds familiar," I sighed, the weight of his words falling over me as I recognised that same teaching from my own father. He'd encouraged me to stand on my own two feet, to be prepared for anything, to face the world alone if I had to. But that didn't mean he wasn't there for me when I needed him most. *And now he never will be again.*

I clenched my jaw and blinked back tears. Saint reached over, taking my hand and squeezing, his cool flesh against mine dragging me back up to the surface. He released me just as fast, opening the book and thumbing through the pages. Then he read a couple of lines to me. "Yet if hope has flown away. In a night, or in a day. In a vision, or in none, is it therefore the less gone? All that we see or seem. Is but a dream within a dream."

"What does it mean?" I whispered, the words making my skin prickle.

"It means that nothing really matters," he mused. "Because we're all just living in a dream."

"Do you believe that?" I asked and he contemplated that.

"I think the world is malleable," he said. "I think our realities can be forged. But that doesn't make it any less real. But I guess there's some comfort in the words because it means whatever fantasy you can dream up could be made true."

I lay back on my pillow, staring up at the ceiling as I thought on that. What did I want my world to look like now that everything had been ripped away from me? What kind of reality was worth moving forward for? And what sweet kind of dreams was I ever going to have now anyway?

"How's the research going then, brother? Have you found out anything interesting?" Kyan asked Saint at breakfast as he used a piece of toast on his plate to shovel up the last remnants of his cooked meal before stuffing it all in his mouth.

Saint watched him with undisguised disgust as Kyan proceeded to suck each of his fingers to remove the grease from them. I laughed softly and Saint shot me a glare that could have melted glass.

"I don't have enough to go on to track Mortez. Not even a first name. And there are fifteen hundred Mortezs in this state alone, let alone the whole of the United States. It is also, most likely, a fake name, especially if he really was working for the CIA which I am currently inconclusive on." Saint leaned back in his chair in thought. There was more light in his eyes today after a decent night's sleep and I was glad to see that the shadows beneath them had disappeared entirely. And it actually made me feel good to be focusing on finding the truth. "It is possible, however, that he would have rented a property or lodged in a hotel somewhere within the vicinity of this school to have been able to arrive at the cabin quickly enough to intercept Tatum's father once he tracked her phone. I have been making calls to the hotels, working grid by grid away from Everlake. There are a surprising amount of inns, B&Bs etcetera out toward the mountains and many didn't answer their phones over the Christmas period no matter how many times I called."

"He was on hold for four hours to one hotel on Christmas day, going through some automated system," Blake supplied with an eyeroll. "Remember when the line cut out and you went apeshit?" he mused like it was a fond memory and Saint's eyes narrowed to slits.

I didn't understand why Saint had been working so tirelessly to find some information on Mortez since I'd left. I knew it was important, but why was *he* so obsessed with it especially?

"It's a shame we didn't take Mortez's phone from his dead body then," Kyan mused, a smirk dancing around his lips and I shook my head at him, knowing he had it. But he was clearly going to mess with Saint before he handed it over.

"A fact I would not have missed if I'd been even semi-conscious," Saint snipped in irritation.

Kyan reached into his blazer pocket and placed down the phone on the table, spinning it around next to his empty plate.

Saint looked over at it with the fires of hell blazing in his eyes. But when he spoke, he was deathly calm. And that was somehow more frightening. "If that is what I think it is, Kyan Roscoe, I will take my knife, castrate you and burn your balls in the fireplace."

"I'm kinda attached to my balls, bro, how about you take a finger instead?" Kyan offered with a chuckle, sliding the phone down the table to Saint.

Saint's hand slammed down on it, his knuckles turning white around it. "Why did you keep this from me?" he hissed like a freaking snake.

Kyan shrugged one shoulder. "I forgot about it."

Saint stood from his chair, practically spitting venom. "You *forgot*? Forgot the one item which could have saved me hours and hours of research into the most minor of details?"

"Yep." Kyan nodded. "Oh, I popped the SIM card out in case there's a tracker on it, but my bet is that's a burner. If not, I know some software you can install which-"

"I know how to block a tracker you infuriating, bushwhacking peasant of a fucking *hick*," Saint snapped, rising from his seat and snatching up his knife as if he was about to see through on his threat and Kyan laughed his head off, placing his hand down on the table.

"You can take my pinky," Kyan offered. "But are you sure you want it? Don't forget how good it feels up your ass, baby. That's a lifetime of pleasure you'll be denying yourself."

Saint growled like an animal. "You won't be laughing when I do it and take your balls too while you're crying like a baby on the floor."

"Saint," I gasped. "Calm down."

"I'll be calm when pieces have been severed from his body," Saint hissed, striding towards all two hundred pounds of Kyan even with a broken arm, fractured ribs and a freaking gunshot wound, but apparently none of those things were enough to deter him. Kyan leaned back in his seat, raising his pinky finger in offering and grinning tauntingly as Saint came at him.

Blake got up, casually stepping between them and snatching the knife from Saint's grip. Saint got up in his face, his teeth bared, his shoulders shaking.

"You have the phone now, dude, so go do your mumbo jumbo to it so we can find out what's on it," Blake said firmly, the voice of reason. Why was that so hot?

"Blake's right," I agreed quickly. "If he was sent by someone, then surely his phone will link us to them," I added hopefully, praying there really was a lead on there. There just had to be. Maybe this was why Saint was so obsessed with his investigations; it was a distraction. And with his current state, he needed one of those almost as keenly as I did.

Saint met my gaze and I sucked my lip, hopeful that he might drop his dismembering threats on Kyan in favour of this. His shoulders slumped and he sighed, heading away towards his room.

"I will disable any tracking software," he muttered, his posture still rigid as he walked upstairs.

Kyan snorted a laugh and I tossed a piece of apple at him from my bowl of fruit and yoghurt. It slapped against his cheek, leaving a white patch of yoghurt by his lips which he licked away before tossing the piece of apple into his mouth too. "Thanks, baby," he mocked. "C'mere. I want a kiss."

Blake frowned, looking at him for the joke. "The closest I've ever seen you get to a kiss is eating a juicy peach. What gives?"

"Things change." Kyan shrugged, but he eyed me hungrily like he was deadly serious about getting his lips on mine.

"Kyan couldn't help himself when he saw me covered from head to toe in blood," I said, my heart beating harder at the memory.

"That's sick, man," Blake commented, but he smirked too.

"I am sick. Really fucking sick. I should be locked up," Kyan drawled then got up, striding towards me on the hunt for that kiss. He leaned down, his hand sliding into my hair and pulling tightly, making me tip my head back so he could claim my mouth. His tongue sank deep between my lips and heat rose in my cheeks as he kissed me unashamedly, branding me as his right in front of Blake.

When he pulled away, I was as breathless as he was and the storm in his eyes said he didn't want to be done with me yet.

"She tastes like sugar laced perfection, right?" Blake grinned, looking hungry to come and claim a kiss for himself and I wasn't wholly against that idea.

"Yeah," Kyan said gruffly just as Saint returned from upstairs with Mortez's phone in hand.

"If there was a tracker it is now disabled, but it's got a passcode," he growled. "I will compile a list of the most common passcodes and use any information I have on Mortez to make some intelligent assumptions."

"If we get locked out of that phone, the information on it will be gone," Kyan warned.

"Congratulations," Saint deadpanned. "You just won the King of Stating the Obvious award. Here's your prize." He punched Kyan's shoulder with his good arm, hard enough to make Kyan wince before he burst out laughing again.

"Are you sure you can break into it?" I asked Saint, worry gnawing at me. Whatever was on that phone had to be able to help us. I was pinning so much on that hope.

"Yes, siren," he said confidently. "Because my name is Saint Memphis."

"And does *the* Saint Memphis want another little side project, because me and Tatum have some vengeance plans and we could use a psycho Sherlock Holmes to help us out with it," Kyan said and despite his jokes, I could see his hesitance to speak this secret in his eyes.

"Go on," Saint encouraged as his brows arched.

"Well, as you know, my family are a bunch of messed up motherfuckers," Kyan began slowly and I squeezed his hand in solidarity.

"Understatement of the year," Blake joked.

"Yeah. Well, I should have told you this when it happened, but back then I guess I was afraid," Kyan said.

"Afraid?" Saint questioned like the thought of that was absurd and I guessed it was kinda hard to think of Kyan fearing anything. But when it came to the love of these men, I knew that meant more to him than anything in the world and I understood why he'd been afraid of altering their opinion of him.

"Last summer, Liam decided that it was time for me to be initiated into this fucked up secret society that him and his rich friends are all a part of. It's called Royaume D'élite. I dunno what that means, but-"

"Elite Kingdom," Saint supplied, because of course he knew that without even trying.

"Right. Makes sense, seeing as every asshole there clearly thinks of themselves as a god," Kyan spat bitterly. "Anyway, it's a place where they meet and arrange business dealings and lord it over all the small folk I guess. They drink fancy alcohol and wear masks and all that shit. But it's not just about business dealings, it's like a place where laws no longer exist. There are men and women there who are bought and sold to be used for anything from fucking to butchering and that's not an exaggeration. The shit I saw there was enough to fuck me up and I've seen a lot of depraved crap in my lifetime."

"Why wouldn't you tell us about this before now?" Blake asked, seeming offended and Kyan hung his head.

"Because... I had to take part in an initiation to earn my membership there and I wasn't given a choice in my participation. They hold this fucked up death game where most of the prospective members just use a proxy – some poor street kid with no idea what they've been put in there for and no choice in the matter. Only one winner can be left at the end of the game which means everyone else has to die. I refused to force some poor bastard to participate in my place, so I..."

"You took part and won," Saint finished for him, his frown deepening. "And you feared we would change our opinion of you when we learned you had been forced to take the lives of innocents?"

I shifted closer to Kyan, fearing the next words that might come from Saint's lips but I was totally thrown as instead of berating him or judging him, Saint stood and moved around the table before enveloping Kyan in his arms. Blake was half a step behind him and the three of them clung to one another fiercely for a long moment as I felt their love for each other like a tangible force in the air.

"You are one of the best men I know, Kyan Roscoe," Saint growled. "Nothing would ever lower my opinion of you."

"I love you, man," Blake added. "And I'm sorry you had to deal with this alone for so long."

Kyan sagged with relief as he clung to the men he'd chosen for his brothers for a little longer before shoving them off playfully.

"Alright, alright, I'm an idiot for doubting you," he said with a relieved laugh. "Now unless one of you wants to suck my cock, I suggest you sit back down and decide whether or not you wanna help me and Tate take those motherfuckers down?"

Kyan dragged me into his lap with a wide grin and I couldn't help but beam back at him as Saint considered what we wanted.

"Yes...I will assist you," Saint agreed. "I'll need to sit with you and go over every single detail you know about their organisation-"

"I was afraid of that," Kyan groaned.

"It may take some time, but I'm sure I'll find a way to unravel their twisted little club." Saint said it with an almost lustful expression and I realised he was totally in his element. And who better to help us take down a bunch of monsters, than the most dangerous monster I knew?

CHAPTER SEVEN

The first day of class after the Christmas break had been a success for the most part. Pearl Devickers had managed not to try and flash me her tits during P.E., none of the little assholes had been sent for a 'chat with the head' and I hadn't even had to give anyone detention.

All in all it was a good day, and it was about to get a hell of a lot better because Tatum was about to come join me for our first kickboxing lesson of the term and I hadn't had her to myself since we'd been in that cabin waiting for her dad to arrive. We'd hung out a lot as a group with the other Night Keepers over the Christmas break, but the risk of them catching onto us had meant that I hadn't so much as touched her in all of that time and now that we'd already crossed that line, I found myself desperate to tear through it again.

Even better than the fact that I had a perfectly valid excuse to be rolling around on the mats with her for the next couple of hours was the fact that I had her all to myself tonight too. And I planned to make damn good use of every single second of that time.

I'd already crossed into forbidden territory with her and there was no way that I could turn back now. So if I was going to go to hell anyway then I wanted to be sure I'd sinned as much as physically possible before then.

The door swung open just as I was drawing the blinds closed over the window. It was dark out anyway so it wouldn't draw suspicion.

As Tatum stepped in, I moved towards her, turning the key in the lock behind her as I crowded her back against the door.

"Fuck, I've missed you this week," I groaned as I leaned close and inhaled the sweet scent of her skin.

"You've seen me every day," she replied with a laugh, swatting my chest and making me groan.

"Yeah, but I can't touch you when the others are there. I feel like I can hardly even look at you either. It's like a slow form of torture which has had my balls aching and me jacking off alone to the memory of your body every damn night." I pressed a kiss to her neck and she moaned softly as she arched into me. "And then I have to watch Kyan and Blake pawing at you all the damn time. It's fucking painful, princess."

"You're the one who told me that you couldn't make me any promises. You can't expect me to be exclusive..."

"I'm not saying that," I ground out, even though truth be told, it was killing me to see her with them and not me. But it wasn't fair of me to try and force promises from her when I knew I couldn't put her first. There would always be that one pressing thing which had to be my priority. And until I'd seen Troy Memphis pay for what he'd taken from me, I couldn't even commit to surviving whatever it was that I'd need to do to bring him down. Let alone make her promises of a future. "But I wish I could."

"I know," she replied, her voice husky as she kept her palms pressed to the door behind her, like she was fighting the urge to touch me. "But even if you did want that, I'm not sure if..."

I pulled back and looked down at her with a slight frown, tilting my head as I looked into her big blue eyes and found guilt waiting there for me.

"Say it, princess, I'm a big boy, I can handle it."

"You know how much I want you," she said, biting her bottom lip as her gaze trailed down my body. "But, I swore to belong to all of the Night Keepers and I kinda...don't hate the idea of that so much recently."

I stilled as I considered that. I mean, it wasn't exactly a surprise that she had something going with Blake and Kyan, but I guessed I'd just thought that if I'd asked her for all of her, then she would have said yes. But maybe that just made me a fucking fool.

"Oh."

"Nash," she breathed, catching my hand to stop me as I started to draw back. "What difference does it make? You're not asking me to be exclusive and what I have with them doesn't have any bearing on how strongly I feel about you." She reached out to press a hand to my heart which leapt at her touch before she skimmed her fingertips down my body. "And you still want me, don't you?"

"Yeah, I want you princess. I want you like I've never wanted anyone before."

"So, take me. The rest of it doesn't make a difference to what we have."

I nodded, because in theory, her words made total sense. It was just a little hard for me to fully comprehend, because there was no chance in hell that I wanted to be seeing anyone other than her. She was it for me. The only girl I thought of or fantasised about. But maybe that didn't matter. So what if she was hooking up with them too? It didn't really make her any less mine, did it? And as a teacher who'd fucked his student, it wasn't like I could really try taking the moral high ground.

"Come on," I said, pulling her over to the corner where our gloves were waiting and reaching out to wrap her knuckles for her. I'd already done mine and I was itching to get in the ring with her.

Tatum watched me as I worked and we both tugged our gloves on in silence before stepping into the ring.

"No holding back," I said, the hint of a smile tugging at the corner of my lips.

"I need this today," she admitted as she rolled her shoulders, her gaze assessing me as I lifted my fists, waiting for her to get ready.

"Then hit me with your best shot, princess. I wanna feel all of that rage in you."

"You might regret that offer," she said, moving to my left and forcing me to match her as we circled each other. "Because I have more rage in me than I think could even be put into words at this point."

"And grief," I pointed out. "I know you're trying not to think about your dad all the time. But I know that grief, that pain. Don't forget I've lived it too. And I know that trying to ignore it won't work in the long term. You really need to-"

Tatum lunged at me so suddenly that I couldn't block it in time, her fist slamming into my chin before she followed up with the other to my gut. Her blue eyes were wild with a reckless kind of savagery and a piece of me knew that she shouldn't really be fighting in this emotional state. But I also knew she needed it. So if she wanted to throw all of that pain my way then I was willing to take it.

I ducked back and took a half assed shot at sweeping her legs out from under her which she managed to jump before leaping at me again.

"Don't go easy on me, Nash. If you won't fight properly then I'll get Kyan down here. He's not afraid to go hard on me."

I gritted my teeth at that insinuation. I'd seen the bruises on her skin after she'd come back from her trip to see Kyan's family at Christmas and I'd also been thoroughly chewed out for trying to insinuate he'd hurt her. Because apparently she'd been begging for every one of them – Kyan's words, not hers, but she hadn't denied it either.

But that didn't mean I was going to let that animal get in the ring with her.

She came at me again and I took a shot to the ribs before returning it with a punch to her gut.

We quickly fell into a brawl, scrapping and punching and fighting with a desperate kind of urgency to her moves like she thought she was on a time limit to do this.

I managed to knock her back a few steps but she quickly rushed me again, ducking low and throwing her shoulder into my gut with enough force to unbalance me. She managed to hook her leg around mine before I could right myself and the two of us crashed down onto the mats.

Tatum was totally lost to her anger and her grief and as she straddled my waist, she threw punch after punch, her breathing ragged and eyes swimming with tears she refused to let fall.

I fought back, but not hard enough to unseat her, taking her anger and grief and letting her throw it into my body until the strength faded from her limbs and she ripped her gloves off, tossing them across the room with a growl of hopeless frustration.

"It hurts so fucking much, Nash," she breathed, her voice a broken, empty thing as she dipped her chin and her blonde hair cascaded forward to curtain her beautiful features.

"I know, princess," I replied, letting my grief show too as it rose up keenly in my chest to meet with hers.

She dropped down and kissed me hard, my breath catching in my throat at the feeling of those full lips against mine and the taste of her heartache on her tongue.

Tatum's hands slid down my shirt which was clinging to me with perspiration from our workout and she ground herself down over my dick, making it hard for me to think of anything aside from her.

I shifted to sit up as I kissed her back and she tugged my shirt over my head with a hard yank, pausing to rip my gloves off too when my shirt got caught on them.

"Wait," I murmured against her mouth as our heavy breathing filled the room and I had to fight to keep hold of my thoughts as I tried to break away from her. I was drunk on this girl. Totally, helplessly, inebriated and out of my damn mind over her, but I needed to try and regain an inch of control because if we did this here then I knew we'd just keep taking risks, hooking up anywhere and everywhere we could. "We could be caught," I panted. "Let's just wait until we get back to mine. I've got a fuck ton of junk food and candles and all kinds of romantic shit-"

"Just fuck me, Nash," she replied, grinding down on me in a way that seriously had me changing my mind about this, but I really had wanted to try and be at least a bit sensible about this.

"Come on. We can be back at my place within like fifteen minutes and then I promise I'll make you-"

"I can't come to your place tonight, Nash," Tatum huffed, pulling back an inch so that she could look at me and we were no longer kissing between every word.

"But it's my night with you," I protested, realising I sounded like a little bitch but unable to stop the way the words came out. "I only get you once every four nights." No need to mention the fact that I'd been counting down the fucking days. We'd missed our last assigned night because Saint was being a fuckwit about taking his pain pills but it had been over a week now and he was well on the mend. Besides, I didn't really give a shit if he took his pills or not. That asshole deserved at least a little pain. It was better than what my brother had got.

"Sorry Nash, but I can't come and stay with you tonight. Saint still needs me. He won't listen to anyone else and I don't want his recovery getting fucked up because he's too stubborn to look after himself."

"Who gives a shit?" I snapped, sexual frustration and my hate of all things Memphis colliding to make me pissier than usual. "That motherfucker did all kinds of fucked up shit to you, not to mention what his family did to mine. Where are your letters, Tatum? Is he still keeping them under lock and key? That whole thing is so fucked up and you know it."

Tatum's jaw set angrily and she leaned back even more, her hands slipping from my chest as she folded her arms and scowled at me.

"Saint almost died trying to protect me. The least I can do is make sure he doesn't end up with permanent injuries," she growled forcefully, leaving no room for argument. But that was bullshit and she knew it. I might have been able to accept her having something with Blake and Kyan, but Saint was cut from the devil's cloth.

"So, what? He takes a bullet for you and now you've lost interest in all of our plans?" I demanded, my heart galloping in my chest at a fierce pace as I considered that. I didn't want to admit to how relieved I'd been to finally have help in my vendetta against the Memphis family, but the idea of her backing out on me felt like having a dagger plunged right into my back and twisted.

"That's not what I said," Tatum growled, shoving to her feet like she wanted to put distance between us and I got up too, glaring as I stood over her and waited to hear what the fuck she had to say on this. "But you do realise that blaming Saint for what his father did is exactly the same as the way the Night Keepers blamed me for the Hades Virus. They believed my dad was responsible and so they made *me* pay. How is you going after Saint any different than that?"

"You can hardly compare yourself to Saint Memphis," I snarled. "He's a fucking monster. He practically enslaved you, he half drowned you, locked you in a coffin, made you believe he destroyed those letters-"

"I know," she all but shouted at me. "I know exactly what he fucking did to me! But I'm also starting to think I know *him*. And I don't think we understand the half of what he's been through in his life. The shit he survived to make him the way he is-"

"I don't give a damn!" I roared, totally losing my cool. "Poor little rich boy had a daddy who didn't love him. Big fucking deal. I bet he cries himself to sleep on his mountain of hundred dollar bills every night. But I had a family who *did* love me. I had a mom who worked herself to the bone to provide for us and a brother with his whole fucking life laid out ahead of him and Troy Memphis just took all of that away from me like it meant nothing at all. He killed them. And unlike you, I haven't had the chance to take my revenge on the man who killed my parent yet, so maybe you just don't have a fucking clue about what I've lived through, or maybe you just don't care."

"Fuck you, Nash," Tatum snarled, her eyes flashing with rage as she stormed towards the door, but there was no fucking way I was letting her walk out on me.

She turned the lock and ripped the door open, but my hand slammed into it above her head as I forced it closed again.

Tatum whirled around as I caged her in, her chin rising as she glared up at me. "You know, I actually thought you were better than them, but you're not, are you? You might have treated me better but you're just as ruthless, just as cruel. You don't even care who you hurt in the process of getting your revenge, just so long as you get it."

"You think I'm as bad as the Night Keepers?" I blanched, staring at her as the fury in her eyes burned right into my soul.

"No, Nash, I don't think you're as bad as the Night Keepers. I think you *are* a Night Keeper. You're just as much of a monster as any of them, maybe even worse. Because their actions were based on grief and shock. Once they realised that I wasn't really the one they should be blaming, they backed off, apologised, even proved they care about me. But you? You've had years to figure out where to aim your grief and how to get your revenge and yet you still chose to aim it at the son of the man responsible as part of your plans."

"I'm nothing like them," I growled, moving so close to her that our chests brushed and she was forced to tilt her chin right back to look up at me.

"No?" Tatum hissed, her rage turning into this deadly kind of coldness that had my entire body tingling with fury. "How come you've got matching tattoos then?"

She shoved me hard enough to knock me back a step, ripped the door open and was gone before I could even reply.

I roared my rage at the empty room, kicking my water bottle hard enough to send it flying into the wall where it broke and sent water spraying everywhere. I marched straight over to the punching bag where I began pounding on it with all the fury of my grief and loss.

I didn't even know how long I stayed there punching it, but my knuckles tore and bled as I went, giving some outward show to the pain which lived inside me. By the time my energy burned out, it was long past midnight and Tatum had never come back.

I sank down to the floor and dropped my head between my knees as the most heart breaking memories of that car crash which had stolen my family overwhelmed me and I just sat there, all alone in the company of my grief.

"You know," Kyan's voice made me look up what must have been at least an hour later, and I scowled as he strode into the gym like he owned the fucking place. "For two people who are taking part in a real life dirty fantasy, you and Tatum sure have been giving off some savage sexual frustration vibes tonight."

"Fuck off, Kyan, I'm not in the mood," I growled.

"Sure." He sat down beside me and pulled a hip flask from his pocket, offering it to me and I took it without a word, tipping it up into my mouth and letting the Jack Daniels burn its way down to my gut as I drank every last drop of it.

We sat in silence for a moment while I pursed my lips and I twisted the empty hipflask between my fingers as I glared at the boxing ring in front of us where I'd been wrestling with Tatum before it had all gone to shit.

"When I was about nine or ten, my grandpa decided to send me to play pee-wee football," Kyan began slowly.

"Is that so?"

"Mmm. I thought for a while that maybe I'd done something to deserve it. Like…I was getting a reward or some shit, but it was all just more of the same old bullshit really, a ploy to get me in the good graces of the children of the most powerful fuckers in the state. Anyway, point is, it didn't take me long to start noticing that my family weren't exactly…normal."

I snorted derisively. He'd told me enough about the O'Briens for that to have become painfully obvious. Besides, a Google search had given me plenty of articles on the biggest crime family in the state if I was interested in looking into it, though I'd stopped snooping after getting a brief overview. Point was, Kyan's family were not nice people.

"Yeah," he agreed even though I hadn't said anything. "Anyway, long story short, I know you don't like to talk about what happened to your family and shit but it's pretty obvious that they're not around anymore. And I guess, maybe you should just try to remember that you were lucky to have them while you did. Because if you miss them this much then I'm guessing they were better people than any I've ever been related to."

"What makes you think I'm thinking about my family?" I muttered, wondering if I should just tell him to fuck off or maybe challenge him to get in the ring with me. I didn't know if him being here was making me feel better or worse.

"Come on, man, we've been hanging out here for years. You might be a grade A asshole when it suits you, but you're also one of a very small group of people who I don't ache to murder through pure irritation at their existence. You might not want to think of a mean motherfucker like me as one of your only friends, but that's what I am. No, in fact, fuck that, you're a Night Keeper now, which means I'm your family. And I take note of the people I give a shit about. So I know what you look like when your grief is eating at you and I figured out a long time ago that you don't really like to talk about it. And that's cool. I'll be your punching bag if you prefer to vent your demons like that."

I pushed my tongue into my cheek as I considered his words. I'd been a loner for so fucking long that I hadn't really considered the fact that I didn't like it that way. And he was right, the two of us had a bond which I didn't easily form with other people. But maybe I had been holding back on account of my family. I didn't want to lose anyone else. But if I was willing to risk letting Tatum get close to me, then what reason did I have to fight a friendship with Kyan or anyone else for that matter?

"I do enjoy punching that face of yours," I joked and he chuckled loudly.

"Give it to me good, baby, you know how I like it," he teased, pushing to his feet and tugging his shirt off, revealing his ink and making me look up at him.

"I had a brother," I said without standing up, feeling like I should give him something true even if I couldn't offer the whole story. "And I guess, I've never really wanted to be close to other guys in any real way since he died because I hate the idea of replacing him or trying to emulate that bond with anyone who isn't him."

Kyan nodded like that actually made sense to him, scratching at his ribs where a tattoo of a raven in flight sat and my gaze trailed across some more of his ink with interest. He really was an artist and he'd made his flesh into his canvas.

"I have no blood brothers," he said slowly. "So I can't really begin to imagine what it might be like to lose one. That said, in my family, chances are any brothers I did have would be conniving sons of bitches anyway. But I did choose two brothers for myself – three now in fact. And I can't say that letting you into the fold has lessened my love for the others." He shrugged. "So maybe stop second guessing what this shit has to mean for you or your past and just do what feels right. If being one of us makes you happy then just…be happy. Fuck knows there's more than enough in this world to make you feel like shit most of the time."

"That's…actually really deep for you," I said, pushing myself to my feet as I looked at him and a smirk tugged at his lips.

"Oh yeah, I'm good at deep. Just ask Tatum. Girl likes it *real* deep. But I guess you figured that out for yourself already, huh?" he taunted and I remembered exactly why I thought of him as an asshole ninety nine percent of the time as jealousy rose up in me, igniting the lingering anger from my argument with the girl in question. "Do you wanna tell me why she came storming back from this little workout the two of you had looking all hot and bothered in all the wrong ways? I had to fuck her through four orgasms before she even began to calm down-"

I threw a punch into his gut with my bare fist and he oomphed out a breath as he laughed through the pain.

"Was it that you couldn't hit the spot?" he choked out as he backed up, clearly baiting me, but I let him do it because I wanted to vent some of my own anger and I knew that was what he was after too.

"I'm guessing all she's got with you is sex then?" I taunted as I hounded after him. "Because there's no way in hell that I can believe she likes being around you for your riveting conversational skills."

"Are you trying to rile me up by suggesting that my girl only wants me for my cock?" he laughed. "Because you wouldn't hear many complaints from me if that was the case."

Kyan took a swing at me which I managed to block before I threw my fist into his ribs, striking that raven right in its smug little face.

"That's not a good thing, idiot," I grunted as he swung a knee into my side and pain ricocheted through my flesh.

"Well, sadly for you she loves everything about me. But I will admit that my cock is pretty high up there on the list. Can't say I'd mind watching you bend her over your desk and give her the cane though. I bet she'd be into it if we asked."

"Stop making student/teacher jokes," I snapped, sweeping his legs out from beneath him with a bark of triumph. "That's got nothing to do with what I have with her."

We fell into a furious battle of fists and power as we rolled across the hard floor and I grunted as he hit me with the force of a fucking sledgehammer. We shouldn't have been doing this without gloves and I knew we'd both be black and blue tomorrow, but it was too late to do anything about that now.

After taking way more hits than I liked, I managed to flip him over beneath me and wrench his arm up his back, driving my knee down into his spine to keep him there.

I counted to three loudly, knowing he was too much of a stubborn bastard to tap out himself then shoved myself to my feet. Kyan rolled onto his back, panting and laughing, his chest glistening with sweat.

"Are you touchy about the student/teacher thing because you don't want me thinking you want to pound me too?" he joked because apparently he was looking for another kicking.

"Fuck off," I growled without any venom as I moved to grab a towel from my bag at the side of the room to mop my brow.

"So… Saint has claimed monopoly of our girl because he's got an itty bitty hole in his shoulder, leaving us on the subs bench until further notice," he said as he got up and followed me across the room. "That leaves us with two options – we either suck each other off to help us get through this dry patch…"

"Or?" I asked, choosing not to dignify that with a response because I certainly wasn't going to fuck another one of my students. Especially not one with stubble, countless tattoos, broad shoulders and a dick.

"Or, we head back to your place and get fucked up while planning ways to get revenge on the Lord of Darkness for breaking his own precious rules." Kyan's eyes glimmered with mischief at that idea and I couldn't help but smirk.

"Option B has a lot of appeal," I agreed, grabbing my shit and turning my back on the gym as I switched off the lights and followed Kyan out.

"Great. Because I already assumed you would say yes and I've already had the perfect idea for how to get under his skin."

"Oh yeah? How?" I asked as we began walking towards the exit.

"I've designed a new tattoo which will drive him in-fucking-sane every time I show him it. And I brought everything I need to add it to my collection. After that, let's sneak back to The Temple and rearrange the food he's got stored down in the catacombs."

"I can log into the school database and drop his GPA to a 3.7?" I suggested with a smirk.

"Fuck yes. His head might actually explode if that happens." Kyan threw an arm around me and howled with laughter and I actually found myself joining in.

Maybe he had a point about me letting him in. It certainly beat sitting around and moping on my own. And if it also equalled Saint Memphis's head exploding then all the better.

CHAPTER EIGHT

I met Mila a few hundred yards from The Temple and walked to English with her while the Night Keepers walked behind us like three dark shadows. I put some distance between us and them so I could chat to my friend in private, but she kept glancing back over her shoulder at them like their presence was unsettling.

"So, what's the real story about Saint's injuries?" she asked and my stomach knotted as I stuck to the story that we'd all decided on.

"There's no other story. He fell off Kyan's dirt bike," I said with a shrug.

Saint had fed the lie to his dad too and a short article had been printed about it in the Sequoia Tribune to cover any students making up their own rumours once they saw his arm in a sling. But there had been plenty this week so far, so it hadn't exactly been effective. Some people believed he'd been beaten up by Kyan and others took to a more elaborate story that he'd been attacked by a bear on Tahoma Mountain before he killed it with his bare hands.

"I've never seen that boy on a bike," she half laughed but I couldn't even muster a smile.

"It was a dare," I answered, the story well memorised by now.

"God, I bet he's been a nightmare to live with."

"He's good so long as I'm around to tend his wounds," I mused.

"Is he making you into his nurse now as well as his slave?" she hissed.

"No...it's not like that," I said, wanting to explain, but how could I? I couldn't even tell Mila about my dad until an official story came out about his death. Otherwise how was I supposed to explain me knowing? And that meant I couldn't go near the truth about Saint nearly dying for me.

"What's it like then?" She narrowed her eyes at me. "Please tell me you're not going all Stockholm on the Night Keepers, girl."

"No," I said quickly, wishing I could explain. And maybe I could a little. I'd never promised to keep my feelings secret. And Mila was my friend. A girl. And it was so nice being around her again. I had so much going on right now that I was seriously gonna go crazy if I didn't get some of it out. And maybe it would distract me enough from Dad and all the bad shit I was trying not to let spill over in my chest. The fact that me and Monroe weren't talking since our fight was playing hard on my mind too. But every time I considered trying to bridge the gap between us, I remembered what he'd said to me and it got my blood boiling all over again. "They aren't who I thought they were though."

Mila arched a brow, but she didn't look judgemental, just curious.

I sighed heavily, tugging her along the path at a quicker pace even though the guys were plenty far behind us now. "Did you know all the terrible shit the Unspeakables did? I mean, *really* terrible shit."

Her eyes swirled with interest. "What do you know?"

I leaned closer to her, telling her everything I knew about them. How Deepthroat had tried to date rape Kyan, how Bait had seduced and manipulated an underage girl and taken her virginity, and every other crime they'd committed. Each story made her lips part wider until she was practically gaping at me. She'd known the rumours, but not the whole story and I could see her disgust as I told her the truth.

"They punish people who deserve it," I finished.

"Except you," she said fiercely and I loved her for that.

"Yeah, except me. But a lot has changed since then. I got my revenge and I think...they really are sorry."

She cast another look over her shoulder. "Even the devil's earth-dwelling cousin?"

I snorted a laugh. "Saint is complicated. Things aren't exactly right between us, but he cares about me. More than I ever thought he could care about anything."

"So what are you saying...you're dating them? *All* of them?" She sounded somewhere between incredibly impressed and totally horrified.

"I guess so," I said, unsure myself. It was easier to put labels on what me and Blake and me and Kyan were. But Monroe I could never mention, and Saint was just...Saint. I wanted them all though, I couldn't deny that. If any of them had asked me to be theirs alone though, I knew I couldn't do it. Belonging to one of them meant belonging to all of them, it was just how it was. Maybe a precedent had been set by the Night Bound legend or maybe it had nothing to do with that at all, but I knew I didn't desire one of them more than the rest. It didn't even make sense to me. I had never wanted anything long term with any guy, now there were four who I desired and yet I could put no label on exactly what it was I wanted from them. Or they from me. We just needed to be together. It was as simple and as confusing as that.

"Tatum, girl, you are the definition of taking on more than one person can handle," she laughed.

"I can handle it," I teased. "I think."

"I can handle one man-snake just fine, but three? Do you like, get with them all together?" she asked, her horror giving way to her desire for the juicy details.

I laughed and it felt good to feel some light in me again. "No. I mean, not *no*. There was one time Kyan and Blake got handsy with me while Saint watched."

"Oh my god," she groaned. "You're gonna be on one of those lifestyle shows aren't you? Like that woman who married her dining table and the six chairs."

I laughed again. "*Mila.* I'm not marrying anyone, trust me. This is just... temporary." Even saying that made my heart clench up into a tight ball. But there was only six months until graduation and then what? Blake, Kyan and Saint had lives waiting for them beyond the walls of this school. And the Hades Virus wasn't going to be around forever keeping us contained here. They'd find a vaccine eventually. They had to. And Monroe...what would he do? He would have made his move on Saint and his father by then or he'd miss his chance. What if he ended up in prison? I cringed at the thought and was glad when I realised Mila was looking down at her phone, not reading my expression.

The idea of losing my men was suffocating. And that made me fear just how deeply my heart was invested in them. It was the one thing I'd sworn they could never have. And I was still trying to guard it. But was it already too late?

"Danny's practising dirty talk," Mila told me. "He legitimately just told me he's getting as hard as an elephant's tusk thinking about what he wants to do to me tonight." She sighed dramatically as I laughed. "I guess that's an improvement on him telling me he wanted to spread open my pomegranate and lick out the seeds the other day. Honestly, that boy. Points for creativity, but minus points for *ew*."

"He's sweet though," I commented and she nodded in agreement.

"*So* sweet. He got me this for Christmas, god knows where he found it or who he bribed to get it in the gate." She pulled a pendant out from under her shirt with a chunky gold heart on it and a thick blue sapphire in the middle of it. "It's the fugliest thing I've ever seen in my life let me tell you. But he's mine so I'll wear it and punch anyone who dares mock me for it." She twisted it over to show me a large engraved D on the back of it. "He told me I can now take his D with me everywhere. Total keeper, right?" Her tone was mocking but there was a glimmer in her eyes that said she meant those words.

"How's the sex training going?" I smirked.

"Girl, I am not cut out for hard labour. I wish someone would just take the boy to a fuck-ya-girl right summer camp or something. Do they have those? They totally should." She narrowed her eyes, a hopeful glimmer entering in them. "Wait a sec, how good are those Night Keepers in bed? The rumours about them are so overblown I dunno what to believe. Don't judge, but I glimpsed Kyan's dick after you fish-dunked him and he went naked swimming in the lake. I legit had to double-take that he wasn't wrangling the loch ness monster between his thighs. And Blake streaked when he won last year's football season so I know he's at least got the equipment. Saint's got that look in his eyes that says he'll murder you viciously but he might just make you come fifty times in a row first."

I breathed another laugh. "What are you saying? You want me to send Danny to Night Keeper Camp?"

"Well, are the rumours true about their performance because Katie Hawkins - who everyone calls Whore-kins now by the way since she has officially blown ninety percent of the football team - said Blake fucked her so good last summer that she's still mourning the rest of her life without sex as good as that. Shrine to his cock and all."

"Mila!" I laughed, losing it completely. It felt so good to talk about something trivial for once. I could keep all the darkness in me at bay and just bathe in her shining aura.

"Well? Come on girl, don't hold out on me," she pushed.

"Kyan and Blake, well…they can fuck you like they're paid to do it. Big money too. I haven't screwed Saint, but sure, the making-you-come-while-he-murders-you thing sounds about right."

"It's official, Danny is totally getting tips from them! Please ask," she implored, clapping her hands together in a prayer.

I smirked, shaking my head at this crazy idea. "Sure, I'll ask. But not Saint, if he gets tips from him Danny will end up attaching his knife to his dick or something and I won't be responsible for the murder of your vagina, Mila."

She burst into hysterics and I felt the guys' eyes burning into our backs. I guessed they'd find out why we were laughing soon enough.

"Get them to talk to him after school today, pinky promise it." She thrust her little finger at me and I hooked mine with hers, grinning.

I wished I could tell her then how much she meant to me, how much I needed her. But I knew that would lead to me unravelling again and I wouldn't be able to explain why I was crying. So I kept smiling and pretended the world wasn't dark and my future wasn't terrifyingly empty.

We made it to English class where Miss Pontus was trying to speak over the babbling students. Blake caught up with us, wrapping his arm around my waist and snatching me away from the seat I was about to drop into beside Mila. I caught her hand, tugging her with me as he stole me away to the back of the class and pulled out a chair for me. I grabbed another seat for Mila and we dropped down side by side. Blake sat next to me with a smug expression, his arm slung over the back of my chair.

Kyan arrived, not leaving Saint's side who was still walking slowly so as not to jolt his wounds and the two of them scowled at Blake for claiming the space beside me.

Miss Pontus cleared her throat as they made it to the back row and dropped into seats beside Blake. "We have an announcement from Headmaster Monroe," she said, trying to speak over everyone while no one listened.

Kyan put his fingers in his mouth, whistling sharply and everyone fell deathly silent. A ripple of fear passed along the front row of the Unspeakables and I spotted Deepthroat glancing back at me, her nose still bandaged from where I'd broken it. A sick kind of satisfaction filled me at the sight. It was less than she deserved and if I could, I would have broken more bones in her body in payment for what she'd done to Kyan. Fuck her. He should have let her rot in prison for it. But then I imagined what he had planned for her after graduation would crush her more thoroughly. So I could wait for that.

Miss Pontus nodded at Kyan in thanks then read the announcement from her iPad. "Headmaster Monroe would like to extend his sympathy to

Saint Memphis after a motorbike accident caused him great injuries during the holidays and asks that everyone in his class treat him with care and offer him plenty of kind words and…blow kisses to warm his heart and help speed up his recovery."

My stomach clenched and I swallowed a laugh at Monroe's joke despite still being angry at him, his words aimed to thoroughly piss Saint off. I glanced at Saint's face, finding him glowering darkly. A few girls in the row ahead of us turned to look at him, their lips parting as if they really were going to offer him sympathetic words.

"Say a single word that suggests I am made of anything but stone and I will ensure your families never find your bodies," Saint said calmly and they quickly turned away, their necks colouring red as they bowed their heads.

"Are you alright, baby?" Kyan asked Saint loudly, locking an arm around his neck and stroking his head like a dog. Saint fought him off as best he could, but with only one arm to fend for himself, he was soon trapped in Kyan's muscles, cursing like a sailor.

Kyan finally released him with a bark of laughter and Saint grabbed his pen and slammed it point down into the back of Kyan's hand on the table. Kyan winced as it drew blood and I gasped as he had to actually pluck it out of his flesh. *Holy shit.*

"Stop it," I snapped at them and they looked to me in surprise. So did Mila and a few other students, their jaws dropping when the two Night Keepers actually obeyed me.

Toby suddenly entered the class with his head ducked low and my heart bunched up into my throat. I couldn't believe he was responsible for stalking me, taking those photos of me through the windows of The Temple. What he'd seen made my skin prickle. It was private. He'd had no right. No fucking *right.*

I realised I'd bared my teeth and Blake's arm had tightened around me, his posture tense. He had a look in his eyes that proved he'd just become a dangerous predator in the room.

Toby hurriedly sat with the rest of the Unspeakables, but he clearly wasn't going to get off that easy as Kyan rose sharply from his chair, pushing his hand into his pocket as he strode up to Toby who started trembling as he approached.

"I just want to make your seat more comfortable, Stalker." Kyan tipped up a pot of thumb tacks onto his seat then shoved Toby down onto it, making him cry out in pain, and half the class winced.

Miss Pontus averted her eyes, sweat beading on her brow as she concentrated on her iPad, gripping it so hard her knuckles were whitening. My gut clenched as Toby squirmed and Kyan leaned down into his face.

"Say thank you, Kyan," Kyan growled and Toby shuddered as he remained in place.

"Th-thank you, Kyan," Toby choked out.

It didn't even make me cringe. Something had changed in me since I'd lost Dad, since I'd murdered Mortez without a flicker of remorse. It wasn't like when I'd driven a knife into Merl's flesh, when I'd watched him die at the hands of my Night Keepers. After that, I'd felt afraid of what I'd become. But now, I embraced it. My choices were justified and I'd seen too much blood spilled before my eyes to shudder at it any more. The dark monster in me wanted to punish Toby for what he'd done to me and I let it feed on his pain as I watched.

"You get it now," Saint said to me, his voice low but still carrying to me from two seats away.

I nodded, eyeing Kyan as he returned to the desk, a smirk on his lips. He walked around our table, moving behind me and lowering his mouth to my ear. "If there's anything in particular you want done to him, just say the word, baby," he purred, his tone sending heat flushing between my thighs. Or maybe it was his words. And I wondered if this twisted creature in me was here to stay or if I'd one day find a way to tame it. With my heart in tatters and my mind still haunted by what I'd been through, I wasn't sure I ever wanted it to leave.

I sat with my Night Keepers in the Oak Common House beside Monroe, the closeness of his thigh against mine on the couch making my heart beat out of rhythm. Saint had insisted he be here and now the two of us were rammed up against one another, trying to hide the anger that lived between us. It may not have shown on my face, but the way it was ripping up the centre of my chest was impossible to ignore. And worse than that, the closeness of him was making desire course through me too, the two emotions colliding inside me and making every inch of my skin blazingly hot.

I kept my eyes off of him as much as possible, but his presence was like a dark spirit only I could see. I noticed every movement he made, every time his hand grazed my thigh as he reached for his beer. He could have just kept it in his grip but instead he kept leaving it on the table and brushing against me again and again. *Fuck*, it was driving me crazy.

Kyan sat on my other side, openly all over me, his hand on my thigh, rubbing circles on the inside of my leg as my school skirt rode up a little too high. This half of the common house was empty since Saint had demanded the Unspeakables keep it that way, like he couldn't stand to be in the proximity of other people today. But that wasn't going to last long. Mila was shooting me looks from across the room, waiting for my signal as she ran her palm up and down Danny's chest beside her.

"So…I have a favour to ask," I said as there was a lull in the conversation and all four of my guys were suddenly as alert as foxes in a chicken pen.

"What is it, Cinders?" Blake asked from the armchair to my right. Saint had taken the one to the left, his back to the crowd of students on the other side of the common house as a party broke out.

"I have a friend who needs some advice," I said, choosing my words carefully.

"You only have one friend," Saint said dryly. "What does she want? I'm not in the most generous of moods."

"You're never in a generous mood," Monroe pointed out, his hand skimming mine as he reached for his beer *again*.

I swear I got half electrocuted whenever he did it. It was infuriating the way my body reacted to his, my thighs clenching together which only served to trap Kyan's hand there and make him growl and force them apart again. I was going to lose my mind if I didn't get some outlet for all this fury and desire.

I wanted to drag Monroe away and smack him for everything he'd said to me and kiss him for how much I hated fighting with him. I had half a mind to drag Kyan away with us too and see how he liked it when I slid my hand between his thighs. Gah, they were all so distracting in general, but the heat of them up close was strong enough to fry my brain and turn my body into a puddle.

"Well he's a friend by association," I said with an eyeroll and all four of them shifted like I'd just told them my friend was God himself and he'd come to smite them all.

"*He?*" Kyan gritted out and I couldn't help a laugh as I realised what had bothered them all so much.

"Jealous, baby?" I mocked him, but the shadow didn't leave his eyes.

"You'd better explain quickly, princess, or it looks like these three are going to start torturing every guy in this room," Monroe taunted, though the underlying ice in his voice told me he wasn't done being pissed at me. And he certainly wasn't going to admit that he was jealous too.

I lowered my voice to a whisper, ignoring him as I looked to the others. "Danny Harper needs some advice. Like, *bedroom* advice. I promised Mila I'd ask for your help. Subtly, obviously," I added as Blake's face split into a shit-eating grin.

He threw his head back, howling like a wolf while Kyan released a low laugh. Saint's face was thoughtful like he was trying to work out if there was anything in it for him and Monroe just sipped his beer.

"I'm not giving sex advice to a student," Monroe tsked. *Pissy asshole.*

"Well the last time you got laid was probably nineteen seventy eight or some shit," Blake tossed at him. "Sex has upgraded since then, old man."

"I'm twenty four, fuckwit, not fucking sixty," Monroe shot back. "And just because you screw girls like it's an Olympic sport doesn't make you good at it."

Kyan smacked Monroe on the back of the head as he leaned behind me and I jammed my elbow into his gut too under the guise of rearranging myself. Monroe's glare said he knew exactly what I was doing and my smirk said I gave no shits.

"Nash gets every girl wet in this school just by being a bossy asshole teacher," Kyan taunted, twisting his fingers into my ponytail. "He could have fucked his way through the daughters of every elite family in Sequoia if he wanted to. But you wouldn't be so naughty would you, Headmaster?"

Monroe gave him an even look across me as my heart thundered like it was trying to give us away. "No. I wouldn't."

"You should really stop looking at our girl like that then," Saint deadpanned, a challenge in his eyes as he dared Monroe to bite back at him and my heart thundered even harder against my chest.

I stole a glance at Monroe and he shrugged. "I'm not looking at shit," he said coldly and my teeth ground together.

"Well are any of you going to help Danny or what?" I asked, wanting to kill this conversation dead before it got any more momentum. Especially with the topic of Monroe screwing students.

"Sure thing, baby. We'll tell Danny how to fuck his girl right," Kyan said, sharing a look with Blake that unnerved me a little. What the hell were they thinking?

"Danny Harper! Come over here!" Blake hollered, his voice carrying above the party.

Danny looked over in surprise and Mila looked to me with a question in her eyes which I answered with a slight nod. Danny headed away from his friends and Kyan scooted up the couch, shoving me half into Monroe's lap to make room on his other side for Danny and crushing me in between them. It wasn't the worst place in the world to be normally, but seeing as Monroe was currently shooting me daggers and my chest was swirling with the fires of hell, it wasn't exactly ideal.

Kyan slung his arm around Danny, tugging him close. "We've got a gift for you."

"A gift?" Danny asked, seeming kind of alarmed and I couldn't really blame him. He had been dragged right into the middle of a pack of wolves. And Mila clearly hadn't tipped him off about this.

"Yeah," Blake took over, leaning forward so his elbows were resting on his knees. "The girls of this school are in a crisis."

I frowned, wondering where the hell he was going with this.

"You see," Blake continued. "I took it upon myself to satisfy as many of them as I could and blow their fucking minds to smithereens. But my dick is now retired from multiple pussy because there's only one pussy I want these days. It's made of diamonds and fucking perfection by the way." He tossed me a dirty wink as I rolled my eyes at him, but a grin pulled at my lips. "And now the girls of Everlake Prep are suffering as they can only experience mediocre dick. They have nothing to aim for. No dick mountain to climb."

"You're boring everyone with your bullshit, Bowman, move the fuck on," Monroe drawled and I snuck another look at him, seeing that his eyes were blazing with a dark kind of energy. Dammit he really got me hot when he looked like that.

"Point is, we wanna impart some knowledge so you can start a revolution of sorts," Blake mused and I snorted a laugh at his ridiculousness. "So your duty now is to listen, absorb and pass on the knowledge to any other guy who needs it. And let's be honest, most of the guys in this school need it."

"What are you talking about?" Danny asked in confusion.

"He wants to teach you how to satisfy a woman in the bedroom," Saint said in exasperation like Blake's theatrical way of explaining this was getting on his nerves.

"Oh," Danny said in surprise. "Well I don't think I need help with that. But thanks."

"Oh, you poor, sad fucking soul," Saint muttered, his upper lip peeling back like he was kind of disgusted with Danny's lack of awareness on the matter. "Blake is trying to be tactful to spare your feelings, but we have it on good authority that you are as useless as a dead worm in a sleeping bag when it comes to fucking women."

"A dead worm?" Danny breathed in horror, glancing over at Mila in accusation. She flushed guiltily, turning away to face her friends and I wondered if this had been the best idea after all. Danny swallowed hard, looking between the Night Keepers. "Well…okay, tell me." There was an edge to his voice like he had something to prove and the flare of heat in his eyes told me how far he was willing to go for my friend. It made me like him even more.

"You've got to get her screaming before you're even close to fucking her. If she's texting while you're going down on her then you ain't doing it right," Kyan growled, gripping my thigh again and digging his fingers into my flesh hard enough to draw a moan from my lips. I wriggled my hips and Monroe cursed as my ass pressed too close to his dick for his liking. Or maybe he did like it, but he wasn't able to admit it right now as he shot me another glare. That was some legit death ray, I swear.

"Did she say that?" Danny gasped, his cheeks pinking a little in embarrassment.

"No, but you just confirmed it," Saint said, a hint of a laugh in his voice. He sat up straighter, more invested now that Danny was squirming and he had someone's discomfort to prey on. "Do you cry when you come, Harper?"

"What?" Danny balked. "Of course not."

"He's just fucking with you," Blake laughed, but Saint's razor blade eyes were clearly making Danny unsure of that.

"Stop being an asshole, Saint," I said sweetly and he looked to me, his

139

vicious expression melting a little.

"That's like asking the sun not to rise, siren," he said coolly.

"Come on, let's go for a drink, Danny boy." Blake stood up, beckoning Freeloader over with some bottles of beers while he broke into a verse of Danny Boy by Glen Miller, replacing half the words with rude ones. "My balls, my balls are tiiingliiing," he warbled and I snorted a laugh.

Freeloader passed me a beer and kept her eyes downcast as I took it. I didn't feel guilty ignoring her, not now I knew what sort of person she really was. But it was still strange to be waited on by her when I would have called her a friend not long ago.

Kyan stood up too and Danny got crowded in between his and Blake's shoulders as they led him outside to the deck ringing the common house overlooking the lake.

"Come on, Saint," Blake called. "He might need the sadist's point of view. And are you sure you don't wanna weigh in, Monroe? Some girls might be into scandalous rollerblade sex or whatever the fuck it is people liked to do in the seventies."

Monroe just glared at him in answer and Saint started to get up to follow them, his face pinching in pain as he did so. I leapt out of my seat to help him and he let me support him as he stood, his breath fanning against my mouth as we got too close to one another. I glanced up at him under my lashes as the scent of apple and danger consumed me. He tucked a lock of hair behind my ear before moving away and his touch left a burn in its wake.

I turned back to my seat, falling down next to Monroe almost as close as we'd been before. I realised too late that I should have taken the opportunity to move away. But now I'd made my bed, I had to lie in it. Monroe's eyes darted to the other students, but no one was looking our way and it wasn't like we were doing anything wrong or even had any intention of doing anything wrong considering the anger blazing between us. Part of me ached to lean into him though, feel the warmth of his body against mine and relive every second of the time we'd spent in that cabin together. Before the whole world had fallen apart. Before what we had had been fractured too.

"I'm going to the bathroom," he told me, his eyes boring into mine for a second before he stood up and walked away, leaving me there alone. My heart crushed as I watched him go, a fundamental piece of me seeming to leave with him.

My throat was thick as he slipped through the door to the restroom and I gripped the edge of the couch as I fought down the pain swelling in me. I took a few measured breaths, knotting my fingers together as I sat there, hating this rift growing between us.

I kept looking over at the bathroom door and suddenly my phone buzzed in my pocket. I took it out, my pulse skipping as I found a message from him.

Nash:

Come here.

I bit down on my lip, his words sparking a wild and expectant energy in me. Was I going to risk going to him? I barely had to think the question before the answer came to me. I needed to see him. We had to sort this shit out between us. But I knew doing it here was risky.

I got to my feet, casually crossing the room and slipping through the door that led into the bathroom. The second I did, Monroe pushed it shut behind me and twisted the lock. His mouth was on mine before I could take a single breath and he lifted me by my ass, planting me down on the vanity unit beside the sink and stepping between my thighs. His kiss was hard and devouring and I could taste his anger on his tongue, but his hunger for me was all consuming beneath it.

I shoved him back as I found my strength, smacking him across the face. His head wheeled sideways from the force I used and he turned back to me with a snarl, grabbing my ponytail and yanking it hard, making me yelp. The party was too loud for someone to hear us, but he immediately glanced at the door as that worry crossed his mind too.

"I thought you didn't want to take risks," I hissed at him, shoving my hands into his chest as he released my ponytail and he pushed back against my hands, forcing his body into them with his superior strength.

"Well maybe if you didn't drive me fucking crazy out there I wouldn't have to." He leaned in close to my face and I fisted my hands in his shirt. "I don't want to fight with you," he snarled.

"Then maybe you should have thought about that before being a hypocritical asshole," I whisper-shouted at him.

He glared at me, capturing my cheeks in both hands, his jaw ticking furiously. "Fine," he spat. "I'm a hypocrite. But if you don't date hypocrites then maybe you should cut off the rest of your little boyfriends."

"And why's that?" I demanded.

"Those assholes take it upon themselves to punish bad people, but they're the worst of the fucking worst, princess," he snarled. "So are you going to cut us all off or just me? Because I'd rather finish it now than let you drag my heart through the sawmill and leave it in two pieces on the other side."

His words stung, but they were laced with jealousy too and I knew he didn't want that. His desperation shone from his eyes and I felt it spearing my heart. The mere suggestion of finishing this made me ache. I clutched onto him, shaking my head as emotion welled inside me. Losing him would be the end of me. I couldn't face it after all I'd lost already.

"No," I gasped. "I don't want that. I need you." The admission brought a blush to my cheeks and he took in the colour with undeniable lust.

His thumbs rubbed my jaw as he gripped my face then he lunged forward and kissed me fiercely, his tongue chasing mine as we held onto each other and my heart tried to pound its way out of my chest. His kiss made me feel weightless, like all the pressure of the world holding my body down just released me. He made me feel safe, secure, but exhilarated too, like we were soaring a thousand miles above the earth and he'd never let me fall.

"Good, because I'm not sure I'd have let you go anyway," he growled against my mouth. "You're bound to me like you are to them. There's no taking that back."

"Nash," I said, breathless. He groaned as he kissed the corner of my lips, working up to my ear then biting and chewing like he wanted to eat me up.

"I've missed you," he said heavily. "I can't stand this. Not being able to touch you, hold you, *be* with you, it's driving me insane."

"I know, I know," I gasped as his mouth moved to my throat and I tilted my head to give him better access, locking my legs around his waist. "I'm going mad without you too."

He stood up straight, pushing me back so my head pressed to the mirror as he admired me beneath him. He growled in frustration, sucking on my lip and biting gently, careful not to break the skin and leave evidence of his touch. "Stay with me tonight. Go back to the old rules."

"I can't," I sighed, running my hands over the firm plains of his back and shoulders. "Saint needs me."

"He has the others," he snarled.

"He won't listen to them," I said, my heart tugging as I was pulled in two directions. But I couldn't abandon Saint. I'd seen what had happened to him without me over Christmas. For whatever reason, I got through to him and it was immeasurably easier on everyone if I continued to care for him and keep him sane.

"Who cares?" Monroe said coldly and I tilted back, a frown pulling at my brow.

"I care," I said, hating to have to keep explaining myself on this. "He's injured because of me."

"It's not your fault," Monroe said fiercely. "None of what happened is your fault."

I glanced away, afraid the tears would come for me again as I was forced to face that night again. "I just need to do this, Nash. I'm sorry, but that's the way it is."

He released a noise of frustration, but gave in, pressing his forehead to mine. "I'll find more ways for us to see each other then," he said, a promise in those words and relief filled me.

"Good, because I hate having to pretend you're not mine." I ran my hand down his shirt until I felt his heart beating solidly beneath my palm. "You are mine right, Nash?"

He gazed at me with the heat of the sun behind his eyes, nodding firmly. "I'm yours, princess. I'll wait to be with you again, but not forever. I'll snatch you away if you're not careful."

I chuckled and he swallowed the sound with another kiss, groaning against my mouth.

"How are you?" he asked as he pulled back and I took in a ragged breath as he cut right to the source of my pain just like that.

"It's hard...pretending it didn't happen, waiting for the news to come out," I said, my throat tight with emotion.

"I know, princess," he said softly. "You're so strong."

"Sometimes I don't want to be. I want to fall apart, let go of all my shattered pieces and just...break." My heart crumpled in my chest and he took my hand, holding it to his lips and kissing my fingers sweetly.

"If you break, I think I'll break with you. I feel your pain like it's a part of me too," he said, his voice gruff. "But you won't break, Tatum Rivers. You will find a way through this. I've seen you do it before."

I thanked him with a lingering kiss and he helped me down off of the counter. I turned and reapplied my lipstick while he watched like a hawk and I knew our time together was already coming to an end.

"You'd better go," I told him, sad that we had to part so soon.

He nodded, running his fingers down my spine and making my whole body tingle before he headed away, exiting the bathroom and disappearing out of sight. I stared at myself in the mirror, finding my eyes thick with shadow. They didn't seem so bright blue anymore. They were like a sea overcast by clouds. And I wasn't sure the sun would ever break through them again.

I headed back into the common house, moving through the crowd and finding everyone parting for me, some even bowing their heads in respect. It was weird as shit and something I was never going to get used to.

As I made it back to the couch, I saw Danny outside with the Night Keepers. Monroe had joined them and was frowning at Blake as he acted out some sort of move on Saint, grinding his hips against him while Saint tried to push him away one-handed. I snorted a laugh, watching as Danny took it so seriously. I started getting slightly mortified though as Blake showed him tongue movements on his own hand and I gazed on in shock as I recognised all of them. *Jesus.*

Kyan weighed in with the odd word or two then caught hold of Danny's throat, apparently showing him how hard to squeeze. Someone dropped down beside me and I turned, finding Mila there, watching the guys with interest.

"What do you think Saint's saying?" she whispered and I glanced back to find he was talking to Danny with no expression on his face while Danny nodded seriously, apparently absorbing what he was saying. Whatever it was, Monroe apparently agreed with it as he weighed in too, nodding his head.

"I have literally no idea," I said just as Blake dropped down to the wooden boards and started humping them with all kinds of hip movements which made my lips pop open.

"Fuck me, that boy has talent," Mila commented. We both huddled closer together, trying not to laugh at Danny as Blake made him get down on the floor and start repeating the actions. But it was impossible not to.

"Do you think this is going to work?" she whispered to me.

I looked at Danny on the floor, grinding his body into it with enthusiasm and considered that. "Umm..."

"Hey Tatum!" Blake called. "We need a willing body."

"I'm not willing," I joked and he leaned through the doorway with a savage expression on his face.

"Come out here, Cinders, or I'll come and get you."

Mila jabbed me in the side in encouragement and I gave her a look of

145

mock annoyance before getting up and heading outside. Blake grabbed me immediately, shoving me back against Kyan who locked an arm around my shoulders to immobilise me. I gasped as Blake gripped my chin between his finger and thumb, smirking at me before leaning in and kissing my ear, my neck, my collar bone. I stopped being embarrassed as I lost myself to his touch, moaning as my eyes fluttered half closed.

"Easy, see?" Blake pulled away and my lips pursed. "Now you try."

Danny took a step towards me and the light atmosphere changed so fast, it was like a lightning bolt had struck the ground.

"Not on her, fuckwit, go try it out on *your* girl," Saint snarled as Kyan tugged me against him protectively and Blake looked like he was about to throw Danny over the railing into the lake. Monroe had taken a purposeful step toward him too and his clenched fist told me Danny was lucky he hadn't come at me any faster.

"Yeah, sorry dude, I wasn't thinking." Danny rubbed a hand over his face, clearly overwhelmed by this situation before he hurried inside to join Mila.

Kyan turned me in his arms and walked me back against the railing to pin me in place. "All this talk of fucking is giving me ideas." He was already hard against my thigh and my heart thumped wildly as I looked up at him, my hands resting on his biceps.

"Why don't we go back to The Temple?" Blake suggested and Saint's eyes sparked at the idea. Monroe's jaw locked and I wished I could just ask him to come with us and forget having to hide this connection between us. Kyan glanced over at him for a second like he was having the exact same thought and an image of the two of them claiming me together sent a needy squeeze through my belly. Yeah…that would be sinful and damn perfect.

Blake's phone dinged and he took it out, glancing at the screen before falling statue still. "What…no. No!" His head snapped up and he gazed out at the water, hunting for something as panic slid over his features.

"What is it?" I slipped away from Kyan in alarm, reaching for Blake's hand and he wordlessly passed me his phone. I gazed down at the message on it from someone who'd called themselves The Justice Ninja.

You'll burn one day too.

Beneath it was a video of a burning boat filled with Blake's trophies out on the lake. Every last one of them, including the damn toilet paper he'd won from Saint.

A splash made me turn and I realised Blake had dived into the lake and was swimming out to a low fire far out in the water.

"Blake!" Kyan yelled, ripping his shirt off and diving in after him.

I hesitated for only a second longer before the urge to go with them snared me. I pulled off my clothes down to my underwear, tossing them on the floor and finding Monroe down to his boxers across from me when I was done, a look of solidarity in his eyes.

We climbed up onto the railing as Saint cursed, unable to follow with his injuries as we jumped into the freezing water. It drew a cry from my lips as the iciness surrounded me, seeming to slice into my skin. Monroe kept to my side as we started moving, swimming hard after Kyan and Blake ahead as panic ran through me. Who would target Blake like that? And why?

It was a long swim, but I didn't slow, needing to be there for Blake as he was always there for me these days. We made it to the burning boat, the fire already having carved a hole through the bottom of it and it was going down fast.

"No!" Blake roared, reaching into the remains and sifting through the ash before the lake consumed it. Anything burnable was already gone and the metal parts of the trophies were half melted, but there seemed to be one he was desperately trying to find as the boat started to get fully submerged. The fire hissed out as the water filled it and Blake grew more frantic.

"What is it Blake?" I begged as I tread water at his side.

"There was a metal plaque from my mom, it was the first trophy I ever got," he said in a panic and Kyan held his phone up, switching on the flashlight, the thing apparently waterproof. He stuck it between his teeth then dove under the water as the boat went down. I took in a deep breath and went after him, the freezing, dark world punctured by the single beam of light from Kyan's phone. The boat was sinking away into the black depths of the lake and the remnants of Blake's trophies were scattering through the water.

A flash of the light against something silver caught my eye and I spotted the engraved metal plaque floating down into the abyss. I swam for it as my lungs began to burn, moving as fast as I could and battling the aching cold as it drove into my bones. I somehow snatched it before it sank too far, turning frantically and kicking my way back to the surface. Kyan came up beside me, moving close as I held up the plaque for Blake. "Is this it?"

Blake grasped for it and sighed in relief as he looked down at the precious item, his hair plastered to his head. "Thank you," he rasped, wrapping his arm around me and hugging me tight.

"Who the fuck did this?" Monroe snarled, his anger clear.

"I don't know, but I'll find them and murder them for this," Blake growled as we started swimming back to the common house. My blood was chilled by the time we got out of the lake and not because of the cold. But because one of my Night Keepers had been targeted and I wouldn't rest until I found out who was responsible.

First a Stalker and now this? Why did it feel like the whole world was out to get us sometimes? And why did I feel like this had barely even begun?

Mila:

Girl, what the shit did those guys say to Danny? I mean, fuuuuuuck. I swear I just came fourteen times. Four. Teen. Times. Screw checking my insta feed ever again, I didn't even realise sex could be this good. I have been wasting my life up until this very moment.

P.S. If you see me being pushed around in a wheelchair today, you know why.

I laughed as I continued eating breakfast and the guys gave me inquisitive looks from across the table. Monroe had started joining us every morning and I liked that a lot. I found myself looking for him while I was making the food each day, glancing at the front door continuously. And when he appeared, I swear my stomach dipped like I was on a roller coaster. Every damn time.

"Mila is pleased," I said in explanation.

"Don't play it down, baby, she's fucking destroyed isn't she?" Kyan smirked and I laughed in answer.

I looked back at my phone just as a news report showed up at the top of the screen. My gut lurched at the sight of the headline and every muscle in my body tensed.

Donovan Rivers found dead after committing suicide.

My pulse thrashed against my eardrums as I clicked on the link, reading the article and feeling sicker and sicker by the second. Rage and pain clawed at the inside of my head as I took in the words that marked the man who'd raised me as irrefutably guilty of leaking the Hades Virus. A man who'd taken his life because he couldn't cope with the weight of the guilt of what he'd done. *No.*

"*No!*" I shouted, standing so fast that I knocked my chair to the floor.

"What's wrong?" Blake asked in alarm and I pointed an accusing finger at Kyan, tossing my phone at him so he could see the article.

It slapped into his broad chest and his eyes flashed over it as it landed on the table before he sighed heavily.

"What did you expect them to do?" Kyan growled. "They had to cover it somehow."

"Suicide?" I practically screamed. "The whole world will see this as an admission of his guilt!"

"Hey, I said you'd get a grave, I didn't promise anything more than that," he snarled, getting to his feet too.

I swiped up the knife from beside his plate, pointing it at him. "You could have told them to make it look like an accident."

"And who would believe that?" he snarled. "He was shot in the head."

I cringed at his words as that image flashed through my mind again. "I don't know, I don't care. But this, this is the worst way they ever could have covered it." I lifted the knife higher, my rage spewing into every inch of my flesh.

"If you're gonna stab me for it then get it fucking over with, baby," Kyan growled, planting his hands down on the table and baring his throat to me. "I won't apologise for protecting you. This is the only way they could cover up his death that made any sense at all. It's better than his body being destroyed in acid, don't you agree?"

I winced away from his words, the knife clattering to the table as I dropped it, turning my back on him as tears stung my eyes. I tried to blink them back, but they wouldn't stop and they soon washed down my cheeks and made my whole body shudder with them. I leaned down, resting my hands on my knees as I dragged in air, trying to shut off this pain. But it was like a switch had been flipped and I could no longer hold it together. It hurt too much. It bit into my skin and cut so deep it was impossible to think of anything but my dad lying dead on the ground beneath me. *No no no.*

Strong arms wrapped around me and I fought against them as Kyan's scent of gasoline and leather surrounded me. He didn't pull back, forcing me into his chest and holding me there until I couldn't fight any more and just came apart, sobbing into his shirt, staining it with mascara and tears.

"I'm sorry," he said in his deep tone that rumbled right through to the centre of my being. "I'm sorry, baby."

I clung to him, letting my anger slide away. It wasn't his fault; he hadn't done this. But it still stung sharply.

"The documents he left behind should prove his innocence," Saint offered and his words helped ease the tension from my body. "I am capable of exposing it all, I just need more time."

"Hurry up," Monroe bit at him.

"A job is not worth doing if it is not done properly," Saint said simply.

Blake suddenly pressed against me from behind and I practically sagged between my two men, their strong bodies holding me up. I didn't want to go to class anymore, I just wanted to stay here surrounded by their warm flesh and drowning in their kisses. But I couldn't hide away from the world.

The worst thing was that everyone in the school would hear this news. My grief would be exposed. And where I'd longed for that before so I didn't have to hide it, now I realised that hiding it had helped me stay together. With everyone looking for my weakness now, how was I going to stop myself falling apart?

"We'll all take the day off from classes so Tatum can have some time to process this news," Saint announced suddenly and I broke free of Blake and Kyan, looking to him in surprise. Of all the people to suggest such a thing, I never would have thought it would come from him.

"Thank you," I breathed, then looked to Monroe. "What about you? Can you stay?"

He nodded firmly, no question about it in his eyes. "I have the morning free for paperwork anyway. And even if I didn't, I'm not leaving you, princess." He moved forward and hugged me, my heart beating steadier at having them all so close.

"What will your family ask in payment for giving her father a grave?" Saint asked Kyan in a tone that made my skin prickle.

"I don't know. And it doesn't matter," Kyan said firmly. "Whatever the price is, I'll pay it."

I reached for him and he stepped forward, winding his fingers between mine. I'd met his family, I knew the sacrifice he'd made for me. And I could never repay him for it.

"I can pay the price," I breathed. "Whatever they want, it shouldn't be on you."

"Naw, baby," he said, knocking his knuckles against my cheek. "It's on me. I wouldn't have it any other way."

The other guys all nodded to Kyan in acknowledgement of what he was offering me and my heart squeezed. I wasn't sure how I'd ended up at the centre of a circle of monsters who'd do anything to protect me, but somehow, it felt like I was right where I was supposed to be.

Saint

CHAPTER NINE

I stood in the old prayer room at the entrance to the catacombs with my right eye twitching as I took count for the fifth time. There was no denying it. We were short twenty three rolls of toilet paper. Someone had either found their way down here and was stealing from us, or there was a culprit living right beneath my roof. And as I knew for a fact that Blake and Kyan didn't give a single shit about the masses being unable to wipe their asses, I had a pretty clear idea of who would be to blame.

My fingers twitched at the edge of the fucking cast I was still cursed to keep on and I shifted against the confines of the sling. I was so sick of wearing the damn thing. *So* fucking sick of it. With a growl, I reached up with my good hand and ripped the knot loose before tearing it off.

My bullet wound no longer needed dressing anyway and I was done with this too. Now all that was left was the infernal cast. Three weeks, six days and fourteen hours remaining until I could banish that as well. And then I could get back to my routine in its fullness.

I stood still in the utter silence of the catacombs and forced myself to count down five full minutes as I got my rage under control.

It was freezing down here, the ice cold air making the bare skin of my chest pebble, but I couldn't bring myself to ask for help pulling on shirts, so this was the standard I lived by aside from when I attended classes.

When the allotted time had finally passed, I headed back through the gym and upstairs where Tatum was working on a school assignment at the dining table.

My teeth clenched at the sound of drilling and I had to force myself not to respond to the incessant noise and remind myself of why it was necessary. Monroe, Blake and Kyan were outside acting like a bunch of hillbilly laymen as they bolted bars over every window in The Temple to make sure that there was no chance of anyone breaking in via them again. Since the so-called Justice Ninja had broken into Blake's room to steal his trophies, we had decided that the only sure fire way to protect our home required this aesthetic sacrifice.

It had taken a fucking week for the bars to be sent which was too fucking close to unacceptable for my liking but with the news of Tatum's father's alleged suicide breaking, this last week had gone to shit anyway. So for one, final day I was going to suck it up and try to ignore the incessant noise of the three of them playing the handyman role with the hopes that after this weekend we could return to our regular routine and the world would be set right once again. I couldn't bear to look at them using tools and doing manual labour though, so I was just trying to pretend it wasn't happening. And it had to be done. There was no way that we could leave this place vulnerable like that, especially now that some fucking little upstart had decided to aim attacks our way.

I already had more than enough plans for how I was going to deal with the *Justice Ninja* just as soon as I got hold of them and they'd better believe that their life wouldn't be worth living when I did.

I crossed the room silently, moving to stand directly behind Tatum as she worked and leaning down carefully until my lips were right beside her ear.

"I know what you've done," I growled and a shriek of alarm escaped

156

her as she leapt up, knocking her glass of water flying as she whirled around to glare at me.

"Saint! What the fuck are you doing creeping up on me like a fucking ghost?"

I lurched forward and spun her around to face the table before pushing her to bend over it with her chest pressing down into the puddle she'd created. My ribs flared with pain at the movement but I gritted my teeth against the agony in favour of fixing this problem.

"This is for making a mess, Tatum," I explained as I reached around her waist with my good hand and fumbled with the fly on her jeans.

Before I could lose my shit over struggling with it, her hands moved over mine and she quickly unbuttoned them before sliding them down over her hips so that her ass was exposed to me in the silky blue panties I'd picked out for her this morning.

"Good girl," I breathed as that act of submission made something in my chest loosen and I rubbed my palm around the curve of her ass.

My dick was rock hard and not for the first time, I found myself imagining what it would be like to take my obsession with this girl further than I had. Not that I would. Unlike Blake and Kyan, I actually respected the fucking rules she'd laid out for us. But sometimes, I was almost certain she would have liked me to break them for her all the same.

My hand clapped down on her ass and a spike of pain burst through my ribs, but the moan that escaped her made it worth it. I was aware that this didn't exactly seem to be much of a punishment for her with the way she lifted her ass and moaned encouragement, but I didn't care. It didn't matter to me if she liked it, because the point was that I was in control of her. I was the one giving her that pleasure or denying her it and she was surrendering the power over her body to me for that purpose. It was probably a fucked up thing for the two of us to enjoy but I didn't care. For some reason, we both needed it and I wasn't strong enough to even attempt to stop this shift in dynamic between us.

I spanked her four more times, sweat breaking out across my brow as the pain in my ribs flared to a burn at the effort and finally stumbling away from her, gripping onto the back of the chair she'd been sitting in as I took a moment to let the agony pass.

"*Saint,*" Tatum gasped as she stood upright, tugging her jeans back up and found me there probably looking like death warmed up. "You shouldn't have done that if you're not strong enough to-"

"I'm more than strong enough to spank you, Tatum, don't go telling me I'm not or I'll be forced to prove it again," I hissed between clenched teeth. I wouldn't admit that the reason I was speaking so quietly was because inhaling any deeper would cause spots of light to blossom across my vision from the pain.

"You need to take it easy," she insisted, reaching out to cup my cheek in her palm and though I'd never admit it, I liked that. I liked having her undivided attention on me. It was the one thing about this insufferable recovery that made it bearable. "It's almost two, you need to take your pills."

"They're due *at* two not at *almost* two and I'm still not done with punishing you," I said, my voice low even as I allowed her to tow me towards the stairs which led up to my room.

Tatum fell still as she made it onto the bottom step and the boost to her height almost put her on eye level with me. That minute shift in the power between us made me want to punish her even more. I wanted her kneeling at my feet, not looking me in the eye.

"What else do you have to punish me for?" she breathed, her eyes flickering with a mixture of fear and what I could have sworn was excitement.

I moved closer to her, so close that our lips were almost touching and the sweet scent of her skin enveloped me. Barely a breath divided us and my treacherous mind went to her rules which were still stuck to the fridge - even though it seemed like I was the only one who took them seriously these days. But I knew them by heart. And I knew that she'd gotten rid of the rule which stopped me from closing this distance between us, from tasting those lips of hers and testing out how far she was willing to dive into this unhealthy obsession of mine.

Because it *was* unhealthy. Not for me, but certainly for her. If she had any comprehension of the way I felt about her, I had no doubt she'd run screaming for the hills. Her stalker had nothing on me. I watched her every move, dissected every comment. I wanted to peel apart her skin and slip inside it and feel every inch of what it was to be her.

That was why I watched her with the others and forced myself to endure the torture of it. Though it ripped me apart with jealousy, I hungered to experience the pleasure she got from them. I needed to see the way her pupils dilated and her breaths grew shallow, I needed to study the arch of her spine and the pitch of her moans. I needed to experience all of her in every moment from her lowest to the highest. I needed to taste her grief and bathe in her joy, suffer in her pain and come apart in her pleasure.

If I ever crossed this line that had been drawn between us, I knew I'd lose control. I'd take every human experience from her, mind, body and soul and devour each and every one of them until she was consumed by me. It was how I was made. To dominate, control, destroy. And I didn't want to destroy her. I wanted to watch her bloom.

"Where are the missing rolls of toilet paper?" I asked her in a low and dangerous voice, my desire for her making me angry, the hard press of my cock growing in my sweatpants at the mere thought of her submitting to whatever I wanted to do to her.

Tatum sucked in a sharp breath and I waited to see if she would lie to me. Heaven help her if she did. But the fucked up, monstrous part of me was hoping for it so that I could punish her even more.

The war in her eyes didn't take long to play out and as that defiance in her blazed through her gaze, I found myself equally thrilled and enraged.

"I gave some to Mila," she said in a strong voice. "And I gave some to the Unspeakables too before I understood about them – clearly I regret that now. The rest I snuck into the school restrooms."

My hands curled into fists, tightening and loosening as I fought against the urge to flip the fuck out.

"Do you understand the concept of power, Tatum?" I asked her. "The man who owns the power rules the world. Do you know why I'm hoarding toilet paper as if I have the demand of it equal to an elephant with the shits?"

"So that you can maintain control with it by being the only one handing out vital resources?" she guessed with a tone to her voice which suggested that I was an asshole for that move.

"Wrong. *Withholding* something that someone desperately needs is where the real power lies. You take it, place it in your possession and then get them to behave in the way you require while keeping the reward they most crave close to your heart. That way, you gain *true* control."

"Like the way you're holding my letters hostage?" she asked with a bitterness to her tone which set the flames of anger in me flaring.

"Well apparently that isn't enough of a hold to have over you. So I think it's time I had you really begging at my mercy to drive the point home." I moved past her on the stairs and caught her hand to make her walk up them at my side.

The clock ticked onto two o'clock as we made it to the top of them and I pointed her towards my nightstand so that she could fetch the pain pills she was so desperate to force upon me.

While she got them, I headed into the closet and selected a set of white lace underwear complete with garter belt and suspenders for her and then chose one of the velvet pouches from the hidden drawer beneath my tie rail.

Tatum was waiting for me as I emerged and I laid the underwear on the bed for her before placing the pouch on the nightstand with a heavy thump so that her attention fell on it.

I beckoned her closer and opened my mouth obligingly so that she could place the pills on my tongue one at a time. Between each, she lifted a glass of water to my lips so that I could wash them down and throughout the entire exchange, I just kept my gaze fixed on hers.

When she finished, she placed the empty glass on the nightstand and looked at me expectantly.

I reached out and brushed my fingertips over her shoulder, slowly skating them down her skin and watching as goosebumps chased the movement until I found the small, silver scar on her forearm. It was no bigger than the pad of my thumb, the swirl of smooth skin looking strangely like a rose. It frustrated me that I hadn't realised what it was sooner. The Hades Virus left marks just like this and with her father's involvement in its creation, it should have been blindingly obvious to me.

I lifted her arm and slowly lowered my mouth to the scar, placing a kiss down on it, running my tongue over it too. I should have hated this blemish on her perfect flesh, but I didn't. This protected her just as thoroughly as I or any of the other Night Keepers were willing to. It was a barrier between her and death.

"I've decided it's time to forward your father's research to my father," I said as I looked up at her, pleased to find her breathing heavier, her teeth sinking into that full bottom lip of hers.

"You...have?" she asked, clearly scrambling to make her mind function on that topic instead of the reaction her body was having to mine.

"I've been over it all. Every last word. And I even read between the lines too. You're immune, aren't you, Tatum?"

"I...how...I know it doesn't mention anything about him testing a vaccine on me in those files," she said, moving to tug her arm out of my grip, but I tightened my fingers on her and refused to let go.

"Of course he didn't. But he detailed the trials he'd been doing and included analysis of the test subjects. There's clear accounts of the successful cases alongside the unsuccessful ones who died." I watched the flash of grief spill through her eyes at the mention of her sister's fate and drank it in. I'd never felt anything as powerful as that emotion which I saw in her. The closest I'd come had been my grandmother's death, but that had left me empty and alone. Not filled with pain and a sense of injustice. I could only imagine ever truly understanding it if I were to lose one of the other Night Keepers...or her.

"So now you want to tell your father about me?" she guessed, giving up any pretence.

"No," I replied firmly. "I won't have that man near you. There is nothing in those documents to give away that you are one of the few successful test subjects. Nothing to give away your part in it at all aside from this scar. And there's no way he will ever find out about that. I believe that the research here will be sufficient to allow the right people to create a vaccine without them ever learning of your existence."

"So, we're just going to keep my immunity secret?" she asked, looking like she was hoping I'd agree.

"We tell the other Night Keepers," I said because I wouldn't keep a secret that big from them. "But it doesn't go beyond our ring of confidence."

"Okay." A smile touched her lips and she moved an inch closer like she thought she might embrace me and I tutted at her.

"Get changed, siren, you have a punishment to endure."

Tatum's eyebrows rose and her gaze strayed to that velvet bag again before she bit into her lip once more and my cock twitched with ideas I wouldn't allow it to fulfil.

I moved across the room, taking hold of the large, cream armchair in the corner and tugging it closer to the bed. A blaze of pain tore across my ribs, but I just gritted my teeth against it and kept going until I had it where I wanted it.

Tatum tried to come and help me, but I shot her a glare to warn her off and she quickly started shedding her clothes instead.

I watched hungrily as she revealed her body to me and I slowly moved to take the velvet bag from the nightstand.

Watching her dress herself in the white lingerie was almost as alluring as watching her strip and when she finally stood before me like a picture of innocence, my heart had shifted to a thundering beat.

I closed in on her, gently brushing her long hair back over her shoulders and skimming my thumbs down her sides in a slow move which had her sucking in a breath as her spine arched beautifully.

"Tell me who owns you," I breathed, hooking a finger beneath one of her suspender straps at the top of her thigh and pulling it away from her bronzed flesh.

"The Night Keepers," she replied and though I'd been looking for her to say my name, I found I liked that answer even better. She was ours. The Night Bound. Sworn to us forever. Which was good, because that was exactly as long as I intended to keep her.

I released the suspender strap with a flick of my finger and it snapped against her skin, making her flinch.

"On the bed, on your back, knees bent, thighs apart," I commanded and I almost groaned aloud as she instantly did as I'd said. I knew I should have questioned my need for control more, worried about what it said about me, but at this point, I'd just accepted that I was my own brand of monster and I wasn't going to make any effort to change it. Especially now that I'd found her so willing to comply to my needs.

The sight of her laid out for me like that had the ache in my throbbing cock consuming my every thought as I watched her, and it took me a moment to remember the bag in my hands.

"You have a choice," I said to her slowly as I drew the strings open and she watched me with a feral hunger in her big blue eyes. "If you would rather I punish you with some menial task then say it now."

"I want this," she replied instantly, still not knowing what I had in mind, but fisting her hands in the sheets in anticipation of it.

"Good. Hold onto the headboard. If at any point you let go, I won't let you come. Understood?"

"Yes," she panted, reaching above her head and curling her fingers around the wrought iron bed frame.

"Tell me how wet you are," I commanded as I drew the thick, egg shaped vibrator from the bag. It had a curved end to it so that once it was inside her, it would stimulate her clit and her g-spot at once and the hungry look she gave it said she wanted that a whole lot. "Do I need to lubricate this?"

"No," she panted. "I'm wet. *Fuck*, Saint."

I should have told her off for saying more than just the answer to my question but the way she panted my name like that had me so fucking hard that I was almost sure I could come in my pants, so I let it slide.

"Good." I moved onto the bed, eyeing the crotch of her panties and seeing that she hadn't been lying about that with a surge of satisfaction. "Now stay perfectly still. I'm not breaking any of your rules and I won't be touching you while you're in this bed."

"The...rules? I don't think the rules really apply anym-"

"The rules will *always* apply to me," I growled, ignoring the twinge of pain that gripped me as I climbed up to stand on the bed. I refused to ever get injured again in my motherfucking life after this. It was utterly unbearable.

I walked towards her until I was standing between her parted thighs, looking down at her panting for me as her gaze raked over my bare chest. I couldn't help but get a serious kick from the power I felt standing over her like that and it certainly seemed like she enjoyed being at my mercy this way too.

I lowered onto my knees slowly, my grip firm on the vibrator as I switched it on and ran it over her panties so that it throbbed against her clit.

Tatum cried out, bucking against it and I snatched it back with a growl, switching it off again.

"What did I say about staying still?" I warned and her eyes widened as her grip on the bed frame tightened.

"Sorry," she breathed and I clucked my tongue at her.

I slowly reached out with my bad hand, using my fingers to pinch the fabric of her panties in my grasp before tugging them back and baring her pussy to me. Fuck, I'd never wanted to slide my cock into anything so much in all my life. It was torture to deny myself. But I lived for the pain of testing my own control, so it was the sweetest kind of ache.

I kept my gaze between her thighs as I moved the vibrator to her entrance but I could feel her eyes on me the entire time.

It sunk in slowly as I made sure not to touch her flesh in any way with my own and she gasped, her toes curling against the sheets, knuckles blanching as she gripped the bed frame as hard as she could and fought with everything she had to stay still.

As I pushed it into her, the curved end slipped into the perfect position against her clit and I withdrew my hand a moment before I would have felt her wetness for myself. It was near to painful to deny myself like that, but the moan that escaped her as I shifted back made it worth it.

"I need to make a phone call," I said to her as I moved off of the bed and took my place in the armchair where I had a perfect view of her. "And you're going to have to stay silent for it."

"What?" she gasped as I pulled the remote from the bag and set the vibrator to a deep, pulsing rhythm and she instantly cried out.

I switched it off again and raised an eyebrow at her. "Remember what I said to you about owning power by withholding something that someone else desperately needs? Well I'm holding the power over your orgasm to teach you the meaning of that sentiment. And I'll either reward you with it or withhold it from you as I please."

Her lips parted as I chose a different rhythm for the vibrator, setting it to a constant buzz and licking my lips as she bucked her hips, moaning again.

When I switched it off this time, her fingers began to uncurl from the headboard and I growled at her. "If you take your hand off of those bars, the game is over. If you make a noise during my phone call, it's over. And to punish you, I'll tie your hands at your back for the rest of the day and night so that you can't even pleasure yourself to finish what I'm starting. Got it?"

"Saint, I don't know if I can-"

I turned the vibrator on again, selecting a rhythm that started out on a gentle buzz and then slowly grew in intensity before dropping off and building again.

Tatum moaned as she writhed on the bed and I gave her a moment to get control of herself as I dialled my father.

She sucked in a breath, biting down on her bottom lip as she fought to stop the noises she was making and a smile tugged at the corner of my lips as she gave in to my game.

"Saint," Father greeted curtly, and I pressed the button for the speakerphone, laying my cell phone down on the arm of my chair.

Tatum's wide eyes fell on it as she realised that meant he'd hear her if she lost control and I smirked at her as I upped the intensity on the vibrator so that her knuckles turned white against the bedposts and she gasped loudly.

"Father. I have come into possession of something that you need to see," I said casually, my voice completely controlled.

"Give me a moment to secure the line," he said.

The sound of bland hold music filled the room and I toyed with the functions on the vibrator remote so that it took up a hard pulsing which vibrated loudly enough for me to hear and Tatum gasped as she writhed uncontrollably on the bed.

"One scream before he comes back on the line," I allowed and Tatum cried out as she pressed her thighs together like she was trying to dampen the feeling taking over her body.

"Good girl. Now keep your legs open, stay quiet and don't come," I commanded, knowing full well my father would be back on the line at any moment and she whimpered as she fought to control herself again.

Tatum's lips parted on a protest to that just as the bland music cut off and my father's voice silenced her.

"Go ahead," he said as Tatum panted through the violent vibrations I was exposing her pussy to.

I took pity on her and lowered the settings to a deep thrum as I forced myself to concentrate on the conversation.

"I have come into possession of Donovan Rivers' research notes," I said, not bothering with any bullshit. "After giving them some analysis, I believe there may be what is required here to develop a vaccine to the Hades Virus. He was certainly on the right track anyway."

A beat of three seconds was the only indication that I would get to say that my father was taken off guard by that and his voice came back following it without a speck of surprise lacing it. He'd trained me well in that much at least.

"Very well, forward it on to me and I'll have it analysed. Do you wish to tell me how you came into possession of it?"

"His daughter belongs to me," I said simply and the moment Tatum cut me an angry look, I upped the power on the vibrations wracking her body so that she gasped and cursed me beneath her breath. "She does everything I say."

"Good. I'll let you know once I have a vaccine for you. Is your new headmaster performing as required?" Father asked conversationally but I knew it was nothing of the sort. He didn't waste time on small talk.

"Yes. Monroe is fitting in quite well," I assured him.

"Well, update me if there's anything else I need to know. I look forward to your email. And make sure you stay safe." To someone else that might have sounded like a touching sentiment from a father to his son, but I knew it was more of a command designed to ensure his heir remained alive and kicking no matter what. We couldn't let the Memphis name die out after all.

"Of course."

The line went dead and Tatum instantly released a moan as she bucked against the bed, a bead of sweat rolling down between her breasts and making me ache to lick it off.

"Please Saint," she panted. "I'm so close."

"Are you now?" I asked in a low tone as I upped the intensity. "Then maybe you should be begging more."

She cried out, her body trembling as her orgasm drew near and I changed the settings to hold it off again.

"I hate you sometimes," she panted, and a dark smile captured my lips as I watched her brought to ruin for me.

"Only sometimes? Then perhaps I'm not trying hard enough. Beg, Tatum and I might give you what you want."

I began changing the settings one after another as she begged and cursed and pleaded, but her hands never once left the bars on the headboard and the more I worked her up, the harder my cock strained with the desire to fill her up and feel every squeeze of that tight pussy for myself.

Her begging turned to pleading, her blue eyes finding mine and locking on them as she moaned and panted.

"What is this, Saint?" she begged, forcing the words out around the dam of need I was building up in her body. "Do you want me too? Or is it just about the control?"

I considered not answering her, but as her gaze slid to the obvious bulge in my pants, that seemed a bit pointless.

"I want to own every single inch of you, Tatum. I want you like I've never wanted any other woman. I want to ravish and destroy you and conquer your body in the most brutal way I can. But I won't break the rules, not ever."

She cried out as I upped the vibrations again for the final time, wanting to watch her come for me as the ache in my body moved beyond desire to something almost too unbearable to deny.

"So don't break them," she gasped. "Just come with me. I want to see you, too."

My jaw clenched at the command even as my cock twitched with pleasure at the mere idea of it. But as I thought on it with her perfect body writhing beneath me, I knew I'd be finishing myself off in the bathroom the moment this was done anyway. And it hadn't actually been a command. She'd been begging me to do it and that was exactly what I'd wanted her doing.

I slowly rose to my feet so that I could stand over her, looking down at the complete and utter perfection of her as she came apart beneath me.

I transferred the remote into the fingers of my bad arm and kept my gaze locked on hers as I pushed my hand into my sweatpants and drew my cock out, fisting it in my hand.

Tatum's eyes widened as they fell on it, her tongue wetting her lips as she bucked on the bed and moaned for me again, seeming even more turned on by the sight of me getting off on this too.

I groaned as I began pumping my cock in just the way I liked, rubbing the moisture from the tip over the head and stroking my hand up and down the full length of my shaft.

"Saint," Tatum gasped again and I was so turned on that I knew it wouldn't take much for me to be coming for her. I upped my pace, pumping myself as I stood over her and giving in to an inch of the all consuming desire I'd held for this girl since the moment I'd first laid eyes on her.

She cried out as her orgasm ripped through her body, her spine arching and the most delicious incarnation of my name spilling from those sinful lips of hers.

Pleasure tore through me and I came hard, my hot cum spilling over her tits where they were close to bursting out of that white bra. A curse of relief and frustration spilled from me as I tried to catch my breath and I switched the vibrator off, dropping the remote to the bed beside her.

"You can let go of the headboard now," I grunted as I looked her over, the sight of my cum on her body making me ache as it marked her out as mine and my cock was practically hard for her again already.

Tatum moaned in a lusty way as she reached down to tug the vibrator out from between her thighs. Her hands began trailing over her body, one teasing her clit as she bathed in the afterglow of what I'd done to her and the other running over her perfect tits, sliding across the cum I'd left on her flesh and smearing it over her nipple as she tugged it free of the material.

For several seconds which dragged on for far too long, I was enraptured by her, aching to grab hold of her and claim her properly, fuck her until she was screaming so loud that she lost her voice. She was temptation personified, this beautiful, alluring, sinful creature designed to command my attention in a way I'd never experienced before.

I took a step closer to her before even realising what I was doing and something in me snapped as she almost made me lose control.

"Stop that," I growled. "Get out of my bed and get yourself cleaned up.

You need a shower and your hair is due a wash. Then I want you to put on the black dress which I hung ready for you in the closet and cook dinner for everyone."

Tatum's lips popped open as she fell still at my tone but I didn't care if I'd hurt her precious feelings. If she tempted me into breaking the rules for her then she would find out exactly how much of a monster I could be and I didn't want to unleash that on her.

I turned away from her and shoved my cock back into my sweatpants as I stalked straight for the stairs.

"Where are you going?" she called after me and I snarled angrily as I headed on down them.

"Out for a run," I snapped.

"Saint you can't! Your ribs will-"

"Do not ever presume to take control of me!" I roared at her as I lost it completely. "You don't tell me what to do and you don't get to make decisions for me!"

I stormed away from the shock and hurt in her big blue eyes, kicking on a pair of sneakers by the front door and trying not to freak out over the lack of socks as I ripped the door open. Even that was enough to send pain searing through my ribs but I didn't care and as I stepped out into the cold, I slammed it as hard as I could.

I'd just allowed her to change the course of my actions. I'd never intended to get myself off with her there. I didn't care how good it had felt or how fucking perfect she'd looked beneath me like that. It wasn't what I'd been planning and if I'd allowed my control to slip like that once then who was to say what would be next?

Would I be eating food with my hands like a savage, wearing pink and red at once, getting up at six *thirteen*? The whole fucking world would burn at my hands before I'd allow it to come to that.

I started jogging up the path that circled the lake, ignoring the immediate blaze of pain which burned through my ribs. But fuck that. I wasn't going to let some fucking bones tell me what I could or couldn't do with my own body. I went for a run around the lake every other day before I was hit by that fucking car and I was done letting that or anything else dictate to me how I had to live my life.

No, broken ribs wouldn't stop me running even if I was half dead by the time I made it back to The Temple. And Tatum Rivers wouldn't take command of my cock even if she was the most irresistible creature I'd ever seen.

CHAPTER TEN

Saint took a morning walk in the winter sun in place of his workout while I accompanied him on it, silence ringing between us. He was still pissed at me and had me come along in nothing but my nightdress and sneakers and I swear my nipples could cut glass right now. Since he'd gone running yesterday and half killed himself, he hadn't spoken a word about it or the way we'd come apart for each other before it either. He had been twitching angrily ever since though, barking orders at all of us while he fought not to collapse from the pain he'd put himself through. Kyan had slipped a sedative in his coffee eventually and he'd passed out in his room for the rest of the day. Blake had told me if I lectured him, he'd start running daily marathons, so I bit my tongue and was glad when he didn't insist on doing it again this morning. But this nightdress stunt was nothing short of childish and I was done with his mood. He needed to get over it.

"Have you made any progress on Mortez's phone?" I asked him, figuring that was pretty neutral ground to break the silence between us.

He glanced at me with narrowed eyes and I gave him an innocent look, fluttering my lashes a little to sweeten him up.

He turned his head away stiffly. "I have one final attempt at entering a passcode. I have tried the most common ones now I am left in a dilemma as I have one final try but two final common passcodes to attempt."

"What if he used something more personal?" I asked with a sigh.

"Then I will be unable to break it. So we must hope that he was not CIA and that his simpleton mind would have lead him to using one of the common passcodes that countless sheeple use in this world on their own phones."

"Sheeple?" I questioned with a snort and his mouth twitched at the corner before he quickly schooled his expression back to a cold wall.

"People who are sheep, blindly walking through life doing as everyone else does," he explained and I laughed. "Knowing your upbringing, your father would have taught you the value of having a random passcode, am I correct?"

"Yeah," I said, bemused.

"Kyan uses one two three four entirely to irritate me, but whenever I get my hands on his phone, I change it and write it in invisible ink on his forehead while he's sleeping. He bought a UV light to ensure he can always find it before it's washed off in the shower."

I smiled at him, knowing that was his way of showing how much he cared about Kyan, protecting his private information. It may as well have been a candle lit dinner and a proposal for how much that meant coming from Saint Memphis.

We arrived back at The Temple and Saint walked away to take his shower while I headed into the kitchenette to make breakfast. By the time everyone sat down, I was anxious to see Saint attempt the final passcode.

"Don't keep us in suspense any longer," Monroe growled, having been badgering Saint to try his decided code all through breakfast. I had a feeling Saint enjoyed holding that power over everyone as he made us all wait. But I was getting pretty sick of it myself.

"Saint," I said sharply and he pursed his lips slightly before reaching into his pocket and taking out Mortez's phone.

Silence fell over us all as we waited for him to try the code.

"Which ones did you decide on trying?" I asked.

"Four four four four, or two two two two," Saint said thoughtfully. "Was Mortez a low numbers man with a flare for the easily reachable four? Or did he extend his thumb enough to hit the two? He did have large hands... perhaps he could reach the two as easily as the four..." Saint frowned.

"Just fucking pick one," Monroe insisted.

"How about we flip a coin?" Blake offered.

Kyan reached across the table, snatching it from Saint's hand and tapping in his own choice.

"No!" Saint roared but Kyan grinned widely.

"Guess he liked those twos," Kyan said, tossing the phone back to Saint. "We're in."

"Oh my god." I got up from my seat, moving around to look over Saint's shoulder and the other guys moved to do the same. Monroe stepped behind me, his hand resting against my back and the pine scent of him reached me. I soaked in the comfort of his closeness, holding my breath as Saint navigated his way to Mortez's messages.

"You're lucky Kyan, if you'd gotten us locked out I'd have had to punish you," Saint growled.

"If you really wanna spank me, Sainty, I'll go lay face down on your bed with my ass out, but don't blame me if I end up liking it," Kyan mocked.

"Don't tempt me," Saint muttered.

"Just show us the damn messages," Monroe said in frustration.

Saint opened them up and flicked through the first couple, clearly passed between his men on the night of the attack as they all got into position. But there was nothing in them more meaningful than that.

The only other messages he'd shared was with someone with the code name 52 and my gut clenched as he scrolled through them.

52:

Have you locked down the target?

Mortez:

We're following his daughter now, boss

52:

Call me when it's done.

52:

Where are you?

52:

Check in.

52:

If you have let me down on this Mortez, I will be revoking your privileges at Royaume D'élite.

"What do you think would happen if we replied pretending to be Mortez? Reckon this asshole will fall for it?" Blake suggested and I nodded in encouragement.

"Can't be worse than doing nothing," I said thoughtfully while Saint drummed his fingers on the table, clearly weighing up the pros and cons.

"What are you thinking?" I asked him.

"I am trying to work out the relevance of their code name '52'," Saint said thoughtfully. "There are fifty two weeks in a year…it's the code number for direct dial calls to Mexico…or there are fifty two cards in a deck – not counting jokers of course-"

"Everyone at the club gets a number," Kyan explained before Saint could come up with any more theories. "I'm 69. Obviously."

I couldn't help but snort a laugh at that despite myself. "Seriously?" I asked and he leaned close to me as if the others weren't all listening too.

"You want me to prove to you that I deserve it? We can ditch our next class…" Kyan leaned down to run his tongue up the side of my neck, making me flush red and Saint elbowed him in the gut to make him back up.

"Maybe later," I said.

"Focus," Saint snapped.

"Check the rest of the phone," Monroe suggested. "If we're going to risk giving ourselves away then at least make sure there isn't a name and address in the contacts list linked to this 52 guy."

"That would be moronic," Saint deadpanned.

"I was exaggerating, but you catch my fucking drift," Monroe urged and Saint nodded, checking the contacts list and the emails, but there was nothing of interest there. There were no other apps on the phone and it was clear this was just a point of contact between Mortez and this 52 person.

"Come on," Kyan urged. "Text back with some bullshit about the phone being broken and having to get it repaired."

"That's not an *entirely* useless idea I suppose," Saint mused, glancing at the clock. "But I need to think on how to phrase it exactly and we only have a minute and fifteen seconds before we have to head to class.

Kyan grabbed the phone from his hand and Saint snarled, twisting sharply around to reach for it and wincing in pain as he did so. I sucked in a breath, moving forward to stop him from getting up.

Kyan tapped something out on the phone and pressed send before Saint could do himself any more damage trying to get to him and I placed a hand on Saint's shoulder to calm him. The tension ran out of his muscles as he looked to me then held his palm out to Kyan for the phone.

"That'll do it," Kyan announced, giving it back to him and Saint's eyes flashed at him as he looked down at it.

I moved closer to read it myself.

Mortez:

My phone broke in the fight so I couldn't get a photo. But the job is done.

I held my breath as I hunted for the dots at the bottom of the message thread that would say someone was replying, but they didn't come.

"There is one other thing we must discuss," Saint said, looking to me and my heart pounded as I caught on to what he was going to say. "Tatum is immune to the Hades Virus."

The other guys sucked in breaths, looking to me in confusion.

"What? How?" Blake demanded, his eyes full of hope and it made my heart squeeze.

Saint leaned back in his chair, letting me explain and I wet my lips. "Well…my father trialled a vaccine on me. It was supposed to have gone through proper testing but apparently corners were cut and…it wasn't safe. That's how my sister died," I said, my throat tight as they gazed at me with a mixture of awe and pity. "Anyway, I guess it worked on me somehow. My dad told me when I saw him and, well…" I shrugged, not wanting to dwell on that memory a second longer.

"Thank fuck for small miracles," Kyan said heavily, staring at me intently.

"This must be kept secret," Monroe said darkly.

"Yes, this knowledge will not leave our home," Saint growled. "Not a word of it."

"We'll take it to the grave," Blake swore.

The others nodded as one, a vow shining in their eyes that I was sure none of them would break

"We must leave," Saint said firmly as he glanced at the clock on the wall, rising from his seat and turning to me, realising I was still in my nightdress and his whole world looked ready to crumble.

"Your first class is with me so your chances of detention are low." Monroe glanced between the others with a smirk. "But never zero."

"That isn't the point," Saint spat and I could see he was about to pop a blood vessel.

"I'll be ready on time." I flew away from him, racing upstairs, knowing that another Saint outburst could lead to him injuring himself even further.

I pulled on my uniform in record time, taming my hair and adding minimal makeup to my face before sprinting back downstairs again. The guys were just stepping out the door as Saint barked at them to leave when I fell into step between Saint and Monroe with a smug smile, blowing a loose lock of hair from my face.

"You didn't shower," Saint grumbled.

"Don't nit pick," I insisted and surprisingly, he didn't. "Did 52 reply?"

"Not yet," Saint said. "But if they *do* fall for this, we must be prepared."

"I'm sure you're working out a ten point plan in your head right now," Monroe said, sounding hopeful instead of mocking him for it.

"Eighteen points," Saint corrected and Monroe smiled, making Saint almost smile too.

We made it to the Acacia Sports Hall and I split away from the guys into the girls' changing room, finding Mila already in her dark green shorts and t-shirt with the Everlake crest on the breast. I realised I should have just dressed in my gym clothes before I left The Temple, but I guessed Saint wouldn't have been able to accept that.

"Hey girl," Mila said with a sad smile. She often gave me that look since the news had come out about my dad's death. "How are you doing?" she asked with genuine empathy and it cut into my chest, splitting the wound wide.

"I'm better," I said, which wasn't untrue. I was still deeply hurting, but it wasn't the viciously keen pain of the first couple of weeks. Part of me hated finding any reprieve from his loss though. I was caught between not wanting to feel this devouring ache, and not wanting to let go of it. "I just need constant distractions."

"Well, that I can do," she said firmly. "I can offer you mindless chat, cookies and hot chocolate on a girl's night at mine tonight? I can even throw in a cheesy movie or two and upgrade the hot chocolate to hard liquor, if you prefer."

"Yeah, that sounds like a dream," I agreed, my heart lifting.

"Great, do you need to like...ask permission?" she lowered her voice to a whisper and my stomach clenched at her words. Things had shifted between me and the Night Keepers, but between Saint's rules and all of their possessive ways, I knew they were going to be difficult about this. But I wasn't going to let them cage me anymore.

"I'll be there, don't worry about it," I said firmly and she beamed.

We filed out of the changing room with the rest of the girls and I had the feeling this day was going to be one of the easier ones. I just had to find a way to convince my jealous little tribe that I needed a few hours off from them tonight for girl time. Easy.

We headed into the sports hall where Monroe was waiting with the guys in our class. He was chatting with Kyan, the two of them chuckling about something as we approached and my lips tugged up at the sight. He always seemed to smile so much more these days since he'd joined the Night Keepers, and though I knew he'd never admit it, it was clear he'd found a place amongst them that felt natural. I shared in that secret too. Because I would never have thought I'd not only fit in with the Night Keepers, but feel like I belonged with them on a base level, like we were always meant to find each other.

"Today we're going to be completing a fitness test to see how you have improved since the start of the school year," Monroe announced.

I hungered for that kind of challenge, I wanted to push myself until I couldn't feel anything anymore. There was nothing like the sweet burn of exercise to drown out every other feeling in my body.

"Line up on both sides of the hall," Monroe instructed and the class split up.

I moved to stand beside Mila at the far end of the hall, but we soon had company as Blake, Kyan and Saint all walked over to stand to my right.

"Memphis!" Monroe barked. "Sit your ass out. You're excused from this class like I've said a thousand times."

Saint scowled, standing there in his P.E. uniform with his arm in a sling.

"I'll watch then," he seethed, snapping his fingers at Freeloader further down the line who came running his way. He murmured something to her and she raced out of the room even when Monroe shouted after her to stop. She returned a minute later with a chair and a cushion, positioning them in front of me. Saint sat down on it, taking his phone from his pocket. A smirk danced around his mouth as he suddenly had a front row seat to my fitness test. *Asswit.*

"Do you really have to sit right there?" I huffed, placing my hands on my hips.

"Yes," he said simply. "I will encourage you."

"And stare at her tits bouncing about," Blake pointed out and Saint didn't deny it.

"It's called a sports bra, doucheberries, and thanks to Saint, it's the best one available so bounceage is minimised to the max," I said, tossing my hair.

"But it can never be *totally* eradicated," Kyan pointed out with a smirk.

Monroe called out to the class, ending our back and forth. "Each exercise will last one minute with fifteen second breaks in between sets. You will count how many of each movement you do. If you lie, you are only lying to yourself. Ready. Jumping jacks. Go!"

I started jumping beside Mila, and Saint watched me closely, correcting my form and making me angrier and angrier by the second. Kyan and Blake were working furiously to outdo each other beside me, grunting and growling as they desperately tried to out jump each other. Monroe shouted *stop* on the minute and I panted as the fifteen second break set in.

"If you fall into the top fitness bracket in the class, I will reward you," Saint told me and my mind spiked with an idea.

"Okay, if I win, I can spend a few hours this evening with Mila in her room," I said and Saint considered that, running a finger over his lips.

"Deal. But if you don't fall into the top bracket, I will punish you."

"Deal," I agreed just as easily and Monroe shouted out for us to start on jump squats.

"What the hell?" Mila hissed at me, her eyes rounding, but we were too deep into the set already for me to explain. Not that I had much of an explanation for that except that Saint liked to spank me or drive me crazy with sex toys. Totally normal shit. Shit I would definitely discuss with her when I secured our girl's night.

I fell into a rhythm, pushing myself harder and harder as I relished the burn in my thighs. It made me forget everything, made the hurt in my body feel sweet in comparison to the raking pain over my dad. Blake and Kyan were throwing punches at each other between every jump, trying to throw the other off and I tried not to get distracted by their display of testosterone. It was especially hard when both of them took their shirts off and tossed them on the floor.

Saint watched us all with approval in his eyes, tapping intermittently on his phone and smiling like we were attractions performing well in his circus.

By the final round, everything ached and I was coated with sweat, my own shirt discarded so I was just in my sports bra and Saint's eyes devoured me. The final round was burpees and everyone groaned, half the class barely getting through each one while me, Kyan and Blake fell into a furious rhythm with each other, somehow in perfect time. Mila was kicking ass beside me, but she was starting to slow and I urged her on as she groaned in pain.

Monroe finally called time and I fell to the floor beside Kyan on his back as his whole chest heaved and Blake's golden skin glinted beyond him. Part of me wanted to climb into the space between them and curl up there as we bathed in the aftermath of our workout.

"Holy shit," I panted.

"We're almost as out of breath as when I fuck you and you're hardly able to tell me how much more you like me than the other Night Keepers," Kyan said, roaring a laugh as Blake punched him.

"Wait," Saint snapped suddenly, standing and walking forward to stare down at Kyan. He pointed at the inner side of his left arm with a look of horror on his face and I rolled over, pushing myself up to see what had caught his attention. "What the fuck is that?!" Saint snapped and Kyan turned his arm out further so Saint could see it better. I burst into hysterics as I saw the brand new tattoo there of a squid, the tentacles perfectly defined as they flared out across his forearm.

"When the hell did you get that?" Blake snorted.

"Is this why you've been wearing long-sleeved shirts all the time lately?" I asked as Saint's shadow seemed to grow around Kyan as he seethed.

"Maybe," Kyan said, tossing me a grin. "I wanted it to heal up before the big reveal. Do you like it? I think the depth of meaning to it really makes it special."

"No she doesn't fucking like it. Who could like that? It's hideous!" Saint snarled. "You will have it removed just as soon as this lockdown is lifted."

Kyan blew out a derisive breath. "Make me."

"Oh I will, I assure you of that." Saint smiled vindictively and I could almost hear the cogs in his brain working as he figured out what leverage he could come up with to make Kyan do what he wanted.

"Has everyone got their results?" Monroe called to the room.

"Shit, I lost count," I muttered.

"I have complied each of your results," Saint said, holding up his phone.

"Of course you did," Kyan laughed through his heavy breathing.

How the hell did he manage that??

Monroe wrote out a chart on the whiteboard and everyone added up their numbers to work out which bracket they fell in. I beamed when Saint announced that me, Kyan and Blake were top of the class above several members of the football team.

"Congratulations," Saint said to me, his eyes glinting. "You have earned a night with your friend. You can be with her from seven until ten tonight."

"How nice of you," Mila said under breath, not loud enough for him to hear. I knew she'd never understand this, but really I was just playing Saint at his own game. And I'd freaking won.

I grinned, not even giving a shit that he was designating times for me. That was just how Saint worked.

Monroe didn't let up all lesson, forcing us to work on whichever exercises we found hardest until we were all dripping with sweat. As mine had been burpees, I especially wanted to punch him in the dick. But as the endorphins kicked in on my way out, I guessed I could forgive him.

After class, we headed out of the hall and Blake slung his sweaty arm around me, pressing a hot kiss to my temple. He smelled of man and heat and deliciousness. I turned toward him, fisting a hand in his hair and tip-toeing up to press my lips to his. He growled demandingly, grabbing my waist and hoisting me up so I wrapped my legs around him. I laughed as he made a show of pinning me against the wall and I heard Kyan cursing somewhere behind us and a bunch of girls gasping and muttering.

His hot, sweaty chest pressed to mine and I loved it, drawing him closer as he kissed me like I was the prom queen and he was the monster who'd stolen me away from my king. I was deep into that wild fantasy when Monroe barked at us.

"Rivers, Bowman! You have a fucking audience, please stop dry humping each other in the corridor."

Blake put me down reluctantly, smirking at me and I looked to Monroe with my cheeks flushing. He had his arms folded and was playing a good game at looking like a stern teacher as he ordered the rest of the students into the changing room. But I could see beneath all of that to the jealousy swirling in his eyes and that got me even hotter. I was quietly conjuring up a scenario where he came over here, fighting for me, then Blake would fight back...Kyan would get all caveman about it too and they'd all just start brawling and-

"Meeting. Now." Saint strode toward the exit without explanation and we all frowned at each other as he left.

"I think we've been summoned," Kyan said, his eyes still pinned to me

184

like he was considering grabbing me and stealing me away from Blake. Or maybe he'd do whatever he was thinking about right here in front of him and Monroe. I shook my head to clear it, figuring it was probably best not to get into an orgy right now and turned, following Saint outside.

The others were right on my heels as we spilled through the double doors and Saint turned to us, taking out Mortez's phone. My heart skipped and jumped and all my heated ideas were forgotten as I focused on it.

"We've had a message," Saint announced, showing it to us.

I read it with my pulse hammering.

52:

Who the fuck is this?

"Shit," I breathed.

"Busted," Blake laughed.

"It's not funny, asshole." Monroe punched him in the arm and Blake's smile fell.

"I believe we are at a dead end," Saint said simply and Kyan strode forward, snatching the phone from him before he could stop him. He hit dial then the speaker phone button and a ringing sound blared from it.

Saint parted his lips as if to rebuke him then slowly nodded. "I suppose this train of action isn't total insanity."

"So what you're saying is that I came up with a plan before you did?" Kyan taunted and Saint's eyes froze to hard blocks of ice.

He opened his mouth to retort when someone answered the call. *Holy shit.*

"You sure have some fucking balls," the gruff male voice said.

"Yeah, they weigh about fifty pounds more than yours do," Kyan said cockily, holding the phone to his mouth, but Saint snatched it from him.

"We've got a few questions for you," Saint said, his voice calm yet holding a deadly threat in it.

The man on the line laughed obnoxiously. "Well I have a few for you too, you piece of shit."

"I assure you, calling me a shit is like calling the devil naughty."

"So are you gonna tell me what you did with my men, you fucking asshole because that many guys don't go off the radar all at once unless they ain't breathing anymore."

"You at least have a few brain cells to rub together then," Saint answered. "So I will offer you a deal that even a reasonably clever man would take. Fifty thousand dollars for the name of your boss."

"And who says I ain't the boss?" the man growled dangerously.

"The first rule of running any kind of illegal operation is to associate yourself with it as little as possible by using lackies to do all the heavy lifting. So if it goes to hell they'll take the fall for it."

"Pah," the man spat. "And who are you then? Some fucking vigilante bounty hunter?"

"If I wanted to collect the bounty on Donovan Rivers' head, his death wouldn't have been announced as a suicide, would it you imbecile?"

My gut twisted at his words, but I wasn't going to let my grief spill out now. Hate and revenge were all I was concentrating on.

"Don't you speak to me like that you fucking cunt," the man snarled. "You think your bribes can sway my loyalty? I get far more than money outta my position, more than you could ever offer me. So when I get my hands on you, I'm gonna pull out your intestines and wear 'em as a necklace."

"A colourful, yet pointless threat," Saint said calmly and I had to admire him for how unshaken he was by this obviously powerful and violent man talking to him like that. "There is no tracker on this phone any longer and I'm sure you and your boss are scratching your heads right now over who may have murdered so many of your men."

"We got you pegged," the man hissed. "We're gonna come for your head and your family's heads and your fucking pet dog's head."

"I don't have a dog but if I did it would be so well trained that a single flick of my finger would turn it from the most docile creature you ever met into the most vicious. It would maul you before you ever got near to hurting it, or me for that matter," Saint mused, examining his nails like facing down death threats was a daily occurrence for him. "Your shortcomings are showing quite vividly now. And I am well aware I am talking to the wrong person. Do give my regards to your boss though."

"He'll have your eyes plucked out and your nose ripped off. He'll-"

Saint cut the line, tucking the phone neatly into his pocket.

"Why'd you hang up?" Blake balked as I just stood there panting for Saint and his psycho ways. Man, why was that so hot? Him taking control like that, talking to that guy like he was nothing and Saint was the king of the world...*gah*.

"We now know his boss is male," Saint said. "He won't ever have met his employer face to face though, so I doubt there is much more he knows that is of use."

"So what now?" I asked, biting my lip as I tried to stop myself eye-fucking Saint. God why was I so into bad boys? No, scrap that. Why was I into cold blooded, *sadistic* boys? Mother nature was obviously fucking high when she built my libido.

"Now, I will deliberate on what I have learned," Saint said even though knowing this guy's boss was male wasn't exactly a significant clue that could lead us anywhere.

"I love you, brother. Especially when your crazy is showing," Kyan said.

"It is one of my finer qualities," Saint smirked and I couldn't help but agree.

CHAPTER ELEVEN

I sat on the picnic benches outside Aspen Halls, watching while Danny, Chad and the rest of the football team made the Unspeakables line up before the wall of the enormous stone building while they threw handfuls of mud at them and I waited to see if any of them were going to crack and give us some information on the Justice Ninja.

This morning, we'd woken up to find a giant brown cock scrawled on the stained glass window in what we were pretty fucking sure was human shit. Honest to fuck, someone in this school had taken a shit, picked it up and used it to draw a cock on our home alongside the initials J.N. Saint had almost gone full Saint and not one of us had been willing to get close enough to clean it off, so he'd ended up calling his maid, Rebecca, and offering her five grand to get her ass down to the house and scrub it off while we were in class.

As the most likely suspects in this fun game of who hated us enough to make a shit mural on our house, the Unspeakables had needed interrogating so I'd volunteered to oversee it. But we'd been at this for over an hour and they had nothing to offer me, so I was giving up hope.

Deepthroat had taken a face full of mud a few seconds ago and I laughed like it was hilarious, snapping a photo to forward on to Kyan before letting the fake smile slip from my face as they all gave their attention back to the game. It felt like clapping for a bunch of kids who needed constant reassurance that they were doing a good job from their daddy all the damn time. But I wasn't their fucking daddy. I was just a miserable son of a bitch with a painted on smile.

I sighed as I lay back on the table, ignoring the bite of cold in the air as I looked up at the stormy sky. It wasn't raining yet, but it was clearly on its way. Just another thing to make this gloomy bastard of a day less enjoyable. I'd already had to sit through double math and geometry today, did the sky really have to start pissing on me too?

I tapped my fingers against the wooden tabletop as Freeloader started crying and begging for mercy. Even that didn't make me feel good. In fact, it kinda made me feel like an asshole. And even though I was, I didn't need reminding of it right now.

"All of you Unspeakable motherfuckers," I called without even bothering to look over at them. "You've got ten seconds to run the fuck away from here as fast as you can. Anyone who is still within sight after that will have the pleasure of having rocks thrown at you instead of mud."

"Aww come on, Blake, it was just getting good," Chad begged, but I ignored his desperate ass. If he was bored that wasn't my problem to solve.

"Ten," I called. "Nine, eight-"

The shrieks and pounding feet of the Unspeakables making their escape reached me and it sounded like most of the football team had chased after them. But that wasn't my problem either. I didn't even bother to finish my countdown.

I released a slow breath and stared up at the ever darkening sky before letting my gaze trail to the huge building beside me. Aspen Halls was old, the grey stone weathered by time and the endless rain that always seemed only moments from falling in this place.

It was four floors of faux gothic beauty designed to make prospective parents of the richest kids in the world gasp and coo at its impressive architecture as they signed over thousands of dollars in fees for the privilege of sending their little darlings here. I'm sure they thought it was the best that money could buy. That their kids would much prefer to be left here in the middle of nowhere than spend time with their families. I mean, I supposed most people had no reason to believe that time might be precious, so it made sense. And it wasn't like I was unhappy here. I loved spending my time with the other Night Keepers and now Tate too. But if I'd realised that my time with my mom was running out, I would have made the most of every day I had with her.

I watched as the forest green Everlake Prep flag flapped hard in the breeze that preceded the rising storm up on the top of the building and I couldn't help but wonder what it would feel like to be way up there when the storm hit.

"You alright, dude?" Danny Harper's voice drew my attention and I glanced around to find him standing there beside me, looking like he gave altogether too many shits about me.

Danny was strange in that respect. Everyone else at this school flocked around me, kissed my ass and wanted to spend time in my company because of the status I held and the protection that might be offered if I saw them as a friend. But Danny actually seemed to give a fuck about me. He was the only one who ever seemed to notice that I painted half of my smiles on these days. The only one who ever asked if I was alright without looking half terrified that if I wasn't, I might use my power in this place to punish him for it. Maybe he really was my friend. I couldn't say I had a whole lot of genuine ones of those though, so it was hard to be certain.

"I heard that lightning struck that flagpole during a storm over the summer," I said, pointing up to the top of the building. "Apparently the flag set alight and was burned to a crisp and they had to get a new one before term started up again."

"Oh yeah?" he asked curiously, turning to look up at it and the dark clouds beyond.

"What do you think it would feel like to stand up there while the rain was crashing down on us and the lightning was burning through the sky?"

He considered that for a moment then turned to look at me with a grin. "I'd say it would feel like being alive," he replied, already knowing what I was getting at and clearly sensing my mood.

I needed some kind of rush today if I was going to break this hopeless bullshit cycle I was descending into.

"I'm pretty sure there's a roof access door inside," Danny suggested as he began to lead the way to the double doors which led into the building, but I shook my head as I shoved myself upright.

"Nah. I say we take the more direct route." I pointed at the grey walls beside us and he hesitated as he took in what I meant.

The bricks were old and the mortar crumbling in enough places that I was sure we would be able to find foot and hand holds to make it to the top. It was a long fucking fall if we screwed it up but that was half the fun.

I smirked at the challenge and shrugged out of my blazer before shedding my tie and rolling my shirt sleeves back. Fancy ass loafers probably weren't the best choice for scaling walls but fuck it, that was what made it interesting.

"You're fucking crazy, dude," Danny chuckled nervously but he shed his blazer and tossed it on the picnic bench alongside mine all the same.

"Beats being miserable," I muttered and the look he cut me said he'd heard that, but he had the good sense not to comment.

Thunder rumbled through the clouds and we both looked up, exchanging a glance which acknowledged that this was dumb as fuck and smirking as we moved towards the wall anyway.

"Last one to the top sucks ass," I taunted as I picked out my first handholds.

"I hope you don't mean that literally," he joked and my smile widened.

"I guess we'll find out when you lose."

"Three, two, one-"

I jammed my fingers into the small gap between the bricks and began to climb as fast as I could.

At first there were more than enough gaps and holes to let me heave myself higher, then I used the top of the first floor window to gain even more height, but as I made it to the second floor, I failed to spot my next grip.

Danny laughed as he pulled ahead to my right and I cursed him as I was forced to shuffle in his direction along the side of the lead frame beneath me.

Thunder echoed through the heavens again and the rain spilled from the sky, causing me to laugh as it saturated my shirt and carved icy fingers down my skin.

I managed to reach a spot where there was another gap above me to let me move higher again and I kept climbing, determined to catch up to Danny as I looked up and found him passing the third floor window above me.

I scrunched my eyes against the pounding rain as thunder echoed again and a flash of lightning lit the sky.

The shiny soles of my shoes slipped against the wet bricks as I scrambled higher and for one heart stopping moment, I almost fell.

My gut lurched and I barked a laugh as adrenaline spiked through me and I clung on for dear life while my feet kicked against the grey bricks until I managed to find another spot to jam my toes into.

Danny had slowed above me and I could hear him cursing as either fear or a lack of hand holds slowed him down. I didn't care which so long as it gave me the chance to regain my lead.

I pushed harder, reaching the third floor and climbing higher as my heart raced and the wind howled hard enough to make my wet shirt flutter and slap against my back.

It was fucking freezing with the rain pounding down on me but even the shivers dancing along my skin helped to banish that endless fucking heartache that had been whispering my name all fucking day. This was why I kept taking these stupid risks. Whatever it took to escape my own bullshit, whatever I could do to set myself free of the constant grief for at least a little while.

I made it to the row of windows on the fourth floor and chanced a look down at the ground way below. My gut lurched as I took in the fall awaiting me if I fucked this up. I wondered if it would be enough to kill me outright or just hurt a whole hell of a lot. Probably best not to find out.

A shout carried to me on the wind and I barked a laugh as I spotted Mila down there, yelling at Danny to get his ass down at once. She was hollering like a fishwife and it seriously sounded like he was at risk of castration if he didn't fall to his death.

Danny wasted time shouting back down to her and I grinned as I pulled ahead. With a grunt of effort, I reached the top edge of the building and heaved myself up.

My heart leapt into my throat as the roof tile I was gripping suddenly ripped free and I yelled out in fright as I swung backwards for half a second before managing to save myself by gripping on tight with my other hand.

I cursed as I looked down at the lethal drop below as I let go of the tile and it spun away to smash to pieces on the concrete path.

Mila swore as she leapt away from it even though it hadn't even come close to hitting her and Danny yelled out for her to move back.

I tore my gaze away from the dizzying fall before clambering up onto the roof with a crow of victory as I won.

Danny wasn't far behind me and I offered him a hand, heaving him up over the edge where we grinned like a pair of fucking delinquents and stood there in the storm with the rain crashing down on us and our arms open wide to it.

Lightning flashed through the sky again and I navigated the slippery tiles carefully as I headed for the flagpole where the saturated flag whipped back and forth wetly, looking pretty fucking sorry for itself.

I climbed up onto the low lip of stone that edged the roof beside it and stood with my toes hanging over the edge as I looked out over campus towards the lake which was currently roiling and bubbling beneath the downpour.

I glanced over my shoulder with a manic grin as I locked eyes with Danny before wrapping my hand around the metal flagpole.

"Come on then!" I yelled at the sky as if I could taunt the storm into making the lightning strike while I held it.

My heart was racing a mile a minute and the heady rush of adrenaline had me laughing like a madman as I kept my fist tight around the metal and waited out the storm.

"Shit, man," Danny said, half laughing, half looking terrified as I waited for the next crash of thunder and the lightning which could decide my fate.

The boom that tore through the clouds overhead was enough to make my bones rattle and I tipped my head back just in time to see a bolt of lightning carve the darkness apart right above my head.

My heart leapt and raced and I came about as close to shitting myself as I ever had in my life before the light faded from the sky and I descended into fits of laughter instead.

A door banged open somewhere behind me and Mila's voice carried over the pouring rain.

"Danny Harper, you get your crazy ass inside this building right now or I'm putting you on a pussy ban for a month!" Mila yelled and I barked a laugh as Danny's face paled.

"That sounds pretty serious, dude," I admitted and he nodded.

"Thanks for the high, man, I'd better run." He turned away and headed for the door and I considered whether or not I was going to keep standing in the storm. That was the only thing about these fucking games we played. Whenever they ended, the rush ended too and I was left with the slow descent back into depression again. But it was usually enough to last me a few days at least.

What I really wanted was to head back and find my girl, kiss her until she was breathless and hold her in my arms all fucking night long. But as she'd been staying in with Saint every damn night so that she could look after him while he healed, I knew there was no chance of that. I mean, it was fair enough, the guy took a bullet and broke bones for her and he was incapable of looking after himself properly, but from a purely selfish point of view it still sucked.

"Blake," Mila called when I stayed where I was, my gaze raking over campus again like I was searching for something. "I think you should come inside now too, you've finished your game and...Tatum would be heartbroken if something happened to you."

I turned to look at her, seeing the hesitance in her eyes as she fought against the desire to speak out on behalf of her friend and the desire not to piss me off. I couldn't help but respect her for it. Most people wouldn't dare to even attempt to tell me what to do. And if I was honest, the girl made some valid points. Now that the initial thrill was over, I was just a douchebag standing in the rain freezing my balls off and getting way too fucking wet anyway.

"Well, as you asked so nicely, Mila, I'll be happy to oblige."

Mila smiled widely and moved aside as I crossed the tiles and headed in after her and Danny.

"You wanna come hang out at the common house?" Danny offered as we dripped our way down the stairs and I shrugged.

"I guess so." There was plenty of booze down there for me to consume and I could use it to ride out the end of this buzz I had going. It sure beat a night alone in my room anyway. "Call the others and let's make it a party. If I'm gonna get drunk I might as well do it in style."

Option number two in my quest to avoid my grief: drink myself into oblivion. Well, who was I to refuse an offer as tempting as that?

CHAPTER TWELVE

Today things were back to normal. For Saint anyway. Except for me, it was supposed to be a day I spent in an Applebees with Dad and Jess while we ate until our stomachs nearly burst before the staff brought out a cake and started singing. It had been one of the few constants in our lives as kids. Our birthdays. No matter where Dad was working, every state had an Applebees. Even if we had to drive four hours to get to it. And today, I was eighteen. With no family left to share in the tradition and no chance of spending it the way I once had.

Last year, Dad had taken the day off work and driven me to Six Flags for the day, buying fast passes so we could skip all the queues and go on every single ride in the park. We'd had dinner at Applebees and hadn't left until it closed, losing ourself to the memories of the past. If I'd known that would be my last birthday with my dad, I would have treasured each moment more deeply, memorised it more exactly. The memories I had were chipped like damaged china, the edges scuffed and missing pieces. Had his shirt been blue or grey? Did we go on the Batman ride first or the Superman one?

Saint was quiet during his walk and so was I. It wasn't until we were almost back to The Temple that he took one of his headphones out and spoke.

"It's time to return to the rules, siren," he said firmly. "The schedule will restart today. So tonight you will sleep at Monroe's."

I blinked in surprise. "Are you sure?"

"I'm well enough. I don't need mollycoddling anymore," he said sharply then he caught my hand, pulling me to a firm halt.

I frowned as I waited for him to go on, unable to read the twisting vortex in his eyes. Sometimes I knew what he needed on instinct, other times it was completely impossible to read anything from his face at all.

"I am grateful for your..." he paused, a crease forming between his eyes as he struggled with how to finish that sentence.

"Help?" I offered with a hint of amusement in my tone.

"Company," he decided, evidently unable to admit he'd needed anything from me.

"You're welcome." I shrugged, moving to leave but he tugged on my hand to keep me there as the wind blustered around us on the path, the pine trees groaning as they swayed.

"And I've enjoyed your company immensely," he continued, sounding like some eighteenth century gentleman. Which was the strangest thing because it made a weird kind of sense. He was so proper, but I'd still never made the connection before. I guess he could be classed as a soul devouring demon in the body of Mr Darcy though.

My heart warmed at his words and I slid my fingers out of his, stepping closer. His eyes widened as he tried to predict my next move, but clearly couldn't. I tip-toed up, wrapping my arms around him and hugging him gently, careful not to crush his bad arm or his hurt ribs. His breathing hitched and he stiffened in my hold like this kind of touch was repugnant to him, or maybe just alien. But he surprised me again when he folded his good arm around me and held me close. He didn't have to wear the sling anymore, but the cast was still in place with a covering over it made from one of his shirts. Kyan had drawn a large, grotesque squid with tentacles made out of cocks on the cast while he'd been sleeping one night and the rage that had roused in Saint had barely simmered since. Blake had had to hold him down so he didn't rip the whole thing off and I'd made the covering for it so his brain didn't implode.

I turned my face towards Saint to say I'd enjoyed my time with him too - much to my freaking surprise - but he turned at the same moment and his lips collided with the corner of my mouth. I pulled away in surprise, my mind whirling.

What the fuck? Did he just try to kiss me?

Kissing me surely hadn't been Saint Memphis' intention. Had it? If it had been anyone else, it would have been obvious. But he was an enigma when it came to intimacy. And he didn't kiss people. But fuck, I wanted him to. I wanted to feel the mouth of the devil on me and see if he tasted like sin itself. I didn't second guess that desire. I just let it flood me and take over.

Heat flushed into my cheeks as I awkwardly moved back into his personal space, seeking out his mouth, but he retreated immediately, his eyes pooling with rage.

"Saint," I said breathily, but he wouldn't look at me. He took another step back, carving out a hole of rejection in my chest.

"Make breakfast," he ordered, falling back on his routine and his freaking rules to save him from this awkwardness.

"*Saint*," I said again, stern this time but that clearly wasn't a good choice because although he did look at me, it was with a hard wall behind his eyes and a snarl on his lips.

"The rules are back in place, Plague, so if you don't want to be punished, I suggest you move right fucking now."

I gaped at him, scolded by him using that name against me. My jaw clenched and anger sizzled beneath my flesh. "*Fine by me.*"

I turned my back on him, striding inside with a furious scowl on my face.

"Hey, princess, what's up?" Monroe had arrived while we were gone, sitting on the couch in football shorts and a t-shirt ready for teaching P.E. today. My heart lifted at the sight of him and some of the rage I felt over Saint's words ebbed away.

"The rules are back on, so I'm bunking with you tonight," I told him airily and he beamed, making the rest of my anger fall away.

"Really?" he asked hopefully.

"Really," Saint said from behind me and I jumped. He moved as silently as a ghost sometimes. He took his seat at the dining table, looking at me expectantly and my anger returned just as Monroe schooled his expression, apparently not having noticed him slipping in either.

I started making breakfast and felt Monroe's eyes following me.

My own gaze was drawn to him again and again and electricity coursed up my spine as he followed my movements. I was glad we were returning to Saint's routine, the rules allowing me time with him at last. And today of all days when I felt like the dark sea of grief in me was churning and roiling, begging to drag me down into it, I needed my rock more than ever.

Saint, Blake and Kyan all walked me to Monroe's house in the evening, the three of them surrounding me like bodyguards. I'd thrown myself into my school work all day to try and distract myself from the bittersweet memories of my previous birthdays and the sharp reminders that I would never spend another one with Dad or Jess again.

I hadn't mentioned it to anyone, just wanting this day to pass by without dwelling on it. What made this day worse than ever was that I'd been called by the police to ask whether I wanted Dad's body cremated or buried and they had offered me the choice of a virtual fucking funeral. With the Hades Virus peaking in the country, I wasn't allowed to travel anywhere to hold an official service for him. So I had to make that choice over a phone call. And now his cremated remains were going to be mailed to me in some neatly packaged box and apparently it could take several weeks for it to arrive because the virus was making processing slow. It made me want to scream. And not just because I couldn't have a funeral for my own father, but because this was exactly what Mortez had wanted. For Dad's death to be packaged up with a tidy little bow and the whole world to believe he was guilty.

The fact that Dad had taken the fall for releasing the Hades Virus meant whoever was truly responsible for unleashing the virus was walking free somewhere. It had to have something do with Royaume D'élite. Those psychos were clearly linked to Mortez and it was obvious they had the power and the resources to pull it off. It didn't matter who they were though, I would come for them, find their weaknesses, expose them for what they were to the whole world. I couldn't picture my enemy in my mind's eye, they were just a faceless monster lurking in the shadows, but one day I would have a face and a name to pass to the authorities. And maybe if I was lucky, that face and name would belong to a dead body by then. My plan relied on Saint hunting down whatever he could about them and finding leads for us to follow. So far, he was finding it difficult. But I had faith in him in this single thing. If there was a man on earth obsessive enough over details to find a thread to pull on when it came to these illusive people, it was Saint.

"Mr Monroe!" Blake crowed, chuckling loudly as he hammered his fist on the back door.

Monroe yanked the door open looking furious. "Shut your mouth," he hissed. "Do you want the whole faculty to hear you?"

"Chill out, man," Blake said. "No one can hear us out here."

"Sound carries in these woods," Monroe growled. "I know it's not *your* reputation you're risking, but-"

"Monroe's right," Saint cut in, smacking Blake around the back of his head. "Don't be a fucking idiot."

Blake looked like he was about to punch him back then his eyes fell to the cast on his friend's arm and he just rolled his eyes.

Kyan muscled his way past Monroe to get inside, placing my overnight bag down beside the couch. The rest of us filed in and Kyan flung himself down in a seat with a sigh. "Maybe I'll stay with you guys tonight." He pressed his tongue into his cheek as he looked at me, his eyes glittering with mischief. The expression had my stomach fluttering.

"No. You know I have work for you to do," Saint said harshly from the doorway. "And we're bordering on late already, so get back outside."

"What are you up to?" Monroe asked and Kyan stood up, rubbing his thumb over the corner of his mouth as he smirked.

"We're going hunting," Blake said, his voice rough and dark.

"For the fucking 'Justice Ninja'," Kyan air quoted the words.

"We just have to squeeze the right throats tonight and we might get a name at last," Saint purred, the excitement in his voice clear.

I noticed Kyan had his fucking hunting knife on his hip and everything. They really were taking this seriously.

"Be careful," I said as Blake pulled me in for a tight hug.

His mouth found mine and he kissed me unashamedly in front of them all. The second he pulled away, Kyan took his place, grabbing my waist and dipping me low just to out-do Blake as he drove his tongue into my mouth, swallowing my squeal of surprise. I could taste them both when he released me, pushing me into Monroe's arms and it was the most deadly, enticing concoction. *I wonder what all four of them taste like mixed together...*

My gaze met Saint's and my heart drummed harder as he eyed my lips with heated lust before turning sharply and striding out the door. Blake followed and Kyan was last, taking his sweet time and stepping outside, pulling the door over with his head still poking into the house. "Don't do anything I wouldn't do." He winked.

"That's a short list," Monroe called after him.

"True. There's only one item on it, Nash," he whispered then shut the door mysteriously.

"What do you think that is?" I turned to Monroe and he grinned.

"Anal. Taking, obviously," Monroe said with a shrug.

I snorted then silence fell between us and my stomach swirled as I realised we were alone at last.

"Do you wanna...have something to eat?" he offered and I strode toward him, shaking my head. "Watch TV?"

"No," I breathed, a sideways smile pulling at my lips.

"Oh," he said in realisation then grinned wickedly. He slipped past me, locking the front door before turning fast, grabbing my hand and dragging me across the room and into his bedroom. "Do you have any idea how many times I've thought about having you in this bed, princess?" He shoved me down onto the mattress and I laughed as I bounced on it, kicking my heels off as he took in the tight black long-sleeved dress Saint had picked out for me. I fell back against his sheets, his pine scent everywhere as I took in the room with white walls and dark blue accents. There was a rack of weights against one wall beside a punching bag and a full length mirror on the other which was wide enough that it gave me a view of most of the bed. "Kinky," I teased. "Have you had Mr Helix in here bent to your will as you whisper about erupting volcanoes in his ear?"

"No," he growled, kicking the door shut, his face saying he was in no mood for jokes as he dragged his shirt over his head and tossed it on the floor.

My eyes travelled over his sculpted body, trailing across the tigress tattoo on his chest to the roses curling along his collarbone and the tribal markings winding over his pecs. I sucked on my lip as my core clenched, so ready for him that I was losing my mind.

"Miss Pontus maybe?" I arched a brow and he huffed out a breath.

"Stop talking," he ordered and I did, biting my lip as I focused on this tempting man before me.

I moved up onto my knees at the end of the bed and he reached down, grabbing the hem of my dress and practically tearing it off of my body. He drank in the dark green lingerie combo I wore with desperation in his eyes and I shivered from that look alone. He reached down, unclipping my bra and pulling it off then he pushed my shoulders so I fell back on the bed. Monroe tugged my feet out from under me and ripped my panties down my legs before tossing them aside. I drew my knees up, excited by his furious haste and he growled as he rested his hands on them and spread my legs wide, making my skin blaze like a furnace as he took in every piece of me.

"You're a siren, Tatum," he said, his voice raspy as he leaned over me, pressing my knees harder so they were driven into the sheets. "I'd gladly dive into the ocean and die for a taste of you." He dropped his head down between my legs and I cried out as he feasted on me. There was no other word for it, his mouth drove against me like he was starved of my flesh. He sank his tongue into my heated core and I fisted my hands in the sheets, my back arching as I bucked my hips and offered myself up to him like a sacrifice on his altar.

He spread my thighs wider still, giving him access to every sensitive piece of my body as he licked and sucked, groaning into my pussy with need. When his tongue slid down to my ass, I squirmed like crazy and he slammed a hand to my stomach, keeping me still as he swirled the tip of his tongue over me and I was soon panting and blushing, a new kind of moan escaping me as I stopped wriggling and started begging for more. His mouth dragged up my centre again and landed on my clit as he started another earthquake beneath his tongue. I was going to shatter, crash, *break*. And I wanted to so badly it hurt.

"Nash," I gasped, barely able to take it as he continued to devour me, never letting me fall to ruin.

"You're going to beg for my cock, princess. I want to hear you whimper for me. I want to make you feel how I've felt waiting to have you again," he growled, turning his head to nip my thigh. He was holding back just enough, careful not to mark me, but that made my skin tingle even more. There was a thrill in hiding this wild passion between us from the world, even if it was difficult at times.

He moved up my body, starting up a new torment on my skin as he sucked and licked everywhere he went. He made it to my breasts and started teasing my nipples, one with his tongue and the other with his fingers. I wrapped my legs around him and he pushed his free hand between us, palming my soaking pussy and laughing into my flesh.

"Nash!" I demanded as he continued to coat his fingers in my desire but he never gave me more than that, savouring how much my body craved him.

"Beg," he insisted, taking his hand from between my thighs and smearing my wetness over my nipples. He fell on my breasts with an unholy groan as he lapped the flavour of me away and I swear I was about to come from this alone.

I was stubborn as shit though and he knew that, but this was clearly turning him the fuck on. And if he didn't give me what I needed soon, I really was going to give in and beg. But not yet. I'd see if he'd break first.

I wriggled my hand between us, cupping his solid cock through his jeans and he drew in a breath between his teeth as I rubbed and squeezed him. I fumbled with his zipper and he lifted his hips as he let me push my hand through his fly, my fingers gliding beneath his waistband and wrapping around his thick, waiting length.

"Fuck, your hands are so soft," he groaned as I tightened my grip, sliding my palm up and down him as I bathed in the perfect smoothness of his shaft. I needed to feel it inside me and I was sure he wouldn't wait forever for me to beg, especially when I felt the wet bead of desire on the head of his dick with my thumb. He was close to losing it himself.

"Come on, Nash," I encouraged with a smirk on my face. "You're the one who's about to beg."

He chuckled low in his throat, thrusting his hips slowly as he fucked my hand. "You're all talk, princess."

He grinned down at me, pressing his hands into the sheets as he lifted more of his weight off of me. My heart stumbled at the sight of this Viking warrior above me and my tummy dipped at the same moment. Hell, he was beautiful. He looked like he was plucked straight out of some Norse myth, a god come to claim me. But I was a goddess to match him and I wasn't going to bow. I just had to up my game.

I took my hand from his boxers and massaged my breasts instead, locking my eyes on his as I writhed beneath him, moaning and panting while I waited for him to crack.

His eyes travelled down my body and his expression became purely animal. "Oh...shit," he breathed.

I slid one hand down my stomach, my muscles flexing and tightening beneath my palm before I reached for my clit and started toying with myself. I rolled my head against his sheets, putting on the show of my life for him as I groaned and sighed his name. It wasn't even faked. Not a single second of it. I was high on this man, desperate for his touch. But I would have him come to me. Not the other way around.

I started to fall apart as I stared at him, drinking in the sight of him watching me as I circled my fingers over my throbbing clit.

He slapped my hand away and his jaw clenched. "Enough," he snapped, a warning in his tone.

"If you're not man enough to do it, I'll do it myself," I teased and his eyes flashed with rage.

"Too far, Tatum," he warned and I gasped as he dragged me off the bed, twisting me around to stand in front of him and capturing my chin with one hand. "See that?" He angled my head down toward the white sheets which were darkened by a wet patch in the centre of them. "Your pussy doesn't lie to me, princess, no matter how much *you* do." His teeth grazed my ear and I shivered, a whine escaping my throat which was filled with pure desperation. How long were we going to play this game? I'd already waited so long to be reunited with him like this. Did we have to dance on this line any longer?

An idea came to me, one which was totally low but would also secure my win.

"Are you really going to make me beg...on my birthday?" I asked, my voice husky and full of victory.

He spun me around in his arms, his expression stern as he glared down at me. "What?"

I fluttered my lashes. "It's my eighteenth today." I swallowed the sharp ball in my throat as saying those words threatened to unleash the cutting grief in me again, gazing at him steadily as I asked what I needed of him with my expression alone.

"Since when?" he demanded.

"Er, since always?" I offered with a shrug and his eyes narrowed.

"Why didn't you tell me?"

"I didn't tell anyone," I said, my smile dropping a little. "I just didn't want to dwell on...everything."

He ran his fingers down my back in feather light strokes and I gritted my teeth.

"Don't pity me, Nash. And don't even think about turning this into some love-making bullshit because you think that's what I need," I warned and his lips parted in surprise before he barked a laugh.

"Fine." He bared his teeth at me then shoved me onto the bed.

Monroe pushed his boxers down and grabbed my hips, yanking me toward him and throwing my left leg over his shoulder. He slammed himself inside me, filling me up without giving me a chance to prepare. I cried out and he pressed his hand to my mouth, leaning over me so my leg was stretched to its limit and he started slamming into me with needy, hungry thrusts.

I groaned and growled and fucking screamed against his hand as he tried to keep me quiet, fucking me in my favourite position and hitting that perfect spot deep inside me. He lost himself, becoming nothing but a beast as he possessed my body and we marked his sheets with our combined scents. He hooked up my other leg, throwing that over his other shoulder and pressed his weight down as he started pounding into me, my body tightening around him like this.

He drove into me without mercy and I loved every second, teetering on the edge of bliss. I could see him coming undone too, his eyes hooded, his grunts and groans deepening. He rolled his hips and his cock rubbed me in the perfect way just before he did it again and I lost my mind, moaning and panting into his hand as my body tensed up and pleasure washed through me like sunshine pouring directly into my veins. Monroe stood upright, gripping my ankles and slamming his hips against me a few more furious times before he came, making my toes curl at the feel of him branding me as his.

I realised he had claw marks raked down his shoulders and he cursed as he pulled out of me, noticing them himself. My legs fell to the bed and worry twisted through me.

"I'll keep a shirt on around the others, but the bigger issue is those, princess." He pointed at a line of crescent nail marks over my hip and I sighed as I sat up, running my fingers across them, quietly liking that he'd marked me.

"Kyan will cover for us," I said and Monroe frowned as he rearranged his pants. I stood up, cupping his cheek, sensing my words had upset him. "You are okay with me being with him too, aren't you?"

He sighed, looking down at me as I gently scraped my nails along his jaw. "Yeah...I'm happy that you make him happy. He needs you, like I need you."

I tip-toed up to kiss him and he wrapped his arms around me, tugging me against his chest. I could feel my desire for him rising again already. The roughness of his jeans against my sensitive skin was delicious.

"Sometimes I worry how much I enjoy their company. I was only ever meant to join the Night Keepers to get close to Saint," he growled, an edge of distress in his tone.

I smoothed out the crease in his brow. "His father is your real target," I reminded him and Monroe sighed.

"I know...I guess I just wanted to focus on his son as well seeing as Troy Memphis showed my mother and my brother no mercy. Maybe I wanted to fuck with his entitled little heir."

"But that's hardly fair," I pushed, not wanting to argue again but that didn't mean I was going to back down on this. I'd been targeted for that very same reason by the Night Keepers. I knew the injustice of it first hand. And it wasn't something I could stand by and allow to happen to Saint now that he'd gone to hell and back for me.

Monroe lowered his hands to my ass, squeezing firmly as he held me in place against him and I felt him growing hard for me again. "You're very convincing when you're naked," he mused.

"It's a gift," I said lightly.

He sighed, looking at me for a long moment. "How about a compromise? We use Saint to get to Troy, but he won't be a casualty in the fallout. We could try getting into his laptop again to see if we can find something that'll help us get to his father."

"Sounds good to me," I agreed. "I'll try and get a recording of him typing in his password because knowing Saint, we're never going to guess it."

"It's probably fifty characters long with fucking umlauts on the vowels and a whole Beethoven symphony in the middle of it."

I laughed and he grinned, walking me back towards the bed again.

"I can't believe you didn't tell me it was your birthday," he said in frustration. "I would have-"

"What? Baked me a cake and sung me happy birthday?" I rolled my eyes, falling down on the bed beneath him.

He frowned then darted out of the room, returning a minute later with a box of lemon drizzle cakes under one arm and a slice in his hand with a lit tealight sitting on top of it.

I burst out laughing at the ridiculousness of it and I swear nothing inside me hurt for that one perfect moment. He held it out for me and I sat up, blowing it out.

"Did you make a wish, princess?" he purred, tossing the box of cakes on the bed beside me and throwing the tealight on the floor.

I nodded as he held the small rectangular cake to my lips and I took a bite, devouring half of it. I'd wished for everything to be okay again, as simple and as sad as that was. But I just hoped for a future which held light in it, a good time I could move toward day by day. And here with Monroe, it seemed almost possible.

He moved onto the bed, pushing me down to lay beneath him as he brought the rest of the cake to his mouth. Then he paused, grinning darkly at me. "I think I'll have mine à la Tatum."

I quirked an eyebrow at him which he answered by pushing the cake between my legs and shoving his fingers into me to crush it inside me. I gasped as he dropped his mouth between my thighs to devour it and I was lost to the lap of his tongue and the graze of his teeth, the world fading all around me until it was just me and this beautiful man and a whole night to do as we pleased.

Blake

CHAPTER THIRTEEN

I sat in class with Saint on my left and Kyan on my right while Miss Pontus blathered on about something Shakespeare had supposedly meant in one of his plays and I gave no shits at all. I mean, it seemed a bit presumptuous to me to say that he'd been using his work to make a comment on anything at all. Maybe he just got off on writing characters and ruining their lives? Perhaps he took joy in birthing people with his imagination and then getting an audience to care for them just so that he could bathe in the tears of the people who came to see his work when he killed their favourite character and fucked up everyone else's lives in the process. If I was going to write a story, I had to think that would be at least some of my motivation. Why not fuck with a fictional life just for shits and giggles? And really, even if he did have some deeper meaning to his work, who was Miss Pontus to say that? If Shakespeare himself wanted to rise from the grave to tell me that then great, I was all ears. But I wasn't going to take my facts from a third party interpretation.

Besides, I had my own tragedies to construct and as my gaze slid between Stalker - formally known as Toby, formally known as Punch, formally, *formally* know as Toby again - to Bait, formally known as... Huh, actually I had no fucking idea what that kid's name had been before we'd stripped him of it. I wanted to say...Quentin. Kid looked like a Quentin, or maybe a Sebastian or a Reginald. Whatever, Bait was always going to be Bait now anyway because he was a predatory pervert who had also turned out to be a spineless traitor. Between him and Stalker the fucking twisted, photo snapping, bush wanking, corner perving...*stalker*, I had work to do.

Me, Kyan and Saint had spent last night hunting the Justice Ninja again, following leads and interrogating people but it had come to nothing once more and I was getting really fucking sick of making no progress on figuring out who they were. I needed to vent some of that frustration and I had a fair idea of how I might manage it…

"Anyone up for a little fun with our least favourite people?" I asked in a low tone, glancing between Saint and Kyan and watching as they both perked up.

Tatum turned in her seat to give me a quizzical look and I just grinned innocently back at her.

"What do you have in mind?" Saint asked with a dangerous glint in his eye.

"I think we need them to perform a cleansing ritual for the spirit of the forest to make sure spring comes again," I said thoughtfully.

Class had only just begun and it was a double lesson, but I was already done with it. Saint had talked Miss Pontus into making notes on the lesson for him anyway and she was emailing them over until his arm was back to full use, so it seemed simple enough to me to just go ahead and get her to extend that courtesy to me and Kyan too.

"Miss Pontus?" I called, pushing to my feet and interrupting her as she started on one about prose. Seriously, was that even a thing anymore? Didn't seem like it.

"Oh, erm, yes...Mr Bowman, can I help you?" our teacher asked, flushing red as she looked at me, like she was worried about what I might say or do.

Which was totally offensive really, I was a nice guy. Everyone wanted to be my friend - they'd just do better not to be my enemy.

"Yeah, actually. I'm sorry, Miss, but I totally forgot to say, me, Kyan, Saint, Bait and Stalker have permission from Headmaster Monroe to finish classes early today to take part in the Spring Pine Cleansing."

Bait whipped around to look at me, his eyes wild beneath his white mask which he still wore every fucking day. That shit was still funny. In fact, it *could* be a whole lot funnier...

I plucked a sharpie from Mila's pencil case and winked at her when she frowned at me. It was really her own fault for having a pencil case. We were all given tablets to work on, so why would you need that shit? Made no sense to me. Unless she was hoping to be the go-to girl for Sharpies and in that case, point won.

"The Spring Pine Cleansing?" Miss Pontus asked as Kyan stood up with a throaty chuckle, slinging his bag and Saint's over his shoulder. He'd been doing that since Saint started classes again and neither of them had ever said so much as a word to acknowledge it.

"Yeah, every year on the errr, what's the date someone?" I asked.

"January eighteenth," some helpful little duck supplied.

"Yeah, that," I agreed. "Every year on January whatever, the Night Keepers have to take two willing sacrifices down to the lake to complete the Spring Pine Cleansing otherwise the Night People will come and curse our trees or whatever and they'll all die. It's super important."

"Oh, erm," Miss Pontus looked to Stalker and Bait as the two of them quivered in their fucking boots. Sacrifices was a nice touch.

Why the hell did that feel so good? Oh right, because I was an asshole and they were a pair of deserving little cretins who preyed on girls and put *my girl* in particular at risk. That. Fuck, I was gonna enjoy this.

"We're actually already late," Saint drawled as he started walking for the door. "And you wouldn't want Monroe having to put you on suspension for failing to follow his orders, would you, Miss? He is your boss now, after all."

"Come on, boys," Kyan said excitedly as he crossed the room to the front row and gripped both Bait and Stalker by the backs of their necks, hoisting them out of their seats.

"Oh, and Mr Monroe said you would send me and Kyan the notes for today's class and let us off of the assignments for the weekend, too," I added as I grabbed my blazer from the back of my chair and shrugged into it. "He offered to do the same for Bait and Stalker but they're such eager beavers they decided they'd rather come back in on Saturday to do all of the work instead."

"Okay then..." Miss Pontus agreed, not really having any choice in it as Kyan hauled our prey out of the room and the other Unspeakables muttered frantically between themselves. They should just be grateful that I was feeling generous enough to leave them out of today's shit. Though it was damn tempting to bring Deepthroat, but Kyan wouldn't have as much fun with her there. Sure, he'd make great sport out of making her suffer and everything, but he was always so dark and pissy after he had to spend time in her company and I just wanted us all to have some clean, wholesome, slightly sadistic, fun today. No date-raping, molesting bitches required. That said, I could offer her a parting gift...

I hesitated as I fished around in my pocket and smirked to myself as I found a stick of gum lurking between a few quarters and quickly shoved it into my mouth and began chewing.

I made a move to follow as Saint swept from the room, making an arm cast look like fucking designer wear even while it was wrapped in a shirt to cover up the massive squid cock monster Kyan had drawn on it. But before I could get more than a few steps, a foot kicked me in the shin and I looked down to find Tatum frowning up at me from her spot beside Mila.

"What about me?" she hissed, and I smirked at her as I leaned down to whisper in her ear.

"I'll take a video for you, Cinders," I promised. "But I don't want Stalker so much as looking at you ever again, let alone being near you for hours while we make him stick pine cones up his ass and sing to the clouds."

"What?" she gasped, half laughing and half frowning as she looked up at me. "You're not seriously going to-"

I leaned down and ended her sentence with a kiss that stole the air from her damn lungs. My hand landed on her thigh and I pushed it beneath her skirt as I drove my tongue into her mouth, using my body to hide what I was doing from the rest of the class.

Tatum gripped my lapels in her fists as I groaned into her mouth and made her a silent promise to pick this up again later. It had been seriously too long since I'd had my way with her and I was done playing nice.

"Catch you later, Tater," I teased as I pulled away from her, winking to let her know I meant that literally and she pouted at me as I backed up.

Luckily, I'd managed to keep hold of my gum during that little exchange or my plan would have gone to shit. I paused as I made it to Deepthroat's desk, dropping to one knee as I made a show of tying my shoelace despite the fact that my loafers had no laces, but whatever, no one would dare question me on that shit.

I spat the gum into my hand as I stood, giving Deepthroat my most predatory grin as I leaned close to her and stuck my gum into her hair right at the back, close to her scalp. She squealed in alarm as I tugged on the long, auburn strands, making sure I fisted as much of it as possible into the gum so that it was stuck in there real good.

"Problem?" I questioned in a low voice as she made a move to leap out of her seat and I slapped a hand down on her shoulder to keep her in place.

"No," she squeaked, with honest to god tears in her eyes and my smile darkened as I glanced at Squits beside her.

I reached out and clapped his cheek a couple of times in a patronising gesture which reminded him who owned his ass and he whimpered in alarm, probably shitting himself again. Nice. Or maybe not so nice for the people in the row behind him. *Sorry dudes.*

I straightened as Deepthroat clutched at her hair, whimpering in alarm as her fingers found the gum stuck deep in it and I looked back to Tatum with a grin which she flipped me off for. But I could see the heat in her eyes and the excitement over my little triumph against our good friend, Deepthroat. Our girl wanted to see this bitch punished just as badly as I did. I just wondered if she realised how much that showed she'd become a part of our group. Now she hungered for the blood of our enemies in the same way we did and there was something really fucking hot about that.

When I looked back to the front of the class, I found our teacher conveniently distracted by something on her laptop. Perfect.

"Thanks, Miss, you're a total badass," I called as I tipped Miss Pontus a salute and she just nodded like she didn't know whether to doubt my bullshit or not.

Just to be on the safe side, I shot Monroe a message in the group chat to let him know that he'd just given permission for us to ditch and to tell him to meet us down by the lake for the Spring Pine Whateverthefuck.

Monroe:
You can't just go around making up bullshit about me letting you out of classes whenever you like.

Saint:
Yes he can. This is important.

Tatum:
You're all a bunch of assholes and I'm not going to forget you cutting me out of this.

Kyan:
Sorry baby, I totally would have let you come. I didn't know Blake had a stick up his ass over it. I promise to make you come later to make up for it.

Kyan:

Literally.

Kyan:

With my dick.

Saint:

She caught your less than subtle euphemism the first time, asshole.

Kyan:

eggplant emoji *bagel emoji* *tongue emoji* *taco emoji* *eggplant emoji* *eggplant emoji* *eggplant emoji* *water emoji*

Kyan:

That meant I'm gonna lick you 'til you're screaming and then fuck you 'til you can't breathe btw (I know some people in here are too out of touch to understand emojis)

Monroe:

I mean it. You guys can't just pull this shit whenever you want out of class.

Tatum:

No chance, Kyan. You guys just left me hanging so I intend to do the same to you.

Saint:

I wasn't offering to fuck you anyway, siren, so stop begging for it.

Tatum:

squid emoji

Blake:

Not that shit again

Kyan:

Haha, I totally agree, baby

Saint:

Tell me what the fucking squid means!

Tatum:

It's like when a bunch of assholes leave you in class while they go off to have fun and you just get all *onion emoji* over it but then you think it through and realise it's actually more *squid emoji*

Kyan:

Octopus emoji

Saint:

Stop dicking around and tell me.

Tatum:

squid emoji

Tatum Rivers has left the chat

I barked a laugh and shoved my phone back into my pocket as I jogged down the corridor and outside to catch the guys. Tatum left the group chat at least four times a week and then Saint had to find her, get hold of her phone, put her back into it again and spank her for misbehaving. At this point I was certain she did it half to piss off Saint and half to get the spanking.

Saint and Kyan had already made it down the path and were heading

222

towards the thick pines which lined the north bank of the lake, herding Stalker and Bait ahead of them and bickering as Saint demanded an answer to his burning squid question while Kyan laughed like he was the god of emoji knowledge and refused to tell him. I was fairly sure I got it, but then sometimes they used it in different context and I was lost again. But I didn't care enough to try and force an answer the way Saint did. My squid ignorant self was happy enough to figure it out eventually.

I jogged until I caught them, shoving Bait in the back hard enough that he fell sprawling to the stone path and skinned his palms.

"Shit, sorry, dude," I said as Kyan roared with laughter and Saint smirked like the demon he was. "I didn't realise you were such a weak bitch and would fall down so easy. I bet Stalker wouldn't go down so easy, would you Stalker?"

The asshole formally known as Toby blinked at me with terrified eyes and the most disappointing look of acceptance which really only made me want to punch him more. Sadly for me, Kyan beat me to it, clocking him in the temple so hard that when he hit the ground he actually blacked out.

"Shit, do you think you killed him?" I laughed as Bait looked half inclined to piss himself.

"You'd better not have, he hasn't even begun to suffer enough for what he did to our girl," Saint growled.

Stalker groaned as he came around, so that was the end of that debate and I sighed as I tried to decide if I was disappointed or not. I guessed disposing of another body would have been a pain though. Especially as some people probably would miss Stalker. His family didn't hate him after all. I mean, they were definitely less than impressed when we sent them all of that evidence of his stalking, plus all of the slightly less true evidence of his drug habit. And drug *dealing* habit. But they'd probably still care if he died. At least for now. Maybe not so much by the time we were done with him though.

While Stalker made a big old fuss out of coming around and pushing himself to sit up, I asked Kyan to hold Bait still while I took the pink Sharpie from my pocket and casually drew a dick on his mask complete with cum shot, thick veins and hairy balls which hung down on his cheek.

"Every day, you'll draw the balls back on, hairs and all," I commanded as he just took it, looking at me like I was a monster. But was I the one who tricked an underage girl into sex? No siree, not me. So who was the monster here really? I mean, okay yeah, also me but also, also *him*.

"Yeah, okay," Bait agreed like a little bitch which was a weird combination of satisfying and utterly unsatisfying.

"Right, enough fun." I announced. "You two have a Pine Festival, or Spring Hoo-Ha or-"

"A Spring Pine Cleansing," Saint drawled, because of course even a totally bullshit event that I just made up so that we could cut class and torture some low lives had warranted immediate memorising. In fact, I wouldn't be surprised if this didn't become an annual event from here on out. Assuming the Hades Virus didn't kill us all before then.

"That's the one," I agreed. "Strip down to your boxers and start stuffing them with pine needles until no more can fit so that the Night People don't come and kill the flowers or whatever."

"Trees," Saint snapped irritably, like that even mattered and Kyan smirked in amusement.

Bait and Stalker quickly did as they'd been told and Kyan tossed his blazer aside before rolling his shirt sleeves back to reveal his ink. He turned his wrist Saint's way and flexed his fingers so that the new squid tattoo wriggled a bit like it was taunting him and Saint's jaw locked so hard, I wondered if it would ever unlock again. He held his tongue though, which was really a testament to how determined he was not to lose his shit in front of our victims because every time he'd locked eyes on that thing since Kyan had gotten it, he'd freaked out up until now.

I stifled a laugh and rolled my eyes at Kyan as he smirked in a taunting way which said he wanted Saint to punch him. He really was a dickhead. Good thing I loved him anyway.

Every time one of our victims winced at the prickle of a pine needle sticking them in the dick, I laughed my damn ass off and Kyan shouted at them to go faster, even when they were practically hopping across the floor as their bare feet got pricked with them too.

By the time Monroe showed up, their boxers were bulging and the two of them looked hella uncomfortable with all of those prickles in their dicks. Dickles, if you will.

"What the fuck are you up to now?" Monroe asked, his eyes lighting with amusement.

Turned out he was a savage bastard when it came to punishing these assholes too, headmaster or not. Seemed he took as much offence to them targeting our girl as the rest of us did and as he had gotten the three of us to swear blind he never had a thing to do with any of this shit, I guessed he'd decided to embrace his inner Night Keeper and punish the deserving instead of getting his panties in a twist about his job.

"Now what?" Saint drawled from his sun chair which he'd made one of the Unspeakables go and fetch him when it became clear this wasn't losing its appeal any time soon. He was working on his cunning plan to bring down a secret society run by billionaires all for the sake of our girl and Kyan after all. No biggie apparently. We weren't even allowed to pitch in until he was 'ready for our input' whatever the fuck that meant. I swear I heard him cackling up in his bell tower in the dead of night sometimes as he worked on his plan.

"Now..." I said, casting my mind about for inspiration but Kyan beat me to it.

"It's time for the great pinecone race," Kyan supplied, picking up one of the heavy, brown cones from the forest floor and throwing it at Stalker as hard as he could.

It smacked him in the ass cheek, and he yelped as he leapt into the air and a big, red welt appeared on his flesh.

"Fuck yes," Monroe agreed, his teacher persona well and truly shed for the time being.

"You two need to run back and forth between this pine tree and the one down by the lake," Kyan instructed Bait and Stalker. "And try to avoid getting hit by the pinecones."

"Guys," Stalker pleaded, his eyes actually looking kinda wet. New goal for today - I wanted that big motherfucker to cry. "You have to hear me out, I swear I never did anything to Tatum. She was my friend, I'm not the one who-"

A pinecone hit him in the face with enough force to draw a bit of blood and Kyan roared with laughter as Monroe snatched another from the ground.

"He said *run*," Saint barked, not bothering to rise from his seat as he continued with his work. "Or do you want to explain to your parents why all of the trees here died?"

He was seriously running with this pine festival shit and I was all in. I stooped to grab myself a pinecone and Bait shrieked in alarm as he sprinted away.

"Nothing like the sound of panicked screams in the afternoon," Kyan sighed and Monroe laughed darkly as he threw a perfectly aimed pinecone at Bait's back.

"Sweet, sweet justice," I agreed, laughing with my friends and feeling this perfectly fucked up kind of happiness as we all bathed in our inner asshole together.

By the time we'd finished up our little pine festivities with Bait and Stalker, they'd gotten to know a whole lot about pine trees. Like, how the cones tasted, how it felt to be whipped with their branches, how much it hurt to rub their asses against the bark for half an hour straight and best of all, how fucking sticky the sap was when smeared in their hair. We'd finished up by chasing them into the lake with more well aimed pinecones and though Saint and

Monroe had ditched out after a couple of hours, me and Kyan had made the fun last until sunset.

We headed back down the path toward The Temple and as both of us upped our pace, it wasn't all that hard to guess why we were so keen to get back.

"She's in my room, tonight, asshole," I growled, elbowing Kyan as we half ran up the path towards the front door.

"Pfft, that's for sleeping. She's fair game this evening and now that Saint isn't monopolising her time, I'm ready to make a repeat of Christmas."

"Quit going on about Christmas," I snarled. Mostly because I was sick of hearing about it and seeing the way Tatum bit her lip every time he brought it up, a little bit because I was salty as fuck over it and a big bit because I was sick of being frozen out and I was ready to win my way back into her panties myself.

"You know," Kyan said slowly, reaching out to hold the door closed as I made a move to open it. "She's already pissed about being left in class earlier. There's a good chance neither of us have a shot tonight."

"For fuck's sake," I cursed, realising he was right. That girl didn't just quit the group chat for fun. It was code for 'you're all in the dog house'. "What are we going to do about it then?"

The corner of Kyan's lips twitched and he gave me an assessing look. "Maybe that's the answer. We do something about it *together*. She might not be so quick to shoot us down if we make a compelling enough offer."

The grin that captured my lips in return was dirty as fuck as I wondered if she'd really go for that. She'd certainly been into it when we'd started down that line before and it had been pretty fucking hot.

"You might be able to pick up some tips at the same time," I taunted and Kyan laughed as he released his hold on the door.

"You might beat me at a lot of pointless shit, brother, but I will destroy you in a competition on fucking. You have my word on that."

"It's not really your word that counts though, is it. It's more about who makes her scream the loudest."

Kyan's dirty laugh announced our arrival into The Temple and Saint and Tatum looked up from the dining table where they'd been eating their dinner which we were three minutes late for, so of course Saint hadn't waited.

He scowled at us as we sauntered in and Kyan strolled away to his room without a word as I moved to the table to join them.

"Did you make him cry?" Saint asked curiously.

"Of course I did," I said with an evil smirk. I probably should have felt a bit bad for the shit I was putting Stalker through, but every time I considered that I just thought about him jerking off in the bushes while watching our girl in her most private moments or photographing her while she was changing or scaring her in the woods and I just felt nothing at all aside from the desire to do worse and worse and worse to him.

"Maybe you should just leave it now," Tatum suggested half heartedly, like she felt she should feel bad about what we were doing to him but just didn't. And why the fuck should she?

"Just leave the organisation of the Unspeakables to us, siren," Saint tsked as he ate his pasta and I rolled my eyes for her benefit before diving in to eat mine.

Kyan reappeared in a wifebeater and a pair of stonewashed jeans and fell on his food like a starving man, somehow managing to demolish all of his before the rest of us finished.

"I think we should play a game tonight," he announced, smacking his lips with pleasure. "And to thank Tatum for taking such good care of us, I think she should be the prize."

"What are you talking about?" she asked, arching a suspicious brow at Kyan before looking between me and Saint.

"I call it, getting you over your fear of the catacombs," Kyan said, reaching for his belt and tugging his hunting knife free before banging it down on the table.

"Who says I'm afraid of the catacombs?" she asked, narrowing her eyes at the murder weapon Kyan had decided to keep.

"You haven't been beyond the gate down there since we killed that scumbag," Saint said dryly, like that was a normal subject matter to discuss over dinner.

"Well, I...haven't had any reason to," she said with a shake of her head though there was a little hesitance which suggested she hadn't wanted to either.

"If you're not afraid, then prove it," Kyan dared. "We will give you the key to the gates and a five minute head start. If you can find your way out before we catch you then you can have an entire week of us following your commands instead of the other way around."

"Speak for yourself," Saint scoffed and Kyan huffed irritably, throwing me a look.

"I'm in," I agreed. "But I won't lose, so I'm not worried."

"All I have to do is make it out to the beach before you catch up and I get you both as my personal servants for the week?" Tatum clarified, ignoring Saint as she looked between me and Kyan hungrily.

"Yeah, baby," Kyan agreed.

"And what if I lose?" she asked, realising there was a catch.

"If one of us catches you, we get to fuck you down there in the dark," Kyan said with a feral smile that said the idea of using a crypt where we'd killed someone for a hook up actually turned him on more. Crazy motherfucker. Although...that did sound kind of hot, so I guessed I was a crazy motherfucker too.

Tatum bit her lip as she looked between us and then glanced at the door which led down to the gym and the catacombs below.

"That kinda sounds like I win either way," she joked and my smile widened as I realised I was actually getting a green flag here. "But what if both of you catch me at once?"

I exchanged a grin with Kyan and shrugged lightly. "Same rules apply, sweetheart."

Tatum sucked in a breath as she considered that, looking between the two of us like she wasn't totally sure for a minute, but the way she bit her lip said the idea was tempting her.

"Remember how good it felt when we had you pinned between us before," I purred and Saint huffed irritably, but everyone ignored him. We didn't need a wet blanket dampening our three way plans. He needed to get on board or stop pouting about it.

"Okay then," she agreed, the light in her eyes saying she was at least a little tempted to lose on purpose. Game on.

"Are you even going to *try* and run, baby?" Kyan asked with a cocky laugh and she rolled her eyes as she pushed to her feet.

"Watch me, *baby*," she mocked, her whole demeanour shifting as she got herself into the headspace to win. But she was sorely fucking mistaken if she thought that was going to happen. I never lost at anything. Definitely not something with a prize this fucking good.

"The keys are in my nightstand," Saint said, still looking pissed off, though there was something more to his expression now too. "Your five minutes starts now, siren. So you'd better run."

"Asshole," she cursed as she tore away from us and bolted up the stairs to find the keys.

I grinned as I stood too, heading down into the gym with Kyan at my side, laughing like all his birthdays had just come at once.

We made our way to the gates which led down into the catacombs and as I turned back to look for Tatum, I was surprised to find Saint following us down too.

"I thought you didn't want to play?" Kyan teased as he rolled his shoulders back and I realised why he'd made the effort to change into something easier to run in. Asshole. But I'd beat him even if I had to do it in my school uniform. Tatum was still in hers too, so she would have to deal with it the same as me.

"I don't," Saint drawled. "It's still against the rules to fuck her. But if either of you manages to catch her and does then I want to make sure I know which of you will need to be punished for it in the morning."

"Riiiight, that's why you wanna watch," I mocked and he cut me a glare but before we could say any more, Tatum shot down the stairs and raced towards us with the keys in her grasp.

"Catch me if you can," she taunted, running straight up to the gate and unlocking it as fast as she could.

"Three minutes and twelve seconds, siren," Saint warned and adrenaline spiked through my veins as I prepared to give chase.

"That's more than enough time to win," she swore before ripping the gate open and racing away into the dark.

Kyan moved to the gate and started rattling it against the wall so that the sound of the metal against the stone clanged loudly in the dark passageways, hopefully making her fear for her damn life.

"I am the dark in the dead of the night!" I bellowed, my voice echoing down into the crypt.

"Hear me roar!" Saint and Kyan both yelled in response and the sound of our voices were rewarded by a shriek of fright from Tatum as she raced away.

I cupped my hands around my mouth and began howling so that the sound of my voice would chase her into the dark and Kyan joined me so she knew that two beasts were hunting her tonight.

Shit, this was hot. I was getting hard already and we weren't even chasing her yet.

We got more and more excitable as Saint kept us informed of the time and when he began counting down from ten, we were both literally bouncing up and down with the promise of the chase.

"Three, two, one-"

Kyan shoved me into the gate and I punched him in the kidney as we launched ourselves into the dark with only the faint light from his cell phone to guide us.

We were both howling and shouting, our voices echoing all around us as we raced into the catacombs.

In our freshman year, right after the three of us had laid claim to The Temple and the catacombs beneath it, we'd decided to take on the roles of the Night Keepers officially and we ran our first ever initiation right down here in these tunnels. We had made literally every student in the school run around down here in the dark with us while we used night vision goggles to track them down and scare them shitless. It had been funny as fuck, but better than that, we'd soon learned every nook, cranny, crypt, coffin and dead end down here by heart.

The tunnels went on and on endlessly, but in reality, there was just one main path through the centre of them all and if you veered off you would just take a loop around before being spat back out onto it again. That meant that unless Tatum was damn lucky, she was bound to have taken one of those turnings and all we had to do was stick to the main route to cut her off when she returned to it.

Kyan kept grabbing and shoving me as I tried to break away from him and laughter bubbled in my chest as I pushed back at him, but I soon realised I wasn't trying all that hard to get ahead. Because he'd gone and planted the seed of the two of us claiming her together and now that he had, I found that I liked that idea a damn lot.

My blood was pumping hot in my limbs and as we rounded another corner and caught the faint glow of another cell phone light up ahead, the two of us cut the noise and ran on as silently as we could manage in the stone passageways.

Tatum was damn fast and for several more twists and turns, it almost seemed like we weren't gaining on her at all. But then the light veered left when she should have hooked right and my heart leapt as I realised we had her.

I cupped my hands to my mouth and howled once more, just to let her know we had her scent and then the two of us turned right, tearing on down the cold passages until we finally reached the large crypt where her wrong turn would lead her.

Kyan gave me a look full of fucked up promises a moment before he flicked his cell phone light off and we were plunged into the pitch dark of the catacombs.

The smirk that tugged at my lips was all carnal need, adrenaline pounding through my body at the thrill of the game as I moved to hide in an alcove right beside the archway she'd be passing through the moment she arrived.

For several tense minutes, there was nothing to keep us company in the shadows but the ragged sound of our breaths and the frantic pounding of our hearts. As those slowed, I found my skin prickling with the knowledge that the two of us were waiting to ambush her alone in the dark.

My dick was so hard that it ached and I had to fight the urge to stroke it and gain some relief from the need filling my body. There was something so exciting about this, like it was forbidden to hunt her the way we were, yet altogether irresistible at the same time. I was so confident of our win that I unhooked the buttons of my shirt and tossed it aside in preparation, wanting to feel my skin against hers as soon as physically possible.

The pounding of footsteps reached us first and the anticipation in my body had my limbs trembling with energy desperate for an outlet as I waited to pounce.

The soft glow of light from her cell phone was next and I shrank further into my hidden alcove as I waited, and waited, and waited-

I stepped out half a second before she arrived, blocking the way on and earning a scream of fear from her as she slammed straight into my solid chest, her cell phone flying from her hand and clattering to the flagstones where the light of it cast us in eerie shadows.

I made a move to grab her, but her palms collided with my chest and she shoved me back a step with a yell before whirling around and taking a few running paces back the way she'd come and crashing into Kyan next.

His arms latched around her instantly and the dark and dangerous tone of his laughter echoed off of the stone chamber as he lifted her clean off of her feet and she screamed in fright.

"Looks like we win, baby," Kyan announced as he carried her to a stone sarcophagus in the centre of the chamber and shoved her down face first over it before slapping her ass hard enough to make her cry out again, but there was a distinctly lusty sound to that scream which had my dick as hard as granite for her.

Kyan yanked his hunting knife from his belt, keeping one hand flat on her back to hold her down and quickly sliced straight through her school skirt and panties in one swift movement.

"For the love of hell, Kyan, you're insane," Tatum hissed as she squirmed against his hold on her, but he only laughed as he pinned her down.

He tossed the knife down on the stone beside her and she gasped as he kicked her legs apart, her blonde hair spilling down to cover her face before me as her fingers gripped the edge of the sarcophagus in anticipation.

Kyan yanked his fly open and shoved his jeans down just enough to let his dick spring free before slamming into her with a single, savage thrust which had her screaming out in pleasure and throwing her head back so that her gaze locked with mine.

For several long moments all I did was stand there staring into her eyes and watching the way her lips parted and her pupils dilated as Kyan fucked her hard and rough. He ripped his wifebeater off with one hand and tossed it aside before gripping her hips even tighter as he drove into her again and she moaned and cursed his name with equal fervour.

"What are you waiting for, Bowman?" Kyan snarled, forcing me to lift my gaze to his just as he wrapped her hair in his fist and he tugged her head back further, controlling her movements. "Do you want him at the same time, baby?" He rolled his hips as he asked the question and she moaned loudly before she answered.

"Yes, Blake," she demanded, her gaze capturing mine as she licked her lips and I smiled like a predator as I moved to stand right before her.

"You are so fucking beautiful, Tatum," I murmured as I rolled my fly down and released my dick, a bead of moisture already sliding down the head.

Kyan slowed for a moment as we both watched her lick that moisture away and I groaned at the feeling of her tongue on my flesh. With another circle of her tongue, Tatum slid my cock between her lips and I growled with pleasure as Kyan started moving faster again.

He kept his hand fisted in her hair as he began to drive into her faster and faster, forcing her to take me right to the back of her throat as the two of us matched his rhythm.

I placed my hands on the edge of the sarcophagus next to hers and she instantly wound her fingers into mine, her grip tight enough to bruise and the stifled moans around my cock enough to let me know just how much she was loving this.

Kyan began to curse as he thrust into her harder and harder and with a powerful slap to her ass, he forced an orgasm from her body which had her crying out around my cock and collapsing down over the sarcophagus as he fell over her too, clearly spilling himself into her just as she'd come for him.

I grunted as her lips tightened around my shaft and slowly pushed her back as Kyan released his hold on her hair.

Kyan kissed and bit at her neck as I pulled my dick from her lips and I watched as he drew her up to stand for me and he stepped back so that I could catch her hand and guide her closer.

My mouth found hers and the faint tremble in her limbs felt like a challenge as I lifted her up to sit on the edge of the sarcophagus.

I tugged on her school tie, yanking it off before ripping at the front of her shirt until the buttons spilled and I was gifted access to her tits in the red push up bra that had been taunting me with its silhouette through the white material all day.

Tatum kissed me with growing heat and I hooked her legs around my waist as I dragged her so close to me that every inch of our chests were touching as I drove my dick inside her.

She was so wet from her own arousal and the evidence of Kyan's presence that I was fully seated in her within one thrust and I groaned as she clamped my dick tightly within the hold of her tight pussy for a moment before we started moving.

My hands gripped her hips as we came together in this furious clash of flesh and tongues and passion and heat and the pace we found as one was exhilarating and unstoppable.

Kyan tugged her shirt from her body, quickly followed by her bra and I broke her kiss so that I could look down at her naked flesh. I found his mouth on her neck and her head tipping back against his tattooed shoulder and she looked so fucking hot between us like that that I didn't even feel any jealousy over her attention wavering.

One of his hands tugged and teased at her nipple and the other slid down to toy with her clit.

Tatum moaned and panted, my name and his escaping her lips time and again as I drove myself into her deep and hard. I could feel the back of Kyan's hand against my abs as I ground into her, but the way her pussy clenched and twitched with the curling of his fingers on her clit only made it hotter.

She screamed as she came again, the sound echoing beautifully in the stone chamber and even in the dim light it was one of the most exquisite sights I'd ever seen. I thrust into her pulsing body twice more as hard as I could and groaned as I came too.

The three of us slumped together, panting, sweating, utterly fucking satisfied and smug as all fuck.

"Well, at least the walk down here wasn't a wasted effort," Saint's voice came from the darkness in the tunnel beyond us and a laugh fell from my lips as Tatum gasped in surprise.

"You had to catch her if you wanted in on it, asshole," Kyan growled but he sounded half amused.

"I don't want in on it," Saint snarled totally unconvincingly and as he stepped closer, the hunger in his eyes proved that was clearly a lie. "Like I said, I just wanted to know which of you needed punishing for breaking the rules. Now I do. Come on, Tatum, you need a shower."

He held a hand out to her and I snorted a laugh as she rolled her eyes but obediently slid out from between our bodies. Her clothes were pretty much shredded so Kyan scooped his wifebeater from the floor and offered it to her to pull on.

He was so much bigger than her that it fell to her thighs and she thanked him for it even as Saint looked like he might burst a blood vessel. Weirdly, he seemed to be more enraged about her wearing Kyan's clothing than he had been about watching the two of us with her.

"I still think I'll win next time," Tatum said mockingly as she let Saint tug her down the passageway and I quickly grabbed the scraps of her clothing while Kyan retrieved her phone.

"Next time?" I called after her, not even caring how obvious it was that I wanted that so damn much.

"Yeah," she replied, looking over her shoulder and biting her lip just before Saint tugged her around the corner.

I exchanged a look with Kyan and his smirk let me know he was thinking about next time too. And I was wondering just how soon that might be.

CHAPTER FOURTEEN

Finding a way to get into Saint's laptop for Monroe's revenge plans against his father was a good distraction for everything on my mind. And as the days drifted by, I focused on that and nothing else. But I'd finally slipped. In the early hours of the morning I'd had a dream about Dad. I'd woken up choking on my own breath and had snuck out of Blake's bed into the bathroom and let myself cry until the tears wouldn't come anymore.

Now, I felt tired and hurting this morning, my wounds ripped freshly open and stinging like they'd been doused in alcohol. At least I had this to focus on. While Saint had been preparing to do school work last night, I'd managed to get a recording on my phone of him entering his password. All me and Monroe needed was to decipher it and secure some alone time with his laptop. Which might have been simple for any other target, but Saint was one meticulous asshole. So we had to wait for an opportunity and dive on it the moment it appeared.

I sat on the couch with my head in Kyan's lap, my feet on Blake's legs and my kindle propped up on my knees. It was hard to concentrate on the book I was reading as Blake ran the pad of his thumb around my bare heel and Kyan absentmindedly trailed his fingers through my hair. They were watching a movie about some race car dude that I wasn't really interested in.

Saint sat across from me in his wing back chair, his foot balanced on his knee and his gaze on his phone. He apparently couldn't get into the movie either, but he always spent this hour with us after dinner no matter what, then he'd either do some work or head to Ash Chambers to play piano. I'd never heard him play before but according to Blake he was 'epic as shit' and I was hardly surprised.

Saint kept glancing over at us, his gaze moving from me to where the guys were touching me then back to his phone. Every time he did, the frown on his brow deepened and I wondered what he was thinking. Did he wish he could join us over here?

He had punished them for breaking my rules by making them eat all of their meals without cutlery for two full days, but I was pretty sure that had backfired on him when he'd had to watch them shovel pasta into their mouths with their bare hands. I honestly wished he'd just let the rules go at this point. It felt like a lifetime ago that I'd wanted to implement them and seeing as he'd watched me taking part in the rule breaks, I knew he was well aware of how much I'd enjoyed breaking them. But any time I tried to bring up changing them he refused to even entertain the idea, and if he was content to torture himself over them then that was up to him. They certainly weren't going to stop me from exploring the new perks to my relationship with the two men who were currently caressing me.

Saint's cast was off at last and his ribs finally healed enough for him to return to normal, the doctors having given him the all clear via a video consultation, much to everyone's relief. He was back to working out every morning and late at night, exhausting himself to the point of almost collapsing. I wondered about the demons that must have haunted him to make him the way he was. No one needed to put their body through the wringer like that twice a day unless they were trying to keep something out. Sometimes, I pitied him. Other times, I hated him. And more recently, I liked him far more than I was willing to admit.

I gave up staring at the page of my book and getting nowhere with it, reaching over to put my kindle on the coffee table. I twisted around to sit up between my guys and Kyan turned to whisper in my ear. "Don't look now but the Prince of Darkness has his eye on you." He chewed on my earlobe and I giggled, glancing over at Saint. His lips pressed into a thin line as he watched us, glaring, absorbing. There was an ache in his eyes which I recognised because I felt it myself for him. He wanted me as keenly as I wanted him. Why couldn't he just take me? I didn't mind being controlled during it, in fact, I was more than happy to be bound and spanked and whatever else the fuck he needed to get off. It got me off too. So why wouldn't he just…do it?

"You should just admit you want her, brother," Kyan taunted Saint, sliding a hand between my legs and spreading them so my panties were bared to him beneath my school skirt.

Blake perked up, sensing the game and smirking as he grabbed my other thigh and pulled my legs even wider. I blushed, but didn't push them off, glancing curiously over at Saint and wondering what it would take to make him give in to the desire in his eyes.

"Fuck off, Kyan," Saint said hollowly, but his eyes didn't leave my face, his hand clenching into a fist on the armrest.

"Well you heard him, baby, let's fuck off to my room and let El Diablo listen to your screams," Kyan said with a cruel grin as he goaded Saint.

I smacked his chest, peeling both of their hands off my thighs as I stood up. "I don't want to go anywhere." I approached Saint with measured steps, my thirst for him growing as I got closer, the air seeming to chill as I entered his personal bubble.

He looked up at me from the chair, sliding his ankle from his knee, but making no other move. Somehow, even though he was lower down than me it still felt like he was dominating every ounce of oxygen that made it into my lungs.

"Just touch her," Blake encouraged and I laughed softly, my pulse drumming in my ears as I looked to Saint for his reaction.

He didn't like being told what to do, but his eyes were flaring with a madness that had me craving him even more. He wanted to touch me. But he had to do it on his own terms. He stood up suddenly so he was in my face, staring down his nose at me and making my legs quiver.

He reached out, surprising me as he dragged his fingers along the arc of my jawline, his breathing growing ragged. I saw the weight of his lust behind his eyes, a tsunami held back by his unyielding restraint in all things. I wanted to taste the full brunt of his desire just once to know I wasn't going entirely crazy by craving him back. That this pull I felt toward him really was reciprocated.

I forgot Blake and Kyan were watching, forgot that this had been a game designed to tease Saint as the air between us became utterly magnetic. But still, he resisted. Was it all about control? Was this just another way to make himself feel powerful?

"Move aside, Tatum," he rasped and I tried not to feel the sting of rejection in my chest. Tried not to notice how fiercely I wanted him now. It was humiliating after all he'd done to me. I did as he asked and he stalked away across The Temple. "I have somewhere to be."

I stared after him as he exited. Blake and Kyan laughed at his ways, but my heart twisted and I couldn't find it in me to laugh with them. I realised it was piano night for him, so he'd be gone for an hour. Nothing altered Saint's routine except being shot and hit by a car apparently. But even that had only altered it fleetingly.

"I feel like he's so sad or something," I said with a pout.

"Come here, baby," Kyan purred. "I'll make you forget sad little Saint exists."

"No time." Blake jumped up, kicking Kyan in the leg. "The Unspeakables are waiting for us at Aspen Halls. They've already been there for like…an hour. Oops."

Kyan grunted in annoyance but pushed out of his seat, frowning at me.

"What have you got planned?" I asked.

"We're going to find out if any of them have heard rumours of who this fucking Justice Ninja is. We've had them listening in on everyone in the dorms outside their rooms at night," Blake growled, cracking his knuckles.

"Anyone who has information can go back to bed. Those who don't will get hunted in the woods." Kyan smiled darkly and my heart pounded out of rhythm.

"Can I come?" I asked, biting my lip at the thought of throwing myself into punishing those assholes tonight.

"Naw." Kyan stepped toward me, kissing me hard. "We got you a babysitter."

I pursed my lips as he walked away, but my mood did a U-turn as I spotted Monroe entering The Temple a heartbeat later. *No complaints here.*

"See you later, Tate." Blake kissed me too and the two of them headed off together shoulder to shoulder. The door shut firmly and I grinned at Monroe as I realised we had just gotten crazy lucky.

I pointed at Saint's laptop on the table and he jogged over to it in anticipation. I took my phone from my pocket, running over to join him and bringing up the video of Saint entering his password. We had one hour before Saint came back and that would have to be enough.

I grabbed a pen and paper as Monroe examined the footage then I sat beside him at the table.

"Okay this first part is E...D...hashtag...E, D, hashtag...E, B, D, C, A," Monroe paused, looking to me with a shake of his head. "It's fucking sheet music, I told you he had a symphony in here." He laughed excitedly, continuing on with the password until I had it all written out.

My stomach swirled as I glanced at the door, but Saint wouldn't be back until ten on the dot. We had plenty of time. I opened his laptop, typing in the password, biting my lip in anticipation then it dinged and we were taken to the home screen. "Yes!"

Monroe shifted closer, his shoulder pressing against mine as he took over, hungrily rifling through Saint's files. Everything was perfectly organised unsurprisingly, but that didn't make it easier to find something useful to use against his father. If he had anything at all on here that would be helpful, it was bound to be hidden deep.

We searched his emails, finding a couple from Troy talking about colleges. He'd listed the emails of board members for various Ivy League colleges and my gut clenched as I thought of Saint heading off across the country after graduation. Blake would no doubt head off to one with a great football team and Kyan? I had no idea what Kyan would do. But his family's claws were so deep in him, I wasn't sure he'd ever get away from them.

"What will you do after our graduation?" I blurted at Monroe and he frowned, keeping his gaze on the screen as he continued to work through folder after folder.

"I don't know, princess. It depends..."

"On what you do about Troy?" I guessed.

"Yeah...and other things." He glanced at me from the corner of his eyes and my neck blazed with heat. "What will *you* do?"

"Honestly...I have no idea. I never really saw myself going to college. Maybe I'll go back to California..." My stomach knotted at the thought of leaving the Night Keepers behind, but what else was really going to happen? They might have thought we were bound forever, but that wasn't true. Things would change after this school year was over. Blake, Kyan and Saint would realise they had lives waiting for them beyond Everlake whether it was college or otherwise. We weren't walking the same paths.

"Hm," he grunted, evidently not pleased with my words. "Maybe I'll follow you there."

I elbowed him with a laugh. "If you're not on the run by then."

"Yeah," he said, his tone serious instead of joking and that made my gut clench tightly.

"Nash..."

"I'm taking on the governor of the whole state, Tatum, it's not without risks. I can't promise this won't end badly," he said, his eyes still on the screen. "So long as I take him down in the process, I don't care what happens to me."

"Don't say that," I hissed and he turned to me at last, his eyes blazing with a pain I knew too well.

The fight went out of me because how could I ask him not to take the risk when I would have done it myself a thousand times over? I'd spilled my enemy's blood to avenge my father without a thought for the consequences. If it wasn't for Kyan, I could be rotting in a prison cell right now. We all could be. And it was clear Nash saw that as a possible outcome for whatever way this went. But the idea of him throwing away his life, of him being ripped away from me too just made me hurt.

"Just be smart about it. Have an exit plan," I pushed.

He nodded firmly. "I will. Just as soon as I have an actual way to get to him."

"You've been careful up until now," I agreed. "You've covered your tracks coming here, you changed your name, buried your own identity…I just can't help but worry after everything Troy already did to your family. He's clearly vindictive and ruthless enough to do whatever it takes to silence you and I just can't bear the idea of something happening to you like that…"

I trailed off, biting my lip and Monroe gently caught my chin and turned my gaze up to meet his.

"Did I ever tell you what my name was, once upon a time?" he asked softly, a slight frown tugging at his brow.

I shook my head slowly, looking into his deep blue eyes and feeling all the hurt of that pain and grief which lived in him there. We were the same now, me and him, both orphans who had lost our siblings too. Both lost souls cut adrift with no one who remembered the children we once were or the love our families once felt.

"It was Jase," he said as a little smile tugged at the corner of my lips. "Jase Harrington."

"Jase," I murmured and he released a soft groan, leaning forward to press his forehead to mine.

"A part of me loves the sound of that name on your lips," he breathed. "But I'm not him anymore. I feel like he was this nice, honest, hard working kid and I'm little more than a shell holding his memories tightly like grains of sand in my fist, desperately trying to keep hold of them even while they continue to slip away. The things I've done…the things I plan to do and am willing to do in payment for the lives of my family, they don't belong to him. He had everything to live for. And I just have this one thing."

"Just the one?" I asked softly, trying to ignore the twist of pain in my gut at that statement.

"That was how it was for a hell of a long time, anyway," he replied, pulling back and using his hold on my chin to get me to look up at him again. "But now I have you. Or at least, I hope I do. And I'm starting to think I've got a whole lot more to live for now."

"You do have me," I promised him and some of the darkness in his blue eyes lightened. "And I have you too."

His lips found mine in a soft, sweet promise of that and some of the pain in my heart seemed to loosen its grip on me as I stole a moment in his strong arms. But we didn't have any more time available to linger and I pushed him back gently with a light laugh.

"That said, we do still wanna take down Troy Memphis, so we should really be concentrating on finding some dirt on this laptop."

Monroe smiled hungrily, releasing me as he turned his attention back to the hunt and I couldn't help but smile to myself at the memory of his mouth on mine and the little piece of his soul he'd just offered up to me.

We fell quiet as we hunted through the laptop and I cast looks over at the door and the clock from time to time.

My phone buzzed after a while and my heart leapt a little as I checked it, finding a message on the group chat for all five of us. I swear I'd left this chat a hundred times, but Saint always managed to get me back into it somehow.

Kyan:

Message for Tatum: I'm going to *squid emoji* your *peach emoji* when I get back later.

I snorted a laugh, shooting him a reply quickly.

Tatum:

Not if I *octopus emoji* your *peacock emoji* first.

Blake:

I have an idea for later... *eggplant emoji* x2 + *winky face emoji* + *doughnut emoji*?

Saint:

Fuck you all.

I breathed a laugh and Monroe looked over at his phone, seeing the messages flash up there too. He grabbed it, tossing out his own reply to the conversation.

Nash:

Tatum just explained this conversation to me and frankly I'm disgusted.

Saint:

Did she tell you what the squid means?

Nash:

Everyone knows what that means.

Saint:

Tell. Me.

Nash:

Squid emoji

Kyan:

Octopus emoji

Saint:

Last warning or I'm closing this chat down.

I laughed, knocking my shoulder against Monroe's and he turned and crushed his lips to mine, fisting his hand in my hair. "I'll never miss an opportunity to rile up Saint Memphis." He smirked and I grinned, glancing at the time and figuring we probably didn't have long enough for a quickie considering we'd gotten nowhere with the laptop so far. And we only had fifteen minutes before Saint would be back. *Dammit.*

Monroe clicked through folder after folder, finding nothing of interest. At five to ten, my stomach started to knot and I stood from my seat in exasperation. "We'd better leave it, Nash. There's nothing here."

"Just wait a second," he growled with urgency to his tone as he clicked on another folder marked MAF.

I glanced at the clock nervously as he clicked on the first file and he inhaled long and slow. "Well, look at that..."

"What is it?" I leaned down to see, my pulse hammering in my ears.

"It's a copy of Troy Memphis's bank statement. And it looks like there's more of them." He clicked on another file then another. "Some of the transactions are highlighted." He pointed one out and I frowned at the large sums of money.

"Did Saint highlight these?" I questioned and Monroe shrugged. "What are they for?"

A key twisted in the front door lock and I nearly leapt out of my skin. Monroe dove to his feet, closing down the folder and shutting the laptop firmly before racing across the room to throw himself on the couch.

I walked purposefully towards the kitchenette, not looking back as Saint entered and hoping I looked casual as I opened the fridge and took out the water filter. As I shut the fridge, I glanced over at Saint, finding him standing by his laptop, staring down at it, his entire body rigid. *Oh shit.*

My heart thrashed against my ribcage as I poured myself a glass of water and tried not to freak the fuck out. *Is he smelling our lasting scent near the damn thing like a freaking vampire??*

I sipped my water and his eyes flicked to me, full of a dark and writhing suspicion. "Go home, Monroe," he commanded in a deadly calm voice and I swear my spine turned to a pillar of ice.

Monroe's head popped up from the couch, yawning like he'd just been taking a nap and he looked pretty damn convincing to me. I just hoped Saint bought it. "Thought I might crash here tonight."

"The answer is no. *Leave*," Saint hissed and Monroe tossed me a look, clearly not wanting to leave me alone with him. But better he got out of here and wasn't accused of anything. Because if Saint figured out Monroe was targeting him, I didn't know what kind of terrifying hell he'd rain down on him.

"Goodnight, Nash," I said to Monroe, trying to keep my voice light and when Saint gave the laptop another hard look, I shot Monroe an expression that encouraged him to get out.

"I'll sleep easier without a phantom breathing down my neck anyway." Monroe gave Saint a pointed look before backing up to the door and making a pretend phone with his thumb and little finger, holding it to his ear as he implored me with his eyes to call him if I needed him. I gave him a small nod and he stepped out the door, the tension in the air humming against my ears as he left me with Saint. He said nothing, his muscles still tight and his teeth grinding.

"I think I'll take a shower," I said airily, taking a step forward, but before I could go anywhere, Saint grabbed the chair in front of his laptop, ripped it off the floor and threw it at the wall. It smashed into three pieces with a heart-shuddering crack and I recoiled in alarm as he bared his teeth at me.

"Do you think I'm a fucking fool?!" he bellowed and fear consumed me. I'd never seen Saint angry like this. There was a deep betrayal in his eyes as he pointed at me then to the laptop. "Do you want to explain to me why my laptop has moved an inch to the left of where I put it?"

I stepped closer to him, knowing it was a dangerous move, but I needed to try and convince him of the lie I was about to tell. And if I ran away, I'd only prove my guilt. "Maybe I knocked it?" I said innocently. "I did some school work right beside it, maybe I-"

"Don't lie to me!" he roared, striding forward and I gasped as he got right in my face. I could taste his breath, could feel the burning, twisting inhuman creature inside him that he battled with every day. But I could feel more than that. Could see *more* in his eyes. It was the depth of this betrayal that he feared. That if I had touched his precious laptop, tried to get into it, then I wasn't trustworthy. The girl who he let sleep in his bed, who was so deep into his inner circle that she now had the power to unravel him.

"Don't shout at me," I bit back at him, his tone making my hackles rise. Instead of leaning away, I leaned toward him, tip-toeing up so we were nose to nose.

"What are you after?" he demanded, his voice dropping to a deadly hiss worthy of a viper. "You want my secrets, Tatum? Because you couldn't handle them. You'd cower in the face of my demons."

"I don't cower for anyone or any*thing*," I snarled. "You should know that by now."

"Maybe I don't know you at all," he snapped, his eyes flashing with red hot anger. "Maybe I let a rat into my home and I need to crush its spine beneath my heel."

I slapped him, my fury bubbling over. How dare he speak to me like that?

He snarled furiously, grabbing my arms, wheeling me around and shoving me against the wall so my back impacted with it. My hair fell forward into my face as a breath huffed out of my lungs.

"Let go of me," I growled as he pinned me there, getting so close that my thoughts were harder to grasp. His crisp apple scent was enticing and made my anger blurry at the edges as it bled into lust. I tried to crush that desire away but it only grew sharper as he panted heavily and our breaths mixed.

"Maybe I'll put you down in the crypt and lock you up in one of those stone coffins for the night, maybe *then* you'll talk," he spat, his eyes a deep void of darkness.

I rested my head back against the wall as he leaned in even closer, a craziness in his gaze that made me want to keep pushing and pushing to find out what happened when he finally lost it completely.

"There's nothing to say. Why are you really angry at me, Saint?" I demanded, my heart all but stopping as he pressed his hard chest to mine and crushed me into the wall firmly enough to hurt. I felt his rock hard cock digging into my thigh and I gasped, unblinking as he glared down at me, a tortured soul staring right back into the depths of my being.

"I'm so fucking *sick* of you tormenting me," he snapped, rage spewing from him as his voice rose once again.

"You're not sick of it. You lap it up," I shot back at him, my features twisting. "You're always staring, always watching me with the others. Why don't you man up and own your feelings for once?"

He smacked his hand into the wall beside my head with a thump, making me flinch full bodily and a yelp of alarm escaped me.

"As if I'd strike you anywhere but your peachy little ass," he laughed coldly and I shoved him, hating him, hating wanting him, hating caring for him. "And you can't get enough of it."

"You're the one who can't get enough. You spank me when I'm bad, and drool over me when I'm good. But you can't just own what you really want and fuck me like a man. It's *pathetic*," I snarled, pushing his buttons, unsure why exactly I was goading the devil, but fuck him. I was so done with this game. This back and forth, this blazing fire between us which he always tried to dismiss as nothing. "Let me past." I shoved him back a step, slipping under his arm, but he caught my hair then shoved me back against the wall again, practically snarling in my face.

"I'm done with this!" I yelled, fury eating me alive as he caged me in. "You're just a cruel, heartless monster of a man and I'm done being your play thi-" His mouth landed on mine and suddenly he was kissing me ferociously, passionately, his tongue sinking between my lips, cool and furious against mine as he groaned headily.

I gasped as he caught my hips, lifting me up and driving me back against the wall once more as he consumed me. That was the only word for it. Saint Memphis was kissing me with the hunger of a warrior invading a kingdom. He was conquering each piece of my mouth and claiming me in a wholly new way. I had never been kissed like this. It was rich and intoxicating and almost blasphemous. It was entirely Saint.

He started tearing at my clothes and I moaned in encouragement, pulling at his shirt and dragging it over his head. As he ripped my cami off and his flesh pressed to mine, I gasped at the hardened kiss of his muscles against my soft curves. He yanked up my skirt, breathless and desperate for me as he pushed my panties aside and found me wet and wanting. Just for him. *All* for him. He groaned, feeling what he did to me and sighing my name.

He kissed me again, harder this time, biting at my lower lip with a growl as he unbuckled his pants. He freed his hard length, looking ready to blow already as he squeezed the base in his fist. He forced me against the wall with one arm, the same one he'd broken, showing no sign of pain except the same, absolute agony I was feeling over our bodies not yet being joined. I couldn't wait a second longer. I was clawing at him, reduced to nothing but a sweaty, needy animal as he guided the tip of his twitching cock to my soaking entrance and I took in a breath as I readied for him to brand me as his at long last.

Saint met my gaze, his eyes full of the deepest, blackest shadow I'd ever seen. His lips were parted, his breaths were coming unevenly and there was nothing but chaos in his expression. He'd let himself go and he was about to show me what it was like to be at the mercy of Saint Memphis when he completely lost control.

He released a noise of anguish as he ground against me and he slid the head of his dick against my entrance, making me gasp and claw at him for more. The atmosphere suddenly crackled and he jerked away from me, dropping me so I fell on my ass and I yelped in surprise.

"Fuck!" he roared, twisting away from me, yanking his pants up and throwing the whole dining table over, sending his laptop clattering over the flagstones.

"Saint!" I yelled, pushing to my feet and reaching for him, my hands actually shaking. What the hell was he thinking?

He jammed his fingers into his eyes, backing up further and further. "I can't do this. The rules. The fucking *rules!*"

"Screw the rules!" I cried wildly, marching towards the fridge as my skirt fell back down over my thighs. "I'll strike them off. Who gives a damn?"

"No!" He raced past me, snatching them from the fridge and clutching them to his chest. His eyes were a fortress designed to keep me out and he was building it higher and higher and higher. "*I* give a damn. You can't pick and choose what goes and what doesn't depending on your mood. That's not how the world works, Tatum," he snapped, his anger at me returning.

I stared at him in shock as he strode past me, marching upstairs and walking straight into his bathroom. He slammed the door and my heart lurched at the sound as it echoed up to the cavernous roof then the crash of more shit breaking filled the air.

I held a hand to my frantic heart, trying to process the roiling storm of emotions taking hold of my body. The sharpest one of all was the rejection he'd left me with. I was still hot and wet between my thighs and my ass was still stinging from where he'd dropped me on the floor. Shame was my only companion as I touched my puffy lips and bit back tears of hurt.

I grappled with the knowledge that Saint would never let himself get that close to me again and a part of me was glad of that. While another part of me wept. Fuck him for doing that to me. For making me pine and ache for him and bring me to the point of no return only to leave me there on the precipice. It was humiliating. But as I picked up my clothes, I found myself pitying him. Because he was his own worst nightmare and he didn't even realise it. If I was a prisoner to Saint Memphis, it was nothing to the captive he made of himself.

CHAPTER FIFTEEN

I stood surrounded by the shattered remains of my bathroom shelf and all the broken bottles of wash products which were slowly leaking across the tiles. Aftershave meeting with perfume, toothpaste and mouthwash and filling the small room with the unpleasantly overwhelming combined scent.

I was shaking. Every muscle in my body trembling with need and hurt and a fucking pain that was rooted so deep within me that it felt like something was tearing apart within my damn soul.

I tipped my head back and bellowed to the ceiling as I fought to vent some of this anger in me, but it only seemed to grow and fester and push harder at the confines of my skin with a desperate need to break free.

I whirled on the mirror, hating the sight of myself falling to ruin as it taunted me from the depths of the silvery surface. The words scrawled across the dark skin of my chest mocking me as they were reflected back in reverse. *The days are long, but the nights are dark.* And I was staring down the barrel of another night sent to torture me. To make it worse she was mine tonight, due to sleep in my bed and fucking fool that I was, I'd been looking forward to having her that close, even though I'd known it would equal me aching for her all night long. But I was always aching for her these days and it was a wound that was only getting deeper, burrowing beneath my skin and taking all of my attention like an itch that burned with the desperate need to be scratched.

I yelled out as I slammed my fist into the mirror, the whole thing shattering as shards of glass were driven into my knuckles. Blood flew and a spike of pure agony raced through the bone of my freshly healed arm.

I was shaking even harder now, the finely tuned restraints I'd tied on my mind snapping one after another as I fought against the animal in me who wanted to race back down those stairs and find Tatum Rivers. I just didn't know if wanted to punish her so severely that she would never look at me with lust in her eyes ever again or rip what little remained of her clothes off and fuck her until the beast in me had taken as much from her flesh as I could possibly take. Either way, with the last of my control burning away into less than nothing, I was sure she would hate me for whichever choice I made.

I took a furious step towards the shower then changed my mind and spun away from it. My cock was hard and aching in my pants, even the small friction caused by walking making me groan as I imagined fucking my little siren until she couldn't see straight and she forgot all about Kyan and Blake and any other man who had ever touched her.

I wanted to brand myself all over her body inside and out, mark her as mine so clearly that all that anyone saw when they looked at her was a huge flashing sign saying *Property of Saint Memphis*. I'd tattoo it on that pretty face of hers if I could bear to see her tarnished that way and I'd certainly fuck it into her so deeply that she'd never forget it again.

But I couldn't do that. I couldn't even think about doing it. Because she wasn't mine. Not mine alone. She was Kyan's and Blake's and Monroe's too. If she was fucking one of us then she should have been fucking all of us. But she shouldn't have been fucking any of us. Because *those were the rules*.

I threw the bathroom door open with such fury that it slammed into the wall and carved a dent into the plaster with the door handle.

The list of rules we'd all agreed to were still clutched in my left hand and they needed some fucking work done on them if I was going to have any hope of stopping them from getting destroyed.

I kneeled down at the set of drawers beside my bed and opened the bottom one, taking my laminator from it and setting it on the floor as I fought to stop the trembling in my limbs.

I smoothed out the page which we'd all signed so long ago and closed my eyes as I recited the rules Tatum had listed on it by heart, like they were etched into my being, the first one now struck out.

1. ~~No Kissing~~

2. No foreplay

3. No sex

4. No touching while we share a bed

5. No entering the bathroom while I'm naked or on the toilet

6. I am allowed two hours of undisturbed study time at the library on every weekday

7. I am allowed one friend who you can not be a dick to

8. Once a week we will ALL eat pizza for dinner without cutlery

9. I am allowed to sit wherever I want in classes

Hadn't I eaten the fucking pizza? Hadn't I let her study and have her little friend and watched her choose to sit away from me in class? I'd respected her privacy in the bathroom and I laid pillows between us to make sure I never touched her when we slept in a bed together. I'd stuck to the terms of our agreement, even when she'd flouted them. Even when she'd purposefully tried to lure me into breaking them and damning myself for it.

The rules I'd laid out sat beneath hers and as I went over them, my frustration only grew.

1. You will sleep in a Night Keeper's bed every night on rotation and

they will have priority over you for 24 hours (6pm-6pm the next day).

2. You must cook breakfast for us every day.

3. You will wear whatever we decide on the day you are in our possession.

4. You will do as we say without complaint unless it conflicts with your rules.

That was the most baffling thing of all. She'd stuck to those rules almost to the letter. The only time she had really flouted them had been when she stayed with me every night while I was healing and she'd taken her punishments for that from me daily. So the only rules she was breaking generally speaking were the ones she had laid out herself.

It was like she didn't care about her own limits, or like she had just changed her mind entirely since making those rules, or like...a trap.

A snarl tore from my lips as I considered that. That she was using her body to tempt and lure us, forcing us to break the rules and using her beauty to tear us apart from the inside out. Blake had been smiling a lot more since he'd been fucking her again. He was sweet to her, attentive. Even Kyan did shit for her beyond just fucking her brains out over a coffin like some kind of sex starved incubus who had been waiting for prey in the dark.

In fact, that whole thing had been a trap of its own. She'd encouraged all of us to chase her down there. I bet she'd known I was watching them from the moment she took their cocks inside her and had been hoping to tempt me to take my turn too.

Because if she had us all firmly under the spell of her pussy and grasped by the balls then she could rule over all of us. And fuck knew what she'd do with power like that once she claimed it.

I gritted my teeth and slid the rules through the laminator, watching as the page was coated in plastic and they were rendered a lot less vulnerable to acts of random scribbling. If any of the rules were going to change then there was going to be a proper fucking meeting about it, not a spur of the moment strike of a pen.

But even as I thought on that, my brow furrowed further. Because if she removed that rule then she couldn't punish me or any of us for breaking it. So her plan to have reasons to punish us made no sense. So what was it? What was I missing here?

For a fleeting moment I remembered how wet she'd been against the tip of my cock, how hard she'd kissed me, how certain she'd seemed to want what we were about to share. But it couldn't be that fucking simple. Nothing in this world was that fucking simple. And if all she needed was someone to fuck her then she had two perfectly willing volunteers waiting in the wings.

I took the freshly protected rules and pushed them beneath my pillow before turning and storming downstairs.

I was breathing so hard that the pain in my ribs was reawakened and I welcomed it, needing something to draw my gaze from the girl who was the sole focus of all of my problems recently.

She'd clearly decided against getting any of her own clothes from my closet to replace the ones I'd torn off of her and I was further infuriated to see her wearing one of Kyan's fucking hoodies. It hung down to her mid-thigh and made it impossible for me to tell if she had her skirt still on beneath it or not.

"Saint," she began, moving off of the couch and raising her chin in defiance as she crossed the room to intercept me.

"What?" I snarled at her, the roar in my head almost drowning out the sound of her voice.

"We need to talk about this."

"About the way you seem determined to fuck with everything in my life that keeps me sane?" I demanded as I advanced on her, unable to stop myself from getting close to her again even though I knew she was a poison designed specially to incapacitate me.

"That's not what this is," she replied in a hard tone. "This is you using a few words scrawled on a piece of paper as an excuse to keep away from me. To punish yourself. I just don't understand why."

"You think this is me punishing myself?" I laughed darkly as I came to stand so close to her that I could smell the honey blossom scent of her shampoo. "Do you seriously not realise that in all the times I've punished you, I've never even come close to subjecting you to the things that I've been through? You don't know the *meaning* of punishment. I'm soft on you and you don't even realise it."

"What happened to make you like this, Saint?" she breathed, reaching out for me like she wanted to comfort me, understand me.

I barked a humourless laugh as I let her hand fall on my cheek and I closed my eyes for a moment as I remembered being torn from everything I knew with no notice at all, time and again. Of having all of my possessions removed and replaced, my routine interrupted. Let alone the real punishments. Days in the dark, muscles cramping, white noise blaring, time slipping away from me without me having any way to know how much of it had passed.

"I was raised in a certain way," I said in a low voice as I moved closer to her, dominating her personal space and inhaling the scent of her mixed with Kyan's vile stench of leather and gasoline from his hoodie which made my jaw grind even harder. "A way that perfect little girls like you could never even comprehend."

"I think we both know by now that I'm not perfect, Saint. The difference between you and me is that I don't flinch away from the stains on my soul."

My hand closed around her throat before I'd even made the full decision to move and I squeezed hard as I walked her back across the room until I'd driven her up against the stained glass window at the front of the church. Rain hammered against the other side of it and a shiver raced along Tatum's skin at the contact with the cold glass, but she made no move to try and remove my grip on her.

There was no denying the hard press of my cock against her thigh as I panted heavily and I felt like I was even closer to breaking than I had been earlier.

"You clearly want me, Saint," she hissed, though my grip on her made it hard for her to get the words out. "So why not just get it over with?"

"Because if I were to fuck you right now, I can assure you that nothing about it would be soft or gentle or make you feel like you knew any more about me. It would only confirm in your mind what your instincts have been warning you about from the very first moment we met. There is no good in me, Tatum Rivers. And I'll ruin you in every way that I can if you give me half the chance. If you make me break the rules for you, you'll regret it more keenly than anything else that's ever happened to you in your miserable life, including the deaths of your loving family."

Tatum swung her fist at me with a savage brutality that sent pain bursting through my jaw and knocked me away from her as the taste of blood coated my tongue.

"What the fuck is going on here?" Kyan's voice interrupted us as he and Blake stepped through the front door and I stormed away from Tatum with a pure force of will. There were marks banding her throat where my fingers had dug in and the fury burning between us made it painfully clear that that hadn't been part of some fantasy we'd been playing out.

"I'm just explaining to our resident whore that not every member of the Night Keepers wants to fuck her," I sneered, the words burning on my tongue as my own cock taunted me with its hardness and called me out on my own bullshit from within my pants.

I'd expected Kyan to strike at me but when Blake's fist slammed into my gut, I was taken off guard, stumbling back against the wall just as Kyan leapt at me too.

I didn't even care that these were the most important men in the world to me as every rotten, ruined, tainted piece of me broke loose and I launched myself into the brawl with reckless abandon, bathing in the pain and relishing doling out more of it.

I only realised that Tatum was screaming at all of us to stop when someone hauled Blake off of me and I spotted Monroe standing there looking savage as he tried to piece together what was happening.

263

"What the fuck is this?" he bellowed as I shoved myself to my feet, my ribs aching in a way that said Kyan's fists had just set back the healing process. But I didn't give a fuck. I didn't give a fuck about anything anymore.

I shoved through the press of bodies surrounding me, snarling at all of them as they tried to speak or intercept me or talk about me like I wasn't fucking here and I kept going until I made it outside.

The rain was hammering down over the lake and my bare skin flared with goosebumps as I strode straight down the path that led away from The Temple and kept going towards the water.

The other Night Keepers and Tatum were yelling behind me, but I couldn't hear them over the feral beast that had laid siege to my mind.

I kept walking towards the lake at a fast pace, the hand that had gripped Tatum's throat clenching and unclenching. I could never lose control with her like that again. I'd just come so close to snapping with her and I knew in the depths of my dark and depraved being that if I ever did that there would be no salvation for me.

She was the one person I'd ever met who made me even consider being a better man than the twisted thing I'd been born to become. She made me question things I'd never questioned and made me care about hurting her like I'd never done for another soul. I couldn't let her see the very worst of me. I couldn't bear it if she did.

I strode straight down the bank and out into the freezing water as the rain slammed down on it and the wind howled all around me.

I couldn't feel any of it. My flesh was dead to the pain of the cold and the rage of the storm just like my heart was dead to normal human feelings of love and kindness. There was no saving me. But I could try my hardest not to corrupt her too thoroughly.

I didn't stop walking until the water lapped up over my waist and the shouts of the others and demands for me to return to them were stolen by the wind.

I didn't even suck in a breath before plunging my head beneath the water. I blew out what little air there was in my lungs as I pushed myself down to sit on the lakebed, the freezing water enveloping me and memories of the cold and the dark welcoming me in like an old friend.

I wasn't the kid who had been beaten. I wasn't even the kid who had been yelled at. My father was a cold and controlled man. I'd never even known him to raise his voice. If my behaviour was deemed unsuitable or my emotions too readable, he had simply and effectively punished me. The dark was where I'd learned to find myself. All those hours trapped and confined for one reason or another with nothing but the silence to keep me company had taught me how to lock onto the few things about me that truly mattered. Those that could never be stolen away.

I had my brothers. Men I'd chosen for myself and sworn to stand by through the worst the world might ever throw at us. And I had my music which even now seemed to writhe and pulse beneath my flesh. But there was something else sitting with me in the dark as my lungs burned and strained and I refused to head back up for air. A girl with blue eyes and the strength to tame monsters.

It hurt me to know how close I'd come to losing it with her. It felt like I'd been attacking myself. My own...heart. And I couldn't bear that. Because I needed to keep owning her. I needed to know that she was mine and I was starting to think that I might just be hers, too. I wouldn't have just lain down my life for anyone else the way I had for her when I'd taken that bullet. I knew it. She knew it. I was just too stubborn to voice what that meant, to allow the idea of the rules shifting to accommodate what I ached for so much. Because if I was honest with myself, I was afraid of claiming it. Of claiming her in any more ways than I already had. Just in case I couldn't figure out a way to keep her.

I pushed to my feet and breached the surface, sucking down a breath a moment before I would have started choking on the rancid water at the bottom of the lake.

When I turned back to the shore, I found four silhouettes waiting for me, standing in the thundering rain like it was where they'd always meant to be.

Blake and Kyan were holding Tatum's arms as she fought to get away from them, but as I strode back towards them with my control more firmly leashed at last, they released her.

She ran to me, taking no more notice of the freezing lake water than I had as she moved straight into it and by the time she made it to me, it was over her knees.

Tatum threw her arms around my neck, gripping the back of my hair in tight fists as she stared up at me, Kyan's drenched sweatshirt clinging to her body as it pressed against my bare chest and the rain continued to pound down on us.

"Don't you dare run from me again, Saint Memphis," she snarled like she had any right to tell me what to do.

"I've never run from anything in my damn life," I growled at her as I watched the rain trickle down over her cheeks and her grip in my hair tightened.

"Liar."

I narrowed my eyes, meaning to correct her, punish her, push her away, but the intensity of those blue eyes reflecting the storm up at me had me pausing and the truth spilling from my lips instead.

"I've never felt anything like I do when I'm with you, Tatum Rivers," I breathed and I couldn't even be sure that she could hear me over the rain crashing down on the lake. "And I don't warn you not to push me because I'm angry at you for trying. I warn you because I'm afraid of what I could do to you if my control slips when we're together and I do something to you that I can't come back from. It's too easy for me to be cruel, it's too easy for me to hurt you."

"I'm not afraid of you, Saint," she replied, the flare of passion in her eyes saying she actually meant that.

"That's just because you don't think you have anything to lose anymore."

"Or maybe I think I've got everything to gain."

I stared at her for a long moment wearing Kyan's hoodie with the rain washing lines of mascara down her cheeks, her hair bedraggled by the storm and lipstick smeared from the kisses I shouldn't have stolen from her and I swear she'd never looked so beautiful to me. Her imperfections were her perfections, the fire in her soul which I had ached to douse was now the thing I admired most in her. And the wildness I'd wanted to tame more than anything I'd ever known was making me crave a taste of that freedom instead.

My hands slid around her waist and I leaned closer to her so that the raindrops which ran around the back of my head fell down and splashed against her cheeks, her nose, her lips.

"I can't try and pretend that I'm not the man I am, Tatum," I growled.

"I never asked you to."

I paused as I considered that, and I realised it was true. I'd assumed the desire she showed for me had come with the caveat that she expected me to change if we acted on it, but she'd never once said that.

"It took a long time to turn me into this monster you know. And I don't think I'll ever stop being him now," I told her.

"Saint, I don't think you're-"

"I'm sorry, Tatum. For all of it. And for none of it. Sometimes I can see what I am as clearly as I can now and I know that the things I do, the things I've *done* are unforgivable. But I also know that being that man is all I know how to be. And I'm not going to have some epiphany one day where I fall in love with a girl and realise the error of my ways and dance off into the sunset. My version of a happily ever after is never going to fall into a nice, neat little box that can be tied off with a pretty bow and have me making some girl's dreams all come true."

"I never said I wanted a happily ever after or a Prince Charming," she replied with just as much conviction as me. "I said that I was yours. All four of you. I swore to be your Night Bound. What that means is up to all of us. And right now, I'm not hating it the way I once did."

I released a long and steady breath, leaning forward until my forehead pressed to hers and inhaling heavily as I dug deep to regain some level of control over myself.

I dropped my hands to Tatum's thighs and lifted her out of the freezing lake water until she wound her legs around my waist and tightened her grip on my neck to hold herself up.

"Saint, I really don't think you should be lifting-"

"Don't tell me what to do, siren, or I'll do a whole lot worse than spank you in the morning when I'm ready to face punishing you again."

Tatum swallowed thickly, leaning back so that she could look at me as I carried her out of the lake in the rain and strode up the beach towards the others where they still waited. My ribs were doing a whole lot more than aching now, but I didn't care. I wasn't putting her down until we were back inside and out of this storm.

"Are you good now?" Kyan asked me, eyeing me like I was a wild animal who had escaped from the zoo and gone on a rampage.

"I'm good," I replied in a clipped tone, walking between the three of them and noting Monroe's glare coupled with the way he looked at me carrying Tatum in my arms.

I was well accustomed to my own jealousy by now and if I wasn't mistaken then I was seeing more than a flicker of that same emotion in his eyes too. The question was, how far were his fantasies for our girl going? He'd obviously been concerned enough about her to come back here to check on her, and it didn't take a fool to see the way he watched her all the time.

The three of them formed a ring around me as I strode back to The Temple with Tatum in my arms, but just as I reached the building, I fell still.

The heavy wooden door swung inwards slowly and large, muddy boot prints had been tracked across the flagstones inside.

I stepped over the threshold with Tatum in my arms and slowly lowered her to the ground as the whole fucking world came crashing down on my head.

On all four walls of the central part of the church which made up the living room, some piece of shit had graffitied three giants cocks and the words

The Justice Ninja will take payment in your blood in red spray paint.

"No," I snarled, like refusing to believe that any of this was happening would just make it go away.

"I'm going to enjoy killing this motherfucker when we catch him," Kyan said in a low and dark voice which was a promise of its own.

The only small mercy was that they'd used spray paint instead of human shit this time and I thanked all that was holy for that. I probably would have had to burn this place if they'd wiped their shit all over my walls.

Monroe frowned down at the floor, pointing out the muddy footprints and the way they seemed to have just circled the room to the spots where they'd plastered the graffiti before leaving again.

I wanted to demand to know which one of them had left the fucking Temple last so that I could lay blame at someone's feet for not locking the door, but I knew it was pointless. I was the reason that we'd all been out in that storm. It was on me.

My jaw was grinding and there was a vein throbbing at my temple as I fought against the desire to do more damage to the place than I had in my rampage earlier. What was the fucking point in preserving it now anyway?

"Saint?" Blake demanded, stepping in front of me and filling the space before me so that my view of the destruction was cut off. "We'll sort this out. You need to go and calm the fuck down before you end up on a killing spree tonight. Go play some piano or some shit, okay?"

I wanted to fight him on it, but I knew in my heart that I was barely holding on to my sanity as it was tonight so I just gave him a firm nod and turned away from the damage, catching Tatum's hand as I went and tugging her down the hall towards Kyan's room.

I drew her through to the bathroom and set the water running in the shower while she watched me with eyes that seemed to see too much.

"You need to warm up," I muttered, getting a pair of towels ready for her and then heading back through to Kyan's room to take one of his shirts for her to wear when she was done. It set off a tick in my jaw to think of her wearing it, but I needed as many reasons as I could come up with to stay away from her tonight or I knew I was going to cave into the temptation of her flesh.

It wasn't even like it had been earlier when lust and desire and anger had collided into something hot and carnal and desperate between us. No, right now I felt like the cracks in me were showing and for some reason I got the impression that if I just allowed myself to get lost in her, it would be that much easier to hold them all together.

But I couldn't do that. Even without the rules to bind me, I knew that if I gave into the desire I felt for her body while I was achy and broken and feral like this that it would be all too easy to let her become the reason I got myself together again. And I had never in my life relied on someone that heavily before. I absolutely wouldn't be doing it with a girl who had every reason to hate me.

It didn't matter if I longed to do it or not. That was just the weakness in me talking. The same weakness my father had worked tirelessly to remove from me. And I refused to ever admit that so much as a speck of it remained despite his best efforts.

I waited in Kyan's room, dripping on his carpet as my sodden sweatpants made me shiver. But I wasn't allowed to enter the bathroom while she was naked, that was one of her rules.

"Saint?" Tatum's voice called to me and I tried not to let the sound of my name on her lips do anything to thaw the cold that had set into my bones, but it warmed them a little all the same.

"I'm here," I said in flat tone, retreating so far into myself that I had no room at all left for rage or hate or any petty, human emotions that might cloud my judgement.

"I'm not naked. You can come back in."

I released a slow breath and moved back into the bathroom, finding her standing beneath the flow of hot water in the black underwear I was pawing at not so long ago when I almost lost control with her.

"Get in," she encouraged. "You must be frozen."

I wanted to tell her that I didn't follow anyone's commands and that she needed to watch her tongue unless she was looking to get punished, but instead I just pushed my soaking sweatpants off of my hips and let them fall to the tiles with a splat. I kept my boxers on, though it wasn't like the tight material left much to the imagination.

I moved beneath the hot water, keeping my eyes off of her so that I wouldn't be tempted again as I turned to face the white tiles on the wall.

I flinched minutely as the soft touch of a sponge brushed against my spine but made no other reaction as Tatum slowly rubbed circles over my skin with it, cleaning my body and taking some of the weight off of my soul at the same time.

We said nothing but once she finished washing me, she dropped the sponge and her hands slid up my spine instead.

I opened my mouth to protest, but before any words made it past my lips, her fingers curled around my shoulders and she began to gently massage the tension from my muscles.

A low, deep groan rolled from the back of my throat as she slowly worked her way lower, finding kinks and knots along my spine and easing them with a firm and purposeful touch which had the knots in my soul unfurling just a little too.

When she made it to the base of my spine and her fingers were skimming the waistband of my boxers, I turned to look at her and she pulled her hands back.

I took her jaw in my grip and turned her face up to mine as I shut off the water.

"Do as I say tonight, okay?" I asked and she nodded silently, her eyes filled with questions I had no intention of answering. Certainly not today.

I made a sound of appreciation and released her, stepping out of the shower and pushing my wet boxers off as I went. My cock sprung free, hard and proud and fucking hopeful as ever even though I absolutely wouldn't be giving in to its demands. But at this point it seemed ridiculous to try and hide it from her. I wasn't a slave to my body any more than I was a slave to anything else though, so if she thought my desire for her was some kind of victory over me then she was sorely mistaken. It only made me more dangerous to her.

I dried myself off and then wrapped a towel around my waist, keeping my back to Tatum as she stripped out of her wet underwear and dried off too.

"Get dressed in that," I commanded, pointing at Kyan's shirt without even bothering to hide my distasteful sneer.

"But this is Ky-"

"I thought you were going to do as I say?" I asked in a hard tone.

Tatum bit her lip and pulled the baggy band tee over her head and I nodded once in approval.

"Follow me," I commanded and I led her back out through Kyan's room to the main part of The Temple where the other Night Keepers were well underway scrubbing the walls. The graffiti was thankfully coming off fairly easily and they'd flipped the dining table upright again too. One of them had even managed to fix the chair I'd broken and I spied a drill and some screws sitting on the kitchen counter, fighting off the desire to shudder at the thought of manual labour.

"I gave the whole place a sweep to make sure there's no chance that anyone was still in here. The door down to the gym and the crypt were locked anyway and the rest of the building is clear," Kyan said as we passed through and I nodded my approval.

I didn't miss Tatum's sharp inhale which said she hadn't considered that, but I ignored it as I led her up to my room.

"Get into bed," I commanded, refusing to look towards my bathroom which I knew was still in a state of disrepair since I'd lost the plot earlier. There were still tiny splinters of glass from the mirror lodged in my knuckles but I didn't have the patience to sit with the tweezers and extract them at the moment.

Tatum slipped away from me and moved beneath the covers, eyeing me in a way that said she expected me to punish her and wasn't totally against the idea. But I wouldn't be doing any such thing tonight. I couldn't. I was on the ledge and about to free fall off of it. I was only so calm because my emotions had burned out. But I was going to need to expel the turmoil inside me before I would really be able to function with true control again.

I moved to the closet and changed into a pair of clean sweatpants and a t-shirt before pulling on a waterproof coat and flicking the hood up over my head.

I switched the lights off in my room as I stepped back out and Tatum gasped from the bed like she didn't know what to expect.

"Stay here all night," I commanded her. "You can only leave the bed if you need to use the bathroom and then you must return to it the moment you are done. Don't call me. Don't message me. Don't come looking for me. I'll be back in time for my workout in the morning."

Her lips parted and I could just make out the movement in the dark, but she managed to hold back on the questions.

"Okay," she agreed in a soft voice that had me relaxing minutely. At least I would know where she was while I was gone, and I could picture her here waiting for me easily enough.

I nodded once and then turned away from her, heading down the stairs and glancing at the other Night Keepers as they continued to scrub the walls.

Blake caught my eye and gave me half a smile, knowing exactly where I was going and silently promising to have this place fixed by the time I returned.

I knew full well I would need to go over all of their cleaning myself to get it up to my standard, but I appreciated the fact that they would give it a good start even if I wouldn't ever admit it.

I headed back out into the storm, making sure to lock the door behind me this time and made my way up the hill in the dark, heading for Ash Chambers.

The rain crashed through the canopy of the trees as I stalked through the forest path and my skin prickled as I felt eyes on me.

I kept walking, that sense of being watched growing more and more certain as I climbed the path and moved further and further away from the safety of The Temple.

When I reached the top of the hill, I turned back suddenly and for a moment I was sure I saw movements in the shadows, but it was so dark that I couldn't be certain.

"Come on then!" I bellowed, cupping my hands around my mouth. "If it's justice you're after then come and take it!"

Silence followed my demand and I sneered as the coward remained hidden in the trees, but I felt certain they were out there somewhere, watching me, waiting. A hunter always knew when another predator drew close. But I was the king of beasts and I refused to be frightened by some skulking vulture.

"Then perhaps the next time you strike, you should try and hit me harder?" I suggested. "Because as of right now, the only thing I see when you leave us your little messages and carry out your cowardly plans, is a dead man walking. And you'd better believe I know how to dispose of your corpse once I'm done cutting you apart."

The trees remained silent and the storm howled with more force, so I turned and headed on to Ash Chambers.

I used my key to let myself in as I reached the old building and locked the door behind me again once I was inside, not bothering with the lights as I navigated the familiar hallways in the dark and heading straight for the room set up with my grand piano.

I shed my jacket as I lowered myself onto the bench before the keys and released a slow breath.

When I started playing, Études, Op. 25 by Chopin I threw myself straight into the aggressive, complicated notes. It was a dark and angry piece which spoke to the monster in me all too clearly and helped me vent some of my rage. I intended to stay here all night and play until my fingers were cramping and my bad arm was screaming at me from pushing the muscles too hard.

I wouldn't return to The Temple until the sun had risen and six am had returned. And then I'd start tomorrow with my guard up again and my walls reconstructed with my control over all things thoroughly intact. And I'd be damn certain not to let Tatum Rivers crack it ever again.

But so help me, I was beginning to think her doing so was inevitable. So maybe I was just delaying my fate.

CHAPTER SIXTEEN

"Only if you wear the tutu and stick a corkscrew up your ass while you do a pirouette for me," I muttered, my brain half functioning as a strange noise drove into my skull.

The repetitive scrubbing sound was underlaid with the dulcet tones of some of Saint's music and I groaned as I rubbed at my eyes, rolling upright as I fought to try and wake up. Why was it so fucking difficult to do? My brain was halfway there, but it felt like a battle within myself to even get my eyes to actually open.

"Isn't it funny how you sleep like a baby when people say killers are supposed to be haunted by the memories of the people they've killed and not be able to sleep at all?" Saint's voice came from somewhere close by. His tone was conversational, but the fact that he was talking to me at all right now proved that he was actually still pretty on edge.

I groaned as I swiped a palm down my face and tried to force my eyes open, realising I'd crashed on the couch again last night. "I think it's supposed to be the guilt that keeps people awake," I muttered. "And I've never been one for feeling much of that. Besides, most of the assholes I've killed deserved it and the others...well, they couldn't be avoided. I might not like what I was forced to do to gain my place at Royaume D'élite but I'm not going to feel guilty about surviving."

I opened my eyes just as Saint tossed his scrubbing brush into the bucket of bleach he'd been using to go over our work on the walls that had been graffitied last night. I probably should have been offended by that, but if I was being totally honest, I'd lost interest in scrubbing the walls after an hour and I'd left more than a few spots of red paint behind.

"Well I certainly don't think you should be feeling any guilt. I just find it interesting that sleep evades me and yet it isn't guilt that keeps me up either. It's habit." Saint shrugged and stalked away from me, carrying his bucket of bleach water and dumping it in the sink.

I cast a glance at the gleaming walls and realised he'd given the entire place a go over too. Every inch of the floors, kitchen and even the soft furnishings gleamed and the scent of a mixture of cleaning products perfumed the air. I guessed that was to do with someone else having been in his sanctuary and his need to eradicate all evidence of the fact. No doubt he'd be instructing his maid, Rebecca, to go over it all again later too. That woman had to be a real life saint to be able to keep up with his level of crazy all the time and still have her job. Although he'd once told me that he paid her like five times the going rate for a cleaner and offered up bonuses for extra jobs so I guessed it was worth it for her to deal with a dose of crazy on the side.

I shoved myself off of the couch and headed back to my room as Saint began cleaning the cleaning bucket. And if that wasn't the perfect example of a waste of a fucking life then I didn't know what was, but far be it from me to interrupt his insanity. His brow was furrowed and I could tell something was bothering him, so despite the fact that it was only five thirty in the morning and I never got up at this unholy hour, I decided to head back out and talk to him once I'd taken a piss and cleaned my teeth.

I hooked one of my sketchbooks out from beneath my mattress and grabbed a couple of pencils from my desk before I left my room again, carrying them back to the couch with me.

Saint was standing over the dining table, looking down at his usual spot on it and running his fingers along the grain of the wood thoughtfully.

"If you're wondering whether or not I've fucked our girl on your spot, the answer is no," I taunted as I took my seat. "But now that you've given me the idea, eating her at the table actually makes a lot of sense."

Instead of biting at me, Saint just frowned a little deeper before heading back over to the kitchenette.

He'd clearly been up all night playing piano like some creepy ghost and the exhaustion was weighing on him, but I knew he wouldn't sleep now until his usual time tonight. Maybe being dog tired would work in his favour and let him actually sleep for once anyway.

I flipped open my sketchbook and started drawing while I waited for him to come to me. Dealing with Saint was always a bit like dealing with a feral cat. If you went strolling up to it with kind words and a bowl of fresh fish thinking you were gonna be best buddies, then you were fresh out of luck. Likely it'd just hiss at you, run off and maybe even try to bite you if you persisted. But if you sat quietly and just happened to leave a little fishy morsel down as an invitation beside you, then eventually the kitty would come and nab it.

"This constant rule breaking is going to have to stop," he ground out as he placed two cups of coffee down on the coffee table and dropped into his throne beside me. *Good kitty.*

"Is that so?" I asked in a voice that let him know I had zero plans to keep my dick out of our girl and he was going to have to get used to it.

He pursed his lips, his fist clenching against the arm of the chair and then releasing again slowly before he let the subject drop and moved on to what was clearly bugging him most right now.

I'd already finished the outline of my sketch and I tilted my head, glancing at Saint for a moment before continuing onto the details as the charcoal steadily stained my fingers black.

"Yesterday, before...everything, I found my laptop an inch to the left of its usual position."

"Holy shit, did you call the cops?" I gasped, chuckling loudly as he shot me a death glare.

The music continued to play over the speakers and it slid from one piece to another with perfect synchronicity. Shit, I was starting to really enjoy this classical crap and I swear he'd figured it out because the songs that were playing were all ones I liked. They just seemed to fit me somehow, speaking to me or something. Fuck him.

"Tatum and Monroe had been here alone before that happened," he went on, ignoring my teasing.

"Oh?" I asked casually, hiding a smirk at the corner of my mouth with my thumb. Luckily Saint's gaze was firmly in the depths of his triple espresso, so he didn't notice.

Maybe Monroe had the idea to eat her at the dining table before me.

"I just get the feeling that there's something going on with the two of them that I'm missing," he muttered.

"Mmm." I kept my eyes on the sketch, half tempted to tell him that Monroe had probably been fucking her brains out right over his laptop and advising him to check the keyboard in case any of the keys had been left a bit sticky. But as hilarious as that would have been, I knew it had nothing on what was going to happen when he caught them going at it. Which he would, because this was Saint Memphis and he already smelled a rat. I just hoped it would work out that I'd be there to see his eyes bug out of his head when he found our girl screaming beneath the headmaster, maybe panting 'yes sir' while he promised she wouldn't have to have detention if she just took her punishment like a good girl.

"That's it? You have no further input?" Saint demanded as I started on some shading.

"What do you want me to say, man? Anyone could have knocked your laptop out of its designated position and Nash is one of us now. You're not seriously suggesting him and Tatum are up to something because of that are you?"

Saint released a frustrated breath and shrugged. "I just have an inkling, that's all. I'm missing something here and I know it. When I get to the bottom of it everything will be fine, I'm sure."

"Well, dig deep, brother," I advised him, smirking to myself as he fell into contemplative silence which actually worked out quite well for me as it meant I could check I was getting the angles of his jaw right.

At six fifteen he stood up suddenly and abandoned me where I sat, heading down to the gym to start his morning workout bang on time and no doubt reset the time warp that had made his routine fall to shit last night and make sure that he was in full control again for today. Nice and neat like nothing had ever happened.

I could have headed back to bed, but instead I just stayed where I was, finishing up my sketch and letting my mind focus on the task. I drank the coffee Saint had made me to perk me up a bit more and found I didn't mind the early morning so much for once.

I didn't even notice when Tatum padded down the stairs to make breakfast, her fingers grasping the top of my sketch book the only warning I got of her arrival.

I growled playfully as she tried to tug it from my grip and looked up to find her bare faced and pouting in my black band t-shirt.

"Can I see?" she asked, her voice husky from lack of use and getting me all hot and bothered.

"Anything for you, baby," I agreed with a mocking smile as I released the book and she flipped it around to get a look.

"Kyan...shit, you're crazy talented," she murmured as she took in the sketch of her and Saint standing out in the lake last night, the rain pouring down on them as they stared at each other with so much intensity that I swear I could still feel those emotions rolling off of them now.

"It's yours if you want it, baby," I joked. "I'll even do you a good deal."

"Does the price have something to do with what you've got hiding beneath your pants?" she asked, rolling her eyes like she already knew the answer to that.

"Funnily enough, it does," I agreed, wondering if she might wanna suck me off before starting on breakfast, but the laugh spilling from her lips said not.

Bet I could convince her though.

"Is Saint okay this morning?" she asked, glancing towards the door that led down to the crypt where the sound of his music was much louder.

"Yeah. He just did a full re-boot and is back to his usual fucked up robot self. No need for you to worry."

She pursed her lips at me like she didn't like me making light of Saint going full Saint and almost destroying the world, but in hindsight I felt it was pretty funny really. No real harm done, everyone got some shit off of their chests, The Temple had a good clean, Saint's piano game was no doubt on top form once again, win win.

"Seriously, baby, don't worry about it. Saint has to lose the plot every now and then so that he has the opportunity to take that stick out of his ass for a few hours and just vent his issues. If he didn't then I believe his head would legitimately explode one of these days. It's all good. I think in a fucked up way he actually likes going off his rocker too. It reminds him he isn't a robot after all. He's a big boy with real feelings and a cock that hungers for a taste of his girl just like any normal, red blooded man."

"The way he is about the rules..." she began like she really did want to understand him better and I sighed as I took the sketchbook from her hands and laid it down on the coffee table, still open on the page with the sketch of her and Saint. That was the kind of Saint bait that might just start a war. He hated anything which documented him losing his shit and I was pretty certain that a sketch of him dripping wet and looking at our girl like the whole world began and ended with her would earn me another beating. But I was always up for that. And if he shredded my art for good measure then so be it. Worth it.

"Saint's stories are his own to tell," I said as I got up and followed her over to the kitchenette where she began to prepare breakfast. "But I can say that rules are what he used to make sense of the world when things were taken from him that were out of his control. If you want an easy life with him then just do as he says. Though I personally feel that pushing him to test the rules isn't a bad thing. It helps him to see that things don't always have to be under his control even if he finds life easier when they are."

"I guess it doesn't matter so long as he's okay," she mused as she got the pan ready to start cooking up some eggs. Luckily for Saint, there were still regular food deliveries being made to the school and Monroe had even started adding some of our specific requests to the orders to make sure that we could keep eating the things we liked. There were some shortages which were hard to get hold of, but money talked so Saint had just started paying the extra for any additional items he wanted and that meant his eggs and avocado were still on the menu.

I moved up close behind Tatum as she worked, my fingers brushing up the lengths of her thighs and leaving black trails from the charcoal behind as she laughed and half heartedly swatted me away. But every time she did, I just growled and moved into her space more, my fingers moving to graze the inside of her thighs, sweep down her neck, slipping inside her shirt to seek out her nipple.

It wasn't quite enough to stop her from preparing the food, but as her breaths grew heavier, I knew it was having the desired effect.

Saint emerged from the crypt, shirtless and gleaming with sweat. His gaze slid over the black marks the charcoal had left all over Tatum's thighs and I smirked at him tauntingly as he growled with irritation.

"Good morning," Tatum said, knocking my hands away again as she took a step towards Saint, but he only nodded before turning and heading for his room.

As he went, I noticed the dark bruising over his ribs where I'd punched him last night and had to admit that that might have been a bit of an asshole move. But he'd called our girl a whore, so I wasn't sorry about it. And the fact that he hadn't called me out on it either said that he agreed that he'd deserved it too.

Saint paused as he spotted the sketch on the coffee table, his jaw grinding as he picked it up and tore the page from the book.

"Don't!" Tatum shouted as she raced away from me to save the sketch before Saint could hurl it into the fire and to my surprise, he actually paused.

"You like this?" he asked, sneering down at the irrefutable proof that he was human while I chuckled like the asshole I was.

"Yes. Please don't destroy it, Saint." Tatum held her hand out for the page and I waited to watch Saint throw it into the flames anyway like the piece of shit he was, but instead he just frowned at it and slowly handed it over.

"Let's get a frame and hang it over the mantelpiece," I suggested, my grin widening as I waited for him to flip on me.

"That seems like taking things a step too far," Saint replied dismissively, his gaze on Tatum instead of me. "But as you're so clearly in love with me, Kyan, maybe next time I'll pose for you with my cock out so that you can draw yourself something to jerk off over."

He strode away without another word, hurrying up the stairs so that our little interaction didn't fuck up his schedule and I had to call out to him once I'd gotten over the surprise of him not freaking out.

"Yes please, baby. But remember when I fuck you, I'll be the one on top!" I called after him.

He flipped me off over the railing and then the heavy bang of his bathroom door closing stole him away from us.

Tatum grinned triumphantly as she held her prized sketch between her fingers and I couldn't help but smirk too. There was something so damn intoxicating about making that girl smile.

The sound of the lock turning in the door drew our attention and Monroe stepped into The Temple, shaking his head like a dog to displace the moisture in his hair.

"How are things this morning?" he asked as Tatum moved back to start plating up and I hounded after her with determination.

"All good," I reassured him. "Saint is back to his old chipper self, Blake still hasn't emerged from his cave and Tatum here was just asking if the two of us could make her come before Saint gets out of the shower."

"What?" she squeaked, turning to glare at me. "I said no such thing."

"It was implied," I said, grabbing her by the waist and hauling her around to face Monroe as he scowled at me.

"Can you quit with the fucking comments?" he hissed, like he hated me constantly making innuendos about the two of them all the time, but I gave no shits.

"Sure. You just need to get over here and put something in our girl real quick because Saint has a precise ten minutes in the shower and we've probably used up five of them already." I walked Tatum towards him as she squirmed in my hold and I couldn't help but laugh as she tried to punch me in the balls.

"Kyan, stop. We can't take stupid risks, like-"

I tugged her shirt up to reveal her bare pussy and pushed my hand between her thighs.

Nash growled, Tatum whimpered and Saint shut off the fucking shower.

"Damn," I said with a dramatic sigh, taking my hand back and rearranging my shirt around her thighs. "Next time, you guys need to get into position faster."

"Asshole," Tatum chastised, shoving me away from her and Monroe shook his head and stalked away to take his spot at the table.

Blake appeared, scrubbing sleep from his eyes and we helped Tatum plate up before bringing all of the food over to the table, just as Saint reappeared right on time to eat.

All in all, I had to say that things were looking pretty good in Night Keeper world today.

CHAPTER SEVENTEEN

Everything about this day was perfect until my last class of the day when I was hit with the force of a freight train. There was a parcel waiting for me in reception and Mr Jacobs excused me to collect it. I knew in my gut what was waiting for me there and I was terrified to face it.

I didn't hear anything the Night Keepers said to me as I drifted out of my seat and headed for the door. I didn't take in any of the walk as my feet guided me there. And now I couldn't hear the receptionist, Miss Schmidt, as she passed over the cardboard box and I felt the solid weight of it in my hands. Though it wasn't as heavy as I'd expected.

She said something else, but I was already walking away, heading outside into the wind and drizzle which whirled around me. I clutched the box to my chest to keep it dry and found myself walking down the eastern path beside the lake. My chest was being brutally sliced into with a butcher's knife. Every breath I drew in hurt. Every step I took juddered through my body and made my soul rattle.

I made it to the Willow Boathouse as the clouds started to part in the sky, so the drizzle ebbed away until just a cool wind remained. I headed inside, taking the twisting stairway up to the room above. I needed to just hide away and find a way to deal with this. It hurt so bad. Every time I thought I was starting to get used to his loss, something like this just split me open all over again. This day had been so bright, so good. And just like that, it had all gone to hell.

My hands trembled around the box as I moved to the far corner by the window and slid down with my back to the wall, my knees to my chest as I stared out at the balcony and the choppy water of the lake beyond. Tears rolled down my cheeks as I held my dad's ashes, wishing I could hold him for real. Wishing I could smell his familiar scent and watch him nudge his glasses up his nose as they slid down it. I wanted to see his crooked smile and hear his deep laugh. He had been my only constant my entire life, my best friend. And now he was reduced to ash in this box and it seemed everything he was and everything he could have been was compressed within it. His lasting dreams, regrets, his daily routines, his ambitions and hopes. All of it lived inside this small space, waiting to be discarded. And I was tasked with doing it.

I didn't know how long I sat there, or how long I cried, but it was dark outside by the time I looked up again. I knew I had to deal with the messages and calls that were coming in repeatedly on my phone. I couldn't put it off any longer. So I took it out, tapping on the latest text and finding it was from Kyan.

Kyan:
Where are you? We're losing our minds. Please answer me, baby.

My heart tugged with guilt as I realised I'd been here for a couple of hours. The school day was over and the Night Keepers would no doubt think something awful had happened to me considering everything we'd been through lately.

I tapped out a reply, blinking back my tears as I focused on sending my response.

Tatum:

I'm sorry. My dad's ashes arrived. I just need to be alone.

I tucked my phone away again, clutching the box tighter and drawing in a long breath. I fell into myself again, unable to find that safe place within me anymore to escape this slicing pain. Nothing could save me from this emotional turmoil.

After a while footsteps pounded up the stairs and the door opened across the room. I wiped my tears away, figuring I'd need to leave if students started arriving, but then I saw it was Kyan.

His eyes found me like a magnet, and he strode across the room with a fierce expression on his face. Was he angry for me staying away from them? I couldn't deal with it if he was. I wasn't nearly strong enough to have an argument right now.

"I don't need a lecture," I forced out, my voice cracking as he reached me, his shadow surrounding me.

He leaned down, scooping me into his arms without a word and carrying me over to the large table at the back of the room where there was a model of the school filling it. He knocked over a section of trees and sat me down in the bare space, pressing his hands down either side of me as he leaned close to my face.

"I'm not here to lecture you, baby." He captured my chin, tilting my head up to look at him and he took in my puffy eyes and tear-stained cheeks with his brows knitting tightly together.

"I need to be alone," I croaked but he shook his head.

"No, you don't," he said simply. "You need a good man and a warm hug. But you'll have to compromise and take a son of a bitch and a dirty fuck." His joking tone brought a smile to my lips and he sighed. "Ah, there she is." He leaned forward and kissed me sweetly. It wasn't like the way he usually kissed me, with a possessive heat that blazed directly into my soul. This was all giving, no taking. Was Kyan hurting for me?

He looked down at the box clutched in my arms with a dark frown and I glanced away from him, not wanting pity. But I didn't know what it was I did want. Maybe nothing. Maybe to make him leave, or maybe to curl up in his arms. But I was tired of falling apart and stitching myself back together again. It was never ending, exhausting.

"Cremation always seemed like the better option to me," he said thoughtfully and I frowned, my interest piqued by the strange comment.

"Why?" I asked.

"Beats being put in the ground and eaten by worms." He shrugged. "At least you can be sure you're dead when you're burned to a crisp."

I released a breath of amusement. Typical Kyan to think of death like that. "I guess."

"Doesn't really matter either way, I suppose."

"Because you're dead and gone and you're not around to care anymore?" I questioned, my tone bitter as I held the box even tighter protectively. I'd never attended church or really believed in a god as such, but I had hoped that there was something beyond this life. If only to comfort me when I'd lost Jess, so I could write to her and hope that somehow she was getting those messages. But maybe deep down, I knew that that was all it was. A comfort.

"No," he said, shaking his head. "I mean the only thing that matters is how you went out, right? Like for example, I quite like the idea of dying in a fiery blaze of gunfire. Seems like your old man went out in a pretty epic way."

He was so frank about it all, it somehow worked to stop me falling apart again. Made me see it in a new way I'd never considered, even if it still came to the same thing. "I guess..."

"Naw baby, think about it. There's a million ways to die and he got a Viking's death. If Valhalla exists, he's drinking mead with the gods now out of a golden chalice."

"*Kyan*," my voice broke as more tears spilled over. I was smiling though, the image he painted giving me something good to focus on.

"Tatum," he said heavily, leaning in to kiss my tears away. "You should really stop crying. Your tears make me bloodthirsty and I might go on a killing spree around campus. There'll be so many bodies, baby, and I don't want more blood on your hands."

A laugh bubbled up in my throat and he growled approvingly at that noise, rubbing his nose against mine.

"C'mere." He pulled me to my feet, wrapping his arm around my shoulders and guiding me to the balcony door. We stepped out into the fresh air and I gazed up at the now clear sky, an endless expanse of stars staring down at us from above.

We walked to the edge of the balcony and I just stared up at the impossibly large universe stretching out above me, reminding me of how small I was and yet my pain felt big enough to fill it all up.

"Someone once told me the people you love become stars and watch over you after they die," Kyan said and I glanced at him in surprise. "I beat the crap out of him to prove him wrong and showed him that even his dead grandma didn't care. But I kinda like the concept all the same."

I snorted a laugh and he looked down at me with a smirk. *Oh Kyan.* It was somehow the perfect thing to say because it made the weight in my chest lessen and the crushing grief lose its grip on me a little.

Kyan tugged me closer beneath his arm as the cold wind tore around us. Spring was on its way, but winter was putting up a good fight. I guessed that was how loss was too. Life always kept moving, even when you expected it to stand still or for the world to wither around you. Everything just kept moving forward and dragging you along with it. But letting go of this pain felt like a betrayal. Moving on felt like he didn't matter. And I was determined that he would *always* matter.

I shivered as the cool wind bit at the bare flesh above my knee high socks.

"You cold, baby? I'll get you warmed up," he growled.

"I'm not in the mood, Kyan," I sighed and he stiffened.

"I didn't mean sex." He turned me to face him, opening his blazer and wrapping it around me so his body heat enveloped me. My dad's ashes were held between us and he didn't press too firmly against me, making sure they weren't squashed. "I don't want you to think that's all this is for me."

"I don't think that," I said earnestly, but he was still frowning. "I can feel that it's more than that."

"Well...I wanna prove it too," he said seriously. "I've never felt like this about anyone. I'd die for you, baby. And I don't mean that in some bullshit romance movie kinda way, I mean it. I'd take a knife under my ribs for you all the way to my heart." The fire in his eyes made my lips fall open and I reached up, tracing my fingers over his face to memorise the way he looked right now. Like a monster who'd just been handed back his soul.

"I'd do the same for you, Kyan. If anything ever happened to you, I..." I shook my head, the idea making my heart clench and panic cleave my chest apart.

"Nothing will happen to me," he growled. "I'm ninety nine percent of people's worst nightmare."

"But the last one percent are all the dangerous assholes you've probably pissed off," I teased and he gave me a lopsided grin.

"That's why I carry a knife." He smirked and I shook my head at him.

He leaned down to kiss me and I let myself get lost in the slow movements of his tongue, the gentle way he touched me for once. This was all so new to us both and I could sense how deeply he really wanted to prove that this wasn't just some fling.

"My pa once told me the only things worth loving in life were the things you could rely on to be there forever. Like pay-per-view porn and mediocre coffee."

I breathed another laugh. "Your family really knew how to raise a kid."

"Yeah, luckily Martha took on a hefty chunk of the role or I'd probably be jerking off into a shitty cup of joe right now instead of holding my girl in my arms," he joked and I smiled at him. "Then I'd have to gut him for making me miss out on you."

"You wouldn't realise I was missing from your life if that was the case," I pointed out.

"Naw, I missed you my whole life, Tatum Rivers. That hole in me would have just gotten wider and wider, filled with whiskey and second rate pussy until I put a gun to my head out of sheer boredom."

"Jesus, don't say that." I smacked his arm and he grinned widely.

"I won't sweeten the truth. Not ever." He shrugged then pushed his fingers into my hair as he gazed at me, drinking me in. "And the filthy, rotten core of it is…you're the best thing that's ever happened to me. And I won't let you go. I'm your captor, baby, but you're mine too. And I say we both throw away the key and stay in each other's cages forever."

"I don't even understand how they can be all over her like that. Especially Blake. His mom *died* from the Hades Virus for god's sake," Pearl Devickers' voice carried to me from the stacks as I sat in my favourite spot in the library by the large window that overlooked the lake.

Mila looked up as she heard her too, frowning at me across the table. We were out of sight here, their conversation clearly meant to be private.

"I know," Georgie huffed. "There go my dreams of being prom queen with Kyan Roscoe."

"Firstly, *I'd* be prom queen," Pearl jested. "And Blake would be my king. I'd pick Saint, but I'm not really into freaky stuff and Candice Norrington said he fucked her mouth so hard two years ago that she had to get her tonsils removed after and *still* has problems swallowing. Not my bag."

My hand was tight around my pen and Mila gave me an expression that told me to ignore them. But screw that.

"Maybe this is all some long term plan. Like they're gonna make her fall in love with them then rip her heart out by hosting an orgy for every girl in school at The Temple," Georgie suggested and they both fell into hysterics.

"You're right, it has to be that," Pearl agreed.

"I guess they could be taking pity on her since her dad died though," Georgie said thoughtfully.

"The guy was a psycho who unleashed a fucking plague on the world. She's trapped us all in this place until they find a vaccine. And frankly, I'm not sticking any kind of shit in my body even if they do come up with one. The government will use it as an opportunity to put trackers on all of us."

I stood up, rounding the corner into the stacks as I lost my cool and Georgie's eyes widened as she spotted me, making Pearl wheel around to find me there behind her.

"Why would the government want to track you, Pearl?" I asked icily. "I'm sure they have far more important things to be doing than watching you take multiple trips to the Botox clinic."

"Have you been eavesdropping on us, *Plague*?" Pearl hissed at me.

"It's hard to miss your shrill voice when you're standing within five feet of me." I strode toward her and was pleased when she cowered, backing into Georgie in alarm. "If you talk about my Night Keepers, my dad, or me again, I'll have you outcast into the Unspeakables."

Her powder pink lips fell open. "You don't have the power."

"Want a bet?" I growled, taking my phone from my pocket and making a show of me bringing up Saint's number to call.

"Okay, okay," Pearl blurted. "But it's not like I'm saying anything the whole school doesn't know anyway."

Georgie tried to hush her, but Pearl clearly didn't have as much control over her tongue, even with this threat hanging over her. I wouldn't actually do it. Pearl might have been a rude bitch, but she hadn't done anything that would serve her a place amongst the Unspeakables.

"I'm going to say this once and if I hear you contradicting it again, I'll make the call to Saint and make sure you're named Liar as an Unspeakable."

I got into her personal space, my upper lip peeling back. "My dad is innocent. The Night Keepers know that as well as I do."

I turned my back on her, about to stalk away when her foolish tongue ran away with her once again.

"*Was* innocent," she corrected, her voice biting, aimed to hurt. "You can't talk about dead people in the present tense."

I wheeled towards her with a snarl and she tried to run, shrieking as she shoved Georgie aside and high-tailed it down the aisle. I took chase after her as rage coursed through me, catching a handful of her raven hair and yanking her backwards. She screamed like a banshee as I threw her up against the shelves and books came tumbling down around her.

"Miss Gaskin!" she screamed for the librarian and I smacked her hard across the face, leaving a pink handprint across her cheek.

The librarian appeared in a fluster wearing a garish knitted sweater with a creepy ass looking rhino on the front of it and stared between us in alarm.

"Miss Rivers, what are you doing?" she gasped.

"Nothing," I said simply, lying straight to her face as I stepped away from Pearl.

"She hit her!" Georgie wailed overdramatically and I rolled my eyes.

I looked to Miss Gaskin, folding my arms and waiting for my punishment, refusing to apologise for it.

"Now, now, I'm sure Miss Rivers wasn't doing anything of the sort, were you?" the librarian asked, her eyes flickering with fear. *Holy shit.*

I shrugged and that was apparently good enough as she ushered Georgie and Pearl away. "Go back to work, don't bother Miss Rivers."

My jaw practically hit the floor as they walked away and I was left with a sense of power that could only have been gifted to me because of my association with the Night Keepers.

"Fuck me, girl," Mila's voice came from behind me and I turned, giving her a bemused look. "I want your super powers."

I laughed. "Well, apparently it just takes being Night Bound to do it.

You wanna go touch the Sacred Stone?"

"Hell no," she laughed then checked her watch. "But I do have to head off."

"Oh have you got plans?" I asked.

"Kinda… see you later, girl." She hurried away, seeming distracted and I frowned after her in surprise, wondering what she was up to.

I dropped back into my seat and looked out at the rain hammering against the window. Football practice probably wasn't much fun right now. The guys had told me to wait here to meet them and walk back together, but they wouldn't be done for another forty minutes and I only had a few paragraphs left of my paper to write.

I finished it up soon enough and packed my things away, figuring I'd head back to The Temple and run a bath. I dreamed of sinking into the heated water and got carried away with the idea of the four of them coming home and finding me there, the door open, bubbles foaming over my flesh. Not that Monroe could join in on that fantasy, and Saint clearly would never come close to crossing that line again. But hell, a girl could dream. And Blake and Kyan would certainly be game...

I pulled the hood up on my coat as I headed outside, the librarian waving enthusiastically at me as I went. It made me wonder if the Night Keepers had something on her or if she was just terrified of invoking their ire. Either way, I guessed she had my back.

The rain hammered down on me and I ducked my head as I jogged along to the main path and started heading up the eastern shore of the lake. The trees were swaying hard in the storm and the wind was howling up on the mountain. There were no other students around, everyone taking shelter from this crazy weather.

I gave up trying to keep my hood up as it was blown back again and again, giving in to the rain as it beat down on me and soaked my hair. The bath idea was sounding even better now. Maybe I could get my hands on some chocolate and wine in the crypt too and make a cosy evening out of it.

Movement amongst the trees to my left made my heart judder and I looked over into the shadows dancing between them, increasing my pace even though I saw nothing there. Toby was well under heel now, so I was sure I didn't have to worry about anything…I just had the uncomfortable feeling of being watched.

But there was nothing there and surely my imagination was just getting carried away? I had plenty of reason to fear shifting shadows in the dark nowadays. I just wished I didn't feel so jumpy.

I turned back to face the path and slammed to a halt as I saw a figure a hundred yards ahead, dressed in black with a bone white mask over their face. From here, it was impossible to tell if they were male or female, but their frame looked fairly slight. Fear cascaded through me as they stood statue still, just staring at me. There was something long and curved in their hands, but I couldn't tell what it was. I fumbled my phone out of my pocket, panic racing through me as I brought up Monroe's number and hit dial. He was the only one likely to have his phone on him during practise. I looked up as I held it to my ear and found the path was now vacant. *Shit.*

The rings sounded again and again in my ear and I started walking along the path once more, but slower this time, fearing how close I was coming to the place where that weirdo had just been. If they were trying to scare me, it was working. But why? And who was it? They looked too small to be Toby. So what did that mean? Did I have some other enemy to fear? The freaking Justice Ninja??

My heart thrashed in my chest as I reached the spot where they'd been standing and I turned, looking into the trees, spotting fresh boot prints there in the mud.

I wanted to run and run until I was safe deep inside The Temple. But more than that, I wanted to expose this asshole and stand my ground. I'd faced real demons, looked my death in the eye, lost my only family. I wouldn't run from this creep.

"Who are you?!" I shouted, my voice lost a little to the storm, but if they were close, watching, then they'd hear me. "Come out here and face me!"

The phone suddenly answered and I jumped as Monroe spoke in my ear. "Tatum?" he asked anxiously.

"Hey," I breathed, a shiver gripping my spine. "There's some asshole out here trying to scare me."

"Where are you?" he growled fiercely.

"On the east shore. About a hundred yards from the turning to Beech House."

"Go there, back to your old room. We're coming," Monroe said firmly and I agreed before hanging up.

I started hurrying along the path, my neck prickling with the feeling of being watched. Hunted…

"Taaatuuum," an eerie voice called, the sound distorted like it was played back through some sort of voice changer. My pulse skipped at the horrid, raspy crackle of it coming from behind me.

I glanced over my shoulder and my stomach clenched into a tight knot as I saw the figure standing there again fifty yards away, this time with a bow and arrow raised in their hands, the tip of the arrow alight with flames.

I screamed in fright as they loosed the arrow, diving off the path and a blaze of fire in my periphery told me that it had barely missed me. I raced into the trees, my shoes sinking into the mud as I climbed the hill that led deeper into the forest, desperate to get away. *Oh fuck fuck fuck!*

"Taaatuuum," that awful voice sounded again, the cracking of twigs behind me telling me I was being followed. And for a second it sounded like there was more than one set of footsteps.

A whoosh of another arrow made me scream again and this one slammed into a tree to my left, the flames hissing as it sank into the wet bark. *Holy fuck.*

Terror gripped me as I pushed myself harder, climbing the hill and finally making it to the top before hurrying down the other side. I stumbled down the steep ground in the dark, unable to see where I was going and my foot suddenly caught in a root. I gasped as I tumbled, falling forward and crashing down the hill, getting caked in mud.

I sank into the wet bog at the bottom of it with a groan, shoving myself up onto my knees as I prepared to keep running. A fiery arrow slammed into the ground just beside my hand and I jerked backwards, staring up the hill where the figure stood, another arrow aimed down at me and their bone white mask covering their whole face, the light flickering over it.

"What do you want?!" I snarled, forcing power into my voice so I didn't sound like a scared little mouse as they pointed that arrow at me.

My muscles were coiled. I was ready to leap out of the way the moment they loosed it, but if I moved too soon, they'd predict it and I'd be dead.

They spoke and their voice came out through that horrible voice changer, making a shudder of fear roll through me. "Justice." They shot the arrow and I screamed, diving aside but it scored across my forearm, taking a chunk of skin with it before it hit the earth and the fire went out.

I was on my feet about to run, but a fierce shout cut through the air. "Tatum!?" Monroe bellowed followed by the rest of the Night Keepers calling for me. My phone was buzzing in my pocket and as I looked up, the asshole on the hill turned into the woods and fled.

I started running up the bank, desperate to get to my men, my teeth clenched in fury as hot blood ran down my arm, mixing with the icy rain. As I reached the top, a weight collided with me and I screamed as someone tackled me to the ground, finding myself looking up at Blake. "I got the Justice Ninja!" he cried.

"It's *me* you idiot!" I snapped and he lifted his head, turning his phone towards my face so the flashlight on it illuminated me.

"Oh, fuck," he growled. "Are you okay? You're covered in mud. And shit, are you bleeding?" He got off of me, dragging me upright and aiming the light at my arm, tearing my sleeve open to get a better look.

I hissed as I saw the uneven slice through my forearm just as the other three guys arrived. The look of abject rage in their eyes as they spotted the blood turned into a violent energy that cloaked all of them in hate.

"Someone was hunting me. They had a fucking bow and arrow," I explained, my voice unsteady as they circled around me like wolves.

"Which way did they go?" Saint hissed and I pointed before he and Kyan immediately took off in that direction.

Blake tugged me into his chest, crushing me close for a moment as a dark growl escaped him.

"Did you get a good look at them?" Monroe snarled, venom pouring from him as he stood there, his eyes saying he wanted to rip me out of Blake's arms and hold me himself.

I shook my head. "They wore dark clothes and a white mask."

"Bait?" Blake snapped immediately but I shook my head.

"It was a full mask," I said. "And they weren't too big, but it could have been a guy or a girl. I'm not sure."

"Fuck," Monroe spat as Blake's hand curled over my wound and gripped tight to stem the bleeding. "Let's get back to the path."

They walked either side of me like warriors marching me down the hill and back onto the path beyond the trees. Being in the light of the lanterns made me feel a bit better, but I was thoroughly shaken. Had that asshole been trying to kill me? Or just scare me?

I shuddered, leaning into Blake, while aching to reach out and drag Monroe closer too. Saint and Kyan burst out of the trees a minute later, their eyes full of fury.

Saint strode toward me, fixing me with a hard stare. "Who knew you were at the library tonight? Who saw you?"

"There were plenty of people at the library. Pearl and Georgie were there." I shrugged. "I was working with Mila, but she left."

"Was Pearl still there when you left?" Blake snarled and I nodded, pretty sure of it.

"Pearl hasn't got the braincells to pull this off," Saint hissed. "But Mila...why did she leave before you?"

"I don't know...she left kind of abruptly. But that doesn't mean anything," I said. "It could have been anyone at the library or someone else who saw me heading there earlier." It was still raining and even with my four guys surrounding me, I'd rather have had this conversation while we were walking back to The Temple, but it was clear they weren't going to just let this go. And it wasn't like I wanted to either, but standing out here in the freezing rain wasn't doing us any good.

The four guys shared a look that made my stomach churn.

"So she just happened to leave before you did, for no good reason?" Saint gritted out.

"You can't actually be suggesting she'd do this," I demanded. "It wasn't Mila."

"Seems like there's only one way to be sure," Kyan murmured darkly, turning and heading off down the path at a brisk pace.

We all marched along behind him and anger curled through me at the insinuation that Mila could be responsible for this.

"Listen to me. It wasn't her," I impressed, but none of them responded.

We headed up the path to Beech House and Kyan practically kicked the door down as he shoved his way inside. We were close behind him and my lips parted at the sight of the muddy boot prints in the hall, but whoever had been wearing them had evidently taken them off, perhaps carried them away. Even the fact that they were fresh prints didn't prove anything though. Someone could have just gotten back from a run or detention.

Kyan led the way upstairs and Blake kept me close as they marched up the stairs and stormed down the hall to my old room. Kyan hammered his fist on the door and Mila tugged it open a beat later, her eyebrows shooting up as she found us all standing there, suddenly under the intense scrutiny of the Night Keepers. She had a silver robe wrapped around her and her hair was damp like she'd taken a recent shower...or been out in the rain.

"What's going on?" she gasped as Kyan shouldered her aside and started tearing her room apart. "What the fuck are you doing!?"

I pulled away from Blake, catching Mila's hand and she took in my bedraggled appearance in alarm.

"What the hell happened, Tatum?" she asked, her eyes glimmering with worry as she saw the cut on my arm.

"Some asshole attacked me," I hissed. "They suspect it was you." I rolled my eyes and her jaw dropped in fright as Monroe and Saint headed into her room too, their filthy football cleats trailing mud everywhere.

"I didn't! Why would they think that?" she gasped in horror.

"I'm sorry." I shook my head, my heart tugging. "Just let them search the place and they'll realise it wasn't you, okay?"

Mila agreed, moving closer to me just as Danny came jogging up the stairs, soaked and carrying a rose between his teeth. It fell from his mouth as he spotted us there and Blake turned to him with his eyes narrowed. "Go back to your room, Danny."

"What's going on?" he asked, walking closer instead of listening to Blake's order.

Blake moved in front of him, barring his way to Mila. "Go the fuck home."

"It's okay, Danny," Mila pressed. "They'll be gone soon."

Danny's jaw locked and he stared at Mila with need in his eyes. "I'm not going anywhere. What the fuck is going on?"

"Where did you hide them?" Saint stepped out of the room, his eyes narrowing on Mila, his expression terrifying.

"Hide what?" she gasped.

"Saint, she didn't do it," I snapped, my blood heating. "Let's just go."

"We're not leaving until we get an answer," Kyan growled as he stepped out of the room behind Saint, cracking his knuckles. "Where did you hide the mask and the boots, Mila?"

"What are you talking about?" Mila clung to my arm, evidently thinking I could save her from them, and I hoped I could.

I moved forward to shield her, glaring between the four of them. "She didn't do it. I trust her."

"Says the girl who trusted the Unspeakables." Saint sneered and my upper lip peeled back. "Get her, Kyan."

"Wait!" I cried. "You can't do anything to her, it says so in the rules. I can have one friend you can't target. And that's her."

Saint considered that and Kyan snorted, but he waited for Saint's answer all the same.

"Needs must, Tatum," he growled. "Whoever hurts her can be punished afterwards when it's done."

"No!" I screamed as Mila backed away in fear.

Kyan strode forward, pushing me into Monroe's chest and he treacherously locked his arms around me to keep me from interfering again. Kyan pushed Mila towards the stairs and Blake moved to her other side before Saint took up position behind her like they were arresting a prisoner of war.

"Stop it!" I yelled and a couple of doors opened along the hall as girls ducked their heads out to see what was going on. As soon as they spotted the Night Keepers, they shut their doors again and locks clicked firmly into place.

I wriggled in Monroe's hold and he twisted me around in his arms, holding me close so I was forced to look at him. "They're going to do this, princess. We need to be sure. Let it be."

"She's my friend!" I shouted, yanking out of his grip and running after them.

Monroe was hot on my heels, but he wasn't fast enough to catch me as I made it downstairs and sped outside.

Mila was on her knees in the mud before Saint, Blake and Kyan, the light from the dorms pouring out onto the ground as students gathered at their windows to watch. Mila's robe had fallen half off her shoulders, revealing part of a strappy leather outfit I guessed she'd bought to wear for Danny. Danny was being held away from her by Blake, curses streaming from his lips as he fought to get free.

"Stop it!" I screamed, running forward, but Monroe caught up with me, latching an arm around my stomach and the other across my shoulders, locking his muscles tight so I was immobilised against him.

Kyan unbuckled his belt, staring down at Mila while Saint stood beside him with his arms folded.

"Tell us the truth and you can save yourself a golden shower," Kyan warned and I gasped.

"Kyan!" I screamed as he freed his cock and started pissing on the ground in front of Mila, moving the stream towards her like a damn laser in a James Bond movie. "You fucking asshole, stop it!"

Saint walked behind Mila, resting his hands on her shoulders as she tried to scramble away from the flow, holding her still. "The truth," he snarled. "Or trust me, you will face far worse than a bath in Kyan's piss before the night is through."

"I didn't do it, I swear - I swear it!" she cried and I hated seeing her like that.

"Then why did you leave the library so fast, huh?" Kyan demanded.

"Because…" She glanced at Danny then back to Kyan as she slid her robe further off her shoulders, revealing the leather outfit she was in which was made up entirely of complicated straps. "I wanted to surprise Danny in this. But I knew it would be a bitch to get on."

Kyan laughed darkly and Saint shot him an icy look.

"Can anyone prove you were here the whole time?" Saint demanded.

"I was in the shower five minutes ago. Nancy saw me." She turned her head to scream up at one of the windows. "Nancy! Tell them!"

We all looked up at the building and Danny took the opportunity to jam his elbow into Blake's gut, breaking free of him and tearing towards Mila. Kyan didn't even stop pissing as he turned and floored him with a furious punch to the head, knocking him flat on his back.

"No!" Mila screamed, reaching for Danny but wincing back as Kyan pissed in her direction to keep her away from him.

He sighed as he finally ran out of juice, tucking himself away and beckoning Blake over. "I'm out bro, and there's no sign of Nancy who-fucking-knows."

Blake rolled his zipper down and I jerked against Monroe's hold, stamping on his feet as I tried to force him to let me go, but he just wouldn't.

"We're going to find out who did this to you no matter what it takes," Monroe breathed in my ear. "If it's not her, then she'll be able to prove it."

Blake started pissing on the ground, picking up where Kyan had left off and Saint watched impatiently, clearly irritated by waiting for Mila to be punished.

A window suddenly pushed open somewhere above and a blonde girl stuck her head out. "Mila was in the bathroom a few minutes ago, I saw her!" she called down. "We were talking for like ten minutes before that too."

My shoulders sagged as relief filled me.

Blake stopped pissing and all the Night Keepers shared a look. Saint nodded, stepping back as he released Mila and she lunged towards Danny on the floor as he groaned.

"He'll be fine, he's being a pussy," Kyan said to Mila as if that counted as an apology somehow.

Monroe released me and I rushed forward with a snarl on my lips. Kyan opened his arms as if he actually expected me to dive into them and I threw a hard punch into his face, sending him stumbling back a step.

He stretched out his jaw, rubbing at the mark I'd left on him with a look of surprise on his face.

"That's for Danny," I growled, then grabbed his shoulders and kneed him in the stomach. "And that's for Mila." I stormed past him towards Blake and he opened his arms as he accepted his punishment before I slammed my fist into his gut and he wheezed.

When I turned, hunting for Saint, I found him and Monroe waiting behind me, ready for their punishments too. I frowned, but didn't hesitate as I punched Saint then Monroe as hard as I could in the chest. I stood panting between them all as they circled around me again, nursing their wounds.

Mila had gotten Danny on his feet and the two of them were kissing like there was no tomorrow.

"I'm sorry," I called to them as they broke apart and Mila looked to me, her features softening.

"At least they trust me now, right guys?" she spoke to the Night Keepers, her jaw tensing.

"Yeah," Blake agreed. "We trust you." He looked to Danny. "Sorry dude." He clapped him on the back and Danny scowled at him.

"Don't be butt hurt about it," Kyan mocked, flexing his fingers which were bruised from the punch. "And you're welcome for the best sex of your life by the way. That's what being a hero earns you." He winked and Danny almost smiled as he snatched Mila's hand and towed her back into the girls' common house to cheers from the watching students.

Saint's hand curled around my arm just below the wound left there by the arrow. "This is unacceptable," he hissed. "When I find who did this, I'll have no mercy."

A shiver went through me at his words and the nods from the others said they agreed. The Justice Ninja was a dead man walking. And so help them, when me and my Night Keepers found them, they were going to *bleed*.

CHAPTER EIGHTEEN

The rest of the week passed without any more signs of the Justice Ninja and little to nothing of interest taking place either. I'd had my night with Tatum but she'd been on what she had named 'the period from hell' so instead of me fucking her brains out, we'd cuddled up and watched some shitty romance movie which made her cry 'in a good way' and had demolished an entire carton of chocolate ice cream.

I'd literally never even come close to doing something like that with a girl before and it had been one of the weirdest and sweetest evenings I think I'd ever had. She'd curled up with a hot water bottle tucked against her belly, snuggled herself beneath my arm and practically purred when I'd rubbed her back for her. I should have been pissed about her making me act soft like that, but I had to admit that it had actually been pretty nice. She'd even told me some stories about her and Jess as kids and though I hadn't shared any soft and fuzzy stories back (mostly because my most prominent early memories involved me watching my uncles torture people while letting me know the best places to inflict pain without actually killing them) it was nice to hear about her life before all of this.

Not that I would have changed anything about what had happened to get her to this place. We were only where we were now because of all of it and even though that made me a selfish motherfucker, I wouldn't change a damn thing.

But by the time it rolled around to my turn to have her in with me again, I was more than happy to take on the challenge of doling out double orgasms to make up for the ones she'd missed.

To make matters even better, it was a Saturday so she could totally go without sleep tonight and make all of my dreams come true.

I had half of my mind on coming up with ideas for that and the other on defeating a hoard of zombies on the Xbox when the sound of my phone ringing interrupted me. Monroe, Blake and Saint had all gone for a run, leaving me and Tatum here alone but as she wanted to catch up on some of her assignments, I'd been left to entertain myself.

The call rang out while I continued to play my game then instantly started ringing again and I cursed as I hit pause, fishing it out from between the sofa cushions and checking the caller ID.

"For fuck's sake," I muttered as I saw my grandpa's name and I sighed as I tried to school my temper enough to be able to talk to him without cursing.

Tatum looked up from her work at the table with a questioning frown and I flashed her a look at the phone before sighing and answering it.

"Good afternoon, lad," Liam's rich voice came down the speaker and my gut tightened in response.

"Afternoon, Grandpa." Fuck, I hated calling him that.

"There's been a little problem with the clean up you ordered for all of those bodies you left in the woods," he said, getting right to the point and I stilled.

"What kind of problem?" Damn, I could have used a cigarette right about now. I didn't know why, but I only ever craved them when I had to interact with this motherfucker.

I hopelessly pushed my fingers into my pockets as if I might miraculously find a pack and looked up as the brush of Tatum's fingers in my hair drew my attention from my search.

She perched on the arm of the couch and slowly stroked her fingers through the dark strands until she'd teased the elastic from it and surprisingly, it alleviated my need to light up as I concentrated on what Liam had to say.

"It turns out that those men you butchered weren't just hired thugs," he said. "They were employed by a mutual friend of ours who has been looking for them with rather a lot of determination."

"Are you saying the clean up wasn't good enough to hide us?" I sneered, knowing it would piss him off for me to suggest that but not giving a crap about it. If his men were incompetent then I wasn't going to sugar coat it.

"Of course not. But the problem is that they know those men were after Donovan Rivers. And one of the men, a guy called Mortez, was apparently a fairly important cog in their operation."

"Just spit it out, old man, I don't see the need for the riddles," I growled as Tatum continued to play with my hair.

"Watch your tone with me, lad," Liam growled and I mentally cursed myself and him.

"I just need to understand what all of this means for me, Grandpa," I added placatingly while hating the fact that I had to make that much effort.

"Well, it turns out that the men were sent by the leader of Royaume D'élite," Liam said casually. "And as you know, a lot of our business dealings are held via that club. I don't want to ruin our working relationship with them. So, I've decided to come clean and offer up a prize valuable enough to clear the debt we now owe them."

A cold, hard knot seemed to tie itself in place in my gut even as he began blathering on about it being the best move for the family and making comments about me having my fun already, because I knew that this wasn't good. Not good at all.

"What prize?" I growled, my gaze flicking to Tatum as she watched me while chewing her bottom lip like she could tell what a bad turn this conversation had taken just from my body language alone.

"Don't worry, I have that all sorted out," he assured me. "All I need you to do is to show up at the club tomorrow to make a formal apology. And bring your little toy, too. Everyone likes to see a pretty face like hers during tense times."

My hand landed on Tatum's knee and I gripped hard enough to bruise, but I didn't care. I needed to feel her there beside me, be sure of the fact that she was solidly present at my side.

"I've already sent Niall to collect the two of you, so it might be worth getting an overnight bag together."

"But-" The line went dead before my protests could even form on my lips and I crushed the phone in my fist as I leapt to my feet and launched it across the room where it skidded across the carpet into a corner.

"Kyan?" Tatum gasped as I began pacing, my mind whirling with all of the possible ways this could work out.

It was clear that this wasn't up for negotiation. Liam had already decided that the price he was going to pay for this debt was the life of the girl I loved. And I knew they'd accept. She was one of the most stunning girls I'd ever seen. Couple that with the fact that she was Donovan Rivers' daughter and I knew exactly what they'd do with her once they had her too. They were going to keep her as a toy for sale in that fucking place. Auction her flesh off to whatever dirty old bastard wanted to fuck the daughter of the man who'd released the Hades Virus into the world and then do it again the next night. And the next. And the next.

"Fuck!" I roared as I paced more frantically, my mind whirling. Niall was already on his way. He'd do whatever the fuck he had to to ensure he took her back with him when he left. If those were Liam's orders then he'd follow them and he wouldn't have even bothered to ask why.

I was going to have to kill him. Which wouldn't be easy, but I'd do it. Family or not, I didn't give a fuck. The link of our blood meant less than shit to me. I'd chosen my own family with the Night Keepers and I would kill everyone and anyone who threatened them.

But that wouldn't be the end of it. Even if I managed to kill Niall, I had eight more uncles, countless cousins, endless hired thugs, all of whom would be sent here one after another until one of them managed to take her. And they'd probably kill the other Night Keepers to punish me for trying to stand against them.

"Kyan? Tell me what's going on," Tatum demanded, stepping in front of me and planting her hands on her hips to stop me from pacing anymore.

I stared down at her with my heart pounding and the rage in my flesh prickling with this deep intensity unlike anything I'd ever known as I silently vowed to protect her with everything I was. But it wouldn't be enough. I knew it. I could give everything, and it wouldn't be enough to stand between her and the O'Briens and this fucked up fate my grandpa had chosen for her.

"My family have realised that the men we killed came from Royaume D'élite," I said, moving closer so that I could take her face between my hands and force her to hold my eye as I delivered the worst of it. "And Liam has decided that rather than try and cover up their involvement and mine, he wants to come clean and pay retribution."

"What's the price?" she asked, her breath catching like she'd already guessed.

"I'll die before I let him sell you to those animals," I snarled, my grip on her face tightening. "There has to be another way. I'll think of another way."

"Kyan..." The fear in her eyes was enough to break me in two and I shook my head defiantly, capturing her lips with mine and kissing her like I was drowning.

She bowed to the demands of my mouth against hers, our tongues warring, breaths panting, my grip bruising and yet none of it fucking mattered. It didn't matter if I was willing to burn the world down for her because Liam O'Brien couldn't be convinced to change his mind. I knew it more certainly than I knew my own heart. Once he had decided on a path, nothing would ever turn him from it, unless it became detrimental to the family.

The fucking family I hated so damn much and which he cared about more than anything in the world. Not the individuals though. He didn't care one iota for our happiness or love. All he cared about was our blood. He'd fight tooth and nail to ensure that no member of our family was ever killed unless it was absolutely necessary. The only exceptions he made were for traitors. But I wasn't a traitor. At least not that he knew. I'd agreed to his terms, to being his puppet in exchange for him leaving the people I cared about alone, but I should have known that that wouldn't really extend to Tatum. He never saw partners as valuable unless they were married in.

My breath caught as my mind snagged on that idea and I pulled back from Tatum, breaking our kiss so suddenly that she stumbled forward a step.

"There might be a way," I said to her, my heart pounding as the idea took root in me and I found that it wasn't just some means to an end - I actually fucking wanted it. I'd never felt anything for a girl the way I did for Tatum. I'd never wanted to keep anything or anyone the way I did her. And I was more than eager to tie her to me in more ways if I could. To make it impossible for her to escape me. "Liam won't touch you if you're family, baby."

"What?" she murmured, frowning at me as the idea I'd had captivated me and I couldn't help but smirk at her.

"Look, I know that I'm a dirty, fucked up son of a bitch and pretty much the last man any girl would really want to tie themselves to for life. But I swear to you, if you say yes to me, I'll spend every day making you laugh and scream and moan my name and I'll bathe myself in the blood of any and every motherfucker who ever so much as looks at you wrong."

"What the hell are you going on about, Kyan?" she asked, half a laugh escaping her lips at my words even as her blue eyes were still filled with concern.

I leaned forward and kissed her hard, stealing the breath from her lungs and using it to fuel this madness which had struck me. I moved my mouth to her jaw, carving a line down her throat and biting down on her collar bone before dropping onto one knee before her.

"Marry me," I said as her full lips parted and she stared down at me like I was insane.

"Kyan... What?"

"Marry me, baby, do it because you own me and I own you and you never want it to fucking end. But do it *today* because you wanna live and the only way Liam will spare you now is if you're an O'Brien by marriage."

Tatum half shook her head, biting down on her bottom lip as she considered my insane request. "But if I marry you, I'll be a Roscoe, not an O'Brien-"

"My mom is an O'Brien, that's all Liam cares about. I'd have the name too if they hadn't needed me to take Roscoe from my father so that I can use his businesses to front their money laundering. To him, everyone with his blood is an O'Brien and everyone who marries in is too."

I tugged the ring from my little finger. It was a platinum skull with diamonds set into its eyes which I'd mostly bought because I'd known that Saint would hate it and I'd been utterly correct in that assumption. If she let me marry her with this thing and wore it forevermore, he was going to lose his shit in a spectacular fashion.

I caught Tatum's left hand in mine and looked into her eyes as I pushed it onto her finger, my pulse spiking as I realised she was really letting me do it. I'd never actually imagined I'd ever do this with a girl, let alone give a shit about her answer, but the way it felt to place my ring on her finger was making me smile like a fucking idiot.

"This is fucking crazy," she breathed.

"I'm gonna need a yes from those lips, baby."

She kept me waiting way too fucking long for that answer but when she gave it, my racing heart actually tried to leap out of my goddamn chest.

"Yes."

I growled hungrily as I shoved myself back to my feet and kissed her again, loving the way her arms felt as they wound around my neck and she tugged me closer like she was just as exhilarated about this as I was. Yeah it was insane, it was fucking absurd, but it was also a solid fucking plan.

That kiss was a promise of something so much more than a get out of jail free card. I could taste the want in her and I was sure she could feel the need in me too. This was more than just us signing some piece of paper and exchanging rings and bullshit vows. I was all in with this and it felt like she was too by the way she tugged me closer like she was trying to taste my soul.

I forced myself to pull back, smirking at her like the cockiest asshole who ever lived. "Your aunt is your legal guardian, right? We just need to get her to sign off on it as you're a minor and-"

"I'm not," Tatum interrupted me. "My birthday was actually a few weeks ago. I just didn't want to make a fuss over it."

I narrowed my eyes at her even though this was technically a good thing, but not telling us about her birthday was just plain wrong.

"You just let your birthday slip by without celebrating it?" I asked her, arching an eyebrow and she rolled her eyes at me.

"That seems like the least of our concerns right now," she pointed out as she spun the ring on her finger. It was still too big for her, but I'd do something about getting it resized after I made her my wife. Fuck, the others were gonna flip out. But I didn't even give a shit. This was the only answer to this problem and I had no issue at all with making her mine in another way.

A heavy knock sounded at the door and I cursed as I quickly shoved Tatum away from the windows, pushing her into the shadows in the area beneath Saint's bedroom and pressing a finger to my lips.

I hurried over to the safe hidden beneath a flagstone by the door to the crypt and tugged it open, entering the code and taking Tatum's gun from it.

I tossed the weapon to her and she caught it, quickly checking it was loaded like she'd done it a thousand times before and then holding it ready as I moved to the door.

I had my hunting knife at my belt and if I had to use it on my uncle, I would. But this whole thing would go a lot fucking smoother if I didn't have to. For a start, Liam would be less than pleased if I killed an O'Brien while working to fuck him over with this marriage and that could be a big enough betrayal to sign my death warrant on its own. It wasn't worth the risk. So if I had to stab him, I'd be aiming for something not too vital then hog tying him somewhere out of sight until after the wedding.

But I was hoping it wouldn't come to that. Niall was actually the one member of my family who I might just stand a chance of turning to my side on this and I was going to have to hope I could convince him.

I tugged the door open, not even batting an eye at my uncle's wide grin as he stood there with his arms wide like he expected a hug or something. His frame was as broad as mine though he was fair where I was dark and the tattoos that marked his flesh had more colour than mine in them too. He had a scar over his right eyebrow which I'd never gotten an actual story for and the darkness swirling in his eyes always made me feel like an innocent little choir boy by comparison. Even so, I was going to stand against this hell dog for my girl and make him see my side of this or I'd take my chances against the darkness in him for her if that was what it took.

"Kyan, lad!" he greeted enthusiastically.

"I know why you're here Niall," I said to him, seriously hoping my girl wasn't going to have to splatter his brains on the walls as his smile widened. "And I have a counter offer."

It had taken me less than ten minutes to convince my uncle to agree to my plan to marry my girl instead of selling her to a bunch of filthy old men like a piece of meat. For a deranged psychopath, Niall actually had some seriously strong feelings about rapists and he'd cut off more than a few sets of balls over the years to prove it so as I'd been hoping it hadn't been that hard to sell him on the idea.

I knew it had something to do with what had happened to his wife years ago, but I also knew better than to ask for the details of that story. All it really came down to was that there used to be a family called the Nelsons who went up against the O'Briens at every turn. They'd taken Niall's wife as part of a strike against us and in the resulting backlash, he'd wiped out every last one of them. But she'd already been dead by the time he got to her. I could only imagine that there was enough evidence there to let him know that they'd been raping her before the end and that was where his hatred stemmed.

I couldn't remember him that well from before it had happened but everyone in our family said that was what had unhinged him. And the man I knew was definitely unhinged alright, like the kind of chaotic and unpredictable that often ended with someone getting stabbed with an unexpected object and left to bleed out with no warning.

So despite the fact that I knew that he was absolutely the most likely of my uncles to kill me one day, he was also my favourite. The only one amongst my entire family who gave me any reason at all to believe he had something more to him than just hate and violence.

It also helped that he loved fucking with plans and changing course from the obvious narrative so of course, he'd been more than happy to let me fuck up Liam's scheme so long as I was happy to take the full blame for my decision. Which I was.

I'd decided to do the dishonourable thing as far as the other Night Keepers went and had sent a single text to the group message telling them that we'd be back later and then I'd left my cell phone on the dining table beside Tatum's and walked out before they got back from their run.

We didn't have time to dick around with hurt feelings and arguments over this being fair or any of that shit because it would all come to the same thing anyway. To protect Tatum from Liam she had to be my wife and we only had a few hours to make that happen.

So as we shot down the highway on my bike, Tatum's arms wrapped tight around my waist as we chased Niall's blacked out SUV towards the city,

I couldn't help but laugh at the turn of events.

Niall was leading the way to St Mary's, the huge Catholic Church where every member of our family had gotten married for the last three generations and where I assumed we were going to get the priest to do us a quickie wedding without any notice. Luckily enough, Father Bernard was well used to accepting donations to his church for all kinds of strange situations that the O'Briens threw his way, so I was sure he would be amenable to it.

Before we made it to the church, Niall pulled his car down a side road and drew to a halt outside a bridal shop. That hadn't been in the plans, but as I considered the idea of Tatum putting on a white dress for me, I decided I liked that a hell of a lot, so I made no complaints.

Tatum squeezed my waist tighter as we looked around at the empty streets while Niall made quick work of forcing the door and I turned my attention to check further down the road to make sure no one was coming.

"Wait here a second, baby," I said, climbing off the bike and heading over to the store. All of the businesses were closed due to the lockdown restrictions for the Hades Virus and I kept my helmet on with my visor down as I moved along the front window of the bridal store.

Of course, Tatum ignored me, shoving me aside as I made a move to follow Niall inside. He'd already disabled the alarm and had the door open and I couldn't help but be quietly impressed by his work.

"If I'm getting a dress then I'm going to be the one picking it," Tatum hissed at me. "You go upstairs and find a suit. I'm not marrying you in a pair of jeans and a wifebeater."

I barked a laugh as she moved away into the store and Niall pointed out a sign for menswear that directed me up the stairs.

I made quick work of selecting a suit. It wasn't like I didn't know how to dress up when I had to, it just wasn't really my preference.

Tatum was waiting by the bike when I made it back downstairs and Niall took the suit I'd chosen from me, tossing it in the back of his car alongside a white dress bag that made it impossible for me to get so much as a glimpse of what she'd selected but made my heart beat faster at the idea of finding out.

"You're getting into this, aren't you, baby?" I teased as she slid back onto the bike behind me and she scoffed lightly.

"I only plan on getting married once, Kyan Roscoe, so I'm going to look hot as fuck for it. Besides, you strike me as a secret romantic and I can't wait to see you tear up at the sight of me walking down the aisle."

I barked a laugh as we took off down the street again and her arms closed tight around my waist as I gave the bike a shot of power and raced towards the church behind Niall. The empty streets certainly made speeding a lot easier and we were somehow lucky enough to avoid any patrolling police vehicles who were out to enforce lockdown too. Though I was willing to bet that had a fair bit to do with the police scanner Niall had in his car.

When we pulled up outside the huge, stone church, I found the smile on my face practically branded there. I was about to marry the most beautiful, smart-mouthed, badass girl I'd ever seen, piss Saint off better than ever before and get one up on my miserable motherfucker of a grandfather all in one fell swoop. Not to mention the consummating. There was going to be a fuck ton of consummating for sure.

I took Tatum's hand as I led her towards the front doors of the church, leaving our helmets hanging from the handlebars of my bike while Niall carried our new outfits inside for us.

The doors were unlocked and when we stepped through them, I spotted Father Bernard and the old organist Mrs Presley lighting candles in anticipation of our arrival.

"Ah, my children, what a joyous day this is," Father Bernard called as the heavy doors swung shut behind us and our footsteps echoed up the aisle towards him.

There was no mention of the fact that he'd only had an hour's warning to prepare this and provide us with a second witness - he was professional at least. And Niall had assured me that he would cover all the legal aspects involved too. All we had to do was show up, say our vows, kiss the bride and then go home and consummate the fuck out of it and Tatum Rivers would be mine forevermore.

"Let's get this over with quickly shall we, Father?" Niall said, grinning like a Cheshire Cat. "My pa has eyes and ears all over the city and I'm willing to bet we're on something of a time restraint here."

"Is there somewhere I can get changed?" Tatum asked, plucking the white dress bag from Niall's arms.

"I'll show you to the antechamber," Mrs Presley announced, bustling forward and leading Tatum away. I noticed she was maintaining her distance all the same and I wasn't complaining about that. I had no intention of getting close enough to anyone to risk catching the Hades Virus while we were out here.

"Do you think she's gonna climb out the window and make a run for it, lad?" Niall asked with a laugh as he lay down in the front pew, tucking an arm behind his head.

"Not a chance," I replied cockily and I was surprised to realise that I really was confident in that. And not just because Tatum knew she had to go through with this to be safe from my grandpa, but because I was actually certain that she wasn't going to run from me. Not now. There was a time when I'd been sure she'd run from us one day and never once look back, but I realised that things had changed. We might still be a bunch of assholes who had bound her to our will, but we belonged to her now just as much as she belonged to us. She wasn't going anywhere, and neither were we. One way or another, the five of us just fit.

I stripped down in the middle of the aisle, not giving a shit about the priest's blushes as he flipped through his oversized bible to find the part he needed.

The suit I'd chosen was black with a black shirt to go beneath it. Nothing too unusual. But instead of pulling the jacket on, I tugged my own leather jacket over the dress shirt instead and I kicked my boots back on too. I hardly looked like the catalogue version of a groom, but my girl knew that wasn't what she was signing up for with me anyway.

I began to loop the tie around my neck and then thought better of that as well, tossing it aside and leaving a few buttons undone so that some of my ink was left on show. I wasn't going to pretend during this. I wanted to marry my girl for real, not just for her safety and I wanted to give her a real version of me for it.

Mrs Presley reappeared with a wide smile as she hurried over to take her place at the organ and Father Bernard beckoned me over to stand before him. I chose a spot six feet away just in case and Mrs Presley placed her fingers down on the keys of the organ and started up the traditional bridal march.

My heart was pounding in my chest as I turned at the flash of white which caught my eye and I found Tatum standing at the far end of the aisle, clad in a figure hugging white lace dress which spilled into a long train behind her.

She'd even pinned a veil in her hair and the sheer fabric hiding her face from me made me all kinds of excited to rip it the fuck off and look into her big blues.

She made her way up the aisle while I fought against the urge to grab her and make her move faster, devouring her with my eyes and licking my lips as I took in the way the material clung to her curves.

When she finally made it to me, I stepped forward and flipped the veil back so that I could look down at her.

Tatum bit her lip as she looked up at me and I knew I was smirking at her like the cockiest bastard to ever grace the planet with the presence of my giant balls as the priest started reading out the vows.

I only gave them half of my attention and Niall yelled at him to make it the abridged version which made Tatum laugh. But my ears perked up quick enough when it came to my turn to make my vows to her, though I may not have totally recited them the way he told me to.

"I, Kyan Liam Roscoe, take you, Tatum Rivers to be my wife. I promise to be yours and only yours, to make you laugh and smile and come so often that you never want to get out of my bed. I'll protect you from anyone who might ever try and hurt you with the fury of a mad man and the precision of a butcher and I'll die for you without you even having to ask. I don't know how to love someone, baby, so I'll just promise to give you all of me, every dark, ruined, fucked up piece in any and every way that you might want it. And I swear that my heart won't ever beat for another woman the way that it races for you." I pushed the ring I'd already given her onto her finger for the second time today and the look she gave me had my entire world revolving around her. Every word I'd spoken to her was true and even if this whole thing might have been unplanned and more than a little insane, I knew for a fact that I would never regret this choice we were making.

Tatum reached for me as I finished speaking, winding her arms around my neck even though she wasn't meant to and I smirked at her as I caught her waist and dragged her body flush with mine. But I didn't kiss her, not yet. I wanted to hear her say it too and I wanted our next kiss to be the one that sealed this fate.

"I, Tatum Rivers, take you, Kyan Liam Roscoe to be my husband," she began and I swear the sound of those words on her lips had me fucking shackled to her already. "I promise to stand with you through all the darkness this world throws at us and give myself to you completely. I'll fight for you and with you and I'll beat your ass when you deserve it. And when you worship me with your body, I'll worship you right back. I never thought I'd bind myself to any man in marriage, so it makes sense for me to be joined with a monster instead. My heart beats for you in a way that makes me feel alive and I promise to make you feel alive every day that we spend together."

I didn't wait for the priest's permission to kiss my girl, I just grabbed her and kissed her with a brutal intensity that left no room for breath or thoughts or even fucking prayers. I claimed her with my lips and kissed her with the profound depth of this secret promise we were making to each other. I'd already known that there was no turning back for me when it came to her, but now I'd sworn it before the entire world too.

When we finally broke apart, Niall started whooping and clapping, taking countless pictures on his phone and looking like the maniac I knew he was.

We signed the marriage register and Father Bernard gave us a fancy ass marriage certificate which I was going to hang in pride of place above my bed so that every time I fucked her in it I could look at it and see those words which said she belonged to me.

Niall took on the job of phoning Liam and I gave some of my attention to listening to him explaining what had happened while the rest of my focus was on kissing my bride and running my hands over every inch of that dress.

The lace was rough and smooth against my palms and she kept batting my hands away as I tugged at the tiny buttons securing it in place while she laughed in a way that held pure joy and set my heart alight with my own happiness.

"He wants to talk to you," Niall interrupted me pawing at my girl and I forced myself to take one hand off of her as I leaned back against the pew and pressed the phone to my ear.

"I hear congratulations are in order," Liam's voice came down the line and I couldn't help but laugh like the smug motherfucker I was.

"Yeah. Well, I felt like the easiest way to express my feelings about my girl to you were with actions rather than words," I said. "Is this going to be a problem?"

Tatum's hand curled around the lapel of my leather jacket and she tugged me towards her before running her lips along my neck and making me fight off a groan. I really wanted to be done with this conversation so that I could take her back home and get on with our wedding night.

"Your disobedience hasn't gone unnoticed, but I appreciate your grit. I won't underestimate you again, lad," Liam said and I could have sworn the old bastard was smiling.

"So we're good?" I clarified, not liking the twinge of pride I felt at out foxing him. I shouldn't have given a shit what he thought, but I guessed families were kind of fucked up like that. I might have hated mine but deep down inside, a part of me was still that kid who had ached to fit in with them.

"We're good. I'll find another way to deal with our little problem. And feel free to get a baby in that girl's belly as soon as possible," he added. "There can never be enough O'Brien blood in the world."

He cut the call before I answered that and I laughed with a mixture of relief and excitement as Tatum's teeth bit down on my neck.

"So?" she demanded as I tossed Niall's phone back to him.

"We're free to go," I told her, gripping her ass tightly in both of my hands. "So let's get you back home where I can rip this dress off of you."

Tatum squealed as I lifted her up and tossed her over my shoulder, carrying her out of the church with a salute of thanks to the priest as I went. I dropped her to her feet beside my bike and she tugged on her leather jacket before gathering up the train of her dress in preparation for the ride.

"I'm never letting you go now, baby, you know that don't you?" I purred as I tugged her close and kissed her one last time before we got back onto my bike.

"Maybe I don't want you to," she replied seductively, pulling her helmet on before I could kiss her again. "Now take me home and let's make this union official."

I didn't need telling twice and I leapt onto the bike, loving the feeling of her arms wrapping tight around me as the engine roared to life beneath us.

I turned us around and shot away from the city, heading back towards Everlake Prep and what I was willing to bet was a trio of angry motherfuckers. But I didn't give a single fuck about that because I'd just made our girl my bride. And Tatum Roscoe was going to be mine forever.

CHAPTER NINETEEN

This was possibly the most surreal day of my life and as I walked hand in hand into Everlake Prep with Kyan, the new ring on my finger pressed between us, I had to laugh.

Kyan looked to me in surprise as I lost my shit, laughing until my stomach hurt and he was laughing too.

He twirled me under his arm, dancing me down the path, neither of us knowing the steps or giving a damn what the hell we looked like. I couldn't believe he was my freaking *husband*.

He caught my waist as we took the western path towards The Temple and he walked me backwards as I continued to dance up on my tip-toes, but he fell into stalking me like a predator instead. His smile turned to a deadly thing and I knew I had just married a hunter and I would always be his choice of prey.

"Are you happy, Mrs Roscoe?" he teased, an edge to his voice that gave away the wolf lurking beneath his skin.

"Yes, for the first time in a long time I feel happy," I admitted.

"Your pa would have hated you marrying a piece of shit like me, though," he pointed out and I shook my head in refusal of that.

"He was protective, so he would have liked someone else being protective of me too. I think he would have liked you, Kyan. A lot. Once he got past the leather jackets, the tattoos and the bullshit, that is." I didn't say it with any sadness, not letting in any pain on this day. Crazy as it was, I just wanted to enjoy it. I'd never seen myself getting married. If I had planned it, I probably would have eloped to Vegas. *Nah, screw Vegas actually, I'd pick Hawaii.*

He scoffed like it wasn't possible, but his eyes brightened like he quietly appreciated my words. We made it back to The Temple and I moved to walk beside Kyan, wondering how the other Night Keepers would react to this. Blake and Monroe would probably laugh and Saint would probably be more pissed about the fact that I'd missed making him dinner. Or maybe that was wishful thinking.

Kyan swept me off my feet before I made it to the door, carrying me in his arms like a baby and I gasped in surprise as the skirt of my wedding dress swept up around my legs in the wind.

"What are you doing?" I laughed.

"Carrying you over the threshold, baby. I wanna start this marriage right," he said with grit to his tone. He was taking this pretty damn seriously and I couldn't say I hated that.

He all but kicked the door open, carrying me inside and I tried to wriggle out of his arms, but he wouldn't let me go, rounding into the lounge where Monroe and Blake had gotten up from their seats with their mouths wide. Saint was... "Where's Saint?" I asked.

"Here," he growled, materialising like a freaking spectre from the dark stairway that led to his room as he took in my dress, his eyes calculating, assessing, denying.

"So, we have some news," I said, still laughing.

Kyan placed me down at last, taking my hand and winding his fingers between mine, his expression deadly serious.

"Well? Where the fuck have you been? And why is Tatum wearing that?" Saint snarled, jerking his chin at my beautiful dress.

Monroe and Blake exchanged a glance of horror and confusion, putting two and two together.

"So, basically...Kyan's family have this rule where-" I started but Kyan cut over me.

"We got married. Tatum is my wife," he said possessively and I glanced at him, snorting a laugh as I tried to catch his eye, but he didn't meet my gaze. *O...kay. Way to drop a bomb Kyan.*

"What?" Monroe asked sharply while Blake frowned, looking for the joke. But there wasn't one to find.

"What do you mean *married*?" Saint hissed and Kyan yanked my hand up, showing them all the ring as evidence. Saint physically recoiled like he'd struck him as he took in the skull on it.

"The thing is, we had to-" I started again, but Kyan barrelled over me, taking the carefully folded marriage certificate from his pocket and offering it to Saint.

"Here's the proof. It's iron clad. Catholic service, real nice priest, wasn't he baby?" He looked to me with a smirk, but there was a glint in his eyes which unsettled me.

"Yeah, but we had to rush be-" I started again, but Saint cut over me this time.

"What the fuck is this, Kyan?" Saint waved it at him and Kyan snatched it back, tucking it neatly into his pocket.

"It's proof that Tatum Rivers is now Tatum Roscoe. My wife. *Mine*," he growled and a shiver ran down my spine.

"Kyan..." I tried to catch his eye again, but he wouldn't look at me. His shoulders were like a wall as he glared at the others, waiting for this to sink in. And panic suddenly seized me. Just because I'd married him didn't mean I belonged to the others any less. Did he think I was choosing him over them?

Because I wasn't able to do that.

"You're having us on, right?" Blake released a weak laugh. "She's not - you wouldn't have-"

"I did," Kyan said smugly then grabbed me, lifting me into the air and tossing me over his shoulder. "And now I'm going to make it official."

"Kyan!" I hammered my fists on his back and he slapped my ass hard.

"This isn't funny, asshole," Monroe snapped and Saint shot him a frown that made my pulse skip. Shit, he could not see him freaking out about this. But Monroe was clearly beyond hiding his feelings for me as his expression twisted in rage.

"It's not meant to be," Kyan supplied simply, marching me away into his room and kicking the door shut behind him. He tossed me onto the bed and I yelped as I bounced, nearly falling off the other side of it.

Kyan grabbed his desk, shoving it in front of the door and the guys started banging their fists on it. He hurried to move the whole bed against the bathroom door and I laughed at his ridiculousness.

"Kyan!" Blake barked. "Show me that certificate!"

"Get your asses out here this second," Saint snarled.

"Tatum, tell me it isn't true!" Monroe yelled.

Kyan stood at the end of the bed and my lips parted as he started unbuckling his pants.

"You're taking this a little far, don't you think?" I arched a stern brow at him.

"Taking what too far?" he growled, his expression sharp and his eyes drinking me in.

"This whole marriage thing. I love being bound to you and I really did mean what I said in the church, but I didn't walk down the aisle for you because I want to play happy families, move to the suburbs and pop out two point four kids or whatever the fuck married people do." I got off the bed and walked towards Kyan. As soon as I got close to him, he shoved me down onto the bed again and pulled his shirt off.

"Kyan!" I gasped as the guys continued to shout beyond the door.

He tossed his shirt aside as I got up again and he caught my arm, throwing me back down onto the bed.

"Stop it," I snapped, getting angry now. "You're acting crazy."

"What's crazy about this? You're my wife. You said I do. You're *mine*. I don't give a fuck about the suburbs or the Volvo or whatever the shit it is I'm *supposed* to do with you. What I know is that you swore to be mine and I swore to be yours and to make that shit official I have to fuck you. So that's what we're gonna do. We'll figure out the rest later."

"This doesn't mean you own me, you know that right?" I said passionately. "You can't cut me off from the others."

"Being married to me means no one else can touch you," he mused. "Unless I say so of course, which I'm undecided on currently. I'll let you know when I've had my fill of you." He dropped his pants, standing before me in just his boxers and ran his hand over his solid length pressing through the material.

"Kyan stop being an asshole, we need to talk!" Blake shouted, throwing his weight against the door.

"Better hurry up, baby, or they might break in before we're done," Kyan said, grinning wickedly. "I'm happy to finish claiming you in private, but an audience won't stop me either."

I stood up on the bed, planting my hands on my hips. "I'm not your property, Kyan. Say it." I walked forward and pursed my lips at him.

"I wouldn't use the word property, more like claimed territory. A fuck-hot, sweet as shit, peachy assed dominion if you will." He grabbed the backs of my legs, knocking them out from under me to make me fall onto my knees beneath him. Then he dropped down to a crouch, shoved my dress up over my waist and gripped my thighs. He lifted my knees up onto his shoulders so I was kneeling on them with the large skirt scrunched up by my hips before he stood up again. I screamed in surprise as he carried me to the window and raked his tongue up the centre of my white panties. I clutched his hair for

331

support, afraid he'd drop me, but his grip on me was firm.

He started to suck my clit through the thin material and I moaned, my head hitting the window with a solid thunk.

"Hey!" Blake shouted from outside and started banging his fist on the window.

Kyan laughed darkly, turning his head to kiss and bite my inner thigh.

"Are you enjoying the show, brother?" Kyan called to Blake and Blake smacked his palm against the window in anger.

"Stop being a dick, Kyan," he snarled.

"Do you want me to stop, baby?" Kyan looked up at me and the heat in his eyes made my core liquify.

"I want you to stop being an asshole," I said breathlessly.

"That wasn't what I asked." He raked his tongue up the centre of me again and I moaned, flexing my neck and bucking my hips to give him more access. But I couldn't let him cloud my thoughts with lust. He couldn't just lay his claim on me like some sort of caveman and shut every other Night Keeper out of here without an explanation.

He gripped my ass hard and twisted around, throwing me on the bed again, making me yelp in surprise. He reached into his boxers, rubbing himself as he stared at me. "Are you really going to deny me, wife?"

I sighed. He looked so damn hot and I supposed we could explain ourselves after the fact...

I scrambled up, getting to my feet again and raising my fists.

"Fine, I want you, but you'll have to fight for it," I growled, a dare in my voice. So yes, okay I was clearly one percent into this. And maybe I wanted to see how caveman he could really go.

Blake cupped his hands around his eyes as he stared in at us and Kyan offered him the finger in response. Monroe appeared beside him then Saint, the three of them looking furious. I couldn't even offer them much of my attention as Kyan lunged forward and I screamed in alarm as he caught my legs, trying to uproot me. I kicked at him, but he kept coming, climbing onto the bed and wrestling me down beneath him. He started tearing off my dress and I punched him in the kidney, making him growl in anger. He caught my hands, pinning them above my head, rocking his hard dick into my thigh and heat spread between my legs. *Oh my god.*

I arched my back, wriggling against his hold and he started kissing my neck, biting and teasing me. "God you're beautiful. And you taste like fucking ecstasy."

I yanked a hand free and caught his throat, forcing him back. He lifted his weight off of me, cocking his head to one side, looking cute as shit.

"Come on, wifey," he teased. "Don't you want your husband to make you come all night long?"

He started moving down my body, trying to get the buttons open behind my back before giving up and tearing my dress off, splitting the material right up the middle. I gasped, about to shout at him, but then he kissed his way down my body and I clawed my hands into his hair, giving in.

"Fuck, Kyan," I said breathlessly. He licked just above my panties and looked up at me with a question in his eyes, his hunger for me clear. "I'm gonna fuck the others right out of you," he said, clearly trying to rile me.

I leaned up, slapping him hard and he growled approvingly.

Damn him for looking like that, for pushing my buttons in just the right way. I almost lost my grasp on my anger though as he lowered his head, kissing my thighs again, his breathing heavy like he was desperate to take this further. The shouts of the other guys started to fade in my head as I raked my fingernails over his muscular shoulders, marking him with red scratches. He grinned at me in a way that made my toes curl against the sheets.

"Fuck you," I panted and his eyes swirled with darkness.

"You used the wrong pronoun," he said, running his tongue up the centre of my panties again. "I think what you mean to say was fuck *me*."

I brought my knee up, slamming it into the side of his head as I got a second wave of will power, twisting myself over onto my knees as I tried to get away. He caught my ankles, dragging me back, his teeth sinking into the back of my thigh and making me yelp. I kicked back at him, catching him in the jaw and he caught my foot, sucking all of my toes into his mouth before biting down hard.

"Ah!" I kicked him again, shaking him off and he laughed as I made it off of the bed. I sped to the window, grabbing the curtains and giving the guys an apologetic look before I yanked them closed and they cursed me colourfully. Did they *want* to watch?

I laughed as Kyan grabbed me by the waist, lifting me off of my feet and throwing me down onto the bed again.

"You're enjoying this." He smirked, standing over me and shoving my legs apart. I lifted my hips, pressing my ankles into the bed as I slid further up it. He caught the backs of my thighs, tearing me back down it so my legs fell either side of him off the bed.

"It's a game I can't really lose," I said, smiling wickedly as I lifted my foot and pressed it against his chest. He pushed his weight down on it, making my knee bend up to my chest as he smirked at me.

"You can lose if I don't let you come," he mused.

"That would make you a bad husband," I panted.

"I never claimed to be a good one." He flashed his teeth at me then tore my panties off, shoving them into my mouth with two fingers.

I spat them out, turning my head and in the time I was distracted by disposing of them, he freed his cock and slammed inside me. I cried out as he filled me, shoving my leg aside so I was spread open for him and I immediately wrapped my thighs around his waist, locking my ankles and squeezing hard.

He laughed as he took me roughly, holding my hands down in the sheets above my head. He moved hard and fast, trying to dominate me and take and take, but I kept pace with him, defying him as I glared up at him. He groaned as I dug my heels into his spine and fought against his hold on my wrists.

"You're mine," he said fiercely and my body clenched around him in response to those words.

I gasped, caught between pleasure and pain, his thrusts becoming more powerful as he dared to try and finish this fast, fulfilling his own desires but not mine. Hell if I was going to let him away with that.

I craned my neck up to kiss him and the moment his mouth was on mine, his grip relaxed on my wrists enough that I knew I could get them free. I kissed him deeply and his hips slowed slightly as he fell into the slow rhythm of my tongue against his.

I yanked one hand free, throwing my fist into his jaw and he lurched backwards with a snarl of anger and lust. I took hold of my brief advantage, shoving his shoulders and forcing him to roll beneath me. I had a feeling he let me do it a little as he smirked and I pressed my knees into the sheets either side of him, riding him hard as he grabbed my hips and started controlling my movements. I reached out to caress his chest, but he slapped my hands away, his eyes dark as he half sat up and yanked them behind my back to keep me at his mercy. He ripped the veil from my hair, tying my hands in place with it and I cursed as he tightened the knot.

He continued to thrust into me, sucking on my breasts and branding me with teeth marks and love bites everywhere his mouth touched. I started to come apart, moaning his name and pressing my forehead to his as he tried to outpace me, but I kept going, sweat rolling down my spine as he pushed me to my limits.

"Fuck," he hissed as I tightened around him and tipped my head back, moaning loudly as I came and he fell apart half a second later, grunting as he finished deep inside me.

I started laughing in my victory and he rolled me off of him, his arms closing around me so I was nose to nose with him lying on the bed.

"Don't underestimate me, Kyan Roscoe," I purred, kissing the tip of his nose.

He yanked me closer by the ass, the evidence of our desire sticky against my thighs. "Never again, *Mrs* Roscoe." He grinned and I scowled as he untied the veil from my wrists and rubbed his thumbs over the sore marks.

I realised the guys had stopped trying to get in and I sighed as I curled up in Kyan's arms, hooking one leg over his hip. "How long are you going to keep this up for?" I asked, letting my eyes fall closed as I soaked in the warmth of his body against mine.

"How long are you going to keep refusing you're mine now?" he countered and I tutted.

"I belong to all of you," I said simply.

"I take my vows very seriously and I intend on honouring them," he said, smirking. "I also have a far bigger claim on you now, so we will just have to see how well the guys behave before I decide if I'll share you."

I opened my eyes, frowning at him. Was he for real? "Kyan," I sighed. "I may be your wife, but I'm not just yours. Besides, I'm not exactly wifey material."

He squeezed my ass then my waist, then my breasts. "Naw, you seem like the perfect wifey material to me."

I snorted, noticing he hadn't responded to the first part of what I'd said. "I mean it, asshole."

"Me too, bitch," he tossed back with a smirk.

"God you're infuriating." I rolled back to rest against the pillow and he laid his head down beside mine, his breath on my neck enough to get me turned on again already.

"By the morning you'll be so sated on my cock that you'll never be infuriated with me again," he commented and I rolled my eyes which made a challenge flare in his.

He moved over me, sliding down between my legs and starting to drive me wild again with his tongue, his eyes on mine the whole time. I sighed as I let my thighs widen and he laughed throatily into my flesh like he'd won something. *Damn him to hell.*

I woke to a strange buzzing noise and took in a long breath through my nose as I rolled onto my back, the sheets tangled around me. I cracked an eye, spotting Kyan across the room at the desk in front of the door, hunched over in his chair. He was butt naked and had something laid out on the desk before him.

I slid out of bed, walking across the room and pressing my hand to his shoulder as I leaned over to see what he was doing. He had a tattoo gun in his hand and was finishing up marking something around his ring finger.

"What do you think, baby?" He placed the gun down, showing it to me and I gasped as I realised he'd tattooed my name there with a skull above it that matched the one on my ring. It actually looked pretty cool.

"I guess you can always tattoo over it if we get a divorce," I teased.

He grabbed my waist, yanking me down onto his lap and his hardening dick as he clutched my naked body against his. "We won't," he growled angrily, grabbing my chin between his rough finger and thumb and forcing me to look him in the eye. "Ever. You're mine."

I frowned, brushing my fingers over his cheeks. "It's not like I want to divorce you. But what about after we graduate-"

"So what? Wherever you go, I'll follow," he said fiercely, squeezing my jaw. "You're my wife."

I couldn't deny how good that sounded on his lips and a part of me wished it could last forever. I just wasn't sure how a future for us was going to work out.

He wrapped his hand in my hair, a snarl on his lips. "Stop worrying," he demanded then lowered his hand between my thighs. "I will never let you get away."

I stood up, pushing away from him with a grin as I strode to the bed and started trying to tug it away from the bathroom door. "I need to pee."

Kyan came up behind me, leaning down and rubbing his hard dick against my ass as he dragged the bed out a foot. I shot him a smirk before I jumped onto the bed, heading across it and slipping into the bathroom.

I peed, showered and took in the love bites all over my breasts and neck which were the worst case of Saint bait I'd ever seen.

"Fucking Kyan," I muttered, but I was smiling as I stepped back into his room wrapped in a towel. He had one of his wife beaters waiting for me and a pair of his boxer shorts too, grinning like a savage as he walked forward, tugging my towel off and helping me into them. "Perfect," he announced, admiring the love bites that were on full display with a smug grin.

"You're going to invoke the wrath of the devil before we've even had breakfast," I sing-songed and he shrugged.

"That's my plan, wife." He smacked me on the ass then dragged his desk out of the way of the door, wrapping his arm around my shoulders as we headed out the door.

Saint was waiting in his usual seat at the dining table, his fingers steepled together and rage brimming in his eyes. "You're late," he bit out and Kyan made a show of pressing a messy kiss to my mouth.

"Sorry, brother, consummating a marriage is lengthy work. I had to write my name on the inside of her pussy with a sharpie attached to my dick," Kyan joked and I ducked out from under his arm, shaking my head at him with a smirk as I headed into the kitchen.

Monroe stepped through the front door, looking like a furious heathen as he strode toward us with his jaw ticking. "Explain."

Blake's door slammed just before he arrived too and he stalked into the room with his muscles bunched. He looked seriously tired and I bit my lip guiltily as I realised we'd probably kept him up half the night.

"Fuck you." He pointed at Kyan. "And you." His finger wheeled onto me. "I want an explanation."

"I really don't know what more can be said. She's my wife. Simple as that really," Kyan said, dropping down into his seat and putting his bare feet up on the table.

I sighed, getting some food from the fridge. "His family have some stupid rule that basically means I'm fair game unless I'm married to him. And his crazy grandpa was going to sell me to Royaume D'élite to wipe their debt clean in payment for cleaning up all the murders at my dad's cabin," I explained and Saint's jaw gritted.

"Come on, we got married for more reasons than just the threat," Kyan pushed, grinning at me and I smiled, a blush rising in my cheeks.

"Well yeah…I wanted it too," I admitted, but that clearly wasn't the right thing to say as the tension in the room tripled.

Monroe and Blake strode forward, standing shoulder to shoulder as they glared down at Kyan from the opposite side of the table. Apparently he was getting the blame more than I was.

"And you didn't think this needed to be mentioned before you went ahead and did it?" Monroe growled.

"Nope." Kyan shrugged. "I mean, I'm sure it sucks for you guys now that I own Tatum in a whole other way. A bigger way some might say. A way recognised by everyone in the world. By God and Satan and every angel and demon hiding in the shadows."

"Would you stop with that shit already?" I huffed. "I'm not going to tell you again. You don't own me more than them now just because we're married."

"Calm down, wife," he chuckled and Blake stepped forward as if he was going to hit him.

Saint held up a hand, drawing everyone's attention to him.

"This is unacceptable," he said, deadly calm, the cogs working behind his eyes. "You cannot hold more ownership of Tatum than the rest of us, that is not how it works."

"Sorry bro." Kyan placed his hands behind his head, leaning back in his seat so the front legs came off the floor. "That's the way it is."

"Once an appropriate amount of time has passed, you will divorce one another in secret and we can all allow your family to keep believing the lie," Saint said thoughtfully.

"No," Kyan snapped, fixing Saint with a glare and my gut clenched at the thought too. "I won't. Not ever."

"It's not your choice," Saint hissed, slamming his hand down on the table.

"Oh, but it is," Kyan said with a dangerous edge to his voice.

"I just really don't think it should bother you guys so much," I said gently, pushing some bread in the toaster. "We might be married, but that doesn't take away from what I have with you individually."

"Naw, I think they need to be taking it *more* seriously," Kyan growled. "The fact is by law you are my wife. Simple as fucking that. They need to accept it."

My mouth dried out as I looked over at him, the blazing energy in his eyes making me suck on my lower lip.

"Stop eye fucking each other," Blake demanded. "If Kyan has married her then I'm marrying her too."

"I've already considered that," Saint said in an icy tone. "The closest place we could go to arrange such a thing legally would be Africa, but as travel is suspended-"

"Saint," I snarled. "I am not marrying more of you. This really doesn't need to be such a big deal."

"Not a big deal?" Saint hissed, rising from his seat. "You and Kyan have altered the power balance between us."

"No we haven't," I snapped. "I belong to all of you and you all belong to me. Wholly, entirely. That's how it is." I realised it was the first time I'd actually defended this situation to all of them out loud. But I was offended that he thought me marrying Kyan changed anything I had with any of them. I didn't belong to them any less just because Kyan was my husband.

"I say we take a vote." Monroe folded his arms and Saint looked to him in surprise before nodding keenly.

"A vote on what?" Kyan drawled. "You can't undo our marriage."

"Well I vote that you do," Blake chipped in. "Like Saint said, you can wait long enough for the dust to settle then we'll all pay for lawyers to file the divorce and keep it quiet."

"Seconded," Monroe agreed.

"I third it," Saint said, smiling cruelly then looked to me. "What do you say siren?"

My mouth parted as I looked to Kyan and his brows pulled together, his eyes seeming to morph into those of a puppy dog. I looked down at the ring he'd given me and my heart tugged violently. "I say no."

Kyan beamed, practically bouncing in his seat.

"You're still outnumbered," Saint said harshly. "So it's done."

"Psh." Kyan waved a hand dismissively. "You couldn't make me sign divorce papers unless you cut off my hand and did it for me. Even then I'm pretty sure my dead flesh would fight back and punch you in the dick."

I folded my arms. "If the truth ever came out to Kyan's family it would hardly be worth it, would it? Then they'd just come after me again and for what? So that you guys can feel like the power in the group is still even despite the fact that I'm telling you this hasn't changed it?" I said with a pout and Blake and Monroe looked like whipped dogs, realising their oversight, while Saint narrowed his eyes, ironing out the kinks of this plan in his mind.

"Fire!" someone screamed outside in fear and my heart lurched.

"What the fuck?" Monroe growled, running towards the door and we all raced after him.

The guys kept close to me as we spilled outside and I gasped at the sight of Kyan's dirt bike sitting on the lawn beside the path, flames rising from it and consuming the whole frame. There was a figure made of newspaper stuffed into a white, long-sleeved dress with a pillowcase for a veil sitting on top of it, the whole thing ablaze.

"No!" Kyan roared, stepping toward it, his expression hopeless as his bike was consumed by the flames.

A few students were gathered on the path, gaping at it or recording it on their phones.

Kyan strode up to the bike, kicking the whole thing over with a furious bellow.

"Who the fuck did this?" He started towards the small group of students and they scattered with screams of fright.

Kyan hefted a fallen branch into his arms, chasing them with a growl of rage.

I broke away from the others, running over to him and he wheeled around, the branch poised to hit me before he lowered it, realising it was me standing there.

"Stop," I begged, my heart thundering in my chest.

He looked over my head, jerking his chin to beckon the Night Keepers closer. "Come on, I'm gonna break bones until someone tells me who did this."

"*No*," I demanded, turning to them and pressing my back to Kyan as I clutched his arm to keep him there. "Not like this. We can't just mindlessly attack anyone and everyone. We have to be smart. This is what that stupid Justice Ninja wants. If you hurt innocent students the cops are going to come. You'll be locked up for this."

"I don't give a shit," Kyan gritted out as the others seemed to consider that and Saint started murmuring to Blake and Monroe in a low voice.

I turned to face Kyan again, making him meet my gaze. "Don't be an idiot. We have to deal with this the right way."

His jaw ticked as he stared down at me and the branch suddenly fell from his hand. I wrapped my arms around him, squeezing him tight, his heart pounding furiously in my ear. "We'll find them."

Kyan's arms closed around me and the tension ran out of my body as he gave in.

"Since when are you capable of seeing reason when you're lusting for blood?" Blake balked at Kyan who shrugged and Blake mimed whipping the air while he wasn't looking.

"Tatum's right," Saint said, his voice sharp and clear. "This needs some deliberation, but we will find them. And when we do, we will dispose of them cleanly. There will be no mistakes. Nothing that will link us to their disappearance."

I gaped at him in surprise. "Are you going to kill them?" I whispered, though Kyan had made sure there was no one close enough to hear.

Saint's face became nothing but a cruel, twisted expression. "No siren, I intend on eradicating them entirely."

Monroe

CHAPTER TWENTY

The acrid stink of smoke clung to my skin long after we'd put out the fire and Kyan had to accept that his bike had moved on from this world. The five of us had headed back inside The Temple so that we could discuss our next moves in private. While Saint showered to get the stench from his flesh and Kyan paced and raged like a wild beast with the scent of blood beneath his nose, I took myself to the kitchenette and leaned back against the counter, sinking a tall glass of water.

There was something going on here that we were missing. All of this Justice Ninja shit left a sour taste in my mouth and I was haunted by the certainty that we weren't seeing something glaringly obvious about all of it, but I just couldn't figure it out.

Blake was showering in their bathroom too and while I stood there trying to work out this bugging sensation in my gut, Tatum padded down the stairs from Saint's room with her hair wet and a white silk robe wrapped around her.

I tried not to stare at her as she drew closer, but I couldn't help it. My tongue felt thick with all the words I needed to say to her and all the things I hadn't been able to when I'd been forced to hide the full depths of my feelings over this marriage.

Her gaze met mine as she crossed the room and headed straight for me and I held my ground as I waited for her to approach.

"Are you alright?" I murmured as I looked her over like I was expecting a physical wound to match up to the internal ones that must have been carved into her when she'd seen that fire. It wasn't about the fucking bike. It was the burning bride on top of it that had worry eating me alive.

"I'm okay," she said with a tight smile before tugging the fridge open to look inside.

I shifted along the counter so that I was hidden by the fridge door too and caught her arm to make her look at me.

"No bullshit, princess," I murmured. "Not with me."

Her gaze met mine and she stepped closer to me, the cool air from the open fridge making her skin pepper with goosebumps as we hid behind it. I knew I should have pulled back but instead I leaned in, cupping her jaw in my hand and looking into her blue eyes.

"I'm worried, Nash," she admitted softly. "I haven't told a soul about me and Kyan getting married outside of the Night Keepers and I know he hasn't either. No one but you guys and his family know. So how did that Ninja asshole know about it? I feel...violated or something. Like my skin is crawling with the feeling of being watched and I can't help but think about Toby-"

"I can't believe he would be so stupid as to still be stalking you after everything we've been doing to him," I said as I moved closer to her and she placed her hand on my chest over my pounding heart. "But I promise you I'll look into it. And if it's not him then we will find whoever the fuck it was."

"So how do you think they found out about the wedding?" she pressed and I tried not to let my anger over the fucking wedding show, even though my jaw tightened and the urge to punch Kyan in his smug face rose up in me powerfully.

"You walked back through campus wearing your dress," I said with a shrug. "Anyone could have seen you and realised what had happened."

"So you think someone *has* been watching me again?" she asked, chewing on her bottom lip and making me ache with the desire to kiss her.

"I don't know. But you've got four hell hounds at your beck and call, princess, they won't get close to you even if they are watching."

Tatum released a shaky breath and wrapped her arms around my waist, pressing her ear over my heart and holding me close so that I coiled my arms around her too.

I inhaled the sweet scent of her shampoo from her freshly washed hair and the ache in my chest forced me to speak.

"Marriage though, really?" I asked, my voice rough and barely concealing my anger.

"It was the only way," she replied and I fought the urge to shout and tell her that wasn't good enough because I'd heard all of the clear and valid reasons for why she'd made the vows. I could even understand the dress if they needed to provide some photographic evidence for Kyan's grandfather, but what was getting me was the way she'd been smiling over it, the ring that still sat on her finger and the fact that she clearly had no regrets about making those vows at all.

"So you chose him?" I pushed, needing to hear it for myself. "He's the one you want the most?"

"That's not what this is," she disagreed, pulling back to look up at me. "You don't understand-"

"So make me understand, princess, because from where I'm standing, it looks a whole lot like you've taken on the title of Mrs Roscoe without a single regret. If it's just some arrangement to protect you from the wrath of the O'Briens then why doesn't it feel like that?"

"Because it's not," Kyan growled as he appeared beside us, tossing the fridge door closed and smirking cruelly as he took in the sight of her wrapped in my arms. "It's about me standing up and claiming her as mine in front of the whole world and letting every motherfucker know that she belongs to me and I belong to her. And that's not something you're willing to offer her, is it, coach?"

I released my hold on Tatum as I stepped up into Kyan's face, practically snarling at him as I moved close enough for our chests to brush up against one another.

"If you're looking for someone to fight so that you don't start crying over your precious dirt bike then keep pushing me, Kyan," I dared him. "Because I'll happily take the excuse to kick your ass right now."

"And why is that?" he goaded. "Is my marriage rubbing you up the wrong way, Nash?" he taunted right back, flexing his muscular arms and making the anger in me multiply tenfold.

"Maybe it is," I hissed, knowing that this was dumb as fuck with Blake and Saint in the building but not backing down all the same. If I didn't say this now then I had no idea when I was going to get the chance to say it.

"She deserves better than being married into a family of thugs and cutthroats," I hissed.

"Yeah," Kyan agreed like he knew that full well and that earned him back an inch of my respect. Or at least it did until he opened his big mouth again. "And she deserves better than some low paid fucking teacher who can't keep his dick in his pants too."

"Stop!" Tatum demanded but it was way too late for that.

I threw my fist straight into Kyan's gut and he grabbed hold of me as he wrenched me away from Tatum and shoved me out towards the middle of the room.

I was on him again within moments, punching and cursing and fighting him in a way unlike anything we'd ever done in the ring. This was all savage emotion and hurt and rage and I didn't even know which one of us was feeling it more.

"What the fuck is going on?" Saint's voice carried over the room a moment before strong hands gripped the back of my shirt and ripped me away from Kyan.

I was angry enough to take a swing at Blake too, but Tatum caught my other arm and gave me a firm look as she moved between me and the fucking savage who she had claimed for a husband.

"Nash just wanted to help me vent a bit of my anger is all," Kyan said, offering up a goading smile like he wanted me to deny it.

He reached out for Tatum and pulled her away from me, tucking her beneath his arm and smirking like he actually wanted me to lose my shit and show my cards to everyone here. But I wasn't giving Saint Memphis access to a secret that could destroy me. If he sent me to prison then that would be the end of all my plans and everything I'd been working to achieve for all of these years.

I couldn't afford for that to happen. I needed to get justice for Mom and Michael, even if it fucking killed me to get it. It was all that mattered to me.

My gaze slid to Tatum and a heavy, uncomfortable feeling built in my gut at the lie I'd just told myself. Because that was bullshit now, wasn't it? Vengeance wasn't the only thing I cared about anymore. There was a girl with blue eyes and the power to make my heart race unlike anyone I'd ever met, who I cared about a whole hell of a lot and who I could fucking lose if Saint ever found out about us.

My reasons for wanting to protect our secret weren't about keeping me out of prison so that I could go after his father and finish what I'd started. I couldn't bear to be parted from her. I just didn't want to admit that to myself because doing so meant owning the fact that I was fucking terrified about the idea of something happening to her. And this Justice Ninja asshole coming after her alongside the threat from the members of Royaume D'élite, Kyan's family and the lethal virus plaguing the world and sending everyone crazy meant I had plenty of reason to fear losing her. And I knew it would destroy me if I did, but I couldn't even own that feeling, not publicly.

I couldn't offer her what Kyan had by marrying her and proclaiming to the world that she was mine and I would stand between her and any danger that might come her way. Which left a vile, bitter taste of envy coating my tongue and a desperate feeling of inadequacy flowing through my veins at knowing I couldn't offer her the world in the same way that he could. Or that any of the other Night Keepers could.

I jerked out of Blake's grip and stalked away from all of them, dropping into Saint's chair beside the fire and glaring into the flames as I fought to get a hold of my emotions before I gave myself away.

The others slowly moved to join me, Kyan, Blake and Tatum taking up the couch while Saint stood before the fire, lording it over all of us as he was silhouetted by the orange flames.

"I've put in an order for a network of hidden surveillance cameras which I'm going to install at key points around campus and The Temple to help us figure out who this fucking Justice Ninja is," Saint said, cutting straight to the point. "Tomorrow we will put out a request for information from the students. The prize will be advantageous to their career beyond the walls of this school. I'll offer them a single favour from us which they will be able to call in at any point in the future. Most of them are at least intelligent enough to know that we already have more than enough power and influence to crown kings and destroy empires so they'd be fools not to take us up on that."

"And what are we going to do to the fucking Ninja once we've exposed them?" Blake asked, his eyes lighting up like he had plenty of cruel and twisted ideas himself.

"We'll do our worst," Saint said simply and even I got a chill at that suggestion. Whoever the hell had decided to take on the Night Keepers either had more guts than anyone I'd ever met before or they were seriously confident in their ability to get away with it. Or maybe they were just goddamn stupid. "In the meantime," Saint carried on like this was a board meeting and we were all just here to listen to him lay out the law. "While Kyan and Tatum were running off to get hitched, I've been making more progress on Royaume D'élite."

"And?" Kyan asked, perking up at the idea of having a new target for his wrath and I had to admit that I was curious too.

"The main issue I'm having is in locating the compound. To be honest, the simplest way to find it would be for you to attend one of their events, Kyan. As a member you can gain entry and I could track you there," Saint mused.

"I told you it's not that easy. They don't even let the members know where it is," Kyan replied with a shake of his head. "You have to send a message to say that you want to attend the next meeting. Then they just send you a random location in the city and when you get there, a car picks you up and you ride to the club in the back of it with the windows blacked out and no way to know where you're going. They scan you for cell phones and listening devices before you even get into the car too, so I don't see how we could track shit," he said as he wound his arm around Tatum and then lifted her into his lap. If she had any protests to the way he was manhandling her then she didn't voice them and I had to fight off another wave of jealousy and anger as I gave my attention back to Saint.

"I'll figure out a way around that. But I'm beginning to think that the only way for us to find the compound is by you making an appearance. Because there isn't a single clue anywhere online or via any of my contacts as to its whereabouts, so it's clearly a very well guarded secret." Saint folded his arms over his chest like the fact that he couldn't figure this out was pissing him off and I tried and failed not to be smug about that.

Kyan grimaced at the idea of going to the club, but didn't outwardly refuse which made Saint's eyes flash with triumph.

"How does the membership work?" Tatum asked, turning to look up at Kyan and the way his gaze softened when he looked her way made my gut twist with envy. "Aside from the whole death games bullshit for the entry, I mean. Like, what do you do then? Just turn up at the club whenever you want?"

"Usual old rich dude bullshit," Kyan said with a shrug. "They gave me this dumbass crest thing and a code number in place of my name to hide my identity from the other members if we don't wanna share. Then I was just given a number to message any week when I want to attend so that they can arrange the car-"

"Can't you use that number to trace them or something?" I asked Saint and he gave me a withering look in reply.

"No. It's a dead end. It's not even an actual phone number, just one of those text collector things. It clearly takes the information and then encrypts it before passing it on to the actual recipient. There's nothing there for me to trace," Saint replied scathingly like I was a child trying to understand the inner workings of a supercomputer. God, I wished I could beat his face in sometimes.

"Okay, but what about bringing guests?" Tatum went on and Kyan shrugged.

"Naw, baby, I can't just invite you all to come with me. Members and spouses only. Nothing in life is that easy," Kyan replied.

"Spouses?" Tatum perked up and every man in the room fell utterly still.

"No," I growled.

"No chance in hell," Blake snarled in agreement.

"I'm not taking you to that fucking hell, baby," Kyan growled passionately, but Tatum just turned to look at Saint as he considered that like it wasn't out of the fucking question.

"I have a right to go," Tatum said fiercely. "They have the answers I need about my dad. They're the reason he was set up and the reason he's dead. None of you have any right to claim otherwise. Besides, I'm the only one here who can leave the safety of this place with the confidence that I won't get infected with the Hades Virus while I'm out there. And if Kyan is going into that viper's pit then he'll need someone to watch his back."

"She has a point," Saint conceded, though he didn't look all too pleased about it.

"I said *no*," Kyan snarled.

"Well you either want to take them down or you don't," Saint snapped.

"If you don't then I suggest you look your new wife in the eye and tell her that you've made the executive decision not to pursue the men who set her father up to die. And I'll look forward to the divorce."

Kyan looked like he was about to leap out of his chair and rip Saint's head off, but Tatum turned in his lap so that she was straddling him, gripping his face between her hands and effectively stealing his attention.

"I'm going after them with or without your help, *husband,*" she warned and even though I knew she was calling him that with the aim of softening him, it still set my blood alight.

There was a long pause that followed where it was clear all of us wanted to argue against this further, but none of us could deny that it was her right to go.

"Fine," Kyan ground out, his posture rigid as he placed his hands on her ass and gripped her tightly. "But you won't leave my side for a single second. You'll do everything I say and if I decide it's getting too dangerous you promise to cut our losses and run with me."

"I swear it," she agreed and I bit my tongue against the rest of the protests I wanted to make, my gaze meeting Blake's and seeing the same concern in his eyes. How had this girl won so much loyalty from us four dark creatures in such a short span of time?

"That's settled then. I'll formulate a plan and you can go this week," Saint said like this whole thing wasn't utterly insane. "In the meantime, I'll continue to pursue the club financially. I have already made a list of likely members from my knowledge of the city's worst assholes and the names you remembered from when you were initiated, Kyan - which would be a lot easier if you'd paid more attention I might add-"

"It's not about me paying attention or not," Kyan growled. "I have purposefully spent my life having as little to do with the kinds of mean motherfuckers my grandpa involves himself with as possible. Whenever I've been forced to work with the family, I've focused on the grunt work, the bloody work, not the posturing or money grabbing and I've never cared to make friends with old rich bastards who want to rule the world with their wallets."

"Hail to that," I muttered, giving Saint a look to let him know I thought of him as one of the aforementioned bastards, but he just ignored me.

"The point is not about you making friends with them, Kyan, it's about knowing who your enemies are," Saint said in an exasperated tone. "I know you like to think of yourself as the biggest, baddest beast in the woods but you forget that a thousand wasps can take down a bear if they work together and a pack of wolves would do it with even more efficiency. Sometimes I feel like you refuse to allow my influence to take effect on you out of sheer determination to remain ignorant."

Blake laughed at that and Kyan shrugged like there might be some truth to the statement.

"I'm still getting over the shock of finding out that there are things the great Saint Memphis can't uncover alone," Blake teased as the mood lightened slightly. "And I'm looking forward to Kyan and Tate figuring it all out for you. Will you be awarding them some kind of prize or will the reward just be in knowing they managed to do something you couldn't?"

"I'd like to see you do as much as I have to track down an elite secret organisation with endless funding and countless powerful people working to protect it," Saint snarled at him like casting shade on his capabilities was the worst thing anyone could do to him.

"I still don't like it," I said, earning myself a glare from Tatum, but I ploughed on regardless. I wasn't ever going to apologise for trying to protect her. "Two people in a sea of serpents doesn't sound like good odds to me."

"I wasn't sure if I should suggest this or not," Kyan said hesitantly. "But I think we could get my uncle Niall on side to help us look into this. He... well he's an evil motherfucker with a mean streak that would make even you assholes shit your pants if he turned it on you, but he also has an axe to grind against people like the sadists running Royaume D'élite. He hasn't made any move against them because he also has no intention to stand against his pa for the position of head of the family so he doesn't like to openly defy him, but I think he would help us get the information we need to take them on. He's a member too and he'd have our backs if he attended the club with us."

I considered that, liking the idea of them having someone else there on their side even if it was a member of Kyan's criminal family.

Tatum scrunched her nose up. "I dunno, Kyan, I know he helped us out with the wedding and all, but he also turned up at Christmas dinner with two severed heads in a Santa sack..."

"You people come from fucked up families," I muttered, shaking my head as I tried to figure out if the guy being a psychopath was a good or a bad thing from the point of view of this plan.

"Just them, not me," Blake protested, pointing between Saint and Kyan and I nodded vaguely to placate him.

"If you think we can trust him then I say reach out," Saint decided for all of us and I had to say that just pissed me off more, but I didn't argue. "I have dirt on him anyway so if he becomes a problem, I can easily neutralise him."

"What's that supposed to mean?" I asked and Saint smirked like a smug bastard.

"I've spent years gathering intelligence on every notable member of the O'Brien family and I have more than enough evidence filed away on each of them to send them to prison indefinitely if I so choose. One email to my contact in the FBI would remove them from our lives if needs be. But it wouldn't entirely remove the threat of retribution as their empire is so large, which is why I haven't pulled the trigger on the whole lot of them to free Kyan from his Grandfather's bonds."

"Who the fuck are you?" I muttered and not for the first time since I'd set myself on this mission to destroy Saint's family, I had to wonder if I wasn't way in over my head. What kind of high school kid just casually mentioned the fact that he owned all the information necessary to take down an entire criminal organisation as well as having FBI contacts?

"He's Saint Memphis," Blake said with a cocky grin like he'd just revealed that he was Batman and Saint just kept smirking. *Asshole.*

"Done," Kyan agreed, making his decision while I was distracted by the megalomaniac in the room. "I'll get Niall in on it and we'll go to the fucking club. Whatever it takes to bring them down and get justice for my girl."

"*Our* girl," Blake corrected.

"Sorry," Kyan said, not sounding sorry at all as he dragged Tatum closer to him and pressed a heated kiss to her lips. "I meant to say my *wife.*"

"I'm already sick of that shit and it's only been twenty-four hours," Blake snapped and I wholeheartedly agreed with him on that even if I had to bite my tongue on saying it.

"Yeah," Kyan said as he pushed himself up to his feet, keeping his grip on Tatum's ass as he lifted her and she was forced to wrap her arms and legs around him so that she didn't fall. A laugh fell from her lips but she didn't try to escape him. "Well it sucks to suck but the truth is the truth. See that ring on her finger?"

"As if anyone in their right mind could miss that monstrosity," Saint hissed.

Kyan laughed loudly as he started to walk away from us in the direction of his room with Tatum still in his arms. She was protesting but it was a pretty weak attempt on her part if she really wanted him to let her go.

"I'm glad you like it. Now I need to go consummate my marriage some more, so I'll see you assholes in the morning," Kyan called over her laughter.

"It's not your fucking night with her!" Blake shouted as he got to his feet and tried to follow them, but Kyan's door slammed in his face before he could stop him.

My skin prickled as the sound of Tatum arguing carried through the door followed by more of Kyan's laughter and then a shriek of laughter from her too. She certainly wasn't protesting all that hard to him claiming ownership over her. In fact, it seemed like she was quite happy with the turn of events.

"What the fuck are we going to do about this?" Blake demanded as he strode back into the room and Saint turned up the music so the three of us wouldn't have to sit here listening when the two of them inevitably started fucking again.

I stayed quiet because I was so consumed with jealousy and anger that I knew if I spoke there wouldn't be any hiding it and I needed to calm the fuck down before I gave myself away.

"We give them this week," Saint said thoughtfully, his own face a carefully blank mask which told me he was fucking fuming too. "One week where we put up with this shit and get through this trip to Royaume D'élite. After that we call a meeting and make our decisions over this marriage one way or another."

"I don't like it," I growled, unable to help myself.

"None of us like it, but that isn't going to change it. And we have enough shit on our plates with the fucking Justice Ninja and Royaume D'élite, let alone Kyan's family breathing down our necks. It isn't worth fighting amongst ourselves too. One week for him to play the controlling husband and fuck the life out of her and then we remind him of the oaths we all swore and end this nonsense."

"Perfect," I deadpanned, shoving out of my chair and heading for the door. "Well, if there's no further need for me to be here, I'll head home for a shower."

"See you tomorrow," Blake called, and I couldn't help but notice that his anger had slipped already and in its place was a heavy kind of sadness which I recognised all too well from my own grief.

Saint said goodnight and headed upstairs while I hesitated by the door with my eyes on Blake.

He shifted forward and slowly switched the Xbox on, but the sigh that escaped him as he leaned back in his seat made my mind up for me. I headed for the fridge and pulled out Saint's bottle of disgustingly expensive vodka before unscrewing the cap and taking a long swig of it then moving over to join Blake. There was only about a quarter of the bottle left but that would be enough to get a nice buzz going at least.

"Go easy on me, I haven't played this before," I said to him as I dropped down beside him and offered up the vodka.

He looked at me in surprise before barking a laugh as he accepted Saint's drink and swigged from the neck of it too while I grabbed myself a controller.

"I can't promise to go easy on you, sunshine, but I do swear to take Saint's wrath alongside you when he realises we drank his precious vodka," he teased.

"How about we finish the bottle then refill it with water?" I suggested.

"Fuck yes." He laughed as he swallowed more of it and I grinned at my new ally in the war against Saint.

It didn't take me too long to figure out the basics of the game. It was basically a survival based bloodbath with plenty of zombie skulls to cave in. Blake did me the favour of selecting simple missions while I got used to it and we were soon laughing while we stabbed and slashed our way through the apocalypse and slowly worked our way through Saint's vodka.

"My mom died too," I said as we managed to get our characters back to their camp after stealing a load of shit from some other survivors. "Not that you have to talk about it with me or whatever, but I was alone after that. I know how much it fucking sucks to have no one around when you're dealing with that. And even though you're not in that situation, and you have people here who care about you, I just thought you should know that I get it."

Blake was silent for a long time, finishing the last inch of vodka in the bottle with a grimace before making his character on the game wander aimlessly through a field.

When I'd basically accepted the fact that he wasn't going to reply, he finally did.

"How did she die?" he asked and I cursed myself because I should have expected that, but then again, it wasn't like I had to give him any details. I had a fake name now and I was sure Saint wouldn't remember me among the countless list of people his father had fucked over in his lifetime even if I still went by my old one.

"She was murdered," I replied, my gaze fixed on the game too.

Blake took a moment to digest that before nodding. "Did you get the fucker who did it?"

My hesitation went on longer this time, but I'd already opened up this line of conversation, so it seemed pointless to lie. Besides, despite my better judgement, it was hard to dislike Blake. There was just something about him that drew people in and whether it was charm or bullshit I'd clearly already begun to fall prey to it.

"Not yet."

"Well, if you ever need any help with that, I'm in," he said and I was surprised to find that I believed him. He meant that wholeheartedly and without any reservations.

"Same goes for you," I said. "I know that this whole vendetta against Royaume D'élite is important to Tatum because she needs the truth to come out to clear her father's name. But it's important for you, too. So that you can get vengeance against the people who released the Hades Virus into the world and make the real culprits pay for your mom's death. I just want you to know that I'm willing to do whatever it takes to bring those motherfuckers down."

Blake turned to look at me and I met his gaze with a heaviness in my own which swore to him I meant that.

After a long moment, he cracked a smile. "Looks like you really are a Night Keeper, aren't you?" he teased. "I knew you couldn't keep fighting it forever."

I rolled my eyes, but I couldn't really deny it. Despite my membership to this exclusive club having been meant to do nothing more than get me closer to Saint and put me in a better position to help Tatum, I had to admit that it was more than that now. In a strange way I was starting to feel like I belonged among these monsters. And that might have been one of the most terrifying things I'd had to admit to myself in a long time. Because if I cared about them then that made me vulnerable to the pain of losing them. And that was something I'd never wanted to risk again after my mom and Michael were killed.

"Let's make it official by fucking with Saint then," I joked, breaking the seriousness of our conversation as I jumped up to refill the empty vodka bottle with water before placing it in the fridge. I probably should have measured it to the exact millimetre before we'd started drinking but a guess was going to have to do. Maybe we'd get lucky and he'd be distracted the next time he poured himself a glass and not notice the difference. Either way, I was looking forward to the freak out he was going to have over it.

I stumbled on my way back to the couch and laughter tore from my lips as I dropped back down beside Blake and he laughed too. That expensive vodka was some strong shit.

"I think you might be drunk, sir," Blake teased and I rolled my eyes at him.

"As if I'd ever drink with a student," I scoffed and the two of us started up the game again as we fell into companionable silence.

My heart felt a little lighter as we sat there together, and I realised that I'd probably been in as much need of a friend tonight as he was. My grief might have been older than his, but it wasn't something that ever went away. So maybe I had to accept that Blake Bowman was quickly becoming my friend and becoming a Night Keeper might not have been so bad after all.

CHAPTER TWENTY ONE

Mila had legit screamed when I'd told her I'd married Kyan and the news had spread around the school like wildfire since. I had to answer questions from a hundred different girls while they all cooed over my ring saying it was *so* me. As if they had any idea. Half of them shot me jealous looks once they'd offered me their congratulations and I hadn't missed the whispers in class from girls wondering what made me so 'damn special'. It didn't feel all bad being envied for being Kyan Roscoe's wife. Not that I went around with a smug smile on my face or anything, but I certainly wasn't complaining.

Kyan had made sure the school register was changed to list me as Tatum Roscoe without my permission and I'd genuinely punched him in the dick for it. I'd never agreed to give up my name. My name was what connected me to my dad and Jess, and once he realised why I was angry at him for it, he'd apologised. But he hadn't gotten the school to change it back yet and when I'd emailed the administration about it, they had mysteriously not replied. *Fucking Night Keepers with their all powerful bullshit.*

I couldn't worry about that tonight though. Kyan had been sent a message confirming we would be going to Royaume D'élite and all other thoughts had been pushed out of my mind. He'd been sent a location in Hemlock City and we had to be there at seven pm to be picked up and taken to the club.

Nerves warred in my stomach, but there was a quiet kind of determination which had settled over me too. I hadn't said much since he'd given me the news. I was stewing on my hate for these people and the monster who lurked amongst them who was responsible for dragging my father into the events that had led to his death. The one responsible for releasing the Hades Virus and killing thousands upon thousands of innocents. For dad, for them, for Blake's mom, I'd fight to bring them down.

I dressed in ripped jeans and a black crop top in Saint's closet then took a moment to take out Dad's ashes which I kept wrapped in one of my sweaters behind a rack of coats. Saint never moved it and Rebecca never touched it and that was all I needed to know about Saint's respect for the matter. I tugged open the pink sweater my dad had bought me a few years ago and hugged the urn to my chest.

"I'm gonna find out who's responsible," I whispered, vowing it to him. "And I'm going to fucking destroy them."

I could almost hear my dad's laugh for a moment, the way he grinned at me when I swore like that. He'd had a filthier mouth than me and I was sure if I could speak to him now, he'd be cursing the assholes who caused his death far more colourfully than I could manage.

I placed him back away, wrapping him up in my sweater again before turning and pulling on my bike leathers. I headed out of the closest, walking downstairs and Kyan met me at the base, looking seriously appetising in his own set of leathers.

"Well aren't you a treat," he growled, grabbing me by the hips and yanking me off the bottom step before kissing me hungrily.

Saint cleared his throat in irritation and as Kyan stepped away I found him, Blake and Monroe all lined up by the door.

"What's this, a receiving line?" I teased and Blake smirked, but the other two kept their deadly serious expressions intact.

We approached Saint first and he held out a medical facemask to Kyan. "Don't take stupid risks."

"Yeah...I'm not wearing that. I've got my bike helmet then we'll be wearing masks into the club anyways," Kyan said with a shrug.

Saint narrowed his gaze. "Have you got the earpieces in?" he asked.

"Yeah," I said. He'd gotten us some high-tech, top of the range, military grade, stupidly expensive communication devices which would apparently go undetected by a bug or spyware detector so that we could all stay in touch while we were out there. It made me feel like a real life spy or an operative or like some really badass superhero with a team of agents at my back. Or maybe I was just trying to convince myself of that so that the nerves didn't freak me the fuck out, but either way, knowing we would be in contact with the other Night Keepers throughout this whole thing was weirdly reassuring.

"Good," Saint shoved the face mask at Kyan again. "Take it in case you need it. You could always wear it beneath your mask."

"I could, but that would be overkill." He grinned at Saint, slapping his cheek a few times patronisingly. "Are you worried about me, sweetums?"

Saint glowered at him, saying nothing but it was clear he was worried. As Kyan moved along, punching Blake and Monroe in turn for putting on this line-up for us, I took the mask from Saint's hand and tucked it in my pocket with a wink.

His mouth tugged up at one corner and I reached forward, kissing his cheek before moving on to Blake and leaving his smile growing.

Blake kissed me like we were about to charge into battle and I wasn't going to return. I was breathless and had sore lips by the time he released me and I moved towards Monroe.

"Take care of her," he spoke to Kyan, his expression becoming dark.

"I won't let her out of my sight," he growled and the other three nodded, making me roll my eyes, though it was admittedly kind of cute.

"Nothing bad will happen," I promised, wishing I could kiss Monroe goodbye too. The way he was looking at my mouth said the feeling was mutual.

"Naw, baby, a lot of bad shit will happen tonight. Just not to us. I promise you that," Kyan said protectively, taking my hand and pulling me toward the door.

I glanced back at the others with my stomach twisting, giving them a tight smile that none of them returned. The worry in their eyes was potent and I swore quietly to myself that we'd pull this off. We'd find something to bring down these assholes and I'd return to the rest of my Night Keepers before dawn.

Kyan was silent as we walked and I glanced up at him, the lamps lighting his face in an amber glow. His jaw was ticking and his eyes held dark secrets which scared me, secrets I was sure were about to be unveiled in this horror show of a club tonight.

"It'll be okay," I told him and he blinked out of his stupor, looking to me.

"Nothing about this is okay, baby. I don't want you anywhere near these fucking people."

"I want to see my enemies before we destroy them," I growled and Kyan wet his lips.

"Guess I can understand that. You don't have to make it sound so hot though," he commented as his eyes dropped to my mouth.

"My bad," I teased, lightening the mood and he smirked a little.

We made it to the front gate and the guard on duty let us out, nodding to Kyan like he was his boss and I guessed if you were a Night Keeper at Everlake, that was the case for these guys. I wondered how much money they spent paying them off.

Kyan led me to his bike and took my helmet from the bars, turning and putting it on my head. He snapped the visor down and made sure it was secure, a small crease forming between his eyes. It was kind of endearing the way he treated me sometimes. The two of us were either clashing with the force of two tsunamis or caressing each other like we were worried the other would break.

He put his own helmet on, swinging his leg over the bike and I climbed on behind him, shifting up close and wrapping my arms around his waist, his stomach muscles firming under my touch. He started the engine and turned us around, taking off down the road that led away from the school, the night devouring us as we went. It was eerily quiet out on these roads, the streetlights few and far between so only the headlight on the bike pierced the dark.

The scent of leather and gasoline pulled at my senses as we sailed along and gazed into the shadowy forest beyond the road. The wind was cool, but the bike leathers kept out the worst of the cold and Kyan was so huge that he shielded me pretty damn well from the wind anyway.

It was over an hour to Hemlock City and when we finally circled down from the hills towards the sprawling metropolis, my heart started to beat a little harder. We sailed along brightly lit streets which were almost as quiet as the forest, the bars and restaurants all shut up for lockdown. The few people who were out wore masks and walked briskly along like they were anxious to get to their destinations. It sent a chill down my spine seeing a place which should have been thrumming with life silenced by the threat of the Hades Virus.

A siren somewhere in the distance made my heart judder. We weren't allowed to be out here. The only travel allowed was for essential workers or for those doing grocery shopping and if a cop stopped us, it would be pretty clear we weren't out for either of those reasons.

Kyan took back streets to avoid the main roads and eventually pulled up in an alley, killing the engine and the lights. He pulled his helmet off, hanging it on the bars. "We need to leave the bike here, baby."

I nodded, climbing off and taking my own helmet off. Kyan took it from me to hang it on the bars then pushed his fingers into my hair, messing it up to fix the flat look it no doubt had from the helmet. Then he grabbed my hand and tugged me out of the alley, my heart tripling its pace as we turned onto a street with graffiti on the walls and the general air of a bad neighbourhood about it. We passed a chain link fence and a dog lunged at it from the other side, barking fiercely, practically foaming at the mouth as it tried to break through. I gasped in surprise and Kyan tugged me along quicker then slowed as we made it to the corner of the street.

"This is the meeting point," he murmured and I nodded, glancing up and down the road as I hunted for any sign of a car. There was nothing around, just the drum of music coming from an apartment across the road and smoke pluming from the window as a few teenagers laughed and toked on pot.

The sound of a car approaching made me still and I glanced behind me, spotting it coming up the street, the dark SUV looking completely out of place here. It had blacked out windows and screamed you're-about-to-be-murdered-in-the-back-of-me.

I straightened my spine, schooling my features and slapping on a resting bitch face for good measure. These monsters weren't going to unnerve me. Or, they at least wouldn't see it when they did.

The car pulled up beside us and the driver's window rolled down, revealing a broad chested man wearing a faceless black mask which was creepy as shit.

"The night awaits you," he said in a deep, gravelly tone that set the hairs rising on the back of my neck.

Kyan stepped forward, taking the crest from his pocket and flashing it to the guy. "Set us free of our shackles."

The man nodded. "Stay where you are." He opened the door, stepping out in front of us and revealing how big he really was. He rolled his shoulders, posturing and clearly aiming to intimidate us. Kyan sure as shit didn't look like it was working on him, but a trickle of fear ran through my blood as the guy reached inside his large coat. He didn't take out a weapon as I expected though, he took out a device which looked like a paddle and my breathing came unevenly as he looked to Kyan.

"Arms out either side of you, legs spread," he commanded and Kyan

368

stepped back, doing as he asked with his jaw tight as the guy ran the paddle over him, hunting for weapons and listening devices. I didn't breathe as he ran it past each of Kyan's ears, but the paddle didn't detect the earpiece and I let out a controlled breath as the guy nodded and turned to me.

I spread my arms and legs and he started running the paddle up from my feet, reaching my waist then my sides and along my arms. The tracker in my bra wasn't activated, but what if something about it set off that paddle? Would we run? But if we did, then this guy would report it. Kyan's family would surely hear about it. Then-

He ran the paddle over my breasts and it didn't go off. *Thank fuck.*

I schooled my expression, practically holding my breath until he finished the search. Then he got back in the car and shut the door sharply.

"Get in," he commanded and I released a subtle breath as I tried to calm my racing heart.

Kyan moved to the back door, opening it and ducking his head in as if to check the space was clear of psychos before standing back to let me go first.

"Ever the gentleman," I said with a taunting smile.

"We both know I'm nothing of the fucking sort." He hounded me into the car, tugging the door shut behind him as we sat side by side on the back seats. There was plenty of room in front of us with two seats facing towards us with two neat piles of clothes on them.

"Change into the Royaume D'élite regalia," the driver instructed. "Your clothes will remain here in the car until you return." He held something out for us and I took it from his hand. It was a small silver disk with a button at the centre of it about the size of my thumb. "When you are ready to leave, all you need to do is click that button and I will have the car waiting outside."

"Okay," I agreed, slightly reassured that we didn't have to stay there all night if we didn't want to.

"Now change." The guy put a divider up between us and took off down the road. I realised the car windows in the back weren't just blacked out one way, they were blacked out both ways, meaning we couldn't see where the hell we were going.

I exchanged a look with Kyan and he brought my hand to his mouth, kissing my wedding ring before moving forward and passing me a bundle of clothes then grabbing his own.

I unravelled the black material. It was an all over black catsuit, the material stretchy and opaque in places and it had the number 77+ embroidered on the chest in gold. With it was a black skull mask with gold detailing all over it, the eyes hollow and the mouth filled with gold teeth. It made my skin prickle to look at.

I stripped out of my clothes, wriggling into the super-tight material which clung to my body. Then I put on the high-heeled boots provided with it before I turned to Kyan, finding him in honest to shit robes over a fitted pair of black trousers and a smart black shirt with gold buttons. It looked so strange on him, covering his tattoos and making him look like some sort of medieval prince. On his chest was the small number 77.

"What's with the numbers?" I frowned.

"Anonymity," he explained and I remembered he'd said something about that before. "When you're signed up as a member a number is linked to your name so if you wanted to go into business with anybody, it can be arranged through the club. Names and details can be swapped privately then or you can remain entirely anonymous depending on people's preferences."

"You told me you were 69," I said, raising an eyebrow at him.

"I will be later if that's what you want, baby," he said, but the joke didn't quite land as we looked at each other fearfully, knowing we were about to walk right into a snake pit.

"So why does mine have a plus symbol on it?" I asked, running a finger over the gold embroidery to point it out.

"Because you're only allowed to come with me. Your membership is spousal and I'm responsible for you while you're here. If you do anything out of line, it's on me."

"I'll behave," I promised and he nodded.

Kyan reached forward, tugging up a hood on my catsuit which I hadn't noticed. "Every part of you has to be covered." He tucked my hair into it before putting up his own hood and I shivered as we shared an intense look. This was getting realer and realer by the second. We were risking so much by being out here. The virus alone was enough reason to stay away, let alone what terrors awaited us at Royaume D'élite. But I wouldn't have been able to stop Kyan from coming here even if I hadn't wanted to come myself. We were doing this for reasons beyond ourselves but knowing that didn't stop me being afraid.

Kyan brushed his rough thumb across my jaw then leaned in and kissed me. There were so many words that passed between us in that kiss, I couldn't count them. But all of them said the same thing. That we had each other's back, that we were going to face this together and return home safe.

When we broke apart, I tucked myself up against him, our fingers interlacing. I rested my head against his shoulder and took comfort in the solid strength of him as we were driven somewhere off into the night.

It was over an hour before the car finally slowed to a halt and the clamour of a party reached us beyond the car.

The driver put the partition down, peering at us through the eyeholes of his mask. "Put your masks on," he instructed sharply.

I put mine on, securing it in place and keeping the hood tight around it, looking to Kyan and shuddering at the sight of the skull covering his face.

The driver gave a signal to someone beyond the car and my heart lurched as the side door opened and another man in a black mask ushered us out. Kyan went first, taking my hand, his grip iron as he guided me from the car and kept me close to his side.

We were at the foot of an impressive stone stairway that led up to what looked like a huge old hotel. The walls were faux gothic and sheer, rising up to steeples and towers, the enormous building casting a massive shadow thicker than the night.

Lights glittered in the windows, but many of the curtains were drawn and my instincts told me I didn't want to know what lay behind them.

"Welcome to Royaume D'élite," the man said, walking ahead of us up the stairs. "You have a guest waiting for you."

He led us through the enormous arching glass doors and I noticed a huge man in the same robes as Kyan waiting to one side of the entrance hall, the number *230* gleaming on his chest. He strode forward at the beckon of our escort and clasped Kyan's hand in greeting.

"Uncle," Kyan said curtly and I realised this must be Niall. He glanced my way and I recognised the green colour of his eyes beneath his skull mask. I was surprised when he reached for me next, squeezing my arm.

"Hello, lass," he purred.

"Please remember not to use each other's names or titles," the escort said with an edge to his voice. "We all go by a single name here."

"And what's that?" I asked, lifting my chin.

"Master," he breathed, the word sending a chill through me. "For we are all the masters of our own destiny at Royaume D'élite. Here we are free to become our truest selves. We shed our skins at the door and step into a realm where anything is possible."

"Great, lad," Niall said. "Now where can my truest self get a stiff drink?"

"Down the hall and to your left," he answered, bowing his head to us. "Have an exhilarating evening." He swept away with that freaky statement, heading back out the front door and leaving us there on the bone white floor.

Niall nodded to us then led the way down the hall and Kyan's grip on my hand only tightened.

"I assume you've arrived?" Saint drawled in my ear suddenly and I nearly leapt out of my skin. *Jesus Christ.*

"Yeah," Kyan answered in a murmur.

"Good. Keep your eyes peeled. Watch the staff's movements and look out for no access areas."

"Okay, over and out," Kyan muttered with a breath of laughter and

Saint cursed him.

Niall turned left into a room under a stone archway and I took in the huge, dark hall spreading out before us. One whole wall at the far end was built of nothing but cages and bile rose in my throat as I saw the men and women inside them, dressed in leather underwear, some of them screaming for help while others curled in on themselves or had haunted expressions on their faces. I realised I wasn't moving, my feet glued to the floor and Kyan was suddenly yanking me along towards a bar, his mouth falling to my ear.

"Don't stare, baby," he reminded me and I jerked my head sideways, my pulse pounding furiously in my head as I tried to calm down.

I noted the people at the bar were drinking through straws, a hole between the teeth in their skull masks allowing them to do so. I had the urge to tear their masks off and throw my fists into their exposed faces and we'd barely even been here a moment.

A shriek caught my ear and I couldn't stop myself from looking as two men in black masks hauled a young girl from one of the cages before injecting her with something. She fell limp and they handed her over to two men who pawed greedily at her skin before they carried her through a black veil out of the room. I found myself moving in that direction, unsure what I could do for her but knowing I needed to try. Kyan yanked me back to his side, fixing me in his gaze and squeezing my wrist hard enough to cut through the fog in my mind.

He didn't say anything, but I knew what he meant. I couldn't go. Even the thought of it now seemed foolish. I couldn't save anyone here. Not tonight anyway. We had to find a way to bring them down. I had to stomach this awful place and not fuck up this chance.

I realised Niall was doing shots through the hole in his mask, throwing them in without the supplied straw on the bar. I held out my hand for one and he placed a clear shot in my palm. I tossed it through the hole in my mask, swallowing thickly and letting the burn of whiskey wash through me, blocking out everything else for a moment.

Then I focused on the movements of the staff as they headed in and out of rooms around the hall. It looked like a lot of them were heading under that black veil.

I nudged Kyan, nodding to it and he sighed like he already knew we'd have to go that way.

"You might want another shot, baby," he murmured, but I shook my head, tugging him along as Niall followed. I didn't want my mind clouded with too much alcohol tonight. We had to focus so we could find a way to destroy this place and the vile people who attended it.

We moved through the crowd who were dancing to rave music and I noticed there were plenty of half naked or even totally naked men and women among them, their eyes glazed like they were high as hell. None of them had masks on and I guessed that they were the poor souls who had been put up for sale in this fucking place.

The masked men and women moved amongst them, pawing at them whenever the desire took them or tugging them out of the room through a door with a sign on it saying it led to the private boudoirs.

Kyan kept me close as we moved through them and I couldn't help but stare as I caught sight of one of the masked men having his cock sucked right in the middle of the fucking room. As my eyes nearly bugged out of my head and I silently thanked my mask for hiding my facial expressions, he pulled out, coming all over the girl's face before punching her hard enough to knock her back on her ass.

The dancers scattered as she fell sprawling to the floor in her leather underwear and I ducked down to help pull her to her feet as the asshole in question moved away like it meant nothing at all to him. My gaze snagged on the golden number *84* on his chest and I gritted my teeth as I committed that to memory, hoping to find a way to pay him back for that move somehow.

More than a few of the masked freaks were looking my way as I helped the beaten hooker to her feet and Kyan tugged my arm roughly, forcing me to release her before I drew too much attention.

"You have to think bigger if you wanna help them, baby," he murmured in my ear. "When we take this place down they'll all be freed. Now slap that guy's ass so that everyone here stops looking at you with so much suspicion."

I was about to ask what guy when he gave me a shove towards a dancer in a leather thong with a ball gag in his mouth. I wanted to protest, but Kyan had a point and I could feel the eyes of the sadistic club members following me, so I reluctantly reached out and slapped the guy's bare ass cheek hard enough to leave a handprint.

He barely even flinched, clearly more than used to being treated like that and it made me feel all kinds of dirty.

"Good girl," Kyan purred, tugging me on as the attention fell off of me and Niall laughed obnoxiously.

We walked through the veil and the first thing I heard were the screams. Doors led off on either side of the corridor which was tinted by red lights. Beyond them, terrible things were happening, things I didn't want to imagine let alone witness. But as we made it to the end of the corridor and walked down a dark stairway, my gut told me I was going to have to see things I didn't want to. Things I might never forget.

At the base of the stone stairway was a corridor bordered by mesh wire walls that ran up to a caged ceiling, beyond which was a high, circular walkway where onlookers were gazing in. Strobe lights flashed intermittently beyond the wire either side of me and I caught sight of passages leading away from here. Kyan quickened his pace as a scream rang out somewhere from within the maze's depths and my spine prickled.

"Viewing point this way!" a man called by a golden door up ahead, ushering us forward.

"We're happy down here," Niall told him, waving him off.

Something collided with the metal wire to my left and I wheeled around in fright.

"Hey!" a half naked girl hissed, trying to force her hand through the wire to reach me. "Are you carrying weapons? Give me something to help!"

She had dark hair and a pretty face, a thousand untold horrors swirling in her brown eyes. She couldn't have been much older than me and a yank in my chest drew me toward her. If it had been me in there, I'd have desperately wanted someone to help me. So how could I just stand here and do nothing?

I reached for her fingers which were threaded through the wire, trying to figure out what I could do, how I could get her out. "I'm sorry, I don't-"

Kyan tugged me away and the attendant by the door strode forward, taking a baton from his hip and whacking it against the wire, making her back away in fright. A shadow moved behind her and a huge man came at her, lunging for her and she twisted away fast, racing off into the maze. He took chase and I stared on as my hands began to shake. *This place is hell.*

A radio crackled behind me and I swallowed thickly as I looked to the worker as a voice came through it.

"More drinks needed on the mezzanine, office twelve," the voice said and the guy bowed to us before striding away down the hall at a swift pace. I shared a look with the others and we took off after him while I tried to drown out the screams carrying from the maze.

"Head to that office," Saint commanded like we weren't already heading there anyway.

"Thanks Captain Obvious," Kyan muttered and I glanced back over my shoulder, my mind still snagged on that horrible caged maze.

"What is that place?" I breathed to Kyan.

"It's a death game," he growled and the edge to his voice told me that it was the very one he'd been in himself. The thought made my throat burn and rage twist violently through my gut.

"How did you survive this hell?" I rasped and he looked down at me with a dark kind of pain in his eyes.

"I had to, baby," he whispered. "So we could return here one day and destroy every last one of them."

Saint

CHAPTER TWENTY TWO

"Is anyone else getting Mission Impossible vibes here?" Blake asked excitedly as the three of us sat at the dining table around my laptop, listening to the feed from Kyan and Tatum's earpieces.

"If the task was impossible, I wouldn't have allowed them to go there," I muttered, glad the microphone was currently off so that the others wouldn't be distracted by this nonsense as they worked to find something of use to us.

"He means like in the movies," Monroe supplied from my left as if the multimillion dollar franchise had escaped my attention and I had no idea about modern culture.

"I am aware of the movies," I said, pinching the bridge of my nose as I fought to contain my frustration. "I just think that comparing the two of them sneaking around in some old manor house full of psychopaths to Tom Cruise dangling from the side of a skyscraper is an unrealistic parallel to draw."

"The tech guy is always grumpy," Blake stage whispered behind my back and Monroe chuckled in appreciation.

"Well if I'm the tech guy then you must be the rookie agent who is too dumb to be allowed on the mission. And if we're really following the script then I will expect you to throw yourself into danger like a moron and get yourself killed shortly," I replied.

"Pfft, I'm not the rookie," Blake protested. "I'm more like James Bond, out on another mission, waiting to be called in for the crossover movie of dreams."

I scoffed, shaking my head at him. "If you're going to start talking about merging fantasy worlds and the entirely unrealistic suggestion that a British MI6 agent would suddenly join forces with a team of-"

"Okay so if he's the rookie, then who am I?" Monroe asked, effectively saving them all from the tirade I was taking off on and I ground my teeth as I tried to decide whether or not I should just kick the two of them out so that I could concentrate.

I cast a cursory look at him sitting there in his sweatpants and wifebeater with his fucking coach whistle hanging around his neck and smirked as I figured it out.

"You're the old timer," I said. "Just one day away from retirement and imparting all of your hard earned knowledge and experience on anyone who will listen. Safe to say, you're doomed to die too. So it's probably for the best that neither of you were deemed necessary for this mission."

"Either that or the three of us are about to fall prey to a strategically placed bomb and the heroes are going to have to go rogue to get themselves out of there," Blake suggested.

A loud knock sounded at the door and we all looked around at it, freezing in our positions like we thought that might actually be an assassin come to kill us all. So help them if it was though.

"You're up, rookie, just try not to die while answering the door," I taunted and Blake cursed me as he shoved out of his seat and headed over to see who the fuck thought it was a good idea to interrupt us. I'd be sure to make their life hell tomorrow to remind them that they were not allowed to come to my fucking house under any circumstances.

"We've found an office," Tatum's hushed voice came through the speakers on my laptop and I cut a look towards the door as Blake hesitated by it before enabling the microphone so I could reply to her.

"Was it locked?" I asked because nothing of value was going to be left sitting in an open room.

"Yeah, but not well enough to count. There's something up with it though, there were a few old dudes who just came out of here, all of them smoking as they congratulated themselves on the deals they'd been making, but the room doesn't really smell of cigars," Kyan put in.

"Riveting," I muttered. "Keep looking, we have an uninvited guest who we need to deal with."

"On it. Over and out," Kyan replied and Tatum sniggered.

"You're not out, it's a live feed," I snarled for what must have been the hundredth time since he'd put that fucking earpiece in and Monroe laughed like his joke was funny. It was not.

I gave Blake a nod and he swung the door open to find Mila and Danny standing there, peering into my private space like they were looking to get their eyes gouged out.

"Oh, hey," Mila began. "Tatum left her English assignment in the library and I haven't been able to get hold of her. It's due tomorrow and it's not finished so I thought-"

"I'll give it to her," Blake said, snatching the page from her hand and moving to close the door.

"Is she here? A few of us are heading down to the common house if you guys wanted to join?" Mila asked quickly while Danny looked inclined to tug her away.

"We do not," I put in and Blake rolled his eyes at me. Apparently Tatum's little friend and her plus one had decided to forgive us for the whole misunderstanding where she almost got a face full of piss which was a pretty smart move on their parts, but it unfortunately left me having to suffer through their company regularly once again. But not here. Never here, goddammit.

I was going to have to make sure Tatum reminded them of the rules before they started to think of themselves as a part of our group or something equally abhorrent.

"Tate and Kyan are in his room, you can probably hear the bed slamming into the wall if you listen for it," Blake deadpanned. "So she can't come out to play right now. If she's got any energy left and wants to head down there later, you'll see us there."

"Okay, catch you later then." Mila stepped back and Danny drew her away as Blake closed the door.

"I will never understand the desire to show up unannounced at someone's house to find out if they're free," I muttered irritably, giving my attention back to the whispered discussion Kyan and Tatum where having while they hunted the office they'd found. "Blake, get me my vodka and a glass, will you? I need a stiff drink."

"Sure thing, boss," Blake agreed too easily and I caught the edge of a smirk on Monroe's lips which had my suspicions rising.

Blake appeared with my bottle of vodka and a tumbler, placing them down beside my laptop like a well trained little puppy. It only took me a cursory glance to realise that there was at least three millimetres too much liquid in the bottle and I blew out a breath of frustration as I felt the two of them tensing up beside me in anticipation of some childish prank they'd set up. Honestly, it was like living with pre-schoolers half the fucking time around here.

I slowly pushed my laptop forward until it was sitting in the middle of the table where it would be safe, keeping most of my attention on the sounds of Kyan and Tatum searching the office as I took the top from the bottle of vodka.

Blake sniggered to himself as I began to fill my glass and I made sure to pour enough to fill it to the top. Unsurprisingly, the tart scent of my favourite alcohol was severely lacking.

I contained my own smirk as I picked up the full glass in one hand and the open bottle in the other, then in one fell swoop, I upended them in both of their laps.

Blake swore as he leapt to his feet and Monroe fell out of his chair in an attempt to escape me while I snorted a laugh in triumph.

"Very funny, asshole," Blake growled while I smirked at him, shoving the glass and bottle away while Monroe muttered curses.

"Try harder next time," I told them as I pulled my laptop close again. "As if I would be fooled by such a sloppy attempt."

Monroe tried to wipe the water from his crotch while Blake jogged away for fresh pants and the sweet taste of victory coated my tongue.

"We'll get you next time," Monroe promised as he righted his chair and dropped into it again, seeming amused by my antics for once.

"If you say so."

"This bookcase has scratches on the floor in front of it," Tatum said in a low voice and Kyan's heavy footsteps made me believe he was crossing the room to join her. My attention instantly snapped back to them and I gritted my teeth in frustration.

"I thought you were supposed to be sneaking?" I hissed, enabling the microphone again as Blake took his seat on my right once more. "Why are you stomping about like an elephant in stilettos?"

"Are you worried about me, Saint, baby?" Kyan mocked and I had to grit my teeth against answering. He knew damn well that I was concerned for the two of them and sitting here helplessly listening in on what they were doing was fucking painful.

"Don't force it Kyan, there must be something to release it," Tatum muttered and I could practically picture him trying to rip the hidden door off of the damn wall.

It took them another few minutes of scrambling about before she announced that they'd found their way in and I was seriously starting to consider medication to stop my heart from thundering in my ears the way it was.

I didn't like this at all. It was too far out of my control. But it was also the only lead we had.

"Okay, we're in a big office with a desk and a bunch of fancy chairs. It stinks of cigars so I'm guessing this is where the old assholes were hanging out," Kyan said.

"That description leaves much to be desired," I muttered, wishing I could have gotten a camera onto them too, but it was too risky. An earpiece I could hide from detectors, but a camera would have been too high of a risk.

"There are cabinets and a computer," Tatum added a little more helpfully. "But I don't even know where to begin."

"Start with the desk," I suggested. "The Hades Virus is the biggest issue globally right now. If they were in there discussing things of importance then there's a good chance that came up, especially if they are working on it in any way."

"Be careful, princess," Monroe added and I shook my head at the pointless addition to the conversation.

"Okay...so there's a laptop here," she said slowly and I could just picture her sitting down before it and opening it up. "Password protected," she added, sounding disappointed.

"Forget it," I instructed. "No one who goes to this much trouble to hide their business dealings is going to have a predictable password. See if there's anything else in the drawers."

I could hear the sounds of her rummaging about and then the rustling of paper. "This looks like stock market stuff," she said.

"Are any particular companies mentioned?" I asked. Stocks and shares were one of my many talents and my fingers twitched with the desire to actually see what she was looking at, but a brief overview of the company names would give me some insight.

"Dresdon Hydraulics, Kingdom Construction, Beuford Corp," she read out and I quickly typed out each company she listed on the document I was using to make notes about their observations. " Serenity Pharmaceuticals-"

"That one," I interrupted her. "My father has been buying up shares in that company recently. Far more than the profit margins would suggest make it a worthy investment."

"You just know all of your father's stock portfolio by heart?" Monroe asked sceptically.

"I keep a close eye on the man most likely to uproot my life, yes," I replied. "And I take note when he makes purchases that seem to make no financial sense. He's been purchasing shares in that company for months even when there were other investment opportunities that would have seen a better return. I assumed he had some insider information on the company which he was waiting to cash out on but the fact that it's a pharmaceutical company rings some alarm bells given our current situation."

"Okay, let me see if I can find any more about Serenity Pharmaceuticals," Tatum said and the sounds of her searching returned to me.

My mind was racing as I waited for them to find something else of use and I quickly pulled up my own stock portfolio, followed by my father's, followed by the company website for Serenity Pharmaceuticals.

Blake leaned in close enough that I could feel his breath feathering on my neck but I didn't even bother to snap at him over it as I quickly started skimming through the information they had on their site.

They were a big company, but not one of the biggest. Obviously they were in the midst of trialling vaccinations for the Hades Virus like every other Pharmaceutical company in the world. All of them taking part in a race to be the first to provide it and cash out on the billions they'd get from worldwide governments for it if they succeeded. Their site was full of overreaching promises of a vaccine within a few months but nothing to say they were really any closer than anyone else to success.

I pulled up a list of the people running the company and added them to my list of assholes to check up on and then Kyan interrupted my hunt.

"I've got something that might be nothing," he said slowly. "It was in the trash."

"Go on," I urged.

"It's a note with a name on it. Dr Henry Singh and a number," he explained.

"Singh was the name of the guy my dad worked for in the lab that developed the Hades Virus," Tatum said urgently.

"Is it a phone number?" Blake asked.

"Naw. It's like a reference number," Kyan replied. "P247T9."

My brain was firing on all cylinders but that meant less than nothing to me and my jaw tightened in frustration.

"Wait," Tatum said suddenly. "There was a number like that on a file I found in the desk drawer. But the stuff inside it was to do with the next elections, so I discarded it."

We were forced to wait while they moved around the office again and Monroe clawed a hand though his blonde hair as the tension built around us.

"The drawers here are locked, shall I force them?" Kyan suggested and I cursed beneath my breath. We needed to investigate this properly, but if they made it obvious someone had been in there then it would put them at risk of discovery.

"I can pick it with a hair pin," Tatum said confidently and I could have kissed her father for teaching her all of that prepper survivalist bullshit.

"Shit, baby, do you know how hot it is to see you going all spy girl on me?" Kyan purred.

"Focus on what you're there to do," Monroe snapped before I could and Kyan chuckled like an asshole.

"Got it!" Tatum announced in excitement and the sound of drawers rolling open followed her words.

I waited patiently as they rifled through more paperwork. Or perhaps it wasn't so patiently because my jaw was grinding and I was moving my fingers to the notes of the most complicated piano piece I could think of on my thigh beneath the table.

"I've got it - P247T9," Kyan said triumphantly and we were forced to wait while they read whatever was in that file.

"Okay, it looks like a breakdown of Singh's research into the creation of the Hades Virus," Tatum explained. "There are some pretty fucked up photographs of test subjects and...nothing else."

"Fuck," Kyan cursed before I could.

"There's another reference number though. Y684E1," she said.

"On it, baby," Kyan replied and we waited again.

"This is taking too fucking long," Blake growled and I couldn't help but agree. They couldn't stay in there much longer. Every moment that passed was another second that could equal their discovery.

"Got it," Tatum said. "Okay, this one is a...it's a lot of test data which looks kinda like the things my dad used to work on..."

"It's about the Hades Virus," Kyan said. "Look."

"Oh yeah," she replied. "Shit, okay, there's a lot of negative results here, it's kinda hard to decipher what..."

I forced myself to remain silent throughout their nonsensical ramblings, waiting for them to figure out what they were looking at and give me the proper information, but it felt like chewing on glass.

"Fuck," Tatum breathed.

"Shit, baby," Kyan said, the two of them sounding like they'd seen a fucking ghost.

"Tell us what you're looking at, or so help me-" I began and Blake slapped a hand down on my shoulder to try and keep me calm.

"Sorry," Tatum said. "My dad's name is on here. These are the results for the vaccine he stole alongside the Hades Virus. The ones he gave to Mortez."

"And?" Blake pressed.

"And it...failed. The vaccine didn't work. It seemed like it did at first but around a month after the Hades Virus had been released into the world some of the people who had been given it were infected and they died. It looks like their bodies couldn't produce the antibodies required to fight it off despite the supposed vaccine in their systems."

We fell silent as the sound of more pages turning came over the speakers.

"Serenity Pharmaceuticals," Kyan said. "Their name is in here on this research. They're the company who produced the vaccine. They're the ones who it ended up with after it was stolen from Singh."

"So they're the ones who stole it? They're responsible for putting the Hades Virus out into the world?" Blake asked.

"They're certainly involved," I muttered because all of this had the stench of a much bigger fish about it. "My guess is that they were just the engineers to the plan. But the man in charge of Royaume D'élite is the one who orchestrated it. That's why there's whispers of Serenity Pharmaceuticals stocks being ready to take a spike. Whoever has shares in the company who creates the vaccine for this will make millions. Fuck that actually, more like billions. I'm willing to bet that the whole thing was set up for that very purpose. Set the virus loose, let the world get desperate and then sweep in with a vaccine and make a fortune off the back of the desperate souls who need it."

"They did all of this - killed all of those people - for *money?*" Blake snarled, staring at me like he couldn't believe that that was the motivation, but of course it was. Money was the root of all evil. I should know, I'd been bathing in it since before I could walk and look at me.

"Obviously," I replied and he shoved out of his chair angrily, stalking away from the table as his grief bubbled up to the surface and rage consumed him.

I kept my focus on Kyan and Tatum, needing to keep my head clear to help them if required while Monroe moved away to comfort Blake.

"But this says they don't have the vaccine," Tatum protested. "So why the hell would they be so stupid as to release the virus anyway?"

"Greed, siren," I pointed out. "They believed they had it and they wanted to reap the rewards of that. The fact that they turned out to be wrong about all of it really just means they made a bad investment as far as they're concerned. No doubt they're working tirelessly to produce a vaccine that really does work so that they can still cash out though."

"Fuck," Kyan muttered and I had to agree with him there.

"You need to put everything back where you found it and get out of there," I instructed. "I have more than enough to go on now. I'll be able to figure out who's running that place and I know where to aim my research next. I want you back home as soon as possible."

"Okay," Tatum agreed and it was clear from the tone of her voice that though this information had shaken her, she wasn't going to be put off of her game by it.

"No more risks," I warned. "Just get out of there."

"Aye aye, captain," Kyan replied and I cursed beneath my breath.

Why did it sound like he intended to do the exact opposite of my commands? And why was I even surprised?

CHAPTER TWENTY THREE

We made sure everything was back in place and my heart thrashed against my chest as we closed the last drawer and shared an intense look.

"Heeeey buddy!" Niall shouted from outside, giving us a cue that someone was headed this way. "Which way to the bar? I'm totally fucking lost."

"Down the hall and to the right," a guy answered Niall.

A feminine laugh came from beyond the door and the handle twisted. I grabbed Kyan's hand, ducking down behind the desk and he dropped into place beside me just as the door flew open. Our masks were still on the desk where we'd left them and I shared an alarmed look with Kyan, praying they wouldn't be spotted.

"Oh woops, I don't think we should be in here, master," a woman's voice sounded.

"Well they shouldn't have left the door open, should they?" an older man's voice sounded, a slur to his words telling me he was drunk.

"What's happening?" Saint spoke in my ear, but I couldn't answer him.

"You're right," she giggled. "Do it to me right here."

"Naughty girl," he laughed and I cringed, sharing a look with Kyan at the sound of the guy's zipper rolling down. "We'll make a terrible mess."

"I love mess," she said breathily.

"Don't I know it," he chuckled then spluttered a cough that made my gut clench. I reached out to cover Kyan's mouth and nose and his lips twitched beneath my palm. "Hurry then, on your knees and open your mouth."

She giggled again and I frowned as I realised we were probably going to have to sit here listening to this old guy getting sucked off for however long it took.

"Take your mask off, " he instructed and she hummed anxiously before the sound of her mask hitting the floor reached me.

"Do it, master," she begged. "Soak me."

Soak? I grimaced then the distinctive sound of a guy pissing filled the room along with the tang of urine in the air. *Oh fuck no.*

"What's that noise?" Saint demanded.

The girl cried out with her joy and the guy laughed while I tried not to throw up in my mouth.

"Make me dirty!" she cried.

"You're filthy," he grunted before the sound of his zipper thankfully did up again. "Let's go before someone comes and finds this mess. We wouldn't want to upset the Grand Master." He started coughing again and my heart began to hammer.

"But he encourages us to be free," she cooed before they stepped out of the room.

"Probably not in his private rooms though," he laughed and the door clicked shut.

"Fucking hell," Kyan growled, getting up and pulling me after him.

"God it stinks. Let's get out of here," I hissed, grabbing our masks and handing Kyan his before I put mine on. "Keep your face covered."

"What happened?" Saint pushed.

"You don't wanna know," I said, but his frustrated growl said that wasn't good enough. Kyan put his mask on and I relaxed a little.

We hurried across the room, avoiding the large stain on the carpet before slipping out the door and shutting it again. We started walking down the corridor and I drew in slow breaths to calm my racing heart.

A group of people walked toward us in an arrowhead formation with a tall man at the front and the rest of them fanning out behind them in a triangle. He was particularly noticeable as his mask was purely gold and a shining crest on his lapel marked him as the Grand Master.

"Good evening," he said to us, nodding and his deep voice made me pause for a moment as I swear I knew it from somewhere.

"Good evening, Grand Master," Kyan supplied, tugging me out of his way and dragging me along as soon as the group passed us.

"That's the leader?" I whispered to Kyan, but Saint answered in my ear.

"You saw him?" Saint asked sharply.

"He wore a solid gold mask," I breathed.

"Big guy," Kyan muttered.

"Tall or broad? What precise height?" Saint demanded.

"I dunno man, I could've used my dick as a tape measure but figured it was inappropriate," Kyan said with a dark laugh.

"You fuckin-"

"He was as tall as Kyan," I told Saint before he burst a blood vessel. "Give or take an inch."

"An inch up or down?" Saint hissed.

"Down," I said.

"Good girl," Saint said and for some reason that made me smile. "Now get the fuck home."

"Not until I've had a smoke," Kyan said as we rounded the corner and Niall stepped forward from the shadows.

"Hey," he grunted. "You kids get what you need?"

"Maybe," Kyan answered. "Where's the nearest smoking room?"

"Do you really need to smoke right now?" I hissed. "Let's just leave."

"Naw, baby," Kyan murmured. "I *really* need a smoke." He gave me an intense look through his mask and I heard Saint cursing in my ear.

"Don't do anything stupid, asshole," Saint warned and I realised what Kyan was suggesting. He wanted to cause trouble, and after what I'd seen here, it was enough for me to want in on that too.

"Yeah, you know what, I fancy a smoke too," I said firmly. "Which way Niall?"

"This way, pretty lass." He turned on his heel and walked along with a swagger.

He led us to a smoking room that was decked out in a Moroccan theme, everyone sitting in groups on decorative cushions on the floor with large hookah vases between them. The group members took it in turns to toke on the pipe and clouds of scented smoke plumed up around them. The scent of fruits, drugs and tobacco all clouded in the room and made my throat burn.

Kyan took the lead through the darkened room to the bar at the back of it, swiping a box of matches out of a large bowl. Then he ordered a hookah and an attendant led us to a ring of cushions before setting up the vase at the middle of it.

"What flavours would you like?" she asked, handing us a menu and Kyan promptly passed it to me.

"Pick your poison, baby," he instructed and I glanced down at the menu, picking out a couple at random.

"Bubblegum and orange," I said.

"Oh, are you sure?" the attendant asked. I had zero intention of smoking this shit either way so I nodded, thrusting the menu at her.

"My girl has particular tastes – oh and I'll have a shot of tequila," Kyan told her and she chuckled before heading away to fetch the flavourings before setting it up for us.

When the hookah was ready and Kyan had his shot in hand, Niall swiped up the pipe and sucked deeply on it, coughing heavily and making a show of pounding his fist on his chest.

"Holy Mary mother of god," he coughed. "That's fucking arsenic."

The attendant reached for it to take it away with profuse apologies and Niall waved a hand.

"I didn't say I didn't like it, missus," he laughed his booming laugh and it was hard not to join in as he sucked hard on the pipe again. Smoke plumed around us and the strong scent of orange and bubblegum made my nose wrinkle.

Kyan pulled me into his lap suddenly and arranged my legs so I was covering what he was doing. It was weird how I could practically see him smirking beneath his mask.

He tipped up his tequila shot onto the end of a curtain that was hanging down the wall beside us so it soaked into it. I held my breath as he struck a match beneath my legs then held it against the material. It went up in flames with a whoosh and I gasped. Kyan dragged me to my feet and I kicked over the hookah as we went, knocking the burning charcoals out of it so it set another fire. I stifled a laugh as we pretended to run away with the rest of the crowd, leaping over cushions while Kyan 'accidentally' knocked people over.

I spotted the asshole, number *84* who had hit that girl earlier amongst the runners and pointed him out to Kyan. With a dark laugh, my man slammed into him hard enough to send the guy crashing to the floor and I not so accidentally stepped on him as we kept running, kicking him in the ribs with my heel as hard as I could.

Niall cackled with glee, less than subtly slamming his boot down on the asshole's hand and grinding it down, breaking fingers as the guy screamed in pain beneath him.

Before anyone else could notice what we'd done, the three of us raced for the door, Kyan's hand firmly locked around mine as a savage grin lifted my lips beneath my mask.

Niall ran behind us, laughing wildly as screams rang out and the whole wall went up in flames. Panic filled the air and my heart swelled at the sound as we all ran away. They deserved to be afraid just like the prisoners in this place were afraid. And we weren't done setting fires yet.

CHAPTER TWENTY FOUR

The screams of the people closest to the fire chased us away as I dragged Tatum out into the corridor bellowing, "Fire!" at the top of my lungs to cause more panic.

Three of the black-masked workers ran past us in the opposite direction with fire extinguishers in their arms though, so I guessed our little party trick wouldn't be out of hand for long. Still, it felt good to strike back at these twisted motherfuckers in some small way.

"You've had your fun, now get the fuck out of there," Saint demanded over the earpiece and I chuckled.

"All in good time," I muttered.

I'd suffered too long in this monstrous place to let them off easy now I was back. I wanted to strike at them, needed to. Just a little to show they hadn't broken me and to prove to myself and my girl that I was dedicated to making this whole fucked up club and every single member of it burn, no matter what it took.

Niall caught my elbow and tugged me out of the corridor we were moving down, through another veiled doorway and onto a raised mezzanine level that looked over the death game taking place on the lower floor.

I tugged Tatum close as we slowed our pace, the screams of the people running from the fire quickly drowned out by the agony laced screams of a man in the maze of death beneath us.

I didn't want to look, didn't want to be forced to think about what it had been like to take part in the carnage of that twisted game, but I wasn't going to allow something as irrelevant as fear hold me back in any way. It was just an emotion designed to cripple. And I refused to let anything like that take root in me.

My hand gripped the railing as I looked down at the game taking place below, watching as the screaming man fought a losing battle for his life against a girl who was stabbing him with all the fury and injustice that I'd felt when I'd been put in that cage.

Tatum stayed close to me, tucking herself beneath my arm and looking out over the carnage too, taking in what I'd lived through in silent disgust. Niall kept walking, but I knew he wouldn't go far so I didn't pay too much attention. No doubt he was up to something, wreaking a little havoc of his own, and I certainly wasn't going to stop him.

It was dark up here, the spectators little more than shadows where we stood above the game. I remembered looking up from within that maze and seeing the glint of black and gold masks peering down at me, knowing not a single one of the people hidden behind them cared if I lived or died and wishing I could drag them down there with me to feel the kiss of my blade themselves.

"My money is on the girl," a man said as he came and took up position to my left and it took me a moment to realise he was speaking to me.

"Oh yeah?" I grunted, watching as the girl in question stood, covered in the blood of the guy she'd just killed and turned to run further into the maze with the bloody knife in her hand.

She was probably a year or two older than me, her long, black hair sticking to her tanned shoulders as the heat of this place made her sweat. She ducked into a shadowy corner just before another guy rounded the other end of the tunnel she was in and I watched with a sneer on my face which was thankfully hidden beneath my mask.

The guy beside me didn't reply as we all watched the big dude draw closer to the girl's hiding place. He clearly hadn't seen her and for some reason, I found myself rooting for her, even though I doubted her opponent was any more deserving of death. Ninety percent of the contestants in the games were proxies plucked off of the street and offered money to take part in a contest without ever being given the full details until they were here with no other choice but to fight for their lives. And even the winners didn't have much prospect of a better life beyond that cage.

I was one of a very few members here who had refused the offer of taking on a proxy and had chosen to fight my own battle for my membership to this fucked up club. If I'd had any real choice, I would have told them to stick their membership up their gold coated assholes and cut their shrivelled ball sacks off for good measure. But of course I hadn't been offered that luxury. Once I was here, someone had to go into that game one way or another so I'd chosen to play with my own life rather than a stranger's. And like most people in this sorry world when faced with the option to fight or die, I'd chosen to bloody my hands and taint my soul in favour of my own survival.

The guy strode straight past the girl's hiding place and she crept out behind him, leaping up onto his back and swiping her blade across his throat before he had the chance to fight her off.

Tatum sucked in a sharp breath beside me as his blood sprayed out and I clenched my teeth as I drew her closer to me, my arm tight around her waist.

"Oh yes. I just placed a bet for fifty grand on her, and you wanna know the best bit?" the man beside me asked, leaning in so the acrid stench of stale sweat and brandy sailed beneath my nose.

"What's that?" I asked, my muscles tightening with the desire to shove him back a fucking step.

"I told them I don't even want any money for a prize. If she wins, I get *her,* for the whole night," he laughed throatily and my spine straightened as I felt a shudder run through Tatum at my side.

"What do you mean you *get* her?" Tatum asked, her voice hard but void of emotion so it wasn't totally clear how disgusted she was to someone who didn't know her.

"I mean, I get her to myself in one of the private rooms to do as I please until dawn," the guy chuckled. "And with only two contestants left in the game, I'm pretty sure I'm in for a good night."

"I thought the winners got membership?" Tatum asked, leaning forward to see him better.

The guy's gaze was fixed on the fighting beneath us so he didn't return her look, but he did laugh loudly at her words.

"I can tell you're new," he said, slapping me on the back like we were sharing a joke and a fierce kind of anger coursed down my spine at the contact. "Maybe next time leave your wife at home, eh? Then you could get in on some of this action too? Or do you like to play with them together?"

"Naw, that's not the kind of monster I am," I said in a low tone which would have been warning enough to most people but not this drunk, entitled son of a bitch.

"Well, I'll happily enlighten you then, my dear," he chuckled, seemingly oblivious to the danger lurking right beside him. "Every person in this fine establishment who is not wearing one of these masks is up for sale. That means that for the right price you can do anything you want to them. Think of them like sex toys or slabs of meat, mice in a trap, whatever you want. Point is, they're nothing. Not unless we decide they are. That girl is just fighting as a proxy and the man whose membership she's playing for has happily agreed to my terms of the bet because once she wins for him, she will have served his purpose."

"So her prize for winning is serving *your* purpose?" Tatum asked and that time the disgust was more than clear in her voice, but our revolting companion only seemed egged on by that.

"Yeah. And she looks like the kind of girl who wants to be fucked in the ass, don't you think?"

The asshole didn't even get the chance to fight as I grabbed him by the back of his cloak and launched him over the railing. But his scream as he fell drew the attention of every screwed up motherfucker in the area.

He fell on top of the cage where the death match was taking place with a sickening crack that said he'd most definitely broken something and chaos broke out around the walkways as he shrieked and screamed for help.

"Holy fuck, Kyan," Tatum gasped but as she looked up at me, I found her blue eyes alight with excitement and I grinned even though she couldn't see it beneath the mask. "Do we need to run?"

"Naw, baby, everything here has a price. I'm sure my trust fund can take the hit for that little misunderstanding," I assured her.

"What the hell is going on?" Saint demanded angrily in my ear, but he didn't need to know that right now, so I ignored him. Tatum took pity on him though and muttered an explanation.

"Kyan just tossed that piece of shit over the balcony and now he's crying like the little bitch he is," she said proudly.

"For the love of Christ, just get the hell out of there before you get yourselves into the kind of trouble you can't get out of," Saint demanded and I could just about hear Monroe saying something too, but I couldn't catch it over the shouts in the room.

Niall's raucous laughter drew my attention and he slapped me on the back as he reappeared, leaning over the railing to watch as the asshole tried to crawl off the top of the cage.

"This is fucking perfect, lad," he howled as he leaned forward to get a better look.

The guy kept trying to crawl along while cradling his arm and whimpering and I couldn't help but laugh too.

Movement from the cage beneath us drew my attention and Tatum caught my hand, squeezing my fingers as we watched the girl who was taking part in the fights below running towards the masked man through the maze.

My eyes were glued to her as she ran with determined strides, leapt up, grabbed the wire at the top of the cage and thrust her knife through the gaps in the metal, sinking it deep into the bastard's gut.

He shrieked in pain as the game organisers raced around the edge of the cage, yelling at the girl to back off but she just kept stabbing and stabbing, the masked man's blood spilling down on her as he collapsed above her and his screams cut out.

"Ho-ly fuck, I think I'm in love," Niall announced, cackling like a hyena as the guards finally made it to the side of the cage where the girl was contained and shot her with stun guns.

She fell to the ground, twitching and convulsing beneath the jolts of electricity and I cursed beneath my breath as the final contestant in the game rounded the corner and spotted her incapacitated on the ground.

The guy ran forward as she scrambled to her knees, her hands sweeping the ground around her as she hunted for the knife she'd dropped.

"No," Tatum gasped as the guy swung a length of rusty metal at her head but the girl somehow managed to roll beneath the blow, grabbing her knife and sweeping it up at him as she stabbed him in the groin.

He fell back with a scream of agony, dropping the rusty pole he'd been using for a weapon and she grabbed it swiftly, finishing him off with a savage blow to the head.

"We have a winner!" someone yelled on the far side of the viewing area and I watched as the girl stood, coated in blood and panting heavily as she tossed the length of metal aside and looked around with a hopeless kind of victory. Yes she'd survived, but she knew she hadn't even come close to winning her freedom from this hell. At least when I won my round, I'd known that I could leave this slice of hell and never come back.

"Well lad, that's my cue," Niall said happily, clapping a hand to my shoulder and drawing my attention to the group of robed men approaching from the other end of the walkway. Their attention was clearly locked on the three of us and I had no doubt they were coming to deal with the fact that a member of the club had just been murdered right before their eyes.

"Shit," I muttered, my grip tightening on Tatum's fingers.

"What do we do now?" she asked.

"What the fuck is going on?" Saint demanded over the earpiece.

"Just leave this to me," Niall said firmly, leaving no room for arguments. "I haven't spent nearly enough of Pa's money recently and I think that beautiful little specimen down there is worth the gold."

"What's that supposed to mean?" Tatum demanded.

"Just get out of here, lad, and take your sweet girl with you. Let's hope neither of you ever have to come back," Niall said authoritatively.

I opened my mouth to protest, but he strode away from us, his arms wide as if offering up an embrace to the men who were clearly looking to make someone pay for this mess as he called out to them.

"Sorry lads! But that asshole had it coming, he was refusing to pay up on a debt he owed me. And I couldn't have known the lass would stick him full of holes now, could I? What say we get together over a whiskey and discuss what reparations you need me to pay to make this right again. And while we're in discussions, I'll be wanting a price for ownership of that girl down there."

I couldn't hear what the men had to say in response to that, but some of the tension seemed to leak from their posture as they accepted Niall into their group and the whole lot of them turned away.

"What does he mean he wants to buy that girl?" Tatum demanded like she thought I may have been wrong about Niall being one of the good ones - at least by my fucked up sense of reasoning.

"Exactly what he said, baby. She's about to get herself a crazy ass motherfucker of a fairy godmother," I explained as I turned her around and pulled the silver button to call for the car out of my pocket.

"You mean he's just going to buy her freedom?" she asked hopefully and I snorted a laugh.

"I seriously doubt that, baby. Nothing in this life is free. If Niall thinks she's worth buying then he has plans for her. All I can say is that it'll be better than being fucked in the ass by that disgusting excuse for a man." I tossed a final look at the corpse of the guy I'd had a hand in killing and smirked to myself as I led Tatum back through the veil and away from the death games.

"Please tell me you're leaving now?" Saint demanded and the pissy tone of his voice let me know that he was less than pleased about the fact that we'd been ignoring him so much.

"Your wish is my command, my lord," I taunted and I swear I could hear him grinding his teeth but he decided not to respond.

"Good. Then it's time to activate the tracking device," Saint growled and my heart leapt at that suggestion, knowing it was the most likely part of our plan to get us caught. "I need you to switch it on and allow it to ping your location. The moment I have it, destroy it before anyone has a chance to pick up on the signal," he explained as if he hadn't already told us how to do this fifty thousand times today.

"Yeah, yeah," I muttered, grasping Tatum by the waist and pushing her back into a darkened alcove.

"I've got it," she murmured, glancing up at me as I slowly slid her zipper down with a smirk dancing around my lips.

"Naw, baby, that's okay, I can grab it for you," I assured her, tossing her a wink as I slid my hand inside her clothes and she bit her lip against a laugh as she coiled her arms around my neck.

"Are you ready?" Saint growled, clearly not appreciating the way I was taking my time to feel her up as I hunted down the little device she'd stored in her bra.

"Almost," I replied, slipping my hand beneath the full weight of her breast and tugging the little black device free. Her rosy nipple taunted me as I dropped my gaze to it and I dipped my head, pushing my mask up a few inches so that I could suck it into my mouth, nipping down hard enough to elicit a surprised gasp from her sweet lips before dutifully releasing her again.

"He's switching it on now," Tatum said in a low voice as Saint began cursing me.

I gave her a dirty laugh as I did as she'd commanded and a little green light appeared on the tracker.

The seconds seemed to drag as we waited for Saint to get the signal and Tatum held her breath as my muscles tensed and I half expected some detector to be triggered.

"Got it," Saint crowed triumphantly and Blake and Monroe whooped in the background. "Now destroy that thing before anyone else catches the signal."

I didn't need telling twice and I flicked the tracker back off before snapping it in two and then tucking it back into Tatum's bra with a hungry growl that made her giggle like a blushing virgin. But my girl was no virgin, I'd made damn sure of that.

I helped her fix her clothes and lifted her mask so that I could steel a kiss because I was aching for one.

"So where is this place?" Tatum whispered to Saint.

"One moment," Saint said, anticipation brimming in his tone. "You're in the middle of fucking nowhere an hour north of Hemlock City."

"Not exactly a revelation," I murmured.

"It will be when I figure out how to get my hands on a military drone and drop a bomb on their heads," Saint said manically like he was actually hopeful he could manage such a thing. And to be fair to the fucker, he probably could.

When it was clear that no one was about to sweep down and drag us away for activating the tracker, I grinned widely, fixed our masks and moved out of our hidden spot in search of an exit.

I kept Tatum close beneath my arm as we made our way back out of the horror house that was Royaume D'élite and as we stepped out into the cool air, we found our driver already waiting to take us back to my bike.

He opened the rear door and we wordlessly slipped inside, a breath of relief passing my lips as he closed the door behind us again and we found ourselves alone in the blacked out rear of the car.

Tatum tugged her mask off as the engine started up, tossing it into the footwell like she was more than glad to be rid of the damn thing before shoving her hood back to reveal her blonde waves.

When I didn't move to do the same, she climbed into my lap and slowly tugged the mask from my face, throwing it down on the seat beside us and pushing my hood back too.

"We're going to destroy them all," she breathed so quietly that I could barely even hear the words as she traced the lines of my face with her fingertips.

I curled my hands around her waist, only noticing the slight tremble in them as I felt the warmth of her flesh beneath my palms.

Memories of fighting in that fucking cage were rising up in me, trying to conquer me and pull me into fear and despair, but instead an insatiable kind of rage was ripping through me, demanding payment in blood for what I'd been forced to do. What others were still being forced to do.

Tatum's mouth found mine in the dark and I kissed her with a powerful kind of need which felt strong enough to consume both of us and she kissed me with all the desire to set the world to rights and burn down anything that stood in our way.

I reached for the zip which secured her catsuit in place and tugged it down, not wanting any piece of that fucking place to be touching her perfect flesh.

She shrugged out of it without breaking our kiss, kicking it to the floor and leaving her in her underwear as she straddled me once more.

I groaned as she yanked my shirt off too, loving the way her soft skin felt beneath the callouses which lined my palms as I explored the curves of her body in the dark. Hardly any light found us in here and something about that just made it hotter as every touch of her flesh against mine took all of my attention and sent need flooding through my skin.

Her hands travelled down my chest and a shiver rode along my spine as I tried to fight against the urge to restrain her, wanting to enjoy the way she was touching me without letting my fucking demons get the better of me as always.

But as she reached between us and unbuckled my belt, my muscles tightened and flexed and a growl escaped my throat which was equal parts need and pain.

All of the fucked up shit that I'd endured in my lifetime seemed determined to push in on me tonight and as much as I cared about this girl in my lap, it was taking everything I had to let her take control of my body like this.

Ever since that bitch, Deepthroat, had drugged me and pawed at me without my permission, I'd taken my pleasure from girls on my own terms and tying them up wasn't just some kink I was into. I needed to have all the power in this exchange or I would lose my fucking mind. But Tatum wasn't just any girl. She was *my* girl. My *wife*. I knew I could trust her even if my body was aching with the need to restrain her with every touch she gifted me and I fought the urge to rip my belt off and use it to bind her.

I groaned as she pushed her panties aside and lined herself up on top of me, the head of my cock pushing against the slick wetness between her thighs as she panted with need.

My gaze met her blue eyes in the dim light as she slowly pushed herself down on top of me and I watched her pupils dilate as she laid her hands on my shoulders and moaned as she took all of me in inch by inch.

"Fuck," I groaned as I wound my hands around her hips, holding her down on me and a needy moan escaped her as my cock filled her. "You know I'll never let anyone hurt you, don't you, baby?" I murmured as she began to move her hips in a torturously slow rhythm and I watched her ride me like she had me under a damn spell.

"I'll never let anyone hurt you either," she swore and it was like those words had been loosed from a bow aimed directly at my dark heart as the truth of them pierced right through me and made me bleed for her.

I leaned forward and kissed her hard as I began to move my hips to meet with hers and she moaned as her hands shifted down my chest and she explored the hard ridges of my abs.

With a grunt of anger aimed entirely at myself, I snatched her wrists into my grasp and tugged them behind her back. Tatum moaned in encouragement as I was rough with her and I cursed myself for having more reason for it than just her pleasure. I shifted my grip so that I could hold both of her wrists in my left hand and thrust into her harder as I moved my right hand between us to tease her clit.

It was hot and fast and sweaty, this desperate claiming of each other in the dark which we both needed more than any words following that fucking night. I just needed to own her and let her own me.

As her body clamped tight around me and she cried out, with her back arching I came hard and deep inside her, biting down on her nipple through her bra and marking her body once again. I couldn't help it. Every time I had her, I was overwhelmed with the need to mark her flesh and paint her body with the evidence of my presence like a beast.

She fell against me, panting and cursing and I chuckled as I released my hold on her wrists and ran my hands up her spine, enjoying the feeling of our bodies being joined too much to let her move away just yet.

"I fucking hate you, Kyan," Saint snarled in my ear and I burst out laughing as I realised he'd been listening to that entire thing.

"Stop listening in on us if you don't like it, asshole," I taunted as Tatum fought against a laugh of her own. "If I'm alone with my wife I'm going to end up fucking her. It's a foregone conclusion, so suck it up."

Saint cursed us but I just pulled the earpiece out and shoved it into the pocket of my jeans which were folded on the seat beside us.

The car was clearly moving down streets with streetlights now and the orange glow of them made it in through the blacked out windows just enough for me to see a bit better and I looked up at my girl with a smile on my face.

"Didn't I say we'd be fine, baby?" I teased her and she rolled her eyes at me.

"Let's just wait until we've finished this before we start gloating," she suggested, cocking her head in a way that was so fucking cute that it made me want to eat her up like the big bad wolf.

I claimed her lips and kissed her deeply, trying to tell her exactly how much she meant to me with that kiss alone, because I knew that there was no fucking way I could put it into words.

Her hands slid onto my chest again and this time instead of pulling them away, I let myself enjoy the way her fingers moved against my skin, the brush of the ring I'd given her when I married her making me smile as she continued to wear it. Every day since I'd spoken those vows to her in that church, she'd kept it on her finger and every time I saw it, I couldn't help but grin like the smug bastard I was for making her mine.

I had no fucking idea how we were going to do any of the things we would need to do to take down the people who had wronged us. But when I was in her arms like that, I found I didn't care. I'd do whatever it took to tear them apart and I'd give everything I had to protect this girl in my arms.

My life was hers and she could have my death too if she needed it. I'd made a vow to that anyway. 'Til death do us part. And for every moment that my heart remained beating, I knew it would belong to her.

CHAPTER TWENTY FIVE

My adrenaline levels were still high as we walked back to The Temple. Saint had left a basket outside full of new clothes, hand gel and freaking watered down bleach so we were as fresh as a daisy by the time we walked inside.

Monroe rushed at me, crushing me into his chest without a care and I sighed, breathing in his comforting scent. My guardian angel. I had no doubt he'd been going crazy with worry here and it hurt me to see him looking at me like that. Like he had feared I wouldn't come back.

Monroe released me, clapping Kyan on the shoulder, but I pushed him away from him. "Don't get too close," I said in alarm. "He needs to quarantine."

"Yeah, she's right," Kyan said firmly and Monroe nodded, backing up. "Not that the Hades Virus could ever really take down Kyan Roscoe." He smirked like a cocky bastard and I rolled my eyes at him.

Saint approached me next and my brows shot up when he dragged me against him, one hand on the back of my head and the other on the base of my spine. He released me just as fast, then nodded to Kyan who returned the nod, some silent conversation passing between them. Though I could hazard a guess at what it was.

I knew I wasn't just some possession to them anymore, but with Saint it was always hard to tell exactly what he thought of me. An asset that he'd die for, or a girl that he'd actually let into his ice-cold heart?

"Where's Blake?" I asked, hunting for the final member of our tribe.

"He's in his room," Monroe said with a frown. "I think he's processing the fact that he has a new enemy to blame. One without a face. For now, anyway."

I nodded, my heart squeezing. "Kyan, you should go to your room. I can bring you food and stuff for the next couple of days."

"Thanks, baby." He kissed my head then the others moved back to let him through and he walked away across the room. He staggered a little as he headed down the corridor and I frowned. He must have been exhausted. Or possibly drunk. But I hadn't seen him drinking a whole lot...

"I'm gonna go home," Monroe said, giving me a longing look and my gut knotted. I wished he could stay, but there was nowhere for him to sleep here except the couch and that wasn't ideal.

"See you tomorrow?" I asked, unable to disguise the hope in my tone even when I felt Saint's eyes drilling into me.

"Yeah," he promised, smiling tightly and lingering there a moment too long before heading out the door.

A weight dropped inside me as he left and I had the urge to run after him, but I couldn't with Saint watching me. We just had to continue living from one private moment to the next, but they never seemed to come often enough.

I tossed Saint a casual smile then headed to the kitchen, grabbing some supplies for Kyan before taking them to his room. He was already falling asleep on his bed as I set him up for quarantine so I slipped back out of his room and knocked on Blake's door. He grunted in answer and my gut tugged.

"Can I come in?" I asked.

"Tatum?" The door yanked open and he pulled me into his arms, hugging me hard enough to drive the breath from my lungs. I clung to him equally hard, sensing his pain and it cut me apart too.

"I'm glad you're home," he said gruffly.

"I'd always come back," I breathed, realising I meant that. That leaving the Night Keepers was no longer an option for me. It might happen one way or another eventually, by fate or grand design. But it wouldn't happen because I was running away. Not anymore.

"Those monsters," Blake snarled. "How could you stand being around them without tearing their throats out?"

"Because I know we have to play the long game and that's something I've learned a bit about," I said and his grip on me firmed.

"Because of us?"

"You're a tamer kind of monster, but…yeah," I admitted.

"You think you've tamed me?" he purred, releasing me and giving me a dark look that made my heart pound.

I tickled his chin like he was a dog, grinning at him. "A little."

He smirked, catching my hand and pulling me down to sit beside him on the bed with a heavy sigh.

"I thought it would feel good to have the right target at last, but somehow it just drags up all that hate and anger again," he growled. "It makes me worry that I'll hurt the wrong person...like I hurt you."

"You won't," I swore, looking into his eyes as I vowed it. "You won't, Blake."

"Do you really have that much faith in me after what I did to you?" he asked, his voice rough.

"Yeah, I do. Because even if you destroyed every member of Royaume D'élite, they deserve it Blake. I saw what they are. I saw what they do," I seethed. "It wouldn't matter which one of them you destroyed, none of them are innocent." His jaw ticked furiously and I reached out to brush my thumb over his cheek to calm him. "So don't worry that you'll hurt the wrong people, because you won't. We've found a bee hive and we need to destroy them all until we find the queen."

"Or the king," he pointed out and I nodded.

"Yeah. Whichever bastard of a monarch runs that place is responsible for releasing the Hades Virus. For everything that happened to my dad...to your mom."

He swallowed hard, his adam's apple bobbing and I leaned in to kiss him.

"Stay," he murmured against my lips and I nodded, wrapping my arms around him. It had been too long since I'd lost myself in my golden boy and after the night I'd had I wanted to drown in his light, the two of us battling the shadows away together.

He fell back on the bed and I curled up in his arms, tiredness dragging at me already as he stroked my hair.

"You're the best Bond girl there ever was," he murmured into my hair and I breathed a laugh.

"What?"

He chuckled softly and the sound made me grin. He started telling me about how him and the others had assigned each other action movie roles and I was giggling as he told me about Saint calling Monroe the old timer.

"He's not old," I laughed, slapping his chest.

"And I'm not the rookie," he said firmly.

"You're *such* a rookie," I snorted and he clutched me tighter with a growl.

"I'm James Bond dammit," he insisted and I gave in.

"Alright, so what would my Bond girl name be?"

"Your first pet and your mother's maiden name," he said simply.

"Isn't that your porn name?" I frowned and he shrugged. "Well...I don't know what my mother's maiden name is and I don't really care either so I'm going to stick with Rivers for the second part. But I never had a pet, we moved around too much for it to be possible. I did go to a school that had a class goldfish for a while though…"

"That'll do. What was it called?" He prodded me, still grinning.

"Jeremy," I announced and Blake burst out laughing. He grabbed my hips, wheeling me on top of him.

"Come here Jeremy Rivers, I'm gonna ravage you," he growled and I laughed, leaning down to kiss him so a curtain of my golden hair fell around us.

"Ravage me in the morning, James Bond, I'm exhausted." I flopped down beside him and he wrapped me back in his arms.

"That's a promise." He kissed me sweetly and I sighed as my eyes fluttered closed.

"I'll even make sure your cocktini is shaken not stirred," I murmured and he snorted a laugh.

"Just you wait for me to plough into your Octopussy," he said before switching the light off. I had the biggest smile on my lips as I fell asleep in Blake's arms and I knew no one but him could have made me feel this way after a night in that hell hole.

I woke to a heavy cough coming from Kyan's room and my heart juddered as I blinked against the light pouring in from the window. *Maybe I imagined it…*

Another loud cough made chills run through me and I pulled away from Blake, getting up.

"What's going on?" he asked as he woke.

Kyan coughed again and my heart thumped out a frantic tune against my ribcage.

"Brother," Blake gasped, jumping up and stepping toward the bathroom door to make his way through to Kyan's room. I snatched his arm to hold him back and realised I was shaking, panic ripping up the centre of me.

"I'll check. It's not safe for you to go in there if -if-" I couldn't get the end of that sentence out, my throat clogged with worry.

Blake nodded stiffly and I stepped past him, opening the door to the bathroom and closing it behind me before I headed to Kyan's door and pushed it open.

"Kyan?" I asked gently, my stomach churning as I saw him lying on the bed on his back, shirtless with sweat collecting on his brow. He coughed heavily and I shoved the door closed behind me, panic bleeding through me as I spotted the rose-shaped rash on his arm, swirling across his skin.

"*No*," I denied this was happening as my whole world crumpled in on itself. *He can't have the virus, he can't be sick!*

"I'm alright," he said, his voice raspy and I shook my head, climbing onto the bed and pressing the back of my hand to his forehead.

"You're burning up," I said, blinking back tears, trying not to let him see the fear in my eyes.

"Is he okay?" Blake called anxiously from the bathroom.

Kyan coughed heavily again, pushing himself up to sit. "I'm fine," he insisted, but I took his hand, turning it over and finding the rash there across his wrist.

I didn't want to voice it, couldn't bear to say it, but Blake called in again, desperate to know if his friend was alright.

"Kyan," I breathed in horror. "You're sick."

His jaw gritted and he cupped my cheek as his eyes darkened, a cold acceptance filling them that terrified me even more.

I climbed into his lap, clutching his face and making him look at me. "You won't die," I growled and the fog cleared from his eyes. "Kyan Roscoe doesn't die like this."

He nodded, giving me a smirk despite the virus taking hold of him and promising him a single week of life at most if he was one of the unlucky ones.

Sixty percent of infected people die from the virus. I could hear the news reels in my head, the death toll growing every day. But I never thought it would strike here. I never wanted to believe it could touch my Night Keepers.

"It would take more than the Hades Virus to kill me, baby," he vowed and I nodded several times, not letting myself entertain the idea of losing him.

Tears ran hot and thick down my cheeks as I held him and kissed him to seal that promise between us. He would *not* die from this.

"Tate!" Blake barked in desperation.

"What's going on?" Saint called from beyond the other door and I jumped off the bed, throwing my weight against it as he tried to open it.

"Kyan's sick," I half sobbed, but drew in a deep breath for my strength so the next words came out slightly steadier. Though when they did, they were so final that they resounded through to my soul. "He's got the Hades Virus."

Blake

CHAPTER TWENTY SIX

I paced back and forth before the fire, clawing my hands through my hair as my breaths came hard and fast and I fought against the urge to scream my fury and frustration at the injustice in the world at the top of my damn lungs.

I wanted to reach out and grab the nearest thing and smash it and then grab the next and smash that too. An endless cycle of carnage to vent some of this hopelessness worming its way beneath my skin.

The entirety of the last three days had been like this, ever since we'd realised that our brother was infected and my world had constricted around me so tightly that I could barely even think anymore.

"Breathe, Blake," Saint commanded as he typed away on his damn computer like the world we knew wasn't burning down around our ears. Like he actually believed he could research a way out of this.

"I knew this would happen," I snarled, still carving a path into the carpet as I spoke, unable to stop. It felt like if my body was no longer in motion then every atom in me might just tear themselves apart from each other just to avoid this crushing pain that was consuming me.

"Kyan is in the top bracket for recovery from this," he said calmly. Too fucking calmly, like he was a creature without a heart or a soul. And if I'd actually believed that he cared as little as it seemed then I would have been beating the shit out of him myself, but I knew this was just how Saint functioned. The more his body demanded an emotional reaction from him, the more the conditioning his father had put him through would force him to retreat into himself. When Saint was deadly calm, his face a blank mask and his words cold and calculated that was actually when he was closest to breaking himself. It was like the calm before the storm. "He's male, between the ages of sixteen and twenty five, has no previous underlying medical history of heart or respiratory conditions, he's strong and fit and healthy. Instead of the widely publicised mortality rate of sixty-three point four percent, someone in his bracket actually only has a forty seven point nine percent chance of succumbing to this virus."

"Only?!" I roared, losing my shit for the hundredth time today and Monroe pushed himself up off the couch, moving to intercept me as I started charging towards Kyan's door. "If it's so fucking low then I want to be in there with him," I demanded. "I want to face my fate at my brother's side and go with him if he leaves me."

"Don't be moronic," Saint hissed as he got to his feet too and snarled at me, standing shoulder to shoulder with Monroe to block my progress. "Forty seven point nine percent chance of death is in no way good odds and you know it. I was merely stating the fact that his chances are better than the publicised average. Are you really so afraid of your own grief that you would risk making all of us suffer it over you if you infect yourself and die from it? What if Kyan survives only to find he passed it on to you and killed you? Is that a burden you wish to place on his head?"

I gritted my teeth in determination and took another step towards Kyan's room, but Monroe's arms encircled me before I could go any further.

"This won't help him," Monroe insisted, tugging me back a step.

"Giving him reasons to worry about you will only mean he is less focused on fighting this thing. Is that what you want?"

My heart was racing and the pain spiking through my body was unbearable as I fought to draw breath. I was sucking air down hard and fast, the week leading up to my mom's death playing on repeat in my mind. I'd made three video calls to her and only one of them had included any actual conversation. After that, the doctors set it up to let us say goodbye twice. That was a cruelty in itself. After the first time I'd been crushed, expecting the worst and dreading the call to say it had happened. But then she'd made it through the night and the next night too, they'd told us she was fighting and I'd been fool enough to believe she would win. The second time they'd connected the video for us, I'd truly believed she'd be there, sitting up in bed telling us how shitty she felt and promising to be home soon. Instead they'd informed us that this really was the end and I'd sat beside my father, his hand wrapped so tight around mine that it felt like my bones would break as we watched her take her final, laboured breath and slip into oblivion.

"I can't go through that again," I choked out as I stared down the hallway towards Kyan's room and stopped fighting Monroe's grip on me.

At least he had Tatum with him, looking after him, holding him, showing him that he was loved while he fought for his damn life. My mom had been all alone.

I still wasn't sure if we'd made the right call by not sending him away to hospital, but I knew as well as the others that there was no real treatment for the Hades Virus.

Saint had managed to get a supply of the recommended steroids and painkillers sent to us and he had a doctor consulting with Tatum on Kyan's at home care eight times a day and we'd all agreed that he was better off here getting full one to one attention rather than in an overrun hospital.

The few times I'd seen Tatum, she'd sworn to me that he was doing as well as could be expected. She only left his room to collect the food and water we left out for her and each time she retreated, Saint approached the short hallway which led to mine and Kyan's rooms in a full face mask and gloves and bleached everything within an inch of its life.

My room had been deemed too close to Kyan's for safety, so I hadn't been back there since his isolation had begun but the camp bed that Monroe had made up for me on the couch had gone unused for the last three nights.

I'd only slept once. Face down over the toilet in Saint's bathroom after drinking myself into a near coma. The fact that he hadn't forced me out was more than enough to let me know how much he cared. But it didn't change anything. My love for my mom hadn't been enough to save her and our combined love for the asshole in that room down the corridor wouldn't help him either.

"You need to get control over yourself," Saint snapped at me as I slumped in Monroe's arms and I was almost certain he was just holding me for support at this point. "He is on day four of the infection already. This is the crucial day. If he makes it through today without bursting any blood vessels in his lungs from the cough, then his chances of survival go up to eighty one percent."

"How the fuck will we know if he bursts a blood vessel in his damn lungs?" I snapped.

"Because he will either start coughing up blood or he won't," Saint snarled.

"And if he does?" I demanded.

"Then his odds don't improve but they don't worsen either. Not unless that goes on for a second day. Or a third." His delivery was so cold and uncaring that if I didn't know him, I would have wanted to tear his throat out for it.

I'd bet Saint would have made an excellent surgeon, perfectly able to put aside any trace of emotion and calculate the odds involved in survival with a steady hand while carving into human flesh. Of course, most people who go into the medical professions did it out of a desire to help other people, so that wouldn't attract him at all.

"Well excuse me if I'm not jumping for fucking joy at the prospect of spending a day waiting to find out if one of the few people I love in this world is going to start literally coughing his lungs up or not," I snarled, wrenching myself out of Monroe's grip as I stormed towards the door.

I needed to get out of this fucking place. I needed to get the fuck away from here so that I could just breathe.

My chest was tightening to the point of pain and there was a ringing in my ears which was only getting louder.

"Blake!" Monroe called out as I kicked my sneakers on, and I looked up to find him charging my way with the clear intention to stop me from running.

"Leave him," Saint snapped, catching his arm as he made to move past him. "Blake needs to learn that the whole world won't just come rushing in to save him whenever things get tough. His daddy taught him to be a winner, but he never learned how to take a beating and we have enough real worries to concern us today without us trying to soothe his childlike sense of injustice at the world."

"Fuck you," I hissed, his words hitting home like the strike of an arrow and Saint's glare only darkened.

"We'll be here, waiting on Kyan while he fights for his life and supporting Tatum with anything she needs to help him when you decide to stop pouting and come home," he said icily.

Monroe was looking at me like my pain hurt him too, but I just sneered in response. I wasn't the one who needed his pity or concern right now, Saint was right about that.

"I just need some air," I snapped. "I'll be back when I've cleared my head."

"I can come if you want me to?" Monroe offered even as Saint shook his head in disgust and sat back down before his laptop.

"No," I replied. "Saint's right, the others need you more than I do. I'll get my own shit together."

I stumbled outside and slammed the door behind me as the pounding of my heart made my head spin and I sucked down lungfuls of the cool air.

Birds were singing in the trees and I tried to focus on that instead of this all consuming fear that was threatening to destroy me. I wouldn't survive this a second time. I couldn't. The fragile scraps of my battered soul which I'd managed to salvage in the wake of my mom's death were held together too loosely. And the things securing them in place all had names. Four names which would break me if they left me too.

I sank down with my back to the heavy wooden door, drawing in a deep breath of air and holding it in my body for as long as I could before slowly releasing it again.

I did that a second time. Then a third. When my legs felt strong enough to hold my weight again, I pushed myself to my feet, battling against this fear until I'd buried it deep enough inside me to function again.

I needed to see him. I had to see for myself that he wasn't as pale as my mom had been, that he wasn't falling prey to the cruel hands of fate and that death didn't already have its claws in him.

I circled the building, moving around it until I reached Kyan's window where I stopped a few feet back from it and stared at the thick material of his curtains which blocked my view inside.

I stooped low and grabbed a couple of pebbles from the forest floor before tossing them at the glass to gain Tatum's attention.

It only took her a few moments to pull the curtains wide and her face split into a relieved smile as she found me standing there between the trees.

"Is he okay?" I called, loud enough for her to hear me through the glass.

"He can talk," Kyan's voice came from behind her and she rolled her eyes mockingly, stepping aside so that I was gifted a view of him propped up in bed on a mountain of pillows. His chest was bare and his tattoo covered flesh was gleaming with a layer of perspiration. Along his right arm I could just make out a series of red rose-shaped marks where the rash had spread but they didn't seem to have appeared anywhere else for the time being. "I'm not dead yet."

Kyan broke out into a series of hacking coughs and Tatum hurried to his

426

side, climbing into the bed beside him and running her hand down his back as he rode out the coughing fit and I forgot to breathe.

He finally slumped back against the pillows and I found myself standing right up against the glass, wishing I could reach through it and do something to help.

"Don't go looking at me like I'm dying, Bowman," Kyan growled as he looked up at me with his chest heaving and a fresh sheen of sweat on his skin. "My life recently got exponentially better. I'm not making my girl into a widow for you to sweep in and steal her from me."

"Damn right you're not," Tatum agreed.

I managed a weak laugh as he smirked at me and Tatum collected a damp cloth, swiping it over his brow and stealing his attention from me. For a moment I didn't even have any words as I just watched them together, taking in the softness in his eyes as he looked up at her. And while I watched them, I couldn't help but feel glad that he'd found her, that he had her there to care for him like that, the way I doubted anyone in his life ever had before. I wanted that for him. I wanted him to live and love and be fucking happy, and if that girl in there was the key to that for him the way she was to me then I saw no reason why we couldn't both have her.

Tatum took a nebuliser from his nightstand and encouraged him to place his mouth and nose over it and I watched as he breathed in and out, following her commands like a good patient. Saint had bought that thing alongside four humidifiers which were all plugged in around the room emitting eucalyptus scented steam from the essential oils added to the water. He'd researched everything said to have any kind of positive effect on the outcome of this virus plus about a hundred other things said to help with anything even remotely similar to it and Tatum had diligently implemented them all. Anything to give Kyan an advantage against the virus fighting to steal him from us.

Kyan had drunk more honey tea, consumed more ginger and gargled more salt water in the last few days than anyone should have to endure in their lifetime. Not to mention the amount of probiotics and vitamins he'd been ingesting alongside the pain killers, anti-inflammatories and steroids.

To my surprise, Tatum had been saying what a good patient he'd been too, but as I looked in at the two of them, it was fairly obvious to me that his nurse was a pretty high factor in his cooperation.

Tatum was wearing a pair of booty shorts and one of Kyan's shirts with a knot tied at the waist to combat the heat in the room which had been cranked up when Kyan started shivering. As I watched them, she moved to straddle him, reaching behind his head to rearrange his pillows before massaging some menthol Vaporub onto his bare chest for him.

Even while he was laying there fighting for his life against a deadly virus, Kyan still managed to raise his hand to squeeze her ass before looking back over at me with a smug grin.

"Asshole," I called and his smile widened.

I tried not to pay attention to the sickly pallor of his skin and focus on him flipping me off instead. He was still the same dickhead who had been my partner in crime for as long as I could remember. He'd been kicking asses for a hell of a long time before this virus came along and no doubt he planned on beating the shit out of this too.

"I hear blowjobs are real good for coughs," he said, loud enough for me to hear him through the glass and Tatum laughed, though I could see how hard she was fighting to remain calm and hide her fear for him.

"I think that's meant to be *giving* them, not receiving them," she replied teasingly. "But if you make it through today without coughing up any blood then maybe I'll give it a try."

"Deal, baby," Kyan said, grinning even bigger and looking my way again. "I just need to-"

A series of violent coughs cut him off and Tatum helped him lean forward, rubbing his back again and meeting my gaze as I pressed up against the glass to watch as he struggled and she tried to comfort him.

The sound of the coughs was rough and brittle and I could practically feel the strength of them in my own chest as I watched with a desperate wish that I could do anything at all to help him.

When he fell back against the pillows, he swiped a hand over his mouth and my heart stopped dead as I saw the specks of blood that he smeared across his lips.

Tatum sucked in a breath of alarm, her terrified gaze meeting mine as Kyan let his eyes flutter closed and lay panting on the bed.

She grabbed the steamer from the nightstand and Kyan groaned like he was in pain as she encouraged him to lean over it again. I watched them for several minutes as panic rose up in me so sharply I could have sworn that I was bleeding out all over the ground.

When it became clear that they'd forgotten I was even here, I backed away from the window.

I kept backing up until I couldn't see them through the glass anymore and then I turned and bolted.

I ran up the path towards campus as fast as my legs could carry me. I didn't slow down when my lungs began to burn and my muscles ached with the agony of pushing them so damn hard.

I raced through the trees and up the track that led to the cliffs, barely even noticing where I was going until I found myself sprinting towards the edge high up above the lake.

I leapt off of it without even pausing, a yell escaping me as my gut plummeted even faster than I did and I fell towards the grey water of the lake far below with my arms and legs wheeling.

I crashed beneath the surface and shot towards the lakebed as the icy cold water embraced me and adrenaline thundered through my veins, waking me up far more thoroughly than any other feeling in the world ever could.

When I finally stopped sinking, I swam for the surface, sucking in a deep breath as my head breached it and staring up at the sky and cursing each and every star in the heavens.

It wasn't fair. Kyan was too good to die like that. He was worth too much. But it didn't matter. None of it mattered. The Hades Virus didn't discriminate between the people it came for. I just needed to try and keep faith that he could beat it.

The only thing left to me now was the aching sense of certainty that I would make the people responsible for this pay. I'd give my life to gaining retribution for the crimes they'd committed and if I lost my brother for their crimes too then I knew there would be no depths I wouldn't stoop to.

Blood would flow and screams would pour from their throats and I wouldn't stop until I was coated in as much death as they'd caused with their sins.

I might have just been some rich brat with a grudge, but there was one thing my father had taught me which I knew would serve me well in this vendetta. I was made to succeed in all things. So if I went to war, I was destined to win.

And so help the men who fell prey to my wrath.

CHAPTER TWENTY SEVEN

I'd hardly slept. Just stolen hours here and there. But never during the night. I watched him vigilantly then. My Night Keeper. My husband. Sometimes I curled beside him, resting my head on his chest and listening to his heartbeat. But other times his fever was so high that I didn't dare suffocate him with my body heat.

It was the sixth day of his illness. And tonight, everything was ghostly quiet in The Temple. I texted the group chat every couple of hours to promise them Kyan was okay and always got responses from them all, proving how few hours of sleep each of them were getting themselves. I couldn't blame them. This was a crucial day for the virus. We'd know soon if he'd survive it or not, but I couldn't let myself consider him not making it. I *wouldn't*.

I watched from a chair beside the bed as Kyan's chest rose and fell too rapidly and he started to shiver. He coughed heavily and it hurt me to watch.

"Baby?" he murmured and I hurried to his side, clasping his hand.

"I'm here," I said gently.

"Lie with me, I need to hold you," he breathed. He sounded so weak and I had the most terrifying feeling he was giving up. That the virus was taking a firmer grip, daring to take the strongest man with the most powerful heart from this world.

"I don't want to fall asleep," I said as he tugged me closer.

"Please," he rasped, looking up at me with desperation in his eyes. "If I die, I want you as close as you can be."

"Please don't say that," I said, tears threatening to spill over. But I forced them back, not letting him see my pain when he had enough pain of his own to face.

"Just in case," he said, tugging on my hand again and I gave in. How could I refuse?

I climbed across him, pulling the covers up over us and wrapping myself around him so his body could feed on the heat of mine. His shivering eased a little and he sighed, tilting his head down to kiss my forehead.

"I love you, Tatum," he breathed.

"Don't," I pleaded, a choked sob escaping me as I clutched him tighter. "Please don't say goodbye."

"I'd be a bad husband if I left without saying goodbye," he said softly, far too softly for Kyan Roscoe. "And I mean it. I love you. I should have said it before. Should have said it a thousand fucking times and now I might only get to say it this once."

"Stop," I begged, my tears flowing free onto his chest. His skin felt cold against mine and I hugged him tighter, wishing I could give him every drop of warmth in my body. I'd pay any price, strike any deal to save him. If I only knew how to conjure the devil, I'd have sold my soul already. "You're not going anywhere."

He stroked my hair and we fell quiet for a while before he spoke once more. "Our story's been pretty messy hasn't it, baby? But I wouldn't ask for a do-over. Everything I ever earned in life was forged in dirt and blood and pain. I just never expected to earn something as perfect as you."

"*Kyan.*" My tears washed over his skin and there was nothing I could do to stop them anymore. "Our story isn't over. We're going to get through this and the pandemic is going to end. There's a time beyond this just waiting for us."

He sought out my hand, threading his fingers through mine and running his thumb over the ring that bound me to him. "Where will we go when it's over?"

"Anywhere you want," I promised. "Where do you want to go?"

He fell quiet, thinking about that as he continued to trace his thumb over my wedding ring. "High Rocks," he decided.

"The amusement park?" I questioned and he nodded.

"Pa never took me there. Said it was for kids. And apparently being eight years old meant I'd outgrown being a kid already. By the time I was a teenager I figured I was too old and too fucking cool for that shit. But I guess I was an idiot. Because now I never got to go."

"You *will* get to go." I leaned up, pressing my hands to the pillow either side of his head and gazing into his dark eyes. "We'll go together."

He smiled a little, but it was the saddest smile I'd ever seen. I leaned down and kissed him, tasting my own tears on his lips and the lasting flavour of the man who had claimed me as his and who I'd claimed right back. We were walking to the brink of death together in this room, me at his side, and I refused to let him slip away from me. I would pull him back when it counted most.

I slid back down his body to curl up with my leg hooked over his and my head on his chest, trying not to break. Kyan ran his fingers through my hair and my heart started to beat in time with his.

"Sleep with me," he asked and I felt like he was asking so much more than that.

I nodded, squeezing his hand, giving him this, too afraid of refusing it if this was his last wish. But the pain that caused me was unimaginable.

My breathing grew shallow as we held each other, nothing but the hours between now and dawn seeming to exist. And I was sure they would determine everything. This was it for him, life or death. And all I could do was pray for life.

"I love you, Kyan," I told him, meaning it from the depths of my soul.

"I didn't earn that, but maybe I might've if I had a bit longer," he breathed.

"You earned it," I said firmly, squeezing my eyes shut. "Don't ever say otherwise. You're everything, Kyan."

"Good to know, baby. At least I got to make you mine before the end. I can say I had one good thing," he said contentedly, hugging me tight and he soon drifted off to sleep, leaving me with my heart breaking.

I lasted perhaps only another hour watching over him before exhaustion dragged me down into a dark and tortured sleep. One where Kyan's fingers slipped out of mine and I couldn't find him anywhere in an endless maze of eternal night.

CHAPTER TWENTY EIGHT

I'd been in Ash Chambers for most of the night, unable to cope with the silence from Kyan's room as I waited on morning and an update on his progress. According to all of the studies this day was the most likely to be the one that decided his fate and from the ashen look on Tatum's face the last time she'd come out to take some food into the room for the two of them, I was finding it hard to hope for the best.

He hadn't eaten anything in two days and she'd had to start crushing his pills and giving them to him in water now that his throat was so swollen he was hardly able to swallow. I knew she hadn't wanted to deliver that update to me, but she knew better than to lie and it wasn't looking good. His decline had been swift and unrepentant and he'd been asleep for most of the last twenty four hours too, the fever sapping his energy as the virus plagued his body.

The doctors I was video calling daily had started to give me that condescending, patronising look. Their latest advice had been for me to *prepare myself.* Well, fuck them. They were the ones who needed to prepare themselves because I'd spent the evening doing everything I could to ruin their fucking lives for giving up on him and come tomorrow they'd find themselves out of their fucking jobs and under investigation for some pretty serious crimes which had been undeniably linked to their sorry asses. No one gave up on Kyan Roscoe and got away with it.

But despite that minor victory I'd claimed over them, I couldn't deny the hopeless panic which had begun to creep along my limbs.

My life had been a series of unpredictable upheavals and I'd been a fool to fall into the trap of believing that this life I'd been trying to build for myself with the family I'd hand picked would be allowed to exist in the way I'd dreamed for it to.

Of course it was foolish of me to rely on anything at all in this world after my upbringing. But Kyan Roscoe was quite probably the strongest, toughest, meanest motherfucker I'd ever had the fortune to meet. It made no fucking sense for him to get sick and die like some feeble soul or old aged pensioner. He was a mountain of a man, a beast without limitation, an endless well of energy and force and fury and yet somehow, he'd been stopped in his tracks by this.

My fingers were cramping against the keys as I played what must have been the fiftieth piece of the night and I cursed as my notes got sloppy. Beethoven's Moonlight Sonata went to shit beneath my clumsy hands and I cursed loudly as I snatched my hands away from the keys and slammed the fall down over them.

Fuck this.

I stood suddenly in the achingly quiet room, my hands clenching and unclenching as my breaths came powerfully and I stood on the very edge of my self control.

I tipped my head back and roared my frustration and heartache and fucking all consuming fear to the vaulted ceiling, the noise bouncing around me as I found myself paralysed within the moment. I didn't want to go back to The Temple. I couldn't bear how quiet it was while Kyan slept and Tatum comforted him and I had to face each and every minute that ticked by on the clock, knowing that it could be his last.

Monroe and Blake had been sitting before the fire when I'd left, waiting for news. It was a cruel and desperate kind of way to spend the night and when I realised I couldn't take it I'd come here instead, making them swear to call me if there was any news.

It wasn't like I hadn't known that life was fleeting, fragile, unpredictable and cruel. I just hadn't thought that *his* life would be like that. If I had ever imagined that I might lose him to any twist of fate, I always would have guessed it would be a more violent end. Not this lingering, aching, decline into death which no amount of power or money or need could reverse.

And I did need him. I needed Kyan Roscoe like I needed air in my lungs. He was more precious to me than I could ever put into words and I didn't even know if he fully understood that.

He was the first friend I'd ever had. The only person who had looked at the darkness in me and seen it as something worth getting to know more about instead of something to run from.

He'd never once feared me. He'd never cowered or flinched from even the worst of me and he'd been as stoic and reliable as the sun rising every morning, always there for me no matter what I needed, no matter how badly I treated him.

He wasn't one in a million. He was one in seven point eight billion. I could search the entire world and never find a single human being who compared to him. He was a man without morals, fears or regrets. He was my brother in the truest, purest sense of the world. We didn't need blood to bind us, our connection was so much purer and truer than that. He was one of the first people in this world who had made me realise that love was a real emotion.

I loved him in a pure, hateful, selfish way which I knew would destroy everything in me if it was stolen away.

Blake wouldn't survive his death. In my heart I knew it would equal his death too, one way or another. And Tatum and Monroe wouldn't stay with us if our unit was broken either. I didn't know how I knew it, but I just did. I could feel it. This balance the five of us had created held its own special kind of harmony which would be destroyed if any one of us were to be stolen away.

Everything I'd ever wanted or needed hung right here in this moment and yet there was nothing I could do to alter the course of events.

I grabbed my jacket and tore from the room, not even bothering to pull it on and welcoming the cold kiss of the air as I made it out of the building and locked up behind me.

It was almost five in the morning but I knew I wouldn't sleep tonight. I'd hardly slept at all since Kyan had caught the virus. If it wasn't worry for my brother that kept me awake, it was anger at myself for allowing him to go to that club, for encouraging it.

I'd been so caught up in the idea of tearing down Royaume D'élite that I'd allowed him to put himself at risk, my own stupid vanity making me believe that we could pull it off without a hitch just because I believed it should be so. But if I'd really been as powerful as I tried to make out then I shouldn't have needed to ask for their help in uncovering the location of the club or the information on its members.

Even now, I was still struggling to piece everything together to take them down, using the challenge of it to distract me from my fear for my friend, but I wasn't really any closer to the answers we so desperately needed.

And if it turned out that what they'd uncovered for me wasn't enough for us to take the club down and rip apart the people running it, uncover the truth about what had happened to Tatum's father and reveal it to the world, then what had it all been for? Kyan had risked his life for this information. He may even die because of it and I wasn't sure I could even deliver on the promises I'd made him to destroy them.

I strode down the path to The Temple, circling the lake and casting my gaze around, hunting the shadows as I wondered whether the Justice Ninja might leap from the darkness to take me on.

I wished he would. I ached for a fight like that. An opponent I could destroy. Someone who I could make bleed for the pain I felt in my heart and soul.

But of course, all remained silent between the trees and I was left with my impending grief, my overwhelming concern and a total sum of nothing even close to helpful that I could do to change the path of fate that we were on.

When I finally approached the building where I'd made my home with my brothers and our girl, I stepped off of the path and circled through the trees towards Kyan's room at the back of the building.

I came to a halt outside his window, gazing at the closed curtains beyond the glass and moving forward until my forehead was pressed to the cold pane. I exhaled slowly, my breath fogging against the glass as I imagined I was truly with him, like I could feel the heat of his flesh, reach out and press my hand to his chest and know that his strong heart still thumped with a savage stubbornness and a clear refusal to give up.

He wouldn't leave me. He wouldn't leave her. He wouldn't leave any of us. Not if he had even the slightest say in the matter. He'd make a deal with the devil and stab an angel in the back if that was what it took to keep him with us. Because we belonged together. We weren't just a bunch of kids playing games and naming ourselves the Night Keepers to justify our depravity. We were five twisted, blackened souls who had always been destined to meet and come together. I refused to believe any other version of the truth. Each of us was missing something, each of us haunted by something, each of us craving something. And the only answers to those needs were in each other. I'd swear to that fact until my dying breath.

When I couldn't take the excruciation of standing there not knowing any longer, I headed around to let myself inside and then moved down to the gym in the crypt.

I'd bury my fears in exercise until my body was screaming at me to stop and the sun had risen to shine light on the truth.

Tomorrow was another day. I just had to pray that it wasn't the beginning of the end.

CHAPTER TWENTY NINE

"**I**'ll ram a tangerine down your throat and make a fruit juicer outta your asshole...then make your mama drink it."

I jerked awake, finding my flesh warmed by another body. I lifted my head as Kyan murmured some other nonsense and I laughed out loud. He hadn't done that since before the virus had hit. And as I grabbed the thermometer from the nightstand and took his temperature, I found it was normal. Totally, utterly, wonderfully *normal*.

"Kyan!" I gasped, shaking him and he woke with a jerk, flinging me from the bed with the force of a battering ram. I hit the floor, rolling into the wall as he cursed and I fell apart laughing.

"Fuck, baby, I'm sorry." He shoved the covers aside, getting up and striding towards me. He knelt down as I continued to laugh and he gripped my hands.

"Kyan you're better!" I all but shouted and he took a moment as he realised he'd just gotten out of bed without needing me to help him for the first time in days, his strength returned.

"Holy shit," he laughed and I lunged at him, kissing him and devouring him and crying tears of complete relief.

He fell back onto the floor and I pushed my hands into his hair as I climbed on top of him, running them all over him before landing on his chest and feeling that strong and invincible heart of his pounding solidly beneath my palm.

"What's going on?!" Blake suddenly shouted through the door, banging his fist on it.

"Kyan's better!" I cried. "He's going to be okay."

"Fuck, shit, tits," Blake blurted. "Can I come in?"

"Don't be an idiot," Saint snapped then spoke to me. "Take Kyan to the bathroom and make sure he is thoroughly cleaned while I start work on his room. The incubation period has passed so as long as there is no residue of the virus in this corner of the house, he can come see us once he's clean."

"Hear that baby? Saint wants you to wash my balls," Kyan purred, smirking at me.

I rolled my eyes but couldn't stop grinning as I towed him into the bathroom and shut the door.

I ran a bath for him, the whole room steaming up as Kyan took a moment to brush his teeth before I did the same. He gave me a minty fresh kiss before slipping off his boxers and getting into the bath. He dunked fully under the foamy water and I moved to kneel beside him, using a sponge to squeeze water over his soapy hair while he grabbed the bottle of bubble bath, pouring it all over his chest and lathering it up.

"What are you doing?" I laughed.

"Just doing a Saint approved job of cleaning myself to make sure I've got zero chance of giving them that fucking virus." He grinned then grabbed my hands, yanking me into the bath with him and sending water splashing everywhere. I started kissing him and he soon tore my clothes off with a frantic desperation. He pushed himself inside me and I gasped, clutching onto his shoulders as he gripped my hips and we started moving at a furious pace.

I clawed at him as he squeezed and sucked my breasts, biting and marking me. We claimed one another with a desperation that meant it only lasted a few minutes and Kyan groaned heavily as he came the same moment I did. Both of us were branded with scratches and finger marks and I laughed against his shoulder as the strength went out of my body.

The amount of bubble bath Kyan had poured into the tub meant we were covered in suds which were also now floating across the floor in an inch of water.

"We'd better shower off all these bubbles," Kyan said brightly, spanking my ass.

I climbed out of the water, hearing Saint cursing from Kyan's bedroom as Kyan chased me into the shower and my giggles echoed around the room. I couldn't stop myself though. It felt too good knowing Kyan was okay. That I wasn't going to lose another piece of my heart to this wicked virus.

He kissed me deeply in the shower and claimed me slower this time as we savoured every moment, revelling in each other. He was sweet and soft and wholly unlike Kyan as he possessed me lovingly, panting my name and trailing kisses along my jaw.

When we'd been in there for what must have been nearly an hour, Blake banged on the door that led to his bedroom.

"Please come the fuck out, you must be clean by now. I swear to god if I have to listen to you fucking each other again, I'm gonna come in there and join in and I can't promise I won't fuck you too, brother, if my enthusiasm overflows."

"Alright, but I'm gonna pass on the ass fucking," Kyan called.

"I'm also passing on witnessing that," Monroe said from beyond the door. "Just get the fuck out here already."

Kyan wrapped a towel around his waist and took a moment fixing one around my body too before scooping up a handful of bubbles from the floor and jogging to the door. He wrenched it open and slapped the bubbles into Blake's forehead before football tackling him onto his bed and kissing his face everywhere. Monroe dog piled on top of them and he and Blake soon got Kyan beneath them, intermittently punching and kissing him as they all laughed.

I rested my shoulder against the doorway, biting my lip as I watched them, my heart swelling with so much happiness it nearly burst.

The door shoved open across the room and Saint stood there in yellow washing up gloves and a mask over his mouth and nose. I couldn't quite tell beneath the mask, but something in his eyes told me he was smiling.

Kyan extracted himself from the dog pile, his towel getting caught beneath Blake's thigh and yanking it off of him as he strode towards Saint with his arms outstretched.

"Don't you dare," Saint warned, but Kyan kept coming, wrapping him in a full body hug and Saint relented, winding his arms around him and clutching him tight.

"Hey asshole," Kyan said.

"Hey motherfucker," Saint replied and my smile nearly split my cheeks apart.

For now, everything in this moment was right and good. And I just wanted to lose myself to it and bathe in this moment of bliss for as long as I possibly could.

CHAPTER THIRTY

I sprinted up the path which circled Maple Lodge and the rest of the teachers' accommodation with sweat gleaming on my skin and my breaths coming hard and fast as I closed in on a new PB for this run. My muscles burned and flexed as I pushed as hard as I could and I burst from the trees before my bungalow with a growl of triumph before skidding to a halt at the front door and scrambling to stop the timer on my watch as fast as I could.

"Yes!" I barked a triumphant laugh as I saw I'd shaved twelve seconds off of my time and smirked to myself as I headed inside.

I tossed my keys into the little dish beside the door and strode over to my kitchenette where I grabbed a drink filled with electrolytes and quickly chugged the whole thing down.

I tugged my shirt off and tossed it in the vague direction of the bathroom where the laundry hamper lived and rolled my shoulders back a few times to relieve some of the tension in them.

There was a protein shake ready and waiting for me in the fridge so I moved to get that too, pressing the cold shaker bottle to the back of my neck and groaning in appreciation before slowly rolling it down my chest as well.

When I'd taken some relief from the cool bottle, I gave it a good shake to make sure none of the powder had settled in the bottom of it then flipped the cap to take a long drink. It was flavoured to taste like chocolate milkshake so I could almost convince myself that it was junk food. Almost. Though as that thought occurred to me, I wondered if I'd be getting an excuse to eat real junk food with Tatum today. I had some snacks in the cupboard and if I timed it right, I might even be able to get a bit of alone time in The Temple with her while the others weren't around.

I needed a chance to talk to her alone about this whole marriage thing. It wasn't like I couldn't understand the reason for it, I just kinda hated it. Like, I genuinely hated it so much I was grinding my teeth at night. Every time Kyan called her his wifey and made comments about her belonging to him in a way that she would never belong to the rest of us, I just wanted to punch his fucking teeth in.

In fact, that might have been exactly what I needed. I grabbed my cell phone and shot him a message, telling him to meet me for a sparring session later on. It was actually one of the few times that I had ever been the one to suggest it. Normally he was pestering me daily for the opportunity to knock me around the ring but recently, he'd been less inclined to show up at all hours with a desperate thirst for blood coursing through his limbs. Maybe that was because of his wife.

For fuck's sake.

I'd given it a few weeks on account of him nearly dying and all, but it was getting to the point where I needed to get some more clarity on where I stood or I was going to lose my fucking mind.

I finished up on my shake and went for a shower, quickly rinsing off before heading into my room in search of a pair of fresh sweatpants.

I almost leapt out of my fucking skin as I found Saint Memphis lounging on my goddamn bed, fully dressed in his school uniform while reading one of my books on personal training.

"What the fuck are you doing?" I yelled at him as I stood there, balls out and dripping with moisture from my shower.

"I could ask you the same thing," he replied in a calm tone, his gaze straying from my book to my body and skimming down until he was looking my dick right in the eye. And that was fucking disconcerting.

"I'm not the one lounging on *your* bed, so I think my question is more relevant," I snarled.

"Perhaps you should cover your cock before we get into this?" Saint suggested, "It's a little inappropriate for a teacher to be waving their genitalia around at a student while they're lying in their bed. Imagine what the school board might think."

I cursed him colourfully as I stalked over to my closet and grabbed a pair of black sweatpants, pulling them on. When I twisted back around to glare at him with my arms folded over the tigress tattoo on my chest, I spotted something hanging from his neck.

"What are you doing with that?" I demanded, taking a step towards him as I pointed at the necklace which Tatum had asked me to look after for her.

"Again, I could ask you the same thing," Saint said in a deadly calm tone which made my skin prickle. This wasn't just a social call from the devil. There was something more going on here. He was up to something or after something and if he'd found that necklace then that meant he'd been snooping through my things too. That had been inside the box on my mantelpiece. He didn't just happen to see it.

"Give that back," I said, giving him a hard stare which normally had students shitting themselves in my classes, but Saint Memphis was no ordinary teenager, he didn't bow to social pressure. Hell, I doubted he'd even bow to Satan if he showed up here this very moment casting the whole world to ruin.

"I intend to," he purred. "Just not to you. Unless you have a valid reason for having it? I'd say our girl would be quite surprised to find her stoic defender had stolen from her like this, wouldn't you?"

"I didn't steal shit," I snarled. "And you know it. So quit acting like a little bitch and dancing in circles. If you've got something you want to say to me then spit it the fuck out."

Saint shifted forward suddenly on the bed, tossing my book back on the nightstand and getting to his feet right in front of me, standing so close that our chests were brushing. But if he thought I was going to back down, he had another thing coming.

"How did it come into your possession then?" he asked in a low voice. "Because the last time I saw Tatum wearing it was right after she believed I burned her precious letters and she ran off to cry about it. When she came back, you were trotting along at her heels playing the good teacher and telling us all to get to class as if you had no idea what had taken place amongst us. And yet now I find *this*."

"What's your point, Memphis? I've got shit I want to do today."

"My point is that I can only assume she gave this to you then. That she asked you to look after it for her because she was afraid of what we...or *I* might do to it. But you weren't a Night Keeper then. You had no ties to her at all. So why would you leap forward like a knight in shining armour to defend our little Night Bound but then pretend not to know anything about what had taken place? You could have punished us for her then. You could have been the brave defender she needed. But you didn't. You gave us detention for being late to class. You gave *her* detention. But you didn't make a single comment about the letters or the girl you'd no doubt been consoling. And now that's got me wondering, why?"

"Maybe I knew she was strong enough to fight her own battles," I snarled, reaching out to grab the necklace in a tight fist so that the chain cut into his neck as I tightened my hold on it. "Now give this back."

"No," Saint replied, not moving a damn inch as I went nose to nose with him. "If you want it, you'll have to rip it clean off of me and then you can explain to Tatum why you broke it. I'm assuming it has some kind of real significance for her. Probably a gift from her sister or father? Or some token she wears in memory of losing her? Whatever way, I'm certain she wanted it to be protected from harm when she entrusted you with it, so I'm sure she would be less than pleased to discover you'd broken it."

"Maybe I should test the strength of the chain," I warned, turning it in my fist so that it tightened around his neck. "If I use it to strangle you then I can just unclasp it from your corpse once you're dead and hand it back to her."

The motherfucker actually grinned at my threat, his eyes dark on mine with a dare clearly dancing in them alongside something which looked horribly like triumph.

"Tell me, Monroe, did your family leave you wanting when it came to love?" he asked.

"What?" I asked, unable to hide the flinch as this spawn of hell spoke about my family and hating the way his eyes flashed with victory at my reaction.

"It's just a fairly common cause for men like us to come into existence through neglect or violence, so it seems like a simple enough question."

I released my hold on Tatum's necklace and shoved away from him as I turned and stalked out into the front room. "My family weren't monsters like yours."

"I'm sure they weren't," he agreed as he followed me. "There are no monsters like my father."

I cut him a look at those words because for a moment there it had sounded suspiciously like hatred lacing his tone when he mentioned the man who took my family from me.

"But they *did* die and leave you all alone?" he pushed and panic flared through me as I turned an icy glare on him again.

"Who told you that?" I demanded, my mind flitting to Tatum for a moment before I could help it. But I instantly dismissed that idea. She might have been going a little soft on Saint ever since he'd almost given his life for her, but I knew she wouldn't betray my trust like that.

"You just said they *weren't* monsters. Talking about them in the past tense is something of a giveaway," he said with a shrug as he moved to pick up my discarded shirt and place it in the laundry hamper like the sight of it on the floor was causing him physical pain.

I ground my jaw as he cocked his head, eyeing me like I was a fucking puzzle he was trying to piece together and I didn't like that one fucking bit. He was better at this mind game bullshit than me and I didn't want him trying to pry my head open to hunt down my secrets.

"What did your father do to you that was so terrible then?" I asked, trying to deflect the attention back away from me. "Did he knock you about a bit? Call you names? Make you feel undeserving of his love?" I could easily imagine that son of a bitch doing all of that and more to his own kid and for a moment I almost felt bad about goading Saint over it. And then I remembered that he'd been raised in his father's image to be just the same as him and I shouldn't be giving a single fuck about anything he'd been through.

"No," Saint replied easily, picking a piece of lint from his sleeve and dropping it to the ground. "Nothing like that."

"Then what?" I demanded, my voice raising in pitch and possibly giving away the fact that I was more interested in his answer than I had any real right to be.

I had assumed that he wouldn't answer me, so when he gave me an appraising look instead of just shutting me down, I was more than a little surprised.

"When I was six, we spent a few weeks in Barcelona," he said slowly, his gaze darkening as he lost himself in the memory. "Have you ever travelled to Europe?"

"I've only ever been to three states," I deadpanned, offering him a flat look.

"Of course. I forget you come from nothing," he said as if that wasn't offensive as shit. "Well, anyway, Barcelona is an old city. Far older than anything we have here and there are countless old buildings and churches and things of the like. Our family were staying in a building that had originally been used as a monastery and dated back to somewhere in the Middle Ages."

"What has this got to do with-"

"If you wish to have an answer to your question then you will allow me to answer how I see fit," Saint said coolly and I huffed out a breath as I indicated for him to go on.

"Anyway, as you can imagine, there wasn't any modern plumbing in the place originally so to the rear of the property in the shadow of the old abbey there was a stone well. Not anything particularly interesting, just a hole in the ground with an old wooden structure over it to hang a bucket from and a circular piece of wood tossed over the top of it to stop anyone from unintentionally falling in."

"I get the picture, you and your family were off staying in some massive estate in Spain with a fucking well on the grounds. Get to the point, Memphis," I said, still feeling pissy about him breaking in here like he thought he owned the entire goddamn world.

Saint's jaw ticked, but that was the only outward sign I got that he was irritated with my impatience.

"At this point in my upbringing I had already been forced to come to terms with the fact that I would never get any warning of us moving from place to place. Trips were always sprung on me suddenly and instantly. I would quite literally be hauled out of bed, stopped mid meal or even wrenched off of the toilet if I'd chosen the wrong moment to take a shit and then I would be bundled into a car or onto a plane or a boat and taken wherever the fuck my father wanted for an undetermined amount of time. It was rather unsettling, which was of course the point and I was never allowed to bring a single thing with me aside from whatever clothes I'd been wearing at the moment selected. But this time, I happened to overhear my father speaking on the phone with the pilot a few minutes before he came to grab me, so I ran back to my room, lifted the floorboard where I hid the toys my grandmother bought me in secret and took a small, red car from beneath it. I placed the car in my pocket and miraculously, it went unnoticed throughout the flight and for almost an entire week once we had arrived in Spain."

"He wouldn't let you have toys?" I asked with a frown. I'd assumed Saint Memphis had been the kid who had every fucking toy ever created. "Why the fuck not?"

"He didn't allow me to form attachments to anything. Toys, furniture, people. It made me strong."

"I am going to seriously disagree with that logic, but fine, I'll bite. What happened when he found you with the toy car? Did he yell at you? Make you cry?" I could hear the dickish tone to my voice, but I wasn't capable of reining it in.

Saint scoffed and shook his head slightly. "He didn't say a word. That's really not his style. He just clicked his fingers to make me follow him and led me through the property to the well. When we got there, he lifted the cover and pointed at it, telling me to throw the car away." Saint paused for half a beat before he went on, but it was enough of a detraction from his monotone that I noticed it. "I made the foolish mistake of crying and begging him to let me keep it."

"Well, you were six, I imagine that would be a pretty standard reaction to losing a toy at that age. I used to have this Power Ranger action figure which I took literally everywhere with me, so I feel the pain of him making you dump it," I said with a shrug.

Saint sighed like I was seriously testing his patience and I had to admit he really had my curiosity piqued now. Hadn't I wanted dirt on Troy Memphis anyway? Maybe if I got Saint to trust me, I could get enough information from him to use in my vendetta. Though I doubted tales of him not letting his kid play with a toy car would get me very far.

"He waited until I finished my tantrum in silence and eventually, when I realised I had no choice in the matter, I threw the car into the well… I can still remember the sound of it hitting the water at the bottom like it just happened," he mused and though his tone was flat, something about his story made me feel a tug of pity for him. He'd just been a kid with a toy car. Was it really the worst thing in the world for him to want to keep something like that?

"That was pretty shitty of him," I said, hating myself for the fact that some of my anger at Saint was fizzling away, but it was kinda hard to stay mad at a kid who had never been allowed to have his toys.

"It wasn't quite as traumatising as the Action Man incident," he mused. "Or at least it wouldn't have been if he hadn't made me go down after it."

"He threw you down the well?" I balked and he rolled his eyes at me.

"No. He suggested that if I cared for the car so much that I wouldn't wish to be parted from it again and instructed me to climb into the bucket. Once I did, he lowered me down into the dark, all the way until the base of the bucket was just touching the surface of the water. He then gave me a choice. I could either dive in and find my toy and he would return me and it to the surface assuming I could climb back into the bucket. Or I could remain in the bucket until I had learned my lesson."

"How deep was the water?" I asked, unable to hide the horror in my voice at all with that question.

"I have no idea. I was too afraid to find out. Perhaps it was just a few inches deep and all I needed to have done was wade around in it until I found the car. Or perhaps it was several feet and I had no chance of ever finding it, let alone getting back into the bucket to be drawn back up to the surface."

"So you chose to stay in the bucket?" I asked, my muscles bunching as I thought about that, this little six year old kid all alone down in the dark. Troy Memphis really was a monster.

"I did. I believe I was in there for around thirty-one hours before he brought me up. Not that he ever let me see a clock to be sure of the time, but it had been around lunch time when I'd been sent down there and it was almost time for dinner the next day once I was brought up." He delivered it with no emotion at all and I couldn't even tell if it was because he didn't feel anything about it or if it was that he was so practiced in repressing the things he felt that he didn't even know *how* to show it.

"That's fucked up," I muttered, half wanting to hug the asshole for a minute before I remembered I hated him.

"So I've been told. Are you going to tell me what fucked you up then? If your family loved you before you lost them was it the losing them that did it? Or the foster care? Maybe a bit of both?"

"The losing them," I ground out, quickly finding my anger with him again at the reminder of exactly why I hated this son of a bitch and his entire family. The things his father had done to him might have been all kinds of fucked up but they'd been done with the purpose of moulding him into his image and from what I'd seen of the way he treated Tatum, I was willing to bet that was a pretty solid success.

"How did they die?" he asked like we were discussing the weather.

"House fire," I lied quickly, hoping he hadn't noticed the moment of hesitation it took for me to come up with that lie. But the way he raised his chin an inch said he'd noticed it alright.

"I see."

If I'd thought Saint was a guarded bastard before all of that then I was wrong, because I swear I saw the shutters slam down behind his eyes as he looked at me. And for a moment I actually felt shitty about it. He'd just shared a whole lot of truth with me. The kind of truth I was sure he didn't share easily or with many people and I'd straight up lied to his face in return.

The worst thing was that I actually felt like an asshole about it. But that was insane because there was no fucking way I could give him any of my truth. But I guessed he really did take this Night Keeper bond between us seriously. I just had to remember that that was a good thing because it made him vulnerable to me. The tattoo on the back of my neck made him believe that he could trust me and I had to use that to my advantage. I needed to reel him in, not go up against him, so I decided to try and offer him something to distract him from my lies and earn me back an ounce of his trust.

"I offered to take the necklace from Tatum because she swore she wasn't going to let you beat her and she didn't want there to be anything left in her possession that you could use against her. I was protecting her. Even before I made a vow to do so. It just felt like the right thing to do," I said.

Saint's expression loosened marginally at that admission and he nodded thoughtfully. "She does have a knack for getting under our skin, doesn't she?"

"Something like that," I agreed, feeling uncomfortable about discussing my feelings for her too much with him. His obsession with her was obvious enough and with my feelings thrown into the mix, it was just another thing for us to butt heads over.

"Well, far be it from me to upset our girl for no reason." Saint reached behind his neck and unclasped the necklace before handing it over to me.

The warm metal pooled in my palm and I looked at it with a frown as I tried to figure out his angle.

"So, you just changed your mind about stealing it because you don't want to upset her?" I asked, the scepticism clear in my tone.

"Believe it or not, I don't gain pleasure from hurting her," Saint said with a shrug as he walked towards the door.

"Why are you so good at it then?" I called after him.

"Because I'm not a nice person. But that doesn't make it intentional. It's just the way it is. Besides, the only reason I ever craved her pain was because I wanted to use it to gain her compliance. For the most part, she bends to my rules these days. She understands my need for control in ways that no one else I've ever met has. And we have an understanding about each other's limits...or at least we used to. As it stands, I have enough on my plate with her marrying that neanderthal and fucking up the power balance in our little quartet. I don't need to have her angry at me for taking this too. When she's ready to trust me fully, she will wear it again herself."

"If you want her to trust you then maybe you should give her letters back to her," I growled, my protectiveness making it easy for me to find my anger with him again.

"Well, the problem with that is that I don't trust her either," he said smoothly, like that whole situation wasn't totally fucked up. "Those letters give me control over her and I need that control in a way you couldn't possibly comprehend. But feel free to let her know we had this chat, I'm sure she will be interested to know I allowed you to keep the necklace."

He didn't give me the chance to reply before heading outside and closing the door behind him, leaving me there wondering what the fuck it must be like to live inside his screwed up head. I had no idea why the hell he thought it was okay to force control over Tatum, but that was an issue for another day. Once we were done with this place, I was more than ready to grab that girl and run as far away from him and the other Night Keepers as I could get. Just so long as we left Troy Memphis bleeding in the gutter when we went.

Once I was sure that he was gone, I tugged my cell phone from my pocket and called Tatum to let her know what had happened.

"Hey, I was just thinking about you," she said, sounding like she actually meant that and I couldn't help but smirk like an idiot at those words.

I knew I was getting in too fucking deep with this girl. This whole thing we had going on could see me in prison, but from the moment I'd given in to it I'd known that I was a lost cause.

Besides, so long as we kept it secret for long enough for me to take down Troy Memphis, I would be content enough to know that I'd at least managed to claw back some points of happiness in this life that had offered me so little. Although, when I'd thought through all of the issues that might stand in the way of the two of us claiming this happiness, I'd never once considered the idea that I would have to deal with her overbearing husband too. I swear ever since Kyan had gotten her to say I do, he had barely left her alone, certainly not for long enough for me to have a chance to figure out what this meant for us. I mean, they'd had the Royaume D'élite shit to deal with and then he'd gotten sick so I could make some allowances for that, but it was time for all of us to move on and get some clarity about things. Not that I thought it should mean anything at all if I was being honest. I didn't give a shit if she had a husband, it didn't make me want her any less. And it wasn't like I was some asshole creeping in on another man's girl. We'd all gotten into this at the same time.

"Well that makes two of us, because I was thinking about you too.

Mostly because Saint was just here and he found your necklace," I said as I moved across the room to the box on my mantelpiece where the only things I'd kept from my past lay.

If I hadn't known that Saint had been looking through it already then I never would have known he had. Outwardly, everything looked exactly the way I'd left it. I lifted out the old photograph of me with Michael and our mom and looked down at it with my skin prickling as I listened to Tatum's next words.

"What did he do with it?" she asked in a concerned voice and I sighed as I placed the necklace and the photo back in the box alongside my things.

"Nothing, princess. He was wearing it and laying on my bed when I arrived back from my run like some kind of bunny boiling stalker or something, but luckily enough I don't think he had any grand designs of trying to seduce me. So we just had a rather disturbing conversation and then he left. He gave the necklace back into my safekeeping and told me that he knew you'd start wearing it again once you learned to trust him."

She was silent for a long moment on the other end of the line and I had to wonder what she thought of that. Was the idea of her ever trusting him as absurd to her as it was to me? Or was she actually considering that as an option. I knew that her opinion on him had changed a lot since he'd taken that bullet for her, but I was more sceptical than her about that whole turn of events.

Yes, I could admit that he'd clearly been willing to put his life at risk for her. But what I wasn't so convinced of was that that had been some show of his deep feelings and proof that he cared for her. Saint was definitely obsessed with her and I was easily able to imagine that his obsession and imagined ownership of her were what had made him put himself at risk like that. If Mortez had taken her he would have lost all control over her and that was what was most unacceptable to him. Not the fact that she was in danger or that he was secretly harbouring love for her.

I seriously had trouble imagining Saint ever being capable of anything like that for anyone. Although, I did have to admit that when Kyan was sick, I'd seen another side to him. I'd witnessed the fear in his eyes and the way the impending grief had weighed on him as well as the pure, utter relief he's experienced when he'd survived. But I didn't want to focus on the reasons I was starting to have to believe that Saint wasn't a monster because that meant revaluating everything that I was trying to achieve with his father and him.

"Is he on his way back here?" she asked me and I moved to the window to look out at the path, but I couldn't see any sign of Saint on it so I guessed he'd already passed into the trees.

"Yeah. I think so."

"Good. Kyan and Blake are going down to the Oak Common House for a few drinks in a minute and I'll be here alone. When he gets back, I'll distract him in his room and you can come in and check out his laptop. It's on the dining table again, but for the love of god don't move the fucking thing when you touch it."

I snorted a laugh even as I let the idea take root in my mind. Saint had been on high alert ever since our last attempt to get into his computer and we hadn't had any other opportunities to try again. But now that I knew what folder I was looking for, I could get straight to what I needed without having to fuck around.

"Are you sure, princess? He's a cunning bastard, if he realises that you're distracting him on purpose then it will all go to shit fast," I said, wondering how hard I should be trying to talk her out of this.

"Don't worry about that. I have a plan. There's one sure-fire way that I know to throw him off his guard and he's been avoiding it for weeks. I can do this."

"Okay. I'm on my way." We hung up and I couldn't help but grin at the idea of finally gaining access to whatever the hell Saint was hiding on that laptop.

I put my mind into revenge gear, grabbed a hoodie and a pair of sneakers before heading out of my house and running down the path towards

The Temple.

It didn't take long to jog through campus, and I eyed the view of the sun setting over the lake as I came up on the huge church, taking care to keep my steps silent as I went.

I paused outside the heavy doors, looking through the small window beside it as I listened for any sounds of someone inside, but the only thing that carried to me was the haunting chill of one of Saint's requiems playing over the speakers.

I carefully slid my key into the lock, smirking at the little Night Keeper perk I'd been gifted as it offered me free entrance into the dragon's lair. I had tried sneaking back here during the day a few times to check up on the laptop but ever since we'd gotten into it the first time, Saint had taken to hiding it when he wasn't around and I had no doubt that he would instantly catch on to the fact that someone had been rummaging through his belongings if I tried to find it. And seeing as there were now bars over all of the opening windows and only five people who had a key to this place, it would have been pretty obvious who had been snooping if that happened.

I turned the key in the lock as slowly as I could manage and eased the door open with my heart in my throat. It wasn't like I was afraid of Saint Memphis or his wrath if he caught onto me, but I knew that if he did catch us out that this would be the last opportunity we got to do this. The moment he was sure that we were looking into him and his family, he would lock this place up tighter than a duck's ass and quite possibly strike back at me in ways I couldn't imagine. At the very least, his mom was on the school board and solely responsible for getting me the position as head teacher and I was in no doubts that she could just as easily take my job from me again. And this was the only thing I had that kept me in a position to come after Troy. If I was cut off from Saint then I really had no fucking idea of how I was going to get to his father.

I had a backup plan of course. If I really couldn't take Troy down any other way then I had a pistol and a bullet with his name on it just waiting for the excuse for me to pull the trigger. The only reason that I hadn't gone for that course of action as of yet was because I didn't actually want to end up gunned down for assassinating the Governor of State. Or I guessed I could spend the rest of my years rotting in prison as an alternative and I didn't much like the sound of that either. Because as much as I was willing to sacrifice to take my revenge on him for what he had done to my brother and mom, I knew that it would have broken their hearts to know that my life had been stolen by him too. And I refused to offer him that satisfaction even in death until it was the only option left available to me.

The song that was currently playing was only on softly, the relaxing tones of Rêverie by Claude Debussy filling the open space in the former church and making a shiver dance down my spine as I slipped across the flagstones and onto the carpet.

The dining table where Saint had left his laptop was directly beneath the balcony which held his bedroom and my heart was pounding as I made my way over to it, hearing Saint's voice coming from the space above.

"What are you doing?" he asked as I moved to stand before the table and gently eased the laptop open.

"I need this Saint," Tatum replied in a low voice. "And I know you do, too. Why are you denying both of us?"

There was a span of silence where I wondered what the fuck she was doing to have rendered him speechless and I quickly pulled up the text she'd sent me with Saint's ridiculously complicated password on it and began typing it out.

"*Please*, Saint," Tatum said. "It doesn't have to be anything that pushes the boundaries of the rules. Just take control of me. Bend me to your will."

What the actual fuck was going on up there? I almost moved away from the laptop to investigate it, but I knew I couldn't fuck this up. This was our shot. Our one chance to get hold of whatever the hell was on here and see if it could help me in any way at all.

"I need a few moments to think on it. Kneel there until I make up my mind," Saint commanded and I swear I wanted to be a fly on the wall up there so damn much that it was making my skin itch.

The laptop came on and I flinched at the dull sound it made, but after holding my breath for a few seconds it became clear that Saint hadn't heard anything over the music and his attention was still on Tatum.

I quickly opened up the file marked MAF and started clicking through the countless documents within it as I tried to figure out why he had copies of his father's bank accounts while ignoring the amount of zeros on the total figures because they just pissed me the fuck off.

After several minutes of flicking back and forth between documents and cross referencing bank account numbers alongside transactions that Saint had highlighted, I began to figure out that the money going out marked as 'charitable donations' were in fact more often than not being paid to people like judges, the police chief, other members of the government and even prominent businessmen and women from the city. Which meant that this was a documented record of all of the bribes Troy had been paying to keep himself in his cushy position of Governor of State. I doubted it was actually enough for a conviction though. But maybe a juicy newspaper article could be leaked to the press to damage his reputation if I was careful about it.

The next file I clicked on only made my frown deepen though as I found a record of Saint's own finances including his investment portfolio. My mouth actually fell open when I saw the summary of the value of his assets. Somehow, through countless investments and buying and selling of stocks and shares, Saint had managed to accumulate more wealth in his own name than his father held by more than double. He wasn't just rich. He was fucking platinum made. It was insane and kind of sickening. I didn't even realise one man could own so damn much.

And the more I looked into his records, the more confused I got. Because as well as his most profitable investments, Saint had also been slowly but surely accumulating shares in all of his father's companies under a host of different pseudonyms until he was in fact secretly holding a controlling portion of the shares in all of them. Every single one.

If it hadn't seemed totally crazy, I would have thought that Saint was actually working against his father, building up his control over his assets and his supporters and getting himself into a position to take everything from him in one fell swoop.

But that was unthinkable, wasn't it? The amount of work that had gone into this was hard to even fathom and I'd only sorted through a handful of the files he had here. If this really was a takedown plan then it was multi-faceted and entirely convoluted, completely overworked and containing so many details that it was insane to think that one man could have done it alone. Let alone him doing all of that while maintaining perfect grades, working out day and night, attending football practice, haunting the piano room with a skill that was scarily good, obsessing over Tatum and ruling the entire school with an iron fist.

Although now that I thought about it, I had to admit that if anyone was capable of such insane work, then it would have to be Saint Memphis.

"I want you to follow me," Saint's voice came from the balcony and I froze as I looked over at the stairs with my heart leaping at the thought of getting caught.

"Why are we going downstairs?" Tatum asked loudly and I knew that she was giving me a warning.

I quickly shut down the files I'd opened up and slammed the laptop closed, cringing at the sound it made as I ran for the door.

"I'm going to watch while you transfer a kilo of rice from one bowl to another using tweezers," Saint said just as I pulled the door open and I couldn't help but wonder why the fuck he would want her to do that just as I slipped outside and pulled the door closed.

I hesitated there for a long moment, listening to Tatum complaining that that hadn't been the kind of punishment she was imagining while Saint laughed cruelly and told her that she would do as she was told if she didn't want a worse punishment.

It fucked me off to think of her in there sorting grains of rice for the next however long, but I forced myself to walk away. It might have been a tedious task but it wasn't like it would cause her any actual harm and she'd done it to give me the chance to get this information so now all I had to do was figure out how I was going to use it.

I walked up the path while I turned it over in my mind again and again and to my utter frustration, one thought kept coming back to me which was like a damn infection in my brain that wouldn't go away.

If Saint really was working to take down his father, then he must have hated him just as truly as I did. And after the story he'd told me about that toy car, I couldn't exactly blame him for that. But if I was going to accept that Saint had every reason to want to take his father down then I had to consider the option of joining forces with him.

Because the enemy of my enemy could just be my friend.

CHAPTER THIRTY ONE

I could sense that Blake's mood was low today as I sat beside him in classes and he barely said a word to me, even when he claimed a spot at my side. His dark aura was seeping into me too and I drank it in like a Dementor sucking on his soul. But instead of thriving on his pain, I just wanted to take it away and soothe that lasting ache inside him over the loss of a parent. A pain I knew too well myself these days.

"If we don't catch the Justice Ninja soon, I'm gonna lose it," Blake murmured to Saint on his other side, his grip tight around the edge of his iPad. Miss Pontus had set us all an assignment to write out the meaning of some boring ass poem about wheat, which basically meant the whole class were talking loudly to one another, paying little attention to their work.

"Be patient," Saint said, his tone calm. He'd already finished his assignment of course and I'd seen more synonyms for wheat listed on it than I even knew existed. I swear he didn't even use a thesaurus either. Maybe he really was a robot.

"I have been," Blake growled and Kyan nodded his agreement from further down the row of desks. Mila was sitting on my other side listening in. I'd apologised again and again for what the Night Keepers had done to her, but she kept insisting it had been worth it for the best sex of her life and was glad that at least they knew she wasn't guilty now. I guessed she was used to the ways of my men in this school; she'd spent years watching them rule, falling into line with the rest of the students. She took what they'd done in her stride and I didn't know whether to worry about all the shit she must have witnessed for her to not give a damn about being almost pissed on, or impressed that she tossed her hair and moved on with life as simple as that. Still, I'd made it clear to each and every one of them that if they ever went after her like that again, I'd cut them somewhere that counted and that somewhere would be their balls. Fair to say they'd gotten the message.

"I'm still up for the idea that we bring groups of students to the fight pit day after day and eventually, I'll beat an admission of guilt out of one of them," Kyan muttered.

"The problem with that is, that half the students in this school would admit guilt to avoid being beaten," Saint said thoughtfully.

"I still think we should question the Unspeakables again," Blake said.

"Do you really think one of them could be responsible though?" I asked, frowning at the idea. "If one of them did it, you would have gotten it out of them the last time you questioned them."

"Tatum's right," Saint agreed. "Their backbones have been thoroughly melted, but they'll get another reminder soon enough anyway."

"They're the only ones with motive though," Blake said thoughtfully.

"Pfft, what about every girl you've fucked then tossed away faster than an old, piss-ridden shoe?" Kyan suggested and my lip curled back at the reminder of that thrilling fact.

"Well, yeah," Blake shrugged. "I doubt they took it *that* personally though."

"Did you really leave Tiffany Forsythe up in a cabin in the woods so that she had to be rescued from a bear?" I frowned while Saint and Kyan

472

laughed and Mila leaned closer to hear the answer.

Blake looked to me with a dark kind of smile that left my skin tingling. "Yep. I mean the bear wasn't planned, but it was a happy coincidence."

"That's awful," I growled, fixing Blake with a glare.

"The bitch stole from me," Blake said angrily.

"We found Blake's wallet in her locker just before the end of term last year," Saint explained, examining his nails for dirt.

"I dunno if it was revenge for me fucking and ducking her, but either way that shit was shady. I told her it would be a one night thing, by the way. And maybe if she'd wanted it to be more than that she shouldn't have just laid there like a dead frog on its back. All I remember from that fuck was my mouth getting glued together from all her gross lip gloss and feeling like I was dipping my dick in an aquarium while having a bunch of fish nibble on the end of it. Vaguely interesting, but kind of disturbing at the same time."

I gaped at him as the others laughed, but Blake's icy mood today meant he didn't even crack a smile. He deadpanned the whole freaking story. And I was like, kinda horrified.

"After I found out she'd stolen my wallet, I invited her up to my dad's mountain lodge during summer break and of course she agreed. I drove her all the way into the middle of fucking nowhere and dumped her ass at the cabin, figuring she'd have to call for help once she realised I wasn't coming back. Didn't quite factor in that she wouldn't have cell service, but at least the message got driven home. I guess I should write a thank you note to the bear."

"Before you left her, I suppose you dipped your dick in the aquarium again?" Mila chipped in, leaning further forward and arching a brow at him.

"Pfft." Blake waved a hand. "I did no such fucking thing. That's just what she told everyone so she didn't have to admit to why I really brought her up there."

"Holy shit," Mila breathed. "She made you out to be such a monster."

Blake shrugged. "I'm not denying that, Mila. I wanted to scare the bitch. Bet she hasn't stolen from anyone since though, has she?"

Kyan cracked his knuckles, smirking and Saint had a glint in his eye as he drank in the thought of the girl's pain.

"Why didn't you make her an Unspeakable?" Mila asked and the guys exchanged a look.

"Because not everyone deserves that shit. She got punished, it was clear she got the message."

"How comes Punch was in the Unspeakables then if all he did was hit you? Did he just wound your pride?" I asked Blake, narrowing my eyes, wondering how strict they really were on their guidelines or if it just depended on whatever mood they were in at the time.

Blake pressed his tongue into his cheek. "I thought Kyan told you about what they all did."

"Well I already knew what Punch had done, so..." I shrugged and Blake's eyes narrowed as he glanced over at the back of Toby's head.

"The kid has anger issues. He was going around flooring anyone in school who so much as looked at him the wrong way. He broke a kid's jaw once. We'd tried punishing him, which should have been warning enough but when he hit me, that was it. We gave him a timeout in the Unspeakables. I didn't ever think he was a real monster until what he did to you." His fists clenched on the table and I noticed the three of them were all glaring at Toby AKA Stalker like they were thinking up the next awful thing to do to him.

Bait glanced over his shoulder from his spot beside Stalker, taking us in through the half mask on his face which was now sporting a large cock on it with the balls drawn below it on his cheek. His gaze fixed on me for a moment and there was an intense anger there that ate into my flesh like acid. I couldn't really blame him for hating me. I was just another one of his enemies now. But I hated him right back now I knew what he'd done.

The bell rang and the guys stood as one, their shoulders brushing and an air of danger crackling around them that told me they were on the hunt. It was the end of the school day and it was rare that a day passed without them punishing an Unspeakable or two.

"Bait, Deepthroat, Stalker, Freeloader, Squits and Pigs!" Blake hollered. "Your lot has been drawn today. Follow us." He strode across the room and Saint followed while Kyan grabbed my hand and pulled me along with them. I turned to wave goodbye to Mila and she waved too, looking slightly pale as she watched the Night Keepers round up the six Unspeakables and send them out the door ahead of them.

Kyan walked at a fierce pace and I had to practically jog to keep up with him. He looked like he was about to throw me over his shoulder at any second, but I warned him off with my eyes.

I sensed a crowd following behind us, perhaps wondering what fresh hell the Night Keepers were about to unleash and I was kinda curious too.

"Are your little legs slowing you down, baby?" Kyan mocked.

"Just because I don't have giant tree trunks for thighs, doesn't mean my legs are little. You're just abnormally tall," I said, grinning at him.

"And you're abnormally fucking hot, so..."

"So?" I smirked.

"I forgot my point." He tugged me closer with an animalistic growl and I laughed.

We followed Blake and Saint as they herded the Unspeakables to the courtyard in front of Aspen Halls. A crowd was forming there like they'd known this was coming and my lips parted at the sight of the benches pushed to the edges of the courtyard. In the central space was a coiled up chain, a lacrosse stick, a cheerleading pom-pom, a frisbee, a roll of toilet paper, a baseball bat, a pair of football shoulder pads, a pile of pine cones and a wooden stick.

Monroe stood beyond them beside a picnic table with a smug look on his face that suggested he'd been the one to put those items there.

"What the fuck is this?" I muttered to Kyan, but he just grinned in answer.

Blake strode to the front of the group, shoving the Unspeakables toward all the items. He walked through the middle of them, picking up the stick which looked like it had come from a pine tree and jumping up onto a bench beyond the items.

"Welcome to the Picnic Games!" Blake hollered and the gathered students cheered in excitement. How had word even spread about this shit? And why didn't I know about it?

I looked to Monroe with a question in my eyes, but he just shrugged, a grin playing around his lips. He was as crazy as the rest of them. And I totally loved it.

Kyan led me across the courtyard to sit on the bench Blake was standing on and Saint sat down on my other side with a vicious smile as we faced the Unspeakables. Monroe moved to stand behind us, anticipation emanating from him and I turned my head, mouthing a *hey* to him which he mouthed back, making my tummy swirl and flutter. *Damn his beautiful face.*

"You will all have fifteen minutes to get your hands on this immunity stick," Blake explained as I turned back to face him, finding him waving the stick in his hands. "Whoever is holding it when the time is up will be immune from all further punishments for two full weeks!" he cried to another round of cheers.

My jaw dropped as I took in the Unspeakables' fearful faces, but as they looked between each other, that fear quickly turned to determination.

"Saint, set the timer," Blake called and Saint took his iPad out, resting it upright in a stand so it was aimed at the Unspeakables with a fifteen minute timer ready to go on it. "May the odds *never* be in your favour," Blake jeered to a round of laughs, then he raised three fingers, putting them down as he counted and the whole crowd joined in. "Three - two - one - go!"

Blake tossed the immunity stick towards them just as Saint hit start on the timer and my heart pounded out of rhythm as they all dived on it. Everyone except Squits who raced for the baseball bat and the football shoulder pads, pulling them on before running at the five who were wrestling on the ground. He released a roar as he hefted the bat above his head and my heart beat harder as the little guy went surprisingly apeshit.

Stalker got the immunity stick, shoving the rest of them off of him with his superior strength, but Squits wheeled the bat around, smacking him in the back with it. Stalker cried out, twisting around in fury and snatching the bat from Squits' hands.

While he wasn't looking, Pigs snatched the immunity stick from Stalker's grip and started running for the edge of the ring. He squealed like an actual pig as Deepthroat came at him with the lacrosse stick, wailing in rage as she smacked him with it again and again. He fell beneath her and she continued to hit him while the others all sprinted forward to try and get their hands on the immunity stick.

Pigs grabbed the only thing within reach which was the toilet paper, throwing it at Deepthroat with a shriek of fear. Deepthroat snatched the immunity stick and picked up the toilet paper too, hugging it to her chest and turning tail. She tore away as Freeloader and Squits fell over Pigs, and Bait and Stalker came after her with nothing but desperation in their eyes.

My gaze was riveted to the fight as Bait picked up the chain, giving Stalker time to make it to Deepthroat and try to wrestle the stick from her hand. She shrieked like a witch burning at the stake, smacking him with the lacrosse stick as she tried to hold onto the toilet paper as well as the immunity stick. Stalker knocked her to the ground with a hard shove, plucking the immunity stick from her hands and attempting to tug the lacrosse stick from her grip too. She let go of it the same moment she lunged at his legs, sinking her teeth into his calf. *Holy fuck.*

Kyan laughed loudly beside me and Saint's eyes were unblinking as he took in the violence before us. Blake was howling like a wolf and plenty of the football team echoed the sound. I realised Monroe was howling too so I figured fuck it, tipped my head back and released my own long howl. Kyan growled like he liked that, his hand dropping onto my thigh and I poked my tongue out at him before turning to face the game again.

Bait suddenly lunged at Stalker from behind, wrapping the chain around his throat, a bellow tearing from his lips as he hung all of his weight from it and Stalker staggered backwards. Deepthroat leapt up, shoving Stalker in the chest to get him on the floor and Freeloader, Pigs and Squits all ran to help as they bound the chain around him, taking out their strongest opponent as a unit. The second he was immobilised, they all turned on one another again, scratching and tearing and kicking as they tried to get the immunity stick from Stalker's hand.

Bait's mask was knocked flying from his face by an elbow from Freeloader and Blake whistled sharply.

"Get it back on this second, Bait, or you're out of the game!" he snapped and Bait dove forward to retrieve it, jamming it back into place and losing his chance of getting his hands on the immunity stick.

Freeloader had it now and she zoomed around the edge of the ring, trying to keep moving as Pigs launched pinecones at her and Squits threw the frisbee with frightening accuracy, smacking her in the face and making her nose bleed.

"Five minutes!" Blake called in warning and if they'd been desperate before, it was nothing compared to what they became. The Unspeakables were suddenly screaming and fighting with the ferocity of wild animals.

Deepthroat smacked Freeloader's legs with the lacrosse stick, taking her to the floor so hard that a collective *oooh* sounded out from the crowd as she busted her knees and hands open. My heart skipped madly as I took in the carnage. Freeloader curled in on herself, giving up as Deepthroat plucked the immunity stick from her hand and turned to face anyone who dared try to take it from her again, the toilet paper still under one arm as she wheeled the lacrosse stick left and right.

Pigs was limping and Squits was shaking beside him, dancing from foot to foot as he considered what to do. Bait had gotten the baseball bat and he ran at Deepthroat, clearly the only one left who was brave enough to take her on. He released a battle cry as he came at her, swinging the bat hard and it collided with the lacrosse stick as she swung it in defence. A splintering of wood sounded and the lacrosse stick snapped in half, leaving her with a pointy weapon in her hand. She immediately jabbed it at Bait and he narrowly missed being skewered as he gasped and jumped back. His leg caught on Stalker on the ground and he toppled over backwards with a cry of defeat just as the timer rolled down to the final ten seconds.

The crowd started counting down as Deepthroat strode forward and pointed the broken stick at Bait's throat, her teeth bared and her eyes wild as she dared him to make another move. The timer dropped to zero and Deepthroat squealed in delight, racing to pick up the pom-pom and throwing her leg in the air as she cheered and jumped, waving the stick in her other hand. The crowd clapped and she drank in the sound, beaming around at them, her victory shining from her eyes.

I glanced at Kyan with a frown, my gut tightening at the sight of her winning. Of all of them, I'd wanted to see her lose most.

Saint was smiling though, and it was a twisted fucking smile which told me to beware. He rose to his feet, climbing onto the table beside Blake and clapping him on the shoulder.

"This was a test!" Saint called out, his voice cutting and clear, making everyone fall deathly silent instantly. "You have all failed that test."

"What?!" Deepthroat shrieked, the pom-pom falling from her hand as her jaw dropped.

"We hoped to see some improvement in you all, but it seems you are still the same selfish pieces of shits we knew you were all along," Saint mused and I stared between the Night Keepers in surprise.

"Did you know about this?" I whispered to Kyan and he nodded, smirking at me.

Saint went on, "Not once did we tell you to use the items in this game as weapons. Not once did we tell you to turn on each other and draw blood."

"But you said-" Deepthroat cried, but Blake cut her off.

"All I said was that the one holding the immunity stick after the timer ran out would be offered two weeks without punishments. You could have discussed it between you and decided who was most worthy of that prize. Instead, you decided to turn on one another, show how little you really care for each other and prove beyond a shadow of a doubt that you have earned your places in the gutter." Blake stared down at them and they all shared a look, horrified by being tricked this way. But he was right. They had never been told to fight for the stick. And the expression on his face sent a delicious shiver through me. *Damn* he looked hot when he was laying down the law.

The crowd started laughing and jeering the Unspeakables and Blake jumped down from the table, snatching the immunity stick from Deepthroat and snapping it in two. He tossed the pieces on the ground. "Moral of the game: don't be a dick." Blake flicked her between the eyes then strode out of the courtyard.

Saint headed after him and I stood up with Kyan, following along behind them as Monroe moved to my other side, leaving the Unspeakables all licking their wounds and exchanging guilty looks.

"That'll stop any little uprisings they might have had in mind," Kyan murmured to me and I nodded, still shocked by what I'd just watched.

"They're going to second guess any friends they thought they'd made amongst one another," Monroe said with a smirk.

"Clever," I remarked. "And fucking psychotic."

"That pretty much sums up which one of us came up with this idea, baby," Kyan said, chuckling.

"Saint," I said simply, no question in my voice.

"Obviously," Monroe growled, his arm brushing mine and sending electricity rushing along my skin.

Kyan laughed harder. "I love that unbalanced motherfucker."

Blake paused as we reached the path which split around the lake and I realised he was looking out at it with his muscles bunched.

"Did that not cheer you up, brother?" Kyan called, leading me over to him. I glanced at Kyan with a question in my eyes.

"Why? What's wrong?" I asked, stepping to Blake's side.

"It's his mother's birthday today," Saint explained with no emotion to his voice. But I guessed the way he showed he cared was by setting up an elaborate death match for his friend to watch.

"Oh," I breathed, my heart clenching tightly in my chest. I took Blake's hand, squeezing. "I didn't know."

"I didn't say," he countered, looking to me with a shrug, but the pain in his eyes was impossible to miss.

"I'm sorry," I breathed.

"Not your fault, Cinders," he said, tugging me closer.

"You can kiss my wife if you want to," Kyan said seriously, pressing his hand to Blake's back.

"Kyan, you don't get to give permission for that," I growled, glaring at him. Monroe shot him a pissy look that only I caught. I really needed to drive this point home once and for all.

"As your husband, I beg to disagree," Kyan said simply and Saint shot him daggers, not that he would ever lay a hand on me anyway, so I didn't know why it bothered *him* so much.

"I may be your wife, but I say who I kiss and don't kiss," I said firmly, moving to tip-toe up and offer my mouth to Blake. Kyan got between us, tugging me back against his chest and a snarl escaped me as I readied to fight him.

"This isn't funny, Kyan," Blake snarled, reaching out and taking my arms, trying to yank me out of his grip.

"Look, you can kiss her. Just know that I'm *allowing* it. As a gift," Kyan said, smirking like a dickhead and I elbowed him in the gut as he released me, pushing me into Blake's arms.

"Come on Blake, let's go for a walk." I caught his hand, tugging him away from the others and I was sure I heard Kyan saying *you're welcome* as I went, so I tossed him the finger over my shoulder.

We walked in silence, taking in the quiet lap of the lake against the shore. The air was slightly warmer, the promise of spring in it and the sky was a bright blue that was slowly starting to pale with the coming twilight.

Each of us understood the other's pain on a deep level. I knew he didn't

481

want to dwell on his mom's death, but I wondered if he might want to talk about the good times instead.

"What was she like?" I asked him. "Your mom?"

He sighed long and slow. "She was...full of life. She always had so much energy. My dad can be a moody fucker at times, but as soon as she walked into the room, she lifted everyone's spirits. Especially his. She just had one of those personalities that shone."

"Like you," I commented and he frowned at me.

"I don't think I'm like that," he muttered.

"Then you're not seeing yourself right. You make me laugh fifty times a day, Blake. Your smile is like...like a beam of light. You always know how to cheer me up or just make the day brighter just by being you."

"You think so?" he asked hopefully.

"I know so," I said firmly, squeezing his fingers. "You've just been through a lot of bad shit, you're still healing."

"I guess," he sighed. "Sometimes it feels like I'm back to my old self, but half the time it still feels like an act."

"I know what you mean," I said gently, my heart sinking. "Sometimes I worry what people will think of me if I let myself be happy. Like it means that I'm not thinking of him, that I've moved on. But I haven't, I don't think you can ever move on from something like that. It's left a wound in me that will always split open...just less often than it did at the start."

"Yeah that's...exactly how it is. It feels like being happy is a betrayal to her memory," he growled.

"She'd want you to be happy," I promised, his pain feeling as heavy as mine. "But it's okay not to be too."

"I suppose," he muttered. "Mostly I just like to take my mind off of it." He reached into his coat pocket, producing two miniature bottles of rum and holding one out to me. "Want one?" He cracked the lid off of one, downing it in two sips.

I laughed. "Where the hell did you get those?"

"The janitor's closet. Little bastard had a stash. He doesn't anymore though." He smirked, shaking his pocket to show me had more hidden in there. "He'll be on the prowl for the culprit though, that asshole is like an angry Pitbull when he's riled."

I twisted the cap off of the rum with a laugh, figuring what the hell as I tossed the contents down my throat. It burned all the way to my stomach, but the heat swept keenly through my veins too and it felt good.

"Let's head up Tahoma Mountain, I know what we can do." Blake started jogging along and I ran with him, laughing more as he led me all the way down the path to the very edge of Sycamore Beach.

Then he veered off onto the track that curled up the mountain and we started climbing steadily. The view down to the lake was incredible and I couldn't believe I'd never been up here before as we climbed higher and higher. Everlake campus really was something special and I knew when I left here, it would always hold a piece of my soul. Too much had happened in this place. So much bad and yet so much good too. It wasn't what I would have wanted when I came here, but now I had my Night Keepers, it was hard to picture life without them. And I wouldn't have given them up for anything. Even with all the shit they'd done to me and I'd done to them in return. It was messy, imperfect and twisted. But it was also my story. *Our* story. And I loved it in its own fucked up way.

We made it up to a cabin set near a steep cliff which was surrounded by a group of trees. Blake headed around to the back of it, pushing a window open and climbing in. He offered me a hand as I walked up to it and frowned curiously.

"What is this place?" I asked.

"In the summer, Mr Colby holds paragliding classes up here," he explained. "I bribed him to leave the window open for me so I can get in here any time I like. It's a cool place to come. And today seems like the perfect weather for paragliding." He grinned.

"Are you serious?" I gasped as I climbed inside, the space filled with paragliding equipment and a bunch of chairs stacked in one corner beside a whiteboard.

"Yep. If you want to?" he asked excitedly and I nodded keenly. "Have you ever done it before?"

"Yeah, my dad used to love it. We'd rent paragliders and climb to the top of Horse Canyon in San Diego then sail down it at sunset. I always did it tandem with him though, I haven't done it alone before."

"No worries, sweetheart, you can ride with me. I wouldn't have it any other way anyway."

He caught my hand again, tugging me over to all the gear and started pulling a dark green jumpsuit on me which had the Everlake crest on the back of it. He admired me in the fitted suit before pulling on his own and my heart raced at the paragliders folded up in colourful bags hanging from hooks on the wall. He took one down, carrying it outside and setting it up while readying the harnesses, the paraglider matching the colour of our suits. I followed him outside, my excitement turning to a knot of anxiety too as he beckoned me over.

"Ready, Cinders?" he asked and I nodded, biting my lip as I approached him and he got into the harness before securing me against him in my own. The cliff stood before us, ready for us to run and jump off of it and my heart hammered as I waited for his signal.

"You really trust me, huh?" he murmured in my ear before nibbling on it. I shivered against him, nodding and reaching back to clutch his hair and draw him closer for a second.

"It's not the worst way to die if I have to go out today," I breathed and he growled in my ear, offering me another little bottle of rum. I let him tip it down my throat and the scent of it washed over me as he drank his own and turned my head to kiss me. His tongue stroked mine and I could almost taste his adrenaline meeting my own. I was laughing by the time we broke apart, excited butterflies sweeping through my belly.

"Let's go!" he cried then we started running for the cliff.

My heart beat wildly out of rhythm and fear and excitement tangled inside me like a living creature as we reached the edge and the air pushed against our paraglider. A scream escaped me as we stepped off of the cliff and the glider lifted us higher as we sailed over the lake far, far below. I laughed and cried out as the wind took us and Blake used the lines on the glider to steer us on the drafts, circling us around the whole of campus. It was breathtakingly beautiful. The water gleamed like it was made of pure crystal, so blindingly blue that it rivalled the sky.

The endless rain recently had made the forest lush and so green. I could make out the students walking around the paths far below, the whole thing looking like some sort of painting. I reached into my jumpsuit and took my phone from my blazer pocket, knowing I was risking dropping it, but I just *had* to capture this moment. Once I'd taken a bunch of pictures of the incredible view, I flipped the camera and took some selfies of us. Blake kissed my cheek and poked out his tongue and we pulled stupid faces as we snapped a few more until we were both laughing.

It was even more exhilarating as we soared towards the earth and the wind whipped past me fiercely. We tore over the water, getting frighteningly close to it until I thought we were going to splash right into it.

"Blake!" I cried and he answered with a laugh as we sailed lower and lower and made it to Sycamore Beach just in time. We hit the sand and ran several steps as we slowed to a halt. Blake pulled our harnesses off, grabbing my waist and throwing me down beneath him in the sand, making my stomach whoosh.

He dropped down over me and his mouth landed on mine, our hearts pounding furiously against one another's as he kissed me. His tongue moved against mine in passionate strokes and I moaned against his lips as I bathed in the happy glow of this moment, adrenaline still pouring through my veins like a dam had broken inside me and all that was held behind it had been purest sunlight. This was one helluva way to forget the darkness living in us and I found myself giddy as I stared up at my beautiful golden boy.

"I love you," he said gruffly, his mouth moving to my jaw, my throat. "And I won't let you feel that way about me in return. I don't deserve your love, Tatum Rivers, but I'm going to try and deserve it. Until I do, I won't ever let you fall for me."

Our mouths clashed again before I could say anything in answer to that, but my heart was swelling and those words weren't just on my tongue, they lived in me. Deeply. I knew I had fallen for Blake already and I wanted to convince him that he was deserving of that, but I was terrified to say it for more reasons than he could ever understand. Because he wasn't the only one I harboured those feelings for. I'd told Kyan the truth because I'd feared losing him, but telling Blake too meant owning the rest of the feelings living in me for the other Night Keepers and I just wasn't ready to do that. Not when I knew a day was coming when this would all fall apart. That this little bubble we'd contained ourselves within would pop and reality would come pouring in on us like a wave.

He ground me into the sand and our bodies collided, my hips bucking as I groaned in encouragement. I was half aware a bunch of students would be heading here to hang out and watch the sunset. It was a miracle no one was here already.

Blake started panting, his hard on grinding between my thighs. I moaned in encouragement and he dragged his teeth along my lower lip, his hands roaming to the zipper holding my jumpsuit in place.

"Blake," I laughed throatily. "We can't. Not here. Let's head back to The Temple."

"Fuck that." He pulled me to my feet. "I'm keeping you as mine tonight." He tugged me along, leaving the paraglider there on the beach as he pulled me into the trees and threw me back against a solid pine trunk. I gasped as his mouth landed on mine and he pawed at my breasts through my clothes with needy squeezes, making my pulse skip and dance.

"We should head back up the mountain," he growled against my lips. "Do it again."

The wind was whipping around us and I knew from the times I'd spent paragliding with my dad that the weather was turning and it wasn't safe to do it now. "The sun's setting and the wind is picking up. Let's just hang out down here if you don't want to go back to The Temple."

"Come on, Cinders. I wanna do it again." He pulled back a little, the fire in his eyes making me worry suddenly. Was he seriously going to march up that mountain again? It would be dark by the time he made it to the cliff.

"It's not safe," I said firmly.

"Even better," he said fiercely, his eyes flashing and making my heart jolt. "I want to feel like the wind is going to dash me into the rocks this time when I land."

He stepped away from me, his jaw set and I caught his arm. "Blake, don't be stupid, you'll get yourself killed."

"Stay here until I get back," he demanded, looking to the sky as if he realised taking me wasn't a good idea anyway. Which meant it definitely wasn't a good idea for him either. There were students arriving on the beach now, their chatter calling to us so he knew I wouldn't be in danger of any Justice Ninja attacks if he left me here. But I didn't want him to leave.

"Don't put yourself at risk," I snarled, clinging onto him, but he shook me off.

"I'll be fine. Probably." He laughed hollowly, unzipping his jumpsuit and taking out another one of the rum bottles from his blazer pocket. I snatched it from his hand before he could drink it and he scowled darkly.

"Are you crazy?" I snapped, my heart thrashing against my ribcage with worry. He'd already had a couple of shots, and who knew how many more he planned on having walking up there this time?

"Does it matter?" he snapped. "I'll see you when I come down." He turned his back on me, striding onto the beach to fetch the paraglider and I jogged after him in a fury. A few of the football crowd spotted us, but none approached when they realised we were mid-argument.

"Blake!" I snapped. "You can't do this." I caught his arm, but he shrugged me off, turning to me with his jaw gritted.

"I didn't ask for permission, Cinders." He strode away and I took out my phone, calling Saint as my heart beat out a panicked tune.

"Yes?" he answered curtly, but there was an edge to his tone that almost could have been misconstrued as concern.

"Blake's being an idiot. He's going paragliding while the wind is picking up and it's almost dark. He's headed to the mountain trail."

"Fucking moron," he drawled. "I'll send Kyan to get him."

I sighed, relaxing a little at his words. "Just tell him to hurry."

"He will," Saint said firmly. "Where are you? I'll come and meet you."

"I don't need-"

"I'm coming and I will track your phone if you don't simply tell me."

I sighed. "I'm at Sycamore Beach, I'll start taking the west path back." I knew I couldn't take any risks since the Justice Ninja had attacked me with a freaking bow and arrow. It still gave me nightmares, especially since the cut on my arm was definitely going to scar.

Students arrived on the beach as I headed to the path and they shot me curious glances at the sight of me in my jumpsuit. As I walked in the direction of The Temple, leaving the sound of chatter behind, a cold wind sent a chill through me and I upped my pace.

I stopped myself from breaking out into a run as the wind blew through the trees and I felt all too alone on this track. Shadows were flitting through the woodland as dusk fell, but I was sure it was just animals and swaying trees. If I let myself think it was anything else, I'd freak out and I was not gonna do that.

My phone buzzed in my pocket and the noise made my heart jolt before I took it out and found a message from an anonymous number, the words in it making fear slide deep into my bones. *Oh my god.*

Pretty little blondie, all alone in the dark.
How easy it would be for a wolf to snap her up…

I looked around in fear, hunting every space between the trees, searching ahead of me and behind. But I couldn't see anyone. Did they actually know I was here, or were they just messing with me?

A crack of a twig up in the woods made my heart stall and I froze on the path, my hand clenching around my phone.

"Who's there?!" I demanded, ready to run for my life if I had to.

There was no sign of a flaming arrow or a white mask, but I could feel eyes on me. I was sure of it.

When no answer came, I started walking again, forcing myself not to run and give them the fear that they wanted from me.

I soon spotted Saint along the path and relief washed through me as I made it to him.

"What's wrong?" he demanded as he took in my expression and I showed him the message on my phone.

His eyes narrowed and he slid his arm around my shoulders, pulling me close to him protectively. It was something only Blake or Kyan usually did, but it felt good being held against him like that, his fresh apple scent drawing me in.

"Between the two of us they would be bleeding out in a puddle of their own blood and piss within moments if they dared attack you now," he murmured.

I released a laugh, but it was only half hearted as I glanced over my shoulder, unsettled by their watchful eyes somewhere close by. *Creep*.

"Maybe we *should* go after them," I whispered, hating this shit. I wanted to drag this bastard out into the light and beat the living hell out of them.

"No," he said simply. "They will slip up soon enough."

"Do you have a plan?" I asked him and he chuckled low in his throat.

"Oh Tatum, I would've thought you'd have learned by now. I'm Saint Memphis, I *always* have a plan."

Saint

CHAPTER THIRTY TWO

I t might have been suggested once or twice in my life that I was prone to taking on too much. But I always felt that that was a matter of perspective. How much was too much? If I was able to complete the tasks I set myself then was it even valid to say that there was too much work to be completed? It wasn't as though I slept much anyway, and I was always willing to push my mind and body to their limits in the quest for perfection.

So, despite my considerable workload, I had no complaints to make. Aside from the fact that entertaining so many projects at once meant that my progress was somewhat slowed on some of them. But I had finally come across something in my hunt for the names of the organisers of Royaume D'élite that I was sure would help point us in the right direction to track them down. The surprising part about it was what else I had discovered.

Kyan:

If any of you see my wife can you let her know I have a package for her...

I gritted my teeth as I read the message in the group chat and drummed my fingers against the table. It was Saturday afternoon and I was working while the others had all gone down to the lake to frolic. They hadn't specifically called it frolicking when they'd headed down there, but I knew the drill well enough by now. Kyan and Blake would swim, Monroe and Tatum would watch for a while until Monroe was goaded into joining the others in the water and then they'd get out and Tatum would run screaming from them while they chased her, threatening to dunk her in the icy water too.

Right on cue, the front door banged open and Tatum raced inside with a shriek of laughter, darting past me and tossing a wide grin my way as she charged up the stairs to my room.

A smile touched the edges of my lips before I could stop it and I didn't even chastise her for using my private space as her safety zone.

Blake:

If the package is your dick again then we don't need constant messages about it.

Kyan:

It is, and I need her to unwrap it with her teeth

I knew these messages were for my benefit and that they would currently be hastily drying off down at the lake beyond The Temple doors. None of them would have let our girl out of their sight now that we had this Justice Ninja bullshit to deal with which meant the messages were entirely intended to get under my skin. The most infuriating thing about that was the fact that I was unable to stop it from working.

Saint:

I am not surprised your wife went running from your dick and your questionable skills with it.

Kyan:

There's nothing questionable about my dick skills, is there wifey?

Tatum:

Squid emoji

I released a long breath and the inevitable followed that.

Kyan:

Fuck yes. With a side of *onion emoji* *octopus emoji* *otter emoji* please.

Tatum:

Only if you let me tie you up this time, baby ;)

The door banged open again and the three assholes entered all shirtless, all dripping moisture with their hair wet. It looked like a set up for a fucking porn shoot and as they tossed their shoes by the door and dumped their shirts in a heap, I had to fight the urge to physically attack them.

Monroe seemed amused as he pushed his dripping hair out of his eyes and came to sit across from me at the dining table.

Kyan and Blake were clearly on the hunt though.

"First one to find her gets a kiss," Blake suggested as he looked around with narrowed eyes as he tried to figure out where she would have hidden.

"You can't just go around kissing my wife without my permission," Kyan grunted.

"You gave me permission the other day, asshole," Blake replied. "Not that I need it."

"Fine. I extend permission to today. If you find her first that is. Otherwise, I'll grant permission for you to watch me with her."

Tatum:

You'll never find me.

The two of them burst into motion, howling like wild animals as they tore through the building, fighting to be the first to find her while neither of them made any move towards my room.

I cut a look towards Monroe and I was sure I noticed his jaw ticking as he watched them hunt, his muscles tense like he was holding back on the desire to join in.

"You look tempted to try for that prize yourself, Nash," I pointed out and he scoffed as he rolled his eyes at me.

"She's my student."

"And you didn't answer my question."

I gave him a knowing smirk and sent a text of my own.

Saint:

The neanderthals are searching off base. How long are you going to keep them in suspense?

Tatum:

No one will ever find me.

Saint:

Is that a challenge?

Tatum:

squid emoji

My hand tingled with the desire to spank her for that and I growled in frustration as I fought against that idea and tried to remember the rules I'd set for myself regarding her. But it was growing more and more difficult to resist her and it was becoming clear to me that we needed a group discussion about more things than just what I'd managed to discover about Royaume D'élite.

I looked at my messages for a long moment as Kyan and Blake raced down into the gym on their hunt and Monroe gave me a look that said he didn't really believe I'd play.

Saint:

I'll give you a *squid emoji* you'll never forget when I find you, siren.

Tatum:

I have no idea what that means? I feel like you're trying to make a threat there somewhere but the *squid emoji* just makes no sense in that context.

I slammed my phone down on the table with a grunt of frustration. I was sure I'd figured the fucking squid out that time. Fuck them. Fuck them and their fucking squids. Even Google wouldn't give me the fucking answers to it, but I wasn't going to give up until I figured it out.

Monroe tugged his own cell phone from his pocket and pulled up the messages, laughing loudly at me as I stalked away from him and my anger rose a fraction at that. How the fuck did a teacher know what it meant and yet I still didn't? That shit was infuriating.

I headed up to my room and fell still at the top of the stairs as I let my gaze skim over everything until I spotted something out of place which would let me know where she was hiding.

It took me less than three seconds to spot the crease in the duvet cover and I prowled towards the bed with purposeful strides before dropping down suddenly and looking beneath it.

Tatum gasped as her eyes met mine and I smiled darkly before snatching hold of her ankle and dragging her out as she screamed like I was serial killer come to murder her. That really shouldn't have turned me on, but what could I say? I was a fucked up being.

I pinned her to the carpet and leaned close to her as she squirmed beneath me.

"Tell me what the squid emoji means," I growled as she wriggled and laughed and I began to seriously doubt the wisdom of pinning her down like this because it felt like I'd somehow given her the upper hand.

"Never," she swore in a whisper that had my hackles rising, but before I could get any ideas about punishing her for it, she leaned up and pressed a kiss to the corner of my mouth.

My grip on her slackened and I pulled back as she drew away, though my skin burned where her lips had met with it.

"What was that for?" I demanded.

"You won the game. Blake said the prize was a kiss."

I scoffed as I shoved myself upright and offered her a hand to pull her up with me. "We need to talk," I said as I found myself inches from her body, her skin flushed from the excitement of the game and her blue eyes bright.

"We do?" she asked, biting her lip and looking at me like she'd been waiting for this. Which was good, because it was well overdue.

"Yes. I drew up an itinerary. So let's get it dealt with now." I turned away from her and headed for the stairs just as Blake and Kyan bounded up them.

"Get out of my room before I throw you over the balcony," I warned them. I hated having people in my personal space and they damn well knew it.

"How come you don't get mad at Tate for coming up here?" Blake complained as he turned back with a huff and jogged down the stairs obligingly.

"She's special," I said before I could stop myself and Kyan made a wooing noise like a little girl at a slumber party.

For fuck's sake.

"We need to have a meeting," I announced as I moved back over to my laptop at the dining table. I had a notepad and pen ready next to it and I was itching to get started.

"It's pizza night," Tatum reminded me as she headed around the table to put the first round of pizzas in the oven.

As if it wasn't bad enough that we all had to eat the cheese and tomato paste bread with our hands, we had to endure the fact that they couldn't all fit in the oven at once, so the food didn't even all arrive at the same time. It was fucking traumatic every damn week. But unlike every other motherfucker in this group, I actually stuck to the rules, so I had to push through the discomfort of it.

I worked hard at keeping my patience as Monroe moved away to help Tatum put the food on and Kyan grabbed a box of beers and dumped the whole thing on the end of the table. I tried to ignore it. Tried to pretend I couldn't see the fact that the cardboard was torn.

I made it six seconds. And then I got up, grabbed the whole thing and stalked toward the front door with the full intention to throw it out into the trees.

Kyan intercepted me with a dark laugh and snatched the box back from me before taking the beers over to the fridge and stacking them inside instead. He even flattened the cardboard and tossed it in the recycling. *Fucker.*

With a sigh of frustration, I moved back to the table to await my food. Once it was cooking, everyone else came to join me and I opened my notebook to the first page, looking down at my itinerary and ignoring the way they were sniggering like a bunch of assholes. If they were incapable of organising themselves or this group, then I was more than happy to take command for them and I didn't give a shit if they mocked me for my methods. This was how we got things done.

"Drink?" Kyan asked just as I was about to start and I looked up to find him holding out a beer for me with his left hand, wrist twisted *just so,* making that fucking squid tattoo look me in the eye. I swear the thing was smirking like the asshole who'd inked it onto his flesh.

I swallowed my anger at everything about his offer with some difficulty and blew out a harsh breath. "No, thank you. I have not in fact, suddenly developed a taste for piss water brew and become a hick just because I spend too much time in your company."

Kyan laughed loudly, dropping into his chair and sipping on the beer himself while Monroe and Blake joined in. I rolled my eyes at them, but let it slide because that smile on Blake's face looked genuine for the first time since Kyan had hauled his ass back here kicking and cursing on his mom's birthday and we'd locked him down in the crypt to stop him from going paragliding in the dark.

He'd been pissed at us for three days following that but hadn't made an argument out of it, likely because he knew full well that we'd been right to do it. Luckily it seemed like today he was feeling himself again and I could allow a little of their bullshit at my expense in favour of making him smile. Not that I'd ever admit it.

Of course, I had now added more plans for dealing with Blake's issues to my list of chores, but while his mood was improved, it didn't seem to be the most pressing of our issues so I was willing to let it be for now. But sooner or later, Blake Bowman was going to have to deal with his grief.

I glanced around to make sure everyone was paying attention and then began the meeting.

"First off, I think I'm closing the net on Royaume D'élite. I've been tracing the financial movements of the O'Briens to try and locate the organiser of the club through the membership fees, and though they use various shell organisations to collect them each month, the amounts don't change."

"How the fuck are you tracing their finances?" Monroe asked me like he'd never even heard of the concept of corrupt members of law enforcement.

"I have people who I can pay to get me all kinds of information if I want it," I said to him in a bored tone. "Money talks and secrets spill. It's a fairly simple concept to grasp."

He frowned at me like my entitled brat was showing and I smirked because I knew it. But I was so much more than an entitled brat. I knew exactly how to handle all of the advantages that I'd been born to and how to use them to gain even more advantages over every situation I was faced with.

Monroe looked like he had something further to say to that, but the oven timer started bleeping and Tatum hopped up to get the first round of pizzas out of it, stealing his attention so that I could go on without having to listen to him. I truly believed that he was perfect for the position of our final Night Keeper, but sometimes his peasantry grated on me to the point of despair. I'd cut him a check to make him feel better about his lot in life if I didn't know he was too damn proud to take it. Not that it mattered anyway. I firmly believed in the concept of this unit we'd built which meant my money was his money anyway. He just hadn't figured that out yet.

"Regardless of my methods, it's safe to say that I'm at least closing in on how the money is processed so it won't take me much longer to figure out who the eventual benefactor is. Has Niall contacted you with information on any of the other members?"

"He managed to track one down but that's a dead end now," Kyan replied, looking a little guilty.

"How so?" I asked, irritated to only be learning this now.

"Because he was one of the men most involved with the sex trafficking side of the operation and Niall followed him home and cut his dick off before making him watch it burn in his own fireplace while he bled out," Kyan said, hiding a smirk beneath his thumb.

"What?" Tatum gasped but her eyes were alight like her shock was happy rather than horrified.

"Well I wish he would have questioned him first," I snapped, irritated that we'd missed the opportunity.

"I'll pass on the message for him to do so next time," Kyan offered. "But you were pre warned that rapists were a sore subject for him so you really shouldn't be surprised."

Monroe shook his head like he didn't know whether to laugh or not and Blake smirked in amusement.

"Fitting as the death may have been, I insist on the next victim of your uncle's wrath to be fully questioned pre execution," I said firmly.

Kyan grimaced at the idea of that but didn't outwardly refuse it, so I took the opportunity to strike that matter from my list.

"Don't go thinking of Niall as some dog you have on a leash," Kyan warned. "Because he will rip your head off to prove you wrong in the blink of an eye. Anything he does for us on this is because he is choosing to. So offer him the respect he demands because we don't want him turning his anger our way."

"Don't worry yourself about it," I replied dismissively. "I have plenty of practice in bringing wild dogs to heel."

Kyan laughed like that was a compliment and I opened my mouth to continue, but instead Tatum shoved some of the fucking pizza between my lips.

Her eyes sparkled with amusement as my obligation to follow the rules forced me to bite and chew and I gave her a death glare over the cheese to which she rolled her eyes.

"So, basically what you're saying is that you haven't dug up enough info on whoever is running the psycho funhouse yet and we need to keep waiting before we can make any more moves?" Blake interjected while I couldn't speak and my mood darkened further.

"I'd like to see you do half as much as I have to track down the members of an elite secret organisation while the entire country is on lockdown," I snarled at him.

"Thank you, Saint," Tatum interrupted like she could see this descending fast and I was distracted from my anger again as her hand landed on my thigh and she held up another slice of pizza for me to eat. "We do appreciate your criminal mastermind ways," she added and I snorted a laugh at that. Not that it was inaccurate, but I hadn't exactly taken on that title officially. I couldn't say I hated it though.

"Fine," I ground out. "I'll keep all of you updated as I find out more. It's also worth letting you know that some of the locations the payments were made threw up red flags for me which I hadn't expected but probably should have."

"What do you mean?" Blake asked.

"Just that a few of the organisations have ties to my father. Somewhat loose ties which I can't easily prove but I'm more than familiar enough with his finances to have spotted the links. It could just be a case of rich old bastards using the same money launderers coincidentally, but after finding his links to Serenity Pharmaceuticals..."

"What?" Monroe pushed, perking up enough to make my intuition take note. He'd been like that when I'd told him about my father putting me down that well and it hadn't gone unnoticed. For some reason, Nash Monroe had a vested interest in my father. I just couldn't figure out what exactly that meant. Maybe it was time I set aside a few hours to get to the bottom of it though.

"His Spidey senses are tingling," Kyan supplied for me and though I loathed him referencing me as a character from a comic book, I nodded once to show my agreement.

"I have an inkling that there's more of a link there," I admitted. "And I'm not often wrong once I get those kinds of feelings. But I'll look into it more before I make any full assessments."

"So you're saying you think your father is a member of this club for rich psychos?" Monroe pushed. "Why am I not surprised?"

"I am assuming no such thing. Neither am I implying it. I'm just laying out the facts as I find them. The rest will fall into line with further investigation and we will deal with it from there. I'll keep you all updated."

Monroe shot a loaded look Tatum's way and I didn't bother to hide the fact that I'd seen it. If I were inclined to entertain Kyan's suggestions of Spidey senses then I'd have to admit they were tingling again. But I wasn't, because that was bullshit. Still, our girl and our coach had a secret. And I was going to get to the bottom of it.

I looked back down to my list which left me with one more issue to deal with.

"Did you make an itinerary for two topics?" Blake asked me with a snigger as he looked over at my notepad and I resisted the urge to bristle at him as I just shrugged.

"You can never be too organised. Not that that's a concept you seem to have ever gotten familiar with. But I can only hope that if I lead by example for long enough the message may sink in."

He scoffed and I ignored him as I moved the subject on.

"We need to discuss the issues among our unit. Kyan has fucked up the balance of power by marrying our girl. The rules are being flouted on an almost daily basis by certain members of the group and the punishments for such infringements are half assed jokes at best and in no way a deterrent for repeat offences," I said.

"Well she's my wife and she's staying that way," Kyan supplied. "And just so you all know, I took into consideration the suggestion that her name go back to Tatum Rivers on the school register and decided against it. Tatum Roscoe just has too good of a ring to it to change it back."

My fist hit the table just as Blake launched an empty beer bottle at his head and Monroe cursed him. Tatum seemed annoyed over it too, but she wasn't making enough protests for my liking.

"This is unacceptable," I snarled.

"Well it's the only way to keep her safe from my family," Kyan said cockily like having a bloodthirsty son of a bitch threaten the life of the only girl he had ever given a shit about was some kind of win in his books. "Besides, I fucking love having a wife. Never really thought I'd be the type, but it turns out it suits the shit out of me. You can't ask me to give her up. I won't. I can't."

Silence fell and I growled beneath my breath but as infuriating as it was, I had already come to the conclusion that he was right about one thing at least. It was the only way to keep her safe from Liam O'Brien for now and so I wouldn't be forcing a divorce while he was still a problem.

"I think we can all agree, however begrudgingly, that Tatum's safety is our priority, and as such, we will allow her to remain married to you," I said, gritting my teeth throughout.

"You know I'm getting pretty sick of you guys presuming you get to *allow* me to do shit all the damn time," Tatum grumbled.

"Then you shouldn't have sworn yourself to be ours for all of time," I said dismissively. "That is not up for negotiation anyway. The point is that we need to all agree what this marriage means."

"You're such an asshole," she muttered and I ignored her as I went on.

"As far as I am concerned, the marriage contract is a contract which secures Tatum's safety from the O'Brien family. Aside from that it means nothing-"

"Wrong," Kyan interrupted with his cockiest fucking smile. "It means she put on a hot as fuck white dress, walked down the aisle in a big ass church, looked me in the eyes and swore to belong to me for-fucking-ever while I swore the same damn thing to her. In fact, Niall was good enough to forward me the pictures this morning. I'm going to get them blown up." He pulled his cell phone from his pocket and opened up the offending photos before enlarging one where the two of them were kissing before the priest with so much passion that it looked like they were only a few seconds from fucking each other's brains out right then and there.

Rage pooled in my gut and I cursed beneath my breath before shaking my head and shoving his phone off the table with a swipe of my hand.

"It's irrelevant," I barked. "When the four of us swore to become Night Keepers, we swore to stand together in everything. When Tatum swore to be Night Bound, she swore to belong to all of us equally. There is no way to alter that agreement and I don't believe that any of us wish to aside from *you* and that's just because you're pussy blinded over her and want exclusive access for your dick."

"*Hey*," Tatum complained like that was somehow offensive and I turned to her with a dark look, leaning close so that my words were spoken with our lips almost brushing.

"It's not an insult, Tatum," I growled. "I think it's pretty clear that all four of us would like exclusive access to your pussy and every other part of you if we could have it. It's only natural for a man to claim his woman and stamp his name all over her to keep every other motherfucker away. But that's not the situation the four of us are in."

Monroe muttered some asinine comment about her being his student and Kyan laughed like he knew something the rest of us didn't, but I ignored them.

"I...that's..." Tatum actually blushed and it was so fucking adorable that I almost wanted to let her off the hook here, but this needed dealing with.

"I think we need to make it clear that Kyan's status as her husband doesn't give him any sort of say over the things any of the rest of us do with our girl," I said. "Do you agree with that, Tatum?"

I leaned back to give her room to breathe and she licked her lips as she glanced between all of us before finally nodding her agreement.

"That was what I swore to first - to belong to all of you. I think it makes sense that that oath takes priority over the one me and Kyan made," she admitted.

"I agree," Blake said instantly and Monroe nodded too.

"That's four against one," I said, pinning Kyan in my glare. "Are you going to continue to fight us on this or are you ready to agree to stop with your caveman bullshit?"

Kyan looked like he wanted to argue further and I couldn't even fault him for it. If there was a way that I could have come up with to make her mine alone I would have done anything it took to make it so. Well, anything other than turn against the men in this room. Our bond was the single most important thing in the world to me and if the rest of them felt the same then it was obvious that this was the only choice we could make. No matter what jealousy it created or how it might push us to compete for her attention and affection, we had to find a way to do this that wouldn't tear us apart, which meant we had to learn to share without killing each other.

"Fine," Kyan agreed. "But if you're all fucking her then I want in on it. At least some of the time."

Tatum laughed like this conversation was insane but after watching her with Blake and Kyan at once, I couldn't say I was totally against the idea of that. The main point was that nothing was off the table when it came to the five of us. Even Monroe wasn't bothering to make his protests tonight, though I was sure he was still trying to deny to himself that he wanted our girl as much as we all did.

"If I'm supposed to belong to all of you and let you...share me," Tatum said, seeming embarrassed about the idea of that though not flinching away from it either. "Then I want you all to swear that you only belong to me too. I'm not going to be used as some plaything for the four of you only to have to watch you fucking other girls."

"Done," I agreed without thought because I didn't want any other girl anyway. I was happy enough to admit that my obsession with her had gone that far because I was fairly certain it was obvious regardless.

Kyan and Blake agreed quickly too and we all looked at Monroe as he shifted uncomfortably in his seat.

"Just agree, asshole, it's not like there's any other pussy you're chasing anyway, and we're stuck in lockdown here for fuck knows how long, so what difference does it make?" Kyan pushed him and Monroe rolled his eyes but nodded all the same. I didn't miss the blush that coated Tatum's cheeks as we all agreed to that or the smug ass look on her face. But I had to wonder if she had truly considered what she was getting by taking on four tortured souls like us. Either way it was agreed so I wrote it down.

I took a breath and pulled out the laminated set of rules that we'd laid out months ago, laying it on the table where everyone could see it. The first one was struck out, but at least I'd managed to preserve the rest up until now.

1. ~~No Kissing~~

2. No foreplay

3. No sex

4. No touching while we share a bed

5. No entering the bathroom while I'm naked or on the toilet

6. I am allowed two hours of undisturbed study time at the library on every weekday

7. I am allowed one friend who you can not be a dick to

8. Once a week we will ALL eat pizza for dinner without cutlery

9. I am allowed to sit wherever I want in classes

The rules I'd laid out were beneath them too:

1. You will sleep in a Night Keeper's bed every night on rotation and they will have priority over you for 24 hours (6pm-6pm the next day).

2. You must cook breakfast for us every day.

3. You will wear whatever we decide on the day you are in our possession.

4. You will do as we say without complaint unless it conflicts with your rules.

"As for the rest of the rules, I think we need to have a fresh look at the no sex, foreplay and no touching in bed rules as *some* members of the group have been repeatedly flouting them and I am personally sick of being the only fucking person here who seems to give a shit about them," I said seriously while Blake and Kyan high fived each other like dickheads.

"Scrap them," Tatum said without hesitation. "I'm not agreeing to any of you ordering me to have sex with you or anything like that. But if I want to then I don't want it to be off the table."

I fought to keep my composure as she suggested that, my brow furrowing as I wondered if it really might have anything to do with me or if she was just sick of feeling like she was breaking the rules whenever she was with Kyan or Blake. Either way, removing this rule would be good for me. I wouldn't have to deal with the constant rule breaks and I could just focus on all of the projects I was working to complete in my own time without being haunted by it.

The others all agreed without me saying anything and my jaw locked as I looked down the original list of rules.

"Are there any new rules which anyone might like to impose or any other rules which need to be amended?" I asked in a flat tone as I kept my gaze on the page.

"Get rid of the one about entering the bathroom while she's naked too," Blake said, offering Tatum a dirty grin across the table and my grip on my pen tightened as I realised that left us with only four out of her nine original rules.

Kyan and Tatum agreed to that and I fought down the urge to freak out about this casual disbandment of an entire way of life. I had wanted to challenge the pizza night issue but if we dropped down to only three rules from her original list, I was fairly certain I was going to have a heart attack.

"I have issues with the rules about me making all the breakfasts and having no control over my clothes," Tatum began but she paused as she looked my way and I forced myself to hold her gaze as I fought not to crack a tooth. "But...maybe we can just agree that I'll get a bit of help with the breakfast clean up and that I can have some say on the clothes...some days."

I knew that what she was really saying was that she intended to start picking her own clothes on the days the others had control over her and I knew I should have argued against it, but at this point it felt like the world was caving in and I knew the others didn't really give a shit about those things the way I did. Kyan and Blake were so pussy blind that they might vote with her against me, and then I wouldn't even be able to dress her on my own days. That was utterly unthinkable so I just gave a curt nod which was as close to agreeing with the idea of playing fast and loose with the rules as I could get.

No one had anything else to disagree with so I turned the page in my notebook and carefully wrote out the amended rules.

We all belong with each other exclusively.

Tatum is allowed two hours of undisturbed study time at the library on every weekday.

Tatum is allowed one friend who we cannot be a dick towards.

Once a week we all eat pizza for dinner without cutlery.

Tatum may select her own seat in class.

Tatum will sleep in a Night Keeper's bed every night on rotation and they will have priority over her for 24 hours (6pm – 6pm).

Tatum will cook breakfast for us in the mornings.

Tatum will wear the clothes selected for her by the Night Keeper who has possession of her that day.

Tatum will do as we say without complaint unless it conflicts with any of the above rules.

"Are the rules really necessary at all anymore?" Blake asked as I shoved them towards him for his signature.

"Just sign them and let's finish this fucking meeting," I snapped as I pushed myself to my feet.

Kyan made a joke about me keeping my panties on and I snarled at him as I turned and strode away. I could feel their eyes on me as I went but I didn't care. We'd covered the things we needed to discuss.

"Just leave the rules on the table for me once you've all signed them," I commanded as I made it to the door and I pushed my feet into my shoes. "I'll laminate them once I come home."

I stepped out into the cold as Kyan started laughing, the anger in my veins heating to the point where I either needed to find my own outlet for it or I was going to start a damn brawl with all of them and I didn't need that shit right now. I needed to calm down. I needed to get out of my own head and find a way to stop the frantic pounding of my heart.

I knew exactly why it was racing, too. Not that I wanted to think about that too much. But the rules which had been keeping me away from Tatum had just been severed with a finality that I couldn't ignore. The question was, would I take advantage of that?

Clearly I wanted to. No, fuck that, I didn't *want* to. I ached to, hungered to, fucking *needed* to. This obsession I had with her was only growing stronger and I felt like I'd been denying myself of her for far too fucking long already. But I also knew that I was poison. The closer she got to me, the deeper I'd delve into her body and infect her soul. And even I knew that doing so would be the most selfish act I'd ever committed.

I strode up the path to Ash Chambers and made my way inside with a growl of frustration as I headed for the grand piano. I needed to lose myself in the movement of my fingers across the keys and drown this frustration in music.

I flicked on the low lights as I entered the cold room where the grand piano sat waiting for me in the shadows like a constant and stoic old friend looking forward to my return.

There was something undeniably comfortable about the enormous instrument, in knowing that there was little to no chance of someone moving it from this exact position while I was gone. I should have been beyond such small comforts, but I couldn't deny that I had come to rely entirely too much on the predictability of such things. Being here in this school had been like a balm to my wandering soul. I didn't like to admit to enjoying concepts like the idea of feeling at home somewhere, but I had come to accept that that was what I felt at Everlake Preparatory. Graduation was going to be a bitch. I'd wait for us to survive that long before I worried about it though. I already had thirteen different plans in place for what the five of us would do when we left this school, I just wasn't ready to select one yet.

I released a long breath as I situated my fingers on the keys, closing my eyes as I made an effort to banish some of the whirling maelstrom of the thoughts churning around my mind and I started to play.

I began with Nocturne in A Minor by Chad Lawson, the music pouring from my soul as the concentration it took to produce it made my bones ache with all the things I struggled to put into words or deal with in the ways that other people seemed to find so fucking easy.

One song flowed into another and another as my fingers danced over the keys faster and faster and I slowly began to relax.

I felt the faint gust of wind on the back of my neck as the door opened, but I didn't turn. There were only a few people who were foolish enough to interrupt me here and only one who I could imagine might want to. Though I never knew why she put the effort in with me that she did.

I didn't stop as I continued to play Nuvole bianche by Ludovico Einaudi though I felt her eyes on me like a flame scoring marks into my skin, branding me in a way which was irreversible and inexplicable and utterly addictive.

The door closed again but I knew she wasn't the one who had left. I could feel her presence in the room as keenly as if her hands were on my skin.

I didn't make any acknowledgement of her arrival until the piece had finished and I reached out to turn the pages of my sheet music, though it was more to give me something to do than any great need to see the notes laid out on paper. Once I had perfected a piece, I rarely needed to refer to the sheets to perform it. I just knew it, better than I even knew myself. I could feel it living in me, waiting for its chance to burst free and fill the room with its beauty.

"I take it Kyan was the one who encouraged you to come here?" I asked her as I toyed with a few notes, mostly to stop the silence from stealing the air in the room.

"How did you guess?" Tatum asked.

"Because for the one of us who is the most adamant that he has no heart, he is the one who knows how best to show he cares without words," I murmured, still not looking at her, though I could feel her drawing closer behind me.

"How so?" she asked as if she hadn't noticed for herself, but I knew she had. It was why she spent time with him the way she did, why she touched him the way she did, why she looked at him the way I pretended not to be jealous over even though sometimes I felt like it would burn me alive from the inside out.

"He just knows how to make the smallest gesture or concession in the way that counts the most and he doesn't ask for any recognition of it either.

He also knows how much to push me and how often I can tolerate it at just the right level to make sure I'm never too dependant on my foolish belief that I can control the world around me."

It was a self pitying kind of thing to say but maybe I was feeling sorry for myself tonight. The rules had all changed and I didn't know if that was one of the best or worst things that could have happened to me. It had opened up the possibility for me to claim everything I'd dreamed of claiming from the girl who was standing in the shadows behind me, but it had also taken away my excuse not to have it.

"He's a good man," Tatum agreed and I almost smiled at that.

It was funny how we could both come to that conclusion over someone who we knew for a fact took pleasure in violence and had killed more than once. And yet I was certain that it was true right down to the core of my being.

"If you stay here, I'm not sure I'm going to be able to maintain my control with you, Tatum," I warned her. "If you stay, you're making this decision for us."

"I'm not afraid of you, Saint."

"That really only makes this worse," I told her. "Because if you're not afraid then you must be seriously underestimating me."

"Or maybe you're the one who is underestimating *me*," she replied and I couldn't help the small twitch of my lips to her words. Never had a truer word been spoken; I'd been underestimating her since the day we'd first met.

"Come over here then, let's see what you've got." I inclined my head to the bench beside me and my skin prickled as my awareness of her presence sharpened until I felt like I was drowning in it.

When she dropped down onto the bench a few inches from me, I inhaled deeply, relishing the scent of her while never once pausing in the movements of my fingers over the keys.

"Can you play?" I asked her, and from the corner of my eye I saw her shake her head.

"I've had so many hobbies over the years that I couldn't even count them if I tried, but I never once got the feeling I had the aptitude to attempt a musical instrument," she explained.

"It's easier than it looks," I murmured as I slowed the movements of my fingers and slowly played the introduction to Beethoven's Moonlight Sonata for her, making it easy for her to follow the pattern my fingers took across the keys. "You try."

I drew my hand back and the music withdrew from the room as she turned to look up at me, biting down on her lip and forcing my attention to her mouth as she hesitated.

"There's nothing easy about that, Saint," she protested and I sighed, reaching out to take her hand and place it on the keys.

I encouraged her to press down on them in order, but her fingers resisted the movements of mine and she frowned as she tried to concentrate on what I was showing her too damn much and hit the wrong notes.

"It's not supposed to feel like that," I said in a low voice, reaching out to smooth the creases from her brow and giving her a light smile as she stared up at me in surprise like she thought I'd be angry over her doing it wrong. But the piano was where I came to vent my emotions, I wasn't going to be angry at her for attempting to understand that. "You have to *feel* the music. Let it use you as a vessel to travel out into the world. Don't overthink it."

"I don't underst-"

I huffed in irritation as I tried to figure out how else to show her what it felt like to me, the silence of the room offending me now that the piano lay unused before us and I wound my arm around her before hoisting her into my lap.

Tatum gasped as I situated her on top of me and I reached my arms around her as I laid my fingers down on the keys once more.

"Place your hands on top of mine," I instructed, my chin almost leaning on her shoulder. "Rest your fingers on each of mine too and relax, let your hands move with mine. Okay?"

She nodded wordlessly and I began to play Unchained Melody by The

O'Neill Brothers. It was a hauntingly beautiful piece which I'd always loved because of the way it almost made me feel real heartache as I brought it to life. But as I played it with her, her hands caressing mine, the notes coming alive as if it really were both of us playing, I swear I felt something in the music which I'd never noticed before. Something sweet and pure and almost hopeful which had my heart thumping solidly in my chest.

I kept playing and Tatum slowly turned until she was looking at me over her shoulder, our hands still moving in perfect synchronisation as the music came to life all around us.

Something about the way she was looking at me was stealing my concentration from the piece and as it drew close to the end, my hand slipped and I hit the wrong note, a curse spilling from my lips a moment before her mouth met mine.

My hands fell utterly still on the piano and the last echoes of the music died before I gained enough of my senses to kiss her back.

Tatum's lips were soft and hesitant against mine but as I pressed forward, they parted for me so that our tongues could meet and she turned away from the piano so that she could run her hands up the front of my shirt.

Our kiss deepened and I swear I could feel the un-played notes of that music thrumming through my veins as I drew my fingers away from the piano and slid them into her hair.

It wasn't like the kisses we'd shared before which were all hot and needy and desperate. That kiss was like the joining of our fractured souls, the taste of the sweetest kind of deliverance and the promise of something so much better than I deserved.

As our tongues moved together and a soft moan escaped her lips, I felt something deep inside me pull together. Like with her by my side I could take on the whole fucking world and make it burn just to make her smile.

Tatum's hands slid down my stomach and she pushed her fingers beneath the hem of my shirt, but I pulled back.

"Do you think that a hawk ever feels bad the moment before it strikes?"

I asked her in a rough voice, pulling her closer while keeping her back at the same time.

"What?" she murmured, her eyes full of lust but laced with vulnerability too. She wanted something from me that I wasn't sure I was even capable of. And I knew I definitely wouldn't be able to offer her anything with even a semblance of it while her hatred for me still simmered close to the surface and her mistrust in me ran so deep.

My gaze ran over her slowly, taking in everything about the way she was looking at me and the clear offer in her eyes. I could take her now. She wanted it too. She wanted to dive into this fire that blazed between us and let it burn her skin deep, but that was it. And as much as it killed me to admit it to myself, that wasn't enough for me.

This girl had become my one truest and most desperate obsession. When I took her, I wanted to claim all of her. Every deep, damaged, hurting part. I wanted her to give herself to me completely, not just in her flesh. And I wanted that enough that I knew I couldn't just take this from her now.

"I'll walk you back to The Temple," I said, my grip on her tightening as I stood and placed her down on her feet.

"Okay," she agreed, her hand sliding into mine like that was the most natural thing in the world.

I looked down at our clasped fingers with a faint frown before leaving them entwined and walking her back out of Ash Chambers and down the darkened paths towards The Temple.

We walked in silence, our breaths fogging before us and tension filling the air as the point where our hands met drew altogether too much of my attention. This was…sweet. And I didn't know how to do sweet. There wasn't any sweet in me. I was bitter and broken and toxic, but I didn't release her hand all the same.

When we made it back to the door of The Temple, I turned her to face me, my hand sliding from hers until I wasn't touching her anymore and I stood looking at her instead.

I pressed my arm to the door above her head and leaned down until my lips were brushing hers and stayed there as we both just looked at each other like we were questioning whether something had changed between us or not. The tension and want in our bodies rose until it was filling that inch of space that divided us, demanding we close the gap and take what we ached for. It was like causing myself a physical wound to hold myself back, especially as a breathy moan escaped her full lips once more, impatient this time and drawing a smile to my own mouth.

"Goodnight, Tatum," I murmured, the movement of my words making our lips touch the smallest amount as I slid my other hand to the door handle and twisted it.

The look she gave me in the moonlight was all lust and a promise of every wicked thing I'd imagined doing to her. But as I pushed the door behind her open a crack and pulled away, she frowned at me as she caught on.

"Where are you going?" she asked as I backed up another step.

"If I come in there with you then I'm going to lose the battle I've got going with this thin line of control I have right now, Tatum, and I have no intention to do that with you tonight."

"But, the rules are different now. I thought-"

"You thought that all of my self control hinged on something written on a piece of paper?" I teased as I backed up again. "No. Unfortunately for you, I'm not as simple as that to unravel."

"Saint," she called after me like I was insane as I continued to back away from her and I only smiled as Blake appeared in the doorway behind her. He gave me a questioning look and I nodded, causing him to tug her back inside.

I waited until he closed the door and the warmth of the light from within The Temple was stolen, leaving me alone in the darkness again. And then I turned and walked back into the shadows where I belonged.

CHAPTER THIRTY THREE

I hadn't had any time alone with Monroe for so long that I was getting desperate. Tonight, I would be staying with him and I couldn't wait to be in our own private space together where I could tear his clothes off and kiss him as much as I wanted. And it was more than that, we never got to have any kind of real conversation with the others around. We were constantly preoccupied with trying to pretend we meant nothing to each other outside of his Night Bound duties and I was tired of keeping away from him.

I'd often meet Monroe's gaze, my chest filling with longing before Kyan tossed us a smirk or made a suggestive face. Whenever he caught us out, we resolutely stopped looking at each other and that just made me hurt. It was also infuriating. So I wanted to make the most of tonight. I was excited to head to his place and had to try and hide my grin as Blake, Kyan and Saint walked me there in the evening.

"Be a good girl, Tatum," Saint instructed as Kyan and Blake claimed kisses from me and Monroe watched patiently from the door.

After the kiss me and Saint had shared last night, I wondered if he might move to take one from me now. But the wall was back in his eyes today and I got the feeling if I stepped toward him in the hopes of that, he'd only draw away. And I was quite done being rejected by Saint Memphis. It was especially humiliating when I thought of all the hurt he'd put me through, and now he somehow had me panting like a bitch in heat for him. *Goddammit.* I really needed to get a grip. Weren't three guys enough for my libido?

As Saint's muscles flexed against his shirt, my metaphorical panties dropped right down to my ankles and I cursed myself internally. *Nope, apparently three guys just don't cut it.* But I was willing to bet four was the magic number. I wanted the full set of Night Keepers even if the idea of that should have been crazy. *Christ, who am I? Four guys?? What would Jess think?* Actually, she'd probably be whooping and cheering for me while I laughed at her. Besides, I was clearly one lucky bitch, so I certainly wasn't going to ruin this situation by second guessing myself.

I glanced at Monroe again and who didn't even seem annoyed about Kyan and Blake's displays of affection, just anxious for them to leave so he could have me to himself.

I stepped through the door, waving goodbye to the others before pushing it shut and beaming at Monroe. He reached past me to lock the door and his fresh pine scent wrapped around me, making my heart beat even faster. Hell, I'd missed him. It wasn't anywhere close to fulfilling seeing him outside of this house because I couldn't touch him the way I wanted to, kiss him when the desire took me. We were overly cautious to the point of insanity, but we had to be. Now finally, at long last, I had him to myself once more.

"I've been going crazy," he growled, grabbing my hips and tugging me flush against him. "Do you know how frustrating it is watching you with them and not being able to lay a real claim on you myself? Being so close to you without being able to touch you. Really fucking *touch* you." He scored his thumb down my spine and I shivered deeply. He eyed my mouth, leaning close and grazing his lips over mine like he was savouring my taste, the way I felt. I found myself doing the same, reaching up to brush my fingers over his coarse stubble and sighing as his mouth moved in soft and exploring movements against mine. My desire was rising and as I tried to speed this up, he chuckled deep in his throat.

"I'm going to enjoy you slowly tonight," he murmured. "I'm going to make sure every piece of your flesh remembers me."

"I wouldn't forget," I insisted as he wrapped his hand around mine. "I couldn't."

"I just want to be sure," he teased, then checked a clock on the wall. "I've got a three point plan for our date night. You ready for part one?"

A laugh escaped me. "That's very Saint of you."

"Pfft," he waved me off. "I'm nothing like that guy, but I do have a few hours of fun filled entertainment before the plan begins."

"What plan?" I pushed, still grinning as he tugged me over to the couch and pushed me down onto it. I tried to pull him with me, biting on my lip hungrily but he tugged his hand free, giving me an intense look for a moment.

"I really wanna tear your clothes off right now," he half murmured to himself as if debating something and I poked my tongue out at him, leaning back in my seat.

"Then why don't you?" I asked hopefully.

"Because I only get you for one night every four days which means I'm missing out on a hell of a lot of time where I don't get to do all kinds of couple things. And you might not have realised it, but I'm actually an awesome boyfriend." He smirked and I chuckled.

"Boyfriend?" I teased.

"Yeah," he growled possessively and I didn't mind that so much. "I don't give a fuck what you are to the other Night Keepers, I know I've got to accept that. But you and me? We're dating, princess. Get used to it." He turned, marching off into the kitchen and grabbing some bean burgers from the fridge that looked freshly freaking prepared.

I was left in the wake of his words with a shit-eating grin on my face and I tucked my feet up underneath me as I watched him place the burgers in a pan and start frying them. When I couldn't stand being away from him any longer, I stood, walking up behind him and dropping my phone into the Bluetooth speaker on the counter, clicking play on The 1 by Taylor Swift before wrapping my arms around his waist from behind. He caught my hands, unhooking them from his stomach and pulling me around so I was in front of him before guiding my hand onto the frying pan handle. He dropped his mouth to my shoulder, tugging my strap down as he kissed a line along it and sent goosebumps tumbling across my skin.

"I make the best burgers, Tatum. It's a fucking travesty I haven't made you one before, but now I can order whatever I want through the school, I figured I might as well take advantage."

He kissed his way back to my neck and I nearly tugged the pan off the heat as his mouth brushed up to my ear. He chuckled, gripping my wrist and guiding the pan forward. "Careful, princess."

"It's hard to be careful when you're driving me crazy," I said breathily, turning to try and capture his lips but he shook his head, releasing me and stepping away.

"Go sit down," he ordered. "I'm not giving in to your sexy hocus pocus until you're thoroughly dated tonight."

I laughed, shaking my head at him. "My sexy hocus pocus?" I cocked a brow at him, pretending to be stern.

"Yeah, you've cast a spell on me since the moment you walked into this school. My heart would have stood a better chance against a bullet than you."

Heat flooded my cheeks and he swiped a hand over his face when I said nothing.

"That was a terrible analogy," he groaned. "I'm so out of practice with this stuff. And if I'm honest, I never really wanted to date anyone like I want to date you, Tatum. I wanna date you so fucking hard, you'll have teddy bears and fucking love hearts coming out of your ears by the time I'm done tonight."

"You got me a teddy bear?" I asked, only slightly – alright a lot – excited by that.

He shrugged one shoulder, looking embarrassed and it was so freaking cute I wanted to snap a photo and keep it in my pocket forever.

"Maybe," he said, looking away to face the burgers.

"Where is it?" I looked around the house hopefully.

"You'll get it later," he said, his back still to me so I darted away, racing toward his room and pushing the door open. "Tatum!" he half shouted, half laughed.

The soft toy was sitting on his bed, but it wasn't even a teddy bear. It was a unicorn the same golden colour as my hair with a little crown on its head, sitting between two brand new boxing gloves that were a shimmery rose gold with white skeleton hands curling over the back of them.

"You weren't supposed to see those yet," Monroe complained from behind me and I leapt away from him, diving onto the bed and scooping them all up in my arms as I turned to him.

"I love them!" I exclaimed and he grinned like a school kid, running a hand down the back of his neck.

"Good, now get your ass back in here for dinner." He walked away and I took a moment to try my new gloves on, admiring them as I strapped them into place before moving to the punching bag he had hanging in the corner of the room and throwing a few punches. Then I placed them back on the bed but took the unicorn with me as I headed back into the lounge, running my hands over its silken soft coat.

I dropped onto the couch just as Monroe placed a plate with the best looking burger I'd ever seen on it in my lap. He dropped down beside me, switching on the TV.

"What do you wanna watch?" he asked.

"Super Truckers," I said immediately and he frowned.

"Don't you get bored of my trucker shows?"

"Nope, they remind me of you. Of being safe and…home."

His brows pulled together. "I'm no one's home. Not even my own."

My lips parted, my heart hurting at those words. "That's not true. You're home to me. Every time I'm with you it's like…like I belong."

I thought of graduation again and a knot formed in my chest. My inheritance from my dad had come into my bank account and I couldn't even stand to look at a penny of it. But I guessed after I left Everlake I'd have to look at finding somewhere to live. But would that somewhere include Monroe?

He considered my words for a second then his mouth pulled up at one side. "I feel the same about you, princess."

"So give me a beer and put Super Truckers on." I grinned and he smirked before fetching two beers from the fridge and settling in beside me as he passed me mine.

We ate our burgers - which were freaking godly - then drank three beers, devoured a huge slice of chocolate cake and two hours of trucker shows later, I felt seriously relaxed. I'd meant what I'd said to Nash. His company was so easy, so familiar. He really was home to me. And the added bonus of me wanting to tear his clothes off at any given moment meant I'd somehow fallen into the seriously lucky position of dating my mouth wateringly hot best friend.

At quarter past ten, Monroe stood up and gave me a mysterious look. "Time to go."

"To…go?" I frowned. "What stage of your plan are we on? I figured the next bit was sex." I bit my lip, letting my gaze travel down him and he growled, capturing my hands and pulling me to my feet.

"What did I say about dating you tonight?" he said in his teacher tone which had my core liquifying.

"Umm, that you wanna date the fuck out of me?" I said teasingly and he chuckled, walking away and grabbing my shoes and coat.

"Now you're getting it. Put these on." He handed them to me and I laughed as I put them on, watching as he tugged on a hoodie then threw a letterman jacket over the top of it and pulled up the hood.

"You look like a student," I teased.

"That's the point." He smirked then beckoned me after him as he walked to the back door. "All of the staff will be back at the Maple Lodge by now and ninety nine percent of students will be in their dorms as it's a weeknight," he explained.

"So where are we going?" I asked as I followed him outside, finding him pulling a bedsheet off of something large sitting by the wall of the house. A golf cart was revealed with a blanket on the seat and a bottle of champagne in the footwell. He leaned inside it, pressing something and fairy lights illuminated all around the roof, making my lips pop open.

"Oh my god, Nash! This is so – so-" I hurried forward, unable to find the words so I kissed him instead.

He broke it off before either of us could get carried away, grinning darkly at me. He offered me his hand to help me inside and I snorted as he bowed to me with a flourish.

"You're too damn cute, Nash Monroe."

"Only for you, princess," he said in a low tone that reminded me he had a heart as dark as the other Night Keepers, he just kept it better hidden sometimes.

I pulled the blanket off the seat before I sat down and Monroe got in beside me, taking it and laying it across our laps. He popped the cork on the champagne and swigged from the bottle before passing it to me. "I figured glasses would be a hazard. I hope this isn't too informal for her highness," he taunted as I took it.

I had a long drink and the bubbles fizzed down my throat. "I never claimed to be a princess, Nash. That was all you."

He started the engine and took off up the track into the trees. "Nah, you are a princess, just not the type I originally pegged you for."

"So what type am I?" I said, narrowing my eyes at him as we sailed along deeper into the darkness.

"You're the warrior type. Like Princess Zelda." He shot me a grin. "And if you ever wanna dress up as her and lay siege to my empire, just know there'll be no complaints on my side."

"Noted," I laughed, sipping more of the champagne.

Monroe drove us all the way to the far end of campus before taking a track down to the main path. He tugged at his hood a little cautiously and I frowned, hating that we had to hide what we were to each other. I wanted to scream it from the top of every building in campus and declare him as mine. But until I graduated, that shit was totally off the cards.

He drove us around to the east side of the lake, slowing before we reached the dorms and parking the cart to one side of the path. He stepped out, taking the champagne from my grip and drinking a mouthful before placing it in the footwell and grabbing my hand to help me out.

"What are we doing here?" My voice came out hushed as adrenaline rushed through me at the thought of being caught together. It was kinda thrilling though too.

Monroe pulled me into his arms, tucking a lock of hair behind my ear and studying my face. "This is where we met, princess."

I looked around, smiling as I realised he was right.

"That was where you laid your suitcase trap." He pointed. "That was where I fell and nearly busted a tooth. And that was where my headphones smashed." I laughed as he turned me around, pointing to a spot on the other side of the path. "That was where you stood and got mouthy with me and where I put you right back in your box."

"Er, I think it was *me* who put *you* in your box, Nash," I tossed back, although okay I had maybe been way off base with Monroe on that day.

"Pfft." He smirked at me, gripping my chin and tilting my head up. "You thought I was a student."

"You let me continue to believe that," I said sternly and his grin widened.

"Yeah, I did," he growled. "And oh how fucking easy it would be if I really was a student at this school."

I wet my lips, watching the shadows dancing across his face as the clouds shifted above to hide the moon. "And what would you do if you were?"

"The same thing I'm doing now, I guess, just without hiding it," he muttered, his gaze dropping to my lips. "I suppose you were always a forgone conclusion for me."

"I wish there wasn't so much risk for you," I whispered seriously. "I'd break this off if I knew it was the right thing to do, but it doesn't feel right. *You* feel right."

"So do you, princess." He leaned down, his fingers carving lines of fire along my jaw before he pushed them into my hair. "When I first saw you here, I thought you were beautiful, entitled and would be just like every other vapid girl in this school. But fuck me, Tatum, you're none of those things. You're not even beautiful the way I saw you that day, not now I've seen your heart, your strength, your pain. You're fucking radiant. You're miles of light in the endless dark."

He leaned down, kissing me, his tongue sinking between my lips and setting my core on fire. I wrapped my arms around him, gripping his shoulders as his muscles rippled beneath my touch like I was setting off an earthquake in him the way he was with me. He tugged my bottom lip between his teeth and I gasped, arching into him, trying to get closer still.

We finally broke apart and I sucked my swollen lips as he led me back to the golf cart. My heart beat like it was a jet plane about to lift off into the sky and the engines were aflame.

I sipped on the champagne as he turned the cart around and we headed back in the direction of Aspen Halls. We passed the huge building but then he took a track up into the trees, following the line of the lakeshore out of sight. We passed The Temple and I glimpsed lights on in the windows between the thick trunks and found myself wondering what the boys were up to tonight. I pictured Saint sitting quietly in his wingback throne while Kyan and Blake played video games. Or maybe they were busy washing blood from their hands after their latest torture session in their hunt for the Justice Ninja.

Monroe drove all the way down to the gym then parked up around the side of the building. He got out and pulled me after him, a devilish glint in his eyes as I followed with the half empty bottle of champagne hanging loosely in my fingers.

Nash walked around to the window to our usual training room and pushed it up, tossing me a grin. He took the bottle from my hands, placing it on the ground, then lifted me up to help me inside. I stifled a laugh as I climbed into the room that smelled of new leather and cleaning spray before turning to grab the bottle Monroe was holding out for me.

He climbed inside and gently pushed the window shut then grabbed my hand again, practically bounding across the room like an excitable puppy. He led me out of the training room and through to the pool where the warm air wrapped around us. It was dark, but Monroe found a switch to bring on the blue lights at the base of the pool and the water seemed to glow, casting patterns across the ceiling and walls.

"Do you have any idea how much I wanted you when we had to isolate here together?" Monroe growled from behind me and a shiver ran through me.

"Tell me." I took a long swig from the champagne bottle then placed it by my feet as a sweet burn filled my tummy. I pulled off my coat, kicked off my shoes and tugged my cami off next. A thrill ran through me as I felt Monroe watching.

"You're addictive. I wanted to consume every piece of you," he said darkly.

I dropped my jeans, bending forward as I pulled them off so he got a view of my ass and my pale pink panties before standing again and looking over my shoulder at him.

"So why didn't you?" I asked teasingly. "No one was here to see."

I unclasped my bra, shrugging it off and his eyes burned with the heat of a thousand suns. I hooked my fingers into the sides of my panties, raising an eyebrow at him. "Why Nash?"

His throat rose and fell. "I have no fucking idea." He started striding forward as if to grab me and I dove into the pool, arcing under the water before resurfacing and turning to face him. I slid my panties off, biting down on my lip as I held them above the water on one finger. "Aren't you coming in?"

He shrugged out of the letterman jacket and hoodie before he practically ripped off his shirt, revealing every gleaming inch of his chiselled body. My eyes raked over his tattoos then followed the trail of hair from his belly button to his waistband. I walked backwards through the water as I waited for him to follow, starving for him.

He unbuckled his jeans, pulling them off, his eyes fixed on me as he dropped them then his boxers followed, revealing how hard he was for me.

He dove into the pool and swam towards me under the water, grabbing my thighs as he surfaced and wrapping my legs around his waist. I gasped as the head of his cock pressed against my entrance and his breathing grew heavy as he walked me to the edge of the pool and pinned me back against the wall.

"Do you remember me holding you like this before?" he growled and I nodded, a moan escaping me as his length butted between my thighs.

"Nash," I sighed in desperation.

He lined himself up with my core, his eyes pinned on mine as he pushed the head of his cock inside me and I felt him throbbing with need.

"Can you feel how much I want you?" he growled and I nodded, grinding my hips as I tried to steal more from him and he teasingly pushed in deeper only to draw himself out again. It was slow and torturous and I whimpered as he did it again.

"This is how you made me feel every time I couldn't have you," he said heavily, his jaw locking in frustration.

"But you can have me now," I panted.

"I told you I'm going to enjoy you slowly tonight," he said as I clung to his muscular arms, trying not to lose my mind as he continued to push in a little deeper only to pull out again.

I tipped my head back with a groan. "*Nash*," I demanded and he had the cheek to laugh.

He reached down, grabbing my hips and lifting me up to sit on the edge of the pool, slinging my legs over his shoulders. He looked up at me as he watched me quiver, his hot breath on my pussy driving me crazy.

I fisted my hand in his hair, tugging him closer and he laughed into my burning centre before dragging his tongue over my wetness and tasting how much I wanted him. He licked his way up to my clit before teasing it between his teeth and making me gasp with the combined pleasure and pain. I started rocking my hips as he glided his tongue over me, sucking and licking before bringing his hand up and pushing two fingers into my burning core. He drove them in and out at an excruciatingly slow speed, lapping at me in teasing strokes.

My hand tightened in his hair as I moaned his name and his tongue moved faster, driving harder against me. His fingers matched the quicker pace and I dropped my free hand behind me for support as I rocked my hips into his tongue. My stomach clenched as I drew closer and closer to release and his tongue didn't relent, his lips against my sensitive flesh making me start to cry out. I knew I had to be quiet, but I couldn't stop and Monroe didn't seem to want to either as my voice echoed off the ceiling.

I dug my heels into his back, my toes flexing as he sucked my clit and curled his fingers inside me.

"Yes," I gasped and he pumped his hand faster, licking and sucking and- "*Fuck.*" I came hard around his fingers and he continued to move them as he prolonged the pleasure. I rode them shamelessly as my head dropped back and warmth danced through my body.

A door banged somewhere beyond the pool room and I gasped as Monroe pulled his hand from between my thighs.

"You little shitbags, if I catch you smoking pot in here again you're dead!" a gruff voice shouted from somewhere beyond the door and I scrambled to my feet.

"Fuck. Pete – the janitor," Monroe hissed, climbing out of the water and we raced towards our clothes and scooped them into our arms. I darted toward the main door, but Monroe caught my arm, dragging me back across the room past the pool and through a door marked *staff only*. He pushed me against the wall inside, pressing a hand to my mouth and I pressed a hand to his in return as we burst out laughing, trying to keep the sound contained.

"You little fucks," the janitor snarled, his voice reverberating around the pool room. "Oh fuck my fucking life. What kind of sicko would leave their panties in the pool? I oughta write to the school board about this."

Monroe took his hand away from my mouth, tugging on his boxers and pants, holding his hoodie between his teeth as he put on his shoes. I followed suit, tugging on my jeans sans panties and dragging my top on before stuffing my bra into my back pocket. My boots were unlaced and half falling off as Monroe pulled me over to the window as he pulled his hoodie on one-handed and I heard footsteps approaching from the pool room. *Shit shit shit.*

Monroe yanked the window open, grabbing me by the hips and lifting me to help me out. My feet hit the ground and I stumbled, realising I was maybe a little drunk as I swallowed another laugh.

"Hey!" Pete shouted from inside and Monroe jumped down behind me, throwing his letterman jacket on and tugging up the hood on his hoodie.

We raced onto the path as Pete leaned out the window and called profanities after us. "You jumped up, self-entitled little cunts! You're lucky I have a bad knee or I'd hunt you down and pulverise you little shits!" he roared and we gave up trying to stifle our laughter, bursting out into hysterics as we tore up the path and into the woods.

"What about the golf cart?" I asked through my laughter.

"Fuck it. It can't be traced back to us." Monroe tugged me onward and we climbed the hill, disappearing into the dark before reaching the track high up in the trees. We sprinted along it in the direction of the headmaster's house and when I spotted the porchlights, I increased my pace, tugging Monroe along behind me.

We made it to the back door, breathless and still laughing and Monroe shoved me against it, kissing me with the force of a hurricane. The scent of chlorine and bad deeds filled the air as I clung to my guardian angel, tearing my nails down his back as he fumbled with the door handle and we almost fell inside as he got the door open. I gripped his neck as he held me up by the waist and marched me backwards towards the bathroom while we continued to kiss and paw at each other in the dark.

"You need a shower, dirty girl," he said against my mouth and I clawed my fingers into his hair, nodding my agreement.

He pushed the bathroom door open, leaving it wide and flicking the light on as he eyed me again, licking his lips, the sight of that sending my pulse haywire. I wanted to tear into him, eat him up, but he was clearly going to drag out the torture.

Monroe started pulling my damp clothes off and I let him, a smile on my lips as he took in every piece of skin he bared until I was standing naked before him. He dropped his jacket and pulled off his hoodie so he was just standing in black jeans before me with a tempting smile on his lips. He guided me over to the shower and I got in obediently, switching it on and tipping my head back as the heated water rushed over me.

Monroe shed his jeans and boxers then stepped in behind me naked, kissing my shoulder. I sighed as he grabbed a sponge and squeezed some vanilla scented soap onto it. He twisted me around by the hips to face him, starting to lather it all over my body, his eyes dark and revealing the hunter in him.

"Kiss me, princess," he instructed and I leaned in, teasing his lower lip between my teeth as he watched me with undeniable lust in his dark blue eyes.

When he slid the sponge down between my legs, he sucked in a breath at the same moment I did. My back arched and my hips rolled in time with the movements of his hand as he ran the sponge up and down, pleasure making my toes scrunch up and my breathing grow heavy.

"It's your turn," I said firmly, lowering my hand to wrap it around his hard shaft and knocking his hand away from me in the same movement.

The unit was full of steam and water was tumbling over Monroe's chest, making him look like some sort of Viking god and I was more than happy to drop to my knees for this deity. His fingers were flexing like he was trying to keep them off me as I stroked him, slowly tightening my grip. He groaned with need and I lowered to my knees before him, gripping the base of his cock as I ran my tongue all the way along the underside of it.

He panted my name in encouragement, his fingers sliding into my soaking hair as I sucked the tip of him and tasted his arousal on my tongue. I gazed up at him and our eyes locked as I slowly took him into my mouth as far as I could before dragging him out again, my teeth grazing his shaft ever so slightly. He was hard as iron in my hand and I was equally wet for him all over again. The adrenaline from escaping the janitor was still twisting through my veins and making me feel high as hell. I upped my pace, pumping the base of his dick as I sucked and licked him, driving him mad as he started thrusting into my mouth.

"Fuck, Tatum," he gasped. "I'm gonna – *argh*." He came hard, the hot liquid rolling down my throat as I swallowed and hummed my approval.

I stood up and kissed him as he leaned back against the wall and tugged me closer by the hips.

"Tell me I can keep you," he growled, an edge to his tone telling me he needed me to say those words.

"You can keep me," I vowed, tip-toeing up to trace his mouth with mine.

He smiled wickedly then grabbed a bottle of shampoo, squeezing some into his palm and rubbing it into my hair before doing his own. When I rinsed it out, he did the conditioner next, massaging my scalp until I was turning to mush. God, being touched by him felt so good. I never wanted him to stop.

When we were clean, we stepped out of the shower and I took a moment to dry my hair a little with a towel so it didn't drip all over the floor.

"Let's go to my room. I'm gonna make you forget your name and scream mine." Monroe hitched a towel around his waist and dragged me through the open door before I could grab a towel myself to cover up. I laughed as we stepped out into the living room and –

"Which name will she be screaming exactly?" Saint deadpanned.

I shrieked as I spotted Saint sitting on the couch with a direct view into the freaking bathroom, his feet resting on the coffee table, his ankles neatly crossed.

"Holy fuck!" Monroe barked, shoving me behind him to shield my body from Saint, like that was the most important thing right now. My heart raged against my ribs as I grabbed a towel from the bathroom, wrapping it around me quickly and moving to Monroe's side again as he came up with an explanation that not even a half-brained monkey would have believed. Let alone Saint Memphis.

"We just went for a run and the hot water doesn't last in the shower too long, so we had to-"

"Enough," Saint said sharply and Monroe fell quiet, his whole body tensing.

Saint got to his feet, walking to the fridge and dropping down as he opened the freezer and took out a bottle of chilled vodka.

"What the fuck?" Monroe snarled.

"I put it in the freezer when I arrived," Saint explained like that was what Monroe had meant as he poured himself a measure in a tumbler and sipped on it slowly, seeming deep in thought. "Which was about an hour ago by the way. And yes, I was here when you came back. And yes, I could have alerted you to my presence then. And yes, I could see into the shower the entire time. And yes, you should have considered closing the bathroom door. But you really seemed too busy to think of it."

"Saint," I said firmly. "I know what this looks like, but-"

"Yes, I am aware of what it looks like, I am standing here seeing it with my own two eyes, Tatum." He sipped the vodka again then placed it down on the side, leaning back against the worktop as he looked between us, letting us squirm. "I also know what it *is* like because I am not a fool, I watched the whole thing – and might I just add that your use of the shower unit during your tryst was lacking, I expected more use of the shower head for one. But I'm getting off point. If you dare to feed me a lie the next time one of your mouths open, I will take personal offence. And I am very certain that you do not want to offend me right now."

I glanced at Monroe, panic starting to find me in the wake of this shock. What was Saint going to do? He could have Monroe fired, sent to prison. Would he do that? Was he so possessive of me that he would use this secret against us?

"So," Saint said, seeming to be in his element as he held all the cards in the room. "I'd like you both to go and dress appropriately for this conversation. I took the liberty of laying out outfits for each of you in Nash's bedroom." He pointed to the door across the room. "Proceed."

Holy shit.

Monroe wrapped his hand around mine in an act of solidarity and we walked across the lounge together and slipped into his room. Saint had left me a fitted black dress with red roses printed on it and Monroe had a pair of smart cream chinos and a white dress shirt waiting. *Did he bring these freaking clothes with him?*

I was soon in the dress, my heart beating wildly as I looked to Monroe who was lost in thought, a line of tension on his brow. When I put on the strappy black heels Saint had provided, Monroe pulled me against him, gripping my cheeks in his palms. "Whatever happens, we'll figure it out."

My lips opened and I nodded quickly, clutching his hands over my face. "I'm yours," I swore. "Nothing will change that."

"I will fight for you with everything I have," he growled and I just bathed in the closeness of him for a long moment, the two of us feeding on each other's strength.

We strode from the room together, hand in hand and ready to face down the devil.

Saint had moved to sit in an armchair which he'd dragged in front of the couch on the other side of the coffee table like we were about to enter some sort of fucked up couple's therapy session.

"Sit." He gestured to the couch before taking another long sip of his vodka, a sense of smugness about him, though his expression was entirely neutral.

Me and Monroe sat together, our hands still clasped. There was no point denying what we were now, and I found I didn't want to either. I lifted my chin, owning my decision, owning Nash Monroe.

Saint fixed his eyes on Monroe and the intensity of them could have cut glass. "I know who you are," he said, letting a smile curl up his lips. "I know *everything*."

My mind spun and fear slid through me at what he knew about us. About how long this had been going on.

Monroe's grip on my hand tightened, but he said nothing. Saint could be bluffing. We had to let him state what he knew, couldn't give anything away ourselves in case he was fishing for answers.

"Enlighten me," Monroe said, his voice rough and full of hate.

Saint placed his vodka down on the table, taking his sweet time to respond as he raised his leg and balanced his ankle on his knee, leaning back in his seat like the king of the fucking world. "Your real name is Jase Harrington. You are Maria Harrington's son. Brother of Michael Harrington."

Dread filled my gut as I realised Saint hadn't been bluffing and Monroe's spine straightened as Saint went on.

"Your mother was involved in a traffic collision with my father on Lake Street in Elm Grove. Her son, your brother, Michael, was killed in the crash, thrown from the car due to his lack of seatbelt."

"That was becau-" Monroe started, but Saint spoke louder, talking over him, saying it all with a cold detachment that made me deeply fear what he was going to do.

"Your mother was subsequently sent to prison where she later died in a brawl, meaning you were sent into foster care and lost your chance of paying for the partial scholarship you won to attend Lakeview High School. Though that is the official version of events, I happen to know my father is a scheming bastard with far too much money and power, so I did some further digging and discovered the payments he made to cover up his own culpability and ensure your mother's imprisonment. I also found a trail of money which led to Marina Barnes who was one of the women suspected of your mother's murder in the prison. I assume you know that he did all of this and that is why you chose to change your name and come after him via me. You would not give up on your hunt for justice seeing as my father had covered up the incident of his own misdemeanour and ensured your mother took the fall instead." He threaded his fingers together and stacked them on his chest, waiting for Monroe's response.

"I-" Monroe began, but Saint instantly cut him off again.

"I know you have been on my laptop, I know Tatum helped you, I know that you are trying to work against me and my father. I am also now acutely aware that you are also fucking our Night Bound," Saint delivered the killing blow.

"Alright, you know," Monroe snarled, straightening his spine as he refused to cow down in the face of everything he'd done, owning it with the fire of hatred that had driven him for so long. "I get it. So what are you going to do about it, Memphis?"

I gripped his hand tighter, looking to Saint, ready to go to bat for Monroe and use any sway I had with this heathen to ensure Monroe wasn't punished for what he'd done.

"Look, Saint-" I started, but he refused to let me speak, cutting over me too.

"Let's work through this infraction by infraction," Saint said calmly, clearly having rehearsed how this whole thing would go in his head. "The lies," he hissed. "Are what irk me most. However, taking into consideration my father's behaviour and the concern you would have had telling me the truth, Nash, I am willing to let those slide. It is quite understandable that you would assume a false identity, take a job at this school and work tirelessly to get close to me in order to target my father in penance for his crimes against your family."

I shared a look with Monroe, shocked by his acceptance of that. But then again, this was Saint Memphis, convoluted and over constructed plans were kinda his thing, so maybe Monroe's approach to this whole situation actually made perfect sense to him.

"However," Saint said cuttingly and my throat tightened as I looked to him once more. "What I cannot accept is the betrayal on *your* behalf, Tatum." His eyes arrowed onto me and my jaw dropped.

"My betrayal?" I snorted. "You do realise I was working against you, Blake and Kyan for a long time, right? I punished you all for what you did to me. Monroe was the only one who I could confide in. Of course I helped him in return."

Saint nodded slowly as acid seemed to drip down my throat.

"Yes, that makes sense." He agreed like he was more interested in trying to piece this puzzle together than anything else. "And that leads me to my next question. Is this relationship purely sex or is it more than that?"

"Tatum is everything to me," Monroe growled and my heart squeezed.

"He's mine," I said possessively. "And I won't let you take him from me. If he leaves this school, so will I."

Saint's brows arched ever so slightly and I felt Monroe's eyes on me, but I couldn't look away from our judge, jury and executioner.

"I see," Saint said, nodding once. "Well, that settles it then." He looked to Monroe. "We will all keep your secret when it comes to your illegal little affair, and where my father is concerned well...I have a proposal for you."

I stared at him in utter shock and sensed Monroe doing the same thing. Where was the freak out? Where was the lecture about him being my teacher and this going against the rules? Where was the yelling and smashing things and the forcing us to beg?

"What proposal?" Monroe balked and Saint smiled, clearly loving how he was unsettling and confusing us at once. For someone who lived by rigid rules and routines, he was the most unpredictable asshole I'd ever known.

"I have, for quite some years now, been preparing to financially ruin my father in what I suppose you could call my own quest for vengeance. Although I wouldn't put it so colourfully myself. I do, however, wish to destroy him as deeply and irrefutably as a person can be destroyed. First, I shall take his wealth. Which I have been working on for years, slowly buying up shares in his companies under multiple false names so that I am the commanding shareholder in each of them, gaining the names of those he bribes and those he is bribed by and paying them off myself so that their loyalty is turned to me. I am in the prime position to take every single asset he owns from him without him ever even realising that I am coming. And I have made absolutely certain that any friends who he thinks may come to his aid will be less than willing to help when he comes begging. My finger is on the trigger, and once I graduate, I will pull it and set in motion his fall from grace."

"So you're going to take all of his money and run off into the fucking sunset?" Monroe shrugged. "I don't give a fuck about his money. I want him hurt, I want him broken, I want him fucking *bloody* for what he did to my family."

The passion in his voice made my lungs labour and I found myself wanting that more than ever too. I wanted him to get his revenge just like I had on Mortez. I wanted him to be free of this heavy weight he carried on his shoulders day after day.

Saint considered that. "The money of course is not just mine. You will be entitled to it just as I am and the other Night Keepers are, but if that is not enough, then obviously once that has been stripped from him, I will offer up the information of all the corrupt dealings he has had during his time in power to the authorities and have him arrested. His reputation will be dashed to pieces, his name smeared through the muck. He will rot in prison, I will hire the best lawyers to ensure it. And if *that* is not enough, there are always strings that can be pulled after the matter...strings he once pulled against your mother. Would that satisfy you, Jase?"

Monroe's breathing was heavy and I turned to him, placing my hand on his back. His gaze was locked on Saint, his jaw pulsing, his eyes flaring with the pain of his shattered family. Of what Saint's father had done to him. And I felt his pain as powerfully as if it was my own.

"I don't want to be called Jase," Monroe said. "I'm not him anymore.

He died alongside my family and I don't want to taint his name with the things I'm going to do to avenge them."

"Okay, *Nash,*" Saint said like it didn't bother him either way. "Would my proposition satisfy you?"

"Yes," Monroe hissed. "That would satisfy me. But how am I supposed to place my faith in *you* of all people?"

"Trust is something that is earned. Nothing I say now will earn your trust in me...or Tatum's. Only my actions from this day forward will gain that." He glanced at me and my stomach writhed. He knew the truth; I didn't trust him. But I had moved further in that direction. It was just hard to solidify any faith in him with the memories of what he'd done to me still fresh enough to sting.

"You're cutthroat," I told him. "I don't feel I can trust you, because one wrong action against you could mean having my head forced underwater in The Temple's font, or fish stew thrown in my face, or being locked in a freaking coffin."

Saint winced and I saw actual pain in his eyes as I said those words. "No...you will not receive that sort of treatment from me again. Things have changed now. The rules have been re-evaluated. And you must know...you must know that..." he trailed off, shaking his head and shutting his eyes hard, seeming like he was a slave to some nightmare inside him.

"Know what?" I breathed, my heart beating out a fierce tune as I hung on his answer like it mattered more than anything else he'd said tonight.

"The truth is..." he sighed, opening his eyes and I fell into the raging maelstrom within them. "I'm not sorry for what I did, because I was not the man I am today sitting in front of you. I cannot apologise for that man any more than I can apologise for the actions of another. But I will say this, Tatum, I will never do those things to you again. I do not desire it, in fact, it unsettles me greatly to even picture it now."

My cheeks flushed warm at his admission and I found myself letting go of my hurt over that a little more. It wasn't perfect, it wasn't even a guarantee that he wouldn't slide back into being that man and lose himself to the darkness again. But it was something. Something big. Something I could see in Saint almost physically, gleaming out from the depths of his eyes. He had changed. And maybe I could trust this new version of him. But could Monroe find his way to trusting him too?

Blake

CHAPTER THIRTY FOUR

"You see this library full of people?" Tatum demanded while I lingered by her table.

"When you're in a room it's as if no one else is here, babe," I teased as I perched my ass on the edge of her desk and she fought against the smile which was tugging at the corner of her lips.

"You can't just flirt your way around the rules Blake Bowm-"

I leaned down and stole a kiss from that angry little mouth of hers and when she didn't shove me off, I pressed forward instead. I got to my feet and tugged her up too, kissing her demandingly as I led her down between two of the stacks before pushing her back against a shelf lined with heavy books.

I dropped my mouth to her jaw, her throat, the very edge of her school shirt collar and the little gasps of pleasure that escaped her had my heart pounding with this new idea. Fuck watching her work on her physics assignment for hours when I could give her a physical right here anyway.

"Blake," Tatum moaned and it was at least half encouragement as the protests faded so I slid my hands up her golden thighs and made my way beneath the hem of her school skirt.

"I'm helping you with your work," I insisted as I moved into her so that she had to part her thighs a little wider so that I could stand between them. "We could call it a practical lesson with a heavy focus on how thrust combined with the perfect levels of friction can result in explosive energy consuming your entire body."

"You're breaking the rules. I'm supposed to be allowed to study here alone," she reminded me as my fingers reached the edge of her panties and I pulled back just enough to look into her blue eyes as my thumb rode across them and sought out her clit.

"Are you going to punish me then, Cinders?" I teased as she stifled a moan, her fingers curling around the thick spines of the books behind her.

"I'm supposed to be allowed private study time here away from all of you and your distracting bodies," she half complained but as I began circling my thumb, that line of thought seemed to abandon her.

"Is that the only thing you like about me?" I teased as she bit down on her bottom lip to try and fight back another moan. "My body? Because I'm not just a piece of meat for you to use, you know?"

"Well your people skills leave something to be desired," she panted, drawing a laugh from me. "And that competitive streak of yours can be-"

"No fraternising between the shelves!" the librarian shrieked from somewhere behind me and I groaned in frustration as Tatum's eyes widened and she shoved me back a step.

I reluctantly obliged, tugging my hands back out from beneath her skirt as I stepped away. I turned towards the librarian with my winning smile in place as I situated myself before Tatum, blocking off the view of her as she straightened out her uniform.

"Of course not, Miss Gaskin. I was just helping Tate reach a book on the top shelf." I grabbed a random book and held it out as evidence.

Gaskin narrowed her gaze on me but said nothing, knowing the line she was treading by mixing it with a Night Keeper at all. But she was clearly unwilling to just leave me here to try and finish what we'd started all the same. Probably didn't want cum stains on the biology books. So unreasonable.

I half considered telling her to leave us the fuck alone, but one glance my girl's way told me I was well and truly done with this game I'd begun and I heaved a sigh, reaching for her hand and drawing her back through the library to her table instead.

"This is the part where you insist I fuck off, isn't it?" I asked her, giving her my best puppy dog look but she wasn't biting.

"I'll never get my work done with you here," she said. "Just give me a few hours, I won't be going anywhere until you come back to escort me. This place is full of other students plus Miss Gaskin. I'm perfectly safe here and my work won't do itself."

I gave in with a dramatic groan and she rolled her eyes at me teasingly.

"So long as you tell me we can pick up where we left off once you're done?" I asked, linking my fingers in a prayer gesture and earning myself a dirty little smirk.

"If I get everything done then maybe."

"I'll take that maybe as a promise, Cinders," I said, leaning in to kiss her once more and seal that promise before backing away from her through the crowded room.

"See you later, golden boy," she teased and my smile widened.

"You can bet your ass you will," I agreed. "All of me." Her blush made me bark a laugh as a lot of the students around the study space made zero effort to hide their interest in our interaction.

I even heard some little fucker whispering to their companion, pointing out that she was married to Kyan like the idea of us sharing her blew their precious little minds. But fuck them, they knew nothing about the Night Keepers and how we worked. The conventional rules of society had never been made to apply to us and if our girl could satisfy me *and* Kyan then who was I to question that?

In fact, if they really wanted their minds blown then they really should hear about the way Saint had caught her sucking Monroe's cock. I'd been a bit pissed about it at first, but once I'd gotten over the shock – and Kyan had spent several hours goading both me and Saint about how he'd figured it out months ago while making a shit ton of dirty student/teacher jokes before playing a relevant porn clip on the TV for us to see with a naughty school girl getting caned by a professor in a tweed jacket and no pants – it had actually made a lot of sense. I couldn't place my finger on it exactly, but I guess I'd been picking up on that tension between the two of them for a while now.

It had annoyed me before Saint had pointed out that I'd literally agreed to it in the new rules. Besides, I was already sharing her with Kyan and Saint clearly had his eyes on her too so I'd decided that I wasn't going to waste time on jealousy. This was just another competition that I could win. I'd be the best boyfriend who gave her the most orgasms and I'd take my prize in the form of kisses from those sweet vanilla lips of hers. Simple.

I headed away when my cheesy grin was bordering on stalker vibes and strode out into the cool air with a sigh. I now had two hours to kill and nothing to drag me out of the darkness that had been niggling at me today.

Today had been a fairly good day for distractions, we'd spent over an hour chasing Stalker with golf carts earlier while throwing pine cones at him before pouring a bottle of olive oil over his head, coating him in flour and locking him in the maintenance cupboard to think about what he'd done for the night. Classic. But it still wasn't enough to totally crush my concerns.

Ever since Kyan had gotten the Hades Virus, I'd found myself worrying about Saint and Monroe catching it too, fretting over whether or not they'd be strong enough to survive it and freaking myself out over the prospect of losing anyone else the way I'd lost my mom.

Being alone made those concerns swell and darken until I found myself fretting over them no matter how slim the chance of infection was now.

I didn't much like the sound of me spending the next few hours moping about and sinking into those kinds of worries and as I looked out over the lake, my gaze caught on the lights illuminating the Willow Boathouse and an idea came to me instead.

I pulled my phone from my pocket and shot Chad and Danny a text asking them to come meet me if they were free, then started up a swift jog down the path. I'd go have some fun, keep myself on a high until Tatum was ready to leave the library, then take her back to my room and show her all the reasons why she should have let me finish what we'd started in the stacks.

By the time I made it to the boathouse, night had officially fallen and the dark water called out to me with the swift promise of exhilaration. Technically no one was supposed to take any of the boats out onto the water after dark, but as I was confident Monroe wasn't going to be expelling me, I didn't waste any time worrying about that.

I didn't bother heading inside the main building but just went straight down to the covered area at the water's edge and moved along the row of boats which were bobbing beside the narrow jetty until I reached a blue and white jet ski which purred my name.

I pulled my phone out of my pocket to check for messages from the others. Chad hadn't seen my message and Danny had replied to say it was date night for him and Mila but that he could try and rearrange if I really wanted him to. In all honesty date night seemed to be every night for those two recently but I felt like a douche for cock blocking him, so I declined and told him to have fun before texting Chad to tell him to meet me on the water if he got my messages.

I tossed my phone and keys in one of the lockers provided alongside the boats then took the key for the jet ski from the hook. There was a ledger sitting there too which I should have written in to keep a record of the fact that I was taking the vessel out, but I didn't bother.

My feet thumped along the jetty and I quickly untethered the jet ski from its position before hopping onto it and starting up the engine. The throaty purr had a smile on my face before I'd even begun to get going and I kicked off of the jetty as I floated out of the line up before tugging on the throttle and speeding out onto the lake.

The inky water seemed to spread out for miles in the dark and I laughed as I raced out onto it, whooping as I pushed the machine to move faster and sweeping it around in wide circles that had my stomach dipping and the adrenaline flowing freely through my limbs.

I sped up and down the water, pushing the jet ski to its limits as I weaved back and forth, almost tipping it up more than once and soaking myself with spray as I went.

My heart felt lighter with the pounding of my pulse and the grin on my face was full and wide as I kept pushing the jet ski harder, making sharper turns and riding the waves created in my wake.

After around half an hour, the sound of another engine approaching on the water caught my attention and I looked up to see a bright light drawing closer.

"You made it!" I called in excitement, though I doubted Chad would be able to hear me over the engine of the speedboat he'd selected.

I drew the throttle back and whipped the jet ski around as I shot across the water to meet him in the middle of the lake. But as I came up on the brightly lit boat, my heart skipped a beat as instead of Chad, I found a hooded figure wearing a white mask looking directly at me as they turned the speedboat my way.

I cursed as I changed direction, cutting to the left and crashing over several big waves that I'd managed to cause with the doughnuts I'd just been doing in the water and my progress was slowed.

I looked over my shoulder as the roar of the speedboat's engine chased after me and a spike of fear flooded me half a second before the boat crashed into the rear end of my jet ski.

I yelled as I was catapulted off of it, my arms cartwheeling as I was thrown through the air before I came crashing down into the ice cold water.

I kicked for the surface with my heart racing and sucked down a breath the moment my head breached the waves.

I cried out in alarm as I found the speedboat racing straight for me and

I dove beneath the surface again, kicking as hard as I could moments before the dark shadow of it sped by overhead.

The burn in my lungs forced me back up again and real fear found me as I realised that I was nothing more than a sitting duck out here. If they were determined to take me out, then there wasn't anything that I was going to be able to do about it.

As I thrust my head up out of the water again, my thundering heart leapt at the sight of the boat tearing away across the water once more, heading in the direction of the boathouse and I let out a shaky breath of relief.

I was forced to tread water as I looked all around for any sign of my jet ski and a flash of white above the waves drew my attention to it.

I swam as fast as I could, cursing as I reached the jet ski only to find it upside down and dead in the water. The emergency choke would have been wrenched free to cut the engine when I was knocked off of it, but that didn't really mean anything as the acrid stench of fuel filled the air around me. The tank must have split in the crash which meant that there was no point in me even trying to flip the thing over unless I planned on sitting on it until someone figured out I was missing and came to look for me.

I was right out in the middle of the lake, the lights from the buildings which surrounded the water little more than pinpricks on the horizon.

The thought of that motherfucker in the white mask made my skin crawl as I realised he'd just put me out of commission. And as he hadn't circled back to make sure he finished me off, I had to assume that I wasn't his intended target.

My mind instantly went to Tatum alone in the library and I cursed as I began the long swim back to shore. I knew she wouldn't walk back without me and was certain that one of the other Night Keepers would come to meet her once she realised I wasn't coming and called them. But at this moment in time, no one but me and that Justice Ninja bastard knew that I was stuck out here and that had my blood running even colder than the icy water of the lake.

Fuck.

I couldn't focus on the what ifs right now, I just needed to give everything I had into swimming back to shore. I'd figure the rest out by then. I just hoped my girl stayed safe where she was until I got back. But I had the horrible feeling that ditching me in the middle of the lake was only the beginning of the Justice Ninja's plans tonight.

CHAPTER THIRTY FIVE

I'd finished up my Physics paper and was working on an assignment for English, but I couldn't concentrate as I waited for Blake to arrive. I was anxious to see him again, biting on my lip every time I thought of kissing him when he got here, glancing around to see how empty this place was right now and wondering if we really could get away with fooling around down here without the librarian finding us again. I wanted to feel the hard plains of his golden chest against mine, feel him dominating me, holding me down, kissing my throat, my-

Get a grip, Tatum.

I laughed at myself, shaking my head and focusing back on my assignment. I swear I was legit obsessed with the Night Keepers sometimes. The Sacred Stone may have been some bullshit artefact, but it sure did feel like it really had bound me to those boys in some soul-deep way. They were so far under my skin that cutting them out would have been excruciating. And part of me hoped I'd never have to do it. But could this really last forever?

I took a long swig from my water bottle and sighed, leaning back in my seat. I really needed to focus or I was not gonna finish this assignment in time for the deadline tomorrow. Not that Miss Pontus would do anything about it; she'd most likely just give me an extension. But I didn't like playing the Night Bound card. Just because I was one of the little Night Keeper gang now, that didn't mean I wanted to use their sway to get away with stuff. I was way too used to my own independence and I sure as shit didn't want any handouts in life. So I would get this assignment done on time if it killed me.

I managed to get a few more paragraphs written before I checked my phone again, but there was no message from Blake. I got up with a sigh, typing out a message to him as I wound through the stacks and headed through the door into the restroom.

When I'd peed, I washed my hands and stared at the girl in the mirror who had faced too much fucking bullshit this year. I could see Dad's features peering through mine, just glimpses of him in the angles of my face, the shape of my eyes. It felt good knowing he was with me in some way, that I could be reminded of him whenever I saw myself. It made me proud to know he lived in me like that. And I swore I'd never let go of him.

I headed back into the library, realising the place had seriously emptied out. It was quiet, almost eerily so. But this was my safe haven. The one place on campus which I had claimed as my own. Especially in this corner by the window overlooking the dark lake.

I dropped into my seat, gazing at my laptop screen with a pout as I tried to piece together my next paragraph about Othello. I procrastinated a little, checking my emails then reached for my water bottle to my right. I frowned as my hand met nothing and I looked up, leaning forward to grab it further down the table, figuring I must've moved it earlier as I downed the last of it.

Okay so...Shakespeare is trying to say that Iago is a shady bastard and Othello really needs to notice it before he ends up killing his wife. Spoiler alert: he totally kills her just before he finds out Iago has manipulated him this whole time and his wife never cheated on him anyway. I mean really, the fact that Othello killed his wife over her handkerchief being found in another guy's room suggests he was kind of a psycho. Even Saint wouldn't kill me over a handker- no wait, he totally would.

I reached for my keyboard to type something completely respectable, but my vision blurred and I frowned as my hands dropped heavily onto it. I blinked to try and clear the clouds around my mind, but they wouldn't lift. *What's happening?*

I reached for my phone beside my laptop, but knocked it off the table with clumsy fingers and my heart thudded erratically. I leaned after it, falling out of my chair and groaning as drowsiness tried to steal me away. *Oh fuck. What's wrong with me?*

I reached for my phone again, my heart beating too fast and then too slow in my chest but a foot slammed down on the screen before I could reach it and I gasped.

I blinked groggily, looking up to search for the perpetrator, but the room was spinning and all I could see was a bone white mask glaring down at me. Fear crushed my chest, but I didn't have the strength to get up and fight.

Hands slid around me, maybe one set, or two, or more. I couldn't concentrate enough to tell.

"*Getoffme,*" I slurred, then realised I could scream. And I seriously needed to scream.

I opened my mouth, my brain working too slow, and a hand slammed down over it that tasted like gasoline. For a moment I was reminded of Kyan, but it couldn't be him. I'd know if it was him.

My scream was lost the same moment I lost consciousness and the next thing I knew, I was being shoved out of the window beside us. My stomach swooped, I gasped and my back hit wet earth, sending pain jarring through my body.

Get up, Tatum, get the fuck up!

I forced myself to move, the cool air helping my senses sharpen just a little more and I managed to roll and crawl forward. I had to move. Had to run.

"Just carry her," someone hissed. I couldn't tell if it was a girl or a guy, their voice too hushed and my brain too fuzzy. *Fuck, how did they drug me?*

"Get away," I snarled, pressing my hands into the mud as I tried to stand.

Hands grabbed me again and suddenly I was being hauled, pulled and half carried along. My mind wouldn't sharpen and I was falling down into the depths of darkness again. I fell into it once more and when I woke I was on my knees, the dark wood spinning around me and shadowy figures standing in front of me.

"Help," I rasped, but it was too quiet. I had to say it louder. Why was it so hard to make my voice work? "Help!"

Someone kicked me in the jaw. "Shut up!"

A guys' voice for sure this time. But whose? Pain throbbed along my jaw and I found an inch of resilience to hold onto, fighting against the hands on me as someone tried to move me again. I threw an elbow back which landed against soft flesh.

"Just do it here," a guy growled and I was shoved to the muddy ground again. "Hurry up."

Freezing liquid suddenly splashed over me and I coughed heavily as the scent of gasoline caught in the back of my throat and made me heave.

"No!" I half choked, half screamed, my voice loud with desperation as I moved onto my knees. My vision blurred as two masked figures stared down at me while one of them continued to pour the gasoline all over me.

I staggered to my feet as terror overrode some of the drug gripping my body, giving me enough strength to stand, but I immediately wobbled.

I can't pass out. I must not pass out.

The click of a lighter made my heart clench like it was in a vice and I gasped as the flame flickered before me in one of their hands, dancing, my vision tripling so there were three of them threatening me.

I backed up, hitting a tree. "Help!" I screamed, managing to pour more volume into the word this time.

A flaming arrow ignited in front of me in one of their hands and fear made my senses sharpen another inch.

"This time it doesn't matter if you miss," the guy's voice again. And I recognised it. I was sure I recognised it. I just couldn't place it with the drug clogging up my brain. *Who the fuck would do this to me? Think, Tatum, think!*

"Run rabbit run," he spat and the arrow swung toward me.

I screamed, turning and racing into the trees. It was so dark and my legs were leaden as I ran as fast as I could with the drug taking root in my body.

My shoes squelched through mud as I hit a downhill and I almost fell way too many times. A flaming arrow whooshed past me, carving a trail of light through the air before it slammed into a tree ahead of me. I veered away from the flames with a shriek of fear, my mind hooking on the only thing I needed right now. Water. I had to get to the lake.

I ran on, the world a haze ahead of me and I was terrified I was going in the wrong direction. But I was heading downhill, it had to be the right way. It couldn't be far.

Cackles of laughter followed behind me, seeming to echo everywhere through the woods and for a second it seemed like there were more masks peering at me amongst the trees. Monsters lurking, prowling near, hunting for flesh.

Another arrow whipped past me and someone swore. "That was close," they laughed and I couldn't tell if they were relieved or disappointed it had missed.

My foot caught on a root and I stumbled, slamming into a tree as I caught myself, tearing my nails into it as I made sure I didn't fall. Falling would be the end of me.

I pushed myself upright and laboured on, my lungs weighed with lead and my mind thick with the pull of the drug.

Don't give up. Keep running. Stay awake.

My feet suddenly hit flatter ground, but the trees didn't thin. I screamed for help. But hardly anyone would be out this late. What if no one was close enough to hear my screams?

Another arrow speared past me, hitting a tree and splintering into two pieces and sending them flying through the air. The flaming tip careered toward me and I screamed, falling to the ground to try and avoid it. It landed a few inches to my left, hissing in the mud as it went out.

Footsteps pounded closer behind me, drumming into my skull. I gritted my teeth and kept moving, desperate to reach the water and praying I was getting near. I didn't know how much longer I could run. And they were so close, so damn close.

I moved with every last scrap of energy in my veins as the drug worked its way deeper into my body, taking hold of my muscles and trying to freeze them, immobilise me. *No no no.*

I pushed myself on as more laughter called out behind me, distorted and filled with their amusement at watching me trying to escape.

I glanced over my shoulder seeing two, then three, then ten figures amongst the trees with masks covering their faces as my vision blurred and multiplied.

Another arrow speared through the air and I ducked with a scream, terrified I was about to feel the pierce of metal driving deep into my flesh and the raging burn of fire consuming me. But somehow it didn't come. So I kept running. And I wouldn't stop.

I just didn't know how much further I could go before one of those arrows found its target.

Blake

CHAPTER THIRTY SIX

Every muscle in my body burned with a fatigue so deep and relentless that I was almost certain my limbs were about to give out and I was going to drown in this god forsaken lake.

As I swam, my mind played tricks on me, making me believe that I could hear screams on the wind that whipped above the waves which had my heart racing with fear for the girl I loved.

I'd kicked my shoes off and ripped my shirt off too so that I could swim better, but I was starting to feel like I wasn't getting anywhere at all. Like I'd somehow managed to swim myself around in circles out here in the dark and I was going to run out of energy at any moment and succumb to the inevitable call of the deep water beneath me.

Tatum's screams carried to me again and the jolt of fear that shot through my body at that sound had a spark of adrenaline igniting in my veins.

That hadn't sounded like my imagination. It had sounded damn like reality come to sucker punch me in the dick.

I swam harder, faster, the sound of her screaming coming once more and making me feel certain that I hadn't imagined it.

A wholly different kind of panic enveloped me as I powered towards the screams, hoping against hope that I was getting closer to her as I sucked down breaths and my limbs trembled with fatigue.

My toes suddenly scraped against the pebbles on the lake bed and I could have fucking sobbed with relief as I struggled further forward and the shore rose beneath me.

When I could finally regain my feet, I shoved myself upright and found myself at Sycamore Beach, the moonlight shining silver off of the sand and highlighting the girl who was racing towards me from a gap between the trees which marked the edge of the forest.

I broke into a run as I powered out of the lake, sucking down deep breaths as the freezing water dripped from my body, making me shiver in the cold wind.

Tatum stumbled and fell as I ran towards her and my heart leapt with panic as I yelled her name.

Movement in the trees beyond her caught my eye and I looked up, spotting a figure between the trees wearing a bone white mask to conceal their face.

"When I catch you, I'm going to fucking destroy you!" I bellowed as I charged towards them, but Tatum was my main focus.

As I reached her, the pungent scent of gasoline caught in the back of my throat and I dropped down to my knees, rolling her over as I pushed the wet hair out of her face.

"Tate?" I asked desperately as she fell limp against me and I shook her hard, trying to force a reaction from her. "Tatum! Wake up!"

I shook her harder and she groaned, lurching over and heaving until she puked all over the rocks beside us.

Her hand flew out to grip my arm as I looked around for any sign of the Justice Ninja, but the trees before us were empty once more.

The scent of gasoline was overwhelming and I realised that it wasn't water that covered her at all.

"Holy fuck, Tate, what the hell happened?" I demanded as I tugged her against me and her blue eyes widened with panic before she seemed to realise it was me.

"They're going to kill me, Blake!" she cried, throwing her arms around me and sending my pulse skyrocketing as I looked out into the trees again.

I gasped as I spotted a flame igniting between the thick trunks and leapt to my feet, hauling her upright. Her legs gave out as she tried to stand so I lifted her off of her feet, cradling her against my chest as a whimper of fear escaped her.

The lake was closest, but I didn't want to risk staying out here any longer. There was clearly something wrong with her and she began to mutter nonsense and sob, while her limbs seemed to hold no strength.

With a growl of determination, I held her closer in my arms and started running for The Temple, turning my back on the fire between the trees and hoping with everything I had that I could outrun whoever was out there before they got that flame near my girl.

The sand slipped and sank beneath my feet and Tatum clung to me as she sobbed and shivered, seeming to at least know that I had her now and trusting me to keep her safe.

And I would keep her safe. No matter what it took, I'd protect her from whoever the fuck was stalking us through the trees.

As my feet hit the path, I glanced back over my shoulder, spotting more flames igniting in the woods, each fire flickering as if they were being laid out to warn us not to turn that way. But I had zero fucking intention of going anywhere near the psychopath between the trees while they held fire and my girl was drenched in gas.

I broke into a sprint as I somehow managed to find a hidden reserve of strength in my exhausted limbs just for her.

She was cold and fragile in my arms, tucked tight against my chest and murmuring things I couldn't understand.

Footsteps pounded down the path behind me, but I refused to look back.

A burst of orange light flared in the corner of my eye and I sucked in a breath as a flaming arrow shot past me and embedded itself in a tree.

Tatum shrieked in fright as she came to enough to spot it and I cursed as I upped my pace with my heart thundering panic though my limbs.

"I've got you, Tate," I swore as another arrow sped through the trees to my right and made my gut lurch.

The spire of The Temple loomed beneath the moon up ahead and I yelled out as I ran, hoping one of the other Night Keepers might hear me and come running.

"Kyan!" I roared, charging up the path and hoping that he was still home like he'd been the last time I'd seen him.

I had no idea how long it had taken me to swim back from the boat crash in the centre of the lake or if any of them had gone to the library to get Tatum when I hadn't shown up. If they had and they knew she was missing then there was no chance of any of them being out here. They'd all be hunting campus for her, leaving me to face this crazy motherfucker alone.

"Saint!" I bellowed as I turned onto the path which led up to the church doors and another flaming arrow whisked by into the trees.

Either they were a bad shot or they weren't actually trying to kill us. Whatever the reason, I just knew I had to get Tatum the hell away from those flames before any of them got close enough to the gasoline to ignite it.

The door burst open as I raced up the path and Saint lurched aside as I didn't even slow, running straight over the threshold and collapsing on the flagstones with our girl still hooked in my arms.

"What the fuck is going on?" Monroe demanded as he leapt to his feet from the couch alongside Kyan.

"Close the fucking door," I demanded and Saint instantly threw it shut before prowling towards me, his lip curling at the scent of the gasoline which was filling the space.

"What's wrong with her?" Saint asked as Tatum groaned in my arms, her eyes falling closed.

"I think she's been drugged. She was being chased and she's covered in gas-"

"Is someone out there?" Kyan demanded, stalking towards us and grabbing his baseball bat from its position beside the door.

"That fucking Ninja asshole," I admitted as I forced myself to my feet again and heaved Tatum up in my arms. "He was shooting at us with burning arrows-"

The three of them all lurched into action around me, Kyan racing for the door with his bat gripped tightly in his hand while Saint barked orders I couldn't concentrate on and Monroe hounded me to the bathroom.

I was trembling with exhaustion and fear for our girl so I couldn't even answer any more of their questions as I walked her straight into the shower and set the hot water running over us before sitting her down on the floor.

Tatum coughed and heaved, throwing up again as I peeled her uniform from her body and tossed it out onto the tiles at Monroe's feet.

"What the hell happened to her?" he demanded, ripping his own shirt off as he moved into the shower too and pulling her up to stand as the water washed the gasoline from her body. She still seemed barely able to use her limbs but he held her tightly and she leaned on him, murmuring his name as he worked to rinse her hair.

"I don't know," I groaned, slumping back against the tiles and shaking my head as exhaustion crippled me. Now that the adrenaline was subsiding, I felt like I'd run a fucking marathon and I had to fight the urge to close my eyes. "I went out on the lake while she was studying. That motherfucker followed me out there and sank my jet ski. When I swam back to shore, I heard her screaming and found her like this."

Monroe cursed as Tatum wound her arms around his neck, demanding he stay with her while my body practically gave out from exhaustion.

I forced myself out of the over crowded shower, dropping my saturated pants and boxers before wrapping a towel around my waist and setting the bath running for her because the shower wasn't getting rid of that stink.

Monroe was murmuring reassurances to Tatum while she clung to his chest and as I moved away to find some bubble bath to put into the water to help get the stench of gasoline off of her, I noticed a note pinned to her blazer where it lay on the floor.

The paper was wet and the ink had run, but I could still make out the words on it.

> *Roses are red and violets are blue,*
> *You need to realise who really owns you,*
> *I dressed you in flames and I kissed you goodnight,*
> *When will you see what's here in the light?*
> *I gave you a chance and you took too much time,*
> *Now I'll have to show you that you're really MINE.*

My skin chilled as I read the note and I looked up as the bathroom door swung open, finding Saint standing there with the fires of hell burning in his dark eyes.

He silently held his hand out for the note and I passed it over without a word.

I watched him read it with his jaw ticking and his gaze cut to Tatum with concern so clear on his features that it made my gut lurch. I'd never seen Saint look at anyone like that before and I was beginning to wonder what it would mean for all of us when he finally faced up to his feelings for our girl.

"Whoever was out there is long gone," he growled. "But Kyan is still hunting all the same."

"This means we got it wrong," I pointed out. "Toby can't have been the stalker. He's been locked in the janitor's closet all evening."

"I'm well aware of that," Saint said in a clipped tone. "Kyan is going to confirm that he's still there and then we will need to reassess...*everything.*"

We'd chased Toby all around campus while pelting him with pinecones earlier this afternoon before locking him in there. And as there were no windows in the room and we were the only ones with a key, it was pretty obvious that it couldn't be him unless he'd escaped. Besides, I was fairly certain that the figure I'd seen in the trees hadn't been anywhere near as big as Toby.

Shit, if he wasn't the guilty party then we'd really made his life hell for nothing. The idea of that didn't sit well with me and I made a mental note to figure out some way to make it up to the dude before giving my attention back to our girl. Right now, Tatum was our priority, fixing things with Toby could wait.

Saint handed the note back to me and moved past me, filling the bath with bubbles and salts which he took from the back of the cupboard.

"She's barely even able to stay conscious," Monroe snarled from the shower where he was still trying to scrub the gasoline from Tatum's body. "When I catch whoever the fuck did this to her, I'm going to fucking kill them."

"I'm okay now I'm here," Tatum said but her words were slurred and I wasn't buying it. I guessed the drug had stolen the fear from her which was something, or maybe it was just that she actually felt safe here amongst us. Wouldn't that be something.

"I'll rip them apart piece by piece until they're begging for mercy and I'll make it last as long as I can before I end them," Saint hissed, eyeing her for a long moment as she leaned against Monroe. "I'm going to get some vinegar to get that stench off of her."

He turned and stalked from the room and I frowned as I sagged back against the sink, my gaze fixed on Tatum as Monroe pressed kisses to her hair and held her tightly. She barely even seemed conscious and the terrifying thoughts of what could have happened to her if I hadn't found her were consuming me.

None of us questioned Saint when he returned to the room with a bottle of white vinegar and he pulled the door to the shower wide before rubbing it all over Tatum's skin. If he said it would get rid of the gasoline stink, then I was going to believe him. Saint knew way more than anyone I'd ever met about shit like that and I was sure she'd want everything possible done to get rid of that smell.

When he was finished, he shut off the shower then took her from Monroe's arms without letting him protest and carried her over to the bath.

I raised an eyebrow as Saint climbed into it fully clothed with Tatum in his arms and began washing her with the honey blossom body wash she liked as if it was the most normal thing in the world

"You should take your clothes off," Tatum muttered, plucking at his shirt and pulling a few of his buttons open before her hand fell still again like even that was hard for her to manage.

"Stop trying to get me naked and let me look after you," Saint grumbled, but the concerned frown on his face gave away his worry despite his waspish tone.

A smile touched Tatum's lips and she did as he commanded, sighing as he carefully ran the sponge over her body and letting her eyes fall closed again as she leaned against his chest.

I swiped a hand down my face and headed back into my room, quickly drying and pulling on some clean sweatpants before getting some out for Monroe to borrow too. He took them wordlessly when I returned to the bathroom, switching out the damp stuff he was wearing while watching as Saint washed Tatum's hair.

"Heads have to roll for this," I snarled as Tatum muttered something I couldn't hear.

"Obviously. But for now just get her something warm to wear," Saint commanded and I blew out a breath before heading back to my room.

I grabbed one of my biggest hoodies before jogging through the building and up the stairs to Saint's closet where Tatum's clothes were kept. I chose her a pair of soft pyjamas and got Saint some sweatpants too then hurried back down to the bathroom.

Saint already had her out when I made it back and she was wrapped in a towel as she sat on the vanity unit in front of him, looking like she was having trouble staying upright. He silently took the clothes I'd brought for her before dressing her in them carefully while Monroe watched with a heavy frown.

When Saint had finished getting her ready, he leaned forward and pressed a kiss to her forehead before indicating for me to take her from the room.

"I'm okay," Tatum protested weakly as she looked up at me with her big blue eyes, blinking sleepily as I lifted her against me again.

"I've got you, Tate," I swore and her gaze softened at my words as I carried her out to sit on the couch before the fire.

"Well, if you insist," she muttered as if she seriously thought she'd be able to walk herself if she wanted to. And I didn't doubt she was stubborn enough to try if I questioned her on it, so I just offered her a smile instead.

"I'm your Prince Charming, remember? I'm pretty sure rescuing the damsel in distress is a job requirement, so be a good girl and let me do my thing."

She laughed softly but the sound was weak compared to her usual laugh and it made my gut twist with concern. If I hadn't heard her screaming, if I hadn't swum as fast as I had, if I hadn't managed to outrun those arrows... I shook my head to clear it of the what ifs and focused on the girl I held safe in my arms.

Monroe followed close behind me, his silence saying more about his feelings than any words might. As we walked back out through my room, we found Kyan stepping through the front door with a sneer on his face and his bat still in his fist. He tossed the weapon down and locked the door before stalking over to me and plucking Tatum out of my arms.

"I was worried about you, big man," she teased, reaching up to cup Kyan's jaw in her hand and the look he gave her made my chest ache. I wasn't the only one of us who would have been destroyed if something worse had happened to her tonight.

"No need to worry about me, baby," Kyan reassured her. "I'm not that easy to kill."

"That's just because you're too stubborn to die," she muttered and he forced a smile for her, though it was clear that he was still really fucking worried about her.

No doubt she was feeling like some kind of pass the parcel prize at this point with us all snatching her from one another, but as a relieved smile touched her mouth, I found the protests I wanted to make dying on my lips. This was where she belonged, with all of us. And I guessed a bit of pass the parcel was bound to happen from time to time with that being the case.

"I take it you didn't find them?" Monroe asked as we moved over to the couch.

"Not yet," Kyan growled, the promise of violence clear in his tone.

He dropped down on the couch, burying his face against Tatum's neck and breathing in deeply as he pressed a kiss to her skin.

"You have to stop scaring me like this, baby," he growled and she laughed lightly like this was nothing. I had to hope that that was just the drugs in her system making her delirious because this seriously wasn't nothing.

"I'm safe now I'm with all of you," she murmured and the idea of her feeling that way made me smile. She looked around with a frown, glancing between me and Monroe as we moved to sit down either side of her and Kyan, and I pulled her feet into my lap. "Where's Saint?"

"I'm here," Saint's voice came from the short corridor which led down to mine and Kyan's room and I looked around to find him leaning against the wall, watching the four of us.

"Come here," Tatum demanded and to my surprise, he did, moving to stand before us and taking Tatum's hand as she reached for him.

A sleepy smile captured her lips and she wriggled in Kyan's arms until he rearranged her so that she was laying across him with her head in Monroe's lap while I painted circles around her ankles with my fingertips.

"Stay with me," she murmured, her eyes fluttering closed and the four of us glanced between each other as we wondered which one of us she was referring to. "All of you," she added firmly and Kyan chuckled darkly.

"Greedy little thing, aren't you, baby?" he asked as he took her other hand and lifted it to press a kiss to her knuckles.

"I belong to all of you," she said sleepily without opening her eyes. "And you're all mine too. We belong together."

None of us made any objections to that statement and Saint slowly sank down to sit on the floor before the couch, keeping Tatum's hand in his.

Within minutes, it was clear that she'd fallen asleep but none of us moved and I slowly leaned my head back and let my eyes fall closed too.

For now, the four of us just needed to stay with our girl and make sure she was okay.

Later, we'd be out for blood.

Monroe

CHAPTER THIRTY SEVEN

The fire burned low while I stayed where I was, jammed into a corner of the couch by Kyan's huge frame with Tatum's head in my lap and my fingers trailing through her damp hair.

Saint had been watching her in silence this whole time and though at first his attention had made me uncomfortable, I had eventually relaxed, realising he wasn't aiming any venom my way over my clear affection for her.

Blake had fallen asleep almost as soon as Tatum had, their combined heavy breathing the only sounds to have broken the silence while the rest of us sat here seething with anger.

It had been almost two hours since we'd taken up this position on the couch and as much as I wanted to stay here, holding her in my arms all night, my limbs were cramping up and a pure and hateful rage was burning through my flesh, aching for an outlet.

"We can't let this stand," Kyan growled, his thumb twisting Tatum's wedding ring back and forth on her finger as he kept hold of her hand and it was as if he'd spoke my own thoughts aloud.

"I have made a full and detailed report of every incident up to date and will add tonight's attack to the list at the earliest opportunity," Saint said in a low voice. "I have contacts in the police who are just waiting for our word on who the culprit is and they will cart them away and make sure they rot in prison for the rest of their miserable lives."

"What if it's an underage student?" I asked.

"What if I want to gut them instead?" Kyan growled.

"We all want to see blood spill," Saint replied, his jaw ticking. "And I'm sure I can buy us more than a little leeway for a healthy dose of corporal punishment. But I can only assume that it is one of the students here as it seems highly unlikely that it would be a member of staff. That being the case, we must assume they are the child of one of the richest and most influential families in the country. I can't see a way for us to easily get away with murder without at least a little suspicion colouring our reputations after the fact. A miserable existence in some cell is the wise choice for them. A few years down the line, if we're still feeling this level of hatred and anger towards them then maybe something can be arranged. As for their age, if they're not eighteen yet, we can lock them up ourselves until they are. This motherfucker isn't getting away with juvie."

"That all depends on us actually finding them though," I ground out.

"Then let's go find them," Saint announced, getting to his feet and carefully placing Tatum's hand back down to rest on her stomach.

"Fuck yes. I won't sleep tonight until I've spilled some blood anyway," Kyan announced and he stood, lifting Tatum in his arms and releasing me from the couch. She hardly even stirred, the effects of whatever she'd been dosed with clearly keeping her out of it. Bile rose in my throat at the idea of how vulnerable she was right now, of how vulnerable she would have been in that monster's arms if she hadn't managed to run from them.

I got up and Saint moved to clip Blake around the ear to wake him.

"Wassgoinon?" he slurred, blinking up at us sleepily and I had to remind myself that he'd been forced to swim half way across the lake tonight before carrying Tatum all the way back to The Temple from the beach. He must have been feeling near dead from exhaustion.

"We're going hunting," Saint announced. "And we're trusting you with our girl while we're gone."

Blake nodded seriously, rearranging himself to lay back on the couch more comfortably before gesturing to Kyan to place Tatum down with him. He did so, laying her head down on Blake's chest as he wrapped his arm around her to hold her close and she murmured something sleepily.

All of us froze to hear her words and my heart leapt as she spoke them without so much as opening an eye. "I love you."

All four of us looked between each other uncomfortably for a moment as we wondered who she was aiming that at or if it had even been intended for us at all. She could have just been dreaming about her family for all we knew. Though Kyan had been boasting about her saying it to him when he was dying at every opportunity he got too.

"I love you too, baby," he purred, leaning close and kissing her cheek as he tucked a blanket over her and Blake.

"Asshole," I muttered as he gave us a smug grin, but I refused to let it bother me. I'd come to the decision that if I wanted this thing with Tatum to keep going the way it was then I was only going to let myself focus on what she had with *me*. The other Night Keepers and their relationships with her weren't going to fuck this up for us because I let myself get jealous.

Saint took a moment to lean over her, gathering her damp hair and tugging it away from her face to make her more comfortable. His fingers lingered against her cheek as he looked down at her and there was a softness to his features that I'd never seen in him before. He wiped his face to a blank mask again before he stood upright and I was guessing I hadn't been meant to see that, but I had. And the most annoying thing was that it made me question some of the assumptions I'd been clinging to about him.

Because if he was capable of caring about her the way it was starting to look like he did, then I had to accept that there was more to him than I wanted to see.

He stepped away and I took my moment with her, leaning down and kissing her lips softly, the warmth of them banishing some of the worries in my heart. She was breathing deeply, no sign of her feeling unwell aside from the fact that she clearly needed to sleep it off and I took comfort from that. But the dark blue bruise which was growing on her jaw had my anger burning hot with the need to destroy whoever the fuck had hurt her.

Blake had already closed his eyes again and I glanced between Kyan and Saint as the three of us moved away to let them rest.

"Where are we going to start?" Kyan asked hungrily, his eyes alight with the promise of violence in the air.

"Did you let Toby out of the closet when you checked on him?" Saint asked, turning away from us and heading up to his room while we waited at the foot of the stairs.

"No," Kyan replied with a shrug. "I had more pressing shit to deal with and I didn't much feel like offering out explanations."

We waited while Saint disappeared at the top of the stairs and he soon reappeared wearing a shirt and carrying one for me. I took it with a muttered thanks, pulling it on as we all headed for the door and grabbed our coats.

"We'd better go and let him out. Maybe if we give him the chance to speak up, he will have some insight into who might have set him up. There is of course a chance that he was just a convenient patsy, but someone as emotional as the Justice Ninja would have most likely targeted him because he was an enemy of theirs whether he knew it or not." Saint pulled the door open and we all headed out into the cool evening air.

It was gone eleven so there weren't many people about, but it wasn't so late that we'd be waking up the entire campus either. Kyan swung his baseball bat happily as we walked, a dark smile tugging at the corner of his lips which promised someone would end the night screaming at his hand.

We made it to the Redwood Dining Hall where they'd left Toby earlier on and Saint used a key to unlock the dark building. He really shouldn't have had that key and as the headmaster I was pretty sure it was my duty to take it from him alongside the rest of them, but it was really the least of the crimes I was letting him get away with around here so it didn't seem like it was worth mentioning.

We strode down the corridor outside the dining hall until we came to the closet in question and Kyan unbolted the door while whistling the Kill Bill tune, Twisted Nerve by Bernard Herrmann.

"I thought we were meant to be here to say sorry, not scare the shit out of him," I muttered.

"He's covered in flour and olive oil," Saint said flatly. "I think this conversation needs to be had after he's cleaned up. No need to jump the gun."

Kyan swung the door open, illuminating the flashlight on his cell phone and shining it down on the shivering, shirtless, flour and olive oil covered boy inside it.

"It's your lucky day, Stalker," Kyan announced, swinging his baseball bat up to rest over his shoulder. "But King Saint can't bear to look at you while you're in such a god awful state, let alone have a conversation with you in your current condition." He waved a vague hand at Toby's entire being in explanation and the guy just cowered, clearly having no fucking idea what was happening.

"He's saying you need to get your ass up," I supplied. "We're all going to go back to your dorm and have a nice little chat. Saint will lose his shit if he has to look at you in that state for long though, so you're gonna need a shower and some clean clothes before he will lower himself to talk to you."

Saint's lips twitched with amusement as I looked at him and goddammit, I grinned back. Fuck, now we were joking around together. What was next? Was I going to start actually trusting him to do all of that shit to his dad like he'd promised? Why didn't that even seem as crazy as it had when he'd first said it to me? I'd been so relieved that he wasn't going to throw me at the mercy of the law over my relationship with Tatum that I think I'd been in too much shock to fully grasp the rest of what he'd been offering at the time. But it had been a week now and he'd been nothing but…well, not *nice* because this was Saint Memphis, but he'd encouraged Tatum to sit next to me on the couch the other night and when she'd kissed me in front of all of them, he'd smirked like he was pleased about it. He'd also looked half inclined to murder me over his jealousy, but still.

Toby scrambled upright, blinking against the light of the cell phone and Kyan was nice enough to lower it so it wasn't shining right in his face.

"After you," Kyan said, indicating the way out with his bat and Toby nodded as he scurried ahead of us and we fell into line as we followed like a pack of wolves stalking a deer.

We walked behind him all the way back to Hazel House, Saint on one side of me and Kyan on the other, our shoulders brushing companionably and me actually feeling comfortable between them, like I fucking belonged there.

Kyan kept whistling his psycho tune and Toby looked like he was one good scare away from adding shit smears to the flour and oil combo that was already coating him. It seemed a bit cruel of us to be letting him believe we were going to do something else to him when we'd actually come to apologise and set him free, but without a full explanation he wouldn't accept us being nice anyway.

We followed him to his dorm then waited while he scurried away for a shower and Saint sneered at the cleanliness of his room which apparently didn't meet his standards even though it seemed fine to me.

When Toby reappeared, he was washed, dressed and looking utterly fucking terrified. Points to him for walking his ass back here if he was that convinced that we'd been planning something horrible, but then again I guessed he knew it was always worse for those who tried to run.

"Take a seat," Saint commanded, gesturing to the bed and I moved to lean against his dresser while Kyan threw himself down on the other bed in the room which clearly belonged to another student, but they weren't here to complain so I guessed he didn't care.

"Look, I've been doing everything you say," Toby began and the fear in his eyes as they darted between the three of us made me feel kinda shitty. I wasn't about to feel bad for trying to protect my girl from a predator, but he'd never been the one who should have borne the brunt of our anger and for that I really was sorry.

"Forget all of that," Saint commanded. "We are here to inform you that we have evidence that proves you are not in fact, Tatum's stalker."

Toby's eyes widened with hope and he twisted his hands in his lap. "You do?" he breathed.

"We do," Saint agreed. "So. This is a formal apology on behalf of myself and all of the Night Keepers. We were wrong and you have been punished unjustly. You are no longer an Unspeakable and your name is once again Toby Rosner."

"That's it?" Toby asked, looking so fucking happy that I couldn't help but smile for him too. "It's all over?"

"No," Saint said and Toby looked terrified for a moment before he continued. "You have suffered terribly at our hands. Of course it would not be enough for us to merely make an apology and return your name to you. So, I have come up with what I think is a fair offer for reparations, but if you don't agree then you may of course tell us what it is you think you deserve."

"Reparations?" Toby asked, staring between the three of us like this was some kind of crazy joke and he couldn't actually believe a word of it.

Kyan chuckled like this was funny as fuck and I just shrugged. I hadn't realised that Saint intended to make amends for the shit we'd done to this kid, but I had to say I was impressed by his morals even letting him know that that was the right thing to do. And by the fact that he actually had morals. Fuck, was he just about to prove to me once and for all that he wasn't a total son of a bitch? Because if he stood up like a man and owned his shit and tried to make amends for it then that told me all I needed to know about his similarities to his father, the man who had lied and cheated and destroyed my family to cover up his own wrongdoing.

"We got it wrong," I said. "And we've been total cocks to you, so that sounds fair to me."

Toby nodded though I could tell he would be happy if we just left it at giving him his name back and promising not to torture him anymore.

"I think that the mental and physical anguish we caused you was severe enough to equal a financial sum of one hundred thousand dollars," Saint said calmly and I had to fight not to gape at that ridiculous sum of money, but he wasn't done there. "Per week that you were subjected to it."

"A hundred thousand *a week*?" I asked, because surely I hadn't heard him right. We'd been hounding Toby for months, that was a fucking fortune.

Saint cut me a scathing look and went on. "Please ignore the pauper in the room. Does that sum seem fair to you? I will round the final six days up to the full weekly sum too as a show of good faith."

"Err, yeah," Toby agreed and I could see that he was calculating that amount too. That was a fuck ton of money, why didn't I just volunteer to be their punching bag for a few months? I'd be set for fucking life.

"Good." Saint pulled an honest to shit cheque book from his back pocket and wrote out so many zeros that I just stared at the thing before he signed it with a flourish and handed it to Toby. "I will of course make sure your parents understand that those rumours about your drug use and dealing were false as well as reassure them about any other unfortunate rumours which may have reached their notice. Additionally, I happen to know the Dean of admissions at Brown so I can make sure you get that placement you want. I can also arrange several favourable business deals for your father's company, and I am willing to offer you the hand of friendship for life. This means that, assuming you never try to fuck me over, I will gladly offer you my support in any business dealings that we may have in our futures. Is this acceptable to you? Does it make us even?"

"Yeah," Toby breathed. "More than even. I've already forgotten about all of it."

Saint quirked a smile then shot me a look that said it was my turn to speak, but I had no idea what I was meant to be saying so I just raised an eyebrow in question.

Saint sighed like I was testing his patience and inclined his head to Toby but I still wasn't getting it, so he was forced to explain. "Nash has something to offer you in reparations too," he said firmly.

"I do?" I glanced between him and Toby, but I didn't have a small fortune to hand over. Hell, I doubted I owned a single thing he wanted. He might have been at the bottom of the pecking order recently, but he was still a trust fund kid with more money than I'd ever be able to lay claim to. But he was looking at me all expectantly and shit, so I had to think of something. Not least because if I allowed Saint to be the better man in this situation, I was going to have to seriously revaluate the way I looked at the world. "Err, yeah, how about I…put you back on the football team?"

"Really?" he asked hopefully, looking like the idea of that appealed to him more than the megabucks Saint was dropping. *Fuck yes.*

"Yeah. And Blake said he wants you to be captain," I added, hoping that Blake would be okay with that. He would probably be pissed though, because his whole thing was about being the best but we had made this kid's life hell, so it seemed like a minor sacrifice in comparison.

"Wow, yeah, my dad would be so proud, that would be amazing," Toby gushed and I grinned, turning to Kyan and passing the buck to him.

"I will offer you one free shot at me." He rolled upright and moved to stand before Toby so that he could deliver the hit.

"How many times exactly have you punched him during his time served as Stalker?" Saint drawled like he was less than impressed by this offer.

Kyan thought about that for a moment then smirked triumphantly. "I lost count. So to make it fair, he can use the bat." He hooked the baseball bat off of the floor and spun it around to offer Toby the handle before standing there with his arms wide, waiting for the blow to fall.

Toby stared at the bat in his hands for a long moment and I couldn't help but take a step forward in protest.

"He could break bones," I said, shaking my head. "Or cave your damn skull in."

"Is that what you want, Toby?" Kyan taunted. "Are you hungering for my death in payment for my crimes? Come on, I bet you've been aching to make one of us bleed. You'll never get a shot like this again."

Toby got to his feet, his brow furrowed as he hefted the bat in his hand like he was weighing it and Saint placed a hand on my shoulder to hold me back as we waited to see what he'd do.

He gripped it in two hands, swinging it back as he looked at Kyan and my gut knotted in concern at the insanity of this, but Kyan didn't even fucking blink.

"No," Toby said suddenly, dropping the bat so that it clattered to the floor. "I don't want to hurt you. I just want you to find the motherfucker who set me up and make them *pay*. Make them pay for Tatum and make them pay for me too."

Kyan laughed darkly and slapped his hand into Toby's. "You have yourself a deal, brother."

"I'm guessing you've had plenty of time to think about who might have been the one to set you up," I said. "So have you got any ideas for us on where to look?"

Toby sighed and dropped back down onto his bed with a shake of his head. "I wish I fucking did, man. I've thought about it over and over and I just can't think of a single person who hates me enough to inflict all the shit I've been through on me. All I keep thinking is that the night you all turned up here to search our rooms, you took them by surprise and they had to get rid of the evidence that linked them to the stalking fast. So maybe it's someone who lives on this floor and I was just the dumb fucker who left my door unlocked or maybe it's someone more calculating than that who knew me and Tatum were friends and thought you'd believe it was me easily."

I huffed out a breath as I thought on that. "On the night they first shot at Tatum with the bow the evidence conveniently pointed us towards Mila too. What if that wasn't an accident? What if they have purposefully made it look like her friends so that she feels like she can't trust anyone. It would be a good way to try and isolate her. Make her more vulnerable to them."

Kyan growled like a wild beast at that suggestion, sweeping up the baseball bat and swinging it in a savage arc which ended with a dent in the wall.

"A bow?" Toby asked, wincing slightly at the damaged brickwork. "Like the ones the archery club use?"

The three of us exchanged a loaded look and Saint clucked his tongue.

"I've already looked into the seven members of the archery club and come to the conclusions that, A, they don't have the balls to pull this off and, B, none of them have any motivation. They're not even students who would have crossed Tatum's path."

"Well maybe it's someone who isn't in the club officially but still likes to use the equipment?" I suggested. "We could ask if they've seen anyone lurking around down there or if anyone has asked to borrow anything recently?"

"I believe they're a pretty skilled archer," Saint mused. "So it would make sense for them to be keeping their skills sharp by practicing regularly…"

"They seem like a pretty shit archer to me," Kyan contradicted. "They always miss."

"They miss on purpose," Saint growled, rolling his eyes like that was the most obvious thing in the world. "They clearly either don't want a murder investigation taking place on campus or are not ready to elevate their attacks to that level yet. The note that was delivered made it clear that they see our girl as rightfully belonging to them. What they really want is to separate us from her. Tonight they had her at their mercy, they clearly found a way to dose her with something, likely rohypnol or ketamine-"

"Date rape?" I interrupted him, my fists locking tight as the fury in me rose to the surface once more. "You think he was going to-"

"No. That's the point. If he had wanted to, he had his opportunity. I don't believe she could have escaped him without him allowing it which either means he gets off on her fear or this was just a trial run," Saint said and lucky for him I'd figured out how to read his rage in his eyes because the emotionless way he delivered that statement would have had me punching him a few weeks ago.

"No Justice Ninja or stalker or anyone else is going to get close enough to her to ever attempt it again," Kyan snarled fiercely. "From now on, she goes nowhere alone. There are four of us and we can easily take shifts."

Toby was listening to all of this with rapt interest and Saint tsked as he remembered we had an audience.

"Come on," he growled, heading for the door. "Let's start by interrogating some archery assholes and then we can move the hunt on from there. I won't rest until we've gotten some fucking answers. Someone in this school knows something that will lead us to this fucking Ninja and when we find him, his life really won't be worth living."

CHAPTER THIRTY EIGHT

I woke in a sea of soft sheets, the scent of apple reaching to me and making me sigh contentedly. My brain was still foggy and my mouth was too dry as I ran my tongue across the roof of it.

"Mmm," I groaned as I pushed myself up, my eyes immediately locking with Saint's who was sitting in the chair across the room in a grey button down, the sleeves rolled up and his elbows rested on his knees. He looked exhausted, like he hadn't slept a single wink, but his face brightened as he saw me awake.

He stood, wordlessly moving to my nightstand and handing me a full glass of water and two Advil. I thanked him, washing them down and draining the whole glass, feeling a little better as I sated my thirst.

"What time is it?" I murmured.

"Eleven thirty three," Saint answered without even glancing at the clock. How the hell did he do that? It was like he had an inbuilt, finely tuned pocket watch in his brain. "An offensive time, but not quite as disconcerting as eleven thirty seven."

I broke a smile and he surprised me by smiling back. He sat down on the edge of the bed, pushing a lock of hair behind my ear and it didn't feel like he was fixing me for once. It felt like he was consoling me. And coming from Saint Memphis that was akin to him turning into a cartoon character and bounding off on a fun-filled adventure to save the world. It didn't freaking happen.

"Any news on the Justice Ninja?" I asked hopefully. Had they found them? Strung them up by the hair from one of the pine trees with two broken legs and the word monster carved into their forehead?

Saint shook his head minimally like the gesture hurt him to admit. "Whoever they are, they're covering their tracks well. Kyan, Monroe and I were out all night hunting them but we still haven't managed to find anything concrete to lead us to them. But I want you to know I am taking this deadly seriously and if they think they can outwit me any longer, they are wrong." He looked straight into my eyes. "I will destroy them for you. I swear it on every scrap of my sullied soul."

His words lit a bloodlust in me that was yearning to be sated. "I want to be there when that happens," I said firmly, no room for negotiation.

"I guarantee it," he said simply and I knew he'd keep his word. "One thing we have deduced is that Toby Rosner is not and never was your stalker. He was framed."

I gasped, thinking over all the awful things that boy had been through since they'd outcast him into the Unspeakables again. "Are you sure?" I asked desperately.

He nodded simply, no room for error in this decision and I believed him.

"Fuck...that's awful," I said heavily. "We have to make it up to him."

"We have already come to an arrangement which ensures he is well compensated for our mistake. It is unfortunate, but there is always a margin of error in corporal punishment. That does not mean the death sentence should be revoked."

I gaped at him for a long second, the cold detachment in his eyes reminding me that I was in the bed of a killer. But that didn't scare me like it should have. It made me feel like I was right where I belonged. Because I was one too.

"Ok...good," I said, trying to cast my mind back over what had happened last night but everything just seemed so muddled that all I could really remember was running through the woods, fearing for my life while the stench of gasoline overwhelmed me and then...then I was safe again, held in the arms of my Night Keepers. I was almost certain that they'd all been there, holding me close at once. But maybe that had just been a dream. I certainly wasn't going to ask Saint about it to find out.

"Do you remember anything about the man who took you?" he asked, holding my eye and keeping his tone soft.

"I..." I tried to think back on what had happened but all I could really remember was the library before anything had happened and then running. "Maybe a guy's voice," I said but I wasn't sure and it made my head pound to try.

"That's alright," Saint said softly. "Don't force the memories. But if anything comes to you then let me know."

"Thanks. Umm, how did I end up here?" I asked, looking around his room in confusion. "I thought I was sleeping on the couch at one point."

"I carried you up here when it was clear you still needed more sleep after we returned from our hunt," he explained. "And I volunteered to be the one to stay and look after you while the others went to class today in the hopes of flushing the culprit out."

"Oh," I said, which didn't really progress the conversation, but my head was still spinning and I wasn't sure what more to say on the subject while my memories were so hazy.

"So..." Saint got to his feet, striding over to the balcony railing and clasping his hands behind his back as he gazed over The Temple like an emperor gazing across his land. "I have something I would like to discuss

587

with you, siren."

"What's that?" I asked, leaning back against the pile of pillows behind me and letting my eyes flutter closed as I waited for the Advil to take effect on my headache.

"I suppose you have considered the fact that the dynamic between us all might change once we have graduated from Everlake," he said calmly, but there was an undercurrent to his voice that set the hairs prickling across my arms.

I opened my eyes, frowning at him, but he didn't turn to face me. "Yes," I admitted.

"Leaving here unsettles me greatly. As I am sure you have noticed, routine is key to my internal state remaining tranquil. But there is one thing that unsettles me far more than leaving this school does - I already have a plan in place for where me, Blake and Kyan will go and have amended that plan to include both you and Nash - but the question is..." He turned around, his eyes a roiling sea of darkness that made my heart skip a beat. "Will you run from us once we leave here? When the world opens up once more and there are no more chains binding you to us?"

I took a deep breath, needing to be honest and let him know that I'd been grappling with this subject myself. "Saint...I don't want my life decided for me. Whatever plan you have-"

"It is a fairly simple one. All of us will attend Yale together – I would have preferred Princeton all in all as it offers the best music program out of all the Ivy League colleges, but Yale is only second to that and although the sports department is not quite as proficient as Harvard, no doubt Blake will bring their football team up in the rankings with a little investment or two from his father. There is also a fantastic art division for Kyan as he will no doubt refuse to take on anything more academic, but the frat parties alone will be enough to ensure his contentment. From a little research, I have pulled Nash's job application from the school's online server and discovered that he has a surprising aptitude for history, so he may choose their classic Greek civilisation course or perhaps he will opt for a broader spectrum of study. As for you, I am aware you have made little suggestion that you have thought about college, so I decided on Yale as the optimum option as it is within just two miles of New Haven Harbour. And though I am well aware it is no Californian beach-"

"Saint," I tried to stop him, but he barrelled on.

"And don't worry about exam pressure. If our grades don't talk, money will. Nash can attend as a mature student and I have already put an offer in on a newly built fraternity house – to my exact specifications - where the five of us can reside. You will have a choice of courses, I have a course pack you can look through when you're ready, but might I suggest you look at their English division as you have quite the aptitude for-"

"*Saint*," I cut him off more firmly, shaking my head. "Look, I never planned to go college, okay? I don't even know what I want to do with my life yet, but I know there's no school subject I'm passionate enough about that I'd go to college for. All I ever really dreamed about was..." I glanced away, unsure if I wanted to share one of my innermost secrets with Saint. Not when he still held my sister's letters from me. Not when there were still so many trust issues between us that I wasn't sure if I'd ever get past them. But I could see he wasn't going to let this go if I didn't explain myself. I sighed. "I just want something of my own, somewhere I love where I can put down roots and stop moving from state to state. Lately I've been thinking about starting a business...maybe training girls in self-defence. I could purchase a gym by the beach."

He considered my words with a stoic expression before nodding once as he made some assessment then strode into his closet. I took a moment to rub my tired eyes and when I opened them again, Saint was standing before me with Jess's letters in his hand. He held them out to me, his eyes firmly on mine as he gave them up. I hunted for the joke in his eyes, certain he wouldn't really be giving me them, but I didn't waste time staring, I grabbed them from him and hugged them to my chest.

It felt like getting a piece of myself back as I clutched onto them and guilt stirred in my gut over the fact that I hadn't written a letter to Jess in a long time. But it had felt like giving Saint more ammo to use against me if he found them.

He kicked off his shoes and got onto the bed, sitting beside me and I looked to him, waiting for an explanation. Silence stretched and a muscle worked in his jaw as he seemed to be thinking up what to say. Maybe he was struggling with putting it into words. He knew the value of giving these back to me. It didn't make it right that he'd taken them in the first place, or that he'd made me believe he'd burned them, but he'd just handed over his leverage on me.

"When I first met Blake, he irritated the fuck out of me," Saint said, surprising me with the direction of conversation he'd taken, but I stayed quiet to see where he was going with this. "My father thought it would be good for me to join a pee-wee football club growing up and obviously I couldn't just attend *any* club, he had to join me up to one full of the most elite kids in Sequoia state, including the son of the owner of the Redwood Rattlesnakes. He wanted to connect with Blake's dad while he was campaigning for mayor, no doubt offering funding for the various clubs and teams his father had sway with. Kyan attended the team too. We were ten. I already knew him from playdates since my father had been working on building connections with the O'Briens for years. Our friendship had been written for us since the day of our fucking conception. Of course, I hadn't expected to like Kyan, but I had immediately recognised a darkness in him that mirrored my own soul and we'd found enough to bond over. It wasn't like that with Blake. Blake was enthusiastic, loud, obnoxious. All qualities I can't tend to stand in a human being."

I laughed a little and he tossed me a dark grin that made my heart hammer wildly.

"Anyway, Kyan immediately took a liking to Blake, their competitive sides driving them together on the field until they realised taking down the opposition side by side was far more satisfying. I, however, grew jealous of Kyan's relationship with Blake. Kyan was the only friend I had ever had. The only person I'd ever let in. And now he had found a boy he seemed to enjoy the company of more than me. I wasn't like Blake, I didn't offer Kyan easy laughs, I tended to prefer a more regimented kind of fun. Games I was in charge of were my forte. Not rude jokes and fart noises as Blake Bowman seemed to be fond of at that age. And I wanted to *hurt* him for it."

I pictured the three of them at that age, Blake and Kyan playing together and laughing while an angry little Saint Memphis stood watching from the side lines, plotting Blake's downfall.

"And did you hurt him?" I asked, enraptured by the story.

Saint released a low laugh. "Yes. I broke into his locker while he was showering one day and took a signed photograph of him and the Rattlesnakes' linebacker, Dirk Hadley, he'd been flashing around to everyone on the team that day. He searched for it frantically after his shower and I watched with a sweet satisfaction over taking something so precious from him, of wielding that power against my enemy."

Woah, even at ten years old Saint had been an itty bitty psycho. Why is that so freaking cute?

"My plan took a turn when Kyan started hunting for the photograph too, sizing up to all the boys on the team and threatening to beat their heads in if they didn't give it back. That made me angry in a way I couldn't put into words, so I took the photograph from my pocket, showing Blake I had it before marching into a bathroom stall. I ripped it into ten pieces and dropped it in the toilet before pulling the chain."

I gasped. "What did Blake do?"

"He punched me," he said, shrugging one shoulder. "And Kyan threatened to do the same, only…Blake stopped him."

"Why?" I asked in surprise.

"He said…he knew that I was jealous of him and Kyan. And that I could be his friend too if I wanted."

My heart squeezed. Typical Blake. He always knew when I was in pain, and he could clearly sense that in Saint too.

"I said no, obviously," Saint deadpanned and I snorted a laugh. "But then when his father showed up to collect him outside the locker room and started screaming and shouting at him about losing that photo, Blake didn't tell him I'd done it. He took the fall. And the next time we had football together, he kicked a boy who dared to say he hoped Santa Claus brought me a personality for Christmas. That was where our friendship truly started. But the thing is, after that day I became afraid of the idea of losing those two people who made my life good. And after I'd seen Blake's reaction to losing his photograph, I realised he would have done anything to get it back. So I took something important from each of them..." He leaned over and opened the drawer of his nightstand, taking a little silver box from it which I had seen before but had never been able to open. He twisted two little dials until a click sounded and it opened. Inside he revealed a silver zippo lighter and a pen with a hologram of a dinosaur on it. "The lighter is Kyan's. He always played with it, even at ten years old. His family gave zero shits if he accidentally burned the world down I suppose. And Blake loved this stupid hologram pen. He brought it to every single fucking class once we started attending middle school together the following fall. I took these things hostage to ensure they never left me. They both beat me up to try and get them back, but they didn't cut me off. We stayed friends and it became a running joke between us that I had their valued possessions locked away somewhere – they often liked to guess places like my haunted bell tower, the attic where I kept all the bodies of those who'd wronged me, or in a box made of human teeth. Hilarious as always," he deadpanned. "Eventually, they gave up and told me to keep them." A crease formed on his brow. "I guess a part of me thought they remained my friends because I had these items. Stupid really...but effective in the right circumstances." He gestured to the letters and I gazed at him, hurting for the little boy who really thought his friends would leave him if he didn't hold their prized possessions ransom. "I suppose what I'm trying to say is that I kept those letters to ensure you had to stay. But I don't want to use them to make you remain with me anymore. I'd like, very much, if you *chose* to stay with all of us."

I pushed the covers back, crawling into Saint's lap and pushing my fingers into his tight curls. "Why do you make it so hard for me to hate you these days?" I asked.

I swear I was breaking apart inside from that story. It was too real. Too raw. And the honesty in his eyes made me think he really had changed when it came to me, that he was trying to let me see him as more than a devil with no heart.

"Maybe I don't want you to hate me. So…will you?" he asked, his voice raspy. "Stay?"

I kissed him, having no answer but that one right now and I gasped as he kissed me back, leaning in rather than pulling away for once. His tongue pushed into my mouth and I moaned as he wrapped his hand in my hair, tugging tight to take control of the kiss. He explored my tongue with hungry movements and I tasted all the sins he'd ever committed and all those he was yet to. But more than that, I tasted that dark and stormy pain inside him which he concealed so well. I felt his hurt as I slid between the walls he confined himself within. I fell into him so deeply that I could sense all of his demons and I faced them down with all the strength I had, wanting to fight them for him and promise him he didn't have to face them alone anymore.

His strong arms wrapped around my waist and I started to pant as I felt his hard length driving into my leg as I tried to get nearer to him. I could be consumed by the darkness in Saint, it was so potent it seemed to breathe down the back of my neck and push me closer to him. And I wanted it. I revelled in the way he drew me in and every atom in the room seemed to spark with the need to drive us close too, like the earth suddenly revolved around us instead of the sun.

Saint yanked my hair hard enough to break the kiss, his breaths coming heavily as he stared at me, tasting his lips. The rules no longer kept us apart.

He could take this further if he wanted. And I could too. I wanted to so badly that a strained whimper escaped me. He leaned forward, not running away at last and my heart drummed out an exhilarated tune as I wondered if this was the moment he would let his guard fall for me at last.

His phone rang sharply on the nightstand and I jolted at the piercing sound. Saint released my hair with a growl, picking it up, his eyes returning to me as he pressed answer and held it to his ear.

"Father," he said curtly and I was suddenly totally alert. Saint's thumb shifted on the screen and his father's powerful voice suddenly filled the room.

"-calling because my people have finished working through Donovan Rivers' work and there seems to be some files missing."

"Missing?" Saint questioned coolly and I frowned. Had someone tampered with Dad's stuff?

"Yes, there should be documents which detailed a continued analysis of a test subject who had taken a trialled vaccination. Obviously, you can understand the importance of such documentation, son."

My throat thickened as I realised that must have been the vaccination me, Dad and Jess got. There had been paperwork mentioning it amongst the documents he'd given me and it sounded like there'd been more detailed information in his work files.

"I do," Saint said simply. "But I'm unsure why you're calling me about it."

There was a pause where I suspected Troy was calculating his next words and my gut tightened. "Well, if I were to guess, these files have been removed manually."

"Perhaps Donovan deleted them," Saint suggested, taking my hand and threading his fingers between mine.

"Why save the rest of these valuable documents only to remove such vital information as that?" Troy questioned. "It almost seems as though he was protecting somebody..."

My heart clenched in my chest.

"Maybe, or maybe the documents were deleted a long time ago because the data was irrelevant. If there was a working vaccination, then surely it would say so in the rest of his files?" Saint asked.

"Yes...perhaps you're right," Troy said, but it didn't sound like he was convinced.

"Have you made any progress towards exposing this conspiracy, father? It is concerning that a CIA agent could-"

"Mortez was not CIA, that much I have confirmed."

"Why didn't you inform me?" Saint bit out.

"You are a teenager, not an employee," Troy said simply. "I will only inform you of anything that concerns you."

Saint's jaw pulsed angrily but instead of snapping at him like I expected, he just answered in a deadened tone. "Yes, father."

"If you remember anything about those missing files, be sure to call me, son."

"I will," Saint said hollowly.

"And perhaps you could have a word with his daughter to see if she knows anything about them."

"Of course," Saint agreed then the line went dead.

Tense silence spread between us for a moment, then I asked him the question that was tearing through my mind.

"Did you delete those files?"

He nodded, his fingers firming on mine. "I would not share the truth of your immunity from the Hades Virus, Tatum. Even if keeping this secret meant every star in the heavens would fall from the sky and everyone on earth would die in a fiery blaze."

I inhaled deeply in surprise then leaned forward and wrapped my arms around him, hugging him tight. "Thank you."

"I'm your Night Keeper, Tatum," he purred. "And I will keep you safe from anything and everything I can."

I smiled at him and he leaned in again as if to kiss me, my breath catching in my throat. But then the door slammed downstairs and the sound of Kyan, Blake and Monroe talking in concerned voices reached up to us.

"Where's Tate?" Blake asked anxiously and I drew away from Saint, chewing my lip as I gazed at him.

There was a vow in his eyes which told me he was going to show me how deeply he could possess me soon enough. But not now. And that was infuriating, because I was desperate to show him how deeply I could possess him too.

Monroe

CHAPTER THIRTY NINE

I sat at the table opposite Tatum's in the library, not so subtly watching her back while she worked with Mila on their Chemistry assignment. Supposedly I was working through some emails on my fancy new laptop that the school had gifted me alongside my promotion, but as every other one was some complaint from a parent, I was finding it hard to give it my full attention. Why couldn't rich people ever just get to the point? The email I was currently reading had six full paragraphs praising me on the way that I was handling the lockdown situation before reaching the single paragraph outlining the point of this bullshit. Pearl Devickers was in line for a solid C in English and that GPA wasn't what mommy dearest wanted to report back to her country club friends. There was a less than subtle suggestion that her grades be given a second look in case they might have been awarded a little too harshly by mistake and a very generous donation had been made to the school in appreciation of the difficulties we were facing due to the Hades Virus. *Nice.*

I typed out a quick reply, fighting the urge to just hit the entitled bitch with a squid emoji which I felt would have made my point better. Instead I thanked her for her generous contribution and assured her that I could get Pearl into the remedial program to give her a shot at boosting her grades. It meant five additional hours of school work a week for the brat but if she wanted to pull her grades up, then that was the only cure I knew. No doubt mommy would be horrified to realise I hadn't read between the less than subtle lines about the bribe she'd just been offering but if she expected me to take a bribe, she was going to have to offer one more plainly than that to get her way.

The library was emptying out and my gaze slid over to Tatum as she sketched something in her notepad before biting down on the end of her pencil while she concentrated. The sight of her doing that had me coming up with all kinds of things I wanted to do with her the moment I got her back to my place tonight.

There was something about us only getting one night in every four days together that made the anticipation unbearable and yet the night itself so fucking satisfying that it was hard to think of anything else, particularly on the days when I knew she was mine.

I sorted through several more emails, internally muttering about the stuck up douchebags who sent their kids to this school the entire time and when I looked up again, I found that we were the last ones left in the room.

The sun had been shining today, spring most definitely in the air and I'd heard several kids talking about a party down at the Oak Common House. I probably should have reminded them all about social distancing, but really, with all of us locked away from the world in here, it seemed pointless. And I had zero desire to spend my evening following a bunch of horny teenagers around and trying to stop them from hooking up.

No. I had much more appealing plans for tonight.

Tatum looked up at me as she felt my gaze on her and the smile that touched her lips was its own kind of promise which had my dick twitching with ideas.

She faked a long yawn and turned to Mila, suggesting they call it a night and hit the party. Unsurprisingly Mila instantly ditched the books and started up a monologue about some designer dress her mom had sent her which had been waiting for a night like this.

Tatum swore to meet her there and Mila hustled out of the library like a woman on a mission, leaving the two of us alone.

The silence in the room felt heavy with promise and I slowly closed my laptop, leaning back in my chair as I looked at the creature who had been sent here to corrupt me. She was a temptress, a siren, an itch that I could never get enough of scratching and the perfect kind of noose to hang myself with.

What we were doing was insane, but I'd long since gone beyond the point of trying to convince myself to stop. The ache I felt for her was never satisfied by a taste and the demand in my body only grew more potent with each moment we got to share.

Tatum gave me a heated look and slowly slid her tie undone before loosening several of her shirt buttons and offering me a glimpse of the black bra she had on beneath it.

I got up slowly, my gaze fixed on hers as I crossed the room, peering down at her with every dirty thought I was having burning in my eyes for her to see. But it was more than that, too. I wanted her physically like an addict needed their next hit, but I needed to protect her with the ferociousness of a demon because she was the first person who had even come close to knowing the true me since before my family had been taken from me. She was the one person I'd let in fully, knowing that the things I'd told her about me could be weapons in the wrong hands while trusting her never to use them against me.

She wasn't just some girl I wanted to fuck. She was fast becoming everything to me. Even my thirst for vengeance didn't seem so desperate when I was in her arms. It was still a sharp and hungry desire, but it wasn't everything anymore. Maybe she was though. Maybe this girl was everything I'd never wanted to admit I needed and everything I should have been fighting to resist. Because I'd sworn I'd never love anyone ever again after feeling the keen burn of losing that love and having my soul shredded by it. I'd made an oath to myself never to care about someone that deeply again because I knew I wouldn't survive losing it a second time.

But even if I wanted to try and turn back, I knew it was too late now. There was no way that I could do it. I was already in too deep and I knew I'd rather drown in her than surface alone again.

"Fancy seeing you here," she teased, watching me approach with a gleam in her eye that said she was just as excited as I was about our night together.

"I heard there was a student in here causing issues for the staff," I said slowly, reaching out to push her books aside so that I could lean over the desk and get closer to her.

I shoved her things a little too hard and managed to knock one of her books onto the floor, causing her to pout at me.

"I should complain to the administration about that," she teased. "I'll tell them you're harassing me and throwing my shit all over the floor."

"We both know that you're the one harassing *me,* princess," I murmured, placing my hands flat on the desk and leaning over her so that I dominated her space.

Tatum raised her chin, those full lips beckoning me in for a taste and making my heart pound as I considered taking one. But we'd sworn not to make careless moves like that around campus again. Especially when we knew for a fact that the fucking stalker was still watching her at every opportunity.

We really shouldn't have been having sleepovers at my place either, but I wasn't giving that up for anything.

"Aren't you going to pick that up?" she breathed as I got so close to her that not kissing her felt like the most impossible task in the world.

"Sure thing, princess." I smirked at her and drew back, loving the heat in her gaze as she watched me pull the chair opposite hers aside and drop to my knees so that I could reach beneath the desk to find the fallen book.

I spotted it right away, but my gaze snagged on her bare legs beneath the table and a growl of longing caught in my throat.

I moved under the table and reached out to run my fingers over her ankle, earning myself a surprised gasp as I circled the flesh there and slowly began to run my hand higher.

"Nash," she breathed, part warning, part moan of longing.

My fingers made it to the top of her knee length socks and I slid my hand up her inner thigh, dipping it beneath her pleated skirt as my dick swelled and strained within my pants.

I shifted forward so that I could reach higher, my heart pounding at this dangerous game. But no one could see what I was doing down here and if anyone appeared, I only had to grab the book and get up.

As that thought crossed my mind, I looked around for the book so that I'd know where it was if I needed it. But instead of spotting it, my gaze caught on something taped to the underside of the table.

I stilled the movement of my hand between Tatum's legs just as I felt the brush of her panties against my fingertips and a breathy moan of longing escaped her.

I jerked my hand back sharply as I stared at the little listening device.

"Why are you stopping?" she protested with a lusty purr to her voice and I quickly crawled back out from beneath the table before placing a finger to her lips to silence her.

Tatum frowned in confusion but she held her tongue and I slid my cell phone from my pocket before turning on the camera and dipping it beneath the table to take a picture.

When I pulled it back out and showed her the photo of the little microphone, her lips popped open in surprise.

"Come on, Princess," I said loudly, picking up her crap and quickly shoving it into her bag. "The Night Keepers are waiting for us."

"Yeah...okay," she agreed, catching on to the idea that we needed to remain subtle around that thing.

I finished putting her stuff away and swung her bag over my shoulder before grabbing my laptop and leading the way outside.

Tatum fell into step beside me and we wordlessly began to head for The Temple.

We kept our silence all the way down the path and I thanked everything in this fucking universe that I hadn't just done what I'd been considering doing to her beneath that table. A recording of that could have had me sent to prison and the stark reminder of that reality had me twitching with nerves.

Tatum unlocked the door as we arrived back at the repurposed church and the two of us moved inside. We found the others all sitting around the TV while Blake and Kyan destroyed zombies and Saint read something on his iPad.

"We have a problem," I announced as we moved over to join them.

"Oh yeah?" Blake asked, pausing the game to give us his full attention.

Saint had perked up like a Labrador who'd just spotted a tennis ball and I had to wonder if he thrived on bullshit or if he just needed a challenge to take his mind off of his own psychosis.

"We were in the library and I found this taped beneath the desk where Tatum always sits." I offered up my phone as evidence and Saint promptly snatched it from me before the others had a chance to do more than give it a cursory look.

"This cannot go on any longer," Saint growled, narrowing his eyes so that I could practically see the cogs turning in that cunning little brain of his.

"Well you're the one who's supposed to be coming up with an amazing plan to stop this asshole," I growled. "And they clearly still have their sights set on Tatum. We need to deal with it fast."

"I say we just go down to the dorms and start beating the shit out of people until we get a confession," Kyan said in a menacing tone. He reached for Tatum over the back of the couch and when she let him take her hand, he yanked her into his arms, dragging her over it and planting her in his lap.

"Kyan," she protested through a laugh as he placed her back to his front and wrapped his muscular arms around her.

"I want you close right now, baby, don't fight me on it," he growled in a low voice and she gave in to his demands with a half hearted eye roll that said she secretly loved his macho bullshit.

"Yeah. I think I'm with Kyan on this now," Blake said. "This is our girl they're fucking with."

"No," Saint snapped, pushing himself upright. "We've tried intimidation and it clearly isn't working. If we start beating the shit out of innocent idiots we will lose the support of the masses and that's unacceptable too."

"What then, asshole?" I demanded. "You always seem to be so full of all these bright ideas and amazing plans but none of it ever seems to come together. You claim to be able to take down your father, Royaume D'élite, this ninja/stalker motherfucker and no doubt countless other threats besides, and yet I don't see any evidence of you actually doing any of those things."

"Watch your tone with me," Saint snarled, shoving to his feet and getting in my face.

"Or what?" I sneered. I was already pissed over this whole situation and if he wanted to get in my face like a jumped up little asshole then I wasn't afraid to put him in his fucking box. We may have decided to work together now, but that didn't mean I was totally convinced that he didn't have the cruelty and vindictiveness of his father in him. It was just better the devil I knew.

"Guys, stop," Tatum demanded, scrambling out of Kyan's lap and forcing herself between us. "If we start fighting among ourselves then we're just playing into their hands. We need to figure out what to do about this."

Saint scowled at me over her head, but as she placed a hand on his chest, some of the fight drained from him.

"You need to stay here tonight," he said to her, the concern in his gaze clear. "It's not worth the risk of the stalker seeing the two of you sleeping up at the head's bungalow. If they really are following you then they could get all the evidence they need to fuck up both of your lives."

"Don't make out like this is about protecting me," I hissed, hating how much sense he was making and feeling like someone had just dumped a bucket of cold water over my head and iced my balls.

"But we already only get one night-" Tatum began and Saint huffed out a frustrated breath.

"Nash can stay here tonight instead of you going up there. With all of us here there's no reason for anyone to believe anything untoward is going on. The windows are covered and you can just sleep out here on the couch to get your night together."

"That's hardly the same," I muttered bitterly.

"Well I'm sorry if protecting our girl gets in the way of you getting your dick wet, Nash," Saint snarled. "But my priority is her safety and protecting this brotherhood. If the two of you go to your place then it puts you both at an unacceptable level of risk. So suck it up, buttercup. Life isn't fair but it sure as fuck is ours to rule over. And once we've sorted out this little stalker situation you can go right on back to fucking your student in private."

I took an angry step towards him, but Tatum turned to me, placing both hands on my chest and looking up at me imploringly.

"He might be saying it like an asshat, but he has a point," she said. "I can't be the reason your life is ruined, Nash."

I groaned in frustration as I was forced to give in, swiping a hand down my face and sending a silent apology to my blue balls as I was forced to give in.

"Fine," I ground out. "I'll just stay here tonight then."

"Good boy," Saint said patronisingly and Kyan chuckled like a dickwad.

"So how the fuck are we going to deal with this stalker once and for all?" Blake demanded and silence fell heavily between us as we all tried to think of a fresh approach to this shit show.

"I need time to think without you assholes ruining my process," Saint announced as if we'd all been yelling out suggestions at once and he couldn't cope with the noise even though we'd been doing nothing of the sort.

"Go freak some people out in your opera house then," Blake said, rolling his eyes like he'd expected this. "But if you haven't come up with anything by the time you come back then we go with Kyan's plan."

"Kyan doesn't have a plan," Saint hissed. "He just wants to beat the shit out of everyone like usual."

"Even so," Blake said firmly while Kyan chuckled like he was excited about the prospect of following through on that. I couldn't say I was totally against it myself.

"Fine," Saint ground out before turning and wheeling away from us.

He grabbed his phone and threw on a coat before striding to the door. Tatum chased after him and caught his hand.

"Be careful out there alone," she breathed. "And lock yourself in the piano room. And text us to let us know you got there okay-"

"Careful, siren, someone might start thinking you care about me," Saint mocked as he looked down at her, but the way his gaze devoured her told me that the feeling was more than mutual.

Tatum pushed forward, moving onto her tiptoes and placing a kiss on his cheek. "That would be crazy though, right?" she breathed as she moved back again and I could have sworn the smug bastard almost smirked.

"Utterly insane," he agreed.

He headed out and Tatum locked the door behind him, double checking it and making my gut tighten as I watched her. She was doing a good job of covering it up, but I could see she was afraid. And I didn't blame her. I was terrified too. The thought of there being some obsessed psychopath stalking her was keeping me up at night even more than my old demons.

The ache I held in my soul for my family was constant, but after all these years it had dulled somewhat. Besides, there was nothing I could do to save my mom or my brother now. But with Tatum I felt like there could be an axe hanging over her head at any moment, waiting to fall and rip all of us apart. I couldn't bear the idea of something happening to her like that.

So if that meant I had to sacrifice my time alone with her, then so be it.

I didn't have to like it to know it was the right thing to do.

Blake grabbed me a beer from the fridge and tossed it to me before handing more out to Tatum and Kyan and the four of us moved to sit before the TV together.

"So," Blake began, looking between everyone with a playful smirk on his face. "Are we allowed to talk about the elephant in the room yet or do we have to just keep on pretending that Tate isn't banging all three of us?"

"Christ," I muttered as Tatum shrieked at him and threw a cushion in his face.

"It's not like that!" she protested, wriggling back into the cushions as if they might save her from the gazes of the three predators who were all looking her way.

"What is it like then?" Blake teased as I opened my beer and took a long swig.

"It's like she's my wife but I let her fuck other guys because the jealousy makes our sex phenomenal," Kyan supplied, catching Tatum around the waist and hauling her into his lap with a grin. "Because I have to work twice as hard to fuck the memory of you guys out of her body."

I scoffed dismissively. "And how's that working out?" I asked, locking her blue eyes with mine. "Have you forgotten all about me just because that thug keeps pawing at you, princess?"

"I can't say I have," she said through a laugh as Kyan planted her ass right on top of his dick and started kissing her neck.

"Did Tate tell you about the two of us having her together down in the crypt?" Blake asked, grinning provocatively as I raised an eyebrow.

"I think that might have slipped her mind," I replied and Tatum squirmed.

"I'm just pointing out that you both being *here* doesn't have to mean you can't make good on those plans I'm sure you had for her at your place," Blake pushed with a dirty grin. "I'm cool with watching...or joining in."

"Do you think that maybe I should be consulted before you start planning a four way?" Tatum demanded, laughing like this was all some big joke to her but as my gaze hitched on her bare thighs, I found myself considering it.

"Tell me, princess," I said slowly, leaning forward and tucking a lock of that long, blonde hair behind her ear. "When you swore an oath to belong to all of us, was this your goal? Did you have fantasies about screwing three guys at once?"

"Or four," Kyan added with a dark chuckle. "Because I'm pretty sure she's got those naughty little eyes of hers on Saint, too."

"I'm not...that's not...*we're* not a thing. This is just...temporary," she spluttered but the doubt written all over her face said that she didn't even believe that herself.

"Wow, Tate, that hurts me," Blake teased. "Because I'm pretty sure you have all of us hooked and I'm definitely not going anywhere."

"You married me, baby, so you can't think that I'm not serious about you," Kyan murmured, moving his mouth to her throat as he held her tight against him and my heart beat a little faster as a soft moan escaped her.

"I wouldn't risk prison for just any girl," I added, watching as Kyan slid his hand onto her knee, shifting her skirt up her thighs as if there wasn't anyone else in the room. But as he raised his gaze to mine, I realised that wasn't right, he wasn't acting like no one else was here, he was putting on a show for the people who were.

"I didn't mean that I'm not serious about all of you," she backtracked. "It just doesn't seem possible that this could last."

"Why not?" Kyan asked, his fingers moving back and forth along her inner thigh while I watched.

"Are you planning to pick between us at some point?" Blake asked her curiously.

"No," she replied without hesitation. "I know it's a bit...unconventional," she said, biting her lip. "But I don't want to pick. I like what we all have right now and if I get my way then that won't change any time soon. Or ever."

"Ever?" I asked, watching her own that statement with a flare of possessiveness in her eyes. "You want all of us to be involved in some kind of polyamorous relationship with you long term?"

"Technically I think it's called a reverse harem," Blake said with a chuckle. "When a queen claims a bunch of men for herself."

"Is that what you want, baby?" Kyan asked, reaching around her and taking hold of her throat as he made her tilt her head back to look up at him. "A harem of monsters to worship you."

"I can think of worse things," she teased and I couldn't help but laugh.

"So you want to be at our mercy?" Kyan added, dipping his voice low as his fingers flexed against her throat and a soft moan escaped her.

"Or maybe," she said slowly, reaching up to tug his hand away before standing in front of us. "I want you all as mine."

She laughed like this was all some joke and turned towards the kitchenette to get herself another drink, swaying her hips as she went.

All three of us watched her with hungry gazes before exchanging a look.

Blake lurched upright but I was just as fast as him and I shoved him back down into Kyan where they instantly started wrestling to be the first to get off the couch. While they had each other occupied, I vaulted the couch and ran for Tatum.

She squealed in alarm as she saw me coming, a hungry smile on my lips as she turned and bolted with a laugh.

But I wasn't letting her get away that easily. With a growl of longing, I darted after her, circling the dining table and almost catching her before she sprang away from me and raced for the stairs that led up to Saint's bedroom. But if she thought I'd be put off by the idea of running into the devil's territory then she was mistaken.

I took the stairs two at a time and tackled her as we reached the top of them, knocking her back onto his bed.

"Shit, Nash, Saint will freak out if we-"

I silenced her with a punishing kiss as I crushed her body beneath mine on the bed, hooking her legs around my waist and grinding my hard cock down against her clit.

She clawed at my shirt, tugging on the back of the material as I devoured her lips and ground our bodies together with a desperate need.

"Fuck, this is like watching a real life porno," Blake commented from somewhere way too close to us. "The naughty school girl getting punished by the coach."

"Shut the fuck up," I snarled as I reared back so that I could push her forest green blazer off and forget the fact that she was my damn student. "You lost so go wait downstairs like a good boy."

"Naw, I don't think that's how this is playing out," Kyan said from my right and the bed bounced beneath us as he moved onto it too.

I glanced at him, already shirtless and moving closer to us so that he could steal my girl's attention from me. He caught her jaw in his hand and the ring he'd tattooed onto his finger in place of a wedding band caught my attention as he kissed her hard and demandingly.

My hesitation gave Blake a chance to move onto the bed on our other side and I raised my eyebrows as he began to unbutton Tatum's shirt for her.

Jealousy rose its ugly head in me as Tatum writhed between the two of them and I was forgotten where I knelt between her tanned thighs. But fuck that. If they wanted to fight a battle for her attention then I'd more than win it from them.

I shifted back as Blake peeled her shirt off, my fingers hooking around the waistband of her plaid green and black skirt as I tugged it down and she lifted her hips to let me do it.

Within moments she was laying before us in nothing but her black underwear and long school socks while Kyan continued to kiss her like he fucking owned her. But he was about to learn a lesson in how to kiss a girl like you owned her. And it had nothing to do with her mouth.

Blake moved his lips to Tatum's breast, tugging it free of her bra as he took her nipple into his mouth and she moaned in encouragement as her hips bucked with need.

I dropped my hand between her thighs, leaning back so that I could watch the way the others were touching her and the way her toned body writhed between them as I gently traced my fingers down the centre of her panties.

She was so wet that she'd soaked them through and I groaned with need as I slid my fingers around the side of them, tugging the material back so that I could push two fingers straight inside her.

Tatum cried out against Kyan's lips and he chuckled as he moved his hand down to meet with mine, taking control of her clit as he pushed his fingers beneath the waistband of her panties. I drove my fingers in and out of her, curving them and thrusting them deep to hit her G spot with every pump of my hand.

Blake was tugging on the nipple which wasn't in his mouth with his fingers and somehow the three of us found the perfect rhythm together to get her coming for us spectacularly within moments.

"Fuck," she panted, her head falling back against the pillows as she looked between us like she thought we might be done there, but I was barely even getting started.

I smiled at her, tugging my shirt off and tossing it aside then holding her gaze as I dipped my head between her thighs and tugged her panties off for her.

Kyan shifted his attention to kissing her neck as he took her hand in his, threading their fingers together and pushing it down onto the mattress just as my mouth made it to her centre.

She cried out as I lapped at her tingling clit, taking advantage of the orgasm we'd already given her as I circled my tongue against her, tasting her, teasing her, owning her.

I kept moving my tongue in that same pattern, loving the way her hips bucked up to meet me until she was grinding herself against me, fucking my mouth and panting my name so that there was no question as to which one of us had her attention now.

My dick strained with the desperate urge to take more from her and as she reared up off of the bed, coming once more with a scream of ecstasy, I quickly forgot any reasons I may have had to hold back.

I moved off of her for a moment, dropping my sweatpants and boxers so that my cock leapt free, hard and ready for her. Tatum licked her lips as the others stayed either side of her, kissing her neck and toying with her tits so that she moaned and panted, her legs spread wide for me and the pleading look in her eyes saying she needed this just as much as I did.

I moved on top of her and my cock instantly found its place against her opening, the slick wetness of her desire urging me on as I thrust inside her with one hard grind of my hips.

Her legs locked around my waist and I groaned as I began to move inside her, not even caring as my shoulders hit Blake and Kyan's with each thrust because the way she was screaming for us had all of my attention.

I fucked her hard and urgently, dominating her body as I kissed her with a savagery that let her know how jealous this was making me and wanting her to admit that I was the one who was possessing her now.

"Roll over, asshole," Kyan demanded, gripping my shoulder and tugging to make me do it.

I cursed him as I was forced to slow my pace but as I pulled back to glare at him, I found his attention fully fixed on Tatum beneath me.

"You want more, don't you baby?" he asked her and her eyes blazed at the idea of that before she nodded her head in agreement.

I didn't need any more encouragement than that, rolling onto my back and tugging her over too so that she could ride me and I could watch her perfect tits bounce. One of the others must have stripped her bra off of her and the fact that I didn't know who kind of pissed me off. But I definitely wasn't complaining about the view as she placed her hands on my chest and fucked me with a moan of pleasure.

Blake seemed to have disappeared and for a few blissful moments it was just me and my girl as Kyan stepped back and dropped his pants.

Tatum turned her head to look at him as he fisted his cock in his hand and he smirked at her as he toyed with himself while watching us. It should have pissed me off, but something about it was just really fucking hot, knowing that someone could see us doing this, that they liked it. I gripped Tatum's hips and guided her up and down my shaft until she was screaming with every slam of my dick into her.

Blake reappeared just as I was sure she was going to come for me again and he grinned as he dropped his pants and moved onto the bed behind her, kissing her neck and making her arch back into him.

"Slow down a moment, sweetheart," he breathed in Tatum's ear and his gaze shifted to me as I gave in to what he wanted and slowed my pace.

Blake pushed her shoulders so that she leaned down over me, bending forward and lifting her ass while keeping our bodies joined. A curtain of blonde hair tumbled around us and for a moment it was just me and her again as I kissed her softly, our heavy breaths mingling.

Something hit the bed beside me and I spotted the bottle of lube just as Tatum gasped at something Blake was doing behind her. But before I could question what that was, her grip on my shoulders tightened and her pussy clamped around my cock forcefully enough to make me groan.

The tightness only intensified as he drove his dick inside her ass and Tatum panted as she clung to me, taking him in until he growled with satisfaction and I could feel the press of his body behind hers bearing down on me.

"Look at you, baby," Kyan purred in appreciation as the three of us slowly began to move as one.

Blake led the movement as he rocked his hips, driving himself deep into her so that I could feel it through the thin wall of flesh dividing the two of us. She was so tight around me that I had to fight against the urge to come already as I found a rhythm with him and we began moving faster.

Tatum cried out as we fucked her together, her body pinned between us as her nails bit into my chest hard enough to draw blood. But the look of intense pleasure on her face was so fucking hot that I didn't care about that. All I wanted was to see how far we could push her, how much she could take.

We upped our pace and Kyan moved back onto the bed with us, catching her jaw and turning her head so that she could kiss him while we fucked her and he continued to pump his cock with his own hand. Tatum reached for him, taking over the job he'd begun and working to pleasure him too even as her pussy squeezed and tightened around me and she came for us once more. Blake cursed as he slammed into her and the way her body clenched had both of us finishing with her.

I groaned as I came inside her, the weight of her and Blake's bodies falling on top of me for several long seconds as we all collapsed into a tangled mess of ecstasy.

Blake drew back first, pulling out of her and moving to lean back against the pillows with a huge grin on his face and before I could do anything else, Kyan was pulling Tatum away from me.

"Do you trust me, baby?" he asked her as he lifted her from the bed and she wound her arms around his neck.

"Always," she replied, her legs coiling around his waist as he kissed her hard and hungrily like he was trying to replace the memories of what me and Blake had just done to her with fresh ones of him.

As their kiss deepened, Tatum's hands moved down his body and he groaned against her lips, but there was something in the tension in his shoulders as she touched him that made me frown.

He suddenly dropped her back onto the bed in front of me, flipping her over so that she was face down and slapping her ass so hard that it instantly left a hand print on her ass cheek. She moaned so loudly that it was more than clear that she liked it and when he pushed his cock into her, she cried out in pleasure.

Kyan growled as he leaned forward, wrapping his hand around her throat and tugging her up onto her knees as he squeezed tight enough to make her gasp and began fucking her with the same savagery he used when fighting.

It was rough and brutal and angry but the way she moaned as she took his cock, her tits bouncing with every thrust was getting me hard again already.

Blake shifted forward and took one of her pert nipples into his mouth before sliding his fingers onto her clit, using the momentum of Kyan's thrusts to work her up into a frenzy.

Her eyes were on me as the two of them took control of her and I couldn't help but want in on more of it, of her, of this goddess amongst us who had us all fighting to bring her to ruin.

"Nash," she gasped, reaching for me and licking her lips as Kyan's grip on her throat tightened and he fucked her even harder.

She was screaming for him and Blake and yet she still wanted more and I was more than ready to give it to her.

I got to my feet on the bed and moved towards her, my cock already hard again as I watched the perfection of this creature before me taking control of us all.

The moment I was close enough, her fingers curled around my dick and she rubbed her thumb over the bead of moisture there before sucking it into her mouth and giving me a lust filled look.

I didn't need any more encouragement than that and I stepped forward, letting her take my cock into her mouth as she moaned with pleasure.

Kyan fucked her harder and I gripped her hair as I drove my cock into her mouth, loving the way it felt as she moaned around my shaft, the vibrations making my whole body shiver with pleasure.

Her hand was on Blake's dick again and he groaned hungrily as he kept up his work on her clit and I watched our girl taking control of all of us like she really was our queen.

Somehow between the press of all of our bodies and the moans and screams of pleasure, I found myself coming again, spilling my cum down her throat as she rode out her own orgasm.

I drew back just as Kyan thrust into her one last time and growled his release too, using his grip on her throat to pull her hard against his chest. He let her go, slapping her ass one last time as she fell forward onto the mattress between me and Blake, her body trembling with the effects of what we'd just done to her.

The four of us all fell back onto the bed in a heap of panting, aching and seriously satisfied bodies, smirking like a bunch of smug motherfuckers.

"Ho-ly shit, princess," I muttered as I tugged her against me and pressed a kiss to her lips.

"You can say that again," she agreed breathily while Kyan laughed like an asshole.

When his laughter turned gleeful, I rolled until I could fix him in my gaze and arched a brow. "What?"

"Saint is going to lose his fucking mind when he sees what we've done to his bed," Kyan descended into hysterics and I found myself laughing too while Tatum groaned.

"And there was me thinking this night couldn't get much better," I said with a laugh.

As if on cue, the sound of the front door banging came from downstairs and Tatum gasped like a naughty kid about to get caught out breaking the rules.

"Cooey, sweetheart, we're waiting for you!" Kyan called out and Tatum squeaked in protest as he laughed loudly.

"Oh, shit," Blake groaned but he was smirking all the same and I had to say, I wasn't exactly sure how I was supposed to act in this situation. Was there a normal way to behave when you were caught out in someone's bed with two other naked dudes and a seriously satisfied girl? If there was, I didn't have time to figure it out because Saint's footsteps were thumping up the stairs and my dick was most definitely out.

The moment he reached the top of the staircase, he fell still and all four of us froze. There was a lingering moment where Saint's eyes just moved between all of the cocks on his bed and Tatum's state of thoroughly fucked. His jaw ticked, his eyes did this strange angry bugging out thing, a vein in his temple took on a life of its own, had kids and built itself a seven bed mansion because it was definitely there to stay, and Saint looked about ready to explode.

Not start yelling or freaking out, but actually explode, like I was expecting to be hit in the face with copious amounts of brain matter at any moment.

Then Kyan started laughing. Fuck, we all started laughing and I dragged Tatum into my arms so that she could bury her face against my chest and hide from the dark lord who had come to destroy us.

"At least we're going to die with smiles on our faces," I joked and she groaned again.

"Tatum," Saint growled and I looked back to find him standing at the foot of the bed seeming way too fucking calm as he fixed her in his gaze and beckoned with a single finger.

I held her tightly against me but she wriggled away, slipping down the bed between me and Blake before crawling over Kyan who was still laughing as he slapped her ass again on her way by. When she moved to stand before Saint, I reached out and grabbed one of the pillows, tossing it over my junk to make it seem like I was at least trying to appear apologetic for the mess we'd made of his bed.

Tatum bit her lip as Saint looked her up and down before reaching out to touch her.

His fingers brushed against her lips which were swollen from so many pleasure filled kisses, before trailing down to her throat where pink marks showed the position Kyan's fingers had maintained while he fucked her.

Tatum gasped as his fingertips shifted over the bite marks on her neck to a love bite on her left breast and her nipples hardened at the contact, her breath hitching.

I might have wanted to deny the idea of her feeling this way about Saint too, but her body was making the truth painfully obvious and for a moment, it looked like he might have been about to fulfil that desire flaring in her eyes and join us down here on his bed.

Instead of that, his calm mask stayed in place as he found finger marks on her hips and thighs before turning her around to inspect Kyan's handprints on her round ass.

Saint tugged Tatum's hair over her shoulder and leaned close behind her back so that he could speak into her ear.

"I should punish you for each and every one of the marks you let them place on your body in my bed," he growled and Blake bit down on his knuckles to hold back his amusement as we all waited for him to blow.

"That seems fair," Tatum breathed, shivering as her hardened nipples drew my attention and Saint pressed even closer to her.

"I will then," he said in a dark tone. "But not now. Now you can go and clean yourself up and think about what you've done. I'll make you suffer in suspense over how and when that punishment is coming. If you wanted my attention, siren, you really should have just asked for it."

"Maybe this *is* me asking for it," she murmured.

"Be careful what you wish for." He gave her a little push and she bit her lip, throwing the three of us an apologetic glance before heading off to the bathroom for a shower.

The moment the door closed behind her, Saint turned his icy gaze on us and Kyan fell apart laughing, cupping his hands behind his head and just owning the fact that he had his cock out in front of a man who looked more than tempted to rip it off.

Saint's gaze slid to me where I much more respectfully held a pillow over my junk and his eyes narrowed.

"Did you assume I would find the sight of your dick more offensive than the act of you rubbing it all over my pillow?" he asked in a dry tone and Blake burst into laughter too.

"Err," I couldn't quite come up with the appropriate response to that and I was really fighting the urge to start laughing in my mission to be at least a little bit apologetic for what we'd done, but it was damn hard to do.

"I found something outside that I need you all to look at," Saint said in a deadly serious tone, changing the subject abruptly. "I think someone's been trying to get down into the catacombs out there and I'm concerned that The Temple isn't secure."

"Shit," I gasped, shoving the pillow away from me as I got out of the bed, the mood sobering instantly as all three of us quickly tracked down our pants and tugged them back on again.

"When I get my hands on that fucking Justice Ninja, he's gonna wish I would kill him," Kyan snarled and Saint made a sound of agreement before leading us all downstairs.

He set a fast pace, kicking on his shoes and heading out into the dark, the three of us hurrying to follow him as he led the way around the back of the building into the shadows.

"There," he said, pointing at the base of the wall where the ground seemed a little uneven.

I moved forward, trying to get a look as I squinted against the darkness and he told us he was going to get a light.

"Does he mean this?" Blake asked, pointing out an area of the old brickwork that seemed to be crumbling around the mortar and Kyan shoved me aside as he tried to get a look.

I shoved him back, cursing the darkness as I failed to see anything serious enough to have made Saint think the stalker had been trying to break in here and turning to look for him with that damn light.

The moment I turned my head, a spray of ice cold water hit me square in the face and I yelled out as Saint turned the hose on the others too.

He quickly swung the hose back and forth drenching all of us with the freezing water before we had a chance to dive away from it and Kyan bellowed as he launched himself at him.

His shoulder caught Saint in the gut and the hose went flying as the two of them crashed into the mud in a heap of fists and curses.

Blake yelled out a battle cry as he launched himself into the fight too and I only hesitated a moment as they yelled for me to help them pin Saint down before I leapt into the fray as well.

He fought like a demon, kicking and punching as the four of us rolled through the mud until we were utterly covered and Kyan was the first to crack and start laughing.

He fell onto his back as Saint punched him once more before bursting into laughter too and the corners of my lips pulled up until I was gasping with laughter, laying amongst the three of them in the dirt.

"Fuck you guys," Saint cursed, swiping mud from his face as he tried to pull himself together.

"No thanks, brother," Kyan teased. "Tate already did a good job of that before you got here."

We started laughing again while Saint sporadically continued to curse us and I couldn't help but think as I lay there covered in mud, soaking wet with my body freshly bruised and my dick utterly satisfied that I might have actually found somewhere I belonged. The Night Keepers may have been a bunch of assholes with a severely dysfunctional moral compass, but somehow being among them felt right, like I'd found something I'd been searching for without ever even realising I was looking for it.

So maybe it was time I stopped trying to bullshit myself about the way I felt and just accept it. Tatum had called us her tribe before, and I was starting to realise that she was right. Down here in the dirt was where I belonged, and I was ready to accept that with all of my heart.

CHAPTER FORTY

We had a plan. The only plan that made any sense, but one that the Night Keepers weren't entirely happy about. I was going to be bait for the Justice Ninja and we'd lead them to a snare I'd set up in the woods. An honest to god snare that was good enough to catch a mountain lion thank you very much and I hadn't minded one bit when Saint's eyes had bugged out of his head while he'd watched me set it up. Or the way Kyan had suggested we go camping in the woods one time so that I could show him my wild side in action.

I just hoped that asshole was spying on me with his listening device tonight because I was hungry as hell for vengeance.

I sat in the library for a while, pretending to do work when really all I was doing was shooting messages to the guys and chewing my pen so hard that I cracked the plastic.

Saint seemed to be putting my punishment on ice until this was dealt with, but I couldn't help but expect him to spring an attack on me at any moment for defiling his bed with the other Night Keepers. I should have known better than that though. Saint didn't launch attacks with a battle cry, he snuck up behind you and slit your throat so you couldn't scream while he cleaved you apart piece by piece. So whatever his punishment was going to be, I knew I would never predict it. I just wished he'd get it over with so I could stop living in a state of anxiety.

Tatum:

Anyone else feeling *squid emoji* tonight?

Kyan:

Naw, baby, I'm getting real *octopus emoji* though. The Justice Ninja is gonna *onion emoji* while I ram a *pine tree emoji* up his *peach emoji* tonight.

Saint:

I am growing weary of these emoticon conversations. I will likely remove the emoticon keyboards from your phones soon.

Blake:

Who says emoticon??

Saint:

A man with good breeding. Something you would know little about, Bowman.

Blake:

Woah. Did you just have a go at my dead mother?

Saint Memphis is typing

Kyan:

Can't believe you'd go at his dead mom like that bro. That's not something I *can even *squid emoji* about.*

Tatum:

I think Saint was just being *clown emoji*

Saint:

*I am incapable of guilt and Blake is incapable of being offended. So I will
not fall for your tomfoolery.*

P.S.

*Cease and desist with the emoticons or I shall punish you all for them
henceforth.*

Nash:

I bet you love this emoji though Saint >> *list emoji*

Tatum:

*Haha oh yes! There's a whole section for stationary. Saint I really want your
protractor emoji in my *wastepaper basket emoji**

Blake:

shocked emoji

Kyan:

Holy fuck.

Saint Memphis is typing

Nash:

Jesus princess…

Saint:

Give me time to decipher the meaning of this and I shall give you my answer, Tatum.

Tatum:

Okay…
(Psst guys did I just offer Saint anal?)

Kyan:

EXTREME ANAL

Tatum:

What makes it extreme???

Blake:

You don't wanna know, Cinders.

Tatum:

Yes I do!!

Saint:

I need all the details before I make my decision.

Tatum:

Haha you're joking right?

Saint:

I never joke. Expect my answer soon.

Kyan:

Don't worry, baby, he doesn't have the *squid emoji* to go through with it. I *however…*

Nash:

*I won't let them go near your *wastepaper basket emoji* princess.*

Blake:

Only because you'll be too busy filling it yourself with your coach whistle.

Nash:

D minus for a shitty joke badly delivered, Bowman.

Tatum:

You guys are distracting me from important Justice Ninja mission stuff and things…

Kyan:

Turn your earpiece on.

Tatum:

No chance pervert.

The guys started sending me filthier and filthier messages to distract me more and I laughed as I continued pretending to work on an assignment.

After a while, our text chat stopped and I started to get anxious about our plans. I wished I could remember more of the night I'd been drugged. It was all so hazy, the last thing I recalled was sitting here, then falling to the floor as I dropped my phone. Beyond that, there were just snippets of the dark woods, a white mask, fire and then Blake pulling me into his arms.

You're dead meat tonight, Ninja.

At a quarter to ten, I subtly turned on my earpiece. The other guys would all be wearing them too so we could stay in contact tonight. It was like a legit undercover operation.

Kyan called my phone on cue and I answered, ready to act my heart out. "Hey."

"Hey baby, how wet are you for me right now?"

I stifled a laugh and gave my rehearsed answer. "Well that's okay, I'll just walk back on my own tonight."

"God, I wanna stick it in you so hard and deep, you'll feel me tickle your throat," Kyan growled and Saint cursed him through the earpiece.

Jesus fucking Christ. Could he ever behave in life or death situations? But alright, maybe I kinda loved his brand of crazy. "Honestly, I don't mind walking back alone. I'll be quick and I'll call you as soon as I get in."

"Yeah and when you get here you're gonna get on your knees and suck your husband's cock like a good wifey," he purred before bursting out laughing.

"I'll see you soon," I gritted out, swallowing my amusement at Blake cracking up in my ear and Monroe cursing him out.

I killed the call, getting to my feet and taking a steadying breath as I packed my things away.

The plan was simple. The guys would be in their hiding spots now, watching and waiting from the trees. So I just had to walk back to The Temple, take my sweet time and hope for the justice bastard to show up. Then I'd turn tail and lead them to my trap and whoosh, they'd be launched skyward, dangling by one ankle in prime position to face the wrath of my tribe. *You shouldn't have messed with me and my Night Keepers, asshole.*

I put the backpack on – not my usual bag choice - which was heavy as shit because the guys had insisted I carry a ten kilo barbell weight in it from the gym to protect me from any arrows flying at me from behind tonight. It was sweet as shit, so I wasn't exactly complaining. But I'd had to put my foot down when they'd all fallen into a detailed discussion of how they could strap one to my chest under my clothes without it being noticeable. Suffice to say, they weren't happy about my role in this plan tonight, but they also knew it was the only logical way to catch the creep. A fact Saint had begrudgingly backed me on. It had been his plan in the first place, only he'd suggested putting a blonde wig on an Unspeakable and setting the bow-and-arrow-wielding-shitbag on them instead. No matter how much the Unspeakables had done, I simply wasn't going to allow that. Besides, this was *my* fight. And I was glad to be at the heart of it. I wanted to be there when we ripped that mask from their face, to stare into the eyes of my enemy and watch as my men made them scream. I might even partake in a little scream-causing of my own if the notion took me.

"Ready?" Saint asked in my ear.

"Yep," I murmured as I weaved through the stacks towards the exit. "Let's take this motherfucker down."

CHAPTER FORTY ONE

All was quiet between the trees as I waited beneath the shadow of a towering pine, my gaze fixed on the path far below and my bat held loosely in my fist.

It was cold tonight, the warmer days not making much difference to the temperature once the sun went down and my breath still fogged before me a little as I waited. I'd chosen a hoodie with the sleeves cut off so that I could move more easily in it when the time came to run but as a shiver ran along my skin, I was doubting the sense of that decision. Still, the way Tatum's eyes had heated when she'd seen me in it made me think it was worth the sacrifice. And I'd gladly wrap her up tightly in my tattooed arms if that was what she wanted at the end of the night.

But for now, my baby was on the hunt.

I smirked to myself at the thought of that, my muscles twitching with the desire to go prowling through the trees and track down the fucking Justice Ninja myself. But I could admit that when it came to planning things like this out, I tended to be more inclined towards charging in and fucking shit up.

Saint was the one with the patience for this level of cunning and secrecy. And after trying to catch this motherfucker in every conceivable way and failing, I was willing to bet that being a sneaky fuck was more likely to work than anything I could have come up with.

"She's just leaving the library," Monroe's voice came over the earpiece Saint had given me and I twisted the bat in my hand in a slow circle as I kept my gaze on the path between the trees ahead of me.

I was hiding up on the ridge, disguised in the shadows, but I had a pretty clear view of the path and lake beyond. If anyone down there dared to move, I'd see them.

"Direction?" Saint hissed. Each of us were located in the trees along the paths surrounding the library, waiting in the dark in every direction so that there was no chance of the bastard we were hunting escaping us.

"Towards The Temple, obviously," Monroe shot back.

"So you meant to say, *east,*" Saint growled.

"Dick off."

I snorted a laugh and kept watching the path beyond my hiding place. I was to the west of the library, overlooking the path which led down to Sycamore Beach, waiting to see if anyone would appear from this direction. I'd give it a few minutes to make sure they didn't and then I'd be stalking my girl through the trees. I didn't know why the idea of that seemed hot when I was the one doing it, but it probably had something to do with the fact that I was a bit fucked up inside.

Both Saint and Blake were positioned on either side of the path further around the lake in the direction Tatum would be heading. Saint had chosen to stay within view of Beech and Hazel Houses so that he could see anyone who left the dorms - which we were guessing they would once they'd overheard Tatum announce that she was leaving the library alone.

But so far, none of the students who had left had caught his attention. Though I was sure that he would be taking down names as each of them exited and they'd all be having a fun interrogation with him tomorrow if this didn't pan out.

"I see her," Blake said in a low voice and my heart began to pound more solidly in my chest as I started to move.

If Tatum had already made it to his position beyond the Willow Boathouse, then there wasn't much chance of me seeing anyone way back here.

I worked to keep my footsteps silent as I moved between the trees, one eye on the path that ran before the water as I headed on.

It was creepy out here at night. Like all the long dead legends which we'd taken the time to learn actually might have had an ounce of truth to them. If I let my imagination run away with me, I could almost feel the cold chill of the Night People's breath along the back of my neck, the touch of a bony finger running down my spine.

Good thing I wasn't a superstitious fucker, or I'd probably have been crapping my pants.

Besides, I'd embodied one of those legends, marked my flesh with their design and taken on everything that came with that fully. If there were any monsters lurking out here in the dark, then I was just keeping company with my own kind. And I doubted many of them would have a soul as brutal and tainted as mine anyway.

I definitely doubted any of them felt the pull of bloodlust as keenly as I did. Because that was what I was aching for tonight. It was why my muscles were tight and my adrenaline was pumping. I wanted to wet my hands in blood and make someone pay for their crimes. I needed to end this once and for all. To find the person who had been coming after our girl and destroy them so thoroughly that I knew they'd never be the same again.

"Something just moved in the trees ahead of me," Monroe hissed and I stilled for a moment as I scowled out into the dark.

If he hadn't started following Tatum yet then I should be coming up on his position, so if there was anything to see here then there was a good chance I'd spot it too.

"Is it me?" I murmured when I failed to spot anything and started walking again.

"Shit, I think it is," he admitted and I snorted a laugh as Blake sniggered down the earpiece.

"Quit dicking around," Saint growled. "Blake have you still got eyes on our girl?"

"I'm on her tail," he confirmed. "She's coming up on Beech House now."

"Okay, I see her too," Saint said and everything went silent again as the two of them moved after her, watching, waiting.

A soft rustle of leaves had me raising my bat, but as I recognised Monroe's broad form in the dim moonlight, I lowered it again.

"Fancy seeing you here, baby," I teased.

"If you're looking for a kiss, you're going to have to take me on that moonlit stroll you promised first. I'm a good girl," he joked right back, pushing an imaginary pair of tits up at me suggestively.

"Naw, sweet thing, that's not my style. I'm a married man these days," I breathed as we started walking together.

"Have I mentioned that I hate you for that?" he murmured and I chuckled low in my throat.

"Have I mentioned how much I love it?" I shot back.

"Shit, I think they're here," Blake's urgent voice interrupted us and we both shut the fuck up instantly.

"Where?" Saint hissed. "I still have eyes on her from the west of the path closing in on Aspen Halls and I can't see anything."

"I have a clear view of the path over the ridge," Blake whispered back. "And I swear there's someone in the trees near the auditorium."

"Fuck," I growled, exchanging a look with Monroe and the two of us started moving faster. If they were that far ahead of us then we didn't need to worry about staying quiet.

"Guys..." Tatum muttered and hearing her voice for the first time made a knot of tension release inside of me. She'd been keeping quiet to make sure she didn't draw attention but that was probably less important now. "I really hope you're ready for this because I'm pretty sure he has a bow again and-" She cut herself off with a shriek of fright and I cursed as I upped my pace and Saint began barking orders.

I hardly listened to any of what he was saying though, because only one thing mattered right now, and that was getting to our girl.

CHAPTER FORTY TWO

I gazed into the eyes of my nightmare, that flaming arrow raised, pointing directly at my face.

I bared my teeth in a snarl before turning on my heel as I raced away from him. His footsteps pounded behind me as I'd hoped, but that didn't save me from the cloying fear as a flaming arrow whistled past my ear. *Fuck!*

I tore back down the path, my breaths coming unevenly as I weaved left and right to evade any arrows that came my way.

"We're coming, Cinders," Blake promised.

"Keep going, princess," Monroe growled, anxiety filling his voice as he raced to meet us.

My running shoes pounded across the path as I fled, my pulse jackhammering as I pushed myself as fast as possible. I sprinted past the dorms, toward the track that led to the trap I'd laid before I veered off the path and up into the trees to my left.

"We're coming, sweetheart," Blake growled in my ear as the Justice Ninja's footsteps chased after me into the trees. I darted between the boughs as another arrow flew through the air, the arc of fire in my periphery making my heart jerk out of rhythm.

"Holy shit," I cursed.

"Just keep going. Don't stop," Saint growled in my earpiece. "I've got eyes on the fucker," he added and relief swept through me as I fought the urge to look over my shoulder.

Keep running. Never stop. Don't look back.

My father's words ran through my head. I'd played this game with him before, pretending to be hunted in the woods. He'd always been so fast and I'd had to learn how to lose him in the dark. But this time, I needed my pursuer to see me, needed him to follow me to my own trap. Because he hadn't realised that he wasn't the hunter in this situation, *I* was.

"We're right on his heels," Blake growled, determination lacing his face.

"Herd that fucker to the snare," Kyan encouraged.

"Hurry up," Monroe urged.

"I'm coming at him from the left at a forty five degree angle, but Blake will likely reach him first," Saint said, ever fucking accurate. Like it mattered what specific angle he was arriving at.

I crested the hill, my arms pumping back and forth either side of me as I led my enemy towards my trap. It wasn't far now.

"Run motherfucker!" Blake roared and a yelp of fear sounded somewhere behind me as the Justice Ninja increased his pace. That yelp told me it was a guy for sure and a dark and twisted smile pulled at my lips as I pictured ripping that mask off in the next few moments.

Another arrow sailed past me, this one so close it ruffled my hair.

"Stay back or I'll kill her!" the Ninja cried to Saint and Blake.

"You have to aim straight first, asshole!" I shouted back with a manic laugh, tearing on as I drew him closer and closer to his downfall.

Another arrow whipped past my ear and I stifled a scream, trying to stay in control. Flames blurred in the corner of my vision and the arrow embedded in a trunk just as I zig-zagged past it.

"I'm gonna make him bleed, baby," Kyan purred.

My smile grew wider at his words and adrenaline coursed into my veins. "We'll make him bleed together."

Monroe

CHAPTER FORTY THREE

I charged through the trees with Kyan at my side, the two of us making zero effort to hide our approach as we raced to meet the others and take down this stalking ninja motherfucker once and for all.

I was so beyond done with worrying about Tatum every time she wasn't with me, afraid of what this obsessed maniac might try and pull next and I was more than ready to make them pay for every moment of fear and pain they'd caused her. Hell, I'd happily beat the shit out of him for the photos he'd taken of her in her most private moments alone.

Fuck the fact that my job was to look after the little shits who occupied this school. I was meant to protect them first and foremost and removing a predator from their midst was a damn good way to do that in my books. Besides, ever since Tatum Rivers had wound her way into my heart, I'd been filled with the overwhelming urge to protect her from all of the shit in this world. And if there was one piece of shit I wanted to stamp beneath my heel more than any other right now, it was the motherfucker who had been stalking her in the shadows.

"Almost there," Tatum growled, her voice edged with triumph as she led the Ninja closer to the trap she'd set for him.

"We're coming, baby," Kyan purred, swinging his bat in anticipation and decapitating a sapling as we charged past it.

The ground was sloping upwards beneath our feet and just beyond the top of the ridge we were climbing, we should be able to see the others if they were as close as Tatum thought.

"Fuck," Blake cursed over the earpiece just as Saint snarled, "Dammit!"

"What?" I barked at the same time as Kyan, racing up the hill even faster.

"He's made a break for it," Tatum cursed. "He isn't on track for the snare anymore. But he's running your way."

"He's a dead man walking," Kyan promised just as movement caught my eye down the hill to our right.

I pointed as I spotted a flash of white as the Ninja looked back over their shoulder and revealed his mask to the moonlight.

"There!" I yelled and Kyan howled with excitement as he spotted our target too.

"You'd better run fast, asshole!" he hollered, a wild laugh bursting from his lips as the Ninja turned and fled.

"We're coming," Saint growled.

"No need," I replied cockily, though I knew they wouldn't give up the chase that easily.

"This kill is mine," Kyan said excitedly and I shook my head in denial as I upped my pace, using the downward slope of the hill to aid my speed as I managed to pull ahead.

"How many times have I told you to up your cardio training?" I called back tauntingly as I raced on and Kyan cursed me colourfully.

"He's turning back towards the path," Saint growled. "Don't let him get away."

A moment after he said it, the Ninja turned towards the path and I had to wonder how the fuck he'd known that that would happen before it had. But now wasn't the moment to question Saint's psycho skills, now was the time to find out just how fast I could run.

"You'd better pray we don't catch you!" I yelled at the top of my lungs as I sped between the trees, racing downhill with all the speed of an avenging angel.

"Fuck, don't let him get away," Tatum's voice in my ear urged me on and I smiled savagely.

"No chance in hell of that, princess. I've got him now," I swore to her and with a burst of adrenaline through my limbs, I leapt out onto the path, skidding as my muddy sneakers fought for purchase before I took off again.

The Ninja was racing down the path towards Sycamore Beach and a feral smile tugged at my lips as I imagined us catching him right in front of the sacred stone. If that wasn't a perfect sacrifice to the Night People, then I didn't know what would be.

"When I catch you, I'm gonna ram this bat so far up your ass that you'll be tasting your own shit!" Kyan yelled from a few paces behind me and a wild laugh tore from my lips as the Ninja raced on, but we were gaining on him and as he threw a look over his shoulder, the panicked look in his eyes beneath the white mask said he knew it.

"And that'll be the nicest thing we do to you!" I added.

My feet pounded along the path and I raced on with victory sailing through my limbs and the scent of vengeance in the air. Tonight, the so-called Justice Ninja would get a taste of the justice they sought so desperately, and I was more than looking forward to serving it out.

CHAPTER FORTY FOUR

I swore between my teeth as I ran on, furious that that bastard had evaded my snare. My perfect fucking snare.

But Saint's damn forty five degree angle paid off as he veered after the Ninja. "I'm gonna cut him off!" he bellowed, his voice reverberating through the earpiece.

Blake turned tail too and I slowed my pace as they managed to loop around him and herd the asshole back in behind me. I let out a scream which was only half feigned as the Ninja aimed another flaming arrow at me and I took off into the trees, unsure where to lead him now and just praying Blake or Saint would catch him before one of those arrows hit its target.

Sweat was beading on my brow and the weight of the plate on my back was taking its toll as I had to push myself to my limits and keep darting left and right between the trees to avoid the arrows. I counted eight shots so far and there was only ten in a standard quiver so he was almost out. The click of his lighter said he was igniting the next arrow and my heart lurched as I realised we had only a small moment to act.

"He's lighting another one," I told the guys.

"I'm right on him," Blake snarled and I heard his voice behind me as well as in my ear.

I dove behind a tree just as the Ninja released the flaming arrow and it whistled off into the woodland. He shouted out in pain as the weight of Blake's body took him to the ground.

"Yes!" Saint cried and I stepped out from behind the tree, laughing excitedly and jumping up and down as I saw the Ninja pinned beneath Blake as he beat the hell out of him.

Kyan and Monroe were shouting something to each other and clearly weren't getting the message.

"I got him," Blake growled triumphantly, punching the guy in the kidney as he sat back on his legs, dragging the bow off his body with the quiver before tossing them out of reach.

"Who is it?" I demanded.

My heart beat wildly as Blake shifted, forcing the Ninja to roll between his legs, the guy shaking as he gazed up at Blake through his white mask. Saint strode forward like the grim reaper and I swear I could hear bells tolling as he reached down and tore the mask from his face.

I gasped as I recognised the culprit. *"Bait,"* I hissed, striding forward with anger raging through my core. I kicked him in the ribs, unleashing my fury on him and he screamed like an infant, trying to curl in on himself, but Blake grabbed his arms and pinned them down in the mud.

"Looks like we caught ourselves a dirty little rat," Blake spat in his face.

"Get off me!" Bait cried.

"You took those pictures," I hissed. "Didn't you?"

"Fuck you!" Bait spat and my upper lip peeled back as he started laughing like he'd won something.

Saint unbuttoned his shirt cuffs, slowly rolling up his sleeves with a deadly look in his eyes that said Bait was about to be in a world of pain.

Bait looked from me to Blake, to Saint and fury flared through his expression. "You think you're the real power in this school, but who's the one who's been making your girl afraid lately? Who's had her frightened and shaking and-"

Blake punched him hard in the jaw and Saint fell on him too, both of them going full savage as they laid into him like wolves tearing into a carcass.

A sick satisfaction washed through me as I watched, soaking in our combined vengeance as Saint threw a rib-cracking punch into Bait's gut before laughing like a beast.

"What's going on?" Monroe asked in my ear, sounding out of breath.

"We caught him. It's Bait. And he's right here getting what he deserves," I hissed.

"Can't be, baby, we're hot on his heels," Kyan said, clearly still running and I frowned.

"That can't be right..." A vision from the night I'd been drugged snagged in my mind and I gasped as I realised the truth. "Oh shit. There's two of them," I told Blake and Saint, but they weren't listening, too busy making Bait scream as they punched and punched.

"Fuck - look! He's circled back around us onto the main path," Monroe panted, clearly talking to Kyan, but that meant I was ahead of them.

"I'll cut him off!" I told them, tearing away from the others and leaving them pulverising Bait, teaching him a lesson for all the wrongs he'd dealt us.

I raced down the hill through the trees as fast as I could, needing to get to the path.

"Shit," Kyan snarled, but didn't give any more explanation than that so I continued on, the hill dropping away steeply beneath my feet.

I broke through the trees at last, stumbling to a halt on the main path under the light of a lamp and gazing in the direction of the beach.

"Where are you?" I asked, pressing my finger into my ear to try and hear them better as they grunted and cursed.

"They've gone back into the trees, but I think they're heading for

Willow Boathouse," Kyan growled.

I listened for them, hearing cracking twigs and heavy footfalls as the chase headed deeper into the forest.

"For fuck's sake!" Monroe barked and I opened my mouth to respond just as hands grabbed me from behind and an ice cold needle jammed into my neck, making fear spike through me like a lightning bolt.

The drug acted so fast that I was already falling towards the ground, darkness swooping in on me as swiftly as death and a scream faded away on my lips.

CHAPTER FORTY FIVE

"**I**'m going to rip you apart piece by piece, you spineless motherfucker!" I roared, my voice echoing out over the lake as I charged through the trees, following the fucking Justice Ninja as they sped towards the water.

The only thing back in that direction was the boathouse and I knew we'd catch them before they made it that far.

"You still on your way, baby?" I called, glancing over my shoulder to see if I might spot her as she ran to meet us. Not that I was seriously turned on by the idea of hunting down this prey with my girl by my side or anything, but what could I say? I was an animal and I wanted my mate by my side when I went in for the kill.

Tatum didn't reply but I couldn't waste any more time looking back for her as the prey in question ducked to the right, charging straight for the water instead of the boathouse.

"Where the fuck is he going?" Monroe shouted as he darted across my path, his brow furrowed as he sprinted after them.

We were so fucking close to catching them, but we'd lost a few precious seconds when he'd first doubled back into the trees and it had given him the chance to pull ahead again. Couple that with the fact that the fucking clouds had deepened and we could hardly see for shit down here in the woods.

"No!" Monroe yelled, bursting forward and my heart leapt at the pure rage in his voice a moment before I spotted the cause for it.

The cloaked figure ahead of us had just vaulted over the rocks lining the edge of the water and was already half way out to a speedboat moored a few feet from the shore.

"Get him!" I roared as I raced down the last few feet of the bank, before leaping over the rocks and landing knee deep in the water just behind Nash.

The Justice Ninja looked up at us just as the roar of the speedboat's engine ripped through the night and he hastily hoisted the anchor up out of the water.

I ran forward with my heart pounding to the beat of my fury as he lurched for the controls and our hopes of catching him were ripped away from us.

"Stop!" I bellowed, charging further into the lake even as the boat wheeled about and he pulled the throttle back.

A wave of water crashed over us as the powerful engine picked up speed and within moments, our quarry was lost.

"For the love of fuck!" I yelled, swinging my baseball bat down into the water as hard as I could and sending another huge spray of water up over myself.

"I don't fucking believe it," Monroe groaned, bracing his hands on his knees as he leaned forward to catch his breath, watching the boat speed away and leaving us to rot on the water's edge.

"That's one lucky son of a bitch," I snarled, glancing to my left where the Willow Boathouse stood further along the water, but it was no use.

The speedboat was already halfway across the water and by the time we managed to get into another vessel, they'd be moored up somewhere on the opposite side of the lake and long gone.

"Fuck," I cursed again, kicking the water angrily as I turned away from the sickening sight of that boat retreating and started wading back to the shore with Monroe at my side. "I'm sorry, baby, they got away in a fucking boat. We'll just have to make Bait squeal to find out who his little friend is."

Tatum didn't reply but Saint's curses reached me clearly enough.

"You don't need to lay into us, we fucking get it," Monroe snapped. "How were we supposed to know they had a speedboat moored up? Just get Bait talking and we can go round them up anyway."

"Bait isn't in much shape to talk right now," Blake said, sounding half amused and a flash of jealousy poured through me at the knowledge that he'd been able to beat the shit out of someone tonight when I hadn't.

"Fuck my life," I muttered. "Where are you at, baby? I need some consoling between your thighs."

"Shut the fuck up, asshole," Saint growled. "Come on, siren, tell us where you've got to."

Silence followed as we all waited for her response and I clambered back out of the water with Nash at my side.

"Princess?" he asked when the silence seemed to stretch too long.

"Maybe her earpiece is broken?" Blake suggested.

"Those are military grade bits of tech," Saint snarled. "They're the best money can buy and practically indestructible. Civilians shouldn't even have them. So no, I don't think it's broken."

"Then maybe it fell out?" I suggested as we began to walk up the hill towards the path.

I could practically hear Saint grinding his teeth at that insinuation and I chuckled darkly, but a shiver of unease ran down my spine all the same.

"Tatum Roscoe!" I yelled at the top of my voice, cupping my hands around my mouth to make sure the sound carried far and wide. "Get your fine ass down here so I can get my hands on it."

"Real classy, asshole," Monroe muttered and I wanted to wink at him and make some remark about the two of us tag teaming her to make ourselves feel better, but the fact that there was still no reply from her had me on edge.

"You don't think there could have been three of those Ninja assholes, do you?" Blake asked cautiously, but before I could answer that, Saint hissed at all of us to shut up and listen.

I didn't know what I was supposed to be listening for until I realised that I could hear footsteps crunching on gravel over the earpiece.

"Are either of you walking on a gravel path?" Saint hissed and Monroe and I grunted a no as we stood silently beneath the trees.

A shiver of dread shifted beneath my flesh as we stood there and the footsteps continued before the sound of a soft, male curse came next.

"What the fuck?" Blake breathed but Saint shushed him aggressively.

"Tatum?" I demanded forcefully, not giving a shit if Saint wanted to listen in on whatever the fuck was happening on that earpiece because I had all the information I needed. There was only one place on campus with that much gravel and that was up by the main gates.

When she still didn't respond, I took off running and Monroe was right beside me as we ran for the pathway and then raced up it towards Aspen Halls.

As something metallic clanged over the earpiece, I yelled Tatum's name again but she still didn't answer me.

My heart thundered with panic so fiercely that it felt like it might crack my ribs with its ferocity. I didn't know what the hell was happening, only that it didn't feel right one fucking bit.

Monroe was yelling for her too and as we charged up the path, Saint and Blake appeared from the trees, the four of us sprinting for Aspen Halls and the only small clue we had as to where our girl was.

The moon slipped out from beyond the clouds just as we reached the enormous, gothic building and I yelled for her again as we ran towards it in desperation, no sign of anyone near it on the gravel drive. Could we have got it wrong? Maybe the footsteps hadn't been on gravel after all. Maybe they'd been down by the shore or somewhere else, but I just couldn't fucking think where.

I yelled and yelled, the others echoing my cries for our girl as we all sensed the utter wrongness of this situation. But it didn't matter. By the time we made it to the open space outside the building, there was no sign of anyone anywhere in sight and no matter how much we shouted Tatum's name, the only thing we could hear from her earpiece was silence.

The four of us fell still as hopelessness consumed us and I swung my baseball bat at the wall of the building, bellowing my rage and fear from my lungs as my heart disappeared into the night.

CHAPTER FORTY SIX

I woke up like I was resurfacing from a deep, dark pool of water, my mind twisting with memories of the trees, the dark, my enemies, my men. I was disorientated as my eyes flickered open and glaringly bright lights shone down at me from a stark white ceiling.

I was in a single bed, the cushion thin beneath my head and metal rails lining either side of the mattress.

"-don't know, maybe there's more of them, maybe they have her somewhere," Monroe spoke urgently in my ear and I tried to move my lips to answer but couldn't manage it right away. "Fuck, what use are your cameras, Saint, if they don't show us where our girl is?"

"Perhaps our enemy knew how to avoid them," he gritted out. "Or perhaps they got lucky."

"Bait must know who has her," Kyan snarled.

"Bait swears no one has her and as he's missing a few teeth and is gonna be pissing blood for the next few weeks, I'm inclined to believe him," Saint hissed.

"You believe that assfuck?!" Kyan roared. "I say I keep pulling out teeth until he tells us where she is!"

"Getting angry will not resolve this situation any faster, if you can't keep your head, I'll have you locked in the crypt," Saint snapped.

"I don't think putting Kyan in a time out is gonna work right now," Blake said in a furious tone. "We need to keep searching."

"We've been all over campus, where the hell else could she be? We know every part of this place," Monroe snarled.

"Why isn't the fucking tracker on her phone showing up? Bait or any accomplice he might have couldn't have known about that," Saint hissed.

My throat eased up a little and I could finally speak as the haze of the drug I'd been given started to lift, my hand moving as if to reach for them in the room.

"I'm right here," I murmured, turning my head as I searched for them, but I wasn't anywhere I knew and I certainly wasn't with my Night Keepers. I realised with a jolt that it was the fucking earpiece I was hearing them through. *Of course.*

"Tatum?!" all of them cried.

"Where are you?" Saint took over as the rest of them fell into frantic demands and I blinked to try and clear my mind enough to hear them. "Shut the fuck up and let me speak," he barked at them and silence fell, letting my mind sharpen another inch. "Where are you Tatum? Describe it to me."

I pressed my hands into the starchy sheets I was lying on and found my strength coming back a bit more as I sat up. My gut wrenched as I took in the space and I forced myself to describe it. "'I'm in what looks like a room in a hospital. There's no windows. Everything's white. So fucking white. Hang on, there's a door." I pushed myself out of bed, but something metal clinked and my leg was tugged back. I shoved the covers off of me, finding one of my ankles chained to the bed.

"No," I gasped, horror winding its way through me and taking me hostage.

"What is it?" Saint demanded anxiously and the other guys made noises of anguish in the background.

"I'm chained to the bed. Shit, Saint - I think – I think-" the door opened and I shut my mouth instantly, my instincts kicking in. This earpiece was vital to me getting back to my Night Keepers and I could *not* let it be known that I had it in. *Shit how many hours of battery life does this thing have??*

"Hello Miss Rivers," a man said as he stepped into the room. He was tall, well-built with dark skin and a fine navy suit hugging his body. His face was chiselled and familiar and my gut clenched tightly as I tried to understand what the hell Saint's father was doing here. The Governor of fucking State. "I have some good news and some bad news."

The guys had fallen deathly silent in my ear, but I felt them listening in like they were right beside me. *What the fuck is happening right now??*

"The good news is, your antibody test just proved that you're immune to the Hades Virus," he said, a smile pulling at his mouth that made my blood chill. "The bad news is that that officially makes your blood the most valuable blood in the world. Even those who have been infected with the virus do not produce the level of antibodies yours does and it seems they can become re-infected after a time. Though I am not a medical man, I have it on good authority that your blood holds the key to a vaccine that could save us all."

"Fuck fuck *fuck*," I heard Saint cursing, losing it entirely and one of the other guys hushed him.

"Why is that the bad news?" I asked Troy, my mouth parched as fear snaked through every inch of my flesh.

He moved to the end of my bed, examining me like I was a lamb about to be led to slaughter. "Because the country is in dire need of a vaccine as fast as one can possibly be produced."

I stared into his eyes, fighting not to cower. "So you want to make a vaccine from my blood? Fine. I can accept that. I'll give blood for that. Obviously I want this virus gone. But just unchain me." I tried not to sound pleading, but it was hard when I was literally at this man's mercy, about to be

659

used for whatever fucking tests needed to be conducted to make this happen. All without my say so. With a chemical scent filling the room and the bright white, horror movie walls glaring at me, I was barely keeping it together.

He shook his head, brushing a speck of invisible lint off of his sleeve before he tugged it up and checked the time on his glitzy watch. "How noble of you, Miss Rivers, but I believe you're misunderstanding me. So let me explain to the best of my abilities in the few more moments I have to spare. You will be exposed to the Hades Virus on a daily basis to the highest possible level your immune system can handle. Your body will respond by creating antibodies at an accelerated rate which will then be harvested to build a vaccine. I will of course make sure you are kept well as long as possible, but I am afraid there is a chance that your body will succumb to the virus eventually. Especially with how hard we are going to need to push your immune system to get what we need from it. It is a sad but honest truth. And it's a sacrifice I am willing to make for my country." He nodded curtly to me, heading for the door and I realised I was trembling with fear, rage, *hate*.

This man was stealing my life from me. I was sure I was going to die here if I didn't get out. The Night Keepers were shouting again, but I couldn't make out the words, though I felt their pain and desperation through the sound alone.

"Don't lie to me," I spat as rage won out amongst all the toxic emotions bubbling inside me. "I know what you're doing it for and it's not your people. It's for *money*."

Troy glanced over his shoulder at me, raising his eyebrows then slowly nodded. "Alright, you caught me. But perhaps I like the sound of being the man responsible for saving the world as a happy side effect. It does have quite the ring to it. And of course, you will be credited as a hero as well. So your sacrifice will not go unrecognised." He stepped aside as a nurse walked into the room with a Serenity Pharmaceuticals lanyard swinging around her neck and Troy nodded to her. "Proceed."

"No!" I screamed in panic.

"Tatum!" Kyan bellowed in my ear. "I'm coming for you, I'm fucking coming, baby, just hold on."

"Shit, Saint, calm down," Blake gasped and I heard them struggling as Saint bellowed curses that raked against my ears.

"We'll find you," Monroe spoke to me. "Princess, we'll figure out where you are. You have a direct line to four demons of hell and I swear we'll seek you out, even if we have to bleed the world dry to do it."

I couldn't answer, but I found myself clinging to his words. I knew they would do whatever was possible to find me. But what if they couldn't? It was Troy Memphis we were dealing with here; the father of the most calculated person I knew. And from everything I'd heard, he was just as methodical, just as thorough in his dealings. If he didn't want me to be found, then I wouldn't be. It was as simple and as terrifying as that.

The nurse didn't look at me as she drew up a syringe full of some drug across the room and I kicked and thrashed, trying to break the chain that bound me to the bed. I flung myself half out of it, throwing my fists into the bitch as she came at me with the needle, shoving her away so it went flying from her hand.

"Get the fuck away from me!" I screamed.

"Ah – help!" she cried and two male nurses burst into the room a second later.

They dove at me and I bit and clawed and fought them with every scrap of strength in my body as my Night Keepers cried out in fear, having no clue what was going on.

One of the nurses managed to get hold of the needle and ram it into my neck and I hissed and spat like a wild cat just before the drug took effect. For the second time tonight, I was pulled away into a pit of darkness. And I was terrified of what fresh hell would await me when I awoke.

The lasting sound of my Night Keepers screaming my name chased me into the dark, and then I was lost to a sea of endless black.

AUTHOR NOTE

Okay guys, how was that? Are we feeling calm, cool, collected? Shall we all take a moment to celebrate the fact that the guys caught the Justice Ninja?! Woohoo *celebration emoji* *dancing emoji* … oh, that's right there were two of them weren't there…this is a little awkward…

Still, we got one of the bastards and it was none other than old 'balls-on-face' Bait and who doesn't love a nice clean victory at the end of a book like that? No need to throw any devices across the room here, no need to brace yourself for impact falling off of a cliff, no siree, everything is looking up… mostly.

Okay, okay, there is that little itty bitty problem with Tatum being dragged off to some creepy lab to be used as a lab rat for some stuff and cheese but if we look at it objectively, she could very well save the world. And really, what's one life in the face of SAVING THE WHOLE WORLD? So let's not be unreasonable about this. She had her fun (who knew she'd get a three sausage sandwich on the dark lord's bed without him present??) so she really has been living her best life and you can't say fairer than that. If anything Troy Memphis is something of a philanthropist, making the hard call to benefit the whole of mankind. And let's be honest, if Deepthroat was the one who was immune and had to be sacrificed to create a vaccine you'd be okay with it. So maybe this is a good point to leave the story at? No need for book 4, right? Do you agree? No? Fair enough then, we'll be sure to let you know how this pans out in the next and final book which means NO CLIFF HANGER!! So hold on to your tightie whities because I'm sure it will be one hell of a bumpy ride but the 4th and final book in the Brutal Boys of Everlake Prep series is coming soooooon.

Also, out of curiosity, how are you all doing on Saint? We gave ourselves a challenge on that little cream cracker, that's for sure, but is he starting to win you over? Were you screaming yes, yes, yes when it seemed like him and Tate might just get down and dirty and then no, no, no when he went all Saint Memphis over it and imploded? Do you remember when you thought he burned the letters? Are you starting to question some things now?

On a more serious note, I would just like to say that though this year has been one of the most challenging that we have all faced with the virus which won't be named crashing in to wreck the party, I think it has been a great one for us to have found our strength and resilience and really prove to ourselves that we won't let the world knock us down. There have been plenty of times when we all wanted to scream our frustration at the sky (and the people who thought eating raw wild bats was a great shout) but there have been a lot of wonderful family moments too where we have all had the chance to spend quality time with those people closest to us.

For me and Caroline personally, 2020 has been an amazing rollercoaster of a ride with our books and we can't thank you guys enough for jumping onboard with us for all the loop the loops, flips and spins and we can't wait to bring even more literary goodness your way for 2021.

We are working hard to hone our craft, pouring our hearts and souls into every page and making every effort to breathe life into our perfectly imperfect characters so that you guys can hopefully fall in love with them, hate them, rage at them and celebrate with them whenever they manage to triumph over the shit we throw their way – and yeah, I know that we can be kinda dicks with how much we do that.

Thank you for being a part of this amazing journey we are on! Each and every one of you holds a special place in our hearts and knowing that we have wonderful readers like you enjoying our books means the world to us. Not so long ago, we were just a pair of sisters who were always making up stories and saying that we should really write a book one day and thanks to you guys, we are living our dreams.

Love, Susanne and Caroline xxx

P.S.

If you wanna join our own elite club (don't worry, you can volunteer a character as proxy to fight to the death for you – woah woah woah you can't all pick Deepthroat at once! – and those of you who are picking Kyan to fight for you, shame on you. He's already been through this shit once. And you say WE'RE the evil ones)

ALSO BY CAROLINE PECKHAM & SUSANNE VALENTI

Brutal Boys of Everlake Prep

(Complete Reverse Harem Bully Romance Contemporary Series)

Kings of Quarantine

Kings of Lockdown

Kings of Anarchy

Queen of Quarantine

**

Dead Men Walking

(Reverse Harem Dark Romance Contemporary Series)

The Death Club

Society of Psychos

**

The Harlequin Crew

(Reverse Harem Mafia Romance Contemporary Series)

Sinners Playground

Dead Man's Isle

Carnival Hill

Paradise Lagoon

Gallows Bridge

Harlequinn Crew Novellas

Devil's Pass

**

Dark Empire
(Dark Mafia Contemporary Standalones)
Beautiful Carnage
Beautiful Savage

**

Forget Me Not Bombshell
(Dark Mafia Reverse Harem Contemporary Standalone)

**

The Ruthless Boys of the Zodiac
(Reverse Harem Paranormal Romance Series - Set in the world of Solaria)
Dark Fae

Savage Fae

Vicious Fae

Broken Fae

Warrior Fae

Zodiac Academy
(M/F Bully Romance Series- Set in the world of Solaria, five years after Dark Fae)
The Awakening

Ruthless Fae

The Reckoning

Shadow Princess

Cursed Fates

Fated Thrones

Heartless Sky

The Awakening - As told by the Boys

Zodiac Academy Novellas
Origins of an Academy Bully

The Big A.S.S. Party

Darkmore Penitentiary

(Reverse Harem Paranormal Romance Series - Set in the world of Solaria, ten years after Dark Fae)

Caged Wolf

Alpha Wolf

Feral Wolf

**

The Age of Vampires

(Complete M/F Paranormal Romance/Dystopian Series)

Eternal Reign

Eternal Shade

Eternal Curse

Eternal Vow

Eternal Night

Eternal Love

**

Cage of Lies

(M/F Dystopian Series)

Rebel Rising

**

Tainted Earth

(M/F Dystopian Series)

Afflicted

Altered

Adapted

Advanced

**

The Vampire Games

(Complete M/F Paranormal Romance Trilogy)

V Games

V Games: Fresh From The Grave

V Games: Dead Before Dawn

*

The Vampire Games: Season Two

(Complete M/F Paranormal Romance Trilogy)

Wolf Games

Wolf Games: Island of Shade

Wolf Games: Severed Fates

*

The Vampire Games: Season Three

Hunter Trials

*

The Vampire Games Novellas

A Game of Vampires

**

The Rise of Issac

(Complete YA Fantasy Series)

Creeping Shadow

Bleeding Snow

Turning Tide

Weeping Sky

Failing Light

Made in the USA
Columbia, SC
27 July 2025

61059162R00400